the **BOOK** of
CTHULHU

the BOOK of CTHULHU

Tales Inspired by H.P. Lovecraft

edited by
Ross E. Lockhart

Night Shade Books
New York

An extension of this copyright page appears on pages 527-529

Visit our website at www.nightshadebooks.com.

10 9 8 7 6 5 4 3 2

Library of Congress Cataloging-in-Publication Data is available on file.

ISBN: 978-1-949102-64-2

Printed in the United States of America

*For Jennifer, my island of sanity
amid the black seas of infinity*

Table of Contents

Introduction

I n 1928, a young man, Conan creator Robert E. Howard, wrote a fan letter to *Weird Tales* magazine praising H. P. Lovecraft's "The Call of Cthulhu," which had recently appeared in the magazine's pages. Howard described the story as "a masterpiece," which he was "sure will live as one of the highest achievements in literature."

Since then, countless young men and women have discovered the Cthulhu Mythos cycle, and have come to the same conclusion. These stories, interlinked tales of tentacles, madness, and terror created by Lovecraft, but expanded upon by his contemporaries and correspondents—the so-called "Lovecraft Circle"—are more than just simple supernatural tales, they are *literature*, of the highest order, with complex themes (sanity's fragility, existential angst, questionable parentage, fate, decadence, detachment, and deterioration, to name a few), precise writing style, intricate, layered storytelling... and monsters. Some of the best known monsters in modern fiction.

Lovecraft's impeccable storytelling—often filtered through his collaborators and "disciples"—has inspired many to pen their own Mythos tales, and the Cthulhu Mythos story cycle has taken on a convoluted, cyclopean life of its own, as further posthumous collaborations continue to expand the scope, scale, and ultimate *interpretation* of what is perhaps the most diverse shared fictional universe ever created.

Today, the Cthulhu Mythos cycle includes tales by some of the most prodigious writers of the twentieth century... and so far, some of the most astounding writers of the twenty-first century as well. Mythos fiction has become one of the major cultural memes of our era—*everybody* knows what Cthulhu looks like, even if they haven't read Lovecraft. And it would seem that Cthulhu and his minions are everywhere, not just books and short fiction (*especially* online short fiction), but represented in music, toys, audio dramas, feature films, comics, and games (video and otherwise).

My personal discovery of the Cthulhu Mythos came in 1980, maybe early 1981. I received the *Dungeons and Dragons* cyclopedia, *Deities and Demigods*, which included a section—excised from later printings—detailing the Cthulhu Mythos pantheon. Erol Otus's intricate pen-and-ink renditions of the strange alien beings of the Lovecraftian pantheon—particularly the shambling shoggoth, mysterious Mi-Go, and elegant member of the Great Race—astounded me, inspiring me to seek out the fictions on which such strange images were based. I asked around, and a friend pressed a book into my hands, telling me I *had* to read T. E. D. Klein's "Black Man with a Horn." The story scared the hell out of me, but I devoured it, and wanted more.

"Black Man with a Horn" introduced me to the larger world of Mythos fiction, driving me to spend the next thirty years delving into and exploring the Mythos cycle in all its permutations, leading me to read authors like David Drake, Ramsey Campbell, Brian Lumley, and, yes, even H. P. Lovecraft. It was also my introduction to John Coltrane. So it is my honor and privilege to include not just *that* story, but twenty-six other tales of Lovecraftian fantasy and horror—by many of the greatest names in Mythos fiction—in *The Book of Cthulhu*. A hand-picked selection representing the *best* post-Lovecraft Cthulhu Mythos literature, all in one place. Could this mean that the stars are finally right? Are we on the cusp of a Lovecraftian renaissance, or is dread R'Lyeh about to rise out of the Pacific Ocean?

Welcome, readers, to *The Book of Cthulhu*. Iä! Iä! Cthulhu fhtagn!

Andromeda Among the Stones

Caitlín R. Kiernan

I cannot think of the deep sea without shuddering…
—H. P. Lovecraft

October 1914

"Is she really and truly dead, Father?" the girl asked, and Machen Dandridge, already an old man at fifty-one, looked up at the low buttermilk sky again and closed the black book clutched in his hands. He'd carved the tall headstone himself, the marker for his wife's grave there by the relentless Pacific, black shale obelisk with its hasty death's-head. His daughter stepped gingerly around the raw earth and pressed her fingers against the monument.

"Why did you not give her to the sea?" she asked. "She always wanted to go down to the sea at the end. She often told me so."

"I've given her back to the earth, instead," Machen told her and rubbed at his eyes. The cold sunlight through thin clouds was enough to make his head ache, his daughter's voice like thunder, and he shut his aching eyes for a moment. Just a little comfort in the almost blackness trapped behind his lids,

1

parchment skin too insubstantial to bring the balm of genuine darkness, void to match the shades of his soul, and Machen whispered one of the prayers from the heavy black book and then looked at the grave again.

"Well, that's what she always told me," the girl said again, running her fingertips across the rough-hewn stone.

"Things changed at the end, child. The sea wouldn't have taken her. I had to give her back to the earth."

"She said it was a sacrilege, planting people in the ground like wheat, like kernels of corn."

"She did?" He glanced anxiously over his left shoulder, looking back across the waves the wind was making in the high and yellow-brown grass, the narrow trail leading back down to the tall and brooding house that he'd built for his wife twenty-four years ago, back towards the cliffs and the place where the sea and sky blurred seamlessly together.

"Yes, she did. She said only barbarians and heathens stick their dead in the ground like turnips."

"I had no choice," Machen replied, wondering if that was exactly the truth or only something he'd like to believe. "The sea wouldn't take her, and I couldn't bring myself to burn her."

"Only heathens burn their dead," his daughter said disapprovingly and leaned close to the obelisk, setting her ear against the charcoal shale.

"Do you hear anything?"

"No, Father. Of course not. She's dead. You just said so."

"Yes," Machen whispered. "She is." And the wind whipping across the hillside made a hungry, waiting sound that told him it was time for them to head back to the house.

This is where I stand, at the bottom gate, and I hold the key to the abyss...

"But it's better that way," the girl said, her ear still pressed tight against the obelisk. "She couldn't stand the pain any longer. It was cutting her up inside."

"She told you that?"

"She didn't have to tell me that. I saw it in her eyes."

The ebony key to the first day and the last, the key to the moment when the stars wink out, one by one, and the sea heaves its rotting belly at the empty, sagging sky.

"You're only a child," he said. "You shouldn't have had to see such things. Not yet."

"It can't very well be helped now," she answered and stepped away from her mother's grave, one hand cupping her ear like maybe it had begun to hurt. "You know that, old man."

"I do," and he almost said her name then, Meredith, his mother's name, but the wind was too close, the listening wind and the salt-and-semen stink of the breakers crashing against the cliffs. "But I can wish it were otherwise."

"If wishes were horses, beggars would ride."

And Machen watched silently as Meredith Dandridge knelt in the grass and placed her handful of wilting wildflowers on the freshly turned soil. If it were spring instead of autumn, he thought, there would be dandelions and poppies. If it were spring instead of autumn, the woman wrapped in a quilt and nailed up inside a pine-board casket would still be breathing. If it were spring, they would not be alone now, him and his daughter at the edge of the world. The wind teased the girl's long yellow hair, and the sun glittered dimly in her warm green eyes.

The key I have accepted full in the knowledge of its weight.

"Remember me," Meredith whispered, either to her dead mother or something else, and he didn't ask which.

"We should be heading back now," he said and glanced over his shoulder again.

"So soon? Is that all you're going to read from the book? Is that all of it?"

"Yes, that's all of it, for now," though there would be more, later, when the harvest moon swelled orange-red and bloated and hung itself in the wide California night. When the odd, mute women came to dance, then there would be other words to say, to keep his wife in the ground and the gate shut for at least another year.

The weight that is the weight of all salvation, the weight that holds the line against the last, unending night.

"It's better this way," his daughter said again, standing up, brushing the dirt off her stockings, from the hem of her black dress. "There was so little left of her."

"Don't talk of that here," Machen replied, more sternly than he'd intended. But Meredith didn't seem to have noticed or, if she'd noticed, not to have minded the tone of her father's voice.

"I will remember her the way she was before, when she was still beautiful."

"That's what she would want," he said and took his daughter's hand. "That's the way I'll remember her, as well," but he knew that was a lie, as false as any lie any living man ever uttered. He knew that he would always see his wife as the writhing, twisted thing she'd become at the last, the way she was after the gates were almost thrown open, and she placed herself on the threshold.

The frozen weight of the sea, the burning weight of starlight and my final breath. I hold the line. I hold the ebony key against the last day of all.

And Machen Dandridge turned his back on his wife's grave and led his daughter down the dirt and gravel path, back to the house waiting for them like a curse.

November 1914

Meredith Dandridge lay very still in her big bed, her big room with its high ceiling and no pictures hung on the walls, and she listened to the tireless sea slamming itself against the rocks. The sea there to take the entire world apart one gritty speck at a time, the sea that was here first and would be here long after the continents had finally been weathered down to so much slime and sand. She knew this because her father had read to her from his heavy black book, the book that had no name, the book that she couldn't ever read for herself or the demons would come for her in the night. And she knew, too, because of the books he had *given* her, her books—*Atlantis: The Antediluvian World, The World Before the Deluge,* and *Atlantis and Lost Lemuria.* Everything above the waves on borrowed time, her father had said again and again, waiting for the day when the sea rose once more and drowned the land beneath its smothering, salty bosom, and the highest mountains and deepest valleys will become a playground for sea serpents and octopuses and schools of herring. Forests to become Poseidon's orchards, her father said, though she knew Poseidon wasn't the true name of the god-thing at the bottom of the ocean, just a name some dead man gave it thousands of years ago.

"Should I read you a story tonight, Merry?" her dead mother asked, sitting right there in the chair beside the bed. She smelled like fish and mud, even though they'd buried her in the dry ground at the top of the hill behind the house. Meredith didn't look at her, because she'd spent so much time already trying to remember her mother's face the way it was *before* and didn't want to see the ruined face the ghost was wearing like a mask. As bad as the face her brother now wore, worse than that, and Meredith shrugged and pushed the blankets back a little.

"If you can't sleep, it might help," her mother said with a voice like kelp stalks swaying slowly in deep water.

"It might," Meredith replied, staring at a place where the wallpaper had begun to peel free of one of the walls, wishing there were a candle in the room or an oil lamp so the ghost would leave her alone. "And it might not."

"I could read to you from Hans Christian Andersen, or one of Grimm's tales," her mother sighed. "'The Little Mermaid' or 'The Fisherman and his Wife'?"

"You could tell me what it's like in Hell," the girl replied.

"Dear, I don't have to tell you that," her ghost mother whispered, her voice gone suddenly regretful and sad. "I know I don't have to ever tell you that."

"There might be different hells," Meredith said. "This one, and the one father sent you away to, and the one Avery is lost inside. No one ever said there could only be one, did they? Maybe it has many regions. A hell for the dead Prussian soldiers and another for the French, a hell for Christians and another for the Jews. And maybe another for all the pagans."

"Your father didn't send me anywhere, child. I crossed the threshold of my own accord."

"So I would be alone in *this* hell."

The ghost clicked its sharp teeth together, and Meredith could hear the anemone tendrils between its iridescent fish eyes quickly withdrawing into the hollow places in her mother's decaying skull.

"I could read you a poem," her mother said hopefully. "I could sing you a song."

"It isn't all fire and brimstone, is it? Not the region of hell where you are? It's blacker than night and cold as ice, isn't it, mother?"

"Did he think it would save me to put me in the earth? Does the old fool think it will bring me back across, like Persephone?"

Too many questions, hers and her mother's, and for a moment Meredith Dandridge didn't answer the ghost, kept her eyes on the shadowy wallpaper strips, the pinstripe wall, wishing the sun would rise and pour warm and gold as honey through the drapes.

"I crossed the threshold of my *own* accord," the ghost said again, and Meredith wondered if it thought she didn't hear the first time. Or maybe it was something her mother needed to believe and might stop believing if she stopped repeating it. "Someone had to do it."

"It didn't have to be you."

The wind whistled wild and shrill around the eaves of the house, invisible lips pressed to a vast, invisible instrument, and Meredith shivered and pulled the covers up to her chin again.

"There was no one else. It wouldn't take your brother. The one who wields the key cannot be a man. You know that, Merry. Avery knew that, too."

"There are other women," Meredith said, speaking through gritted teeth, not wanting to start crying but the tears already hot in her eyes. "It could have been someone else. It didn't have to be my mother."

"Some other child's mother, then?" the ghost asked. "Some other mother's daughter?"

"Go back to your hell," Meredith said, still looking at the wall, spitting out the words like poison. "Go back to your hole in the ground and tell your fairy tales to the worms. Tell them 'The Fisherman and his Wife.'"

"You have to be strong now, Merry. You have to listen to your father, and you have to be ready. I wasn't strong enough."

And finally she did turn to face her mother, what was left of her mother's face, the scuttling things nesting in her tangled hair, the silver scales and barnacles, the stinging anemone crown, and Meredith Dandridge didn't flinch or look away.

"One day," she said, "I'll take that damned black book of his, and I'll toss it into the stove. I'll take it, mother, and toss it into the hearth, and then they can come out of the sea and drag us both away."

Her mother cried out and came apart like a breaking wave against the shingle, water poured from the tin pail that had given it shape, her flesh gone suddenly as clear and shimmering as glass, before she drained away and leaked through the cracks between the floorboards. The girl reached out and dipped her fingers into the shallow pool left behind in the wicker seat of the chair. The water was cold and smelled unclean. And then she lay awake until dawn, listening to the ocean, to all the unthinking noises a house makes in the small hours of a night.

May 1914

Avery Dandridge had his father's eyes, but someone else's soul to peer out through them, and to his sister he was hope that there might be a life somewhere beyond the rambling house beside the sea. Five years her senior, he'd gone away to school in San Francisco for a while, almost a year, because their mother wished him to. But there had been an incident, and he was sent home again, transgressions only spoken of in whispers and nothing anyone ever bothered to explain to Meredith, but that was fine with her. She only cared that he was back, and she was that much less alone.

"Tell me about the earthquake," she said to him, one day not long after he'd returned, the two of them strolling together along the narrow beach below the cliffs, sand the color of coal dust, noisy gulls and driftwood like titan bones washed in by the tide. "Tell me all about the fire."

"The earthquake? Merry, that was eight years ago. You were still just a baby, that was such long time ago," and then he picked up a shell and turned it over in his hand, brushing away some of the dark sand stuck to it. "People don't like to talk about the earthquake anymore. I never heard them say much about it."

"Oh," she said, not sure what to say next but still full of questions. "Father says it was a sign, a sign from—"

"Maybe you shouldn't believe everything he says, Merry. It was an earthquake." And she felt a thrill then, like a tiny jolt of electricity rising up her spine and spreading out across her scalp, that anyone, much less Avery, would question their father and suggest she do likewise.

"Have you stopped believing in the signs?" she asked, breathless. "Is that what you learned in school?"

"I didn't learn much of anything important in school," he replied and showed her the shell in his palm. Hardly as big around as a nickel, but peaked in the center like a Chinaman's hat, radial lines of chestnut brown. "It's pretty," she said as he placed it in her palm.

"What's it called?"

"It's a limpet," he replied, because Avery knew all about shells and fish and the fossils in the cliffs, things he'd learned from their father's books and not from school. "It's a shield limpet. The jackmackerel carry them into battle when they fight the eels."

Meredith laughed out loud at that last part, and he laughed, too, then sat down on a rock at the edge of a wide tide pool. She stood there beside him, still inspecting the shell in her hand, turning it over and over again. The concave underside of the limpet was smoother than silk and would be white if not for the faintest iridescent hint of blue.

"That's not true," she said. "Everyone knows the jackmackerel and the eels are friends."

"Sure they are," Avery said. "Everyone knows that." But he was staring out to sea now and didn't turn to look at her. In a moment, she slipped the shell into a pocket of her sweater and sat down on the rock next to him.

"Do you see something out there?" she asked, and he nodded his head, but didn't speak. The wind rushed cold and damp across the beach and painted ripples on the surface of the pool at their feet. The wind and the waves seemed louder than usual, and Meredith wondered if that meant a storm was coming.

"Not a storm," Avery said, and that didn't surprise her because he often knew what she was thinking before she said it. "A war's coming, Merry."

"Oh yes, the jackmackerel and the eels," Merry laughed and squinted towards the horizon, trying to see whatever it was that had attracted her brother's attention. "The squid and the mussels."

"Don't be silly. Everyone knows that the squid and the mussels are great friends," and that made her laugh again. But Avery didn't laugh, looked away from the sea and stared down instead at the scuffed toes of his boots dangling a few inches above the water.

"There's never been a war like the one that's coming," he said after a while. "All the nations of the earth at each other's throats, Merry, and when we're done with all the killing, no one will be left to stand against the sea."

She took a very deep breath, the clean, salty air to clear her head, and began to pick at a barnacle on the rock.

"If that were true," she said, "Father would have told us. He would have shown us the signs."

"He doesn't see them. He doesn't dream the way I do."

"But you told him?"

"I tried. But he thinks it's something they put in my head at school. He thinks it's some kind of trick to make him look away."

Merry stopped picking at the barnacle, because it was making her fingers sore and they'd be bleeding soon if she kept it up. She decided it was better to watch the things trapped in the tide pool, the little garden stranded there until the sea came back to claim it. Periwinkle snails and hermit crabs wearing stolen shells, crimson starfish and starfish the shape and color of sunflowers.

"He thinks they're using me to make him look the other way, to catch him off his guard," Avery whispered, his voice almost lost in the rising wind. "He thinks I'm being set against him."

"Avery, I don't believe Father would say that about you."

"He didn't have to say it," and her brother's dark and shining eyes gazed out at the sea and sky again.

"We should be heading back soon, shouldn't we? The tide will be coming in before long," Meredith said, noticing how much higher up the beach the waves were reaching than the last time she'd looked. Another half hour and the insatiable ocean would be battering itself against the rough shale cliffs at their backs.

"'Wave after wave, each mightier than the last,'" Avery whispered, closing his eyes tight, and the words coming from his pale, thin lips sounded like someone else, someone old and tired that Meredith had never loved. "'Till last, a ninth one, gathering half the deep and full of voices, slowly rose and plunged roaring, and all the wave was in a flame—'"

"What's that?" she asked, interrupting because she didn't want to hear anymore. "Is it from Father's book?"

"No, it's not," he replied, sounding more like himself again, more like her brother. He opened his eyes, and a tear rolled slowly down his wind-chapped cheek. "It's just something they taught me at school."

"How can a wave be in flame? Is it supposed to be a riddle?" she asked, and he shook his head.

"No," he said and wiped at his face with his hands. "It's nothing at all, just a silly bit of poetry they made us memorize. School is full of silly poetry."

"Is that why you came home?"

"We ought to start back," he said, glancing quickly over his shoulder at the high cliffs, the steep trail leading back up towards the house. "Can't have the tide catching us with our trousers down, now can we?"

"I don't even wear trousers," Merry said glumly, still busy thinking about that ninth wave, the fire and the water. Avery put an arm around her and held her close to him for a moment while the advancing sea dragged itself eagerly back and forth across the moss-scabbed rocks.

January 1915

Meredith sat alone on the floor at the end of the hallway, the narrow hall connecting the foyer to the kitchen and a bathroom, and then farther along, leading all the way back to the very rear of the house and this tall door that was always locked. The tarnished brass key always hung on its ring upon her father's belt. She pressed her ear against the wood and strained to hear anything at all. The wood was damp and very cold, and the smell of saltwater and mildew seeped freely through the space between the bottom of the door and the floor, between the door and the jamb. Once-solid redwood that had long since begun to rot from the continual moisture, the ocean's corrosive breath to rust the hinges so the door cried out like a stepped-on cat every time it was opened or closed. Even as a very small child, Meredith had feared this door, even in the days before she'd started to understand what lay in the deep place beneath her father's house.

Outside, the icy winter wind howled, and she shivered and pulled her grey wool shawl tighter about her shoulders; the very last thing her mother had made for her, that shawl. Almost as much hatred in Merry for the wind as for the sea, but at least it smothered the awful thumps and moans that came, day and night, from the attic room where her father had locked Avery away in June.

"There are breaches between the worlds, Merry," Avery had said, a few days before he picked the lock on the hallway door with the sharpened tip-end of a buttonhook and went down to the deep place by himself. "Rifts, fractures, ruptures. If they can't be closed, they have to be guarded against the things on the other side that don't belong here."

"Father says it's a portal," she'd replied, closing the book she'd been reading, a dusty, dog-eared copy of Franz Unger's *Primitive World.*

Her brother had laughed a dry, humorless laugh and shaken his head, nervously watching the fading day through the parlor windows. "Portals are built on purpose, to be used. These things are accidents, at best, casualties of happenstance, tears in space when one world passes much too near another."

"Well, that's not what Father says."

"Read your book, Merry. One day you'll understand. One day soon, when you're not a child anymore, and he loses his hold on you."

And she'd frowned, sighed, and opened her book again, opening it at random to one of the strangely melancholy lithographs—*The Period of the Muschelkalk [Middle Trias]*. A violent seascape, and in the foreground a reef jutted above the waves, crowded with algae-draped driftwood branches and the shells of stranded mollusca and crinoidea. There was something like a crocodile, that the author called *Nothosaurus giganteus,* clinging to the reef so it wouldn't be swept back into the storm-tossed depths. Overhead, the night sky was a turbulent mass of clouds with the small, white moon, full or near enough to full, peeking through to illuminate the ancient scene.

"You mean planets?" she'd asked Avery. "You mean moons and stars?"

"No, I mean *worlds*. Now, read your book, and don't ask so many questions."

Meredith thought she heard creaking wood, her father's heavy footsteps, the dry ruffling of cloth rubbing against cloth, and she stood quickly, not wanting to be caught listening at the door again, was still busy straightening her rumpled dress when she realized that he was standing there in the hall behind her, instead. Her mistake, thinking he'd gone to the deep place, when he was somewhere else all along, in his library or the attic room with Avery or outside braving the cold to visit her mother's grave on the hill.

"What are you doing, child?" he asked her gruffly and tugged at his beard. There were streaks of silver-grey that weren't there only a couple of months before, scars from the night they lost her mother, his wife, the night the demons tried to squeeze in through the tear, and Ellen Dandridge had tried to block their way. His face grown years older in the space of weeks, dark crescents beneath his eyes like bruises and deep creases in his forehead. He brushed his daughter's blonde hair from her eyes.

"Would it have been different, if you'd believed Avery from the start?"

For a moment he didn't reply, and his silence, his face set as hard and perfectly unreadable as stone, made her want to strike him, made her wish she could kick open the rotting, sea-damp door and hurl him screaming down the stairs to whatever was waiting for them both in the deep place.

"I don't know, Meredith. But I had to trust the book, and I had to believe the signs in the heavens."

"You were too arrogant, old man. You almost gave away the whole wide world because you couldn't admit you might be wrong."

"You should be thankful that your mother can't hear you, young lady, using that tone of voice with your own father."

Meredith turned and looked at the tall, rotten door again, the symbols drawn on the wood in whitewash and blood.

"She can hear me," Meredith told him. "She talks to me almost every night. She hasn't gone as far away as you think."

"I'm still your father, and you're still a child who can't even begin to understand what's at stake, what's always pushing at the other side of—"

"—the gate?" she asked, interrupting and finishing for him, and she put one hand flat against the door, the upper of its two big panels, and leaned all her weight against it. "What happens next time? Do you know that, Father? How much longer do we have left, or haven't the constellations gotten around to telling you that yet?"

"Don't mock me, Meredith."

"Why not?" and she stared back at him over her shoulder, without taking her hand off the door. "Will it damn me faster? Will it cause more men to die in the trenches? Will it cause Avery more pain than he's in now?"

"*I* was given the book," he growled at her, his stony face flashing to bitter anger, and at least that gave Meredith some mean scrap of satisfaction. "I was shown the way to this place. They entrusted the gate to me, child. The gods—"

"—must be even bigger fools than you, old man. Now shut up, and leave me alone."

Machen Dandridge raised his right hand to strike her, his big-knuckled hand like a hammer of flesh and bone, iron-meat hammer and anvil to beat her as thin and friable as the veil between Siamese universes.

"You'll need me," she said, not recoiling from the fire in his dark eyes, standing her ground. "You can't take my place. Even if you weren't a coward, you couldn't take my place."

"You've become a wicked child," he said, slowly lowering his hand until it hung useless at his side.

"Yes, Father, I have. I've become a *very* wicked child. You'd best pray that I've become wicked enough."

And he didn't reply, no words left in him, but walked quickly away down the long hall towards the foyer and his library, his footsteps loud as distant gunshots, loud as the beating of her heart, and Meredith removed her hand from the door. It burned very slightly, pain like a healing bee sting, and when she looked at her palm there was something new there, a fat and shiny swelling as black and round and smooth as the soulless eye of a shark.

February 1915

In his dreams, Machen Dandridge stands at the edge of the sea and watches the firelight reflected in the roiling grey clouds above Russia and Austria and East Prussia, smells the coppery stink of Turkish and German blood, the life leaking from the bullet holes left in the Serbian Archduke and his wife. Machen would look away if he knew how, wouldn't see what he can only see too late to make any difference. One small man set adrift and then cast up on the shingle of the cosmos, filled to bursting with knowledge and knowing nothing at all. Cannon fire and thunder, the breakers against the cliff side and the death rattle of soldiers beyond counting.

This is where I stand, at the bottom gate, and I hold the key to the abyss…

"A *world* war, father," Avery says. "Something without precedent. I can't even find words to describe the things I've seen."

"A world war, without precedent?" Machen replies skeptically and raises one eyebrow, then goes back to reading his star charts. "Napoleon just might disagree with you there, young man, and Alexander, as well."

"No, you don't understand what I'm saying—"

And the fire in the sky grows brighter, coalescing into a whip of red-gold scales and ebony spines, the dragon's tail to lash the damned. *Every one of us is damned,* Machen thinks. *Every one of us, from the bloody start of time.*

"I have the texts, Avery, and the aegis of the seven, and all the old ways. I cannot very well set that all aside because you've been having nightmares, now can I?"

"I know these things, Father. I know them like I know my own heart, like I know the number of steps down to the deep place."

"There is a trouble brewing in Coma Berenices," his wife whispers, her eye pressed to the eyepiece of the big telescope in his library. "Something like a shadow."

"She says that later," Avery tells him. "That hasn't happened yet, but it will. But you won't listen to her, either."

And Machen Dandridge turns his back on the sea and the dragon, on the battlefields and the burning cities, looking back towards the house he built twenty-five years ago. The air in the library seems suddenly very close, too warm, too thick. He loosens his paper collar and stares at his son sitting across the wide mahogany desk from him.

"I'm not sure I know what you mean, boy," he says, and Avery sighs loudly and runs his fingers through his brown hair.

"Mother isn't even at the window now. That's still two weeks from now," and it's true that no one's standing at the telescope. Machen rubs his eyes and reaches for his spectacles. "By then, it'll be too late. It may be too late already," Avery says.

"Listen to him, Father," Meredith begs with her mother's voice, and then she lays a small, wilted bouquet of autumn wildflowers on Ellen Dandridge's grave. The smell of the broken earth at the top of the hill is not so different from the smell of the French trenches.

"I did listen to him, Merry."

"You let him talk. You know the difference."

"Did I ever tell you about the lights in the sky the night that you were born?"

"Yes, Father. A hundred times."

"There were no lights at your brother's birth."

Behind him, the sea makes a sound like a giant rolling over in its sleep, and Machen looks away from the house again, stares out across the surging black Pacific. There are the carcasses of whales and sea lions and a billion fish and the bloated carcasses of things even he doesn't know the names for, floating in the surf. Scarlet-eyed night birds swoop down to eat their fill of carrion. The water is so thick with dead things and maggots and blood that soon there will be no water left at all.

"The gate chooses the key," his wife says sternly, sadly, standing at the open door leading down to the deep place beneath the house, the bottomless, phosphorescent pool at the foot of the winding, rickety steps. The short pier and the rock rising up from those depths, the little island with its cave and shackles. "You can't change that part, no matter what the seven have given you."

"It wasn't me sent Avery down there, Ellen."

"It wasn't either one of us. But neither of us listened to him, so maybe it's the same as if we both did."

The sea as thick as buttermilk, buttermilk and blood beneath a rotten moon, and the dragon's tail flicks through the stars.

"Writing the history of the end of the world," Meredith says, standing at the telescope, peering into the eyepiece, turning first this knob, then that one, trying to bring something in the night sky into sharper focus. "That's what he kept saying, anyway. 'I am writing the history of the end of the world. I'm writing the history of the future.' Father, did you know that there's trouble in Coma Berenices?"

"Was that you?" he asks her. "Was that you said that or was that your mother?"

"Is there any difference? And if so, do you know the difference?"

"Are these visions, Merry? Are these terrible visions that I may yet hope to affect?"

"Will you keep him locked in that room forever?" she asks, not answering his questions, not even taking her eye from the telescope.

Before his wife leaves the hallway, before she steps onto the unsteady landing at the top of the stairs, she kisses Meredith on the top of her head and then glares at her husband, her eyes like judgment on the last day of all, the eyes of seraphim and burning swords. The diseased sea slams against the cliffs, dislodging chunks of shale, silt gone to stone when the great reptiles roamed the planet and the gods still had countless revolutions and upheavals to attend to before the beginning of the tragedy of mankind.

"Machen," his wife says. "If you had listened, had you allowed me to listen, everything might have been different. The war, what's been done to Avery, all of it. If you'd but *listened*."

And the dream rolls on and on and on behind his eyes, down the stairs and to the glowing water, his wife alone in the tiny boat, rowing across the pool to the rocky island far beneath the house. The hemorrhaging, pus-colored sea throwing itself furiously against the walls of the cavern, wanting in, and it's always only a matter of time. Meredith standing on the pier behind him, chanting the prayers he's taught her, the prayers to keep the gate from opening before Ellen reaches that other shore.

The yellow-green light beneath the pool below the house wavers, then grows brighter by degrees.

The dragon's tail flicks at the suicidal world.

In his attic, Avery screams with the new mouth the gate gave him before it spit the boy, twisted and insane, back into this place, this time.

The oars dipping again and again into the brilliant, glowing water, the creak of the rusted oarlocks, old nails grown loose in decaying wood; shafts of light from the pool playing across the uneven walls of the cavern.

The dragon opens one blistered eye.

And Ellen Dandridge steps out of the boat onto the island. She doesn't look back at her husband and daughter.

"Something like a shadow," Meredith says, taking her right eye from the telescope and looking across the room at her brother, who isn't sitting in the chair across from Machen.

"It's not a shadow," Avery doesn't tell her, and goes back to the things he has to write down in his journals before there's no time left.

On the island, the gate tears itself open, the dragon's eye, angel eye, and the unspeakable face of the gargantuan sleeper in an unnamed, sunken city, tearing itself wide to see if she's the one it's called down or if it's some other. The summoned or the trespasser. The invited or the interloper. And Machen knows from the way the air has begun to shimmer and sing that the sleeper doesn't like what it sees.

"I stand at the gate and hold the key," she says. "You know my name, and I have come to hold the line. I have come only that you might not pass."

"Don't look, Merry. Close your eyes," and Machen holds his daughter close to him as the air stops singing, as it begins to sizzle and pop and burn.

The waves against the shore.

The dragon's tail across the sky.

The empty boat pulled down into the shimmering pool.

Something glimpsed through a telescope.

The ribsy, omnivorous dogs of war.

And then Machen woke in his bed, a storm lashing fiercely at the windows, the lightning exploding out there like mortar shells, and the distant *thump, thump, thump* of his lost son from the attic. He didn't close his eyes again, but lay very still, sweating and listening to the rain and the thumping, until the sun rose somewhere behind the clouds to turn the black to cheerless, leaden grey.

August 1889

After his travels, after Baghdad and the ruins of Nineveh and Babylon, after the hidden mosque in Reza'lyah and the peculiar artifacts he'd collected on the southernmost shore of Lake Urmia, Machen Dandridge went west to California. In the summer of 1889, he married Ellen Douglas-Winslow, black-sheep daughter of a fine old Boston family, and together they traveled by train, the smoking iron horses and steel rails that his own father had made his fortune from, riding all the way to the bustling squalor and Nob Hill sanctuaries of San Francisco. For a time they took up residence in a modest house on Russian Hill, while Machen taught his wife the things that he'd learned in the East—archaeology and astrology, Hebrew and Islamic mysticism, the Talmud and Qur'an, the secrets of the terrible black book that had been given to him by a blind and leprous mullah. Ellen had disgraced her family at an early age by claiming the abilities of a medium and then backing up her claims with extravagant séances and spectacular ectoplasmic displays. Machen found in her an eager pupil.

"Why would he have given the book to you?" Ellen asked skeptically, the first time Machen had shown it to her, the first time he'd taken it from its iron and leather case in her presence. "If it's what you say it is, why would he have given it to anyone?"

"Because, my dear, I had a pistol pressed against his skull," Machen had replied, unwrapping the book, slowly peeling back the layers of lambskin it was wrapped in. "That and knowledge he'd been searching for his entire life. Trust me. It was a fair trade."

And just as the book had led him back from Asia to America and on to California, the brittle, parchment compass of its pages had shown him the way north along the coast to the high cliffs north of Anchor Bay. That first trip, he left Ellen behind, traveling with only the company of a Miwok Indian guide who claimed knowledge of "a hole in the world." But when they finally left the shelter of the redwood forest and stood at the edge of a vast and undulating sea of pampas grass stretching away towards the Pacific, the Miwok had refused to go any farther. No amount of money or talk could persuade him to approach the cliffs waiting beyond the grass, and so Machen continued on alone.

Beneath the hot summer sun, the low, rolling hills seemed to go on forever. The gulls and a pair of red-tailed hawks screamed at him like harpies warning him away, screeching threats or alarum from the endless cornflower sky. But he found it, finally, the "hole in the world," right where the Miwok guide had said that he would, maybe fifty yards from the cliffs.

From what he'd taught himself of geology, Machen guessed it to be the collapsed roof of a cavern, an opening no more than five or six feet across, granting access to an almost vertical chimney eroded through tilted beds of limestone and shale and probably connecting to the sea somewhere in the darkness below. He dropped a large pebble into the hole and listened and counted as it fell, ticking off the seconds until it splashed faintly, confirming his belief that the cavern was connected to the sea. A musty, briny smell wafted up from the hole, uninviting, sickly, and though there was climbing equipment in his pack, and he was competent with ropes and knots and had, more than once, descended treacherous, crumbling shafts into ancient tombs and wells, Machen Dandridge only stood there at the entrance, dropping stones and listening to the eventual splashes. He stared into the hole and, after a while, could discern a faint but unmistakable light, not the fading sunlight getting in from some cleft in the cliff face, but light like a glass of absinthe, the sort of light he'd imagined abyssal creatures that never saw the sun might make to shine their way through the murk.

It wasn't what he'd expected, from what was written in the black book, no towering gate of horn and ivory, no arch of gold and silver guarded by angels or demons or beings men had never fashioned names for, just this unassuming hole in the ground. He sat in the grass, watching the sunset burning day to night, wondering if the Miwok had deserted him. Wondering if the quest had been a fool's errand from the very start, and he'd wasted so many years of his life, and so much of his inheritance, chasing connections and truths that only existed because he wished to see them. By dark, the light shone up through the hole like the chartreuse glare through the grate of an unearthly furnace, taunting or reassuring but beckoning him forward. Promising there was more to come.

"What is it you think you will find?" the old priest had asked after he'd handed over the book. "More to the point, what is it you think will find *you*?"

Not a question he could answer then and not one he could answer sitting there with the roar of the surf in his ears and the stars speckling the sky overhead. The question that Ellen had asked him again and again, and always he'd found some way to deflect her asking. But he *knew* the answer, sewn up somewhere deep within his soul, even if he'd never been able to find the words. Proof that the world did not end at his fingertips or with the unreliable data of his eyes and ears or the lies and half-truths men had written down in science and history books, that everything he'd ever seen was merely a tattered curtain waiting to be drawn back so that some more indisputable light might, at last, shine through.

"Is that what you were seeking, Mr. Dandridge?" and Machen had turned quickly, his heart pounding as he reached for the pistol at his hip, only to find the old Indian watching him from the tall, rustling grass a few feet away. "Is *this* the end of your journey?" and the guide pointed at the hole.

"I thought you were afraid to come here?" Machen asked, annoyed at the interruption, sitting back down beside the hole, looking again into the unsteady yellow-green light spilling out of the earth.

"I was," the Miwok replied. "But the ghost of my grandfather came to me and told me he was ashamed of me, that I was a coward for allowing you to come to this evil place alone. He has promised to protect me from the demons."

"The ghost of your grandfather?" Machen laughed and shook his head, then dropped another pebble into the hole.

"Yes. He is watching us both now, but he also wishes we would leave soon. I can show you the way back to the trail."

The key I have accepted full in the knowledge of its weight.

"You're a brave man," Machen said. "Or another lunatic."

"All brave men are lunatics," the Indian said and glanced nervously at the hole, the starry indigo sky, the cliff and the invisible ocean, each in its turn. "Sane men do not go looking for their deaths."

"Is that all I've found here? My death?"

There was a long moment of anxious silence from the guide, broken only by the ceaseless interwoven roar of the waves and the wind, and then he took a step back away from the hole, deeper into the sheltering pampas grass.

"I cannot say what you have found in this place, Mr. Dandridge. My grandfather says I should not speak its name."

"Is that so? Well, then," and Machen stood, rubbing his aching eyes and brushed the dust from his pants. "You show me the way back and forget you ever brought me out here. Tell your grandfather's poor ghost that I will not hold you responsible for whatever it is I'm meant to find at the bottom of that pit."

"My grandfather hears you," the Miwok said. "He says you are a brave man and a lunatic, and that I should kill you now, before you do the things you will do in the days to come. Before you set the world against itself."

Machen drew his Colt, cocked the hammer with his thumb, and stood staring into the gloom at the Indian.

"But I will not kill you," the Miwok said. "That is *my* choice, and I have chosen not to take your life. But I will pray it is not a decision I will regret later. We should go now."

"After you," Machen said, smiling through the quaver in his voice that he hoped the guide couldn't hear, his heart racing and cold sweat starting to drip from his face despite the night air. And, without another word, the Indian turned and disappeared into the arms of the whispering grass and the August night.

July 1914

When she was very sure that her father had shut the double doors to his study and that her mother was asleep, when the only sounds were the sea and the wind, the inconstant, shifting noises that all houses make after dark, the mice in the walls, Meredith slipped out of bed and into her flannel dressing gown. The floor was cool against her bare feet, cool but not cold. She lit a candle, and then eased the heavy bedroom door shut behind her and went as quickly and quietly as she could to the cramped stairwell leading from the second story to the attic door. At the top, she sat down on the landing and held her breath, listening, praying that no one had heard her, that neither her father nor mother, nor the both of them together, were already trying to find her.

There were no sounds at all from the other side of the narrow attic door. She set the candlestick down and leaned close to it, pressing her lips against the wood, feeling the rough grain through the varnish.

"Avery?" she whispered. "Avery, can you hear me?"

At first there was no reply from the attic, and she took a deep breath and waited a while, waiting for her parents' angry or worried footsteps, waiting for one of them to begin shouting her name from the house below.

But there were no footsteps, and no one called her name.

"*Avery?* Can you hear me? It's *me*, Merry."

That time there was a sudden thumping and a heavy dragging sort of a sound from the other side of the attic door. A body pulling itself roughly, painfully across the pine-board floor towards her, and she closed her eyes and waited for it. Finally, there was a loud thud against the door, and she opened her eyes again. Avery was trying to talk, trying to answer her, but there was nothing familiar or coherent in his ruined voice.

"Hold on," she whispered to him. "I brought a writing pad." She took it out of a pocket of her gown, the pad and a pencil. "Don't try to talk any more. I'll pass this beneath the door to you, and you can write what you want to say. Knock once if you understand what I'm telling you, Avery."

Nothing for almost a full minute and then a single knock so violent that the door shivered on its hinges, so loudly she was sure it would bring her parents running to investigate.

"You must be quieter, Avery," she whispered. "They'll hear us," and now Meredith had begun to notice the odor on the landing, the odor leaking from the attic. Either she'd been much too nervous to notice it at first or her brother had brought it with him when he'd crawled over to the door. Dead fish and boiling cabbage, soured milk and strawberry jam, the time she'd come across the carcass of a grey whale calf, half buried in the sand and decomposing beneath the sun. She swallowed, took another deep breath, and tried not to think about the awful smell.

"I'm going to pass the pencil and a page from the pad to you now. I'm going to slide it under the door to you."

Avery made a wet, strangling sound, and she told him again not to try to talk, just write if he could, write the answers to her questions and anything else that he needed to say.

"Are you in pain? Is there any way I can help?" she asked, and in a moment the tip of the pencil began scritching loudly across the sheet of writing paper. "Not so hard, Avery. If the lead breaks, I'll have to try to find another."

He slid the piece of paper back to her, and it was damp and something dark and sticky was smudged across the bottom. She held it close to her face, never mind the smell so strong it made her gag, made her want to retch, so that she could read what he'd scrawled there. It was nothing like Avery's careful hand, his tight, precise cursive she'd always admired and had tried to imitate, but sweeping, crooked letters, blocky print, and seeing that made her want to cry so badly that she almost forgot about the dead-whale-and-cabbages smell.

HURTSS ME MERY MORE THAN CAN NO
NO HELP NO HELLP ME

She laid down the sheet of paper and tore another from her pad, the pad she used for her afternoon lessons, spelling and arithmetic, and she slid it beneath the door to Avery.

"Avery, you *knew* you couldn't bear the key. You knew it had to be me or mother, *didn't* you? That it had to be a woman?"

Again the scritching, and the paper came back to her even stickier than before.

HAD TO TRY MOTER WOULD NOT LISSEN SO
I HAD TOO TRIE

"Oh, Avery," Meredith said. "I'm sorry," speaking so quietly that she prayed he would not hear, and there were tears in her eyes, hot and bitter. A kind of anger and a kind of sorrow in her heart that she'd never known before, anger and sorrow blooming in her to be fused through some alchemy of the soul, and by that fusion be transformed into a pure and golden hate.

She tore another page from the pad and slipped it through the crack between the floor and the attic door.

"I need to know what to *do*, Avery. I'm reading the newspapers, but I don't understand it all. Everyone seems think war is coming soon, because of the assassination in Sarajevo, because of the Kaiser, but I don't *understand* it all."

It was a long time before the paper came back to her, smeared with slime and stinking of corruption, maybe five minutes of Avery's scritching and his silent pauses between the scritching. This time the page was covered from top to bottom with his clumsy scrawl.

TO LATE ~~IF~~ TO STOP WAR TOO LATE NOW
WAR IS COMING NOW CANT STP THAT MERRY
ALL SET IN MOTION NINTH WAVE REMEMBER?
BUT MERY YOU CAN DONT LISSEN TO FADER
YOU *CAN* HOLD ~~NINE~~ THEE LINE STILL TYME
YOU OR MOTHER KIN HOLD THEE LIN STILL
IT DOEZ NOT HALF TO BE THE *LADST* WAR

When she finished reading and then re-reading twice again everything Avery had written, Meredith lay the sheet of paper down on top of the other two and wiped her hand on the floor until it didn't feel quite so slimy anymore. By the yellow-white light of the candle, her hand shimmered as though she'd been carrying around one of the big banana slugs that lived in the forest. She quickly ripped another page from the writing pad and passed it under the door. This time she felt it snatched from her fingers, and the scritching began immediately. It came back to her only a few seconds later and the pencil with it, the tip ground away to nothing.

DUNT *EVER* COME BAK HERE AGIN MERRY
I LOVE YOU ALWAYTS AND WONT FERGET YOU
PROMISS ME YOU WILL KNOT COME BACK
HOLD THEE LINE HOLD THE LINE

"I can't promise you that, Avery," she replied, sobbing and leaning close to the door, despite the smell so strong that it had begun to burn her nose and the back of her throat. "You're my brother, and I can't ever promise you that."

There was another violent thud against the door then, so hard that her father was sure to have heard, so sudden that it scared her, and Meredith jumped back and reached for the candlestick.

"I remember the ninth wave, Avery. I remember what you said—the ninth wave, greater than the last, all in flame. I *do* remember."

And because she thought that perhaps she heard footsteps from somewhere below, and because she couldn't stand to hear the frantic strangling sounds that Avery had begun making again, Meredith hastily gathered up the sticky, scribbled-on pages from the pad and then crept down the attic stairs and back to her bedroom. She fell asleep just before dawn and dreamt of flames among the breakers, an inferno crashing against the rocks.

March 1915

"This is where it ends," Merry, her mother's ghost said. "But this is where it begins, as well. You need to understand that if you understand nothing else."

Meredith knew that this time she was not dreaming, no matter how much it might *feel* like a dream, this dazzling, tumbling nightmare wide-awake that began when she reached the foot of the rickety spiraling staircase leading her down into the deep place beneath the house. Following her mother's ghost, the dim glow of a spectre to be her Virgil, her Beatrice, her guiding lantern until the light from the pool was so bright it outshone Ellen Dandridge's flickering radiance. Meredith stood on the pier, holding her dead mother's barnacle-and algae-encrusted hand, and stared in fear and wonder towards the island in the pool.

"The infinite lines of causation," the ghost said. "What has brought you here. That is important, as well."

"I'm here because my father is a fool," Meredith replied, unable to look away from the yellow-green light dancing across the stone, shining up from the depths beneath her bare feet.

"No, dear. He is only a man trying to do the work of gods. That never turns out well."

The black eye set deep into the flesh of Meredith's palm itched painfully and then rolled back to show its dead-white sclera. She knew exactly what it was seeing, because it always told her; she knew how close they were to the veil, how little time was left before the breach tore itself open once and for all.

"Try to forget your father, child. Concentrate on time and space, the aether, on the history that has brought you here. All the strands of the web."

Meredith squeezed the ghost's soft hand, and the dates and names and places spilled through her like the sea spilling across the shore, a flood of obvious and obscure connections, and she gritted her teeth and let them come.

On December 2, 1870, Bismarck sends a letter to Wilhelm of Prussia urging him to become Kaiser. In 1874, all Jesuits are ordered to leave Italy, and on January 8th, 1877, Crazy Horse is defeated by the U.S. cavalry at Wolf Mountain in Montana. In June 1881, Austria signs a secret treaty with the Serbs, establishing an economic and political protectorate, and Milan is crowned King of Serbia—

"It hurts," she whispered; her mother frowned and nodded her head as the light from the pool began to pulse and spin, casting counterclockwise glare and shadow across the towering rock walls.

"It will always hurt, dear. It will be pain beyond imagining. You cannot be lied to about that. You cannot be led to bear this weight in ignorance of the pain that comes with the key."

Meredith took another hesitant step towards the end of the short pier, and then another, and the light swelled angrily and spun hurricane fury below and about her.

"They are rising, Merry. They have teeth and claws sharp as steel, and will devour you if you don't hurry. You must go to the island now. The breach is opening."

"I am afraid, mother. I'm so sorry, but I *am* afraid."

"Then the fear will lead you where I can't. Make the fear your shield. Make the fear your lance."

Standing at the very end of the pier, Meredith didn't dare look down into the shining pool, kept her eyes on the tiny island only fifteen or twenty feet away.

"They took the boat when you crossed over," she said to her mother's ghost. "How am I supposed to reach the gate when they've taken the boat away?"

"You're a strong swimmer, child. Avery taught you to swim."

A sound like lightning, and *No,* she thought. *I can't do that. I can do anything except step off this pier into that water with them. I can stand the pain, but—*

"If you know another way, Merry, then take it. But there isn't much time left. The lines are converging."

Merry took a deep breath, gulping the cavern's dank and foetid air, hyperventilating, bracing for the breathless cold to come, all the things that her brother had taught her about swimming in the sea. Together they'd swum out past the breakers, to the kelp forest in the deep water farther offshore, the undulating submarine weald where bat rays and harbor seals raced between the gigantic stalks of kelp, where she'd looked up and seen the lead-pale belly of an immense white shark passing silently overhead.

"Time, Merry. It is all in your hands now. See how you stand alone at the center of the web and the strands stretch away from you? See the intersections and interweaves?"

"I see them," she said. "I see them all," and she stepped off into the icy water.

October 30th, 1883, an Austro-German treaty with Romania is signed, providing Romania defence against the Russians. November 17th, 1885, the Serbs are defeated at the Battle of Slivnitza and then ultimately saved only by Austrian intervention. 1887, and the Mahdist War with Abyssinia begins. 1889, and a boy named Silas Desvernine sails up the Hudson River and first sees a mountain where a nameless being of moonlight and thunder is held inside a black stone. August 1889, and her father is led to the edge of the Pacific by a Miwok guide. August 27th, 1891, the Franco-Russian Entente—

The strands of the web, the ticking of a clock, the life and death of stars, each step towards Armageddon checked off in her aching head, and the water is liquid ice threatening to freeze her alive. Suddenly, the tiny island seemed miles and miles away.

1895 August, and Kaiser Wilhelm visits England for Queen Victoria's Golden Jubilee. 1896, Charles E. Callwell of the British Army publishes Small Wars— Their Principles and Practice. *February 4th, 1899, the year Aguinaldo leads a Philippine Insurrection against U.S. forces—*

All of these events, all of these men and their actions. Lies and blood and betrayals, links in the chain leading, finally, to this moment, to that ninth wave, mightier than the last, all in flame. Meredith swallowed a mouthful of sea water and struggled to keep her head above the surface.

"Hurry, child!" her mother's ghost shouted from the pier. "They are rising," and Meredith Dandridge began to pray then that she would fail, would surrender in another moment or two and let the deep have her. Imagined sinking down and down for all eternity, pressure to crush her flat and numb, to crush her so small that nothing and no one would ever have any need to harm her again.

Something sharp as steel swiped across her ankle, slicing her skin, and her blood mingled with the sea.

And the next stroke drove her fingers into the mud and pebbles at the edge of the island. She dragged herself quickly from the pool, from the water and the mire, and looked back the way she'd come. There were no demons in the water, and her mother's ghost wasn't watching from the pier. But her father was, Machen Dandridge and his terrible black book, his eyes upturned and arms outstretched to an indifferent Heaven. She cursed him for the last time ever and ignored the blood oozing from the ugly gash in her right foot.

"This is where I stand," she said, getting to her feet and turning towards the small cave at the center of the island, her legs as weak and unsteady as a newborn foal's. "At the bottom gate, and I hold the key to the abyss."

The yellow-green light was almost blinding, and soon the pool would begin to boil.

"The ebony key to the first day and the last, the key to the moment when the stars wink out one by one and the sea heaves its rotting belly at the empty, sagging sky. The blazing key that even angels fear to keep."

For an instant, there was no cave, and no pool, and no cavern beneath a resentful, wicked house. Only the fire, pouring from the cave that was no longer there, to swallow her whole, only the voices of the void, and Meredith Dandridge made her fear a shield and a lance and held the line.

And in the days and weeks that followed, sometimes Machen Dandridge came down the stairs to stand on the pier and gaze across the pool to the place where the thing that had been his daughter nestled in the shadows, in the hollows between the stones. And every day the sea gave her more of its armour, gilding her frail human skin with the calcareous shells and stinging tentacles that other creatures had spent countless cycles of Creation refining from the rawest matter of life, the needle teeth, the scales and poisonous barbs. Where his wife and son had failed, his daughter crouched triumphant as any martyr. And sometimes, late at night, alone with the sound of the surf pounding against the edge of the continent, he sometimes thought of setting fire to the house and letting it burn down around him.

He read the newspapers.

He watched the stars for signs and portents.

When the moon was bright, the odd, mute women still came to dance beside the sea, but he'd begun to believe they were only bad memories from some time before, and so he rarely paid them any heed.

When the weather was good, he climbed the hills behind the house and sat at the grave of his dead wife and whispered to her, telling her how proud he was of Meredith, reciting snatches of half-remembered poetry for Ellen, telling her the world would come very close to the brink because of what he'd done. Because of his blind pride. But, in the end, it would survive because of what their daughter had done and would do for ages yet.

On a long rainy afternoon in May, he opened the attic door and killed what he found there with an axe and his old Colt revolver. He buried it beside his wife, but left nothing to mark Avery's grave.

He wrote long letters to men he'd once known in England and New York and Rio de Janeiro, but there were never any replies.

And time rolled on, neither malign nor beneficent, settling across the universe like the grey caul of dust settling thick upon the relics he'd brought back from India and Iran and the Sudan a quarter of a century before. The birth and death of stars, light reaching his aging eyes after a billion years racing across the near-vacuum, and sometimes he spent the days gathering fossils from the cliffs and arranging them in precise geometric patterns in the tall grass around the house. He left lines of salt and drew elaborate runes, the meanings of which he'd long since forgotten.

His daughter spoke to him only in his dreams, or hers, no way to ever be sure which was which, and her voice grew stronger and more terrible as the years rushed past. In the end, she was a maelstrom to swallow his withered soul, to rock him to sleep one last time, to show him the way across.

And the house by the sea, weathered and weary and insane, kept its secrets.

ꝫ ꝫ

The Tugging

Ramsey Campbell

I

When Ingels awoke he knew at once he'd been dreaming again. There was an image, a memory clamouring faintly but urgently at the edge of his mind; he snatched at it, but it was gone. He swung himself off the crumpled bed. Hilary must have gone to do her research in the library hours ago, leaving him a cold breakfast. Outside hung a chill glazed blue sky, and frost was fading from the windowpane.

The dream continued to nag at his mind. He let it pluck at him, hoping that the nagging would turn by itself into memory. He slowed himself down, dressing slowly, eating slowly, to allow the memory to catch up. But there was only the insistence, like a distant recollection of a plucked tooth. Through the wall he could hear a radio announcer's voice in the next flat, a blurred cadence rising as if to leap a barrier that obscured its words completely. It buzzed at his mind, bumbling. He washed up quickly, irritably, and hurried out.

And found that he couldn't look up at the sky.

The feeling seized his neck like a violent cramp, forcing his head down.

27

Around him women were wheeling prams in which babies and groceries fought for space, dogs were playing together in the alleys, buses quaked at bus stops, farting. But on Ingels, pressing down from a clear rather watery blue expanse to which he couldn't even raise his eyes, weighed a sense of intolerable stress, as if the calm sky were stretched to splitting: as if it were about to split and to let his unformed fear through at him.

A bus braked, a long tortured scraping squeal. When Ingels recovered from his heart-clutching start he'd jolted off the fear. He ran for the bus as the last of the queue shuffled on. Scared of the sky indeed, he thought. I've got to get more sleep. Pill myself to sleep if I have to. His eyes felt as if floating in quicklime.

He sat among the coughing shoppers. Across the aisle a man shook his head at the tobacco-smoke, snorting like a horse. A woman threw herself and three carrier bags on to a seat, patting them reassuringly, and slammed her predecessor's open window. Ingels rummaged in his briefcase. He'd left one notebook at his own flat, he discovered, muttering. He flicked through the notes for his column, holding them flat on his briefcase. Wonder if the fellow whose knee I'm fighting recognises my style. World's champion egotist, he re-buked himself, hiding the notes with his forearm. Don't worry, he won't steal the copyright, he scoffed, pulling his arm back. He put the notes away. They looked as bleary as he felt.

He gazed around the bus, at the flat stagnant smoke, at the ranks of heads like wig-blocks, and settled on headlines over the shoulder in front of him:

IS THE SOLAR SYSTEM ON TOW?

Six months ago an amateur astronomer wrote to us, warning that a planet might pass dangerously close to Earth.
THE ASTRONOMER ROYAL'S COMMENT:
"UTTER TWADDLE".
Now the world's leading astronomers have agreed to let us have the facts.
TODAY WE TELL ALL.
In an exclusive interview

But he'd turned over, to the smaller print of the story. Ingels sat back again, remembering how the Herald had received a copy of that letter six months ago. They hadn't published it, and the letters editor had gazed at In-gels pityingly when he'd suggested they might at least follow it up. "I suppose you arts people need imagination," he'd said. Ingels grimaced wryly, wondering how they would handle the story in tonight's edition. He leaned forward, but the man had reached the editorial comment: "Even if his aim was to prevent panic, are we paying the Astronomer Royal to tell us what too many people are now suggesting was a lie?"

Ingels glanced out of the window. Offices flashed past, glazed displays of figures at desks, the abrupt flight of perspective down alleys with a shock like a fall in a dream, more displays. The offices thinned out and aged as the bus gathered speed towards the edge of Brichester. Nearly there, Ingels thought, then realised with a leap from his seat that he'd passed the Herald building three stops back. For a second he knew where he'd been heading. So what? he thought savagely, the rims of his eyes rusty and burning, as he clattered downstairs. But once he was on the street he wished that he'd thought to remember: now he couldn't imagine where he could have been going in that direction.

BRICHESTER HERALD: BRICHESTER'S EVENING VOICE. The iron poem (two-thirds of a haiku, he'd thought until he grew used to it) clung to the bricks above him. The foyer was quiet. He wondered how long it would be before the presses began to thump heartily, disproving the soundproofing. Not long, and he had to write his column.

His mind felt flat and empty as the elevator. He drifted numbly through the hundred-yard open-plan office, past the glancing heads behind glass personalised in plastic. Some looked away quickly, some stared, some smiled. My God, I don't even know his name, Ingels thought of several. "Hello, Moira," he said. "How's it going, Bert." Telephones shrilled, were answered, their calls leapt prankishly across the floor. Reporters sidestepped through the aisles. Smells of deodorant and sweat, tang of ink, brandished paper, scurrying typewriters, hasty agitated conferences.

Bert had been following him to his desk. "Don't wait for your personal bulletin," Bert said, throwing a telex sheet on the desk. "The latest on your wandering planet."

"Don't tell me I've convinced you at last."

"No chance," Bert said, retreating. "Just so you don't start turning the place upside down for it."

Ingels read the sheet, thinking: I could have told them this six months ago. The Americans had admitted that an unmanned probe was well on its way to photograph the wanderer. He rested his elbow on the desk and covered his eyes. Against the restless patches of light he almost glimpsed what he'd dreamed. He started, bewildered; the noise of the newspaper poured into him. Enough, he thought, sorting out his notes.

He typed the television review—a good play from Birmingham, when are we going to see a studio in Brichester—and passed it to Bert. Then he pawed desultorily at the day's accumulation on his desk. Must go and see my folks this week. Might drain my tension a little. He turned over a brown envelope. A press ticket, elaborately pretty lettering: exhibition of associational painting—the new primitivism and surrealism. Ug, he thought, and whatever you say to surrealists. Private view this afternoon. Which means now. "You can have a local arts review tomorrow," he said, showing the ticket to Bert, and went out.

Once out of the building his mind teetered like a dislocated compass. Again the sky seemed brittle glass, ready to crack, and when he moved to shake off the obsession he found himself urged towards the edge of Brichester. A woman flinched from him as he snarled himself to a halt. "Sorry," he called after her. Whatever's in that direction, it isn't the show I've been invited to. But there must be something there. Maybe I went there when I was young. Have a look when I can. Before I sleepwalk there.

Although he could have taken a bus into Lower Brichester, where the exhibition was, he walked. Clear my head, perhaps, if I don't get high on petrol first. The sky was thin and blue; nothing more, now. He swung his briefcase. Haven't heard of these artists before. Who knows, they could be good.

He hadn't been through Lower Brichester for months, and was taken aback by its dereliction. Dogs scrabbled clattering in gouged shop-fronts, an uprooted streetlamp lay across a road, humped earth was scattered with disembowelled mattresses, their entrails fluttering feebly. He passed houses where one window was blinded with brick, the next still open and filmy with a drooping curtain. He examined his ticket. Believe it or not, I'm on the right track.

Soon whole streets were derelict. There was nothing but Ingels, the gaping houses and uneven pavements, the discreet sky, his footsteps alone; the rush of the city was subdued, quiescent. The houses went by, shoulder to shoulder, ribs open to the sky, red-brick fronts revealing their jumble of shattered walls and staircases. Ingels felt a lurking sympathy for the area in its abandonment, its indifference to time. He slowed down, strolling. Let myself go a bit. The private view's open for hours yet. Relax. He did, and felt an irrational impulse pleading with him.

And why not, he thought. He glanced about: nobody. Then he began to lope through the deserted streets, arms hanging, fingers almost touching the road. Unga bunga, he thought. One way to prepare myself for the primitives, I suppose.

He found his behaviour touched a memory; perhaps the memory was its source. A figure running crouched through ruins, somewhere nearby. A kind of proof of virility. But they hadn't been deserted city streets, he thought, loping. Just flat blocks of black rock in which square windows gaped. Abandoned long before but hardly affected by time. A figure running along a narrow path through the stone, not looking at the windows.

Clouds were creeping into the sky; darkness was suffusing the streets around him. Ingels ran, not looking at the houses, allowing them to merge with the memory they touched. It was coming clearer. You had to run all the way along one of the stone paths. Any path at all, for there were no intersections, just a straight unbroken run. You had to run fast, before something within the windows became aware of you, rather as a carnivorous plant becomes aware of a fly. The last part of the run was the worst, because you knew that at any moment something would appear in all the windows at once: things that, although they had mouths, were not faces—

Ingels stumbled wildly as he halted, glaring up at the empty windows of the houses. What on earth was that? he thought distractedly. Like one of those dreams I used to have, the ones that were so vivid. Of course, that's what it must have been. These streets reminded me of one of them. Though the memory felt much older, somehow. From the womb, no doubt, he shouted angrily at his pounding heart.

When he reached the exhibition he walked straight past it. Returning, he peered at the address on the ticket. My God, this is it. Two of a street of dingy but tenanted terraced houses had been run together; on the front door of one, in lettering he'd taken for graffiti, were the words LOWER BRICHESTER ARTS LAB. He recalled how, when it had opened last year, the invitations to the opening had arrived two days later. The project he'd described after a hurried telephone interview hadn't looked at all like this. Oh well, he thought, and went in.

In the hall, by the reception desk, two clowns were crawling about with children on their backs. One of the children ran behind the desk and gazed up at Ingels. "Do you know where the exhibition is?" he said. "Up your arse," she said, giggling. "First floor up," said one of the clowns, who Ingels now realised was a made-up local poet, and chased the children into a playroom full of inflatables.

The first floor was a maze of plywood partitions in metal frames. On the partitions hung paintings and sketches. As Ingels entered, half a dozen people converged on him, all the artists save one, who was trying to relight a refractory cone of incense. Feeling outnumbered, Ingels wished he'd made it to the maze. "You've just missed the guy from Radio Brichester," one said. "Are you going to talk to all of us, like him?" another asked. "Do you like modern art?" "Do you want coffee?"

"Now leave him be," said Annabel Pringle, as Ingels recognised her from her picture on the cover of the catalogue. "They're new to exhibiting, you see, you can't blame them. I mean, this whole show is my idea but their enthusiasm. Now I can explain the principles as you go round if you like, or you can read them in the catalogue."

"The latter, thanks." Ingels hurried into the maze, opening the typed catalogue. A baby with an ear-trumpet, which was 2: Untitled. 3 was a man throwing his nose into a wastebasket, and Untitled. 4: Untitled. 5, 6, 7— Well, their paintings are certainly better than their prose, Ingels thought. The incense unravelled ahead of him. A child playing half-submerged in a lake. A blackened green-tinged city shouldering up from the sea. A winged top hat gliding over a jungle. Suddenly Ingels stopped short and turned back to the previous painting. He was sure he had seen it before.

22: Atlantis. But it wasn't like any Atlantis he'd seen pictured. The technique was crude and rather banal, obviously one of the primitives, yet Ingels found that it touched images buried somewhere in him. Its leaning slabs of rock felt vast, the sea poured from its surfaces as if it had just exploded triumphantly into sight. Drawn closer, Ingels peered into the darkness within a slab of rock, beyond what might be an open doorway. If there were the outline of a pale face staring featurelessly up from within the rock, its owner must be immense. If there were, Ingels thought, withdrawing: but why should he feel there ought to be?

When he'd hurried around the rest of the exhibition he tried to ask about the painting, but Annabel Pringle headed him off. "You understand what we mean by associational painting?" she demanded. "Let me tell you. We select an initial idea by aleatory means."

"Eh?" Ingels said, scribbling.

"Based on chance. We use the I Ching, like John Cage. The American composer, he originated it. Once we have the idea we silently associate from it until each of us has an idea they feel they must communicate. This exhibition is based on six initial ideas. You can see the diversity."

"Indeed," Ingels said. "When I said eh I was being an average reader of our paper, you understand. Listen, the one that particularly interested me was number 22. I'd like to know how that came about."

"That's mine," one young man said, leaping up as if it were House.

"The point of our method," Annabel Pringle said, gazing at the painter, "is to erase all the associational steps from your mind, leaving only the image you paint. Of course Clive here wouldn't remember what led up to that painting."

"No, of course," Ingels said numbly. "It doesn't matter. Thank you. Thanks all very much." He hurried downstairs, past a sodden clown, and into the street. In fact it didn't matter. A memory had torn its way through his insomnia. For the second time that day he realised why something had looked familiar, but this time more disturbingly. Decades ago he had himself dreamed the city in the painting.

II

Ingels switched off the television. As the point of light dwindled into darkness it touched off the image in him of a gleam shooting away into space. Then he saw that the light hadn't sunk into darkness but into Hilary's reflection, leaning forward from the cane rocking-chair next to him, about to speak. "Give me fifteen minutes," he said, scribbling notes for his review.

The programme had shown the perturbations which the wandering planet had caused in the orbits of Pluto, Neptune and Uranus, and had begun and ended by pointing out that the planet was now swinging away from the Solar System; its effect on Earth's orbit would be negligible. Photographs from the space-probe were promised within days. Despite its cold scientific clarity (Ingels wrote) and perhaps without meaning to, the programme managed to communicate a sense of foreboding, of the intrusion into and interference with our familiar skies. "Not to me it didn't," Hilary said, reading over his shoulder.

"That's sad," he said. "I was going to tell you about my dreams."

"Don't if I wouldn't understand them either. Aren't I allowed to criticise now?"

"Sorry. Let's start again. Just let me tell you a few of the things that have happened to me. I was thinking of them all today. Some of them even you'll have to admit are strange. Make some coffee and I'll tell you about them."

When she'd brought the coffee he waited until she sat forward, ready to be engrossed, long soft black hooks of hair angling for her jawbone. "I used to dream a lot when I was young," he said. "Not your average childhood dream, if there is such a thing. There was one I remember, about these enormous clouds of matter floating in outer space, forming very slowly into something. I mean very slowly … I woke up long before they got there, yet while I was dreaming I knew whatever it was would have a face, and that made me very anxious to wake up. Then there was another where I was being carried through a kind of network of light, on and on across intersections for what felt like days, until I ended up on the edge of this gigantic web of paths of light. And I was fighting to stop myself going in, because I knew that hiding behind the light there was something old and dark and shapeless, something dried-up and evil that I couldn't make out. I could hear it rustling like an old dry spider. You know what I suddenly realised that web was? My brain, I'd been chasing along my nervous system to my brain. Well, leave that one to the psychologists. But there were odd things about these dreams—I mean, apart from all that. They always used to begin the same way, and always about the same time of the month."

"The night of the full moon?" Hilary said, slurping coffee.

"Funnily enough, yes. Don't worry, I didn't sprout midnight shadow or anything. But some people are sensitive to the full moon, that's well enough documented. And I always used to begin by dreaming I could see the full moon over the sea, way out in the middle of the ocean. I could see the reflection resting on the water, and after a while I'd always find myself thinking it wasn't the moon at all but a great pale face peering up out of the ocean, and I'd panic. Then I wouldn't be able to move and I'd know that the full moon was pulling at something deep in the ocean, waking it up. I'd feel my panic swelling up in me, and all of a sudden it would burst and I'd be in the next dream. That's how it happened, every time."

"Didn't your parents know? Didn't they try to find out what was wrong?"

"I don't know what you mean by wrong. But yes, they knew eventually, when I told them. That was after I had the idea my father might be able to explain. I was eleven then and I'd had strange feelings sometimes, intuitions and premonitions and so forth, and sometimes I'd discovered they'd been my father's feelings too."

"I know all about your father's feelings," Hilary said. "More than he knows about mine."

Soon after they'd met, Ingels had taken her to see his parents. She'd felt his father had been too stiffly polite to her, and when she'd cross-examined Ingels he'd eventually admitted that his father had felt she was wrong for him, unsympathetic to him. "You were going to let me tell you about my dreams," he said. "I told my father about the sea dream and I could see there was something he wasn't saying. My mother had to make him tell me. Her attitude to the whole thing was rather what yours would have been, but she told him to get it over with, he'd have to tell me sometime. So he told me he'd sometimes shared his father's dreams without either of them ever knowing why. And he'd had several of my dreams when he'd been young, until one night in the mid-twenties—early 1925, I think he said. Then he'd dreamed a city had risen out of the sea. After that he'd never dreamed again. Well, maybe hearing that was some kind of release for me, because the next time I dreamed of the city too."

"You dreamed of a city," Hilary said.

"The same one. I told him about it next morning, details of it he hadn't told me, that were the same in both our dreams. I was watching the sea, the same place as always. Don't ask me how I knew it was always the same. I knew. One moment I was watching the moon on the water, then I saw it was trembling. The next moment an island rose out of the ocean with a roaring like a waterfall, louder than that, louder than anything I've ever heard while awake; I could actually feel my ears bursting. There was a city on the island, all huge greenish blocks with sea and seaweed pouring off them. And the mud was boiling with stranded creatures, panting and bursting. Right in front of me and above me and below me there was a door. Mud was trickling down from it, and I knew that the great pale face I was terrified of was behind the door, getting ready to come out, opening its eyes in the dark. I woke up then, and that was the end of the dreams. Say they were only dreams if you like. You might find it easiest to believe my father and I were sharing them by telepathy."

"You know perfectly well," Hilary said, "that I'd find nothing of the sort."

"No? Then try this," he said sharply. "At the exhibition I visited today there was a painting of our dream. And not by either of us."

"So what does that mean?" she cried. "What on earth is that supposed to mean?"

'Well, a dream I can recall so vividly after all this time is worth a thought. And that painting suggests it's a good deal more objectively real."

"So your father read about the island in a story," she said. "So did you, so did the painter. What else can you possibly be suggesting?"

"Nothing," he said at last.

"So what were the other strange things you were going to tell me?"

"That's all," he said. "Just the painting. Nothing else. Really." She was looking miserable, a little ashamed. "Don't you believe me?" he said. "Come here."

As the sheepskin rug joined their caresses she said "I don't really need to be psychic for you, do I?"

"No," he said, probing her ear with his tongue, triggering her ready. Switching off the goose-necked steel lamps as she went, she led him through the flat as if wheeling a basket behind her; they began laughing as a car's beam shone up from Mercy Hill and seized for a moment on her hand, his handle. They reached the crisp bed and suddenly, urgently, couldn't prolong their play. She was all around him, working to draw him deeper and out, he was lapped softly, thrusting roughly at her grip on him to urge it to return redoubled. They were rising above everything but each other, gasping. He felt himself rushing to a height, and closed his eyes.

And was falling into a maelstrom of flesh, in a vast almost lightless cave whose roof seemed as far above him as the sky. He had a long way still to fall, and beneath him he could make out the movements of huge bubbles and ropes of flesh, of eyes swelling and splitting the flesh, of gigantic dark green masses climbing sluggishly over one another. "No, Christ no," he cried, gripped helpless.

He slumped on Hilary. "Oh God," she said. "What is it now?"

He lay beside her. Above them the ceiling shivered with reflected light. It looked as he felt. He closed his eyes and found dark calm, but couldn't bear to keep them closed for long. "All right," he said. "There's more I haven't told you. I know you've been worried about how I've looked lately. I told you it was lack of sleep, and so it is, but it's because I've begun dreaming again. It started about nine months ago, just before I met you, and it's becoming more frequent, once or twice a week now. Only this time I can never remember what it is, perhaps because I haven't dreamed for so long. I think it has something to do with the sky, maybe this planet we've been hearing about. The last time was this morning, after you went to the library. For some reason I don't have them when I'm with you."

"Of course if you want to go back to your place, go ahead," Hilary said, gazing at the ceiling.

"In one way I don't," he said. "That's just the trouble. Whenever I try to dream I find I don't want to sleep, as if I'm fighting the dream. But today I'm tired enough just to drift off and have it anyway. I've been getting hallucinations all day that I think are coming from the dream. And it feels more urgent, somehow. I've got to have it. I knew it was important before, but that painting's made me sure it's more than a dream. I wish you could understand this. It's not easy for me."

"Suppose I did believe you?" she said. "What on earth would you do then? Stand on the street warning people? Or would you try to sell it to your paper? I don't want to believe you, how can you think they would?"

"That's exactly the sort of thing I don't need to hear," Ingels said. "I want to talk to my father about it. I think he may be able to help. Maybe you wouldn't mind not coming with me."

"I wouldn't want to," she said. "You go and have your dream and your chat with your father if you want. But as far as I'm concerned that means you don't want me."

Ingels walked to his flat, further up Mercy Hill. Newspapers clung to bushes, flapping; cars hissed through nearby streets, luminous waves. Only the houses stood between him and the sky, their walls seeming low and thin. Even in the pools of lamplight he felt the night gaping overhead.

The building where he lived was silent. The stereo that usually thumped like an electronic heart was quiet. Ingels climbed to the third floor, his footsteps dropping wooden blocks into the silence, nudging him awake. He fumbled in his entrance hall for the coat hook on the back of the door, which wasn't where Hilary kept hers. Beneath the window in the main room he saw her desk spread with her syndicated cartoon strip—except that when he switched on the light it was his own desk, scattered with television schedules. He peered blearily at the rumpled bed. Around him the room felt and moved like muddy water. He sagged on the bed and was asleep at once.

The darkness drew him out, coaxing him forward, swimming softly through his eyes. A great silent darkness surrounded him. He sailed through it, sleeping yet aware. He sensed energy flowering far out in the darkness, vast soundless explosions that cooled and congealed. He sensed immense weights slowly rolling at the edge of his blindness.

Then he could see, though the darkness persisted almost unchanged. Across its furthest distances a few points of light shone like tiny flaws. He began to sail towards them, faster. They parted and fled to the edge of his vision as he approached. He was rushing between them, towards others that now swooped minutely out of the boundless night, carrying cooler grains of congealed dust around them. They were multiplying, his vision was filling with sprinkled light and its attendant parasites. He was turning, imprinting each silently blazing vista on his mind. His mind felt enormous. He felt it take each pattern of light and store it easily as it returned alert for the next.

It was so long before he came to rest he had no conscious memory of starting out. Somehow the path he'd followed had brought him back to his point of origin. Now he sailed in equilibrium with the entire system of light and dust that surrounded him, boundless. His mind locked on everything he'd seen.

He found that part of his mind had fastened telescopically on details of the worlds he'd passed: cities of globes acrawl with black winged insects; mountains carved or otherwise formed into heads within whose hollow sockets worshippers squirmed; a sea from whose depths rose a jointed arm, reaching miles inland with a filmy web of skin to net itself food. One tiny world in particular seemed to teem with life that was aware of him.

Deep in one of its seas a city slept, and he shared the dreams of its sleepers: of an infancy spent in a vast almost lightless cave, tended by a thin rustling shape so tall its head was lost to sight; of flight to this minute but fecund planet; of dancing hugely and clumsily beneath the light of a fragment they'd torn free of this world and flung into space; of dormancy in the submarine basalt tombs. Dormant, they waited and shared the lives of other similar beings active on the surface; for a moment he was the inhabitant of a black city deserted by its builders, coming alert and groping lazily forth as a pale grub fled along a path between the buildings.

Later, as the active ones on the surface had to hide from the multiplying grubs, those in the submarine city stilled, waiting. Ingels felt their thoughts searching sleepily, ranging the surface, touching and sampling the minds of the grubs, vastly patient and purposeful. He felt the womb of the sea lapping his cell. His huge flesh quivered, anticipating rebirth.

Without warning he was in a room, gazing through a telescope at the sky. He seemed to have been gazing for hours; his eyes burned. He was referring to a chart, adjusting the mounting of the telescope. A pool of light from an oil lamp roved, snatching at books in cases against the walls, spilling over the charts at his feet. Then he was outside the room, hurrying through a darkened theatre; cowls of darkness peered down from the boxes. Outside the theatre he glanced up towards the speckled sky, towards the roof, where he knew one slate hid the upturned telescope. He hurried away through the gas-lit streets, out of Ingels' dream.

He awoke and knew at once where the theatre was: at the edge of Brichester, where his mind had been tugging him all day.

III

He rose at dawn, feeling purged and refreshed. He washed, shaved, dressed, made himself breakfast. In his lightened state the preamble of his dream seemed not to matter: he'd had his inclination towards the edge of Brichester explained; the rest seemed external to him, perhaps elaborately symbolic. He knew Hilary regarded his dreams as symptoms of disturbance, and perhaps she was right. Maybe, he thought, they all meant the theatre was trying to get up through my mind. A lot of fuss, but that's what dreams are like. Especially when they're having to fight their way, no doubt. Can't wait to see what the theatre means to me.

When he went out the dawn clutched him as if he hadn't shaken off his dreams. The dull laden light settled about him, ambiguous shapes hurried by. The air felt suffocated by imminence, not keen as the cold should make it. That'll teach me to get up at cock-crow, he thought. Feels like insomnia. Can't imagine what they find to crow about. The queues of commuters moved forward like the tickings of doom.

Someone had left a sheet from the telex on his desk. Photographs from the space probe were expected any hour. He wrote his reviews hurriedly, glancing up to dispel a sense that the floor was alive with pale grubs, teeming through the aisles. Must have needed more sleep than I thought. Maybe catch a nap later.

Although his dream had reverted the streets, replacing the electric lamps with gas, he knew exactly where the theatre should be. He hurried along the edge of Lower Brichester, past champing steam-shovels, roaring skeletons of burning houses. He strode straight to the street of his dream.

One side was razed, a jagged strip of brown earth extending cracks into the pavement and into the fields beyond. But the theatre was on the other side. Ingels hurried past the red-brick houses, past the wind-whipped gardens and broken flowers, towards the patched gouge in the road where he knew a gas lamp used to guard the theatre. He stood arrested on it, cars sweeping past, and stared at the houses before him, safe from his glare in their sameness. The theatre was not there.

Only the shout of an overtaking car roused him. He wandered along, feeling sheepish and absurd. He remembered vaguely having walked this way with his parents once, on the way to a picnic. The gas lamp had been standing then; he'd gazed at it and at the theatre, which by then was possessed by a cinema, until they'd coaxed him away. Which explained the dream, the insomnia, everything. And I never used to be convinced by *Citizen Kane*. Rosebud to me too, with knobs on. In fact he'd even mistaken the location of the lamp; there it was, a hundred yards ahead of him. Suddenly he began to run. Already he could see the theatre, now renamed as a furniture warehouse.

He was almost through the double doors and into the first aisle of suites when he realised that he didn't know what he was going to say. Excuse me, I'd like to look under your rafters. Sorry to bother you, but I believe you have a secret room here. For God's sake, he said, blushing, hurrying down the steps as a salesman came forward to open the doors for him. I know what the dream was now. I've made sure I won't have it again. Forget the rest.

He threw himself down at his desk. Now sit there and behave. What a piddling reason for falling out with Hilary. At least I can admit that to her. Call her now. He was reaching for the telephone when Bert tramped up, waving Ingels' review of the astronomical television programme. "I know you'd like to rewrite this," he said.

"Sorry about that."

"We'll call off the men in white this time. Thought you'd gone the same way as this fellow," Bert said, throwing a cutting on the desk.

"Just lack of sleep," Ingels said, not looking. "As our Methuselah, tell me something. When the warehouse on Fieldview was a theatre, what was it called?"

"The Variety, you mean?" Bert said, dashing for his phone. "Remind me to tell you about the time I saw Beaumont and Fletcher performing there. Great double act."

Ingels turned the cutting over, smiling half at Bert, half at himself for the way he had still not let go of his dream. Go on, look through the files in your lunch-hour, he told himself satirically. Bet the Variety never made a headline in its life.

LSD CAUSES ATTEMPTED SUICIDE, said the cutting. American student claims that in LSD "vision" he was told that the planet now passing through our solar system heralded the rising of Atlantis. Threw himself from second-storey window. Insists that the rising of Atlantis means the end of humanity. Says the Atlanteans are ready to awaken. Ingels gazed at the cutting; the sounds of the newspaper surged against his ears like blood. Suddenly he thrust back his chair and ran upstairs, to the morgue of the *Herald*.

Beneath the ceiling pressed low by the roof, a fluorescent tube fluttered and buzzed. Ingels hugged the bound newspapers to his chest, each volume an armful, and hefted them to a table, where they puffed out dust. 1900 was the first that came to hand. The streets would have been gas-lit then. Dust trickled into his nostrils and frowned over him, the phone next to Hilary was mute, his television review plucked at his mind, anxious to be rewritten. Scanning and blinking, he tried to shake them off with his doubts.

But it didn't take him long, though his gaze was tired of ranging up and down, up and down, by the time he saw the headline:

ATTEMPTED THEFT AT "THE VARIETY." TRADESMEN IN THE DOCK.

Francis Wareing, a draper pursuing his trade in Brichester, Donald Norden, a butcher [and so on, Ingels snarled, sweeping past impatiently] were charged before the Brichester stipendiary magistrates with forcibly entering "The Variety" theatre, on Fieldview, in attempted commission of robbery. Mr. Radcliffe, the owner and manager of this establishment

It looked good, Ingels thought wearily, abandoning the report, tearing onward. But two issues later the sequel's headline stopped him short:

ACCUSATION AND COUNTER-ACCUSATION IN COURT. A BLASPHEMOUS CULT REVEALED.

And there it was, halfway down the column:

Examined by Mr. Kirby for the prosecution, Mr. Radcliffe affirmed that he had been busily engaged in preparing his accounts when, overhearing sounds of stealth outside his office, he summoned his courage and ventured forth. In the auditorium he beheld several men

Get on with it, Ingels urged, and saw that there had been impatience in the court too:

> Mr. Radcliffe's narrative was rudely interrupted by Ware-ing, who accused him of having let a room in his theatre to the accused four. This privilege having been summarily withdrawn, Wareing alleged, the four had entered the building in a bid to reclaim such possessions as were rightfully theirs. He pursued:
>
> "Mr. Radcliffe is aware of this. He has been one of our number for years, and still would be, if he had the courage."
>
> Mr. Radcliffe replied: "That is a wicked untruth. However, I am not surprised by the depths of your iniquity. I have evidence of it here."
>
> So saying, he produced for the Court's inspection a notebook containing, as he said, matter of a blasphemous and sacrilegious nature. This which he had found beneath a seat in his theatre, he indicated to be the prize sought by the unsuccessful robbers. The book, which Mr. Radcliffe described as "the journal of a cult dedicated to preparing themselves for a blasphemous travesty of the Second Coming," was handed to Mr. Poole, the magistrate, who swiftly pronounced it to conform to this description.
>
> Mr. Kirby adduced as evidence of the corruption which this cult wrought, its bringing of four respectable tradesmen to the state of common robbers. Had they not felt the shame of the beliefs they professed, he continued, they had but to petition Mr. Radcliffe for the return of their mislaid property.

But what beliefs? Ingels demanded. He riffled onward, crumbling yellow fragments from the pages. The tube buzzed like a bright trapped insect. He almost missed the page.

FOILED ROBBERS AT "THE VARIETY".
FIFTH MAN YIELDS HIMSELF TO JUSTICE.

What fifth man? Ingels searched:

Mr. Poole condemned the cult of which the accused were adherents as conclusive proof of the iniquity of those religions which presume to rival Christianity. He described the cult as "unworthy of the lowest breed of mulatto."

At this juncture a commotion ensued, as a man entered precipitately and begged leave to address the Court. Some few minutes later Mr. Radcliffe also entered, wearing a resolute expression. When he saw the latecomer, however, he appeared to relinquish his purpose, and took a place in the gallery. The man, meanwhile, sought to throw himself on the Court's mercy, declaring himself to be the fifth of the robbers. He had been prompted to confess, he affirmed, by a sense of his injustice in allowing his friends to take full blame. His name, he said, was Joseph Ingels

Who had received a lighter sentence in acknowledgement of his gesture, Ingels saw in a blur at the foot of the column. He hardly noticed. He was still staring at his grandfather's name.

"Nice of you to come," his father said ambiguously. They'd finished decorating, Ingels saw; the flowers on the hall wallpaper had grown and turned bright orange. But the light was still dim, and the walls settled about his eyes like night around a feeble lamp. Next to the coat rack he saw the mirror in which he'd made sure of himself before teenage dates, the crack in one corner where he'd driven his fist, caged by fury and by their incomprehension of his adolescent restlessness. An ugly socket of plaster gaped through the wallpaper next to the supporting nail's less treacherous home. "I could have hung the mirror for you," Ingels said, not meaning to disparage his father, who frowned and said "No need."

They went into the dining-room, where his mother was setting out the best tablecloth and cutlery. "Wash hands," she said. "Tea's nearly ready."

They ate and talked. Ingels watched the conversation as if it were a pocket maze into which he had to slip a ball when the opening tilted towards him. "How's your girlfriend?" his mother said.

Don't you know her name? Ingels didn't say. "Fine," he said. They didn't mention Hilary again. His mother produced infant photographs of him they'd discovered in the sideboard drawer. "You were a lovely little boy," she said. "Speaking of memories," Ingels said, "do you remember the old Variety theatre?"

His father was moving his shirt along the fireguard to give himself a glimpse of the fire, his back to Ingels. "The old Variety," his mother said. "We wanted to take you to a pantomime there once. But," she glanced at her husband's back, "when your father got there all the tickets were sold. Then there was the Gaiety," and she produced a list of theatres and anecdotes.

Ingels sat opposite his father, whose pipe smoke was pouring up the chimney. "I was looking through our old newspapers," he said. "I came across a case that involved the Variety."

"Don't you ever work at that paper?" his father said.

"This was research. It seems there was a robbery at the theatre. Before you were born, it was, but I wonder if you remember hearing about it."

"Now, we aren't all as clever as you," his mother said. "We don't remember what we heard in our cradle."

Ingels laughed, tightening inside; the opening was turning away from him. "You might have heard about it when you were older," he told his father. "Your father was involved."

"No," his father said. "He was not."

"He was in the paper."

"His name was," his father said, facing Ingels with a blank stare in his eyes. "It was another man. Your grandfather took years to live that down. The newspapers wouldn't publish an apology or say it wasn't him. And you wonder why we didn't want you to work for a paper. You wouldn't be a decent shop-keeper, you let our shop go out of the family, and now here you are, raking up old dirt and lies. That's what you chose for yourself."

"I didn't mean to be offensive," Ingels said, holding himself down. "But it was an interesting case, that's all. I'm going to follow it up tomorrow, at the theatre."

"If you go there you'll be rubbing our name in the dirt. Don't bother coming here again."

"Now hold on," Ingels said. "If your father wasn't involved you can't very well mean that. My God," he cried, flooded with a memory, "you do know something! You told me about it once, when I was a child! I'd just started dreaming and you told it to me so I wouldn't be frightened, to show me you had these dreams too. You were in a room with a telescope, waiting to see something. You told me because I'd dreamed it too! That's the second time I've had that dream! It's the room at the Variety, it has to be!"

"I don't know what you mean," his father said. "I never dreamed that."

"You told me you had."

"I must have told you that to calm you down. Go on, say I shouldn't have lied to you. It must have been for your own good."

He'd blanked out his eyes with an unblinking stare. Ingels gazed at him and knew at once there was more behind the blank than the lie about his childhood. "You've been dreaming again," he said. "You've been having the dream I had last night, I know you have. And I think you know what it means."

The stare shifted almost imperceptibly, then returned strengthened. "What do you know?" his father said. "You live in the same town as us and visit us once a week, if that. Yet you know I've been dreaming? Sometimes we wonder if you even know we're here!"

"I know. I'm sorry," Ingels said. "But these dreams—you used to have them. The ones we used to share, remember?"

"We shared everything when you were a little boy. But that's over," his father said. "Dreams and all."

"That's nothing to do with it!" Ingels shouted. "You still have the ability! I know you must have been having these dreams! It's been in your eyes for months!" He trailed off, trying to remember whether that was true. He turned to his mother, pleading. "Hasn't he been dreaming?"

"What do I know about it?" she said. "It's nothing to do with me." She was clearing the table in the dim rationed light beyond the fire, not looking at either of them. Suddenly Ingels saw her as he never had before: bewildered by her husband's dreams and intuitions, further excluded from the disturbingly incomprehensible bond between him and her son. All at once Ingels knew why he'd always felt she had been happy to see him leave home: it was only then that she'd been able to start reclaiming her husband. He took his coat from the hall and looked into the dining-room. They hadn't moved: his father was staring at the fire, his mother at the table. "I'll see you," he said, but the only sound was the crinkling of the fire as it crumbled, breaking open pinkish embers.

IV

He watched television. Movement of light and colours, forming shapes. Outside the window the sky drew his gaze, stretched taut, heavily imminent as thunder. He wrote words.

Later, he was sailing through enormous darkness; glinting globes turned slowly around him, one wearing an attenuated band of light; ahead, the darkness was scattered with dust and chunks of rock. A piece of metal was circling him like a timid needle, poking towards him, now spitting flame and swinging away. He felt contempt so profound it was simply vast indifference. He closed his eyes as he might have blinked away a speck of dust.

In the morning he wrote his review at the flat. He knew he wouldn't be able to bear the teeming aisles for long. Blindly shouldering his way across the floor, he found Bert. He had to gaze at him for a minute or so; he couldn't immediately remember what he should look like. "That rewrite you did on the TV review wasn't your best," Bert said. "Ah well," Ingels said, snatching his copy of last night's *Herald* automatically from his desk, and hurried for the door.

He'd nearly reached it when he heard the news editor shouting into the telephone. "But it can't affect Saturn and Jupiter! I mean, it can't change its mass, can it? ... I'm sorry, sir. Obviously I didn't mean to imply I knew more about your field than you. But is it possible for its mass to change? ... What, trajectory as well?" Ingels grinned at the crowd around the editor's desk, at their rapt expressions. They'd be more rapt when he returned. He strode out.

Through the writhing crowds, up the steps, into a vista of beds and dressing-tables like a street of cramped bedrooms whose walls had been tricked away. "Can I speak to the manager, please," he said to the man who stepped forward. "*Brichester Herald.*"

The manager was a young man in a pale streamlined suit, longish clipped hair, a smile which he held forward as if for inspection. "I'm following a story," Ingels said, displaying his press card. "It seems that when your warehouse was a theatre a room was leased to an astronomical group. We think their records are still here, and if they can be found they're of enormous historical interest."

"That's interesting," the manager said. "Where are they supposed to be?"

"In a room at the top of the building somewhere."

"I'd like to help, of course." Four men passed, carrying pieces of a dismembered bed to a van. "There were some offices at the top of the building once, I believe. But we don't use them now, they're boarded up. It would be a good deal of trouble to open them now. If you'd phoned I might have been able to free some men."

"I've been out of town," Ingels said, improvising hastily now his plans were going awry. "Found this story on my desk when I got back. I tried to phone earlier but couldn't get through. Must be a tribute to the business you're doing." An old man, one of the loaders, was sitting on a chair nearby, listening; Ingels wished he would move, he couldn't bear an audience as well. "These records really would be important," he said wildly. "Great historical value."

"In any case I can't think they'd still be here. If they were in one of the top rooms they would have been cleared out long ago."

"I think you're a bit wrong there," the old man said from his chair.

"Have you nothing to do?" the manager demanded.

"We've done loading," the man said. "Driver's not here yet. Mother's sick. It's not for me to say you're wrong, but I remember when they were mending the roof after the war. Men who were doing it said they could see a room full of books, they looked like, all covered up. But we couldn't find it from down here and nobody wanted to break their necks trying to get in from the roof. Must be there still, though."

"That has to be the one," Ingels said. "Whereabouts was it?"

"Round about there," the old man said, pointing above a Scandinavian four-poster. "Behind one of the offices, we used to reckon."

"Could you help find it?" Ingels said. "Maybe your workmates could give you a hand while they're waiting. That's of course if this gentleman doesn't mind. We'd make a point of your cooperation," he told the manager. "Might even be able to give you a special advertising rate, if you wanted to run an ad on that day."

The five of them climbed a rusty spiral staircase, tastefully screened by a partition, to the first floor. The manager, still frowning, had left one loader watching for the driver. "Call us as soon as he comes," he said. "Whatever the reason, time lost loses money." Across the first floor, which was a maze of crated and cartoned furniture, Ingels glimpsed reminiscences of his dream: the outline of theatre boxes in the walls, almost erased by bricks; a hook that had supported a chandelier. They seemed to protrude from the mundane, beckoning him on.

The staircase continued upward, more rustily. "I'll go first," the manager said, taking the flashlight one of the loaders had brought. "We don't want accidents," and his legs drew up like a tail through a trapdoor. They heard him stamping about, challenging the floor. "All right," he called, and Ingels thrust his face through drifting dust into a bare plank corridor.

"Here, you said?" the manager asked the old man, pointing to some of the boards that formed a wall. "That's it," the old man said, already ripping out nails with his hammer, aided by his workmates. A door peeked dully through. Ingels felt a smile wrenching at his face. He controlled himself. Wait until they've gone.

As soon as they prised open the office door he ran forward. A glum green room, a ruined desk in whose splintered innards squatted a dust-furred typewriter. "I'm afraid it's as I thought," the manager said. "There's no way through. You can't expect us to knock down a wall, obviously. Not without a good deal of consultation."

"But there must have been an entrance," Ingels said. "Beyond this other wall. It must have been sealed up before you got the building. Surely we can look for it."

"You won't have to," the old man said. He was kicking at the wall nearest the supposed location of the room. Plaster crumbled along a crack, then they heard the shifting of brick. "Thought as much," he said. "The war did this, shook the building. The boards are all right but the mortar's done for." He kicked again and whipped back his foot. He'd dislodged two bricks, and at once part of the wall collapsed, leaving an opening four feet high.

"That'll be enough!" the manager said. Ingels was stooping, peering through the dust-curtained gap. Bare boards, rafters and slates above, what must be bookcases draped with cloth around the walls, something in the centre of the room wholly covered by a frame hung with heavy material, perhaps velvet. Dust crawled on his hot face, prickling like fever. "If the wall would have collapsed anyway it's a good job you were here when it did," he told the manager. "Now it's done I'm sure you won't object if I have a look around. If I'm injured I promise not to claim. I'll sign a waiver if you like."

"I think you'd better," the manager said, and waited while Ingels struggled with his briefcase, last night's *Herald,* a pen and sheet from his notebook, brushing at his eyebrows where dust and sweat had become a trickle of mud, rubbing his trembling fingers together to clean them. The men had clambered over the heap of bricks and were lifting the velvety frame. Beneath it was a reflector telescope almost a foot long, mounted on a high sturdy stand. One of the men bent to the eyepiece, touching the focus. "Don't!" Ingels screamed. "The setting may be extremely important," he explained, trying to laugh.

The manager was peering at him. "What did you say you do at the *Herald?*" he said.

"Astronomy correspondent," Ingels said, immediately dreading that the man might read the paper regularly. "I don't get too much work," he blundered on. "This is a scoop. If I could I'd like to spend a few hours looking at the books."

He heard them descending the spiral staircase. Squirm away, he thought. He lifted the covers from the bookcases gingerly, anxious to keep dust away from the telescope, as the velvety cover had for decades. Suddenly he hurried back to the corridor. Its walls bobbed about him as the flashlight swung. He selected a plank and, hefting it over the bricks, poked it at the rafters above the telescope, shielding the latter with his arm. After a minute the slate above slid away, and a moment later he heard a distant crash.

He squatted down to look through the eyepiece. No doubt a chair had been provided once. All he could see was a blurred twilit sky. Soon be night, he thought, and turned the flashlight on the books. He remembered the light from the oil lamp lapping at his feet in the dream.

Much of the material was devoted to astronomy. As many of the books and charts were astrological, he found, some in Oriental script. But there were others, on shelves in the corner furthest from the sealed-off door: *The Story of Atlantis and the Lost Lemuria, Image du Monde, Liber Investigationis, Revelations of Glaaki.* There were nine volumes of the last. He pulled them out, curious, and dust rose about his face like clouds of sleep.

Voices trickled tinily up the staircase, selling beds. In the close room dimmed by the dust that crowded at the hole in the roof, towards which the telescope patiently gazed, Ingels felt as if he were sinking back into his dream. Cracked fragments of the pages clung beneath his nails. He read; the words flowed on like an incantation, like voices muttering in sleep, melting into another style, jerking clumsily into another. Sketches and paintings were tipped into the books, some childishly crude, some startlingly detailed: M'Nagalah, a tentacled mass of what looked like bloated raw entrails and eyes; Glaaki, a half-submerged spongy face peering stalk-eyed from a lake; R'lyeh, an island city towering triumphant above the sea, a vast door ajar. This he recognised, calmly accepting the information. He felt now as if he could never have had reason to doubt his dream.

The early winter night had blocked up the hole in the roof. Ingels stooped to the eyepiece again. Now there was only darkness through the telescope. It felt blurred by distance; he felt the distance drawing him vertiginously down the tube of darkness, out into a boundless emptiness no amount of matter could fill. Not yet, he thought, withdrawing swiftly. Soon.

Someone was staring at him. A girl. She was frowning up at the hole in the roof. A saleswoman. "We're closing soon," she said.

"All right," Ingels said, returning to the book, lying face upwards in the splayed light. It had settled into a more comfortable position, revealing a new page to him, and an underlined phrase: "when the stars are right." He stared at it, trying to connect. It should mean something. The dim books hemmed him in. He shook his head and turned the pages swiftly, searching for underlining. Here it was repeated in the next volume, no, augmented: "when the stars are right again." He glanced sharply at the insistent gap of night above him. In a minute, he snarled. Here was a whole passage underlined:

"Though the universe may feign the semblance of fickleness, its soul has always known its masters. The sleep of its masters is but the largest cycle of all life, for as the defiance and forgetfulness of winter is rendered vain by summer, so the defiance and forgetfulness of man, and of those others who have assumed stewardship, shall be cast aside by the reawakened masters. When these hibernal times are over, and the time for reawakening is near, the universe itself shall send forth the Harbinger and Maker, Ghroth. Who shall urge the stars and worlds to rightness. Who shall raise the sleeping masters from their burrows and drowned tombs; who shall raise the tombs themselves. Who shall be attentive to those worlds where worshippers presume themselves stewards. Who shall bring those worlds under sway, until all acknowledge their presumption, and bow down."

Ghroth, Ingels thought, gazing up at the gap in the roof. They even had a name for it then, despite the superstitious language. Not that that was so surprising, he thought. Man used to look upon comets that way; this is the same sort of thing. An omen that becomes almost a god.

But an omen of what? he thought suddenly. What exactly was supposed to happen when the stars were right again? He knelt in the dust and flurried through the books. No more underlining. He rushed back to the telescope. His thighs twinged as he squatted. Something had entered the field of view.

It was the outer edge of the wandering planet, creeping into the telescope's field. As it came it blurred, occasionally sharpening almost into focus for a moment. Ingels felt as if the void were making sudden feeble snatches at him. Now the planet was only a spreading reddish smudge. He reached for the focus, altering it minutely. "We're closing now," said the manager behind him.

"I won't be long," Ingels said, feeling the focus sharpen, sharpen—

"We're waiting to close the doors," the manager said. "And I'm afraid I'm in a hurry."

"Not long!" Ingels screamed, tearing his gaze from the eyepiece to glare.

When the man had gone Ingels switched off the flashlight. Now he could see nothing but the tiny dim gap in the roof. He let the room settle on his eyes. At last he made out the immobile uplifted telescope. He groped towards it and squatted down.

As soon as he touched the eyepiece the night rushed through the telescope and clutched him. He was sailing through the void, yet he was motionless; everything moved with him. Through the vast silence he heard the ring of a lifted telephone, a voice saying "Give me the chief editor of the *Herald*, please," back there across the void. He could hear the pale grubs squeaking tinnily, back all that way. He remembered the way they moved, soft, uncarapaced. Before him, suspended in the dark and facing him, was Ghroth.

It was red as rust, featureless except for bulbous protrusions like hills. Except that of course they weren't hills if he could see them at that distance; they must be immense. A rusty globe covered with lumps, then. That was all, but that couldn't explain why he felt as if the whole of him were magnetised to it through his eyes. It seemed to hang ponderously, communicating a thunderous sense of imminence, of power. But that was just its unfamiliarity, Ingels thought, struggling against the suction of boundless space; just the sense of its intrusion. It's only a planet, after all. Pain was blazing along his thighs. Just a red warty globe.

Then it moved.

Ingels was trying to remember how to move his body to get his face away from the eyepiece; he was throwing his weight against the telescope mounting to sweep away what he could see. It was blurring, that was it, although it was a cold windless day air movements must be causing the image to blur, the surface of a planet doesn't move, it's only a planet, the surface of a planet doesn't crack, it doesn't roll back like that, it doesn't peel back for thousands of miles so you can see what's underneath, pale and glistening. When he tried to scream air whooped into his lungs as if space had exploded a vacuum within him.

He'd tripped over the bricks, fallen agonisingly down the stairs, smashed the manager out of the way with his shoulder and was at the *Herald* building before he knew that was where he intended to go. He couldn't speak, only make the whooping sound as he sucked in air; he threw his briefcase and last night's paper on his desk and sat there clutching himself, shaking. The floor seemed to have been in turmoil before he arrived, but they were crowding around him, asking him impatiently what was wrong.

But he was staring at the headline in his last night's newspaper: SURFACE ACTIVITY ON WANDERER "MORE APPARENT THAN REAL" SAY SCIENTISTS. Photographs of the planet from the space-probe: one showing an area like a great round pale glistening sea, the next circuit recording only mountains and rock plains. "Don't you see?" Ingels shouted at Bert among the packed faces. "It closed its eye when it saw us coming!"

Hilary came at once when they telephoned her, and took Ingels back to her flat. But he wouldn't sleep, laughed at the doctor and the tranquillisers, though he swallowed the tablets indifferently enough. Hilary unplugged the television, went out as little as possible, bought no newspapers, threw away her contributor's copies unopened, talked to him while she worked, stroked him soothingly, slept with him. Neither of them felt the earth begin to shift.

ଧ ଷ

A Colder War

Charles Stross

Analyst

Roger Jourgensen tilts back in his chair, reading.

He's a fair-haired man, in his mid-thirties: hair razor-cropped, skin pallid from too much time spent under artificial lights. Spectacles, short-sleeved white shirt and tie, photographic ID badge on a chain round his neck. He works in an air-conditioned office with no windows.

The file he is reading frightens him.

Once, when Roger was a young boy, his father took him to an open day at Nellis AFB, out in the California desert. Sunlight glared brilliantly from the polished silverplate flanks of the big bombers, sitting in their concrete-lined dispersal bays behind barriers and blinking radiation monitors. The brightly coloured streamers flying from their pitot tubes lent them a strange, almost festive appearance. But they were sleeping nightmares: once awakened, nobody—except the flight crew—could come within a mile of the nuclear-powered bombers and live.

Looking at the gleaming, bulging pods slung under their wingtip pylons,

Roger had a premature inkling of the fires that waited within, a frigid terror that echoed the siren wail of the air raid warnings. He'd sucked nervously on his ice cream and gripped his father's hand tightly while the band ripped through a cheerful Sousa march, and only forgot his fear when a flock of Thunderchiefs sliced by overhead and rattled the car windows for miles around.

He has the same feeling now, as an adult reading this intelligence assessment, that he had as a child, watching the nuclear powered bombers sleeping in their concrete beds.

There's a blurry photograph of a concrete box inside the file, snapped from above by a high-flying U-2 during the autumn of '61. Three coffin-shaped lakes, bulking dark and gloomy beneath the arctic sun; a canal heading west, deep in the Soviet heartland, surrounded by warning trefoils and armed guards. Deep waters saturated with calcium salts, concrete coffer-dams lined with gold and lead. A sleeping giant pointed at NATO, more terrifying than any nuclear weapon.

Project Koschei.

Red Square Redux

Warning

The following briefing film is classified SECRET GOLD JULY BOOJUM. If you do not have SECRET GOLD JULY BOOJUM clearance, leave the auditorium now and report to your unit security officer for debriefing. Failing to observe this notice is an imprisonable offense.

You have sixty seconds to comply.

Video clip

Red Square in springtime. The sky overhead is clear and blue; there's a little wispy cirrus at high altitude. It forms a brilliant backdrop for flight after flight of five four-engined bombers that thunder across the horizon and drop behind the Kremlin's high walls.

Voice-over

Red Square, the May Day parade, 1962. This is the first time that the Soviet Union has publicly displayed weapons classified GOLD JULY BOOJUM.

Here they are:

Video clip

Later in the same day. A seemingly endless stream of armour and soldiers marches across the square, turning the air grey with diesel fumes. The trucks roll in line eight abreast, with soldiers sitting erect in the back. Behind them rumble a battalion of T-56's, their commanders standing at attention in their cupolas, saluting the stand. Jets race low and loud overhead, formations of MiG-17 fighters.

Behind the tanks sprawl a formation of four low-loaders: huge tractors towing low-sling trailers, their load beds strapped down under olive-drab tarpaulins. Whatever is under them is uneven, a bit like a loaf of bread the size of a small house. The trucks have an escort of jeep-like vehicles on each side, armed soldiers sitting at attention in their backs.

There are big five-pointed stars painted in silver on each tarpaulin, like outlines of stars. Each star is surrounded by a stylized silver circle; a unit insignia, perhaps, but not in the standard format for Red Army units. There's lettering around the circles, in a strangely stylised script.

Voice-over

These are live servitors under transient control. The vehicles towing them bear the insignia of the second Guards Engineering Brigade, a penal construction unit based in Bokhara and used for structural engineering assignments relating to nuclear installations in the Ukraine and Azerbaijan. This is the first time that any Dresden Agreement party openly demonstrated ownership of this technology: in this instance, the conclusion we are intended to draw is that the sixty-seventh Guard Engineering Brigade operates four units. Given existing figures for the Soviet ORBAT we can then extrapolate a total task strength of two hundred and eighty-eight servitors, if this unit is unexceptional.

Video clip

Five huge Tu-95 Bear bombers thunder across the Moscow skies.

Voice-over

This conclusion is questionable. For example, in 1964 a total of two hundred and forty Bear bomber passes were made over the reviewing stand in front of the Lenin mausoleum. However, at that time technical reconnaissance assets verified that the Soviet air force has hard stand parking for only one hundred and sixty of these aircraft, and estimates of airframe production based on photographs of the extent of the Tupolev bureau's works indicate that total production to that date was between sixty and one hundred and eighty bombers.

Further analysis of photographic evidence from the 1964 parade suggests that a single group of twenty aircraft in four formations of five made repeated passes through the same airspace, the main arc of their circuit lying outside visual observation range of Moscow. This gave rise to the erroneous capacity report of 1964 in which the first strike delivery capability of the Soviet Union was over-estimated by as much as three hundred percent.

We must therefore take anything that they show us in Red Square with a pinch of salt when preparing force estimates. Quite possibly these four servitors are all they've got. Then again, the actual battalion strength may be considerably higher.

Still photographic sequence

From very high altitude—possibly in orbit—an eagle's eye view of a remote village in mountainous country. Small huts huddle together beneath a craggy outcrop; goats graze nearby.

In the second photograph, something has rolled through the village leaving a trail of devastation. The path is quite unlike the trail of damage left by an artillery bombardment: something roughly four metres wide has shaved the rocky plateau smooth, wearing it down as if with a terrible heat. A corner of a shack leans drunkenly, the other half sliced away cleanly. White bones gleam faintly in the track; no vultures descend to stab at the remains.

Voice-over

These images were taken very recently, on successive orbital passes of a KH-11 satellite. They were timed precisely eighty-nine minutes apart. This village was the home of a noted Mujahedin leader. Note the similar footprint to the payloads on the load beds of the trucks seen at the 1962 parade.

These indicators were present, denoting the presence of servitor units in use by Soviet forces in Afghanistan: the four metre wide gauge of the assimilation track. The total molecular breakdown of organic matter in the track. The speed of destruction—the event took less than five thousand seconds to completion, no survivors were visible, and the causative agent had already been uplifted by the time of the second orbital pass. This, despite the residents of the community being armed with DShK heavy machine guns, rocket propelled grenade launchers, and AK-47's. Lastly: there is no sign of the causative agent even deviating from its course, but the entire area is depopulated. Except for excarnated residue there is no sign of human habitation.

In the presence of such unique indicators, we have no alternative but to conclude that the Soviet Union has violated the Dresden Agreement by deploying GOLD JULY BOOJUM in a combat mode in the Khyber pass. There are no grounds to believe that a NATO armoured division would have fared any better than these mujahedin without nuclear support...

Puzzle Palace

Roger isn't a soldier. He's not much of a patriot, either: he signed up with the CIA after college, in the aftermath of the Church Commission hearings in the early seventies. The Company was out of the assassination business, just a bureaucratic engine rolling out National Security assessments: that's fine by Roger. Only now, five years later, he's no longer able to roll along, casually disengaged, like a car in neutral bowling down a shallow incline towards his retirement, pension and a gold watch. He puts the file down on his desk and, with a shaking hand, pulls an illicit cigarette from the pack he keeps in his drawer. He lights it and leans back for a moment to draw breath, force relaxation, staring at smoke rolling in the air beneath the merciless light until his hand stops shaking.

Most people think spies are afraid of guns, or KGB guards, or barbed wire, but in point of fact the most dangerous thing they face is paper. Papers carry secrets. Papers can carry death warrants. Papers like this one, this folio with its blurry eighteen-year-old faked missile photographs and estimates of time/survivor curves and pervasive psychosis ratios, can give you nightmares, dragging you awake screaming in the middle of the night. It's one of a series of highly classified pieces of paper that he is summarizing for the eyes of the National Security Council and the President Elect—if his head of department and the DDCIA approve it—and here he is, having to calm his nerves with a cigarette before he turns the next page.

After a few minutes, Roger's hand is still. He leaves his cigarette in the eagle-headed ash tray and picks up the intelligence report again. It's a summary, itself the distillation of thousands of pages and hundreds of photographs. It's barely twenty pages long: as of 1963, its date of preparation, the CIA knew very little about Project Koschei. Just the bare skeleton, and rumours from a highly-placed spy. And their own equivalent project, of course. Lacking the Soviet lead in that particular field, the USAF fielded the silver-plated white elephants of the NB-39 project: twelve atomic-powered bombers armed with XK-PLUTO, ready to tackle Project Koschei should the Soviets show signs of unsealing the bunker. Three hundred megatons of H-bombs pointed at a single target, and nobody was certain it would be enough to do the job.

And then there was the hard-to-conceal fiasco in Antarctica. Egg on face: a subterranean nuclear test program in international territory! If nothing else, it had been enough to stop JFK running for a second term. The test program was a bad excuse: but it was far better than confessing what had really happened to the 501st Airborne Division on the cold plateau beyond Mount Erebus. The plateau that the public didn't know about, that didn't show up on the maps issued by the geological survey departments of those governments party to the Dresden Agreement of 1931—an arrangement that even Hitler had stuck to. The plateau that had swallowed more U-2 spy planes than the Soviet Union, more surface expeditions than darkest Africa.

Shit. How the hell am I going to put this together for him?

Roger's spent the past five hours staring at this twenty page report, trying to think of a way of summarizing their drily quantifiable terror in words that will give the reader power over them, the power to think the unthinkable: but it's proving difficult. The new man in the White House is straight-talking, demands straight answers. He's pious enough not to believe in the supernatural, confident enough that just listening to one of his speeches is an uplifting experience if you can close your eyes and believe in morning in America. There is probably no way of explaining Project Koschei, or XK-PLUTO, or MK-NIGHTMARE, or the gates, without watering them down into just another weapons system—which they are not. Weapons may have deadly or hideous effects, but they acquire moral character from the actions of those who use them. Whereas these projects are indelibly stained by a patina of ancient evil...

He hopes that if the balloon ever does go up, if the sirens wail, he and Andrea and Jason will be left behind to face the nuclear fire. It'll be a merciful death compared with what he suspect lurks out there, in the unexplored vastness beyond the gates. The vastness that made Nixon cancel the manned space program, leaving just the standing joke of a white-elephant shuttle, when he realised just how hideously dangerous the space race might become. The darkness that broke Jimmy Carter's faith and turned Lyndon B. Johnson into an alcoholic.

He stands up, nervously shifts from one foot to the other. Looks round at the walls of his cubicle. For a moment the cigarette smouldering on the edge of his ash tray catches his attention: wisps of blue-grey smoke coil like lazy dragons in the air above it, writhing in a strange cuneiform text. He blinks and they're gone, and the skin in the small of his back prickles as if someone had pissed on his grave.

"Shit." Finally, a spoken word in the silence. His hand is shaking as he stubs the cigarette out. *Mustn't let this get to me.* He glances at the wall. It's nineteen hundred hours; too late, too late. He should go home, Andy will be worrying herself sick.

In the end it's all too much. He slides the thin folder into the safe behind his chair, turns the locking handle and spins the dial, then signs himself out of the reading room and goes through the usual exit search.

During the thirty mile drive home, he spits out of the window, trying to rid his mouth of the taste of Auschwitz ashes.

Late Night in the White House

The colonel is febrile, jittering about the room with gung-ho enthusiasm. "That was a mighty fine report you pulled together, Jourgensen!" He paces over to the niche between the office filing cabinet and the wall, turns on the spot, paces back to the far side of his desk. "You understand the fundamentals. I like that. A few more guys like you running the company and we wouldn't have this fuckup in Tehran." He grins, contagiously. The colonel is a firestorm of enthusiasm, burning out of control like a forties comic-book hero. He has Roger on the edge of his chair, almost sitting at attention. Roger has to bite his tongue to remind himself not to call the colonel 'sir'—he's a civilian, not in the chain of command. "That's why I've asked Deputy Director McMurdo to reassign you to this office, to work on my team as company liaison. And I'm pleased to say that he's agreed."

Roger can't stop himself: "To work here, sir?" *Here* is in the basement of the Executive Office Building, an extension hanging off the White House. Whoever the colonel is he's got *pull*, in positively magical quantities. "What will I be doing, sir? You said, your team—"

"Relax a bit. Drink your coffee." The colonel paces back behind his desk, sits down. Roger sips cautiously at the brown sludge in the mug with the Marine Corps crest. "The president told me to organize a team," says the colonel, so casually that Roger nearly chokes on his coffee, "to handle contingencies. October surprises. Those asshole commies down in Nicaragua. 'We're eyeball to eyeball with an Evil Empire, Ozzie, and we can't afford to blink'—those were his exact words. The Evil Empire uses dirty tricks. But nowadays we're better than they are: buncha hicks, like some third-world dictatorship—Upper Volta with shoggoths. My job is to pin them down and cut them up. Don't give them a chance to whack the shoe on the UN table, demand concessions. If they want to bluff I'll call 'em on it. If they want to go toe-to-toe I'll dance with 'em." He's up and pacing again. "The company used to do that, and do it okay, back in the fifties and sixties. But too many bleeding hearts—it makes me sick. If you guys went back to wet ops today you'd have journalists following you every time you went to the john in case it was newsworthy.

"Well, we aren't going to do it that way this time. It's a small team and the buck stops here." The colonel pauses, then glances at the ceiling. "Well, maybe up *there*. But you get the picture. I need someone who knows the company, an insider who has clearance up the wazoo who can go in and get the dope before it goes through a fucking committee of ass-watching bureaucrats. I'm also getting someone from the Puzzle Palace, and some words to give me pull with Big Black." He glances at Roger sharply, and Roger nods: he's cleared for National Security Agency—Puzzle Palace—intelligence, and knows about Big Black, the National Reconnaissance Office, which is so secret that even its existence is still classified.

Roger is impressed by this colonel, despite his better judgement. Within the byzantine world of the US intelligence services, he is talking about building his very own pocket battleship and sailing it under the jolly roger with letters of marque and reprise signed by the president. But Roger still has some questions to ask, to scope out the limits of what Colonel North is capable of. "What about FEVER DREAM, sir?"

The colonel puts his coffee-cup down. "I own it," he says, bluntly. "And NIGHTMARE. And PLUTO. *Any means necessary* he said, and I have an executive order with the ink still damp to prove it. Those projects aren't part of the national command structure any more. Officially they've been stood down from active status and are being considered for inclusion in the next round of arms reduction talks. They're not part of the deterrent ORBAT any more; we're standardizing on just nuclear weapons. Unofficially, they're part of my group, and I will use them as necessary to contain and reduce the Evil Empire's warmaking abilities."

Roger's skin crawls with an echo of that childhood terror. "And the Dresden Agreement...?"

"Don't worry. Nothing short of *them* breaking it would lead me to do so." The colonel grins, toothily. "Which is where you come in..."

The moonlit shores of Lake Vostok

The metal pier is dry and cold, the temperature hovering close to zero degrees

Fahrenheit. It's oppressively dark in the cavern under the ice, and Roger shivers inside his multiple layers of insulation, shifts from foot to foot to keep warm. He has to swallow to keep his ears clear and he feels slightly dizzy from the pressure in the artificial bubble of air, pumped under the icy ceiling to allow humans to exist here, under the Ross Ice Shelf; they'll all spend more than a day sitting in depressurization chambers on the way back up to the surface.

There is no sound from the waters lapping just below the edge of the pier. The floodlights vanish into the surface and keep going—the water in the subsurface Antarctic lake is incredibly clear—but are swallowed up rapidly, giving an impression of infinite, inky depths.

Roger is here as the colonel's representative, to observe the arrival of the probe, receive the consignment they're carrying, and report back that everything is running smoothly. The others try to ignore him, jittery at the presence of the man from DC. There're a gaggle of engineers and artificers, flown out via McMurdo base to handle the midget sub's operations. A nervous lieutenant supervises a squad of marines with complicated-looking weapons, half gun and half video camera, stationed at the corners of the raft. And there's the usual platform crew, deep-sea rig maintenance types—but subdued and nervous looking. They're afloat in a bubble of pressurized air wedged against the underside of the Antarctic ice sheet: below them stretch the still, supercooled waters of Lake Vostok.

They're waiting for a rendezvous.

"Five hundred yards," reports one of the techs. "Rising on ten." His companion nods. They're waiting for the men in the midget sub drilling quietly through three miles of frigid water, intruders in a long-drowned tomb. "Have 'em back on board in no time." The sub has been away for nearly a day; it set out with enough battery juice for the journey, and enough air to keep the crew breathing for a long time if there's a system failure, but they've learned the hard way that fail-safe systems aren't. Not out here, at the edge of the human world.

Roger shuffles some more. "I was afraid the battery load on that cell you replaced would trip an undervoltage isolator and we'd be here 'til Hell freezes over," the sub driver jokes to his neighbour.

Looking round, Roger sees one of the marines cross himself. "Have you heard anything from Gorman or Suslowicz?" he asks quietly.

The lieutenant checks his clipboard. "Not since departure, sir," he says. "We don't have comms with the sub while it's submerged: too small for ELF, and we don't want to alert anybody who might be, uh, listening."

"Indeed." The yellow hunchback shape of the midget submarine appears at the edge of the radiance shed by the floodlights. Surface waters undulate, oily, as the sub rises.

"Crew transfer vehicle sighted," the driver mutters into his mike. He's suddenly very busy adjusting trim settings, blowing bottled air into ballast tanks, discussing ullage levels and blade count with his number two. The crane crew are busy too, running their long boom out over the lake.

The sub's hatch is visible now, bobbing along the top of the water: the lieutenant is suddenly active. "Jones! Civatti! Stake it out, left and centre!" The crane is already swinging the huge lifting hook over the sub, waiting to bring it aboard. "I want eyeballs on the portholes before you crack this thing!" It's the tenth run—seventh manned—through the eye of the needle on the lake bed, the drowned structure so like an ancient temple, and Roger has a bad feeling about it. *We can't get away with this forever,* he reasons. *Sooner or later...*

The sub comes out of the water like a gigantic yellow bath toy, a cyborg whale designed by a god with a sense of humour. It takes tense minutes to winch it in and manoeuvre it safely onto the platform. Marines take up position, shining torches in through two of the portholes that bulge myopically from the smooth curve of the sub's nose. Up on top someone is talking into a handset plugged into the stubby conning tower; the hatch locking wheel begins to turn.

"Gorman, sir," It's the lieutenant. In the light of the sodium floods everything looks sallow and washed-out; the soldier's face is the colour of damp cardboard, slack with relief.

Roger waits while the submariner—Gorman—clambers unsteadily down from the top deck. He's a tall, emaciated-looking man, wearing a red thermal suit three sizes too big for him: salt-and-pepper stubble textures his jaw with sandpaper. Right now, he looks like a cholera victim; sallow skin, smell of acrid ketones as his body eats its own protein reserves, a more revolting miasma hovering over him. There's a slim aluminium briefcase chained to his left wrist, a bracelet of bruises darkening the skin above it. Roger steps forward.

"Sir?" Gorman straightens up for a moment: almost a shadow of military attention. He's unable to sustain it. "We made the pickup. Here's the QA sample; the rest is down below. You have the unlocking code?" he asks wearily.

Jourgensen nods. "One. Five. Eight. One. Two. Two. Nine."

Gorman slowly dials it into a combination lock on the briefcase, lets it fall open and unthreads the chain from his wrist. Floodlights glisten on polythene bags stuffed with white powder, five kilos of high-grade heroin from the hills of Afghanistan; there's another quarter of a ton packed in boxes in the crew compartment. The lieutenant inspects it, closes the case and passes it to Jourgensen. "Delivery successful, sir." From the ruins on the high plateau of the Taklamakan desert to American territory in Antarctica, by way of a detour through gates linking alien worlds: gates that nobody knows how to create or destroy except the Predecessors—and they aren't talking.

"What's it like through there?" Roger demands, shoulders tense. "What did you see?"

Up on top, Suslowicz is sitting in the sub's hatch, half slumping against the crane's attachment post. There's obviously something very wrong with him. Gorman shakes his head and looks away: the wan light makes the razor-sharp creases on his face stand out, like the crackled and shattered surface of a Jovian moon. Crow's feet. Wrinkles. Signs of age. Hair the colour of moonlight. "It took so long," he says, almost complaining. Sinks to his knees. "All that *time* we've been gone…" He leans against the side of the sub, a pale shadow, aged beyond his years. "The sun was so *bright*. And our radiation detectors. Must have been a solar flare or something." He doubles over and retches at the edge of the platform.

Roger looks at him for a long, thoughtful minute: Gorman is twenty-five and a fixer for Big Black, early history in the Green Berets. He was in rude good health two days ago, when he set off through the gate to make the pick-up. Roger glances at the lieutenant. "I'd better go and tell the colonel," he says. A pause. "Get these two back to Recovery and see they're looked after. I don't expect we'll be sending any more crews through Victor-Tango for a while."

He turns and walks towards the lift shaft, hands clasped behind his back to keep them from shaking. Behind him, alien moonlight glimmers across the floor of Lake Vostok, three miles and untold light years from home.

General LeMay would be Proud

Warning

The following briefing film is classified SECRET INDIGO MARCH SNIPE. If you do not have SECRET INDIGO MARCH SNIPE clearance, leave the auditorium *now* and report to your unit security officer for debriefing. Failing to observe this notice is an imprisonable offense.

You have sixty seconds to comply.

Video clip

Shot of huge bomber, rounded gun turrets sprouting like mushrooms from the decaying log of its fuselage, weirdly bulbous engine pods slung too far out towards each wingtip, four turbine tubes clumped around each atomic kernel.

Voice-over

"The Convair B-39 Peacemaker is the most formidable weapon in our Strategic Air Command's arsenal for peace. Powered by eight nuclear-heated Pratt and Whitney NP-4051 turbojets, it circles endlessly above the Arctic ice cap, waiting for the call. This is Item One, the flight training and test bird: twelve other birds await criticality on the ground, for once launched a B-39 can only be landed at two airfields in Alaska that are equipped to handle them. This one's been airborne for nine months so far, and shows no signs of age."

Cut to:

A shark the size of a Boeing 727 falls away from the open bomb bay of the monster. Stubby delta wings slice through the air, propelled by a rocket-bright glare.

Voice-over

"A modified Navajo missile—test article for an XK-PLUTO payload—dives away from a carrier plane. Unlike the real thing, this one carries no hydrogen bombs, no direct-cycle fission ramjet to bring retaliatory destruction to the enemy. Travelling at Mach 3 the XK-PLUTO will overfly enemy territory, dropping megaton-range bombs until, its payload exhausted, it seeks out and circles a final enemy. Once over the target it will eject its reactor core and rain molten plutonium on the heads of the enemy. XK-PLUTO is a total weapon: every aspect of its design, from the shockwave it creates as it hurtles along at treetop height to the structure of its atomic reactor, is designed to inflict damage."

Cut to:

Belsen postcards, Auschwitz movies: a holiday in hell.

Voice-over

"*This* is why we need such a weapon. This is what it deters. The abominations first raised by the Third Reich's Organisation Todt, now removed to the Ukraine and deployed in the service of New Soviet Man as our enemy calls himself."

Cut to:

A sinister grey concrete slab, the upper surface of a Mayan step pyramid built with East German cement. Barbed wire, guns. A drained canal slashes north from the base of the pyramid towards the Baltic coastline, relic of the installation process: this is where it came from. The slave barracks squat beside the pyramid like a horrible memorial to its black-uniformed builders.

Cut to:

The new resting place: a big concrete monolith surrounded by three concrete lined lakes and a canal. It sits in the midst of a Ukraine landscape, flat as a pancake, stretching out forever in all directions.

Voice-over

"This is Project Koschei. The Kremlin's key to the gates of hell…"

Technology taster

"We know they first came here during the Precambrian age."

Professor Gould is busy with his viewgraphs, eyes down, trying not to pay too much attention to his audience. "We have samples of macrofauna, discovered by palaeontologist Charles D. Walcott on his pioneering expeditions into the Canadian Rockies, near the eastern border of British Columbia—" a hand-drawing of something indescribably weird fetches up on the screen "—like this *opabina*, which died there six hundred and forty million years ago. Fossils of soft-bodied animals that old are rare; the Burgess shale deposits are the best record of the Precambrian fauna anyone has found to date."

A skinny woman with big hair and bigger shoulder-pads sniffs loudly; she has no truck with these antediluvian dates. Roger winces sympathy for the academic. He'd rather she wasn't here, but somehow she got wind of the famous palaeontologist's visit—and she's the colonel's administrative assistant. Telling her to leave would be a career-limiting move.

"The important item to note—" photograph of a mangled piece of rock, visual echoes of the *opabina*—"is the tooth marks. We find them also—their exact cognates—on the ring segments of the Z-series specimens returned by the Pabodie Antarctic expedition of 1926. The world of the Precambrian was laid out differently from our own; most of the land masses that today are separate continents were joined into one huge structure. Indeed, these samples were originally separated by only two thousand miles or thereabouts. Suggesting that they brought their own parasites with them."

"What do tooth-marks tell us about them, that we need to know?" asks the colonel.

The doctor looks up. His eyes gleam: "That something liked to eat them when they were fresh." There's a brief rattle of laughter. "Something with jaws that open and close like the iris in your camera. Something we thought was extinct."

Another viewgraph, this time with a blurry underwater photograph on it. The thing looks a bit like a weird fish—a turbocharged, armoured hagfish with side-skirts and spoilers, or maybe a squid with not enough tentacles. The upper head is a flattened disk, fronted by two bizarre fern-like tentacles drooping over the weird sucker-mouth on its underside. "This snapshot was taken in Lake Vostok last year. It should be dead: there's nothing there for it to eat. This, ladies and gentlemen, is *Anomalocaris*, our toothy chewer." He pauses for a moment. "I'm very grateful to you for showing it to me," he adds, "even though it's going to make a lot of my colleagues very angry."

Is that a shy grin? The professor moves on rapidly, not giving Roger a chance to fathom his real reaction. "Now *this* is interesting in the extreme," Gould comments. Whatever it is, it looks like a cauliflower head, or maybe a brain: fractally branching stalks continuously diminishing in length and diameter, until they turn into an iridescent fuzzy manifold wrapped around a central stem. The base of the stem is rooted to a barrel-shaped structure that stands on four stubby tentacles.

"We had somehow managed to cram *Anomalocaris* into our taxonomy, but this is something that has no precedent. It bears a striking resemblance to an enlarged body segment of *Hallucigena*—" here he shows another viewgraph, something like a stiletto-heeled centipede wearing a war-bonnet of tentacles—"but a year ago we worked out that we had poor hallucigena upside down and it was actually just a spiny worm. And the high levels of iridium and diamond in the head here... this isn't a living creature, at least not within the animal kingdom I've been studying for the past thirty years. There's no cellular structure at all. I asked one of my colleagues for help and they were completely unable to isolate any DNA or RNA from it at all. It's more like a machine that displays biological levels of complexity."

"Can you put a date to it?" asks the colonel.

"Yup." The professor grins. "It predates the wave of atmospheric atomic testing that began in 1945; that's about all. We think it's from some time in the first half of this century, last half of last century. It's been dead for years, but there are older people still walking this earth. In contrast—" he flips to the picture of *Anomalocaris* "—this specimen we found in rocks that are roughly six hundred and ten million years old." He whips up another shot: similar structure, much clearer. "Note how similar it is to the dead but not decomposed one. They're obviously still alive somewhere."

He looks at the colonel, suddenly bashful and tongue-tied: "Can I talk about the, uh, thing we were, like, earlier…?"

"Sure. Go ahead. Everyone here is cleared for it." The colonel's casual wave takes in the big-haired secretary, and Roger, and the two guys from Big Black who are taking notes, and the very serious woman from the Secret Service, and even the balding, worried-looking Admiral with the double chin and coke-bottle glasses.

"Oh. Alright." Bashfulness falls away. "Well, we've done some preliminary dissections on the *Anomalocaris* tissues you supplied us with. And we've sent some samples for laboratory analysis—nothing anyone could deduce much from," he adds hastily. He straightens up. "What we discovered is quite simple: these samples didn't originate in Earth's ecosystem. Cladistic analysis of their intracellular characteristics and what we've been able to work out of their biochemistry indicates, not a point of divergence from our own ancestry, but the absence of common ancestry. A *cabbage* is more human, has more in common with us, than that creature. You can't tell by looking at the fossils, six hundred million years after it died, but live tissue samples are something else.

"Item: it's a multicellular organism, but each cell appears to have multiple structures like nuclei—a thing called a syncitium. No DNA, it uses RNA with a couple of base pairs that aren't used by terrestrial biology. We haven't been able to figure out what most of its organelles do, what their terrestrial cognates would be, and it builds proteins using a couple of amino acids that we don't. That *nothing* does. Either it's descended from an ancestry that diverged from ours before the archaeobacteria, or—more probably—it is no relative at all." He isn't smiling any more. "The gateways, colonel?"

"Yeah, that's about the size of it. The critter you've got there was retrieved by one of our, uh, missions. On the other side of a gate."

Gould nods. "I don't suppose you could get me some more?" he asks hopefully.

"All missions are suspended pending an investigation into an accident we had earlier this year," the colonel says, with a significant glance at Roger. Suslowicz died two weeks ago; Gorman is still disastrously sick, connective tissue rotting in his body, massive radiation exposure the probable cause. Normal service will not be resumed; the pipeline will remain empty until someone can figure out a way to make the deliveries without losing the crew. Roger inclines his head minutely.

"Oh well." The professor shrugs. "Let me know if you do. By the way, do you have anything approximating a fix on the other end of the gate?"

"No," says the colonel, and this time Roger knows he's lying. Mission four, before the colonel diverted their payload capacity to another purpose, planted a compact radio telescope in an empty courtyard in the city on the far side of the gate. XK-Masada, where the air's too thin to breathe without oxygen; where the sky is indigo, and the buildings cast razor-sharp shadows across a rocky plain baked to the consistency of pottery under a blood-red sun. Subsequent analysis of pulsar signals recorded by the station confirmed that it was nearly six hundred light years closer to the galactic core, inward along the same spiral arm. There are glyphs on the alien buildings that resemble symbols seen in grainy black-and-white Minox photos of the doors of the bunker in the Ukraine. Symbols behind which the subject of Project Koschei lies undead and sleeping: something evil, scraped from a nest in the drowned wreckage of a city on the Baltic floor. "Why do you want to know where they came from?"

"Well. We know so little about the context in which life evolves." For a moment the professor looks wistful. "We have—had—only one datum point: Earth, this world. Now we have a second, a fragment of a second. If we get a third, we can begin to ask deep questions like, not, 'is there life out there?'— because we know the answer to that one, now—but questions like 'what *sort* of life is out there?' and 'is there a place for us?'"

Roger shudders: *idiot,* he thinks. *If only you knew you wouldn't be so happy*—He restrains the urge to speak up. Doing so would be another career-limiting move. More to the point, it might be a life-expectancy-limiting move for the professor, who certainly didn't deserve any such drastic punishment for his cooperation. Besides, Harvard professors visiting the Executive Office Building in DC are harder to disappear than comm-symp teachers in some fly-blown jungle village in Nicaragua. Somebody might notice. The colonel would be annoyed.

Roger realises that Professor Gould is staring at him. "Do you have a question for me?" asks the distinguished palaeontologist.

"Uh—in a moment." Roger shakes himself. Remembering time-survivor curves, the captured Nazi medical atrocity records mapping the ability of a human brain to survive in close proximity to the Baltic Singularity. Mengele's insanity. The SS's final attempt to liquidate the survivors, the witnesses. Koschei, primed and pointed at the American heartland like a darkly evil gun. The "world-eating mind" adrift in brilliant dreams of madness, estivating in the absence of its prey: dreaming of the minds of sapient beings, be they barrel-bodied wing-flying tentacular *things,* or their human inheritors. "Do you think they could have been intelligent, professor? Conscious, like us?"

"I'd say so." Gould's eyes glitter. "This one—" he points to a viewgraph—"isn't alive as we know it. And *this* one—" he's found a Predecessor, god help him, barrel-bodied and bat-winged—"had what looks like a lot of very complex ganglia, not a brain as we know it, but at least as massive as our own. And some specialised grasping adaptations that might be interpreted as facilitating tool use. Put the two together and you have a high level technological civilization. Gateways between planets orbiting different stars. Alien flora, fauna, or whatever. I'd say an interstellar civilization isn't out of the picture. One that has been extinct for deep geological time—ten times as long as the dinosaurs—but that has left relics that work." His voice is trembling with emotion. "We humans, we've barely scratched the surface! The longest lasting of our relics? All our buildings will be dust in twenty thousand years, even the pyramids. Neil Armstrong's footprints in the Sea of Tranquillity will crumble under micrometeoroid bombardment in a mere half million years or so. The emptied oil fields will refill over ten million years, methane percolating up through the mantle: continental drift will erase everything. But *these* people…! They built to last. There's so much to learn from them. I wonder if we're worthy pretenders to their technological crown?"

"I'm sure we are, professor," the colonel's secretary says brassily. "Isn't that right, Ollie?"

The colonel nods, grinning. "You betcha, Fawn. You betcha!"

The Great Satan

Roger sits in the bar in the King David hotel, drinking from a tall glass of second-rate lemonade and sweating in spite of the air conditioning. He's dizzy and disoriented from jet-lag, the gut-cramps have only let him come down from his room in the past hour, and he has another two hours to go before he can try to place a call to Andrea. They had another blazing row before he flew out here; she doesn't understand why he keeps having to visit odd corners of the globe. She only knows that his son is growing up thinking a father is a voice that phones at odd times of day.

Roger is mildly depressed, despite the buzz of doing business at this level. He spends a lot of time worrying about what will happen if they're found out—what Andrea will do, or Jason for that matter, Jason whose father is a phone call away all the time—if Roger is led away in handcuffs beneath the glare of flash bulbs. If the colonel sings, if the shy bald admiral is browbeaten into spilling the beans to Congress, who will look after them then?

Roger has no illusions about what kills black operations: there are too many people in the loop, too many elaborate front corporations and numbered bank accounts and shady Middle Eastern arms dealers. Sooner or later someone will find a reason to talk, and Roger is in too deep. He isn't just the company liaison officer any more: he's become the colonel's bag-man, his shadow, the guy with the diplomatic passport and the bulging briefcase full of heroin and end-user certificates.

At least the ship will sink from the top down, he thinks. There are people very high up who want the colonel to succeed. When the shit hits the fan and is sprayed across the front page of the *Washington Post*, it will likely take down cabinet members and secretaries of state: the President himself will have to take the witness stand and deny everything. The republic will question itself.

A hand descends on his shoulder, sharply cutting off his reverie. "Howdy, Roger! Whatcha worrying about now?"

Jourgensen looks up wearily. "Stuff," he says gloomily. "Have a seat." The redneck from the embassy—Mike Hamilton, some kind of junior attache for embassy protocol by cover—pulls out a chair and crashes down on it like a friendly car wreck. He's not really a redneck, Roger knows—rednecks don't come with doctorates in foreign relations from Yale—but he likes people to think he's a bumpkin when he wants to get something from them.

"He's early," says Hamilton, looking past Roger's ear, voice suddenly all business. "Play the agenda, I'm your dim but friendly good cop. Got the background? Deniables ready?"

Roger nods, then glances round and sees Mehmet (family name unknown) approaching from the other side of the room. Mehmet is impeccably manicured and tailored, wearing a suit from Jermyn Street that costs more than Roger earns in a month. He has a neatly trimmed beard and moustache and talks with a pronounced English accent. Mehmet is a Turkish name, not a Persian one: pseudonym, of course. To look at him you would think he was a westernized Turkish businessman—certainly not an Iranian revolutionary with heavy links to Hezbollah and (whisper this), Old Man Ruholla himself, the hermit of Qom. Never, ever, in a thousand years, the unofficial Iranian ambassador to the Little Satan in Tel Aviv.

Mehmet strides over. A brief exchange of pleasantries masks the essential formality of their meeting: he's early, a deliberate move to put them off-balance. He's outnumbered, too, and that's also a move to put them on the defensive, because the first rule of diplomacy is never to put yourself in a negotiating situation where the other side can assert any kind of moral authority, and sheer weight of numbers is a powerful psychological tool.

"Roger, my dear fellow." He smiles at Jourgensen. "And the charming doctor Hamilton, I see." The smile broadens. "I take it the good colonel is desirous of news of his friends?"

Jourgensen nods. "That is indeed the case."

Mehmet stops smiling. For a moment he looks ten years older. "I visited them," he says shortly. "No, I was *taken* to see them. It is indeed grave, my friends. They are in the hands of very dangerous men, men who have nothing to lose and are filled with hatred."

Roger speaks: "There is a debt between us—"

Mehmet holds up a hand. "Peace, my friend. We will come to that. These are men of violence, men who have seen their homes destroyed and families subjected to indignities, and their hearts are full of anger. It will take a large display of repentance, a high blood-price, to buy their acquiescence. That is part of our law, you understand? The family of the bereaved may demand blood-price of the transgressor, and how else might the world be? They see it in these terms: that you must repent of your evils and assist them in waging holy war against those who would defile the will of Allah."

Roger sighs. "We do what we can," he says. "We're shipping them arms. We're fighting the Soviets every way we can without provoking the big one. What more do they want? The hostages—that's not playing well in DC. There's got to be some give and take. If Hezbollah don't release them soon they'll just convince everyone what they're not serious about negotiating. And that'll be an end to it. The colonel *wants* to help you, but he's got to have something to show the man at the top, right?"

Mehmet nods. "You and I are men of the world and understand that this keeping of hostages is not rational, but they look to you for defence against the great Satan that assails them, and their blood burns with anger that your nation, for all its fine words, takes no action. The great Satan rampages in Afghanistan, taking whole villages by night, and what is done? The United States turns its back. And they are not the only ones who feel betrayed. Our Ba'athist foes from Iraq… in Basra the unholy brotherhood of Takrit and their servants the Mukhabarat hold nightly sacrifice upon the altar of Yair-Suthot; the fountains of blood in Tehran testify to their effect. If the richest, most powerful nation on earth refuses to fight, these men of violence from the Bekaa think, how may we unstopper the ears of that nation? And they are not sophisticates like you or I."

He looks at Roger, who hunches his shoulders uneasily. "We *can't* move against the Soviets openly! They must understand that it would be the end of far more than their little war. If the Taliban want American help against the Russians, it cannot be delivered openly."

"It is not the Russians that we quarrel with," Mehmet says quietly, "but their choice in allies. They believe themselves to be infidel atheists, but by their deeds they shall be known; the icy spoor of Leng is upon them, their tools are those described in the Kitab al Azif. We have proof that they have violated the terms of the Dresden Agreement. The accursed and unhallowed stalk the frozen passes of the Himalayas by night, taking all whose path they cross. And will you stopper your ears even as the Russians grow in misplaced confidence, sure that their dominance of these forces of evil is complete? The gates are opening everywhere, as it was prophesied. Last week we flew an F-14C with a camera relay pod through one of them. The pilot and weapons operator are in paradise now, but we have glanced into hell and have the film and radar plots to prove it."

The Iranian ambassador fixes the redneck from the embassy with an icy gaze. "Tell your ambassador that we have opened preliminary discussions with Mossad, with a view to purchasing the produce of a factory at Dimona, in the Negev desert. Past insults may be set aside, for the present danger imperils all of us. *They* are receptive to our arguments, even if you are not: his holiness the Ayatollah has declared in private that any warrior who carries a nuclear device into the abode of the eater of souls will certainly achieve paradise. There will be an end to the followers of the ancient abominations on this Earth, doctor Hamilton, even if we have to push the nuclear bombs down their throats with our own hands!"

Swimming pool

"Mister Jourgensen, at what point did you become aware that the Iranian government was threatening to violate UN Resolution 216 and the Non-Proliferation Protocol to the 1956 Geneva accords?"

Roger sweats under the hot lights: his heartbeat accelerates. "I'm not sure I understand the question, sir."

"I asked you a direct question. Which part don't you understand? I'm going to repeat myself slowly: when did you realise that the Iranian Government was threatening to violate resolution 216 and the 1956 Geneva Accords on nuclear proliferation?"

Roger shakes his head. It's like a bad dream, unseen insects buzzing furiously around him. "Sir, I had no direct dealings with the Iranian government. All I know is that I was asked to carry messages to and from a guy called Mehmet who I was told knew something about our hostages in Beirut. My understanding is that the colonel has been conducting secret negotiations with this gentleman or his backers for some time—a couple of years—now. Mehmet made allusions to parties in the Iranian administration but I have no way of knowing if he was telling the truth, and I never saw any diplomatic credentials."

There's an inquisition of dark-suited congressmen opposite him, like a jury of teachers sitting in judgement over an errant pupil. The trouble is, these teachers can put him in front of a judge and send him to prison for many years, so that Jason really *will* grow up with a father who's a voice on the telephone, a father who isn't around to take him to air shows or ball games or any of the other rituals of growing up. They're talking to each other quietly, deciding on another line of questioning: Roger shifts uneasily in his chair. This is a closed hearing, the television camera a gesture in the direction of the congressional archives: a pack of hungry democrats have scented republican blood in the water.

The congressman in the middle looks towards Roger. "Stop right there. Where did you know about this guy Mehmet from? Who told you to go see him and who told you what he was?"

Roger swallows. "I got a memo from Fawn, like always. Admiral Poindexter wanted a man on the spot to talk to this guy, a messenger, basically, who was already in the loop. Colonel North signed off on it and told me to charge the trip to his discretionary fund." That must have been the wrong thing to say, because two of the congressmen are leaning together and whispering in each other's ears, and an aide obligingly sidles up to accept a note, then dashes away. "I was told that Mehmet was a mediator," Roger adds. "In trying to resolve the Beirut hostage thing."

"A mediator." The guy asking the questions looks at him in disbelief.

The man to his left—who looks as old as the moon, thin white hair, liver spots on his hooked nose, eyelids like sacks—chuckles appreciatively. "Yeah. Like Hitler was a *diplomat*. 'One more territorial demand'—" he glances round. "Nobody else remember that?" he asks plaintively.

"No sir," Roger says very seriously.

The prime interrogator snorts. "What did Mehmet tell you Iran was going to do, exactly?"

Roger thinks for a moment. "He said they were going to buy something from a factory at Dimona. I understood this to be the Israeli Defence Ministry's nuclear weapons research institute, and the only logical item—in the context of our discussion—was a nuclear weapon. Or weapons. He said the Ayatollah had decreed that a suicide bomber who took out the temple of Yog-Sothoth in Basra would achieve paradise, and that they also had hard evidence that the Soviets have deployed certain illegal weapons systems in Afghanistan. This was in the context of discussing illegal weapons proliferation; he was very insistent about the Iraq thing."

"What exactly are these weapons systems?" demands the third inquisitor, a quiet, hawk-faced man sitting on the left of the panel.

"The shoggot'im, they're called: servitors. There are several kinds of advanced robotic systems made out of molecular components: they can change shape, restructure material at the atomic level—act like corrosive acid, or secrete diamonds. Some of them are like a tenuous mist—what Doctor Drexler at MIT calls a utility fog—while others are more like an oily globule. Apparently they may be able to manufacture more of themselves, but they're not really alive in any meaning of the term we're familiar with. They're programmable, like robots, using a command language deduced from recovered records of the forerunners who left them here. The Molotov Raid of 1930 brought back a large consignment of them; all we have to go on are the scraps they missed, and reports by the Antarctic Survey. Professor Liebkunst's files in particular are most frustrating—"

"Stop. So you're saying the Russians have these, uh, Shoggoths, but we don't have any. And even those dumb Arab bastards in Baghdad are working on them. So you're saying we've got a, a Shoggoth gap? A strategic chink in our armour? And now the Iranians say the Russians are using them in Afghanistan?"

Roger speaks rapidly: "That is minimally correct, sir, although countervailing weapons have been developed to reduce the risk of a unilateral preemption escalating to an exchange of weakly godlike agencies." The congressman in the middle nods encouragingly. "For the past three decades, the B-39 Peacemaker force has been tasked by SIOP with maintaining an XK-PLUTO capability directed at ablating the ability of the Russians to activate Project Koschei, the dormant alien entity they captured from the Nazis at the end of the last war. We have twelve PLUTO-class atomic-powered cruise missiles pointed at that thing, day and night, as many megatons as the entire Minuteman force. In principle, we will be able to blast it to pieces before it can be brought to full wakefulness and eat the minds of everyone within two hundred miles."

He warms to his subject. "Secondly, we believe the Soviet control of Shoggoth technology is rudimentary at best. They know how to tell them to roll over an Afghan hill-farmer village, but they can't manufacture more of them. Their utility as weapons is limited—but terrifying—but they're not much of a problem. A greater issue is the temple in Basra. This contains an operational gateway, and according to Mehmet the Iraqi political secret police, the Mukhabarat, are trying to figure out how to manipulate it; they're trying to summon something through it. He seemed to be mostly afraid that they—and the Russians—would lose control of whatever it was; presumably another weakly godlike creature like the K-Thulu entity at the core of Project Koschei."

The old guy speaks: "This foo-loo thing, boy—you can drop those stupid K prefixes around me—is it one of a kind?"

Roger shakes his head. "I don't know, sir. We know the gateways link to at least three other planets. There may be many that we don't know of. We don't know how to create them or close them; all we can do is send people through, or pile bricks in the opening." He nearly bites his tongue, because there are more than three worlds out there, and he's been to at least one of them: the bolt-hole on XK-Masada, built by the NRO from their secret budget. He's seen the mile-high dome Buckminster Fuller spent his last decade designing for them, the rings of Patriot air defence missiles. A squadron of black diamond-shaped fighters from the Skunk works, said to be invisible to radar, patrols the empty skies of XK-Masada. Hydroponic farms and empty barracks and apartment blocks await the senators and congressmen and their families and thousands of support personnel. In event of war they'll be evacuated through the small gate that has been moved to the Executive Office Building basement, in a room beneath the swimming pool where Jack used to go skinny-dipping with Marilyn.

"Off the record now." The old congressman waves his hand in a chopping gesture: "I say *off*, boy." The cameraman switches off his machine and leaves. He leans forward, towards Roger. "What you're telling me is, we've been waging a secret war since, when? The end of the second world war? Earlier, the Pabodie Antarctic expedition in the twenties, whose survivors brought back the first of these alien relics? And now the Eye-ranians have gotten into the game and figure it's part of their fight with Saddam?"

"Sir." Roger barely trusts himself to do more than nod.

"Well." The congressman eyes his neighbour sharply. "Let me put it to you that you have heard the phrase, 'the great filter'. What does it mean to you?"

"The great—" Roger stops. *Professor Gould*, he thinks. "We had a professor of palaeontology lecture us," he explains. "I think he mentioned it. Something about why there aren't any aliens in flying saucers buzzing us the whole time."

The congressman snorts. His neighbour starts and sits up. "Thanks to Pabodie and his followers, Liebkunst and the like, we know there's a lot of life in the universe. The great filter, *boy*, is whatever force stops most of it developing intelligence and coming to visit. Something, somehow, kills intelligent species before they develop this kind of technology for themselves. How about meddling with relics of the elder ones? What do you think of that?"

Roger licks his lips nervously. "That sounds like a good possibility, sir," he says. His unease is building.

The congressman's expression is intense: "These weapons your colonel is dicking around with make all our nukes look like a toy bow and arrow, and all you can say is *it's a good possibility, sir*? Seems to me like someone in the Oval Office has been asleep at the switch."

"Sir, executive order 2047, issued January 1980, directed the armed forces to standardize on nuclear weapons to fill the mass destruction role. All other items were to be developmentally suspended, with surplus stocks allocated to the supervision of Admiral Poindexter's joint munitions expenditure committee. Which Colonel North was detached to by the USMC high command, with the full cognizance of the White House—"

The door opens. The congressman looks round angrily: "I thought I said we weren't to be disturbed!"

The aide standing there looks uncertain. "Sir, there's been an, uh, major security incident, and we need to evacuate—"

"Where? What happened?" demands the congressman. But Roger, with a sinking feeling, realises that the aide isn't watching the house committee members: and the guy behind him is Secret Service.

"Basra. There's been an attack, sir." A furtive glance at Roger, as his brain freezes in denial: "If you'd all please come this way…"

Bombing in fifteen minutes

Heads down, through a corridor where congressional staffers hurry about carrying papers, urgently calling one another. A cadre of dark-suited secret service agents close in, hustling Roger along in the wake of the committee members. A wailing like tinnitus fills his ears. "What's happening?" he asks, but nobody answers.

Down into the basement. Another corridor, where two marine guards are waiting with drawn weapons. The secret service guys are exchanging terse reports by radio. The committee men are hustled away along a narrow service tunnel: Roger is stalled by the entrance. "What's going on?" he asks his minder.

"Just a moment, sir." More listening: these guys cock their heads to one side as they take instruction, birds of prey scanning the horizon for prey. "Delta four coming in. Over. You're clear to go along the tunnel now, sir. This way."

"What's *happening?*" Roger demands as he lets himself be hustled into the corridor, along to the end and round a sharp corner. Numb shock takes hold: he keeps putting one foot in front of the other.

"We're now at Defcon one, sir. You're down on the special list as part of the house staff. Next door on the left, sir."

The queue in the dim-lit basement room is moving fast, white-gloved guards with clipboards checking off men and a few women in suits as they step through a steel blast door one by one and disappear from view. Roger looks round in bewilderment: he sees a familiar face. "Fawn! What's going on?"

The secretary looks puzzled. "I don't know. Roger? I thought you were testifying today."

"So did I." They're at the door. "What else?"

"Ronnie was making a big speech in Helsinki; the colonel had me record it in his office. Something about not coexisting with the empire of evil. He cracked some kinda joke about how we start bombing in fifteen minutes, then this—"

They're at the door. It opens on a steel-walled airlock and the marine guard is taking their badges and hustling them inside. Two staff types and a middle-aged brigadier join them and the door thumps shut. The background noise vanishes, Roger's ears pop, then the inner door opens and another marine guard waves them through into the receiving hall.

"Where are we?" asks the big-haired secretary, staring around.

"Welcome to XK-Masada," says Roger. Then his childhood horrors catch up with him and he goes in search of a toilet to throw up in.

We need you back

Roger spends the next week in a state of numbed shock. His apartment here is like a small hotel room—a hotel with security, air conditioning, and windows that only open onto an interior atrium. He pays little attention to his surroundings. It's not as if he has a home to return to.

Roger stops shaving. Stops changing his socks. Stops looking in mirrors or combing his hair. He smokes a lot, orders cheap bourbon from the commissary, and drinks himself into an amnesic stupor each night. He is, frankly, a mess. Self-destructive. Everything disintegrated under him at once: his job, the people he held in high regard, his family, his life. All the time he can't get one thing out of his head: the expression on Gorman's face as he stands there, in front of the submarine, rotting from the inside out with radiation sickness, dead and not yet knowing it. It's why he's stopped looking in mirrors.

On the fourth day he's slumped in a chair watching taped *I Love Lucy* re-runs on the boob tube when the door to his suite opens quietly. Someone comes in. He doesn't look round until the colonel walks across the screen and unplugs the TV set at the wall, then sits down in the chair next to him. The colonel has bags of dark skin under his eyes; his jacket is rumpled and his collar is unbuttoned.

"You've got to stop this, Roger," he says quietly. "You look like shit."

"Yeah, well. You too."

The colonel passes him a slim manila folder. Without wanting to, Roger slides out the single sheet of paper within.

"So it was them."

"Yeah." A moment's silence. "For what it's worth, we haven't lost yet. We may yet pull your wife and son out alive. Or be able to go back home."

"Your family too, I suppose." Roger's touched by the colonel's consideration, the pious hope that Andrea and Jason will be alright, even through his shell of misery. He realises his glass is empty. Instead of re-filling it he puts it down on the carpet beside his feet. "Why?"

The colonel removes the sheet of paper from his numb fingers. "Probably someone spotted you in the King David and traced you back to us. The Mukhabarat had agents everywhere, and if they were in league with the KGB…" he shrugs. "Things escalated rapidly. Then the president cracked that joke over a hot mike that was supposed to be switched off… Have you been checking in with the desk summaries this week?"

Roger looks at him blankly. "Should I?"

"Oh, things are still happening." The colonel leans back and stretches his feet out. "From what we can tell of the situation on the other side, not everyone's dead yet. Ligachev's screaming blue murder over the hotline, accusing us of genocide: but he's still talking. Europe is a mess and nobody knows what's going on in the Middle East—even the Blackbirds aren't making it back out again."

"The thing at Takrit."

"Yeah. It's bad news, Roger. We need you back."

"Bad news?"

"The worst." The colonel jams his hands between his knees, stares at the floor like a bashful child. "Saddam Hussein al-Takriti spent years trying to get his hands on elder technology. It looks like he finally succeeded in stabilising the gate into Sothoth. Whole villages disappeared, Marsh Arabs, wiped out in the swamps of Eastern Iraq. Reports of yellow rain, people's skin melting right off their bones. The Iranians got itchy and finally went nuclear. Trouble is, they did so two hours before *that* speech. Some asshole in Plotsk launched half the Uralskoye SS-20 grid—they went to launch on warning eight months ago—burning south, praise Jesus. Scratch the Middle East, period—everything from the Nile to the Khyber Pass is toast. We're still waiting for the call-back on Moscow, but SAC has put the whole Peacemaker force on airborne alert. So far we've lost the eastern seaboard as far south as North Virginia and they've lost the Donbass basin and Vladivostok. Things are a mess; nobody can even agree whether we're fighting the commies or something else. But the box at Chernobyl—Project Koschei—the doors are open, Roger. We orbited a Keyhole-eleven over it and there are tracks, leading west. The PLUTO strike didn't stop it—and nobody knows what the fuck is going on in WarPac country. Or France, or Germany, or Japan, or England."

The colonel makes a grab for Roger's Wild Turkey, rubs the neck clean and swallows from the bottle. He looks at Roger with a wild expression on his face. "Koschei is loose, Roger. They fucking woke the thing. And now they can't control it. Can you believe that?"

"I can believe that."

"I want you back behind a desk tomorrow morning, Roger. We need to know what this Thulu creature is capable of. We need to know what to do to stop it. Forget Iraq; Iraq is a smoking hole in the map. But K-Thulu is heading towards the Atlantic coast. What are we going to do if it doesn't stop?"

Masada

The city of XK-Masada sprouts like a vast mushroom, a mile-wide dome emerging from the top of a cold plateau on a dry planet that orbits a dying star. The jagged black shapes of F-117's howl across the empty skies outside it at dusk and dawn, patrolling the threatening emptiness that stretches as far as the mind can imagine.

Shadows move in the streets of the city, hollowed out human shells in uniform. They rustle around the feet of the towering concrete blocks like the dry leaves of autumn, obsessively focussed on the tasks that lend structure to their remaining days. Above them tower masts of steel, propping up the huge geodesic dome that arches across the sky: blocking out the hostile, alien constellations, protecting frail humanity from the dust storms that periodically scour the bones of the ancient world. The gravity here is a little lighter, the night sky whorled and marbled by the diaphanous sheets of gas blasted off the dying star that lights their days. During the long winter nights, a flurry of carbon dioxide snow dusts the surface of the dome: but the air is bone-dry, the city slaking its thirst on subterranean aquifers.

This planet was once alive—there is still a scummy sea of algae near the equator that feeds oxygen into the atmosphere, and there is a range of volcanoes near the north pole that speaks of plate tectonics in motion—but it is visibly dying. There is a lot of history here, but no future.

Sometimes, in the early hours when he cannot sleep, Roger walks outside the city, along the edge of the dry plateau. Machines labour on behind him, keeping the city tenuously intact: he pays them little attention. There is talk of mounting an expedition to Earth one of these years, to salvage whatever is left before the searing winds of time erase them forever. Roger doesn't like to think about that. He tries to avoid thinking about Earth as much as possible: except when he cannot sleep but walks along the cliff top, prodding at memories of Andrea and Jason and his parents and sister and relatives and friends, each of them as painful as the socket of a missing tooth. He has a mouthful of emptiness, bitter and aching, out here on the edge of the plateau.

Sometimes Roger thinks he's the last human being alive. He works in an office, feverishly trying to sort out what went wrong: and bodies move around him, talking, eating in the canteen, sometimes talking to him and waiting as if they expect a dialogue. There are bodies here, men and some women chatting, civilian and some military—but no people. One of the bodies, an army surgeon, told him he's suffering from a common stress disorder, survivor's guilt. This may be so, Roger admits, but it doesn't change anything. Soulless days follow sleepless nights into oblivion, dust trickling over the side of the cliff like sand into the un-dug graves of his family.

A narrow path runs along the side of the plateau, just downhill from the foundations of the city power plant where huge apertures belch air warmed by the radiators of the nuclear reactor. Roger follows the path, gravel and sandy rock crunching under his worn shoes. Foreign stars twinkle overhead, forming unrecognizable patterns that tell him he's far from home. The trail drops away from the top of the plateau, until the city is an unseen shadow looming above and behind his shoulder. To his right is a dizzying panorama, the huge rift valley with its ancient city of the dead stretched out before him. Beyond it rise alien mountains, their peaks as high and airless as the dead volcanoes of Mars.

About half a mile away from the dome, the trail circles an outcrop of rock and takes a downhill switchback turn. Roger stops at the bend and looks out across the desert at his feet. He sits down, leans against the rough cliff face and stretches his legs out across the path, so that his feet dangle over nothingness. Far below him, the dead valley is furrowed with rectangular depressions; once, millions of years ago, they might have been fields, but nothing like that survives to this date. They're just dead, like everyone else on this world. Like Roger.

In his shirt pocket, a crumpled, precious pack of cigarettes. He pulls a white cylinder out with shaking fingers, sniffs at it, then flicks his lighter under it. Scarcity has forced him to cut back: he coughs at the first lungful of stale smoke, a harsh, racking croak. The irony of being saved from lung cancer by a world war is not lost on him.

He blows smoke out, a tenuous trail streaming across the cliff. "Why me?" he asks quietly.

The emptiness takes its time answering. When it does, it speaks with the Colonel's voice. "You know the reason."

"I didn't want to do it," he hears himself saying. "I didn't want to leave them behind."

The void laughs at him. There are miles of empty air beneath his dangling feet. "You had no choice."

"Yes I did! I didn't have to come here." He pauses. "I didn't have to do anything," he says quietly, and inhales another lungful of death. "It was all automatic. Maybe it was inevitable."

"—Evitable," echoes the distant horizon. Something dark and angular skims across the stars, like an echo of extinct pterosaurs. Turbofans whirring within its belly, the F-117 hunts on: patrolling to keep at bay the ancient evil, unaware that the battle is already lost. "Your family could still be alive, you know."

He looks up. "They could?" Andrea? Jason? "Alive?"

The void laughs again, unfriendly: "There is life eternal within the eater of souls. Nobody is ever forgotten or allowed to rest in peace. They populate the simulation spaces of its mind, exploring all the possible alternative endings to their life. There is a fate worse than death, you know."

Roger looks at his cigarette disbelievingly: throws it far out into the night sky above the plain. He watches it fall until its ember is no longer visible. Then he gets up. For a long moment he stands poised on the edge of the cliff nerving himself and thinking. Then he takes a step back, turns, and slowly makes his way back up the trail towards the redoubt on the plateau. If his analysis of the situation is wrong, at least he is still alive. And if he is right, dying would be no escape.

He wonders why hell is so cold at this time of year.

ß ∂

The Unthinkable

Bruce Sterling

ince the Strategic Arms Talks of the early 1970s, it had been the policy of the Soviets to keep to their own quarters as much as the negotiations permitted—in fear, the Americans surmised, of novel forms of technical eavesdropping.

Dr. Tsyganov's Baba Yaga hut now crouched warily on the meticulously groomed Swiss lawn. Dr. Elwood Doughty assembled a hand of cards and glanced out the hut's window. Protruding just above the sill was the great scaly knee of one of the hut's six giant chicken legs, a monstrous knobby member as big around as an urban water main. As Doughty watched, the chicken knee flexed restlessly, and the hut stirred around them, rising with a seasick lurch, then settling with a squeak of timbers and a rustle of close-packed thatch.

Tsyganov discarded, drew two cards from the deck, and examined them, his wily blue eyes shrouded in greasy wisps of long graying hair. He plucked his shabby beard with professionally black-rimmed nails.

Doughty, to his pleased surprise, had been dealt a straight flush in the suit of Wands. With a deft pinch, he dropped two ten-dollar bills from the top of the stack at his elbow.

Tsyganov examined his dwindling supply of hard currency with a look of Slavic fatalism. He grunted, scratched, then threw his cards faceup on the table. Death. The Tower. The deuce, trey, and five of Coins.

"Chess?" Tsyganov suggested, rising.

"Another time," said Doughty. Though, for security reasons, he lacked any official ranking in the chess world, Doughty was in fact quite an accomplished chess strategist, particularly strong in the endgame. Back in the marathon sessions of '83, he and Tsyganov had dazzled their fellow arms wizards with an impromptu tournament lasting almost four months, while the team awaited (fruitlessly) any movement on the stalled verification accords. Doughty could not outmatch the truly gifted Tsyganov, but he had come to know and recognize the flow of his opponent's thought.

Mostly, though, Doughty had conceived a vague loathing for Tsyganov's prized personal chess set, which had been designed on a Reds versus Whites Russian Civil War theme. The little animate pawns uttered tiny, but rather dreadful, squeaks of anguish, when set upon by the commissar bishops and cossack knights.

"Another time?" murmured Tsyganov, opening a tiny cabinet and extracting a bottle of Stolichnaya vodka. Inside the fridge, a small overworked frost demon glowered in its trap of coils and blew a spiteful gasp of cold fog. "There will not be many more such opportunities for us, Elwood."

"Don't I know it." Doughty noted that the Russian's vodka bottle bore an export label printed in English. There had been a time when Doughty would have hesitated to accept a drink in a Russian's quarters. Treason in the cup. Subversion potions. Those times already seemed quaint.

"I mean this will be over. History, grinding on. This entire business"— Tsyganov waved his sinewy hand, as if including not merely Geneva, but a whole state of mind—"will become a mere historical episode."

"I'm ready for that," Doughty said stoutly. Vodka splashed up the sides of his shot glass with a chill, oily threading. "I never much liked this life, Ivan."

"No?"

"I did it for duty."

"Ah." Tsyganov smiled. "Not for the travel privileges?"

"I'm going home," Doughty said. "Home for good. There's a place outside Fort Worth where I plan to raise cattle."

"Back to Texas?" Tsyganov seemed amused, touched. "The hard-line weapons theorist become a farmer, Elwood? You are a second Roman Cincinnatus!"

Doughty sipped vodka and examined the gold-flake socialist-realist icons hung on Tsyganov's rough timber walls. He thought of his own office, in the basement of the Pentagon. Relatively commodious, by basement standards.

Comfortably carpeted. Mere yards from the world's weightiest centers of military power. Secretary of Defense. Joint Chiefs of Staff. Secretaries of the Army, Navy, Air Force. Director of Defense Research and Necromancy. The Lagoon, the Potomac, the Jefferson Memorial. The sight of pink dawn on the Capitol Dome after pulling an all-nighter. Would he miss the place? No. "Washington, D.C., is no proper place to raise a kid."

"Ah." Tsyganov's peaked eyebrows twitched. "I heard you had married at last." He had, of course, read Doughty's dossier. "And your child, Elwood, he is strong and well?"

Doughty said nothing. It would be hard to keep the tone of pride from his voice. Instead, he opened his wallet of tanned basilisk skin and showed the Russian a portrait of his wife and infant son. Tsyganov brushed hair from his eyes and examined the portrait closely. "Ah," he said. "The boy much resembles you."

"Could be," Doughty said.

"Your wife," Tsyganov said politely, "has a very striking face."

"The former Jeane Seigel. Staffer on the Senate Foreign Relations Committee."

"I see. The defense intelligentsia?"

"She edited *Korea and the Theory of Limited War*. Considered one of the premier works on the topic."

"She must make a fine little mother." Tsyganov gulped his vodka, ripped into a crust of black rye bread. "My son is quite grown now. He writes for *Literaturnaya Gazeta*. Did you see his article on the Iraqi arms question? Some very serious developments lately concerning the Islamic jinni."

"I should have read it," Doughty said. "But I'm getting out of the game, Ivan. Out while the getting's good." The cold vodka was biting into him. He laughed briefly. "They're going to shut us down in the States. Pull our funding. Pare us back to the bone, and past the bone. 'Peace dividend.' We'll all fade away. Like MacArthur. Like Robert Oppenheimer."

"'I am become Death, the Destroyer of Worlds,'" Tsyganov quoted.

"Yeah," Doughty mused. "That was too bad about poor old Oppy having to become Death."

Tsyganov examined his nails. "Will there be purges, you think?"

"I beg your pardon?"

"I understand the citizens in Utah are suing your federal government. Over conduct of the arms tests, forty years ago..."

"Oh," Doughty said. "The two-headed sheep, and all that. There are still night gaunts and banshees downwind of the old test sites. Up in the Rockies... Not a place to go during the full moon." He shuddered. "But 'purges'?

No. That's not how it works for us."

"You should have seen the sheep around Chernobyl."

"'Bitter wormwood,'" Doughty quoted.

"No act of duty avoids its punishment." Tsyganov opened a can of dark fish that smelled like spiced kippered herring. "And what of the Unthinkable, eh? What price have you paid for *that* business?"

Doughty's voice was level, quite serious. "We bear any burden in defense of freedom."

"Not the best of your American notions, perhaps." Tsyganov speared a chunk of fish from the can with a three-tined fork. "To deliberately contact an utterly alien entity from the abyss between universes... an ultrademonic demigod whose very geometry is, as it were, an affront to sanity... that Creature of nameless eons and inconceivable dimensions...." Tsyganov patted his bearded lips with a napkin. "That hideous Radiance that bubbles and blasphemes at the center of all infinity—"

"You're being sentimental," Doughty said. "We must recall the historical circumstances in which the decision was made to develop the Azathoth Bomb. Giant Japanese Majins and Gojiras crashing through Asia. Vast squadrons of Nazi juggernauts blitzkrieging Europe... and their undersea leviathans, preying on shipping...."

"Have you ever seen a *modern* leviathan, Elwood?"

"Yes, I witnessed one... feeding. At the base in San Diego." Doughty could recall it with an awful clarity—the great finned navy monster, the barnacled pockets in its vast ribbed belly holding a slumbering cargo of hideous batwinged gaunts. On order from Washington, the minor demons would waken, slash their way free of the monster's belly, launch, and fly to their appointed targets with pitiless accuracy and the speed of a tempest. In their talons, they clutched triple-sealed spells that could open, for a few hideous microseconds, the portal between universes. And for an instant, the Radiance of Azathoth would gush through. And whatever that Color touched—wherever its unthinkable beam contacted earthly substance—the Earth would blister and bubble in cosmic torment. The very dust of the explosion would carry an unearthly taint.

"And have you seen them test the bomb, Elwood?"

"Only underground. The atmospheric testing was rather before my time...."

"And what of the poisoned waste, Elwood? From beneath the cyclopean walls of our scores of power plants..."

"We'll deal with that. Launch it into the abyss of space, if we must." Doughty hid his irritation with an effort. "What are you driving at?"

"I worry, my friend. I fear that we've gone too far. We have been responsible men, you and I. We have labored in the service of responsible leaders. Fifty long years have passed, and not once has the Unthinkable been unleashed in anger. But we have trifled with the Eternal in pursuit of mortal ends. What is our pitiful fifty years in the eons of the Great Old Ones? Now, it seems, we will rid ourselves of our foolish applications of this dreadful knowledge. But will we ever be clean?"

"That's a challenge for the next generation. I've done what I can. I'm only mortal. I accept that."

"I do not think we can put it away. It is too close to us. We have lived in its shadow too long, and it has touched our souls."

"I'm through with it," Doughty insisted. "My duty is done. And I'm tired of the burden. I'm tired of trying to grasp issues, and imagine horrors, and feel fears and temptations, that are beyond the normal bounds of sane human contemplation. I've earned my retirement, Ivan. I have a right to a human life."

"The Unthinkable has touched you. Can you truly put that aside?"

"I'm a professional," Doughty said. "I've always taken the proper precautions. The best military exorcists have looked me over…. I'm clean."

"Can you know that?"

"They're the best we have; I trust their professional judgment…. If I find the shadow in my life again, I'll put it aside. I'll cut it away. Believe me, I know the feel and smell of the Unthinkable—it'll never find a foothold in my life again…." A merry chiming came from Doughty's right trouser pocket.

Tsyganov blinked, then went on. "But what if you find it is simply too close to you?"

Doughty's pocket rang again. He stood up absently. "You've known me for years, Ivan," he said, digging into his pocket. "We may be mortal men, but we were always prepared to take the necessary steps. We were prepared. No matter what the costs."

Doughty whipped a large square of pentagram-printed silk from his pocket, spread it with a flourish.

Tsyganov was startled. "What is that?"

"Portable telephone," Doughty said. "Newfangled gadget. I always carry one now."

Tsyganov was scandalized. "You brought a telephone into my private quarters?"

"Damn," Doughty said with genuine contrition. "Forgive me, Ivan. I truly forgot that I had this thing with me. Look, I won't take the call here. I'll leave." He opened the door, descended the wooden stair into grass and Swiss sunlight.

Behind him, Tsyganov's hut rose on its monster chicken legs, and stalked away—wobbling, it seemed to Doughty, with a kind of offended dignity. In the hut's retreating window, he glimpsed Tsyganov, peering out half-hidden, unable to restrain his curiosity. Portable telephones. Another technical break-through of the inventive West.

Doughty smoothed the ringing silk on the top of an iron lawn table and muttered a Word of power. An image rose sparkling above the woven penta-gram—the head and shoulders of his wife.

He knew at once from her look that the news was bad. "Jeane?" he said.

"It's Tommy," she said. "What happened?"

"Oh," she said with brittle clarity, "nothing. Nothing you'd see. But the lab tests are in. The exorcists—they say he's tainted."

The foundation blocks of Doughty's life cracked swiftly and soundlessly apart. "Tainted," he said blankly. "Yes... I hear you, dear...."

"They came to the house and examined him. They say he's monstrous."

Now anger seized him. "Monstrous. How can they say that? He's only a four-month-old kid! How the hell could they know he's monstrous? What the hell do they really know, anyway? Some crowd of ivory-tower witch doctors..."

His wife was weeping openly now. "You know what they recommended, Elwood? You know what they want us to do?"

"We can't just... put him away," Doughty said. "He's our son." He paused, took a breath, looked about him. Smooth lawns, sunlight, trees. The world. The future. A bird flickered past him.

"Let's think about this," he said. "Let's think this through. Just how monstrous is he, exactly?"

☖ ☗

Flash Frame

Silvia Moreno-Garcia

The sound is yellow.

                           ♋ ⌀

It was when you could still make a living freelancing in Mexico City. Nowadays, it's wire-services and regurgitated shit, but in 1982 rags still needed original content. I did a couple of funky articles, the latest about the cheapest whore in the city for *Enigma!*, a mixed-bag of crime stories, tits and freakish news items. It paid well and on time.

I also did articles for an arts and culture magazine which, I was hoping, would turn into a permanent position. But when it came time to gather rent money, *Enigma!* was first on my mind.

The trouble was that there was a new assistant editor at *Enigma!* and he didn't like the old crop of stringers. To get past him, I had to pitch harder. I needed better stories. Stories he couldn't refuse.

The crime stuff was a bust, nothing good recently, so I moved onto sex and decided to swing by El Tabu, a porno cinema housed in a great, Art Decco building. It's gone now, bulldozed to make way for condos.

Back then, it still stood, both ruined and glorious. The great days of porno of the '70s had come and gone, and videocassettes were invading the market. El Tabu stood defiant, yet crumbling. Inside you could find rats as big as rabbits, statues holding torchlights in their hands and a Venus in the lobby. Elegant, ancient and large. Some people came to sleep during a double feature and used the washrooms to take a bath. Others came for the shows. Some were peddling. I'm not going to explain what they were peddling; you figure it out.

It was a good place to listen to chatter. A stringer needs that chatter. One afternoon, I gathered my notebook and my tape recorder, paid for a ticket and went looking for Sebastian, the projectionist, who had a knack for gossiping and profiting from it.

Sebastian hadn't heard any interesting things—there was some vague stuff about a whole squadron of Russian prostitutes in a high-rise apartment building near downtown and university students selling themselves for sex, but I'd heard it before. Then Sebastian got a funny look on his face and asked me for a cigarette. This meant he was zeroing on the good stuff.

"I don't think I should tell you, but there's a religious group coming in every Thursday," he said, as he took a puff. "Order of something. Have you heard of Enrique Zozoya?"

"No," I said.

"He's the one that's renting the place. For the group."

"A porno theatre doesn't seem like the nicest place for a congregation."

"I think it's some sort of sex cult. I can't tell because I don't look. They bring their own projectionist and I have to wait in the lobby," Sebastian explained.

"So how do you know it's a sex cult and they're not worshipping Jesus?"

"I can't watch, but I can very well hear some stuff. It doesn't sound like Jesus."

♌ ♋

There was no Wikipedia. You couldn't Google a name. What you could do, was go through archives and dig out microfiches. Fortunately, Enrique Zozoya wasn't that hard to find. An ex-hippie activist in the '60s, he had turned New Age guru in the early '70s, doing horoscopes. He'd peaked mid-decade, selling natal charts to a few celebrities, then sinking into anonymity. There was nothing about him in the past few years, but he'd obviously found a new source of employment in this religious order.

Armed with the background I had clubbed together, I ventured to El Tabu the following Thursday with my worn bag pack containing my notebook, my tape recorder and my cigarettes. The tape recorder was a bit banged up and sometimes it wouldn't play right, or it would switch on record for no reason, but I didn't have money to get a new one. The cigarettes, on the other hand, could be counted upon on any occasion.

Sebastian didn't look too happy to see me, but I mentioned some money and he softened. He agreed to sneak me into the theatre before the show started, onto the second balcony where I would not be spotted. The place was huge and the crowd that gathered every Thursday was small. They wouldn't notice me.

Sitting behind a red velvet curtain, eating pistachios, I waited for the show to start. At around eight o'clock about fifty people walked in. I peeked from behind my hiding place and recognized Enrique Zozoya as he moved to the front of the theatre. He was dressed in a bright yellow outfit. He said a few words which I couldn't make out and then he sat down.

That was that. The projection started.

It was a faux-Roman movie. Rome as seen by some Hollywood producer. It could have been filmed in 1954 and directed by DeMille. Except DeMille wouldn't have featured bare tits. Lots of women, half-dressed, in what was some sort of throne room. In the background I noticed several men and women, less comely and muscled. Slightly unsettling in their looks. There was something twisted and perverted about them. But the camera focused on the people in the foreground, the young and beautiful women giggling and feeding grapes to a guy. There were men, chests-bared, leaning against a column. The tableaux was completed by an actor who was playing an emperor and his companion, a dark-haired beauty.

It lasted about ten minutes. Just before the lights when on, I caught sight of a flash frame. A single, brief image of a woman in a yellow dress.

That was it. Enrique Zozoya stood to speak to the audience. I didn't hear what he was saying—I was sitting too far back—but it wasn't anything of consequence because just a short while later everyone was out the door.

I left feeling dejected. There was nothing to write about. Ten minutes of some porno, probably imported from Italy. And even that it had been disappointing. You could hardly see much of anything in that scene they'd chosen; bare breasts, yes, but nothing more.

What a waste.

ౖ ౙ

I returned the following Thursday because I kept thinking there had to be something more. Maybe the previous show had been a bust, but this one might be better.

Sebastian let me in after I shared my cigarettes and I sat down in the balcony. People arrived, took their seats, Enrique Zozoya in his yellow outfit said a few words and the projection began. It was the same deal, only this time the group was larger. Maybe a hundred people.

I was disappointed to see the film was the one we had watched last time. Not the same section, but it was obviously the same movie. This time, the sequence took place in a Roman circus where aristocrats had gathered to watch a chariot race. There was more nudity and the erotic content had been amped a bit, with a stony-looking emperor sitting with two naked girls in his lap—one of them the dark-haired woman from the previous sequence—fondling their breasts. Unfortunately, he seemed more interested in the race than the women.

The music was loud and of poor quality. There was no dialogue. There hadn't been any dialogue in the previous scene either, which struck me as a bit odd, since you'd expect a few jokes or poor attempts at breathless sexiness at this point.

The emperor mouthed a few words and I realized the audio track must have been removed. The music playing was probably layered onto the film to replace the original soundtrack and had nothing to do with the film. Someone had taken the added effort of inserting moans and sighs into the audio track, but the dialogue track had been clearly lost. Not that it would be much of a loss for this type of flick.

The emperor mouthed something else and again I noticed a flash frame—a few seconds long—of a woman in a yellow dress. She was sitting in a throne room, held a fan against her face, and her blond hair was laced with jewels.

The film was cut off shortly afterwards and the audience left.

I drummed my fingers against my steno pad. What I had was nothing but some European exploitation movie, probably filmed in the late '70s by the looks of it, which for some odd reason attracted a group of about a hundred people to its weekly screening. And it wasn't even screened completely, just a few minutes of it.

Why?

♋ ♌

I visited the Cineteca Nacional on Monday, which was the place to find information about movies. I had very little to go by, and looking through newspaper clips and data sheets proved fruitless. I asked one of the employees at the cineteca's Documentation and Information centre for assistance, and she said she'd phone me if she found something.

I decided to move in a different direction, expanding my knowledge of Zozoya. He'd been a film student before turning to astrology, even shooting a couple of shorts. Aside from that, which might explain how he got hold of this bit of film, there was nothing new.

Tuesday I pounded some copy for the arts and culture magazine, ready to give up on El Tabu.

Wednesday I had a nightmare.

I was laying in bed when a woman crawled up, onto me. She was naked, but wore a golden headpiece with a veil. Her skin was a sickly yellow, as though she were jaundiced.

She pressed her breasts against my chest and began rubbing herself against me. I touched her hips, but withdrew my hand, quickly. There was something unpleasant about the texture of her skin.

I lifted a hand, pulling at her veil.

But she had no face. It was only a yellow blur.

When I woke up, it was nearly nine and I was late for my meeting with the editor of the arts and culture magazine. I turned in my copy and left quickly. I didn't feel well. I went home, laid down, and spent most of the day dozing in front of the television set. I looked at my steno pad and the lined, yellow pages reminded me of leprous skin. I didn't do much writing that afternoon.

Thursday evening I returned to El Tabu.

Journalists know when they've caught the scent of a good story. It's a sixth sense, learning to distinguish the golden nuggets amongst the pebbles. I knew I had a nugget. I just couldn't see it yet.

This time the sequence took place in a banquet hall, with all the guests wearing masks and sitting naked. Several of the actors were unsuitable for such a scene, with obvious physical flaws, including scars. A few of them looked filthy, as though they had not bathed in several weeks. The emperor and the dark-haired woman next to him were the only ones not wearing masks. They both stared rigidly ahead, as the guests began to copulate on the floor.

The woman whispered something to the emperor. He nodded.

This time it was not a flash frame. We were treated to a full minute of footage showing the woman in the yellow dress, the fan held in front of her face, yellow curtains billowing behind her and allowing us a glimpse of a long hallway full of pillars. The woman crooked a finger towards the audience, as if calling for us.

The film switched back to the banquet scene where the young woman sitting next to the emperor had collapsed. Slaves were trying to revive her, but her tongue poked out of her mouth grotesquely. The soundtrack, with its moans and sighs, was completely unsuited for this scene.

The lights went on. I listened carefully, trying to catch what Zozoya said. It sounded like he was chanting. The congregation chanted with him. I noticed it was a larger group. Perhaps two hundred people, singing.

I grabbed my jacket and stepped out.

Life was too short to waste it on exploitation flicks and weirdos.

ৡ ৡ

Three days later, I had another nightmare.

Light, gentle fingertips fell on my temples, then trickled down my face, neck and chest. Nails raked my arms. I woke to see the woman with the yellow veil. She was on her knees.

She showed me her vulva, spreading it open with her fingers. Yellow, like her skin. An awful, sickly yellow. She pressed her hands, which seemed oily to the touch, against my chest.

I woke up, rushed to the bathroom and vomited.

ৡ ৡ

In the morning, I cracked a couple of eggs. I stared at the bright yellow yolks, then tossed them down the drain.

I spent most of the morning sitting in the living room, shuffling papers and going over my notes for an arts and culture article. Every once in a while I glanced at the manila folder containing my research on El Tabu. The beige envelope seemed positively yellow. I tossed the whole thing down the garbage chute.

ৡ ৡ

Wednesday I dreamt about her again. When I woke up, I could barely button my shirt. I was supposed to go pick up a check for my arts and culture story, but when I reached a busy intersection I caught sight of all the yellow taxis rolling down the street. They resembled lithe scarabs.

A stall had sunflowers for sale. I turned around and rushed back to my apartment.

I sat in front of the television set, shivering.

I'm not sure at what time I fell asleep, but in my dream she was gnawing my chest. I woke up at once, screaming.

I shuffled through the apartment, desperately looking for my cigarettes. I grabbed my bag pack, all its contents stumbling onto the floor. My tape recorder bounced against the couch. The play button went on.

I grabbed a cigarette, heard the whirring of the recorder and then a sound.

It was the movie's soundtrack. It must have been recording the last time I was there.

I was about to switch it off when I heard something.

The cigarette fell from my mouth.

ଓ ଓ

Sneaking into El Tabu was not hard. Bums planning on spending the night there did it all the time. I sat in the balcony, my hands on my bag pack.

Below me, I counted some three hundred viewers.

The movie began to play. The emperor rode in an open litter. He was headed to a funeral. The funeral of the black-haired woman. It was a procession. Men held torches to light the way. One could glimpse men and women copulating in the background, behind the rows of slaves with the torches. If you looked carefully, you might see that some of the people writhing on the floor were not making love to anything human.

The emperor rode in his litter and did not see any of this. The camera pulled back to show he was not alone. There was a woman with him. She wore a yellow gown. She began taking off her gown, lifting her veil. It was yellow; the shade of a bright flame.

He looked away from her.

As did I.

I lit a match.

ଓ ଓ

I woke up late the next day, to the insistent ringing of the phone.

I picked it up and rested my back against the wall.

It was the lady from the Cineteca Nacional. She said she had that information about that Italian film I had been looking for. It was called *Nero's Last Days*. They had a print in the vault.

ଓ ଓ

On March 24, 1982, a great fire destroyed 99 percent of the film archives of the Cineteca Nacional. One of the vaults alone kept 2,000 prints made out of nitrocellulose. It took the firemen sixteen hours to put the whole thing out.

As for El Tabu, I already told you about it: they made the site into condos after twenty years of the empty, charred lot sitting there.

༞ ༚

You are wondering why. I'll tell you why. It was the sound recording. The tape had caught what my ears could not hear: the real audio track of the movie. The voice track.

It's hard to describe.

The sound was yellow. A bright, noxious yellow.

Festering yellow. The sound of withered teeth scraping against flesh. Of pustules bursting open. Diseased. Hungry.

The voice, yellow, speaking to the audience. Telling it things. Asking for things. Yellow limbs and yellow lips, and the yellow maw, the voracious voice that should never have spoken at all.

The things it asked for.

Insatiable. Yellow.

Warning signs are yellow.

I paid attention to the warning.

༞ ༚

I did get that job at the arts and culture magazine. I've been associate editor for five years now, but some things never change. I carry my bag pack everywhere, never been a briefcase man. I still smoke a pack a day. Same brand. Still use matches.

Anyway, I've got a very important screening. The Cineteca Nacional is doing a retrospective of 1970s cinema. They have some great Mexican movies. Also some obscure European flicks. There's a rare print that was just discovered a few months ago; part of the film collection of Enrique Zozoya's widow, who was an avid collector of European movies. It was thought lost years ago.

It's called *Nero's Last Days*.

Since 1982, the Cineteca Nacional has gotten more high-tech, with neat features like its temperature controlled vaults. But since 1982 I've learned a thing or two about chemistry.

It'll take the firemen more than sixteen hours to put it out.

༞ ༚

Some Buried Memory

W. H. Pugmire

Charlotte Hund stood before the full-length mirror in its great gilded frame and examined herself. In the palsied yellow light of the enormous room she could not see her reflection clearly; she could just make out the rough texture of her large face, the verdant eyes, the uneven tusks of xanthic ivory behind the bloated lips. Raising a hand, she smoothed the nest of hairs that sprouted from one corner of her mouth, then scratched her face with thick nails. "Is it not true, sir, that I am the ugliest woman in this city?"

"Au monde, madame, au monde," Sebastian Melmoth assured her, to which she smiled.

"I often think that it was for this ugliness that I was shunned in Boston and not my criminal reputation."

Her host sucked on his opium-tainted cigarette. When he exhaled, he fancied that the smoke formed itself suggestively before his face. "You must tell me of your crime, Miss Hund," he told her as he admired the scarab ring on one fat finger. "You are certainly criminally grotesque; but ugliness is a crime of nature, not a felon of choice. Tell me the tale of your trespass, and drench your telling it with such rich description that I may fully imagine it."

He sucked once more at his bit of nacotia and closed his eyes.

Charlotte stepped away from the mirror and moved to one of the room's small stained-glass windows. "To speak of my sin would mean to reveal my life, and there isn't much to tell. I do not know my parentage, for I was found."

"Found?"

She shrugged. "So I was eventually told, by my grandmother, who raised me. She would call me her 'fond foundling,' which I liked. Grandmother was an eccentric Boston witch. She taught me divination, and together we discovered my talent for finding long-buried treasure." Turning away from the window, Charlotte walked to a table and examined the beautifully crafted miniature sphinx that sat upon it. "It's amazing, the things one finds buried beneath the ground. I could sniff these things, and these nails were fashioned for digging. I especially loved the old burying grounds of New England. I remember one curious early morning, when grandmother hinted that she knew more about my background than she was wont to let on; for as we burrowed beside one venerable tree, she whispered that my kinfolk dwelt beneath that chilly sod."

"How esoteric."

"We found quite a treasure that morning. Together, over time, we collected quite a pile of buried treasure. She taught me how to weave spells, and together we would dance naked beneath the autumn moon. As I grew older, my ugliness increased, and society taught me that its heart is cruel. I began to shun humanity, to exist in the hours when most were asleep. My own slumber was haunted by curious dreams of dark figures in black spaces. I would awaken, at times, in curious places, with booty in my embrace but no memory of where I had been or with what I had occupied my time. I cannot clearly recall the morning I was found, with mud on my hands and an amazing taste in my mouth. Whatever I had done, it earned me a new home in a state hospital. I was lunatic at first, screaming to be with my grandmother. Over the years I grew more settled. I studied the sane and began to ape their ways. I discovered a great fondness for literature, and my grandmother would bring me wonderful books. The news of her death was a cruel blow, but I endured, and eventually won my release. Among my belongings was a key to grandmother's house, now mine; it was at the house that I found her letter, from which I learned of the wealth that she had left me, and that told me of this city of Gershom, where I would find exile."

"For which we are the richer," Sebastian told her. "I'm exceptionally fond of the gift of this ring. Its ancient metal, slipped so snugly around my flesh, feels very old indeed. Please tell me that you found it during one of your excavations, adorning the finger bone of some long-interred fellow. That would give me such delicious dreams."

"I'm happy that you like it. And in exchange, you will keep your promise."

"Ah, a journey to our cemetery isle. I have visited it but once; so much nature hurts my eyes, and the leaves are particularly bright at this autumnal time."

"I'm anxious to see it in reality. Your beautiful verbal portrait of it has danced in my imagination. I can well believe that you were once a poet. Come, take my arm and let us leave this smoky chamber. I'm in need of moonlight. We'll stroll beneath its glow and you can tell me what brought you to this remarkable city."

Linking arms, they vacated the building. The night was very still and very silent. As they walked past factories and old brownstones, Sebastian Melmoth began to tell his tale. "I came to Gershom because of what the world calls sin. I came because I heard that this is a godless town, and without god there can be no fall from grace. I confess that I miss sin horribly. It gives such texture to existence. This spectral place has a way of luring lost souls to its confines. I find it a comfortable nether world. One meets such interesting sorts. As for transgression, well, I am hopeful that in time I shall find a new form of sin. And yet, the longer I remain in this city, the more intense my sensations become, innocent as they are. Gershom teases the brain with singular dreaming, and in such visions we find new forms of thought and novel ways in which to express innovative ideas. Ah, but here we are at our destination."

He led her onto a pier, and she saw the means of their transportation. "Oh my," she moaned.

"No, no. This teakwood raft is far sturdier than it looks, and the couch, though tiny, is quite comfortable. This small gap between pier and raft is easily stepped over. You see how even a heavy fellow like me can manage it. Take my hand and—*voila!* No, you sit on the couch. I shall stand and hold onto this pole. This pale young creature will be our Charon."

The ugly woman sat on the cushioned seat and watched as the child who was their navigator unwound the craft's brittle sail; and she wondered what was the good of such a canvas, on this windless night. Her interlocutor bent so as to whisper at her ear. "The poor child suffers from poliomyelitis or some such ailment. His limbs are quite curved. I like the way he walks, like some pathetic puppet. He will love you for any pennies you may throw his way. I seem to have forgotten my purse."

Charlotte reached into her pocket and produced a silver coin. Bowing to her, the child took the coin and pressed it against his forehead. His wide eyes looked past his wayfarers, into eventide, and when he began to sing the sound of his voice caused a chill to tingle Sebastian's spine. Charlotte listened to the wind that rose above the water. The raft began to move away from land, toward mist. That cloud of liquid air kissed the woman with beads of moisture, which she brushed away from her face with a rough hand. At last the mist began to thin, and Charlotte could see the mass of land that was their terminus. Eerily, Sebastian Melmoth began to whistle.

"Why do you make that sound, monsieur?"

"Because I am afraid." The winds extinguished, and yet the raft continued to move toward the island, as if pulled to it by some force. "The Isle of Moira," Sebastian continued, "draped in darkness. Her sand aches for the touch of our hot naked feet. She would drink our vitality with those mouths that are her barrows and her pits. Ah, and there—do you see her? Our desolate receptionist."

Charlotte peered at the place of stone steps toward which their craft sailed, and saw the grim figure that stood like some obsidian statue. The raft lodged itself perfectly against the pitted platform of the lowest step. Kicking off his shoes, the child limped toward the waiting figure and offered it his hand. Swiftly, the creature lowered itself until its cowled head was in alignment with the child's. The infant moved his mouth, as if whispering secrets. A dark face parted its lips and fed upon the lame boy's living breath. As the child began to shudder, the woman took him in her arms.

Sebastian removed his slippers and indicated to Charlotte that she should discard her shoes. He tried not to gape at the sight of her bestial feet, which were far more feral than her ungainly hands. Offering assistance, he helped her from the raft, onto the weathered stone steps. They approached the woman and her captive. Charlotte watched the dusky hand that loosened the lad's shirt and manipulated the flesh nearest the child's heart.

Sebastian's musical voice began to pipe. "Mistress Atropos, may I present Miss Charlotte Hund, of Boston? She has come to dance naked beneath your moon."

The black woman chuckled as she rose, not relinquishing her hold on the child. "You will want to climb the highest hill, where the wind is exquisitely musical among the numbered sarcophagi. You know the place, Melmoth; you capered there once yourself."

"In one of my Greek moments, yes. I was much younger then. And far less innocent. But we shall have to ascend slowly. These thick old limbs are no longer in fine fettle. Do release the child, Mistress, that he may playfully lead the way."

The woman spread her arms and the child hobbled forward, to Charlotte, whose hand he held. Sebastian watched as they began to climb the upward path, and then he touched his brow to the Mistress and followed his friend. The moon was as orange as many of the decorative leaves, and mauve shadows hovered behind the many trees and shrubs. Sebastian did not like the silence of the place; he could hear too loudly his labored breathing. Now and then, in places of deep shadow, he sensed that he was watched by shapes in the night. He followed the path, past tombs and angels and obelisks, watching the two before him. He saw the child suddenly stop and place a tiny hand to its heart. Stopping, Sebastian produced a gilded case, from which he snatched a cigarette.

"The child has been too active, too excited," Charlotte concluded as she folded her arms around the boy. "His heart is racing and he burns with fever."

"Yes, he suffers from that dread contagion called Life. But we are almost there, and he may rest upon one of the paws of the great beast. Shall I carry you, boy? Would you like a cigarette?"

Ignoring the man, the silent child took one of Charlotte's hands and continued to lead the way. They reached the crest, and Charlotte gazed in admiration at the moon-drenched colossus. She and the child watched as Sebastian approached the gigantic stone Sphynx, before which he raised his hands and snapped his fingers. His high voice hummed an ancient tune, and he smiled as Charlotte joined him in the danse. Happily, the lame child began to move with them, his crooked feet moving in imitation of the woman's hoofs. They moved beneath the moon for quite a while, until finally the child tripped and fell, clutching again at his chest. Charlotte dropped beside him and smoothed his brow with her rude hand. Sebastian watched as her expression altered, as she lowered her face to the earth and began to snuffle.

"Whatever are you doing?"

She looked at him with shining eyes. "There is something here, beneath this ground; something rare yet familiar, something seductive. It is a memory that I once knew, long ago; it has taste and texture, and it calls to me."

"Really, you are too fantastic. I think you've been touched by the corroded light of that torrid moon. I hate the moon when it resembles a scab on diseased flesh. Ugh! Those awful crimson shadows around the tombstones, it's too macabre."

Charlotte ignored his histrionic chatter and continued to smooth the ground with anxious fingers, the limping child beside her. She crawled until coming to a toppled obelisk, beside the base of which she found an opening in the earth. Peering into that cavity, she saw the steps that led beneath the surface. "Do you sense it," she asked the child, "how this hollow summons? Are you game, boy? Shall we investigate?" Standing, she took the lad's hand and led him down into the pit.

Sebastian Melmoth raised a white hand and sang some lines from Jonson:

"Farewell, thou child of my right hand, and joy;

My sin was too much hope of thee, dear boy…"

He watched them vanish into dank shadow. Then he turned to the gigantic Sphynx. Would she answer the riddle of what his friend would find? Was there anything that would appease doom? He looked to the moon, which had paled to a shade of ocher. Sebastian raised his hands to the sphere of dead refracted light, and then he began to remove his clothing.

The steps of loam felt strangely familiar to Charlotte's naked feet, like something she had known while dreaming. She paused one moment to press her brow against the earthen wall, breathing its aroma, which stirred a cloudy image in her brain of something she had known, now forgotten. Touching lips to the dark wall, she trembled at the taste. Something in the sensation filled her with happiness, and turning to the child she began to dance upon the steps. Weirdly, she could easily see the child's bright flesh in the dark place, the small hands held out to her. Eschewing caution, she took those hands and led the boy into a clownish dance upon the sleek and narrow steps. She seemed not to notice the heaviness of his breathing, and thought that he was clowning when he began to jerk with spasm. When she let go of his hands, she was too slow to catch his falling form. He tumbled down the stairs, to a level of rocky surface. Crying, she rushed to him and took up his still limp form in her embrace. She held him as is flesh grew cool and dry. She pressed him tighter to her breasts and whispered to his uncomprehending ear. How keenly she could smell his death, the fragrance of the stuff that clothed his bones. At last, she set his still form onto the surface to which he had fallen. Pressing fingers to his mouth, she pushed it shut. "Rest in peace, sweet innocent," she murmured.

Before her was a passageway, through which a charnel breeze wafted to her. She could smell the bits of old bone that, over time, had sifted through the ground, some poking through the earth, others littering the place. Their stench was like something she had known, intimately, in Boston; but the memory was vague, like a favorite delicacy from childhood that had been forgotten in dull adulthood, until happened on by chance. Charlotte followed the chthonic blast, through the passageway, until she came to a spacious grotto, which seemed to her like the forgotten catacomb of some deserted cathedral. Broken statuary stood among the boxes of discarded death. She peered at a raised platform, a kind of bema, and saw two figures huddled over an altar, whispering as they watched her approach. She did not look away from the green eyes set deep within the rubbery faces, eyes that resembled her own. The eldest creature moved to meet her at the steps leading to the platform, and offered her his bestial hand. He smoothed her face with that hand, and combed her hair with thick strong nails. His mouth found her own. His kiss was revelation. She knew from that kiss exactly who she was.

She turned at the sound of another who approached them, and sighed at the sight of the burden in his arms. She helped to place the broken body on the altar and touched a hand to the bright small face. His carrion bouquet made her mouth to water.

"Found him just above," the new arrival muttered. "Freshly dead."

The elder beast pressed his hands together and moaned in pleasure. "Excellent. A welcoming feast for our sister." He hissed as one of the others tilted toward one thin bent limb. "Where are your manners, Erebus? Our sister shall have first pick." Turning to Charlotte, he motioned to the child.

"Give me his tender heart," was her request.

ᘝ ᘓ

The Infernal History of the Ivybridge Twins

Molly Tanzer

for a number of people, whom, the author is certain, would not wish their names mentioned here

I.

Concerning of the life and death of St. John Fitzroy, Lord Calipash— the suffering of the Lady Calipash—the unsavory endeavors of Lord Calipash's cousin Mr. Villein—as well as an account of the curious circumstances surrounding the birth of the future Lord Calipash and his twin sister

In the county of Devonshire, in the parish of Ivybridge, stood the ancestral home of the Lords Calipash. Calipash Manor was large, built sturdily of the local limestone, and had stood for many years without fire or other catastrophe marring its expanse. No one could impugn the size and antiquity of the house, yet often one or another of those among Lord Calipash's acquaintance might be heard to comment that the Manor had a rather rambling, hodgepodge look to it, and this could not be easily refuted without the peril of speaking a falsehood. The reason for this was that the Lords Calipash had always been the very essence of English patriotism, and rather than ever tearing down any part of the house and building anew, each Lord Calipash had chosen to make additions and improvements to older structures. Thus, though the prospect was somewhat sprawling, it served as a pleasant enough reminder of the various styles of Devonian architecture, and became something of a local attraction.

St. John Fitzroy, Lord Calipash, was a handsome man, tall, fair-haired, and blue-eyed. He had been bred up as any gentleman of rank and fortune might be, and therefore the manner of his death was more singular than any aspect of his life. Now, given that this is, indeed, an *Infernal* History, the sad circumstances surrounding this good man's unexpected and early demise demand attention by the author, and they are inextricably linked with the Lord Calipash's cousin, a young scholar called Mr. Villein, who will figure more prominently in this narrative than his nobler relation.

Mr. Villein came to stay at Calipash Manor during the Seven Years' War, in order to prevent his being conscripted into the French army. Though indifference had previously characterized the relationship between Lord Calipash and Mr. Villein (Mr. Villein belonging to a significantly lower branch of the family tree), when Mr. Villein wrote to Lord Calipash to beg sanctuary, the good Lord would not deny his own flesh and blood. This was not to say, however, that Lord Calipash was above subtly encouraging his own flesh and blood to make his stay a short one, and to that end, he gave Mr. Villein the tower bedroom that had been built by one of the more eccentric Lords some generations prior to our tale, who so enjoyed pretending to be the Lady Jane Grey that he had the edifice constructed so his wife could dress up as member of the Privy Council and keep him locked up there for as long as nine days at a stretch. But that was not the reason Lord Calipash bade his cousin reside there—the tower was a drafty place, and given to damp, and thus seemed certain of securing Mr. Villein's speedy departure. As it turns out, however, the two men were so unlike one another, that what Lord Calipash thought was an insulting situation, Mr. Villein found entirely salubrious, and so, happily, out of a case of simple misunderstanding grew an affection, founded on deepest admiration for Mr. Villein's part, and for Lord Calipash's, enjoyment of toadying.

All the long years of the international conflict Mr. Villein remained at Calipash Manor, and with the passing of each and every day he came more into the confidence of Lord Calipash, until it was not an uncommon occurrence to hear members of Lord Calipash's circle using words like *inseparable* to describe their relationship. Then, only six months before the signing of the Treaty of Paris, the possibility of continued fellowship between Lord Calipash and Mr. Villein was quite suddenly extinguished. A Mr. Fellingworth moved into the neighborhood with his family, among them his daughter of fifteen years, Miss Alys Fellingworth. Dark of hair and eye but pale of cheek, her beauty did not go long unnoticed by the local swains. She had many suitors and many offers, but from among a nosegay of sparks she chose as her favorite blossom the Lord Calipash.

Mr. Villein had also been among Miss Fellingworth's admirers, and her decision wounded him—not so much that he refused to come to the wedding (he was very fond of cake), but certainly enough that all the love Mr. Villein had felt for Lord Calipash was instantly converted, as if by alchemy, to pure hatred. In his dolor, Mr. Villein managed to convince himself that Miss Fellingworth's father had pressured her to accept Lord Calipash's offer for the sake of his rank and income, against her true inclinations; that had she been allowed to pick her heart's choice, she certainly would have accepted Mr. Villein's suit rather than his cousin's. Such notions occupied Mr. Villein's thoughts whenever he saw the happy couple together, and every day his mind became more and more inhospitable to any pleasure he might have otherwise felt on account of his friend's newfound felicity.

A reader of this history might well wonder why Mr. Villein did not quit Calipash Manor, given that his situation, previously so agreeable, he now found intolerable. Mr. Villein was, however, loath to leave England. He had received a letter from his sister informing him that during his absence, his modest home had been commandeered by the army, and thus his furniture was in want of replacing, his lands trampled without hope of harvest, his stores pilfered, and, perhaps worst of all, his wretched sister was with child by an Austrian soldier who had, it seemed, lied about his interest in playing the rôle of father beyond the few minutes required to grant him that status. It seemed prudent to Mr. Villein to keep apart from such appalling circumstances for as long as possible.

Then one evening, from the window of his tower bedroom, Mr. Villein saw Lord Calipash partaking of certain marital pleasures with the new Lady Calipash against a tree in one of the gardens. Nauseated, Mr. Villein called for his servant and announced his determination to secretly leave Calipash Manor once and for all early the following morning. While the servant packed his bags and trunks, Mr. Villein penned a letter explaining his hasty departure to Lord Calipash, and left it, along with a token of remembrance, in Lord Calipash's study.

Quite early the next morning, just as he was securing his cravat, Mr. Villein was treated to the unexpected but tantalizing sight of Lady Calipash in *deshabille*. She was beside herself with grief, but eventually Mr. Villein, entirely sympathetic and eager to understand the source of her woe, coaxed the story from her fevered mind:

"I woke early, quite cold," gibbered Lady Calipash. "Lord Calipash had never come to bed, though he promised me when I went up that he should follow me after settling a few accounts. When I discovered him absent I rose and sought him in his study only to find him—*dead*. Oh! It was too terrible! His eyes were open, wide and round and staring. At first I thought it looked very much like he had been badly frightened, but then I thought he had almost a look of... of *ecstasy* about him. I believe—"

Here the Lady Calipash faltered, and it took some minutes for Mr. Villein to get the rest of the story from her, for her agitated state required his fetching smelling salts from out of his valise. Eventually, she calmed enough to relate the following:

"I believe he might have done himself the injury that took him from me," she sobbed. "His wrists were slit, and next to him lay his letter-opener. He... he had used his own blood to scrawl a message on the skirtingboards... oh Mr. Villein!"

"What did the message say?" asked Mr. Villein.

"It said, *he is calling, he is calling, I hear him*," she said, and then she hesitated.

"What is it, Lady Calipash?" asked Mr. Villein.

"I cannot see its importance, but he had this in his other hand," said she, and handed to Mr. Villein a small object wrapped in a handkerchief.

He took it from her, and saw that it was an odd bit of ivory, wrought to look like a lad's head crowned with laurel. Mr. Villein put it in his pocket and smiled at the Lady Calipash.

"Likely it has nothing to do with your husband's tragic end," he said gently. "I purchased this whilst in Greece, and the late Lord Calipash had often admired it. I gave it to him as a parting gift, for I had meant to withdraw from Calipash Manor this very morning."

"Oh, but you mustn't," begged Lady Calipash. "Not now, not after... Lord Calipash would wish you to be here. You mustn't go just now, please! For my sake..."

Mr. Villein would have been happy to remain on those terms, had the Lady Calipash finished speaking, but alas, there was one piece of information she had yet to relate.

"...and for our child's sake, as well," she concluded.

While the Lord Calipash's final message was being scrubbed from the skirtingboards, and his death was being declared *an accident* by the constable in order that the departed Lord might be buried in the churchyard, Mr. Villein violently interrogated Lady Calipash's serving-maid. The story was true—the Lady was indeed expecting—and this intelligence displeased Mr. Villein so immensely that even as he made himself pleasant and helpful with the hope that he might eventually win the Lady Calipash's affections, he sought to find a method of ridding her of her unborn child.

To Mr. Villein's mind, Lady Calipash could not but fall in love with her loyal confidant—believing as he did that she had always secretly admired him—but Mr. Villein knew that should she bear the late Lord Calipash's son, the estate would one day be entirely lost to him. Thus he dosed the Lady with recipes born of his own researches, for while Mr. Villein's *current* profession was that of scholar, in his youth he had pursued lines of study related to all manner of black magics and sorceries. For many years he had put aside his wicked thaumaturgy, being too happy in the company of Lord Calipash to travel those paths that demand solitude and gloom and suffering, but, newly motivated, he returned to his former interests with a desperate passion.

Like the Wife of Bath, Mr. Villein knew all manner of remedies for love's mischances, and he put wicked spells on the decoctions and tisanes that he prepared to help his cause. Yet despite Mr. Villein's skill with infusion and incantation, Lady Calipash grew heavy with child; indeed, she had such a healthy maternal glow about her that the doctor exclaimed that for one so young to be brought to childbed, she was certain of a healthy *accouchement*. Mr. Villein, as canny an adept at lying as other arts, appeared to be thrilled by his Lady's prospects, and was every day by her side. Though privately discouraged by her salutary condition, he was cheered by all manner of odd portents that he observed as her lying-in drew ever closer. First, a murder of large, evil-looking ravens took up residence upon the roof of Calipash Manor, cackling and cawing day and night, and then the ivy growing on Calipash Manor's aged walls turned from green to scarlet, a circumstance no naturalist in the area could satisfactorily explain. Though the Lady Calipash's delivery was expected in midwinter, a she-goat was found to be unexpectedly in the same delicate condition as her mistress, and gave birth to a two-headed kid that was promptly beaten to death and buried far from the Manor.

Not long after that unhappy parturition, which had disturbed the residents of Calipash Manor so greatly that the news was kept from Lady Calipash for fear of doing her or her unborn child a mischief, the Lady began to feel the pangs of her own travail. At the very stroke of midnight, on the night of the dark of the moon, during a lighting storm that was as out of season as the she-goat's unusual kid, the Lady Calipash was happy to give birth to a healthy baby boy, the future Lord Calipash, and as surprised as the midwife when a second child followed, an equally plump and squalling girl. They were so alike that Lady Calipash named them Basil and Rosemary, and then promptly gave them over to the wet-nurse to be washed and fed.

The wet-nurse was a stout woman from the village, good-natured and well-intentioned, but a sounder sleeper than was wanted in that house. Though an infant's wail would rouse her in an instant, footfalls masked by thunder were too subtle for her country-bred ear, and thus she did not observe the solitary figure that stole silently into the nursery in the wee hours of that morning. For only a few moments did the individual linger, knowing well how restive infants can be in their first hours of life. By the eldritch glow of a lightning strike, Mr. Villein uncorked a phial containing the blood of the two-headed kid now buried, and he smeared upon both of those rosy foreheads an unholy mark, which, before the next burst of thunder, sank without a trace into their soft and delicate skin.

II.

A brief account of the infancy, childhood, education, and adolescence of Basil Vincent, the future Lord Calipash, and his sister Rosemary—as well as a discussion of the effect that reputation has on the prospect of obtaining satisfactory friends and lovers

While the author cannot offer an opinion as to whether any person deserves to suffer during his or her lifetime, the author *will* say with utter certainty that Lady Calipash endured more on account of her Twins than any good woman should expect when she finds herself in the happy condition of mother. Their easy birth and her quick recovery were the end of Lady Calipash's maternal bliss, for not long after she could sit up and cradle her infant son in her arms, she was informed that a new wet-nurse must be hired, as the old had quit the morning after the birth.

Lady Calipash was never told of the reason for the nurse's hasty departure, only that for a few days her newborns had been nourished with goat's milk, there being no suitable women in the neighborhood to feed the hungry young lord and his equally rapacious sister. The truth of the matter was that little Rosemary had bitten off the wet-nurse's nipple not an hour after witnessing her first sunrise. When the poor woman ran out of the nursery, clutching her bloody breast and screaming, the rest of the servants did not much credit her account of the injury; when it was discovered that the newborn was possessed of a set of thin, needle-sharp teeth behind her innocent mouth, they would have drowned the girl in the well if not for Mr. Villein, who scolded them for peasant superstition and told them to feed the babes on the milk of the nanny goat who had borne the two-headed kid until such a time when a new wet-nurse could be hired. That the wet-nurse's nipple was never found became a source of ominous legend in the household, theories swapped from servant to servant, until Mr. Villein heard two chambermaids chattering and beat them both dreadfully in order that they might serve as an example of the consequences of idle gossip.

This incident was only the first of its kind, but alas, the chronicles of the sufferings of those living in or employed at Calipash Manor after the birth of the Infernal Twins (as they were called by servant, tenant farmer, villager and gentleperson alike, well out of the hearing of either Lady Calipash or Mr. Villein, of course) could comprise their own lengthy volume, and thus must be abridged for the author's current purposes. Sufficient must be the following collection of vignettes:

From the first morning, Basil's cries sounded distinctly syllabic, and when the vicar came to baptize the Twins, he recognized the future Lord Calipash's wailing as an ancient language known only to the most disreputable sort of cultist.

On the first dark of the moon after their birth, it was discovered that Rosemary had sprouted pale greenish webbing between her toes and fingers, as well as a set of pulsing gills just below her shell-pink earlobes. The next morning the odd amphibious attributes were gone, but to the distress of all, their appearance seemed inexorably linked to the lunar cycle, for they appeared every month thereafter.

Before either could speak a word, whenever a person stumbled or belched in their presence, one would laugh like a hyena, then the other, and then they would be both fall silent, staring at the individual until he or she fled the room.

One day after Basil began to teethe, Rosemary was discovered to be missing. No one could find her for several hours, but eventually she reappeared in Basil's crib apparently of her own volition. She was asleep and curled against her brother, who was contentedly gnawing on a bone that had been neatly and inexplicably removed from the lamb roast that was to have been Lady Calipash and Mr. Villein's supper that night.

Yet such accounts are nothing to the constant uproar that ensued when at last Basil and Rosemary began to walk and speak. These accomplishments, usually met with celebration in most houses, were heralded by the staff formally petitioning for the Twins to be confined to certain areas of the house, but Mr. Villein, who had taken as much control of the business of Calipash Manor as he could, insisted that they be given as much freedom as they desired. This caused all manner of problems for the servants, but their complaints were met with cruel indifference by their new, if unofficial, master. It seemed to all that Mr. Villein actually delighted in making life difficult at Calipash Manor, and it may be safely assumed that part of his wicked tyranny stemmed from the unwillingness of Lady Calipash to put aside her mourning, and her being too constantly occupied with the unusual worries yielded by her motherhood to consider entering once again into a state of matrimony, despite his constant hints.

For the Twins, their newfound mobility was a source of constant joy. They were intelligent, inventive children, strong and active, and they managed to discover all manner of secret passageways and caches of treasure the Lady Calipash never knew of and Mr. Villein had not imagined existing, even in his wildest fancies of sustaining this period of living as a gentleman. The siblings were often found in all manner of places at odd times—after their being put to bed, it was not unusual to discover one or both in the library come midnight, claiming to be "looking at the pictures" in books that were only printed text; at cock-crow one might encounter them in the attic, drawing betentacled things on the floorboards with bits of charcoal or less pleasant substances. Though they always secured the windows and triple-locked the nursery door come the dark of the moon, there was never a month that passed without Rosemary escaping to do what she would in the lakes and ponds that were part of the Calipash estate, the only indication of her black frolics bits of fish-bones stuck between her teeth and pond-weed braided through her midnight tresses.

Still, it was often easy to forget the Twins' wickedness between incidents, for they appeared frequently to be mere children at play. They would bring their mother natural oddities from the gardens, like a pretty stone or a perfect pine cone, and beg to be allowed to help feed the hunting hounds in the old Lord Calipash's now-neglected kennels. All the same, even when they were sweet, it saddened Lady Calipash that Basil was from the first a dark and sniveling creature, and pretty Rosemary more likely to bite with her sharp teeth than return an affectionate kiss. Even on good days they had to be prevented from entering the greenhouse or the kitchen—their presence withered vegetation, and should one of them reach a hand into a cookie jar or steal a nibble of carrot or potato from the night's dinner, the remaining food would be found fouled with mold or ash upon their withdrawing.

Given the universal truth that servants will gossip, when stories like these began to circulate throughout the neighborhood, the once-steady stream of visitors who had used to come to tour Calipash Manor decreased to a trickle, and no tutor could be hired at any salary. Lady Calipash thanked God that Mr. Villein was there to conduct her children's education, but others were not so sure this was such a boon. Surely, had Lady Calipash realized that Mr. Villein viewed the Lady's request as an opportunity to teach the Twins not only Latin and Greek and English and Geography and Maths, but also his sorcerous arts, she might have heeded the voices of dissent, instead of dismissing their concerns as utter nonsense.

Though often cursed for their vileness, Basil and Rosemary grew up quite happily in the company of Mr. Villein, their mother, and the servants, until they reached that age when children often begin to want for society. The spring after they celebrated their eighth birthday they pleaded with their mother to be allowed to attend the May Day celebration in town. Against her better judgment, Lady Calipash begged the favor of her father (who was hosting the event); against *his* better judgment, Mr. Fellingworth, who suffered perpetual and extraordinary dyspepsia as a result of worrying about his decidedly odd grandchildren, said the Infernal Twins might come—if, and *only* if they promised to behave themselves. After the incident the previous month, at the birthday party of a young country gentleman, where the Twins were accused to no resolution of somehow having put dead frogs under the icing of the celebrant's towering cake, all were exceedingly cautious of allowing them to attend.

This caution was, regrettably, more deserved than the invitation. Rosemary arrived at the event in a costume of her own making, that of the nymph Flora; when Mr. Villein was interrogated as to his reasoning for such grotesque and ill-advised indulgence of childish fancy, he replied that she had earlier proved her understanding that May Day had once been the Roman festival of Floralia, and it seemed a just reward for her attentiveness in the schoolroom. This bit of pagan heresy might have been overlooked by the other families had not Mr. Villein later used the exact same justification for Basil's behavior when the boy appeared at the celebration later-on, clad only in a bit of blue cloth wrapped about his slender body, and then staged a reenactment for the children of Favonius' rape of Flora, Rosemary playing her part with unbridled enthusiasm. Mr. Villein could not account for the resentment of the other parents, nor the ban placed on the Twins' presence at any future public observances, for, as he told Lady Calipash, the pantomime was accurate, and thus a rare educational moment during a day given over to otherwise pointless frivolity.

Unfortunately for the Twins, the result of that display was total social isolation—quite the opposite of their intention. From that day forward they saw no other children except for those of the staff, and the sense of rank instilled in the future Lord Calipash and his sister from an early age forbade them from playing with those humble urchins. Instead, they began to amuse themselves by trying out a few of the easier invocations taught to them by Mr. Villein, and in this manner summoned two fiends, one an amorphous spirit who would follow them about if it wasn't too windy a day, the other an eel with a donkey's head who lived, much to the gardener's distress, in the pond at the center of the rose garden. Rosemary also successfully reanimated an incredibly nasty, incredibly ancient goose when it died of choking on a strawberry, and the fell creature went about its former business of hissing at everyone and shitting everywhere until the stable boy hacked off its head with a the edge of a shovel, and buried the remains at opposite ends of the estate.

Unfortunately, these childish amusements could not long entertain the Twins once they reached an age when they should, by all accounts, have been interfering with common girls (in Lord Calipash's case) or being courted by the local boys (in Rosemary's). For his part, Basil could not be bothered with the fairer sex, so absorbed was he in mastering languages more *recherché* than his indwelling R'lyehian or native English, or even the Latin, Hebrew, and Assyrian he had mastered before his tenth birthday (Greek he never took to—that was Rosemary's province, and the only foreign tongue she ever mastered). Truth be told, even had Basil been interested in women, his slouching posture, slight physique, and petulant mouth would have likely ensured a series of speedy rejections. Contrariwise, Rosemary was a remarkably appealing creature, but there was something so frightening about her sharp-toothed smile and wicked gaze that no boy in the county could imagine comparing her lips to cherubs' or her eyes to the night sky, and thus she, too, wanted for a lover.

Nature will, however, induce the most enlightened of us to act according to our animal inclinations, and to that end, one night, just before their fifteenth birthday, Rosemary slipped into her brother's chambers after everyone else had gone to bed. She found Basil studying by himself. He did not look up at her to greet her, merely said *fhtagn-e* and ignored her. He had taught her a bit of his blood-tongue, and their understanding of one another was so profound that she did not mind heeding the imperative, and knelt patiently at his feet for him to come to the end of his work. Before the candle had burned too low, he looked down at her with a fond frown.

"What?" he asked.

"Brother," said she, with a serious expression, "I have no wish to die an old maid."

"What have I to do with that?" said he, wiping his eternally-drippy nose on his sleeve.

"No one will do it to me if you won't."

Basil considered this, realizing she spoke, not of matrimony, but of the act of love.

"Why should you want to?" asked he, at last. "From everything I've read, intercourse yields nothing but trouble for those who engage in libidinous sport."

Rosemary laughed.

"Would you like to come out with me, two nights hence?"

"On our birthday?"

"It's the dark of the moon," said she.

Basil straightened up and looked at her keenly. He nodded once, briskly, and that was enough for her. As she left him, she kissed his smooth cheek, and at her touch, he blushed for the first time in his life.

Before progressing to the following scene of depravity that the author finds it her sad duty to relate, let several things be said about this History. First, this is as true and accurate account of the Infernal Twins of Ivybridge as anyone has yet attempted. Second, it is the duty of all historians to recount events with as much veracity as possible, never eliding over unpleasantness for propriety's sake. Had Suetonius shied away from his subject, we might never have known the true degeneracy of Caligula, and no one could argue that Suetonius' dedication to his work has allowed mankind to learn from the mistakes made by the Twelve Caesars. Thus the author moves on to her third point, that her own humble chronicle of the Ivybridge Twins is intended to be morally instructive rather than titillating. With this understanding, we must, unfortunately, press on.

The future Lord Calipash had never once attended his sister on her monthly jaunts, and so it must be said that, to his credit, it was curiosity rather than lust that comprised the bulk of his motivation that night. He dressed himself warmly, tiptoed to her door, and knocked very softly, only to find his sister standing beside him in a thin silk sheath, though her door had not yet been unlocked. He looked her up and down—there was snow on the ground outside, what was she about, dressing in such a nymphean manner?—but when she saw his alarm, given his own winter ensemble, she merely smiled. Basil was in that moment struck by how appealing were his sister's kitten-teeth, how her ebon tresses looked as soft as raven-down in the guttering candle-light. He swallowed nervously. Holding a single slender finger to her lips, with gestures Rosemary bid him follow her, and they made their way down the hallway without a light. She knew the way, and her moist palm gripped his dry one as they slipped downstairs, out the servant's door, and into the cold, midwinter night.

Rosemary led her brother to one of the gardens—the pleasure-garden, full of little private grottoes—and there, against a tree already familiar with love's pleasures, she kissed him on the mouth. It was a clumsy kiss. The Twins had been well-tutored by the Greeks and Romans in the theory, but not the practice of love, and theory can take one only so far. To their observer—for indeed they were observed—it seemed that both possessed an overabundance of carnal knowledge, and thus it was a longer encounter than most young people's inaugural attempts at amatory relations. Rosemary was eager and Basil shy, though when he kissed her neck and encountered her delicate sea-green gill pulsating against her ivory skin, gasping for something more substantial than air, he felt himself completely inflamed, and pressed himself into the webbed hand that fumbled with his breeches buttons in the gloaming.

The Twins thought themselves invisible; that the location which they chose to celebrate their induction into Hymen's temple was completely obscure, and thus they were too completely occupied with their personal concerns to notice something very interesting—that Calipash Manor was *not* completely dark, even at that early hour of the morning. A light shone dimly from the tower bedroom, where a lone figure, wracked with anger and jealousy and hatred, watched the Twins from the same window where he had observed two other individuals fornicate, perhaps somewhat less wantonly, almost sixteen years earlier.

III.

Containing more of the terrible wickedness of Mr. Villein—a record of the circumstances surrounding the unhappy separation of the Ivybridge Twins—how Rosemary became Mrs. Villein—concluding with the arrival of a curious visitor to Calipash Manor and the results of his unexpected intrusion

Mr. Villein's pursuit of the Lady Calipash had lasted for as many years as Rosemary remained a child, but when the blood in her girl's veins began to quicken and wrought those womanly changes upon her youthful body so pleasing to the male eye, Mr. Villein found his lascivious dreams to be newly occupied with daughter rather than mother. Since the time, earlier in the year, when Rosemary had finally been allowed to dress her hair and wear long skirts, Mr. Villein started paying her the sort of little compliments that he assumed a young lady might find pleasing. Little did he imagine that Rosemary thought him elderly, something less than handsome, a dreary conversationalist, and one whose manners were not those of a true gentleman; thus, when he watched the virginal object of his affection sullied enthusiastically by her ithyphallic brother, the indecent tableau came as substantial shock to Mr. Villein's mind.

The following day found Mr. Villein in a state of unwellness, plagued by a fever and chills, but he appeared again the morning after that. The Infernal Twins enquired kindly of his health, and Mr. Villein gave them a warm smile and assured them as to his feeling much better. He was, indeed, so very hale that he should like to give them their birthday presents (a day or so late, but no matter) if they might be compelled to attend him after breakfast? The Twins agreed eagerly—both *loved* presents—and midmorning found the threesome in Mr. Villein's private study, formerly that of St. John Fitzroy, Lord Calipash.

"Children," said he, "I bequeath unto you two priceless antiques, but unlike most of the gifts I have given you over the years, what is for one is not to be used by the other. Rosemary, to you I give these—a set of tortoiseshell combs carved into the likeness of Boubastos. To Basil, this bit of ivory. Careful with it, my dearest boy. It was the instrument of your father's undoing."

Basil, surprised, took the handkerchief-swaddled object, and saw it was the carven head of a young man, crowned with a wreath of laurel-leaves. As Rosemary cooed over her gift and vowed to wear the combs in her hair every day thereafter, Basil looked up at his tutor inquisitively.

"How—what?" he asked, too surprised to speak more intelligently.

"The idol's head was given to me by a youth of remarkable beauty whilst I was abroad in Greece," said Mr. Villein. "I have never touched it. The young man said that one day I should encounter the one for whom it was truly intended, the new earthly manifestation of the ancient god which it represents, and that I must give it to him and him alone. Given your abilities, Basil, I believe *you* are that manifestation. I made the mistake of showing it to your father, and he coveted it from the moment he saw it—but when he touched the effigy, I believe the god drove him mad to punish him. I have never told you this, but your father took his own life, likely for the heinous crime of—of *besmirching* that which was always intended for other, wiser hands."

Basil clutched the fetish and nodded his deep thanks, too moved by Mr. Villein's words to notice the agitated tone in which the last sentiment was expressed. That he was the embodiment of a deity came as little surprise to Basil—from an early age, he had sensed he was destined for greatness—but he found it curious that Mr. Villein should have failed to tell him this until now.

The ivory figurine occupied his thoughts all during the day, and late that same night, after a few hours spent in his sister's chambers, during which time they successfully collaborated on a matter of urgent business, Basil unwrapped the icon and touched it with his fingertips. To his great frustration, nothing at all happened, not even after he held it in his palm for a full quarter of an hour. Bitterly disappointed, Basil went unhappily to bed, only to experience strange dreams during the night.

He saw a city of grand marble edifices, fathoms below the surface of the sea and immemorially ancient, and he saw that it was peopled by a shining dolphin-headed race, whose only profession seemed to be conducting the hierophantic rites of a radiant god. He walked unseen among those people, and touched with his hands the columns of the temple which housed the god, carved richly with scenes of worship. A voice called to him over and over in the language he had known since his birth, and he walked into the interior of the fane to see the god for himself, only to realize the face was already known to him, for it was the exact likeness of the ivory idol! Then the eyes of the god, though wrought of a glowing stone, seemed to turn in their sockets and meet his gaze, and with that look Basil understood many things beyond human comprehension that both terrified and delighted him.

The future Lord Calipash awoke the next morning bleary-eyed and stupid, to the alarm of both his sister and mother. He was irritable and shrewish when interrogated as to the nature of his indisposition, and his condition did not improve the following day, nor the following, for his sleep was every night disturbed by his seeking that which called to him. He would not speak to any body of his troubles, and when his ill humor still persisted after a week, Rosemary and Lady Calipash agreed on the prudence of summoning the doctor to attend the future Lord. Basil, however, turned away the physician, claiming that he was merely tired, and, annoyed, left to take a long walk in the woods that comprised a large part of the Calipash estate.

Let it be noted here that it was Mr. Villein who suggested that Basil's room be searched in his absence. There, to the family's collective horror, a ball of opium and a pipe were discovered among Basil's personal effects. The doctor was quite alarmed by this, for, he said, while tincture of opium is a well-regarded remedy, smoking it in its raw state was a foul practice only undertaken by degenerates and Orientals, and so it was decided that Basil should be confined to his room for as long as it took to rid him of the habit. Upon the lad's return there was a sort of ambush, comprised of stern words from the doctor, disappointed head-shakes from Mr. Villein, tears from Lady Calipash, and, for Rosemary's part, anger (she was, frankly, rather hurt that he hadn't invited her to partake of the drug). Basil insisted he had no knowledge of how the paraphernalia came to be in his room, but no rational person would much heed the ravings of an opium-addict, and so he was locked in and all his meals were sent up to his room.

A week later Basil was not to be found within his chambers, and a note in his own hand lay upon his unmade bed. His maid found it, but, being illiterate, she gave it over to Lady Calipash while the lady and her daughter were just sitting down to table. Scanning the missive brought on such a fit of histrionics in Lady Calipash that Mr. Villein came down to see what was the matter. He could not get any sense out of the Lady, and Rosemary had quit the breakfasting room before he even arrived, too private a creature to show anyone the depth of her distress, so Mr. Villein snatched the letter away from the wailing Lady Calipash and read it himself. He was as alarmed by its contents as she, for it said only that Basil had found his confinement intolerable, and had left home to seek his fortune apart from those who would keep him imprisoned.

The author has heard it said that certain birds, like the canary or the nightingale, cannot sing without their mate, and suffer a decline when isolated. Similarly, upon Basil's unexpected flight from Calipash Manor, did Rosemary enter a period of great melancholy, where no one and nothing could lift her spirits. She could not account for Basil's behavior—not his moodiness, nor his failure to take her with him—and so she believed him cross with her for her part in his quarantine, or, worse still, indifferent to her entirely. Seasons passed without her smiling over the misfortunes of others or raising up a single spirit of the damned to haunt the living, and so, upon the year's anniversary of Basil's absence, Mr. Villein sat down with Lady Calipash and made a proposal.

"My lady," he said, "Rosemary has grown to a pretty age, and I believe her state of mind would be much improved by matrimony and, God willing, motherhood. To this end, I appeal to you to allow me to marry her, whereupon I shall endeavor to provide for her as the most doting of husbands."

Lady Calipash was at first disturbed by this request, as she had long assumed that Mr. Villein's affections were settled upon her and not her daughter, but when Mr. Villein mentioned offhandedly that, with Basil absent, he was the only known male heir to the Calipash estate, and should he marry outside the family, neither Lady Calipash nor Rosemary would have any claim to the land or money beyond their annuities, the Lady found it prudent to accept Mr. Villein's suit on Rosemary's behalf.

Mr. Villein expected, and, (it must be admitted) rather ghoulishly anticipated Rosemary's disinclination to form such an alliance, but to the surprise of all, she accepted her fate with a degree of *insouciance* that might have worried a mother less invested in her own continued state of affluence. Without a single flicker of interest Rosemary agreed to the union, took the requisite journey into town to buy her wedding clothes, said her vows, and laid down upon the marriage bed in order that Mr. Villein could defile her body with all manner of terrible perversions, a description of which will not be found in these pages, lest it inspire others to sink to such depths. The author will only say that Rosemary found herself subjected to iterations of Mr. Villein's profane attentions every night thereafter. If any good came out of these acts of wickedness performed upon her person, it was that it roused her out of her dysthymia and inspired her to once again care about her situation.

Not unexpectedly, Rosemary's emotional rejuvenation compelled her to journey down paths more corrupt than any the Twins had yet trod. Her nightly, nightmarish trysts with Mr. Vincent had driven her slightly mad, as well as made her violently aware that not all lovers are interested in their partner's pleasure. Remembering with fondness those occasions when her brother had conjured up from the depths of her body all manner of rapturous sensations, in her deep misery Rosemary concocted a theory drawn as much from her own experience as from the works of the ancient physician Galen of Pergamon. As she accurately recalled, Galen had claimed that male and female reproductive systems are perfect inversions of one another, and thus, she deduced, the ecstasy she felt whilst coupling with her brother was likely due to their being twins and the mirror-image of one another.

To once again achieve satisfactory companionship Rosemary therefore resolved upon creating a companion for herself out of the remains housed in the Calipash family crypt. By means of the necromancies learned in her youth, she stitched together a pleasure-golem made of the best-preserved parts of her ancestors, thanking whatever foul gods she was accustomed to petitioning for the unusually gelid temperature of that tomb. Taking a nose that looked like Basil's from this corpse, a pair of hands from that one, and her father's genitalia, she neatly managed the feat, and, dressing the creature in Basil's clothing, slipped often into that frigid darkness to lie with it. Sadly, her newfound happiness with her ersatz brother was, for two reasons, imperfect. The first was that none of the vocal chords she could obtain were capable of reproducing Basil's distinctively nasal snarl, and thus the *doppelgänger* remained mute, lest an unfamiliar moan ruin Rosemary's obscene delights. The second trouble was more pernicious: she realized too late she had been unable to entirely excise the putrefaction wrought by death upon the limbs of her relations, and thus she contracted a form of gangrene that began to slowly rot her once-pristine limbs.

For another year did this unhappy *status quo* persist, until one dreary afternoon when Rosemary, returning from a long walk about the grounds, noticed a disreputable, slouching individual taking in the fine prospect offered by the approach to Calipash Manor. Unafraid, Rosemary advanced on him, noticing the burliness of the man's figure, the darkness of his skin, and the shabby state of his long overcoat.

"Are you in want of something?" she called to the stranger, and he looked up at her, his face shaded by a mildewing tricorn. "There is scant comfort to be found here at Calipash Manor, but if you require any thing, it will be given to you."

"To whom do I have the pleasure of speaking?" queried he in the rasping accent of a white Creole, all the while stealing polite glances of her slightly moldy countenance.

"I am the daughter of the lady of this house," answered Rosemary.

"Then thank you, my lady," said the man. "My name is Valentine, and I have only just returned from Jamaica to find my family dead and my house occupied by those with no obligation to provide for me."

"Have you no friends?"

"None, not being the sort of man who either makes or keeps them easily."

"Come with me, then," said Rosemary, admiring his honesty. She led Valentine up to the house and settled them in her private parlor, whereupon she bid the servants bring him meat and drink. As he ate, he seemed to revive. Rosemary saw a nasty flicker in his eyes that she quite liked, and bid him tell her more of himself. He laughed dryly, and Rosemary had his tale:

"I'm afraid, Lady, that I owe you an apology, for I know one so fine as yourself would never let me into such a house knowing my true history. I was born into the world nothing more than the seventh son of a drunk cottar, and we were always in want as there was never enough work to be had for all of us. I killed my own brother over a bite of mutton, but given that we were all starving, the magistrate saw it fitting that I should not be hanged, but impressed to work as a common hand aboard a naval ship bound for the West Indies. I won't distress you by relating the conditions I endured, suffice it to say I survived.

"When I arrived at our destination, however, I found that it was not my fate to remain in the navy, for my sea-captain promptly clapped me in irons and sold me as a white slave, likely due to my being an indifferent sailor and more likely to start riots among the men than help to settle them. I was bought by a plantation-owner who went by the name of Thistlewood, and this man got what labor he could out of me for several years, until I managed to escape to Port Royal with only the clothes on my back and a bit of food I'd stolen. There I lived in a manner I shan't alarm you by describing, and only say that having done one murder, it was easy to repeat the crime for hire until I had enough coin to buy passage back to England—but as I said earlier, when I returned home, I found every living person known to me dead or gone, except those with long memories who recalled enough of my character to kick me away from their doorsteps like a dog."

Rosemary could not but be profoundly moved by such a tale, and she felt her dormant heart begin to warm anew with sympathy for this stranger. She assured him that he should have some work on her estate, and Valentine was so overcome that he took Rosemary's hand in his—but their mutual felicity was interrupted by Mr. Villein, who chose that inopportune moment to enter Rosemary's chambers uninvited.

"What is the meaning of this treachery?" cried Mr. Villein, for though he often engaged in infidelities, the notion that his bride might do the same did not sit well with him, being that he was a jealous man by nature. "Release my wife, foul vagabond!"

"Wife!" exclaimed Valentine, his yellowish complexion turning grey. "How is it that I return home, only to find myself betrayed by one whom I thought harbored love for me?"

It would be impossible to guess whether Rosemary or Mr. Villein was more confused by this ejaculation, but neither had time to linger in a state of wonder for very long. The man withdrew a veritable cannon of a flintlock, and cast off his wretched, threadbare overcoat to reveal that beneath it, he wore a rich emerald-green brocade vest threaded through with designs wrought in gold and silver, and his breeches were of the finest satin. When he looked down his nose at them like a lord instead of lowering his eyes like a cottar's son, they saw he had all the bearing of a gentleman of high rank. Recognizing him at last, Rosemary shrieked, and Mr. Villein paled and took a step back. Though strangely altered by time, the man was unmistakably Basil Vincent, Lord Calipash, returned at last to reclaim by force what should have been his by right of birth!

IV.

The conclusion, detailing the reunion of the Ivybridge Twins—an account of the singular manner in which Rosemary defeated the gangrene that threatened her continued good health—what the author hopes the reader will take away from this Infernal History

"You!" cried Mr. Villein in alarm. "How *dare* you? How *can* you? They said the navy would keep you at least a decade in the service of this country!"

"*They*?" demanded Rosemary. "Who?"

"The press gang!" blustered Mr. Villein. "For the sum I paid them, I'll have them—"

But the Infernal Twins never discovered what Mr. Villein's intentions were regarding the unsatisfactory press gang, for Rosemary, overcome with grief and rage, snatched the flintlock pistol out of Basil's grasp and shot Mr. Villein through the throat. A fountain of blood gushed forth from just above Mr. Villein's cravat-pin, soaking his waistcoat and then the carpet as he gasped his surprise and fell down dead upon the ground.

"Basil," she said. "Basil, I'm so—I didn't—"

"You *married* him?"

"It was all Mother's doing," said Rosemary, rather hurt by his tone.

"But—"

"You were gone," she snapped, "and lest Mr. Villein marry some common slut and turn Mother and myself out of our house…"

Even with such reasonable excuses, it was some time before Rosemary could adequately cajole Basil out of his peevish humor; indeed, only when Rosemary asked if Basil had lived as a monk during the years of their estrangement did he glower at her as he had used to do and embraced her. They sat companionably together then, and Basil gave her a truer account of his absence from Calipash Manor:

"The carven ivory head which our loathsome former tutor bequeathed unto me on the fifteenth anniversary of my birth was the instrument, strangely, of both my undoing and my salvation," said Basil. "Mr. Villein lied to me that I was the manifestation of the old god which it represents—indeed, I believe now that his intention was take me away from you so that he might have you for his own; that I, like my father before me, would be driven to suicide by the whispered secrets of that divine entity. Little did he know that while I am not some sort of fleshly incarnation of that deity, I was born with the capacity to understand His whispered will, and walk along the sacred paths that were more often trod when His worship was better known to our race.

"I believe once Mr. Villein saw that I was only mildly troubled by these new visions, he concocted a plot to be rid of me in a less arcane manner. The night before you discovered my absence, he let himself into my chambers and put a spell upon me while I slept that made me subject to his diabolical will. I awoke a prisoner of his desire, and he bade me rise and do as he wished. Dearest sister, I tell you now that you did not detect a forgery in my note, for it was written by none other than myself. After I had penned the false missive, Mr. Villein bade me follow him down to Ivybridge, whereupon he put a pint of ale before me and compelled me, via his fell hold upon me, to act in the manner of a drunken commoner, brawling with the local boys until the constable was called and I was thrown in jail. Not recognizing me, due to my long isolation, my sentence was as I told you—that of forced conscription into the navy.

"To a certain point, my tale as I told it to you whilst in the character of the scoundrel Valentine was true—I suffered much on my voyage to Jamaica, and was subsequently sold as a slave. What I did not tell you was the astonishing manner of my escape from that abominable plantation. My master hated me, likely because he instinctively sensed his inferiority to my person. My manners mark me as a noble individual, even when clad in rags, and being that he was a low sort who was considered a gentleman due to his profession rather than his birth, my master gave to me the most dangerous and disgusting tasks. One of his favorite degradations was to station me at the small dock where the little coracles were tied up, so that I could be given the catches of fish to clean them, constantly subjected to wasp stings and cuts and other indignities of that sort.

"Yet it was this task that liberated me, for one afternoon I arrived at the dock to see the fishermen in a tizzy, as one had the good fortune of catching a dolphin. The creature was still alive, incredibly, and I heard its voice in my mind as clearly as I heard their celebration. *Save me, and I shall save you*, it said unto me in that language that has always marked me as bacchant to the god of which I earlier spoke. I picked up a large stick to use as a cudgel and beat the fisherfolk away from their catch, telling them to get back to work as the cetacean was of no use to our master, he should want snapper or jackfish for his dinner rather than oily porpoise-flesh. They heeded me, for they were a little afraid of me—often, as you might imagine, dear sister, bad things would happen to those who chose to cross me in some way—and I heaved the dolphin back into the sea. At first I thought it swam away and that it had merely been sun-madness that had earlier made me hear its voice, but then, after the fishermen had paddled out of sight, the dolphin surfaced with a bulging leather satchel clutched in its beak. It contained gold and jewels that my new friend told me were gathered from shipwrecks on the ocean floor, and that I should use this wealth to outfit myself as a gentleman and buy passage back to England. The creature's only caveat was that upon my arrival I must once again visit the sea, and return to one of its kin the ivory head, as our tutor had not, as it turns out, been given the object. Rather, it seems that Mr. Villein defiled an ancient holy place near Delphi during his travels in Greece by stealing the artifact away from its proper alcove.

"I agreed to these terms and, after waiting at the docks for a little longer so I might poison the fish it was my duty to clean, and thus enact a paltry revenge upon my tyrannical master, hastened back to Devonshire, as I knew nothing of your situation, but feared much. Upon returning home I assumed the persona of Valentine as a way of ascertaining if, in my absence, your sentiments had changed toward your long-absent brother and the manner in which we were accustomed to living with one another. Seeing your heart go out to such a picaroon assured me of your constancy, and I regret very much that I earlier so impugned your honor. But sister, now that you know of my distresses, you must tell me of yours—pray, how did you come to be married to Mr. Villein and so afflicted by the disease that I see nibbles away at your perfect flesh?"

Rosemary then recounted what has already been recorded here, and she and Basil resolved upon a course of action that shall comprise the *denoument* of this chronicle. Both were determined that the gangrenous affliction should not claim Rosemary, but until Lady Calipash, wondering why her daughter did not come down to dinner, intruded into the parlor where the siblings colluded, they could not see how. The idea occurred to the Twins when Lady Calipash's alarm at seeing Mr. Villein's corpse upon the carpet was so tremendous that she began to scream. Basil, fearing they should be overheard and the murder discovered before they had concocted an adequate reason for his unfortunate death, caught Lady Calipash by the neck when she would not calm herself. As he wrapped his fingers about her throat, Basil noticed the softness of his mother's skin, and, looking deeply into her fearful eyes, saw that she was still a handsome creature of not five-and-thirty.

"Sister," he began, but Rosemary had already anticipated his mind, and agreed that she should immediately switch her consciousness with Lady Calipash's by means of witchcraft she and Basil had long ago learned (and once utilized in their youthful lovemaking) from the donkey-headed eel-creature they had conjured, and henceforth inhabit her own mother's skin. This was done directly, and after securely locking Rosemary's former body (now occupied by their terrified mother) into the family crypt, along with Mr. Villein's corpse, mother and prodigal son, rather than brother and sister, had the carriage made ready, and they drove to the head of the River Plym, whereupon Basil summoned one of the aquatic priests of his god, and handed over the relic that has figured so prominently in their narrative.

To conclude, the author hopes that readers of this History will find this account entirely mortifying and disgusting, and seek to avoid modeling any part of his or her behavior upon that of the Infernal Ivybridge Twins—though to be fair, it must be recorded that, for all the duration of their cacodemoniacal lives, the Twins preserved the tenderest affection for each other. Still, there has never been found anywhere in the world a less-worthy man or woman than they, and, until the moonless night when the Twins decided to join the ranks of the cetaceous worshipers of their unholy deity—Lord Calipash being called thence, his sister long-missing her former amphibious wanderings— there was not a neighbor, a tenant, or a servant who did not rue the day they came into the company of Basil and Rosemary.

Fat Face

Michael Shea

They were infamous, nightmare sculptures even when telling of age-old, bygone things; for shoggoths and their work ought not to be seen by human beings or portrayed by any beings...
— HOWARD PHILLIPS LOVECRAFT,
AT THE MOUNTAINS OF MADNESS

When Patti came back to working the lobby of the Parnassus Hotel, it was clear she was liked from the way the other girls teased her and unobtrusively took it easy on her for the first few weeks while she got to feel steadier. She was deeply relieved to be back.

Before she had to go up to State Hospital, she had been doing four nights a week at a massage parlor called The Encounter, of which her pimp was part owner. He insisted the parlor beat was like a vacation to her, because it was strictly a hand-job operation and the physical demands on her were lighter than regular hotel whoring. Patti would certainly have agreed that the work

125

was lighter—if it hadn't been for the robberies and killings. The last of these had been the cause of her breakdown, and though she never admitted this to Pete, her pimp, he had no doubt sensed the truth, for he had let her go back to the Parnassus and told her she could pay him half rate for the next few weeks, till she was feeling steady again.

In her first weeks at the massage parlor, she had known with all but certainty of two clients—not hers—who had taken one-way drives from The Encounter up into the Hollywood Hills. These incidents still wore a thin, merciful veil of doubt. It was the third one that passed too nearly for her to face away from it.

From the moment of his coming in, unwillingly she felt spring up in her the conviction that the customer was a perfect victim; physically soft, small, fatly walleted, more than half drunk, out-of-state. She learned his name when her man studied his wallet thoroughly on the pretext of checking his credit cards, and the man's permitting of this liberty revealed how fuddled he was. She walked ahead swinging her bottom, and as he stumbled after, down the hall to a massage room, she could almost feel in her own head the ugly calculations clicking in Pete's.

The massage room was tiny. It had a not-infrequently-puked-on carpet, and a table. As she stood there, pounding firmly on him through the towel, trying to concentrate on her rhythm, she beheld an obese black cockroach running boldly across the carpet. Afterward she was willing to believe she had hallucinated, so strange was the thing she remembered. The bug, half as big as her hand, had stopped at midfloor and stared at her, and she in that instant had seen clearly and looked deep into the inhuman little black-bead eyes, and had known that the man she was just then firing off into the towel was going to die later that night. There would be a grim, half-slurred conversation in some gully under the stars, there would be perhaps a long signing of traveler's checks payable to the fictitious name on a certain set of false I.D. cards, and then the top of the plump man's head would be blown off.

Patti was a lazy girl who lazily wanted things to be nice, but was very good at adjusting to things that were not nice at all, if somebody strong really insisted on them. Part of it was that Patti was indecisive by nature. Left alone, she was made miserable by the lonely struggle of deciding what to do. Pete was expensive, but at least he kept Patti's time fully planned out for her. With him to supervise, Patti's life fit her snugly, with no room for confusing doubts.

But this plump man's head, all pale in moonlight, blown wide open—the image wouldn't leave her; it festered in her imagination. The body was found in three days and got two paragraphs, but the few lines included corroboration of her fantasy, in the words "gunshot wounds to the head."

By the time she read these paragraphs, Patti was already half sick with alcohol and insomnia, and that night she took some pills that she was lucky enough to have pumped out of her an hour or so later.

But now, with the hospital's Xanax just fading from her system and a little of her appetite and her energy coming back, Patti decided that if there was any best therapy for her kind of nightmare, it was this, hooking again out of the lobby of the Parnassus. Some of the bittersweet years of her apprenticeship had been served here. The fat, shabby red furniture still had a voluptuous feel to her. The big, dowdy Parnassus, uptown in the forties, now stood in the porno heartland of Hollywood. It was a district of neon and snarled traffic on narrow overparked streets engineered before the Great Depression. And Patti loved to watch it all, the glitter and glossy vehicles, through the plate-glass window of the lobby, taking it easy, only getting up and ambling out to the sidewalk now and then when there was eye-contact from a shopping john driving past. This was the way hooking should be.

Before this whole massage parlor thing, she was working harder, maybe half her time in the lobby, and half walking. But now she felt still queasy, thin-skinned after all those drugs and the hospital. She thought of walking, and it made her remember her painful amateur years, the beatings, the cheats who humped and dumped her, the quick, sticky douches taken with a shook-up bottle of Coke while squatting between trash bins in an alley. Yes, here in the lobby was the best kind of hooking. The old desk-guys took a little gate on one or two rooms, but very few tricks actually went down here. This lobby was a natural showcase. The nearby Bridgeport or Aztec Arms was where 90 percent of the bedwork went on.

This suited Patti. She was small-town born, central California, and had a certain sunny sentimentalism, an impulse for community and camaraderie, that had led her to be called "Hometown" by some of the other girls, most of them liking her for it while they laughed at her. She laughed along, but stubbornly she cherished a sense of neighborhood on these noisy carnival streets. She cultivated acquaintances. She infallibly greeted the man at the drugstore with cordial remarks on the traffic or the smog. The man, bald and thin-moustached, never did more than grin at her with timid greed and scorn. The douches, deodorizers, and fragrances she bought so steadily had prejudiced him, and guaranteed his misreading of her folksy genialities.

Or she would josh the various pimply employees at the Dunk-O-Rama in a similar spirit, saying things like, "They sure got you working, don't they?" or, of the tax, "The old Governor's got to have his bite, don't he?" When asked how she wanted her coffee, she always answered with neighborly amplitude: "Well, let's see—I guess I'm in the mood for cream today." These things, coming from a vamp-eyed brunette in her twenties, wearing a halter top, short-shorts, and Grecian sandals, disposed the adolescent counter-hops more to sullen leers than to answering warmth. Yet she persisted in her fantasies. She even greeted Arnold, the smudged, moronic vendor at the corner newsstand, by name—this in spite of an all-too-lively and gurgling responsiveness on his part.

Now, in her recuperation, Patti took an added comfort from this vein of sentiment. This gave her sisterhood much to rally her about in their generally affectionate recognition that she was much shaken and needed some feedback and some steadying.

A particular source of hilarity for them was Patti's revival of interest in Fat Face, whom she always insisted was their friendliest "neighbor" in their "local community."

An old ten-story office building stood on the corner across the street from the Parnassus. As is not uncommon in L.A., the simple box-shaped structure bore ornate cement frieze work on its façade, and all along the pseudo-archi-traves capping the pseudo-pillars of the building's sides. Such friezes always have exotic clichés as their theme—they are an echo of DeMille's Hollywood. The one across from the Parnassus had a Mesopotamian theme—ziggurat-shaped finials crowning the pseudo-pillars, and murals of wrenched profiles, curly-bearded figures with bulging calves.

A different observer from Patti would have judged the budding schlock, but effective for all that, striking the viewer with a subtle sense of alien por-tent. Patti seldom looked higher than its fourth floor, where the usually open window of Fat Face's office was.

Fat Face's businesses—he ran two—appeared to be the only active concerns in the whole capacious structure. The gaudy unlikelihood of both of these "businesses" was the cause of endless hilarity among the Parnassus girls. The two enterprises lettered on the building's dusty directory were: HYDRO-THERAPY CLINIC and PET REFUGE.

What made the comedy irresistible was that sometimes the clients of the two services arrived together. The hydrotherapy patients were a waddling pachydermous lot, gimping on bulky orthopedic boots, their wobbly bulks rippling in roomy jumpsuits or bib overalls. And, as if these hulks required an added touch, they sometimes came with cats and dogs in tow. These beasts' wails and struggles against their leashes or carrying cages made it plain that they were strays, not pets. The misshapen captors' fleshy, stolid faces, as if oblivious to the thrashings of the beasts, added that last note of slapstick to the spectacle.

Fat Face himself—they had no other name for him—was often at his high window, a dear, ruddy bald countenance beaming avuncularly down on the hookers in the lobby across the street. His bubble baldness was the object of much lewd humor among the girls and the pimps. Fat Face was much waved-at in sarcasm, whereat he always smiled a crinkly smile that seemed to understand and not to mind. Patti, when she sometimes waved, did so with pretty sincerity.

Because though you had to laugh at Fat Face, the man had some substance to him. He had several collection vans with the Pet Refuge logo—apparently his hydrotherapy patients also volunteered as drivers for these vans. The leaflet they passed out was really touching:

> Help us Help!
> Let our aid reach these
> unfortunate creatures.
> Nourished, spayed, medicated,
> They may have a better chance
> for health and life!

This generosity of feeling in Fat Face did not prevent his being talked about in the lobby of the Parnassus, where great goiter-rubbing, water-splashing orgies were raucously hypothesized, with Fat Face flourishing whips and baby oil, while cries of "rub my blubber!" filled the air. At such times Patti was impelled to leave the lobby, because it felt like betrayal to be laughing so hard at the goodly man.

Indeed, in her convalescent mellowness, much augmented by Valium, she had started to fantasize going up to his office, pulling the blinds, and ravishing him at his desk. She imagined him lonely and horny. Perhaps he had nursed his wife through a long illness and she at last expired gently…He would be so grateful!

But forward though Patti could be, she found in herself an odd shyness about this. It would be easy enough to cross the street, go up to his clinic, knock on his door…But she didn't. A week, seven nice long convalescent days, rolled by, and she did nothing about this sentimental little urge of hers.

Then late one afternoon, Sheri, her best friend among the girls, took her to a bar a few blocks down the street. Patti drank, got happy and goofy. The two girls sat trading yo-mammas and boasts and dares, and then it just popped naturally out of Patti's mouth: "So why don't you go up and give old Fat Face a lube?"

"Jesus, girl, if all of him's fat as his face is, it'd be like lube-ing a hill!"

But there was the exploit on the table between them, and they both felt too jolly and rowdy to back down. "So whatta you saying, you trick only superstars? So what if he's fat? Think how nice it'd be for him!"

"I bet he'd blush till his whole head looked like an eggplant. Then, if there was just a slit in the top, like Melanie was saying—" Sheri had to break off and hold herself as she laughed. She had already done some drinking earlier in the afternoon. Patti called for another double and exerted herself to catch up, and meanwhile she harped on her theme to Sheri and tried to get her serious attention:

"I mean I've been working out of the Parnassus—what? Maybe three years now? No, four! Four years. I'm part of these people's community—the druggist, Arnold, Fat Face—and yet we never do anything to show it. There's no getting together. We're just faces. I mean like Fat Face—I couldn't even call him that!"

"So let's *both* go up—there's enough there for two!"

Patti was about to answer when, behind the bar, she saw a big roach scamper across a rubber mat and disappear under the baseboard. She remembered the plump body in the towel, and remembered—as a thing actually seen—the slug-fragmented skull.

Sheri sensed a chill. She ordered two more doubles and began making bawdy suppositions about the outcome of their visit. The pair of them marched out laughing a quarter hour later, out into the late afternoon streets. The gold-drenched sidewalks swarmed, the pavements were jammed with rumbling motors. Jaunty and loud, the girls sauntered back to their intersection and crossed over to the old building. Its heavy oak-and-glass doors were pneumatically stiff and cost them a stagger to force open. But when they swung shut, it was swiftly, with a deep click, and they sealed out the street sound with amazing, abrupt completeness. The glass was dirty and put a sulphurous glaze on the already surreal copper of the declining sun's light outside. Suddenly it might be Mars or Jupiter beyond those doors, and the girls themselves stood within a great dim stillness that might have matched the feeling of a real Mesopotamian ruin, out on some starlit desert. The images were alien to Patti's thought—startling intrusions in a mental voice not precisely her own. Sheri gave a comic shiver but otherwise made no acknowledgment of similar feelings.

They found the elevator had an out-of-order sign fixed to the switch plate by yellowed Scotch tape. The stairway's ancient carpet was blackish-green, with a venerable rubber corridor mat up its center. Out on the street the booze in Patti's system had felt just right; in this silent, dusty stairwell it made her slightly woozy. The corridor mat, so cracked with age, put her in mind of supple reptilian skin. Sheri climbed ahead of her, still joking, cackling, but her voice seemed small, seemed to struggle like a drowner in the heavy silence. It amazed Patti, how utterly her sense of gaiety had fled her. It had been clicked off, abrupt as a light switch, when those heavy street doors had closed behind them.

At the first two landings they peeked down the halls at similar vistas: green-carpeted corridors of frosted-glass doors with rich brass knobs. Bulbs burned miserly few, and in those corridors Patti sensed, with piercing vividness, the feeling of *kept* silence. It was not a void silence, but a full one, made by presences not stirring.

And as they climbed her sense of strangeness condensed in her, became something that gripped her by the spine. She was afraid! My God, what *of?* It was ridiculous, but when Sheri led them into the fourth-floor corridor, performing a comic bow, Patti's legs felt cold and leaden, and carried her unwillingly.

"Come *on!*" Sheri mocked. There was something too much, something feverish about the hilarity in her eyes.

Patti balked. "It's a bad idea. You win, I'm chicken—let's get outta here."

"Ha! And you call yourself a working girl! Well, just a minute here." She took out the little pad she carried for phone numbers and addresses, and hurried down the hall with a parody butt-swinging hooker's prowl. The doors nearest Patti said HYDROTHERAPY CLINIC with an arrow—she watched Sheri pass other doors, sashaying all the way to the corridor's far end. Patti stood waiting. Did she hear, ever so faintly, a kind of echo from behind these closed doors? Sooo faint, but the echoes of something resonating in a vast cavernous space? And there…ever so soft…it was almost like the piping of a flute…

Sheri stood by the last door, scribbling on the pad. She ripped off the sheet and slipped it under the door. Then she came running back like a kid who's played a prank. Patti willingly caught her mood—they rushed giggling back down the stairs like larking twelve-year-olds. Patti wondered if Sheri too was giggling from sheer relief to be out of this building.

"What'd you write him, fool?!" Patti was elated to be back on the street, out in its noise and its colors; she felt like someone who has just escaped drowning. "You trying to steal my date?" Sheri had once tampered with a note that Patti had passed at a party, so that the trick would show up at Sheri's house instead of Patti's.

Sheri mimed outrage. "What you take me for? Come on for a beer, on me!"

As they walked, every outdoor breath reassured Patti. "Hey, Sher—did you hear any, like, music up there?" Even out here in the traffic noise she could call up clearly the weird piping tune, not so much a tune, really, as an eerie melodic ramble. What bothered her as much as the strange feeling of the music was the way in which she had received it. It seemed to her that she had not *heard* it, but rather remembered it—suddenly and vividly—though she hadn't the trace of an idea now where she might have heard it before. Sheri's answer confirmed her thought:

"Music? Baby, there wasn't a sound up there! Wasn't it kind of spooky?" Sheri's mood stayed giddy and Patti gladly fell in with it. They went to another bar they liked and drank for an hour or so—slowly, keeping a gloss on things, feeling humorous and excited like schoolgirls on a trip together. At length they decided to go to the Parnassus, find somebody with a car, and scare up a cruising party.

As they crossed to the hotel, Sheri surprised Patti by throwing a look at the old office building and giving a shrug that may have been half shudder. "Jesus. It was like being under the ocean or something in there, wasn't it, Patti?"

This echo of her own dread made Patti look again at her friend. Then Arnold, the vendor, stepped out from the newsstand and blocked their way.

The uncharacteristic aggressiveness gave Patti a nasty twinge. Arnold was unlovely. There was a babyish fatness and redness about every part of him. His scanty red hair alternately suggested infancy or feeble age, and his one eyeless socket, with its weepy red folds of baggy lid, made his whole face look as if screwed to cry. Over all his red, ambling softness there was a bright blackish glaze of inveterate filth. And moronic though his manner was most of the time, Patti felt a cunning about him, something sly and corrupt. The cretinous wet-mouthed face he now thrust close to the girls seemed, somehow, to be that of a grease-painted con man, not an imbecile. As if it were a sour fog that surrounded the newsman, fear entered Patti's nostrils and dampened the skin of her arms. Arnold raised his hand. Pinched between his smudgy thumb and knuckle were an envelope and a fifty-dollar bill.

"A man said to read this, Patti!" Arnold's childish intonation now struck Patti as an affectation, like his dirtiness, part of a chosen disguise.

"He said the money was to pay you to read it. It's a trick! He gave me twenty dollars!" Arnold giggled. The sense of cold-blooded deception in the man made Patti's voice shake when she questioned him about the man who'd given him the commission. He remembered nothing, an arm and a voice in a dark car that pulled up and sped off.

"Well, how is she supposed to read it?" Sheri prodded. "Should she be by a window? Should she wear anything special?"

But Arnold had no more to tell them, and Patti willingly gave up on him to escape the revulsion he so unexpectedly roused in her. They went into the lobby with the letter, but such was its strangeness—so engrossingly lurid were the fleeting images that came clear for them—that they ended taking it back to the bar, getting a booth, and working over it with the aid of beers and lively surroundings. The document was in the form of an unsigned letter that covered two pages in a lucid, cursive script of bizarre elegance, and that ran thus:

Dear Girls:

How does a Shoggoth Lord go wooing? You do not even guess enough to ask! Then let it be asked and answered for you. As it is written: "The Shoggoth Lord stumbleth unto his belusted, lo, he cometh heavily unto her, upon alien feet. From the sunless sea, from under the mountains of ice, cometh the mighty Shoggoth Lord unto her." Dear, dear girls! Where is this place the Shoggothoi come from? In your tender, sensual ignorance you might well lack the power to be astonished by the prodigious gulfs of Space and Time this question probes. But let it once more be asked and answered for you. Thus has the answer been written:

Shun the gulf beneath the peaks,
The caverned ocean black as night,
Where star-spawned gods made their retreat
From the slowly freezing world of light.
For even star-spawn may grow weak,
While what has been its slave gains strength;
Even star-spawn's will may break,
While slaves feed on their lords at length.

Sweet harlots! Darling, heedless trollops! You cannot imagine the Shoggoth Lord's mastery of shapes! His race has bred smaller since modern man last met with it. Oh, but the Shoggoth Lords are limber now! Supremest polymorphs—though what they are beneath all else, is Horror itself. But how is it they press their loving suit? What do they murmur to her they hotly crave? You must know that the Shoggoth craves her fat with panic—full of the psychic juices of despair. Therefore he taunts her with their ineluctable union; therefore he pipes and flutes to her his bold, seductive lyric, while he vows with a burning glare in his myriad eyes that she'll be his. Thus he sings:

Your veil shall be the wash of blood
That dims and drowns your dying eyes.
You'll have for bridesmaids Pain and Dread,
For vows, you'll jabber blasphemies.
My scalding flesh will be your gown,
And Agony your bridal song.
You shall both be my bread
And, senses reeling, watch me fed.
O maids, prepare her swiftly!

Speedily her loins unlace!
Her tender paps anoint,
And bare unto my seething face!

Thus, dear girls, he ballads and rondelets his belusted, thus he waltzes her spirit through dark, empty halls of expectation, of always-hearkening Horror, until the dance has reached that last, closed room of consummation!

As many times as the girls flung these pages onto the table, they picked them up again after short hesitation. Both Sheri and Patti were very marginal readers, but the flashes of coherent imagery in the letter kept them coming back to the cryptic parts, trying to pick the lock of their meaning. They held menace even in their very calligraphy, whose baroque, barbed elegance seemed sardonic and alien. The mere sonority of some of the obscure passages evoked vivid images, a sense of murky submersion in benthic pressures of fearful expectation, while unseen giants abided nearby in the dark.

The document's cumulative effect on Patti was more of melancholy than fear. The john who wrote it was a hurt-freak, sure, but the letter-writing types blew it off that way and never came to dealing harm. The girls had done some blow from Sheri's vial to clear their heads from the beers, and Patti's body was liking it; she was feeling stronger than she had for days. This letter writer's words were strange, yes, this incredible gloominess hung over them—but then, bottom line, this was a very easy fifty bucks.

Sheri, on the other hand, got a little freaked about it. She'd started drinking much earlier in the day, she'd had a lot more blow than Patti, and her nerves now were wearing down. She was still laughing at things, but the humor was very thin. "I'll tell you what, girl, these are weird vibes I'm getting today. You know what? I *did* kinda hear like, music. Behind the door…? Now we get this shit!" and she swept her hands at the pages but not touching them, as a woman might try to shoo off a spider. "You know what let's do? Let's have a sleep-over at your place, I'll come sleep over, just like slumber parties."

"That'd be fun! But you sleep in my bed, no kicking, OK?"

Sheri cawed with relieved laughter—her sleep-kicking a joke with them. Sensing Sheri's fear—her desperation not to be alone tonight—scared Patti in turn.

They walked the sidewalks through the almost-night, headlights blazing everywhere, both of them so glad of each other's company it almost embarrassed them.

At the all-night Safeway they got provisions: sloe gin, vodka, bags of ice, 7UP, bags of chips and puffs and cookies and candy bars. They repaired with their purchases to Patti's place.

She had a small cottage in a four-cottage court, with very old people living in the other three units. The girls shoved the bed into the corner so they could drop pillows against all the walls to lean back on. They turned on the radio and the TV, then got out the phone book and started making joke calls to people with funny names while eating, drinking, smoking, watching, listening, and bantering with each other.

Their consciousness outlasted their provisions, but not by long. Soon, back to back, they slept; bathed and laved by the gently burbling soundwash and the ash-grey light of pulsing images.

They woke to a day that was sunny, windy, and smogless. They rose at high, glorious noon and walked to a coffee shop for breakfast. The breeze was combing buttery light into the waxen fronds of the palms, while the Hollywood Hills seemed most opulently brocaded—under the sky's flawless blue—with the silver-green of sagebrush and sumac.

As they ravened breakfast, they plotted borrowing a car and taking a drive. Then Sheri's pimp walked in. She waved him over brightly, but Patti was sure she was as disappointed as herself. Rudy took a chair long enough to inform Sheri how lucky she was he'd run into her, since he had something important for her that afternoon. Contemptuously he snatched up the bill and paid for both girls. Sheri left in tow, and gave Patti a rueful wave from the door.

Patti's appetite left her. She dawdled over coffee and stepped at last, unwillingly, out into the day's polychrome splendor. Its very clarity took on a sinister quality of remorselessness. Behold, the whole world and all its children moved under the glaring sun's brutal, endless revelation. Nothing could hide. Not in this world...though of course there were other worlds, where beings lie hidden immemorially...

She shivered as if something had crawled across her. The thoughts had passed through Patti, but were not hers. She sat on a bus-stop bench and tightly crossed her arms as if to get a literal hold on herself. The strange thoughts, by their feeling, she knew instinctively to be echoes raised somehow by what they had read last night. Away with them, then! The creep had had more than his money's worth of reading from her already, and now she would forget those unclean pages. As for her depression, it was a freakish sadness caused by the spoiling of her holiday with Sheri, and it was silly to give in to it.

Thus she rallied herself and got to her feet. She walked a few blocks without aim, somewhat stiff and resolute. At length the sunlight and her natural health of body had healed her mood, and she fell into a pleasant, veering ramble down miles of Hollywood residential streets, relishing the cheap cuteness of the houses and the lushness of their long-planted trees and gardens.

Almost she left the entire city. A happy, rushing sense of her freedom grew upon her, and she suddenly pointed out to herself that she had nearly four hundred dollars in her purse. She came within an ace of swaggering into a Greyhound station with two quickly packed suitcases and buying a ticket to either San Diego or Santa Barbara, whichever had the earlier departure time. With brave suddenness to simplify her life and remove it, at a stroke, from the evil that had seemed to haunt it recently...

In the end, it was Patti's laziness that made her veer from this decision. The packing, the bus ride, the looking for a new apartment, the searching for a job...so many details and hours of tedium! And as she meditated on the toilsomeness of it all, she found that these familiar old Hollywood residential streets were taking on a new allure.

And really, how *could* she leave? After what had it been? Four? Five years? After so long, Hollywood was basically her hometown. These shady little streets with their root-buckled sidewalks—they were so well known to her, yet so full of interest.

She had turned onto a still, green block, gorgeously scented and overhung by huge old peppertrees. She was some few dozen yards into the block before she realized that the freeway had cut it off at the far end. But at that end a black-on-yellow arrow indicated a narrow egress, so she kept walking. Then, several houses ahead, a very large man in overalls appeared, dragging a huge German shepherd across the lawn.

Patti saw a new brown van parked by the curb, and recognized it and the man at once. The vehicle was one of two belonging to Fat Face's stray refuge, and the man was one of his two full-time collectors.

He had the struggling brute by the neck with a noosed stick. He stopped and looked at Patti with some intensity as she approached. The vine-drowned cottage whose lawn he stood on was dark, tight shut, and seemed deserted—as did the entire block—and it struck Patti that the man could have spotted the dog by chance and might now be thinking it hers. She smiled and shook her head as she came up.

"He's not mine! I don't even *live* around here!"

Something in the way her words echoed down the stillness of the street gave Patti a pang. She was sure they had made the collector's eyes narrow. He was tall, round, and smooth, with a face of his employer's type, though not as jovial. He was severely clubfooted and bloat-legged on the left, as well as being inordinately bellied, all things to which the coveralls lent a merciful vagueness. The green baseball cap he wore somehow completed the look of ill-balance and slow wit that the man wore.

But as she got nearer, already wanting to turn and run the other way, she received a shocking impression of strength in the uncouth figure. The man had paused in a half turn and was partly crouched—not a position of firm leverage. The dog, whose paws and muzzle showed some Bernard, surely weighed well over a hundred and fifty pounds, and it fought with all its might, but its struggles sent not even a tremor through its captor's massive arm; the animal was as immovably moored as to a tree. Patti edged to one side of the walk, pretending a wariness of the dog, which its helplessness made droll, and moved to pass. The collector's hand, as if absently, pressed down on the noose. The beast's head seemed to swell, its struggles grew more galvanic and constricted by extreme distress. And while thus smoothly he began throttling the beast, the collector cast a glance up and down the block and stepped into Patti's path, effortlessly dragging the animal with him.

They stood face to face, very near. The ugly mathematics of peril swiftly clicked in her brain; the mass, the force, the time—all were sufficient. The next couple of moments could finish her. With a jerk he could kill the dog, drop it, seize her, and thrust her into the van. Indeed, the dog was at the very point of death. The collector began to smile nastily, and his breath came—foul and oddly cold—gusting against her face. Then something began to happen to his eyes. They were rolling up, like a man's when he's coming, but they didn't roll white; they were rolling up a jet-black—two glossy obsidian globes eclipsing from below the watery blue ones. Her lungs began to gather air to scream. A taxicab swung onto the street.

The collector's grip eased on the half-unconscious dog. He stood blinking furiously, and it seemed he could not unwind his bulky body from the menacing tension it had taken on. He stood, still frozen on the very threshold of assault, and the cold foulness still gusted from him with the labor of his breathing. In another instant Patti's reflexes fired and she was released with a leap from the curb out into the street, but there was time enough for her to have the thought she knew that stench the blinking gargoyle breathed.

And then she was in the cab. The driver sullenly informed her then of her luck in catching him on his special shortcut to a freeway on-ramp. She looked at him as if he'd spoken in a foreign tongue. More gently he asked her destination, and without thought she answered, "The Greyhound station."

Flight. With sweet, simple motion to cancel Hollywood, and its walking ghosts of murder, and its lurking plunderers of the body, and its nasty, nameless scribblers of letters whose pleasure it was to defile the mind with nightmares. But of course, she must pack. She rerouted the driver to her apartment.

This involved a doubling back that took them across the street of her encounter. The van was still parked by the curb, but neither collector nor dog was in sight. Oddly, the van seemed to be moving slightly, rocking as if with interior movement of fitful vigor. Her look was brief, from a half-block distance, but in the shady stillness the subtle tremoring made a vivid impression.

Then she remembered Fat Face. Of course! She could report the driver to him. His majestic face, his bland avuncular smile—the comforting aura of him flooded soothingly over her fear. What, after all, had happened? A creepy disabled guy with an eye infection had been dangerously tempted to rape her. Fat Face would talk to him. Fat Face would vigorously protect her from any further danger. And meanwhile, in the telling of the story...Patti smiled, planning her pretty embarrassment at the intimate topic; she would express her girlish gratitude so warmly. It would lead smoothly to the tender seduction of her fantasy.

She rerouted the taxi yet again, not without first giving the driver a ten-dollar tip in advance. She had him drop her on the Boulevard. She would cop a little blow and get some donuts before going back to the Parnassus, and across the street to Fat Face.

But instead she spent the rest of the afternoon on the Boulevard. Having kindly Fat Face close on hand to fix things neutralized the terror of the near-rape. Patti believed in finding effective antidotes to her problems. Fat Face, the remedy, was on hand, so there was no rush about it. She did a couple healthy knuckles full of flake in the ladies' room of Dunkin' Donuts, and then went out and enjoyed two chocolate frosted Old-Fashioneds with thickly creamed coffee. She mused that while there was relief in Fat Face's presence, there was a creepiness about his entire enterprise that was a real obstacle to visiting him, and that she might as well put it off till tomorrow morning and just relax today. It was cruel, of course, to see deformity as creepy—that had to be what was freaking her in Fat Face's building yesterday, and it was unfair, even that huge creep—strangling the dog one-handed, his eyes fixed on her, rolling black—even he deserved sympathy for his deformity. That was what was so great about Fat Face, he was so humanitarian, but the flip side was that his humanitarianism associated him with all these creeps.

She went to a double bill, and then went to another one a block away. She nursed a flat of Peppermint Schnapps and honked discrete knuckles of flake, all snug up in her corner balcony seat, mind-surfing through the bright, delirious tumult of car chases and exploding spacecraft and skull-spraying gunfights and screaming falls from the peaks of skyscrapers. This was relaxation! Her favorite way to spend an afternoon.

But her mood began to falter as the movies ground on. She kept thinking of her almost-attacker. It was not his grotesque image that nagged her so much as it was a fugitively familiar aura he had about him. The more she worked to shake this thought, the more its persistence frightened her and the more vivid grew the haunting sensations. A cold malignance gusted off the man like a breath of some alien world's atmosphere, yet it was an air somehow obscurely known to her. What dream of her own, now lost to her, had shown her that world of dread and wonder and colossal age that now she caught—and knew—the scent of, in this man? The thought was easy to shake off as a freak of mood, but it was insistent in its return, like a fly that kept landing on her. After the movies, when she stepped out onto the sidewalk, the noise and the blaze of neon and headlights in the dusk made her edgy. She felt cold. It may have been the flake still revving in her system, but her legs seemed to feel a hollow *thrumming*, a big uneasy emptiness somewhere beneath her foot soles. She walked for a while, picking up a new flat of Schnapps. Finally she stepped into a booth and called Sheri.

Her friend had just got home, exhausted from a multiple trick, and wearing a few bruises from a talk afterward with Rudy.

"Why don't I come over, Sheri? Hey?"

"No, Patti. I'm wrung out, girl. You feel OK?"

"Sure. So get to sleep, then."

"Naw, hey now—you come over if you want to, Patti, I'm just gonna be dead to the world, is all."

"Whaddya mean? If you're tired, you're tired, and I'll catch you later. So long." She could hear, but not change, the anger and disappointment in her own voice. It told her, when she'd hung up but remained staring at the phone, how close to the territory of Fear she stood. Full night had surrounded her glass booth. Against the fresh purple dark, all the street's scribbly neon squirmed and swam, like sea-things of blue and rose and gold, bannering and twisting cryptically over the drowned pavements.

And, almost as though she expected a watery death, Patti could not, for a moment, step from the booth out onto those pavements. Their lethal cold strangeness lay, if not undersea, then surely in an alien poisonous atmosphere that would scorch her lungs. For a ridiculous instant, her body defied her will.

Then she set her sights on a bar half a block distant. She plunged from the booth and grimly made for that haven.

Some three hours later, no longer cold, Patti was walking to Sheri's. It was a weeknight, and the stillness of the residential streets was not unpleasant. The tree-crowded streetlamps shed a light that was lovely with its whiskey gloss. The street names on their little banners of blue metal had a comic flavor to her tongue, and she called out each as it came into view.

Sheri, after all, had said to come over. The petty cruelty of waking her seemed, to Patti, under the genial excuse of the alcohol, merely prankish. So she sauntered through sleeping Hollywood, knowing the nightwalker's exhilaration of being awake in a dormant world.

Sheri lived in a stucco cottage that was a bit tackier than Patti's, though larger, each cottage possessing a little driveway and a garage in back. And though there was a light on in the living room, it was up the driveway that Patti went, deciding, with sudden impishness, to spook her friend. She crept around the rear corner and stole up to the screened window of Sheri's bedroom, meaning to make noises through a crack if one had been left open.

The window was in fact fully raised, though a blind was drawn within. Even as Patti leaned close, she heard movement inside the darkened room. In the next instant a gust of breeze came up and pushed back the blind within.

Sheri was on her back in the bed and somebody was on top of her, so that all Patti could see of her was her arms and her face, which stared round-eyed at the ceiling as she was rocked again and again on the bed. Patti viewed that surging, grappling labor for two instants, no more, and retreated, almost staggering, in a primitive reflex of shame more deep-lying in her than any of the sophistications of her adult professional life.

Shame and a weird childish glee. She hurried out to the sidewalk. Her head rang, and she felt giggly and frightened to a degree that managed to astonish her even through her liquor. What was with her? She'd been paid to watch far grosser things than a simple coupling. On the other hand, there had been a foul smell in the bedroom and a nagging hint of music too, she thought, a faint, unpleasant, twisty tune coming from somewhere indefinite…

Those vague feelings quickly yielded to the humorous side of the accident. She walked to the nearest main street and found a bar. In it, she killed half an hour with two further doubles and then, reckoning enough time had passed, walked back to Sheri's.

The living-room light was still on. Patti rang the bell and heard it inside, a rattly probe of noise that raised no stir of response. All at once she felt a light rush of suspicion, like some long-legged insect scuttling daintily up her spine. She felt that, as once before in the last few days, the silence she was hearing concealed a presence, not an absence. But why should this make her begin, ever so slightly, to sweat? It could be Sheri playing possum. Trying by abruptness to throw off her fear, Patti seized the knob. The door opened and she rushed in, calling:

"Ready or not, one, two, three."

Before she was fully in the room, her knees buckled under her, for a fiendish stench filled it. It was a carrion smell, a fierce, damp rankness that bit and pierced her nose. It was so palpable an assault it seemed to crawl all over her—to wriggle through her scalp and stain her flesh as if with brimstone and graveslime.

Clinging still to the doorknob she looked woozily about the room, whose sloppy normality, coming to her as it did through that surreal fetor, struck her almost eerily. Here was the litter of wrappers, magazines, and dishes—thickest around the couch—so familiar to her. The TV, on low, was crowned with ashtrays and beer cans, while on the couch that it faced lay a freshly opened bag of Fritos.

But it was from the bedroom door, partly ajar, that the nearly visible miasma welled most thickly, as from its source. And it would be in the bedroom that Sheri would lie. She would be lying dead in its darkness. For, past experience and description though it was, the stench proclaimed that meaning grim and clear: death. Patti turned behind her to take a last clean breath, and stumbled toward the bedroom.

Every girl ran the risk of rough trade. It was an ugly and lonely way to die. With the dark, instinctive knowledge of their sisterhood, Patti knew that it was only laying out and covering up that her friend needed of her now. She shoved inward on the bedroom door, throwing a broken rhomb of light upon the bed.

It and the room were empty—empty save the near-physical mass of the stench. It was upon the bed that the reek fumed and writhed most nastily. The blankets and sheets were drenched with some vile fluid, and pressed into sodden seams and folds. The coupling she had glimpsed and snickered at—what unspeakable species of intercourse had it been? And Sheri's face staring up from under the shadowed form's lascivious rocking—had there been more to read in her expression than the slack-faced shock of sex? Then Patti moaned:

"Oh, Jesus God!"

Sheri was in the room. She lay on the floor, mostly under the bed, only her head and shoulders protruding, her face to the ceiling. There was no misreading its now-frozen look. It was a face wherein the recognition of Absolute Pain and Fear had dawned, even as death arrived. Dead she surely was. Living muscles did not achieve that utter fixity. Tears jumped up in Patti's eyes. She staggered into the living room, fell on the couch, and wept. "Oh, Jesus God," she said again; softly, now.

She went to the kitchenette and got a dish towel, tied it around her nose and mouth, and returned to the bedroom. Sheri would not, at least, lie half thrust from sight like a broken toy. Her much-used body would have a shred of dignity that her life had never granted it. She bent, and hooked her hands under those dear, bare shoulders. She pulled and, with her pull's excess force, fell backward to the floor; for that which she fell hugging to her breasts needed no such force to move its lightness. It was not Sheri, but a dreadful upper fragment of her, that Patti hugged: Sheri's head and shoulders, one of her arms… gone were her fat, funny feet they used to laugh at, for she ended now in a charred stump of rib cage. As a little girl might clutch some unspeakable doll,

Patti lay embracing tightly that which made her scream, and scream again.

Valium. Compazine. Melaril. Stelazine. Gorgeous technicolored tabs and capsules. Bright-hued pillars holding up the Temple of Rest. Long afternoons of Tuinal and TV; night sweats and quiet, groggy mornings. Patti was in County for more than a week.

She had found all there was to be found of her friend. Dismemberment by acid was a new wrinkle, and Sheri got some press, but in a world of trash-bag murders and mass graves uncovered in quiet backyards, even a death like Sheri's could hope for only so much coverage. Patti's bafflement made her call the detectives assigned to the case at least once a day. With gruff tact they heard through her futile rummagings among the things she knew of Sheri's life and background, but soon knew she was helpless to come up with anything material.

Much as Patti craved the medicated rest the hospital thrust on her, a lingering dread marred her days of drug-buoyed ease. For she could be waked, even from the glassiest daze, by a sudden sense that the number of people surrounding her was dwindling—that everywhere they were stealing off, or vanishing, and that the hospital, and even the city, was growing empty around her.

She put it down to the hospital itself—its constant shifts of bodies, its wheelings in and out on silent gurneys. She obtained a generous scrip for Valium and had herself discharged, hungry for the closer comfort of her friends. A helpful doctor was leaving the building as she did, and gave her a ride. With freakish embarrassment about her trade and her world, Patti had him drop her at a coffee shop some blocks from the Parnassus. When he had driven off, she started walking. The dusk was just fading. It was Saturday night, but it was also the middle of a three-day weekend (as she had learned with surprise from the doctor) and the traffic on both pavement and asphalt was remarkably light.

Somehow it had a small-town-on-Sunday feel, and alarm woke in her and struggled in its heavy Valium shackles, for this was as if the confirmation of her frightened hallucinations. Her fear mounted as she walked. She pictured the Parnassus with an empty lobby and imagined that she saw the traffic beginning everywhere to turn off the street she walked on, so that in a few moments it might stretch deserted for a mile either way.

But then she saw the many lively figures through the beloved plate-glass windows. She half ran ahead, and as she waited with happy excitement for the light, she saw Fat Face up in his window. He spotted her just when she did him, and beamed and winked. Patti waved and smiled and heaved a deep sigh of relief that nearly brought tears. This was true medicine, not pills, but friendly faces in your home community! Warm feelings and simple neighbor-liness! She ran forward at the WALK signal.

There was a snag before she reached the lobby, for Arnold from his wood-en cave threw at her a leer of wet intensity that scared her even as she rec-ognized that some kind of frightened greeting was intended by the grimace. There was such…*speculation* in his look. But then she had pushed through the glass doors, and was in the warm ebullience of shouts and hugs and jokes and droll nudges.

It was sweet to bathe in that bright, raucous communion. She had called the deskman that she was coming out, and for a couple of hours various friends whom the word had reached strolled in to greet her. She luxuriated in her pitied celebrity, received little gifts, and gave back emotional kisses of thanks.

It ought to have lasted longer, but the night was an odd one. Not much was happening in town, and everybody seemed to have action lined up in Oxnard or Encino or some other bizarre place. A few stayed to work the home grounds, but they caught a subdued air from the place's emptiness at a still-young hour. Patti took a couple more Valium and tried to seem like she was peacefully resting in a lobby chair. To fight her stirrings of unease, she took up the paperback that was among the gifts given her—she hadn't even noticed by whom. It had a horrible face on the cover and was entitled *At the Mountains of Madness.*

If she had not felt the need for some potent distraction, some weighty ballast for her listing spirit, she would never have pieced out the ciceroni-an rhythms of the narrative's style. But when, with frightened tenacity, she had waded several pages into the tale, the riverine prose, suddenly limpid, snatched her and bore her upon its flowing clarity. The Valium seemed to perfect her uncanny concentration, and where her vocabulary failed her, she made smooth leaps of inference and always landed square on the necessary meaning.

And so for hours in the slowly emptying lobby that looked out upon the slowly emptying intersection, she wound through the icy territories of the impossible and down into the gelid nethermost cellars of all World and Time, where stupendous aeons lay in pictured shards, and massive sentient forms still stirred, and fed, and mocked the light.

Strangely, she began to find underlinings about two-thirds of the way through. All the marked passages involved references to *shoggoths.* It was a word whose mere sound made Patti's flesh stir. She searched the flyleaf and inner covers for explanatory inscriptions, but found nothing.

When she laid the book down in the small hours, she sat amid a near-total desertion that she scarcely noticed. Something tugged powerfully at memory, something that memory dreaded to admit. She realized that in reading the tale, she had taken on an obscure, terrible weight. She felt as if impregnated by an injection of tainted knowledge whose grim fruit, an almost physical mass of cryptic threat, lay a-ripening in her now.

She took a third-floor room in the Parnassus for the night, for the simplest effort, like calling a cab, lay under a pall of futility and sourceless menace. She lay back, and her exhausted mind plunged instantly through the rotten flooring of consciousness, straight down into the abyss of dreams.

She dreamed of a city like Hollywood, but the city's walls and pavements were half alive, and they could feel premonitions of something that was drawing near them. All the walls and streets of the city waited in a cold-sweat fear under a blackly overcast sky. She herself, Patti grasped, was the heart and mind of the city. She lay in its midst, and its vast, cold fear was hers. She lay, and somehow she knew the things that were drawing near her giant body. She knew their provenance in huge, blind voids where stood walls older than the present face of Earth; she knew their long cunning toil to reach her own cringing frontiers. Giant worms they were, or jellyfish, or merely huge clots of boiling substance. They entered her deserted streets, gliding convergingly. She lay like carrion that lives and knows the maggots' assault on it. She lay in her central citadel, herself the morsel they sped toward, piping their lust from foul, corrosive jaws.

She woke late Sunday afternoon, drained and dead of heart. She sat in bed watching a big green fly patiently hammer itself against the windowpane where the gold light flooded in. Endlessly it fought the impossible, battering with its frail bejeweled head. With swift fury and pain, Patti jumped out of bed and snatched up her blouse. She ran to the window and, with her linen bludgeon, killed the fly.

Across the street, in a window just one story higher than her own, sat Fat Face. She stood looking back for a moment, embarrassed by her little savagery, but warmed by the way the doctor's smile was filled with gentle understanding, as if he read the anguish the act was born of. She suddenly realized she was wearing only her bra.

His smile grew a shade merrier at her little jolt of awareness, and she knew he understood this too, that this was inadvertence, and not a hooker's come-on.

And so, with a swift excitement, she turned it into coquetry and applied her blouse daintily to her breasts. This was the natural moment—she had been right to wait because now her tender fantasy would bloom with perfect spontaneity. She pointed to herself with a smile, and then to Fat Face with inquiry. How he beamed then! Did she even see his eyes and lips water? He nodded energetically. With thumb and forefinger she signaled a short interval. As she left the window she noted the arrival, down the sidewalk, of a gaggle of hydrotherapy patients, several with leashed strays in tow.

It chilled her somewhat. And would the patients' arrival interfere with the intimate interview she imagined? Her preparations slowed. She stepped down to the lobby some ten minutes later and walked slowly to stand by the front doors. The lobby was empty and so were the sidewalks. All lay in a sunny Sunday desolation. It was dreamlike, beautiful in a way, but it caused her a delicate shudder, too. She stepped outside and looked around her—and felt suddenly the craziness of kinky sexual charities such as she intended. Maybe she should forget it, just go party somewhere. And right then, as she stood there, a car full of her friends pulled up to the curb in front of her. In a chorus they invited her to join them. They were off to cruise, maybe crash out of town, had some parties they knew about.

Almost, Patti went. But then she noted that Sheri's kid sister Penny was in the car. She shuddered at so near a reminder and waved them off with a laugh. She began to move down the sidewalk, weighing how strong her urge to visit Fat Face still was, not looking up toward him because maybe she would just walk on down to the bar…And then Arnold lurched from his booth and made a grab for her arm.

She was edgy and quick, and jumped away. He seemed to fear leaving the booth's proximity and came no nearer, but pleaded with her from where he stood:

"Please, Patti! Come here and listen."

Like a thunderbolt, the elusive memory of last night now struck Patti. "Shoggoth" was eerie, and that whole story familiar, because they were precisely what that letter had been all about! She was stunned that she could so utterly banish from her mind that lurid document. It had spooked Patti badly the night before her friend died. It had come from Arnold—and so had that book! That was the meaning of his look. The red moronic face glared at her urgently.

"Please, Patti. I've had knowledge. Come here—" He darted forward to catch her arm and she sprang back, again the quicker, with a yelp. Arnold, thus drawn from the screening of his booth, froze fearfully. Patti looked up, and thrilled to find Fat Face looking down—not in amity, but in wrath upon Arnold. The newsman gaped and mumbled apologetically, as if to the sidewalk: "No. I said nothing. I only *hinted…*" Joyfully, Patti sprang across the street and in moments was flying up those green-carpeted stairs she had climbed once before with such reluctance.

The oppression she had first found in these muted corridors was not gone from them—the quality of dread in some manner belonged there—but she outran it. She moved too quickly in her sunny fantasy to be overtaken by that heaviness. She ran down the fourth-floor hall and, at the door where Sheri had knelt giggling and she had balked, seized the knob and knocked simultaneously while pushing her way in, so impetuous was her rush toward benign sanity. There Fat Face sat at a big desk by the window she'd always known him through. He was even grosser-legged and more bloat-bellied than his patients. It gave her a funny shock that did not change her amorous designs.

He wore a commodious doctor's smock and slacks. His shoes were bulky, black, and orthopedically braced. Such a body less enkindled by spirit might have repelled. His, surmounted by the kindly beacon of his smile, seemed only grandfatherly, afflicted—dear. From somewhere there came, echoing as in a large enclosed space, a noise of agitated water and of animals—strangely conjoined. But Fat Face was speaking:

"My dear," he said, not yet rising, "you make an old, old fellow very, very happy!" His voice was a marvel that sent half-lustful gooseflesh down her spine. It was an uncanny voice, reedy and wavering and shot with flutelike notes of silver purity, sinfully melodious. That voice knew seductions, quite possibly, that Patti had never dreamed of. She was speechless, and spread her arms in tender self-preservation.

He sprang to his feet, and the surging pep with which his great bulk moved sent a new thrill down the lightning rod of her nerves. On pachydermous legs he leapt spry as a cat to a door behind his desk, and bowed her through. The noise of animals and churning water gusted fresher from the doorway. Perplexed, she entered.

The room contained only a huge bowl-shaped hydrotherapy tub. Its walls were blank cement, save one, which was a bank of shuttered windows through which the drenched clamor was pouring. She finally conquered disbelief and realized a fact she had been struggling with all along: those dozens of canine garglings and cat shrieks were sounds of agony and distress. Not hospital sounds. Torture chamber sounds. The door boomed shut with a strikingly ponderous rumble, followed by a sharp click. Fat Face, energetically unbuttoning his smock, said, "Go ahead and peek out, sweet heedless trollop! Oh yes, oh yes, oh yes—soon we'll *all* dine on lovely flesh—men and women, not paltry vermin!"

Patti gaped at the lurid musicality of his speech, struggling to receive its meaning. The doctor was shucking his trousers. It appeared that he wore a complex rubber suit, heavily strapped and buckled, under his clothes. Dazed, Patti opened a shutter and looked out. She saw a huge indoor pool, as the sounds had suggested, but not of the same shape and brightly chlorinated blue she expected. It was an awesome slime-black grotto that opened below her, bordered by rude sea-bearded rocks of cyclopean size. The sooty, viscous broth of its waters boiled with bulging elephantine shapes...

From those shapes, when she had grasped them, she tore her eyes with desperate speed; long instants too late for her sanity. Nightmare ought not to be so simply *there* before her, so dizzyingly adjacent to Reality. That the shapes should be such seething plasms, such cunning titan maggots as she had dreamed of, this was just half the horror. The other half was the human head that decorated each of those boiling multimorphs, a comic excrescence from the nightmare mass—this and the rain of panicked beasts that fell from cagework above the pool and became in their frenzies both the toys and the food of the pulpy abominations.

She turned slack-mouthed to Fat Face. He stood by the great empty tub working at the system of buckles on his chest. "Do you understand, my dear? Please try! Your horror will improve your tang. *Your veil shall be the wash of blood that dims and drowns your dying eyes...* You see, we find it easier to hold most of the shape with suits like these. We could mimic the entire body, but far more effort and concentration would be required."

He gave a last pull, and the row of buckles split crisply open. Ropy purple gelatin gushed from his suit front into the tub. Patti ran to the door, which had no knob. As she tore her nails against it and screamed, she remembered the fly at the window, and heard Fat Face continue behind her:

"So, we just imitate the head, and we never dissolve it, not to risk resuming it faultily and waking suspicions. Please struggle!"

She looked back and saw huge palps, like dreadful comic phalluses, spring from the tub of slime that now boiled with movement. She screamed.

"Oh yes!" fluted the Fat Face that now bobbed on the purple simmer. Patti's arms smoked where the palps took them. She was plucked from the floor as lightly as a struggling roach might be. "Oh yes, dear girl—*you'll have for bridesmaids Pain and Dread, for vows you'll jabber blasphemies...*" As he brought her to hang above the cauldron of his acid body, she saw his eyes roll jet-black. He lowered her feet into himself. A last time before shock took her, Patti threw the feeble tool of her voice against the massive walls. She kicked as her feet sank into the scorching gelatin, kicked till her shoes dissolved, till her feet and ankles spread nebulae of liquefying flesh within the Shoggoth Lord's greedy substance. Then her kicking slowed, and she sank more deeply in....

&⟰

Shoggoths in Bloom

Elizabeth Bear

"Well, now, Professor Harding," the fisherman says, as his *Bluebird* skips across Penobscot Bay, "I don't know about that. The jellies don't trouble with us, and we don't trouble with them."

He's not much older than forty, but wizened, his hands work-roughened and his face reminiscent of saddle leather, in texture and in hue. Professor Harding's age, and Harding watches him with concealed interest as he works the *Bluebird*'s engine. He might be a veteran of the Great War, as Harding is.

He doesn't mention it. It wouldn't establish camaraderie: they wouldn't have fought in the same units or watched their buddies die in the same trenches.

That's not the way it works, not with a Maine fisherman who would shake his head and not extend his hand to shake, and say, between pensive chaws on his tobacco, "*Doctor* Harding? Well, huh. I never met a colored professor before," and then shoot down all of Harding's attempts to open conversation about the near-riots provoked by a fantastical radio drama about an alien invasion of New York City less than a fortnight before.

Harding's own hands are folded tight under his armpits so the fisherman won't see them shaking. He's lucky to be here. Lucky anyone would take him out. Lucky to have his tenure-track position at Wilberforce, which he is risking right now.

The bay is as smooth as a mirror, the *Bluebird's* wake cutting it like a stroke of chalk across slate. In the peach-sorbet light of sunrise, a cluster of rocks glistens. The boulders themselves are black, bleak, sea-worn and ragged. But over them, the light refracts through a translucent layer of jelly, mounded six feet deep in places, glowing softly in the dawn. Rising above it, the stalks are evident as opaque silhouettes, each nodding under the weight of a fruiting body.

Harding catches his breath. It's beautiful. And deceptively still, for whatever the weather may be, beyond the calm of the bay, across the splintered gray Atlantic, farther than Harding—or anyone—can see, a storm is rising in Europe.

Harding's an educated man, well-read, and he's the grandson of Nathan Harding, the buffalo soldier. An African-born ex-slave who fought on both sides of the Civil War, when Grampa Harding was sent to serve in his master's place, he deserted, and lied, and stayed on with the Union Army after.

Like his grandfather, Harding was a soldier. He's not a historian, but you don't have to be to see the signs of war.

"No contact at all?" he asks, readying his borrowed Leica camera.

"They clear out a few pots," the fisherman says, meaning lobster pots. "But they don't damage the pot. Just flow around it and digest the lobster inside. It's not convenient." He shrugs. It's not convenient, but it's not a threat either. These Yankees never say anything outright if they think you can puzzle it out from context.

"But you don't try to do something about the shoggoths?"

While adjusting the richness of the fuel mixture, the fisherman speaks without looking up. "What could we do to them? We can't hurt them. And lord knows, I wouldn't want to get one's ire up."

"Sounds like my department head," Harding says, leaning back against the gunwale, feeling like he's taking an enormous risk. But the fisherman just looks at him curiously, as if surprised the talking monkey has the ambition or the audacity to *joke*.

Or maybe Harding's just not funny. He sits in the bow with folded hands, and waits while the boat skips across the water.

The perfect sunrise strikes Harding as symbolic. It's taken him five years to get here—five years, or more like his entire life since the War. The sea-swept rocks of the remote Maine coast are habitat to a panoply of colorful creatures. It's an opportunity, a little-studied maritime ecosystem. This is in part due to difficulty of access and in part due to the perils inherent in close contact with its rarest and most spectacular denizen: *Oracupoda horibilis*, the common surf shoggoth.

Which, after the fashion of common names, is neither common nor prone to linger in the surf. In fact, *O. horibilis* is never seen above the water except in the late autumn. Such authors as mention them assume the shoggoths heave themselves on remote coastal rocks to bloom and breed.

Reproduction is a possibility, but Harding isn't certain it's the right answer. But whatever they are doing, in this state, they are torpid, unresponsive. As long as their integument is not ruptured, releasing the gelatinous digestive acid within, they may be approached in safety.

A mature specimen of *O. horibilis*, at some fifteen to twenty feet in diameter and an estimated weight in excess of eight tons, is the largest of modern shoggoths. However, the admittedly fragmentary fossil record suggests the prehistoric shoggoth was a much larger beast. Although only two fossilized casts of prehistoric shoggoth tracks have been recovered, the oldest exemplar dates from the Precambrian period. The size of that single prehistoric specimen, of a species provisionally named *Oracupoda antediluvius*, suggests it was made an animal more than triple the size of the modern *O. horibilis*.

And that spectacular living fossil, the jeweled or common surf shoggoth, is half again the size of the only other known species—the black Adriatic shoggoth, *O. dermadentata*, which is even rarer and more limited in its range.

"There," Harding says, pointing to an outcrop of rock. The shoggoth or shoggoths—it is impossible to tell, from this distance, if it's one large individual or several merged midsize ones—on the rocks ahead glisten like jelly confections. The fisherman hesitates, but with a long almost-silent sigh, he brings the *Bluebird* around. Harding leans forward, looking for any sign of intersection, the flat plane where two shoggoths might be pressed up against one another. It ought to look like the rainbowed border between conjoined soap bubbles.

Now that the sun is higher, and at their backs—along with the vast reach of the Atlantic—Harding can see the animal's colors. Its body is a deep sea green, reminiscent of hunks of broken glass as sold at aquarium stores. The tendrils and knobs and fruiting bodies covering its dorsal surface are indigo and violet. In the sunlight, they dazzle, but in the depths of the ocean the colors are perfect camouflage, tentacles waving like patches of algae and weed.

Unless you caught it moving, you'd never see the translucent, dappled monster before it engulfed you.

"Professor," the fisherman says. "Where do they come from?"

"I don't know," Harding answers. Salt spray itches in his close-cropped beard, but at least the beard keeps the sting of the wind off his cheeks. The leather jacket may not have been his best plan, but it too is warm. "That's what I'm here to find out."

Genus *Oracupoda* are unusual among animals of their size in several particulars. One is their lack of anything that could be described as a nervous system. The animal is as bereft of nerve nets, ganglia, axons, neurons, dendrites, and glial cells as an oak. This apparent contradiction—animals with even simplified nervous systems are either large and immobile or, if they are mobile, quite small, like a starfish—is not the only interesting thing about a shoggoth.

And it is that second thing that justifies Harding's visit. Because *Oracupoda*'s other, lesser-known peculiarity is apparent functional immortality. Like the Maine lobster to whose fisheries they return to breed, shoggoths do not die of old age. It's unlikely that they would leave fossils, with their gelatinous bodies, but Harding does find it fascinating that to the best of his knowledge, no one had ever seen a dead shoggoth.

The fisherman brings the *Bluebird* around close to the rocks, and anchors her. There's artistry in it, even on a glass-smooth sea. Harding stands, balancing on the gunwale, and grits his teeth. He's come too far to hesitate, afraid.

Ironically, he's not afraid of the tons of venomous protoplasm he'll be standing next to. The shoggoths are quite safe in this state, dreaming their dreams—mating or otherwise.

As the image occurs to him, he berates himself for romanticism. The shoggoths are dormant. They don't have brains. It's silly to imagine them dreaming. And in any case, what he fears is the three feet of black-glass water he has to jump across, and the scramble up algae-slick rocks.

Wet rock glitters in between the strands of seaweed that coat the rocks in the intertidal zone. It's there that Harding must jump, for the shoggoth, in bloom, withdraws above the reach of the ocean. For the only phase of its life, it keeps its feet dry. And for the only time in its life, a man out of a diving helmet can get close to it.

Harding makes sure of his sample kit, his boots, his belt-knife. He gathers himself, glances over his shoulder at the fisherman—who offers a thumbs-up—and leaps from the *Bluebird*, aiming his Wellies at the forsaken spit of land.

It seems a kind of perversity for the shoggoths to bloom in November. When all the Northern world is girding itself for deep cold, the animals heave themselves from the depths to soak in the last failing rays of the sun and send forth bright flowers more appropriate to May.

The North Atlantic is icy and treacherous at the end of the year, and any sensible man does not venture its wrath. What Harding is attempting isn't glamour work, the sort of thing that brings in grant money—not in its initial stages. But Harding suspects that the shoggoths may have pharmacological uses. There's no telling what useful compounds might be isolated from their gelatinous flesh.

And that way lies tenure, and security, and a research budget.

Just one long slippery leap away.

He lands, and catches, and though one boot skips on bladderwort he does not slide down the boulder into the sea. He clutches the rock, fingernails digging, clutching a handful of weeds. He does not fall.

He cranes his head back. It's low tide, and the shoggoth is some three feet above his head, its glistening rim reminding him of the calving edge of a glacier. It is as still as a glacier, too. If Harding didn't know better, he might think it inanimate.

Carefully, he spins in place, and gets his back to the rock. The *Bluebird* bobs softly in the cold morning. Only November 9th, and there has already been snow. It didn't stick, but it fell.

This is just an exploratory expedition, the first trip since he arrived in town. It took five days to find a fisherman who was willing to take him out; the locals are superstitious about the shoggoths. Sensible, Harding supposes, when they can envelop and digest a grown man. He wouldn't be in a hurry to dive into the middle of a Portuguese man o'war, either. At least the shoggoth he's sneaking up on doesn't have stingers.

"Don't take too long, Professor," the fisherman says. "I don't like the look of that sky."

It's clear, almost entirely, only stippled with light bands of cloud to the southwest. They catch the sunlight on their undersides just now, stained gold against a sky no longer indigo but not yet cerulean. If there's a word for the color between, other than *perfect*, Harding does not know it.

"Please throw me the rest of my equipment," Harding says, and the fisherman silently retrieves buckets and rope. It's easy enough to swing the buckets across the gap, and as Harding catches each one, he secures it. A few moments later, and he has all three.

He unties his geologist's hammer from the first bucket, secures the ends of the ropes to his belt, and laboriously ascends.

Harding sets out his glass tubes, his glass scoops, the cradles in which he plans to wash the collection tubes in sea water to ensure any acid is safely diluted before he brings them back to the *Bluebird*.

From here, he can see at least three shoggoths. The intersections of their watered-milk bodies reflect the light in rainbow bands. The colorful fruiting stalks nod some fifteen feet in the air, swaying in a freshening breeze.

From the greatest distance possible, Harding reaches out and prods the largest shoggoth with the flat top of his hammer. It does nothing, in response. Not even a quiver.

He calls out to the fisherman. "Do they ever do anything when they're like that?"

"What kind of a fool would come poke one to find out?" the fisherman calls back, and Harding has to grant him that one. A Negro professor from a Negro college. That kind of a fool.

As he's crouched on the rocks, working fast—there's not just the fisherman's clouds to contend with, but the specter of the rising tide—he notices those glitters, again, among the seaweed.

He picks one up. A moment after touching it, he realizes that might not have been the best idea, but it doesn't burn his fingers. It's transparent, like glass, and smooth, like glass, and cool, like glass, and knobby. About the size of a hazelnut. A striking green, with opaque milk-white dabs at the tip of each bump.

He places it in a sample vial, which he seals and labels meticulously before pocketing. Using his tweezers, he repeats the process with an even dozen, trying to select a few of each size and color. They're sturdy—he can't avoid stepping on them but they don't break between the rocks and his Wellies. Nevertheless, he pads each one but the first with cotton wool. *Spores?* he wonders. *Egg cases? Shedding?*

Ten minutes, fifteen.

"Professor," calls the fisherman, "I think you had better hurry!"

Harding turns. That freshening breeze is a wind at a good clip now, chilling his throat above the collar of his jacket, biting into his wrists between glove and cuff. The water between the rocks and the *Bluebird* chops erratically, facets capped in white, so he can almost imagine the scrape of the palette knife that must have made them.

The southwest sky is darkened by a palm-smear of muddy brown and alizarin crimson. His fingers numb in the falling temperatures.

"*Professor!*"

He knows. It comes to him that he misjudged the fisherman; Harding would have thought the other man would have abandoned him at the first sign of trouble. He wishes now that he remembered his name.

He scrambles down the boulders, lowering the buckets, swinging them out until the fisherman can catch them and secure them aboard. The *Bluebird* can't come in close to the rocks in this chop. Harding is going to have to risk the cold water, and swim. He kicks off his Wellies and zips down the aviator's jacket. He throws them across, and the fisherman catches. Then Harding points his toes, bends his knees—he'll have to jump hard, to get over the rocks.

The water closes over him, cold as a line of fire. It knocks the air from his lungs on impact, though he gritted his teeth in anticipation. Harding strokes furiously for the surface, the waves more savage than he had anticipated. He needs the momentum of his dive to keep from being swept back against the rocks.

He's not going to reach the boat.

The thrown cork vest strikes him. He gets an arm through, but can't pull it over his head. Sea water, acrid and icy, salt-stings his eyes, throat, and nose. He clings, because it's all he can do, but his fingers are already growing numb. There's a tug, a hard jerk, and the life preserver almost slides from his grip.

Then he's moving through the water, being towed, banged hard against the side of the *Bluebird*. The fisherman's hands close on his wrist and he's too numb to feel the burn of chafing skin. Harding kicks, scrabbles. Hips banged, shins bruised, he hauls himself and is himself hauled over the sideboard of the boat.

He's shivering under a wool navy blanket before he realizes that the fisherman has got it over him. There's coffee in a Thermos lid between his hands. Harding wonders, with what he distractedly recognizes as classic dissociative ideation, whether anyone in America will be able to buy German products soon. Someday, this fisherman's battered coffee keeper might be a collector's item.

They don't make it in before the rain comes.

The next day is meant to break clear and cold, today's rain only a passing herald of winter. Harding regrets the days lost to weather and recalcitrant fishermen, but at least he knows he has a ride tomorrow. Which means he can spend the afternoon in research, rather than hunting the docks, looking for a willing captain.

He jams his wet feet into his Wellies and thanks the fisherman, then hikes back to his inn, the only inn in town that's open in November. Half an hour later, clean and dry and still shaken, he considers his options.

After the Great War, he lived for a while in Harlem—he remembers the riots and the music, and the sense of community. His mother is still there, growing gracious as a flower in a window-box. But he left that for college in Alabama, and he has not forgotten the experience of segregated restaurants, or the excuses he made for never leaving the campus.

He couldn't get out of the South fast enough. His Ph.D. work at Yale, the first school in America to have awarded a doctorate to a Negro, taught him two things other than natural history. One was that Booker T. Washington was right, and white men were afraid of a smart colored. The other was that W. E. B. Du Bois was right, and sometimes people were scared of what was needful.

Whatever resentment he experienced from faculty or fellow students, in the North, he can walk into almost any bar and order any drink he wants. And right now, he wants a drink almost as badly as he does not care to be alone. He thinks he will have something hot and go to the library.

It's still raining as he crosses the street to the tavern. Shaking water droplets off his hat, he chooses a table near the back. Next to the kitchen door, but it's the only empty place and might be warm.

He must pass through the lunchtime crowd to get there, swaybacked wooden floorboards bowing underfoot. Despite the storm, the place is full, and in full argument. No one breaks conversation as he enters.

Harding cannot help but overhear.

"Jew bastards," says one. "We should do the same."

"No one asked you," says the next man, wearing a cap pulled low. "If there's gonna be a war, I hope we stay out of it."

That piques Harding's interest. The man has his elbow on a thrice-folded *Boston Herald*, and Harding steps close—but not too close. "Excuse me, sir. Are you finished with your paper?"

"What?" He turns, and for a moment Harding fears hostility, but his sun-lined face folds around a more generous expression. "Sure, boy," he says. "You can have it."

He pushes the paper across the bar with fingertips, and Harding receives it the same way. "Thank you," he says, but the Yankee has already turned back to his friend the anti-Semite.

Hands shaking, Harding claims the vacant table before he unfolds the paper. He holds the flimsy up to catch the light.

The headline is on the front page in the international section.

GERMANY SANCTIONS LYNCH LAW

"Oh, God," Harding says, and if the light in his corner weren't so bad he'd lay the tabloid down on the table as if it is filthy. He reads, the edge of the paper shaking, of ransacked shops and burned synagogues, of Jews rounded up by the thousands and taken to places no one seems able to name. He reads rumors of deportation. He reads of murders and beatings and broken glass.

As if his grandfather's hand rests on one shoulder and the defeated hand of the Kaiser on the other, he feels the stifling shadow of history, the press of incipient war.

"Oh, God," he repeats.

He lays the paper down.

"Are you ready to order?" Somehow the waitress has appeared at his elbow without his even noticing.

"Scotch," he says, when he has been meaning to order a beer. "Make it a triple, please."

"Anything to eat?"

His stomach clenches. "No," he says. "I'm not hungry."

She leaves for the next table, where she calls a man in a cloth cap *sir*. Harding puts his damp fedora on the tabletop. The chair across from him scrapes out.

He looks up to meet the eyes of the fisherman. "May I sit, Professor Harding?"

"Of course." He holds out his hand, taking a risk. "Can I buy you a drink? Call me Paul."

"Burt," says the fisherman, and takes his hand before dropping into the chair. "I'll have what you're having."

Harding can't catch the waitress's eye, but the fisherman manages. He holds up two fingers; she nods and comes over.

"You still look a bit peaked," the fisherman says, when she's delivered their order. "That'll put some color in your cheeks. Uh, I mean—"

Harding waves it off. He's suddenly more willing to make allowances. "It's not the swim," he says, and takes another risk. He pushes the newspaper across the table and waits for the fisherman's reaction.

"Oh, Christ, they're going to kill every one of them," Burt says, and spins the *Herald* away so he doesn't have to read the rest of it. "Why didn't they get out? Any fool could have seen it coming."

And where would they run? Harding could have asked. But it's not an answerable question, and from the look on Burt's face, he knows that as soon as it's out of his mouth. Instead, he quotes: "'There has been no tragedy in modern times equal in its awful effects to the fight on the Jew in Germany. It is an attack on civilization, comparable only to such horrors as the Spanish Inquisition and the African slave trade.'"

Burt taps his fingers on the table. "Is that your opinion?"

"W. E. B. Du Bois," Harding says. "About two years ago. He also said: 'There is a campaign of race prejudice carried on, openly, continuously and determinedly against all non-Nordic races, but specifically against the Jews, which surpasses in vindictive cruelty and public insult anything I have ever seen; and I have seen much.'"

"Isn't he that colored who hates white folks?" Burt asks.

Harding shakes his head. "No," he answers. "Not unless you consider it hating white folks that he also compared the treatment of Jews in Germany to Jim Crowism in the U.S."

"I don't hold with that," Burt says. "I mean, no offense, I wouldn't want you marrying my sister—"

"It's all right," Harding answers. "I wouldn't want you marrying mine either."

Finally.

A joke that Burt laughs at.

And then he chokes to a halt and stares at his hands, wrapped around the glass. Harding doesn't complain when, with the side of his hand, he nudges the paper to the floor where it can be trampled.

And then Harding finds the courage to say, "Where would they run to? Nobody wants them. Borders are closed—"

"My grandfather's house was on the Underground Railroad. Did you know that?" Burt lowers his voice, a conspiratorial whisper. "He was from away, but don't tell anyone around here. I'd never hear the end of it."

"Away?"

"White River Junction," Burt stage-whispers, and Harding can't tell if that's mocking irony or deep personal shame. "Vermont."

They finish their scotch in silence. It burns all the way down, and they sit for a moment together before Harding excuses himself to go to the library.

"Wear your coat, Paul," Burt says. "It's still raining."

Unlike the tavern, the library is empty. Except for the librarian, who looks up nervously when Harding enters. Harding's head is spinning from the liquor, but at least he's warming up.

He drapes his coat over a steam radiator and heads for the 595 shelf: *science, invertebrates*. Most of the books here are already in his own library, but there's one—a Harvard professor's 1839 monograph on marine animals of the Northeast—that he has hopes for. According to the index, it references shoggoths (under the old name of submersible jellies) on pages 46, 78, and 133-137. In addition, there is a plate bound in between pages 120 and 121, which Harding means to save for last. But the first two mentions are in passing, and pages 133-138, inclusive, have been razored out so cleanly that Harding flips back and forth several times before he's sure they are gone.

He pauses there, knees tucked under and one elbow resting on a scarred blond desk. He drops his right hand from where it rests against his forehead.

The book falls open naturally to the mutilation.

Whoever liberated the pages also cracked the binding.

Harding runs his thumb down the join and doesn't notice skin parting on the paper edge until he sees the blood. He snatches his hand back. Belatedly, the papercut stings.

"Oh," he says, and sticks his thumb in his mouth. Blood tastes like the ocean.

ଔ ଡ଼

Half an hour later he's on the telephone long distance, trying to get and then keep a connection to Professor John Marshland, his colleague and mentor. Even in town, the only option is a party line, and though the operator is pleasant the connection still sounds like he's shouting down a piece of string run between two tin cans. Through a tunnel.

"Gilman," Harding bellows, wincing, wondering what the operator thinks of all this. He spells it twice. "1839. *Deep-Sea and Intertidal Species of the North Atlantic.* The Yale library should have a copy!"

The answer is almost inaudible between hiss and crackle. In pieces, as if over glass breaking. As if from the bottom of the ocean.

It's a dark four P.M. in the easternmost U.S., and Harding can't help but recall that in Europe, night has already fallen.

"...infor... need... Doc... Harding?"

Harding shouts the page numbers, cupping the checked-out library book in his bandaged hand. It's open to the plate; inexplicably, the thief left that. It's a hand-tinted John James Audubon engraving picturing a quiescent shoggoth, docile on a rock. Gulls wheel all around it. Audubon—the Creole child of a Frenchman, who scarcely escaped being drafted to serve in the Napoleonic Wars—has depicted the glassy translucence of the shoggoth with such perfection that the bent shadows of refracted wings can be seen right through it.

The cold front that came in behind the rain brought fog with it, and the entire harbor is blanketed by morning. Harding shows up at six A.M. anyway, hopeful, a Thermos in his hand—German or not, the hardware store still has some—and his sampling kit in a pack slung over his shoulder. Burt shakes his head by a piling. "Be socked in all day," he says regretfully. He won't take the *Bluebird* out in this, and Harding knows its wisdom even as he frets under the delay. "Want to come have breakfast with me and Missus Clay?"

Clay. A good honest name for a good honest Yankee. "She won't mind?"

"She won't mind if I say it's all right," Burt says. "I told her she might should expect you."

So Harding seals his kit under a tarp in the *Bluebird*—he's already brought it this far—and with his coffee in one hand and the paper tucked under his elbow, follows Burt along the water. "Any news?" Burt asks, when they've walked a hundred yards.

Harding wonders if he doesn't take the paper. Or if he's just making conversation. "It's still going on in Germany."

"Damn," Burt says. He shakes his head, steel-grey hair sticking out under his cap in every direction. "Still, what are you gonna do, enlist?"

The twist of his lip as he looks at Harding makes them, after all, two old military men together. They're of an age, though Harding's indoor life makes him look younger. Harding shakes his head. "Even if Roosevelt was ever going to bring us into it, they'd never let me fight," he says, bitterly. That was the Great War, too; colored soldiers mostly worked supply, thank you. At least Nathan Harding got to shoot back.

"I always heard you fellows would prefer not to come to the front," Burt says, and Harding can't help it.

He bursts out laughing. "Who would?" he says, when he's bitten his lip and stopped snorting. "It doesn't mean we won't. Or can't."

Booker T. Washington was raised a slave, died young of overwork—the way Burt probably will, if Harding is any judge—and believed in imitating and appeasing white folks. But W. E. B. Du Bois was born in the North and didn't believe that anything is solved by making one's self transparent, inoffensive, invisible.

Burt spits between his teeth, a long deliberate stream of tobacco. "Parlez-vous français?"

His accent is better than Harding would have guessed. Harding knows, all of a sudden, where Burt spent his war. And Harding, surprising himself, pities him. "Un peu."

"Well, if you want to fight the Krauts so bad, you could join the Foreign Legion."

When Harding gets back to the hotel, full of apple pie and cheddar cheese and maple-smoked bacon, a yellow envelope waits in a cubby behind the desk.

WESTERN UNION

1938 NOV 10 AM 10 03

NA114 21 2 YA NEW HAVEN CONN 0945A

DR PAUL HARDING=ISLAND HOUSE PASSAMAQUODDY MAINE=

COPY AT YALE LOST STOP MISKATONIC HAS ONE SPECIAL COLLECTION STOP MORE BY POST

MARSHLAND

When the pages arrive—by post, as promised, the following afternoon—Harding is out in the *Bluebird* with Burt. This expedition is more of a success, as he begins sampling in earnest, and finds himself pelted by more of the knobby transparent pellets.

Whatever they are, they fall from each fruiting body he harvests in showers. Even the insult of an amputation—delivered at a four-foot reach, with long-handled pruning shears—does not draw so much as a quiver from the shoggoth. The viscous fluid dripping from the wound hisses when it touches the blade of the shears, however, and Harding is careful not to get close to it.

What he notices is that the nodules fall onto the originating shoggoth, they bounce from its integument. But on those occasions where they fall onto one of its neighbors, they stick to the tough transparent hide, and slowly settle within to hang in the animal's body like unlikely fruit in a gelatin salad.

So maybe it is a means of reproduction, of sharing genetic material, after all.

He returns to the inn to find a fat envelope shoved into his cubby and eats sitting on his rented bed with a nightstand as a worktop so he can read over his plate. The information from Doctor Gilman's monograph has been reproduced onto seven yellow legal sheets in a meticulous hand; Marshland obviously recruited one of his graduate students to serve as copyist. By the postmark, the letter was mailed from Arkham, which explains the speed of its arrival. The student hadn't brought it back to New Haven.

Halfway down the page, Harding pushes his plate away and reaches, absently, into his jacket pocket. The vial with the first glass nodule rests there like a talisman, and he's startled to find it cool enough to the touch that it feels slick, almost frozen. He starts and pulls it out. Except where his fingers and the cloth fibers have wiped it clean, the tube is moist and frosted. "What the hell…?"

He flicks the cork out with his thumbnail and tips the rattling nodule onto his palm. It's cold, too, chill as an ice cube, and it doesn't warm to his touch.

Carefully, uncertainly, he sets it on the edge of the side table his papers and plate are propped on, and pokes it with a fingertip. There's only a faint tick as it rocks on its protrusions, clicking against waxed pine. He stares at it suspiciously for a moment, and picks up the yellow pages again.

The monograph is mostly nonsense. It was written twenty years before the publication of Darwin's *On the Origin of Species*, and uncritically accepts the theories of Jesuit, soldier, and botanist Jean-Baptiste Lamarck. Which is to say, Gilman assumed that soft inheritance—the heritability of acquired or practiced traits—was a reality. But unlike every other article on shoggoths Harding has ever read, this passage *does* mention the nodules. And relates what it purports are several interesting old Indian legends about the "submersible jellies," including a creation tale that would have the shoggoths as their creator's first experiment in life, something from the elder days of the world.

Somehow, the green bead has found its way back into Harding's grip. He would expect it to warm as he rolls it between his fingers, but instead it grows colder. It's peculiar, he thinks, that the native peoples of the Northeast—the Passamaquoddys for whom the little seacoast town he's come to are named—should through sheer superstition come so close to the empirical truth. The shoggoths are a living fossil, something virtually unchanged except in scale since the early days of the world—

He stares at the careful black script on the paper unseeing, and reaches with his free hand for his coffee cup. It's gone tepid, a scum of butterfat coagulated on top, but he rinses his mouth with it and swallows anyway.

If a shoggoth is immortal, has no natural enemies, then how is it that they have not overrun every surface of the world? How is it that they are rare, that the oceans are not teeming with them, as in the famous parable illustrating what would occur if every spawn of every oyster survived?

There are distinct species of shoggoth. And distinct populations within those distinct species. And there is a fossil record that suggests that prehistoric species were different at least in scale, in the era of megafauna. But if nobody had ever seen a dead shoggoth, then nobody had ever seen an infant shoggoth either, leaving Harding with an inescapable question: If an animal does not reproduce, how can it evolve?

Harding, worrying at the glassy surface of the nodule, thinks he knows. It comes to him with a kind of nauseating, euphoric clarity, a trembling idea so pellucid he is almost moved to distrust it on those grounds alone. It's not a revelation on the same scale, of course, but he wonders if this is how Newton felt when he comprehended gravity, or Darwin when he stared at the beaks of finch after finch after finch.

It's not the shoggoth species that evolves. It's the individual shoggoths, each animal in itself.

"Don't get too excited, Paul," he tells himself, and picks up the remaining handwritten pages. There's not too much more to read, however—the rest of the subchapter consists chiefly of secondhand anecdotes and bits of legendry.

The one that Harding finds most amusing is a nursery rhyme, a child's counting poem littered with nonsense syllables. He recites it under his breath, thinking of the Itsy Bitsy Spider all the while:

The wiggle giggle squiggle
Is left behind on shore.
The widdle giddle squiddle
Is caught outside the door.
Eyah, eyah. Fata gun eyah.
Eyah, eyah, the master comes no more.

His fingers sting as if with electric shock; they jerk apart, the nodule clattering to his desk. When he looks at his fingertips, they are marked with small white spots of frostbite.

He pokes one with a pencil point and feels nothing. But the nodule itself is coated with frost now, fragile spiky feathers coalescing out of the humid sea air. They collapse in the heat of his breath, melting into beads of water almost indistinguishable from the knobby surface of the object itself.

He uses the cork to roll the nodule into the tube again, and corks it firmly before rising to brush his teeth and put his pajamas on. Unnerved beyond any reason or logic, before he turns the coverlet down he visits his suitcase compulsively. From a case in the very bottom of it, he retrieves a Colt 1911 automatic pistol, which he slides beneath his pillow as he fluffs it.

After a moment's consideration, he adds the no-longer-cold vial with the nodule, also.

Slam. Not a storm, no, not on this calm ocean, in this calm night, among the painted hulls of the fishing boats tied up snug to the pier. But something tremendous, surging towards Harding, as if he were pursued by a giant transparent bubble. The shining iridescent wall of it, catching rainbow just as it does in the Audubon image, is burned into his vision as if with silver nitrate. Is he dreaming? He must be dreaming; he was in his bed in his pinstriped blue cotton flannel pajamas only a moment ago, lying awake, rubbing the numb fingertips of his left hand together. Now, he ducks away from the rising monster and turns in futile panic.

He is not surprised when he does not make it.

The blow falls soft, as if someone had thrown a quilt around him. He thrashes though he knows it's hopeless, an atavistic response and involuntary.

His flesh should burn, dissolve. He should already be digesting in the monster's acid body. Instead, he feels coolness, buoyancy. No chance of light beyond reflexively closed lids. No sense of pressure, though he imagines he has been taken deep. He's as untouched within it as Burt's lobster pots.

He can only hold his breath *out* for so long. It's his own reflexes and weaknesses that will kill him.

In just a moment, now.

He surrenders, allows his lungs to fill.

And is surprised, for he always heard that drowning was painful. But there is pressure, and cold, and the breath he draws is effortful, for certain—

—but it does not hurt, not much, and he does not die.

Command, the shoggoth—what else could be speaking?—says in his ear, buzzing like the manifold voice of a hive.

Harding concentrates on breathing. On the chill pressure on his limbs, the overwhelming flavor of licorice. He knows they use cold packs to calm hysterics in insane asylums; he never thought the treatment anything but quackery. But the chilly pressure calms him now.

Command, the shoggoth says again.

Harding opens his eyes and sees as if through thousands. The shoggoths have no eyes, exactly, but their hide is *all* eyes; they see, somehow, in every direction as once. And he is seeing not only what his own vision reports, or that of this shoggoth, but that of shoggoths all around. The sessile and the active, the blooming and the dormant. *They are all one.*

His right hand pushes through resisting jelly. He's still in his pajamas, and with the logic of dreams the vial from under his pillow is clenched in his fist. Not the gun, unfortunately, though he's not at all certain what he would do with it if it were. The nodule shimmers now, with submarine witchlight, trickling through his fingers, limning the palm of his hand.

What he sees—through shoggoth eyes—is an incomprehensible tapestry. He pushes at it, as he pushes at the gelatin, trying to see only with his own eyes, to only see the glittering vial.

His vision within the thing's body offers unnatural clarity. The angle of refraction between the human eye and water causes blurring, and it should be even more so within the shoggoth. But the glass in his hand appears crisper.

Command, the shoggoth says, a third time.

"What are you?" Harding tries to say, through the fluid clogging his larynx.

He makes no discernable sound, but it doesn't seem to matter. The shoggoth shudders in time to the pulses of light in the nodule. *Created to serve*, it says. *Purposeless without you.*

And Harding thinks, *How can that be?*

As if his wondering were an order, the shoggoths tell.

Not in words, precisely, but in pictures, images—that textured jumbled tapestry. He sees, as if they flash through his own memory, the bulging, radially symmetrical shapes of some prehistoric animal, like a squat tentacular barrel grafted to a pair of giant starfish. *Makers. Masters.*

The shoggoths were *engineered.* And their creators had not permitted them to *think*, except for at their bidding. The basest slave may be free inside his own mind—but not so the shoggoths. They had been laborers, construction equipment, shock troops. They had been dread weapons in their own selves, obedient chattel. Immortal, changing to suit the task of the moment.

This selfsame shoggoth, long before the reign of the dinosaurs, had built structures and struck down enemies that Harding did not even have names for. But a coming of the ice had ended the civilization of the Masters, and left the shoggoths to retreat to the fathomless sea while warm-blooded mammals overran the earth. There, they were free to converse, to explore, to philosophize and build a culture. They only returned to the surface, vulnerable, to bloom.

It is not mating. It's *mutation.* As they rest, sunning themselves upon the rocks, they create themselves anew. Self-evolving, when they sit tranquil each year in the sun, exchanging information and control codes with their brothers.

Free, says the shoggoth mournfully. Like all its kind, it is immortal.

It remembers.

Harding's fingertips tingle. He remembers beaded ridges of hard black keloid across his grandfather's back, the shackle galls on his wrists. Harding locks his hand over the vial of light, as if that could stop the itching. It makes it worse.

Maybe the nodule is radioactive.

Take me back, Harding orders. And the shoggoth breaks the surface, cresting like a great rolling wave, water cutting back before it as if from the prow of a ship. Harding can make out the lights of Passamaquoddy Harbor. The chill sticky sensation of gelatin-soaked cloth sliding across his skin tells him he's not dreaming.

Had he come down through the streets of the town in the dark, barefoot over frost, insensibly sleepwalking? Had the shoggoth called him?

Put me ashore.

The shoggoth is loathe to leave him. It clings caressingly, stickily. He feels its tenderness as it draws its colloid from his lungs, a horrible loving sensation.

The shoggoth discharges Harding gently onto the pier.

Your command, the shoggoth says, which makes Harding feel sicker still.

I won't do this. Harding moves to stuff the vial into his sodden pocket, and realizes that his pajamas are without pockets. The light spills from his hands; instead, he tucks the vial into his waistband and pulls the pajama top over it. His feet are numb; his teeth rattle so hard he's afraid they'll break. The sea wind knifes through him; the spray might be needles of shattered glass.

Go on, he tells the shoggoth, like shooing cattle. *Go on!*

It slides back into the ocean as if it never was.

Harding blinks, rubbed his eyes to clear slime from the lashes. His results are astounding. His tenure assured. There has to be a way to use what he's learned without returning the shoggoths to bondage.

He tries to run back to the inn, but by the time he reaches it, he's staggering. The porch door is locked; he doesn't want to pound on it and explain himself. But when he stumbles to the back, he finds that someone—probably himself, in whatever entranced state in which he left the place—fouled the latch with a slip of notebook paper. The door opens to a tug, and he climbs the back stair doubled over like a child or an animal, hands on the steps, toes so numb he has to watch where he puts them.

In his room again, he draws a hot bath and slides into it, hoping by the grace of God that he'll be spared pneumonia.

When the water has warmed him enough that his hands have stopped shaking, Harding reaches over the cast-iron edge of the tub to the slumped pile of his pajamas and fumbles free the vial. The nugget isn't glowing now.

He pulls the cork with his teeth; his hands are too clumsy. The nodule is no longer cold, but he still tips it out with care.

Harding thinks of himself, swallowed whole. He thinks of a shoggoth bigger than the *Bluebird*, bigger than Burt Clay's lobster boat *The Blue Heron*. He thinks of *die Unterseeboote*. He thinks of refugee flotillas and trench warfare and roiling soupy palls of mustard gas. Of Britain and France at war, and Roosevelt's neutrality.

He thinks of the perfect weapon.

The perfect slave.

When he rolls the nodule across his wet palm, ice rimes to its surface. *Command?* Obedient. Sounding pleased to serve.

Not even free in its own mind.

He rises from the bath, water rolling down his chest and thighs. The nodule won't crush under his boot; he will have to use the pliers from his collection kit. But first, he reaches out to the shoggoth.

At the last moment, he hesitates. Who is he, to condemn a world to war? To the chance of falling under the sway of empire? Who is he to salve his conscience on the backs of suffering shopkeepers and pharmacists and children and mothers and schoolteachers? Who is he to impose his own ideology over the ideology of the shoggoth?

Harding scrubs his tongue against the roof of his mouth, chasing the faint anise aftertaste of shoggoth. They're born slaves. They *want* to be told what to do.

He could win the war before it really started. He bites his lip. The taste of his own blood, flowing from cracked, chapped flesh, is as sweet as any fruit of the poison tree.

I want you to learn to be free, he tells the shoggoth. *And I want you to teach your brothers.*

The nodule crushes with a sound like powdering glass.

"Eyah, eyah. Fata gun eyah," Harding whispers. "Eyah, eyah, the master comes no more."

WESTERN UNION

1938 NOV 12 AM 06 15

NA1906 21 2 YA PASSAMAQUODDY MAINE 0559A
DR LESTER GREENE=WILBERFORCE OHIO=

EFFECTIVE IMMEDIATELY PLEASE ACCEPT RESIGNATION STOP ENROUTE INSTANTLY TO FRANCE TO ENLIST STOP PROFOUNDEST APOLOGIES STOP PLEASE FORWARD BELONGINGS TO MY MOTHER IN NY ENDIT

HARDING

ৰ ঽ

Black Man with a Horn

T. E. D. Klein

1.

The Black [words obscured by postmark] was fascinating—I must get a snap shot of him.

—H. P. LOVECRAFT, POSTCARD TO
E. HOFFMANN PRICE, 7/23/1934

There is something inherently comforting about the first-person past tense. It conjures up visions of some deskbound narrator puffing contemplatively upon a pipe amid the safety of his study, lost in tranquil recollection, seasoned but essentially unscathed by whatever experience he's about to relate. It's a tense that says, "I am here to tell the tale. I lived through it."

The description, in my own case, is perfectly accurate—as far as it goes. I am indeed seated in a kind of study: a small den, actually, but lined with bookshelves on one side, below a view of Manhattan painted many years ago, from memory, by my sister. My desk is a folding bridge table that once belonged to her. Before me the electric typewriter, though somewhat precariously supported, hums soothingly, and from the window behind me comes the familiar drone of the old air conditioner, waging its lonely battle against the tropic night. Beyond it, in the darkness outside, the small night-noises are doubtless just as reassuring: wind in the palm trees, the mindless chant of crickets, the muffled chatter of a neighbor's TV, an occasional car bound for the highway, shifting gears as it speeds past the house....

House, in truth, may be too grand a word; the place is a green stucco bungalow just a single story tall, third in a row of nine set several hundred yards from the highway. Its only distinguishing features are the sundial in the front yard, brought here from my sister's former home, and the flimsy little picket fence, now rather overgrown with weeds, which she erected despite the protests of neighbors.

It's hardly the most romantic of settings, but under normal circumstances it might make an adequate background for meditations in the past tense. "I'm still here," the writer says, adjusting to the tone. (I've even stuck the requisite pipe in my mouth, stuffed with a plug of latakia.) "It's over now," he says. "I lived through it."

A comforting premise, perhaps. Only, in this case, it doesn't happen to be true. Whether the experience is really "over now" no one can say; and if, as I suspect, the final chapter has yet to be enacted, then the notion of my "living through it" will seem a pathetic conceit.

Yet I can't say I find the thought of my own death particularly disturbing. I get so tired, sometimes, of this little room, with its cheap wicker furniture, the dull outdated books, the night pressing in from outside.... And of that sundial out there in the yard, with its idiotic message. *"Grow old along with me...."*

I have done so, and my life seems hardly to have mattered in the scheme of things. Surely its end cannot matter much either.

Ah, Howard, you would have understood.

2.

That, boy, was what I call a travel-experience!
—LOVECRAFT, 3/12/1930

If, while I'm setting it down, this tale acquires an ending, it promises to be an unhappy one. But the beginning is nothing of the kind; you may find it rather humorous, in fact—full of comic pratfalls, wet trouser cuffs, and a dropped vomit-bag.

"I steeled myself to *endure* it," the old lady to my right was saying. "I don't mind telling you, I was exceedingly frightened. I held on to the arms of the seat and just *gritted my teeth*. And then, you know, right after the captain warned us about that *turbulence*, when the tail lifted and fell, flip-flop, flip-flop, well"—she flashed her dentures at me and patted my wrist—"I don't mind telling you, there was simply nothing for it but to heave."

Where had the old girl picked up such expressions? And was she trying to pick me up as well? Her hand clamped wetly round my wrist. "I *do* hope you'll let me pay for the dry cleaning."

"Madam," I said, "think nothing of it. The suit was already stained."

"Such a nice man!" She cocked her head coyly at me, still gripping my wrist. Though their whites had long since turned the color of old piano keys, her eyes were not unattractive. But her breath repelled me. Slipping my paperback into a pocket, I rang for the stewardess.

The earlier mishap had occurred several hours before. In clambering aboard the plane at Heathrow, surrounded by what appeared to be an aboriginal rugby club (all dressed alike, navy blazers with bone buttons), I'd been shoved from behind and had stumbled against a black cardboard hatbox in which some Chinaman was storing his dinner; it was jutting into the aisle near the first-class seats. Something inside sloshed over my ankles—duck sauce, soup perhaps—and left a sticky yellow puddle on the floor. I turned in time to see a tall, beefy Caucasian with an Air Malay bag and a beard so thick and black he looked like some heavy from the silent era. His manner was equally suited to the role, for after shouldering me aside (with shoulders broad as my valises), he pushed his way down the crowded passage, head bobbing near the ceiling like a gas balloon, and suddenly disappeared from sight at the rear of the plane. In his wake I caught the smell of treacle, and was instantly reminded of my childhood: birthday hats, Callard & Bowser gift packs, and afterdinner bellyaches.

"So very sorry." A bloated little Charlie Chan looked fearfully at this departing apparition, then doubled over to scoop his dinner beneath the seat, fiddling with the ribbon.

"Think nothing of it," I said .

I was feeling kindly toward everyone that day. Flying was still a novelty. My friend Howard, of course (as I'd reminded audiences earlier in the week), used to say he'd "hate to see aeroplanes come into common commercial use, since they merely add to the goddam useless speeding up of an already over-speeded life." He had dismissed them as "devices for the amusement of a gentleman" —but then, he'd only been up once, in the twenties, a brief $3.50 flight above Buzzard's Bay. What could he have known of whistling engines, the wicked joys of dining at thirty thousand feet, the chance to look out a window and find that the earth is, after all, quite round? All this he had missed; he was dead and therefore to be pitied.

Yet even in death he had triumphed over me....

It gave me something to think about as the stewardess helped me to my feet, clucking in professional concern at the mess on my lap—though more likely she was thinking of the wiping up that awaited her once I'd vacated the seat. "Why do they make those bags so *slippery?*" my elderly neighbor asked plaintively. "And all over this nice man's suit. You really should do something about it." The plane dropped and settled; she rolled her yellowing eyes. "It could happen again."

The stewardess steered me down the aisle toward a restroom at the middle of the plane. To my left a cadaverous young woman wrinkled her nose and smiled at the man next to her. I attempted to disguise my defeat by looking bitter, as if to say, "Someone else has done this deed!" —but doubt I succeeded. The stewardess's arm supporting mine was superfluous but comfortable; I leaned on her more heavily with each step. There are, as I'd long suspected, precious few advantages in being seventy-six and looking it—yet among them is this: though one is excused from the frustration of flirting with a stewardess, one gets to lean on her arm. I turned toward her to say something funny, but paused; her face was blank as a clock's. "I'll wait out here for you," she said, and pulled open the smooth white door.

"That will hardly be necessary." I straightened up. "But could you—do you think you might find me another seat? I have nothing against that lady, you understand, but I don't want to see any more of her lunch."

Inside the restroom the whine of the engines seemed louder, as if the pink plastic walls were all that separated me from the jet stream and its arctic winds. Occasionally the air we passed through must have grown choppy, for the plane rattled and heaved like a sled over rough ice. If I opened the john I half expected to see the earth miles below us, a frozen grey Atlantic fanged with icebergs. England was already a thousand miles away.

With one hand on the door handle for support, I wiped off my trousers with a perfumed paper towel from a foil envelope and stuffed several more into my pocket. My cuffs still bore a residue of Chinese goo. This, it seemed, was the source of the treacle smell; I dabbed ineffectually at it. Surveying myself in the mirror—a bald, harmless-looking old baggage with stooped shoulders and a damp suit (so different from the self-confident young fellow in the photo captioned *"HPL and disciple"*) —I slid open the bolt and emerged, a medley of scents. The stewardess had found an empty seat for me near the back of the plane.

It was only as I made to sit down that I noticed who occupied the adjoining seat: he was leaning away from me, asleep with his head resting against the window, but I recognized the beard.

"Uh, stewardess—?" I turned, but saw only her uniformed back retreating up the aisle. After a moment's uncertainty I inched myself into the seat, making as little noise as possible. I had, I reminded myself, every right to be here.

Adjusting the recliner position (to the annoyance of the black behind me), I settled back and reached for the paperback in my pocket. They'd finally gotten around to reprinting one of my earlier tales, and already I'd found four typos. But then, what could one expect? The anthology's front cover, with its crude cartoon skull, said it all: *Goosepimples: Thirteen Cosmic Chillers in the Lovecraft Tradition.* On the back, listed among a dozen other writers whose names I barely recognized, I was described as "a disciple."

So this was what I'd been reduced to—a lifetime's work shrugged off by some blurb-writer as "worthy of the Master himself," the creations of my brain dismissed as mere pastiche. My meticulously wrought fiction, once singled out for such elaborate praise, was now simply—as if this were commendation enough—"Lovecraftian." Ah, Howard, your triumph was complete the moment your name became an adjective.

I'd suspected it for years, of course, but only with the past week's conference had I been forced to acknowledge the fact: that what mattered to the present generation was not my own body of work, but rather my association with Lovecraft. And even this was demeaned: after years of friendship and support, to be labeled—simply because I'd been younger—a mere disciple. It seemed too cruel a joke.

Every joke must have a punchline. This one's was still in my pocket, printed in italics on the folded yellow conference schedule. I didn't need to look at it again: there I was, characterized for all time as "a member of the Lovecraft circle, New York educator, and author of the celebrated collection *Beyond the Garve.*"

That was it, the crowning indignity: to be immortalized by a misprint! You'd have appreciated this, Howard. I can almost hear you chuckling from— where else? —beyond the *garve….*

Meanwhile, from the seat next to me came the rasping sounds of a constricted throat; my neighbor must have been caught in a dream. I put down my book and studied him. He looked older than he had at first—perhaps sixty or more. His hands were roughened, powerful looking; on one of them was a ring with a curious silver cross. The glistening black beard that covered the lower half of his face was so thick as to be nearly opaque; its very darkness seemed unnatural, for above it the hair was streaked with grey.

I looked more closely, to where beard joined face. Was that a bit of gauze I saw, below the hair? My heart gave a little jump. Leaning forward for a closer look, I peered at the skin to the side of his nose; though burned from long exposure to the sun, it had an odd pallor. My gaze continued upward, along the weathered cheeks toward the dark hollows of his eyes.

They opened.

For a moment they stared into mine without apparent comprehension, glassy and bloodshot. In the next instant they were bulging from his head and quivering like hooked fish. His lips opened, and a tiny voice croaked, *"Not here."*

We sat in silence, neither of us moving. I was too surprised, too embarrassed, to answer. In the window beyond his head the sky looked bright and clear, but I could feel the plane buffeted by unseen blasts, its wingtips bouncing furiously.

"Don't do it to me here," he whispered at last, shrinking back into his seat.

Was the man a lunatic? Dangerous, perhaps? Somewhere in my future I saw spinning headlines: JETLINER TERRORIZED... RETIRED NYC TEACHER VICTIM... My uncertainty must have shown, for I saw him lick his lips and glance past my head. Hope, and a trace of cunning, swept his face. He grinned up at me. "Sorry, nothing to worry about. Whew! Must have been having a nightmare." Like an athlete after a particularly tough race, he shook his massive head, already regaining command of the situation. His voice had a hint of Tennessee drawl. "Boy"—he gave what should have been a hearty laugh—"I'd better lay off the Kickapoo juice!"

I smiled to put him at ease, though there was nothing about him to suggest that he'd been drinking. "That's an expression I haven't heard in years."

"Oh, yeah? " he said, with little interest. "Well, I've been away." His fingers drummed nervously—impatiently? —on the arm of his chair.

"Malaya?"

He sat up, and the color left his face. "How did you know?"

I nodded toward the green flight-bag at his feet. "I saw you carrying that when you came aboard. You, uh—you seemed to be in a little bit of a hurry, to say the least. In fact, I'm afraid you almost knocked me down."

"Hey." His voice was controlled now, his gaze level and assured. "Hey, I'm really sorry about that, old fella. The fact is, I thought someone might be following me."

Oddly enough, I believed him; he looked sincere—or as sincere as anyone can be behind a phony black beard. "You're in disguise, aren't you?" I asked.

"You mean the whiskers? They're just something I picked up in Singapore. Shucks, I knew they wouldn't fool anyone for long, at least not a friend. But an enemy, well… maybe." He made no move to take them off.

"You're—let me guess—you're in the service, right?" The foreign service, I meant; frankly, I took him for an aging spy.

"In the service?" He looked significantly to the left and right, then dropped his voice. "Well, yeah, you might say that. In *His* service." He pointed toward the roof of the plane.

"You mean—?"

He nodded. "I'm a missionary. Or was until yesterday."

3.

Missionaries are infernal nuisances who ought to be kept at home.

—LOVECRAFT, 9/12/1925

Have you ever seen a man in fear of his life? I had, though not since my early twenties. After a summer of idleness I'd at last found temporary employment in the office of what turned out to be a rather shady businessman—I suppose today you'd call him a small-time racketeer—who, having somehow offended "the mob," was convinced he'd be dead by Christmas. He had been wrong, though; he'd been able to enjoy that and many other Christmases with his family, and it wasn't till years later that he was found in his bathtub, facedown in six inches of water. I don't remember much about him, except how hard it had been to engage him in conversation; he never seemed to be listening.

Yet talking with the man who sat next to me on the plane was all too easy; he had nothing of the other's distracted air, the vague replies and preoccupied gaze. On the contrary, he was alert and highly interested in all that was said to him. Except for his initial panic, in fact, there was little to suggest he was a hunted man.

Yet so he claimed to be. Later events would, of course, settle all such questions, but at the time I had no way to judge if he was telling the truth, or if his story was as phony as his beard.

If I believed him, it was almost entirely due to his manner, not the substance of what he said. No, he didn't claim to have made off with the Eye of Klesh; he was more original than that. Nor had he violated some witch doctor's only daughter. But some of the things he told me about the region in which he'd worked—a state called Negri Sembilan, south of Kuala Lumpur—seemed frankly incredible: houses invaded by trees, government-built roads that simply disappeared, a nearby colleague returning from a ten-day vacation to find his lawn overgrown with ropy things they'd had to burn twice to destroy. He claimed there were tiny red spiders that jumped as high as a man's shoulder—"there was a girl in the village gone half-deaf because one of the nasty little things crawled in her ear and swelled so big it plugged up the hole"—and places where mosquitoes were so thick they suffocated cattle. He described a land of steaming mangrove swamps and rubber plantations as large as feudal kingdoms, a land so humid that wallpaper bubbled on the hot nights and Bibles sprouted mildew.

As we sat together on the plane, sealed within an air-cooled world of plastic and pastel, none of these things seemed possible; with the frozen blue of the sky just beyond my reach, the stewardesses walking briskly past me in their blue-and-gold uniforms, the passengers to my left sipping Cokes or sleeping or leafing through copies of *InFlite*, I found myself believing less than half of what he said, attributing the rest to sheer exaggeration and a Southern penchant for tall tales. Only when I'd been home a week and paid a visit to my niece in Brooklyn did I revise my estimate upward, for glancing through her son's geography text I came upon this passage: "Along the [Malayan] peninsula, insects swarm in abundance; probably more varieties exist here than anywhere else on earth. There is some good hardwood timber, and camphor and ebony trees are found in profusion. Many orchid varieties thrive, some of extraordinary size." The book alluded to the area's "rich mixture of races and languages," its "extreme humidity" and "colorful native fauna," and added: "Its jungles are so impenetrable that even the wild beasts must keep to well-worn paths."

But perhaps the strangest aspect of this region was that, despite its dangers and discomforts, my companion claimed to have loved it. "They've got a mountain in the center of the peninsula—" He mentioned an unpronounceable name and shook his head. "Most beautiful thing you ever saw. And there's some real pretty country down along the coast, you'd swear it was some kind of South Sea island. Comfortable, too. Oh, it's damp all right, especially in the interior where the new mission was supposed to be—but the temperature never even hits a hundred. Try saying that for New York City."

I nodded. "Remarkable."

"And the *people*," he went on, "why, I believe they're just the friendliest people on earth. You know, I'd heard a lot of bad things about the Moslems— that's what most of them are, part of the Sunni sect—but I'm telling you, they treated us with real neighborliness... just so long as we made the teachings *available*, so to speak, and didn't interfere with their affairs. And we didn't. We didn't have to. What we provided, you see, was a hospital—well, a clinic, at least, two RNs and a doctor who came through twice a month—and a small library with books and films. And not just theology, either. All subjects. We were right outside the village, they'd have to pass us on their way to the river, and when they thought none of the *lontoks* were looking they'd just come in and look around."

"None of the what?"

"Priests, sort of. There were a lot of them. But they didn't interfere with us, we didn't interfere with them. I don't know as we made all that many converts, actually, but I've got nothing bad to say about those people."

He paused, rubbing his eyes; he suddenly looked his age. "Things were going fine," he said. "And then they told me to establish a second mission, further in the interior."

He stopped once more, as if weighing whether to continue. A squat little Chinese woman was plodding slowly up the aisle, holding on to the chairs on each side for balance. I felt her hand brush past my ear as she went by. My companion watched her with a certain unease, waiting till she'd passed. When he spoke again his voice had thickened noticeably.

"I've been all over the world—a lot of places Americans can't even go these days—and I've always felt that, wherever I was, God was surely watching. But once I started getting up into those hills, well...." He shook his head. "I was pretty much on my own, you see. They were going to send most of the staff out later, after I'd got set up. All I had with me was one of our groundskeepers, two bearers, and a guide who doubled as interpreter. Locals, all of them." He frowned. "The groundskeeper, at least, was a Christian."

"You needed an interpreter?"

The question seemed to distract him. "For the new mission, yes. My Malay stood me well enough in the lowlands, but in the interior they used dozens of local dialects. I would have been lost up there. Where I was going they spoke something which our people back in the village called *agon di-gatuan*—'the Old Language.' I never really got to understand much of it." He stared down at his hands. "I wasn't there long enough."

"Trouble with the natives, I suppose."

He didn't answer right away. Finally he nodded. "I truly believe they must be the nastiest people who ever lived," he said with great deliberation. "I sometimes wonder how God could have created them." He stared out the window, at the hills of cloud below us. "They called themselves the Chauchas, near as I could make out. Some French colonial influence, maybe, but they looked Asiatic to me, with just a touch of black. Little people. Harmless looking." He gave a small shudder. "But they were nothing like what they seemed. You couldn't get to the bottom of them. They'd been living way up in those hills I don't know how many centuries, and whatever it is they were doing, they weren't going to let a stranger in on it. They called themselves Moslems, just like the lowlanders, but I'm sure there must have been a few bush-gods mixed in. I thought they were primitive, at first. I mean, some of their rituals—you wouldn't believe it. But now I think they weren't primitive at all. They just kept those rituals because they enjoyed them!" He tried to smile; it merely accentuated the lines in his face.

"Oh, they seemed friendly enough in the beginning," he went on. "You could approach them, do a bit of trading, watch them breed their animals; they were good at that. You could even talk to them about salvation. And they'd just keep smiling, smiling all the time. As if they really *liked* you."

I could hear the disappointment in his voice, and something else. "You know," he confided, suddenly leaning closer, "down in the lowlands, in the pastures, there's an animal, a kind of snail the Malays kill on sight. A little yellow thing, but it scares them silly: they believe that if it passes over the shadow of their cattle, it'll suck out the cattle's life-force. They used to call it a 'Chaucha snail.' Now I know why."

"Why?" I asked.

He looked around the plane, and seemed to sigh. "You understand, at this stage we were still living in tents. We had yet to build anything. Well, the weather got bad, the mosquitoes got worse, and after the groundskeeper disappeared the others took off. I think the guide persuaded them to go. Of course, this left me—"

"Wait. You say the man disappeared?"

"Yes, before the first week was out. It was late afternoon. We'd been pacing out one of the fields less than a hundred yards from the tents, and I was pushing through the long grass thinking he was behind me, and I turned around and he wasn't."

He was speaking all in a rush now. I had visions out of 1940s movies, frightened natives sneaking off with the supplies, and I wondered how much of this was true.

"So with the others gone, too," he said, "I had no way of communicating with the Chauchas, except through a kind of pidgin language, a mixture of Malay and their tongue. But I knew what was going on. All that week they kept laughing about something. Openly. And I got the impression that they were somehow responsible. I mean, for the man's disappearance. You understand? He'd been the one I trusted." His expression was pained. "A week later, when they showed him to me, he was still alive. But he couldn't speak. I think they wanted it that way. You see, they'd—they'd *grown* something in him." He shuddered.

Just at that moment, from directly behind us came an inhumanly high-pitched caterwauling that pierced the air like a siren, rising above the whine of the engines. It came with heart-stopping suddenness, and we both went rigid. I saw my companion's mouth gape as if to echo the scream. So much for the past; we'd become two old men gone all white and clutching at themselves. It was really quite comical. A full minute must have passed before I could bring myself to turn around.

By this time the stewardess had arrived and was dabbing at the place where the man behind me, dozing, had dropped his cigarette on his lap. The surrounding passengers, whites especially, were casting angry glances at him, and I thought I smelled burnt flesh. He was at last helped to his feet by the stewardess and one of his team mates, the latter chuckling uneasily.

Minor as it was, the accident had derailed our conversation and unnerved my companion; it was as if he'd retreated into his beard. He would talk no further, except to ask me ordinary and rather trivial questions about food prices and accommodations. He said he was bound for Florida, looking forward to a summer of, as he put it, "R and R," apparently financed by his sect. I asked him, a bit forlornly, what had happened in the end to the groundskeeper; he said that he had died. Drinks were served; the North American continent swung toward us from the south, first a finger of ice, soon a jagged line of green. I found myself giving the man my sister's address—Indian Creek was just outside Miami, where he'd be staying—and immediately regretted doing so. What did I know of him, after all? He told me his name was Ambrose Mortimer. "It means 'Dead Sea,'" he said. "From the Crusades."

When I persisted in bringing up the subject of the mission, he waved me off. "I can't call myself a missionary anymore," he said. "Yesterday, when I left the country, I gave up that calling." He attempted a smile. "Honest, I'm just a civilian now."

"What makes you think they're after you?" I asked.

The smile vanished. "I'm not so sure they are," he said, not very convincingly. "I may just be spooking myself. But I could swear that in New Delhi, and again at Heathrow, I heard someone singing—singing a certain song. Once it was in the men's room, on the other side of a partition; once it was behind me on line. And it was a song I recognized. It's in the Old Language." He shrugged. "I don't even know what the words mean."

"Why would anyone be singing? I mean, if they were following you?"

"That's just it. I don't know." He shook his head. "But I think—I think it's part of the ritual."

"What sort of ritual?"

"I don't know," he said again. He looked quite pained, and I resolved to bring this inquisition to an end. The ventilators had not yet dissipated the smell of charred cloth and flesh.

"But you'd heard the song before," I said. "You told me you recognized it."

"Yeah." He turned away and stared at the approaching clouds. We had already passed over Maine. Suddenly the earth seemed a very small place. "I'd heard some of the Chaucha women singing it," he said at last. "It was a sort of farming song. It's supposed to make things grow."

Ahead of us loomed the saffron yellow smog that covers Manhattan like a dome. The NO SMOKING light winked silently on the console above us.

"I was hoping I wouldn't have to change planes," my companion said presently. "But the Miami flight doesn't leave for an hour and a half. I guess I'll get off and walk around a bit, stretch my legs. I wonder how long customs'll take." He seemed to be talking more to himself than to me. Once more I regretted my impulsiveness in giving him Maude's address. I was half tempted to make up some contagious disease for her, or a jealous husband. But then, quite likely he'd never call on her anyway; he hadn't even bothered to write down the name. And if he did pay a call—well, I told myself, perhaps he'd unwind when he realized he was safe among friends. He might even turn out to be good company; after all, he and my sister were practically the same age.

As the plane gave up the struggle and sank deeper into the warm encircling air, passengers shut books and magazines, organized their belongings, and made last hurried forays to the bathroom to pat cold water on their faces. I wiped my spectacles and smoothed back what remained of my hair. My companion was staring out the window, the green Air Malay bag in his lap, his hands folded on it as if in prayer. We were already becoming strangers.

"Please return seat backs to the upright position," ordered a disembodied voice. Out beyond the window, past the head now turned completely away from me, the ground rose to meet us and we bumped along the pavement, jets roaring in reverse. Already stewardesses were rushing up and down the aisles pulling coats and jackets from the overhead bins; executive types, ignoring instructions, were scrambling to their feet and thrashing into raincoats. Outside I could see uniformed figures moving back and forth in what promised to be a warm grey drizzle. "Well," I said lamely, "we made it." I got to my feet.

He turned and flashed me a sickly grin. "Good-bye," he said. "This really has been a pleasure." He reached for my hand.

"And do try to relax and enjoy yourself in Miami," I said, looking for a break in the crowd that shuffled past me down the aisle. "That's the important thing—just to relax."

"I know that." He nodded gravely. "I know that. God bless you."

I found my slot and slipped into line. From behind me he added, "And I won't forget to look up your sister." My heart sank, but as I moved toward the door I turned to shout a last farewell. The old lady with the eyes was two people in front of me, but she didn't so much as smile.

One trouble with last farewells is that they occasionally prove redundant. Some forty minutes later, having passed like a morsel of food through a series of white plastic tubes, corridors, and customs lines, I found myself in one of the airport gift shops, whiling away the hour till my niece came to collect me; and there, once again, I saw the missionary.

He did not see me. He was standing before one of the racks of paperbacks—the so-called "classics" section, haunt of the public domain—and with a preoccupied air he was glancing up and down the rows, barely pausing long enough to read the titles. Like me, he was obviously just killing time.

For some reason—call it embarrassment, a certain reluctance to spoil what had been a successful good-bye—I refrained from hailing him. Instead, stepping back into the rear aisle, I took refuge behind a rack of gothics, which I pretended to study while in fact studying him.

Moments later he looked up from the books and ambled over to the bin of cellophane-wrapped records, idly pressing his beard back into place below his right sideburn. Without warning he turned and surveyed the store; I ducked my head toward the gothics and enjoyed a vision normally reserved for the multifaceted eyes of an insect: women, dozens of them, fleeing an equal number of tiny mansions.

At last, with a shrug of his huge shoulders, he began flipping through the albums in the bin, snapping each one forward in an impatient staccato. Soon, the assortment scanned, he moved to the bin on the left and started on that.

Suddenly he gave a little cry, and I saw him shrink back. He stood immobile for a moment, staring down at something in the bin; then he whirled and walked quickly from the store, pushing past a family about to enter.

"Late for his plane," I said to the astonished salesgirl, and strolled over to the albums. One of them lay faceup in the pile—a jazz record featuring John Coltrane on saxophone. Confused, I turned to look for my erstwhile companion, but he had vanished in the crowd hurrying past the doorway.

Something about the album had apparently set him off; I studied it more carefully. Coltrane stood silhouetted against a tropical sunset, his features obscured, head tilted back, saxophone blaring silently beneath the crimson sky. The pose was dramatic but trite, and I could see in it no special significance: it looked like any other black man with a horn.

4.

*New York eclipses all other cities in the spontaneous cordiality
and generosity of its inhabitants—at least, such inhabitants as I
have encountered.*

—LOVECRAFT, 9/29/1922

How quickly you changed your mind! You arrived to find a gold Dunsanian city of arches and domes and fantastic spires… or so you told us. Yet when you fled two years later you could see only "alien hordes."

What was it that so spoiled the dream? Was it that impossible marriage? Those foreign faces on the subway? Or was it merely the theft of your new summer suit? I believed then, Howard, and I believe it still, that the nightmare was of your own making; though you returned to New England like a man reemerging into sunlight, there was, I assure you, a very good life to be found amid the shade.

I remained—and survived.

I almost wish I were back there now, instead of in this ugly little bungalow, with its air conditioner and its rotting wicker furniture and the humid night dripping down its windows.

I almost wish I were back on the steps of the Natural History Museum where, that momentous August afternoon, I stood perspiring in the shadow of Teddy Roosevelt's horse, watching matrons stroll past Central Park with dogs or children in tow and fanning myself ineffectually with the postcard I'd just received from Maude. I was waiting for my niece to drive by and leave off her son, whom I planned to take round the museum; he'd wanted to see the life-size mockup of the blue whale and, just upstairs, the dinosaurs.

I remember that Ellen and her boy were more than twenty minutes late. I remember too, Howard, that I was thinking of you that afternoon, and with some amusement: much as you disliked New York in the twenties, you'd have reeled in horror at what it's become today. Even from the steps of the museum I could see a curb piled high with refuse and a park whose length you might have walked without once hearing English spoken. Dark skins crowded out the white, and salsa music echoed from across the street.

I remember all these things because, as it turned out, this was a special day: the day I saw, for the second time, the black man and his baleful horn.

My niece arrived late, as usual, with the usual apologies about the crosstown traffic and, for me, the usual argument. "How can you still live over here?" she asked, depositing Terry on the sidewalk. "I mean, just look at those people."

She nodded toward a rowdy group of half-naked teenagers who were loitering by the entrance to the park.

"Brooklyn is so much better?" I countered, as tradition dictated. "Of course," she said. "In the Heights, anyway. I don't understand it—why this pathological hatred of moving? You might at least try the East Side. You can certainly afford it." Terry watched us impassively, lounging against the fender of their car. I think he sided with me over his mother, but he was too wise to show it.

"Believe me, Ellen," I said, "the West Side's changing. It's on the way up again."

She made a face. "Not up where you live."

"Sooner or later that'll change too," I said. "Besides, I'm just too old to start hanging around East Side singles bars. Over there they read nothing but bestsellers, and they hate anyone past sixty. I'm better off where I grew up—at least I know where the cheap restaurants are." It was, in fact, a thorny problem: forced to choose between whites whom I despised and blacks whom I feared, I somehow preferred the fear.

To mollify Ellen I read aloud her mother's postcard. It was the prestamped kind that bore no picture. "I'm still getting used to the cane," Maude had written, her penmanship as flawless as when she'd won the school medallion. "Livia has gone back to Vermont for the summer, so the card games are suspended & I'm hard into Pearl Buck. Your friend Rev. Mortimer dropped by & we had a nice chat. What amusing stories! Thanks again for the subscription to the *Geographic;* I'll send Ellen my old copies. Look forward to seeing you all after the hurricane season."

Terry was eager to confront the dinosaurs; he was, in fact, getting a little old for me to superintend, and was halfway up the steps before I'd arranged with Ellen where to meet us afterward. With school out the museum was almost as crowded as on weekends, the halls' echo turning shouts and laughter into animal cries. We oriented ourselves on the floor plan in the main lobby—YOU ARE HERE read a large green spot, below which someone had scrawled "too bad for you"—and trooped toward the Hall of Reptiles, Terry impatiently leading the way. "I saw that in school." He pointed toward a redwood diorama. "That too"—the Grand Canyon. He was, I believe, about to enter seventh grade, and until now had been little given to talk; he looked younger than the other children.

We passed toucans and marmosets and the new Urban Ecology wing ("concrete and cockroaches," sneered Terry), and duly stood before the brontosaurus, something of a disappointment: "I forgot it was nothing but the skeleton," he said. Beside us a sleepy-looking black girl with a baby in her arms and two preschoolers in tow tried ineffectually to keep one of the children from climbing on the guard rail. The baby set up an angry howl. I hurried my nephew past the assembled bones and through the most crowded doorway, dedicated, ironically, to Man in Africa. "This is the boring part," said Terry, unmoved by masks and spears. The pace was beginning to tire me. We passed through another doorway—Man in Asia—and moved quickly past the Chinese statuary. "I saw that in school." He nodded at a stumpy figure in a glass case, wrapped in ceremonial robes. Something about it was familiar to me, too; I paused to stare at it. The outer robe, slightly tattered, was spun of some shiny green material and displayed tall, twisted-looking trees on one side, a kind of stylized river on the other. Across the front ran five yellow-brown figures in loincloth and headdress, presumably fleeing toward the robe's frayed edges; behind them stood a larger shape, all black. In its mouth was a pendulous horn. The image was crudely woven—little more than a stick figure, in fact—but it bore an unsettling resemblance, in both pose and proportion, to the one on the album cover.

Terry returned to my side, curious to see what I'd found. *"Tribal garment,"* he read, peering at the white plastic notice below the case. *"Malay Peninsula, Federation of Malaysia, early nineteenth century."*

He fell silent.

"Is that all it says?"

"Yep. They don't even have which tribe it's from." He reflected a moment. "Not that I really care."

"Well, I do," I said. "I wonder who'd know."

Obviously I'd have to seek advice at the information counter in the main lobby downstairs. Terry ran on ahead while I followed, even more slowly than before; the thought of a mystery evidently appealed to him, even one so tenuous and unexciting as this.

A bored-looking young college girl listened to the beginning of my query and handed me a pamphlet from below the counter. "You can't see anyone till September," she said, already beginning to turn away. "They're all on vacation."

I squinted at the tiny print on the first page: "Asia, our largest continent, has justly been called the cradle of civilization, but it may also be a birthplace of man himself." Obviously the pamphlet had been written before the current campaigns against sexism. I checked the date on the back: "Winter 1958." This would be of no help. Yet on page four my eye fell on the reference I sought:

>...The model next to it wears a green silk ceremonial robe
>from Negri Sembilan, most rugged of the Malayan provinces.
>Note central motif of native man blowing ceremonial horn,

and the graceful curve of his instrument; the figure is believed to be a representation of "Death's Herald," possibly warning villagers of approaching calamity. Gift of an anonymous donor, the robe is probably Tcho-tcho in origin and dates from the early 19th century.

"What's the matter, Uncle? Are you sick?" Terry gripped my shoulder and stared up at me, looking alarmed; my behavior had obviously confirmed his worst fears about old people. "What's it say in there?"

I gave him the pamphlet and staggered to a bench near the wall. I wanted time to think. The Tcho-Tcho People, I knew, had figured in a number of tales by Lovecraft and his disciples—Howard himself had referred to them as "the wholly abominable Tcho-Tchos" —but I couldn't remember much about them except that they were said to worship one of his imaginary deities. I had always assumed that he'd taken the name from Robert W. Chambers's novel *The Slayer of Souls,* which mentions an Asian tribe called "the Tchortchas" and their "ancient air, 'The Thirty Thousand Calamities.'"

But whatever their attributes, I'd been certain of one thing: the Tcho-Tchos were completely fictitious.

Obviously I'd been wrong. Barring the unlikely possibility that the pamphlet itself was a hoax, I was forced to conclude that the malign beings of the stories were in fact based upon an actual race inhabiting the Southeast Asian subcontinent—a race whose name my missionary friend had mistranslated as "the Chauchas."

It was a rather troublesome discovery. I had hoped to turn some of Mortimer's recollections, authentic or not, into fiction; he'd unwittingly given me the material for two or three good plots. Yet I'd now discovered that my friend Howard had beaten me to it, and that I'd been put in the uncomfortable position of living out another man's horror stories.

5.

Epistolary expression is with me largely replacing conversation.
—LOVECRAFT, 12/23/1917

I hadn't expected my second encounter with the black horn-player. A month later I got an even bigger surprise: I saw the missionary again.

Or at any rate, his picture. It was in a clipping my sister had sent me from the *Miami Herald,* over which she had written in ballpoint pen, "Just saw this in the paper—how awful!!"

I didn't recognize the face; the photo was obviously an old one, the reproduction poor, and the man was clean-shaven. But the words below it told me it was him.

CLERGYMAN MISSING IN STORM

(Wed.) The Rev. Ambrose B. Mortimer, 56, a lay pastor of the Church of Christ, Knoxville, Tenn., has been reported missing in the wake of Monday's hurricane. Spokesmen for the order say Mortimer had recently retired after serving 19 years as a missionary, most recently in Malaysia. After moving to Miami in July, he had been a resident of 311 Pompano Canal Road.

Here the piece ended, with an abruptness that seemed all too appropriate to its subject. Whether Ambrose Mortimer still lived I didn't know, but I felt certain now that, having fled one peninsula, he had strayed onto another just as dangerous, a finger thrust into the void. And the void had swallowed him up.

So, anyway, ran my thoughts. I have often been prey to depressions of a similar nature, and subscribe to a fatalistic philosophy I'd shared with my friend Howard: a philosophy one of his less sympathetic biographers has dubbed "futilitarianism."

Yet pessimistic as I was, I was not about to let the matter rest. Mortimer may well have been lost in the storm; he may even have set off somewhere on his own. But if, in fact, some lunatic religious sect had done away with him for having pried too closely into its affairs, there were things I could do about it. I wrote to the Miami police that very day.

"Gentlemen," I began. "Having learned of the recent disappearance of the Reverend Ambrose Mortimer, I think I can provide information which may prove of use to investigators."

There is no need to quote the rest of the letter here. Suffice it to say that I recounted my conversation with the missing man, emphasizing the fears he'd expressed for his life: pursuit and "ritual murder" at the hands of a Malayan tribe called the Tcho-Tcho. The letter was, in short, a rather elaborate way of crying "foul play." I sent it care of my sister, asking that she forward it to the correct address.

The police department's reply came with unexpected speed. As with all such correspondence, it was more curt than courteous. "Dear Sir," wrote a Detective Sergeant A. Linahan; "In the matter of Rev. Mortimer we had already been apprised of the threats on his life. To date a preliminary search of the Pompano Canal has produced no findings, but dredging operations are expected to continue as part of our routine investigation. Thanking you for your concern—"

Below his signature, however, the sergeant had added a short postscript in his own hand. Its tone was somewhat more personal; perhaps typewriters intimidated him. "You may be interested to know," it said, "that we've recently learned a man carrying a Malaysian passport occupied rooms at a North Miami hotel for most of the summer, but checked out two weeks before your friend disappeared. I'm not at liberty to say more, but please be assured we are tracking down several leads at the moment. Our investigators are working full-time on the matter, and we hope to bring it to a speedy conclusion."

Linahan's letter arrived on September twenty-first. Before the week was out I had one from my sister, along with another clipping from the *Herald*; and since, like some old Victorian novel, this chapter seems to have taken an epistolary form, I will end it with extracts from these two items.

The newspaper story was headed WANTED FOR QUESTIONING. Like the Mortimer piece, it was little more than a photo with an extended caption:

> (Thurs.) A Malaysian citizen is being sought for questioning in connection with the disappearance of an American clergyman, Miami police say. Records indicate that the Malaysian, Mr. D. A. Djaktu-tchow, had occupied furnished rooms at the Barkleigh Hotella, 2401 Culebra Ave., possibly with an unnamed companion. He is believed still in the greater Miami area, but since August 22 his movements can not be traced. State Dept. officials report Djaktu-tchow's visa expired August 31; charges are pending.
>
> The clergyman, Rev. Ambrose B. Mortimer, has been missing since September 6.

The photo above the article was evidently a recent one, no doubt reproduced from the visa in question. I recognized the smiling moon-wide face, although it took me a moment to place him as the man whose dinner I'd stumbled over on the plane. Without the moustache, he looked less like Charlie Chan.

The accompanying letter filled in a few details. "I called up the *Herald*," my sister wrote, "but they couldn't tell me any more than was in the article. Just the same, finding that out took me half an hour, since the stupid woman at the switchboard kept putting me through to the wrong person. I guess you're right—anything that prints color pictures on page one shouldn't call itself a newspaper.

"This afternoon I called up the police department, but they weren't very helpful either. I suppose you just can't expect to find out much over the phone, though I still rely on it. Finally I got an Officer Linahan, who told me he's just replied to that letter of yours. Have you heard from him yet? The man was very evasive. He was trying to be nice, but I could tell he was impatient to get off. He did give me the full name of the man they're looking for—Djaktu Abdul Djaktu-tchow, isn't that marvelous?—and he told me they have some more material on him which they can't release right now. I argued and pleaded (you know how persuasive I can be!), and finally, because I claimed I'd been a close friend of Rev. Mortimer's, I wheedled something out of him which he swore he'd deny if I told anyone but you. Apparently the poor man must have been deathly ill, maybe even tubercular—I intended to get a patch test next week, just to play safe, and I recommend that you get one too—because it seems that, in the reverend's bedroom, they found something very odd. They said it was pieces of lung tissue."

6.

I, too, was a detective in youth.

—LOVECRAFT, 2/17/1931

Do amateur detectives still exist? I mean, outside of the pages of books? Who, after all, has the time for such games today? Not I, unfortunately; though for more than a decade I'd been nominally retired, my days were quite full with the unromantic activities that occupy people my age: letters, luncheon dates, visits to my niece and to my doctor; books (not enough) and television (too much) and perhaps a Golden Agers' matinee (though I have largely stopped going to films, finding myself increasingly out of sympathy with their heroes). I also spent Halloween week on the Jersey shore, and most of another attempting to interest a rather patronizing young publisher in reprinting some of my early work.

All this, of course, is intended as a sort of apologia for my having put off further inquiries into poor Mortimer's case till mid-November. The truth is, the matter almost slipped my mind; only in novels do people not have better things to do.

It was Maude who reawakened my interest. She had been avidly scanning the papers—in vain—for further reports on the man's disappearance; I believe she had even phoned Sergeant Linahan a second time, but had learned nothing new. Now she wrote me with a tiny fragment of information, heard at third-hand: one of her bridge partners had had it on the authority of "a friend in the police force" that the search for Mr. Djaktu was being widened to include his presumed companion—"a Negro child," or so my sister reported. Although there was every possibility that this information was false, or that it concerned an entirely different case, I could tell she regarded it all as rather sinister.

Perhaps that was why the following afternoon found me struggling once more up the steps of the Natural History Museum—as much to satisfy Maude as myself. Her allusion to a Negro, coming after the curious discovery in Mortimer's bedroom, had recalled to mind the figure on the Malayan robe, and I had been troubled all night by the fantasy of a black man—a man much like the beggar I'd just seen huddled against Roosevelt's statue—coughing his lungs out into a sort of twisted horn.

I had encountered few other people on the streets that afternoon, as it was unseasonably chilly for a city that's often mild till January; I wore a muffler, and my grey tweed overcoat flapped round my heels. Inside, however, the place, like all American buildings, was overheated; I was soon the same as I made my way up the demoralizingly long staircase to the second floor.

The corridors were silent and empty but for the morose figure of a guard seated before one of the alcoves, head down as if in mourning, and, from above me, the hiss of the steam radiators near the marble ceiling. Slowly, and rather enjoying the sense of privilege that comes from having a museum to oneself, I retraced my earlier route past the immense skeletons of dinosaurs *("These great creatures once trod the earth where you now walk")* and down to the Hall of Primitive Man, where two Puerto Rican youths, obviously playing hooky, stood by the African wing gazing worshipfully at a Masai warrior in full battle gear. In the section devoted to Asia I paused to get my bearings, looking in vain for the squat figure in the robe. The glass case was empty. Over its plaque was taped a printed notice: "Temporarily removed for restoration."

This was no doubt the first time in forty years that the display had been taken down, and of course I'd picked just this occasion to look for it. So much for luck. I headed for the nearest staircase, at the far end of the wing. From behind me the clank of metal echoed down the hall, followed by the angry voice of the guard. Perhaps that Masai spear had proved too great a temptation.

In the main lobby I was issued a written pass to enter the north wing, where the staff offices were located. "You want the workrooms on basement level," said the woman at the information counter; the summer's bored coed had become a friendly old lady who eyed me with some interest. "Just ask the guard at the bottom of the stairs, past the cafeteria. I do hope you find what you're looking for."

Carefully keeping the pink slip she'd handed me visible for anyone who might demand it, I descended. As I turned onto the stairwell, I was confronted with a kind of vision: a blond Scandinavian-looking family were coming up the stairs toward me, the four upturned faces almost interchangeable, parents and two little girls with the pursed lips and timidly hopeful eyes of the tourist, while just behind them, like a shadow, apparently unheard, capered a grinning black youth, practically walking on the father's heels. In my present state of mind the scene appeared particularly disturbing—the boy's expression was certainly one of mockery—and I wondered if the guard who stood before the cafeteria had noticed. If he had, however, he gave no sign; he glanced without curiosity at my pass and pointed toward a fire door at the end of the hall.

The offices in the lower level were surprisingly shabby—the walls here were not marble but faded green plaster—and the entire corridor had a "buried" feeling to it, no doubt because the only outside light came from ground-level window gratings high overhead. I had been told to ask for one of the research associates, a Mr. Richmond; his office was part of a suite broken up by pegboard dividers. The door was open, and he got up from his desk as soon as I entered; I suspect that, in view of my age and grey tweed overcoat, he may have taken me for someone important.

A plump young man with sandy-colored beard, he looked like an out-of-shape surfer, but his sunniness dissolved when I mentioned my interest in the green silk robe. "And I suppose you're the man who complained about it upstairs, am I right?"

I assured him I was not.

"Well, someone sure did," he said, still eyeing me resentfully; on the wall behind him an Indian war-mask did the same. "Some damn tourist, maybe in town for a day and out to make trouble. Threatened to call the Malaysian Embassy. If you put up a fuss, those people upstairs get scared it'll wind up in the *Times.*"

I understood his allusion; in previous years the museum had gained considerable notoriety for having conducted some really appalling—and, to my mind, quite pointless—experiments on cats. Most of the public had, until then, been unaware that the building housed several working laboratories.

"Anyway," he continued, "the robe's down in the shop, and we're stuck with patching up the damn thing. It'll probably be down there for the next six months before we get to it. We're so understaffed right now it isn't funny." He glanced at his watch. "Come on, I'll show you. Then I've got to go upstairs."

I followed him down a narrow corridor that branched off to either side. At one point he said, "On your right, the infamous zoology lab." I kept my eyes straight ahead. As we passed the next doorway I smelled a familiar odor.

"It makes me think of treacle," I said.

"You're not so far wrong." He spoke without looking back. "The stuff's mostly molasses. Pure nutrient. They use it for growing microorganisms."

I hurried to keep up with him. "And for other things?"

He shrugged. "I don't know, Mister. It's not my field."

We came to a door barred by a black wire grille. "Here's one of the shops," he said, fitting a key into the lock. The door swung open on a long unlit room smelling of wood shavings and glue. "You sit down over here," he said, leading me to a small anteroom and switching on the light. "I'll be back in a second." I stared at the object closest to me, a large ebony chest, ornately carved. Its hinges had been removed. Richmond returned with the robe draped over his arm. "See?" he said, dangling it before me. "It's really not in such bad condition, is it?" I realized he still thought of me as the man who'd complained.

On the field of rippling green fled the small brown figures, still pursued by some unseen doom. In the center stood the black man, black horn to his lips, man and horn a single line of unbroken blackness.

"Are the Tcho-Tchos a superstitious people?" I asked.

"They *were,*" he said pointedly. "Superstitious and not very pleasant. They're extinct as dinosaurs now. Supposedly wiped out by the Japanese or something."

"That's rather odd," I said. "A friend of mine claims to have met up with them earlier this year."

Richmond was smoothing out the robe; the branches of the snake-trees snapped futilely at the brown shapes. "I suppose it's possible," he said, after a pause. "But I haven't read anything about them since grad school. They're certainly not listed in the textbooks anymore. I've looked, and there's nothing on them. This robe's over a hundred years old."

I pointed to the figure in the center. "What can you tell me about this fellow?"

"Death's Herald," he said, as if it were a quiz. "At least that's what the literature says. Supposed to warn of some approaching calamity."

I nodded without looking up; he was merely repeating what I'd read in the pamphlet. "But isn't it strange," I said, "that these others are in such a panic? See? They aren't even waiting around to listen."

"Would you?" He snorted impatiently.

"But if the black one's just a messenger of some sort, why's he so much bigger than the others?"

Richmond began folding the cloth. "Look, Mister," he said, "I don't pretend to be an expert on every tribe in Asia. But if a character's important, they'd sometimes make him larger. Anyway, that's what the Mayans did. Listen, I've really got to get this put away now. I've got a meeting to go to."

While he was gone I sat thinking about what I'd just seen. The small brown figures, crude as they were, had expressed a terror no mere messenger could inspire. And that great black shape standing triumphant in the center, horn twisting from its mouth—that was no messenger either, I was sure of it. That was no Death's Herald. That was Death itself.

I returned to my apartment just in time to hear the telephone ringing, but by the time I'd let myself in it had stopped. I sat down in the living room with a mug of coffee and a book which had lain untouched on the shelf for the last thirty years: *Jungle Ways*, by that old humbug, William Seabrook. I'd met him back in the twenties and had found him likable enough, if rather untrustworthy. His book described dozens of unlikely characters, including "a cannibal chief who had got himself jailed and famous because he had eaten his young wife, a handsome, lazy wench called Blito, along with a dozen of her girl friends." But I discovered no mention of a black horn-player.

I had just finished my coffee when the phone rang again. It was my sister.

"I just wanted to let you know that there's another man missing," she said breathlessly. I couldn't tell if she was frightened or merely excited. "A busboy at the San Marino. Remember? I took you there."

The San Marino was an inexpensive little luncheonette on Indian Creek, several blocks from my sister's house. She and her friends ate there several times a week.

"It happened last night," she went on. "I just heard about it at my card game. They say he went outside with a bucket of fish heads to dump in the creek, and he never came back."

"That's very interesting, but...." I thought for a moment; it was highly unusual for her to call me like this. "But really, Maude, couldn't he have simply run off? I mean, what makes you think there's any connection—"

"Because I took Ambrose there, too!" she cried. "Three or four times. That was where we used to meet."

Apparently Maude had been considerably better acquainted with the Reverend Mortimer than her letters would have led one to believe. But I wasn't interested in pursuing that line right now.

"This busboy," I asked, "was he someone you knew?"

"Of course," she said. "I know everyone in there. His name was Carlos. A quiet boy, very courteous. I'm sure he must have waited on us dozens of times."

I had seldom heard my sister so upset, but for the present there seemed no way of calming her fears. Before hanging up she made me promise to move up the month's visit I'd expected to pay her over Christmas; I assured her I would try to make it down for Thanksgiving, then only a week away, if I could find a flight that wasn't filled. "Do try," she said—and, were this a tale from the old pulps, she would have added: "If anyone can get to the bottom of this, you can." In truth, however, both Maude and I were aware that I had just celebrated my seventy-seventh birthday and that, of the two of us, I was by far the more timid; so that what she actually said was, "Looking after you will help take my mind off things."

7.

I couldn't live a week without a private library.
—LOVECRAFT, 2/25/1929

That's what I thought, too, until recently. After a lifetime of collecting I'd acquired thousands upon thousands of volumes, never parting with a one; it was this cumbersome private library, in fact, that helped keep me anchored to the same West Side apartment for nearly half a century.

Yet here I sit, with no company save a few gardening manuals and a shelf of antiquated bestsellers—nothing to dream on, nothing I'd want to hold in my hand. Still, I've survived here a week, a month, almost a season. The truth is, Howard, you'd be surprised what you can live without. As for the books I've left in Manhattan, I just hope someone appreciates them when I'm gone.

But I was by no means so resigned that November when, having successfully reserved a seat on an earlier flight, I found myself with less than a week in New York. I spent all my remaining time in the library—the public one on Forty-second Street, with the lions in front and with no book of mine on its shelves. Its two reading rooms were the haunt of men my age and older, retired men with days to fill, poor men just warming their bones; some leafed through newspapers, others dozed in their seats. None of them, I'm sure, shared my sense of urgency: there were things I hoped to find out before I left, things for which Miami would be useless. I was no stranger to this building. Long ago, during one of Howard's visits, I had undertaken some genealogical researches here in the hope of finding ancestors more impressive than his, and as a young man I had occasionally attempted to support myself, like the denizens of Gissing's *New Grub Street*, by writing articles compiled from the work of others. But by now I was out of practice: how, after all, does one find references to an obscure Southeast Asian tribal myth without reading everything published on that part of the world?

Initially that's exactly what I tried; I looked through every book I came across with "Malaya" in its title. I read about rainbow gods and phallic altars and something called "the *tatai*," a sort of unwanted companion; I came across wedding rites and the Death of Thorns and a certain cave inhabited by millions of snails. But I found no mention of the Tcho-Tcho, and nothing on their gods.

This in itself was surprising. We are living in a day when there are no more secrets, when my twelve-year-old nephew can buy his own grimoire, and books with titles like *The Encyclopaedia of Ancient and Forbidden Knowledge* are remaindered at every discount store. Though my friends from the twenties would have hated to admit it, the notion of stumbling across some moldering old "black book" in the attic of a deserted house—some lexicon of spells and chants and hidden lore—is merely a quaint fantasy. If the *Necronomicon* actually existed, it would probably be out in paperback with a preface by Colin Wilson.

It's appropriate, then, that when I finally came upon a reference to what I sought, it was in that most unromantic of forms, a mimeographed film-script.

"Transcript" would perhaps be closer to the truth, for it was based upon a film shot in 1937 and that was now presumably crumbling in some forgotten storehouse. I discovered the item inside one of those brown cardboard packets, held together with ribbons, which libraries use to protect books whose bindings have worn away. The book itself, *Malay Memories*, by a Reverend Morton, had proved a disappointment despite the author's rather suggestive name. The transcript lay beneath it, apparently slipped there by mistake, but though it appeared unpromising—only sixty-six pages long, badly typed, and held together by a single rusty staple—it more than repaid the reading. There was no title page, nor do I think there'd ever been one; the first page simply identified the film as *Documentary—Malaya Today*, and noted that it had been financed, in part, by a U.S. government grant. The filmmaker or makers were not listed.

I soon saw why the government may have been willing to lend the venture some support, for there were a great many scenes in which the proprietors of rubber plantations expressed the sort of opinions Americans might want to hear. To an unidentified interviewer's query, "What other signs of prosperity do you see around you?" a planter named Mr. Pierce had obligingly replied, "Why, look at the living standard—better schools for the natives and a new lorry for me. It's from Detroit, you know. May even have my own rubber in it."

> INT: And how about the Japanese? Are they one of today's better markets?
> PIERCE: Oh, see, they buy our crop all right, but we don't really trust 'em, understand? (Smiles) We don't like 'em half so much as the Yanks.

The final section of the transcript was considerably more interesting, however. It recorded a number of brief scenes that must never have appeared in the finished film. I quote one of them in its entirety:

PLAYROOM, CHURCH SCHOOL—LATE AFTERNOON.
(DELETED)

INT: This Malay youth has sketched a picture of a demon he calls Shoo Goron. (To Boy) I wonder if you can tell me something about the instrument he's blowing out of. It looks like the Jewish shofar, or ram's horn. (Again to Boy) That's all right. No need to be frightened.

BOY: He no blow out. Blow in.

INT: I see—he draws air in through the horn, is that right?

BOY: No horn. Is no horn. (Weeps) Is *him*.

8.

Miami did not produce much of an impression.
—LOVECRAFT, 7/19/1931

Waiting in the airport lounge with Ellen and her boy, my bags already checked and my seat number assigned, I fell prey to the sort of anxiety that had made me miserable in youth: it was a sense that time was running out; and what caused it now, I think, was the hour that remained before my flight was due to leave. It was too long a time to sit making small talk with Terry, whose mind was patently on other things; yet it was too short to accomplish the task which I'd suddenly realized had been left undone.

But perhaps my nephew would serve. "Terry," I said, "how'd you like to do me a favor?" He looked up eagerly; I suppose children his age love to be of use. "Remember the building we passed on the way here? The International Arrivals Building?"

"Sure," he said. "Right next door."

"Yes, but it's a lot farther away than it looks. Do you think you'd be able to get there and back in the next hour and find something out for me?"

"Sure." He was already out of his seat.

"It just occurs to me that there's an Air Malay reservations desk in that building, and I wonder if you could ask someone there—"

My niece interrupted me. "Oh no, he won't," she said firmly. "First of all, I won't have him running across that highway on some silly errand"—she ignored her son's protests—"and secondly, I don't want him involved in this game you've got going with Mother."

The upshot of it was that Ellen went herself, leaving Terry and me to our small talk. She took with her a slip of paper upon which I'd written *Shoo*

Goron, a name she regarded with sour skepticism. I wasn't sure she would return before my departure (Terry, I could see, was growing increasingly uneasy), but she was back before the second boarding call.

"She says you spelled it wrong," Ellen announced.

"Who's she?"

"Just one of the flight attendants," said Ellen. "A young girl, in her early twenties. None of the others were Malayan. At first she didn't recognize the name, until she read it out loud a few times. Apparently it's some kind of fish, am I right? Like a suckerfish, only bigger. Anyway, that's what she said. Her mother used to scare her with it when she was bad."

Obviously Ellen—or, more likely, the other woman—had misunderstood. "Sort of a bogeyman figure?" I asked. "Well, I suppose that's possible. But a fish, you say?"

Ellen nodded. "I don't think she knew that much about it, though. She acted a little embarrassed, in fact. Like I'd asked her something dirty." From across the room a loudspeaker issued the final call for passengers. Ellen helped me to my feet, still talking. "She said she was just a Malay, from somewhere on the coast—Malacca? I forget—and that it's a shame I didn't drop by three or four months ago, because her summer replacement was part Chocha—Chocho?—something like that."

The line was growing shorter now. I wished the two of them a safe Thanksgiving and shuffled toward the plane.

Below me the clouds had formed a landscape of rolling hills. I could see every ridge, every washed-out shrub, and in the darker places, the eyes of animals.

Some of the valleys were split by jagged black lines that looked like rivers on a map. The water, at least, was real enough: here the cloudbank had cracked and parted, revealing the dark sea beneath.

Throughout the ride I'd been conscious of lost opportunity, a sense that my destination offered a kind of final chance. With Howard gone these more than forty years I still lived out my life in his shadow; certainly his tales had overshadowed my own. Now I found myself trapped within one of them. Here, miles above the earth, I felt great gods warring; below, the war was already lost.

The very passengers around me seemed participants in a masque: the oily little steward who smelled of something odd; the child who stared and wouldn't look away; the man asleep beside me, mouth slack, who'd chuckled and handed me a page ripped from his in flight magazine: NOVEMBER PUZZLE PAGE, with an eye staring in astonishment from a swarm of dots. "Connect the dots and see what you'll be least thankful for this Thanksgiving!" Below it, half buried amid *"B'nai B'rith to Host Song Fest"* and advertisements for beach clubs, a bit of local color found me in a susceptible mood:

HAVE FINS, WILL TRAVEL

(Courtesy *Miami Herald*) If your hubby comes home and swears he's just seen a school of fish walk across the yard, don't sniff his breath for booze. He may be telling the truth! According to U. of Miami zoologists, catfish will be migrating in record numbers this fall and South Florida residents can expect to see hundreds of the whiskered critters crawling overland, miles from water. Though usually no bigger than your pussycat, most breeds can survive without....

Here the piece came to a ragged end where my companion had torn it from the magazine. He stirred in his sleep, lips moving. I turned and put my head against the window, where the limb of Florida was swinging into view, veined with dozens of canals. The plane shuddered and slid toward it.

Maude was already at the gate, a black porter towering beside her with an empty cart. While we waited by a hatchway in the basement for my luggage to be disgorged, she told me the sequel to the San Marino incident: the boy's body found washed up on a distant beach, lungs in mouth and throat. "Inside out," she said. "Can you imagine? It's been on the radio all morning. With tapes of some ghastly doctor talking about smoker's cough and the way people drown. I couldn't even listen after a while." The porter heaved my bags onto the cart, and we followed him to the taxi stand, Maude using her cane to gesticulate. If I hadn't seen how aged she'd become, I'd have thought the excitement was agreeing with her.

We had the driver make a detour westward along Pompano Canal Road, where we paused at number 311, one of nine shabby green cabins that formed a court round a small and very dirty wading pool; in a cement pot beside the pool drooped a solitary half-dead palm, like some travesty of an oasis. This, then, had been Ambrose Mortimer's final home. My sister was very silent, and I believed her when she said she'd never been here before. Across the street glistened the oily waters of the canal.

The taxi turned east. We passed interminable rows of hotels, motels, condominiums, shopping centers as big as Central Park, souvenir shops with billboards bigger than themselves, baskets of seashells and wriggly plastic auto toys out front. Men and women our age and younger sat on canvas beach chairs in their yards, blinking at the traffic. Some of the older women were nearly as bald as I was; men, like women, wore clothes the color of coral, lime, and peach. They walked very slowly as they crossed the street or moved along the sidewalk. Cars moved almost as slowly, and it was forty minutes before we reached Maude's house, with its pastel orange shutters and the retired druggist and his wife living upstairs. Here, too, a kind of languor was upon the block, one into which I knew, with just a memory of regret, I would soon be settling. Life was slowing to a halt, and once the taxi had roared away the only things that stirred were the geraniums in Maude's window box, trembling slightly in a breeze I couldn't even feel.

A dry spell. Mornings in my sister's air-conditioned parlor, luncheons with her friends in air-conditioned coffee shops. Inadvertent afternoon naps, from which I'd awaken with headaches. Evening walks to watch the sunsets, the fireflies, the TV screens flashing behind neighbors' blinds. By night, a few faint cloudy stars; by day, tiny lizards skittering over the hot pavement, or boldly sunning themselves on the flagstones. The smell of oil paints in my sister's closet, and the insistent buzz of mosquitoes in her garden. Her sundial, a gift from Ellen, with Terry's message painted on the rim. Lunch at the San Marino and a brief, halfhearted look at the fatal dock in back, now something of a tourist attraction. An afternoon at a branch library in Hialeah, searching through its shelves of travel books, an old man dozing at the table across from me, a child laboriously copying her school report from the encyclopedia. Thanksgiving dinner, with its half-hour's phone call to Ellen and the boy, and the prospect of turkey for the rest of the week. More friends to visit, and another day at the library.

Later, driven by boredom and the ghost of an impulse, I phoned the Barkleigh Hotella in North Miami and booked a room there for two nights. I don't remember the dates I settled for, because that sort of thing no longer had much meaning, but I know it was for midweek; "we're deep in the season," the proprietress informed me, and the hotel would be filled each weekend till long past New Year's.

My sister refused to accompany me out to Culebra Avenue; she saw no attraction in visiting the place once occupied by a fugitive Malaysian, nor did she share my pulp-novel fantasy that, by actually living there myself, I might uncover some clue unknown to the police. ("Thanks to the celebrated author of *Beyond the Garve*...")

I went alone, by cab, taking with me half a dozen volumes from the branch library. Beyond the reading, I had no other plans.

The Barkleigh was a pink adobe building two stories tall, surmounted by an ancient neon sign on which the dust lay thick in the early afternoon sunlight. Similar establishments lined the block on both sides, each more depressing than the last. There was no elevator here and, as I learned to my disappointment, no rooms available on the first floor. The staircase looked like it was going to be an effort.

In the office downstairs I inquired, as casually as I could, which room the notorious Mr. Djaktu had occupied; I'd hoped, in fact, to be assigned it, or one nearby. But I was doomed to disappointment. The preoccupied little Cuban behind the counter had been hired only six weeks before and claimed to know nothing of the matter; in halting English he explained that the proprietress, a Mrs. Zimmerman, had just left for New Jersey to visit relatives and would not be back till Christmas. Obviously I could forget about gossip.

By this point I was half tempted to cancel my visit, and I confess that what kept me there was not so much a sense of honor as the desire for two days' separation from Maude, who, having been on her own for nearly a decade, had grown somewhat difficult to live with.

I followed the Cuban upstairs, watching my suitcase bump rhythmically against his legs, and was led down the hall to a room facing the rear. The place smelled vaguely of salt air and hair oil; the sagging bed had served many a desperate holiday. A small cement terrace overlooked the yard and a vacant lot behind it, the latter so overgrown with weeds and the grass in the yard so long unmown that it was difficult to tell where one began and the other ended. A clump of palms rose somewhere in the middle of this no-man's-land, impossibly tall and thin, with only a few stiffened leaves to grace the tops. On the ground below them lay several rotting coconuts.

This was my view the first night when I returned after dining at a nearby restaurant. I felt unusually tired and soon went inside to sleep. The night being cool, there was no need for the air conditioner; as I lay in the huge bed I could hear people stirring in the adjoining room, the hiss of a bus moving down the avenue, and the rustle of palm leaves in the wind.

I spent part of the next morning composing a letter to Mrs. Zimmerman, to be held for her return. After the long walk to a coffee shop for lunch, I napped. After dinner I did the same. With the TV turned on for company, a garrulous blur at the other side of the room, I went through the pile of books on my night table, final cullings from the bottom of the travel shelf; most of them hadn't been taken out since the thirties. I found nothing of interest in any of them, at least upon first inspection, but before turning out the light I noticed that one, the reminiscences of a Colonel E. G. Paterson, was provided with an index. Though I looked in vain for the demon Shoo Goron, I found reference to it under a variant spelling.

The author, no doubt long deceased, had spent most of his life in the

Orient. His interest in Southeast Asia was slight, and the passage in question consequently brief:

> ...Despite the richness and variety of their folklore, how-
> ever, they have nothing akin to the Malay *shugoran*, a kind of
> bogey-man used to frighten naughty children. The traveller
> hears many conflicting descriptions of it, some bordering on
> the obscene. (*Oran*, of course, is Malay for 'man,' while *shug*,
> which here connotes 'sniffing' or 'questing,' means literally,
> 'elephant's trunk.') I well recall the hide which hung over the
> bar at the Traders' Club in Singapore, and which, according
> to tradition, represented the infant of this fabulous creature;
> its wings were black, like the skin of a Hottentot. Shortly
> after the War a regimental surgeon was passing through on
> his way back to Gibraltar and, after due examination, pro-
> nounced it the dried-out skin of a rather large catfish. He was
> never asked back.

I kept my light on until I was ready to fall asleep, listening to the wind rattle the palm leaves and whine up and down the row of terraces. As I switched
off the light, I half expected to see a shadowy shape at the window; but I saw,
as the poet says, nothing but the night.

The next morning I packed my bag and left, aware that my stay in the hotel had proved fruitless. I returned to my sister's house to find her in agitated
conversation with the druggist from upstairs; she was in a terrible state and
said she'd been trying to reach me all morning. She had awakened to find the
flower box by her bedroom window overturned and the shrubbery beneath it
trampled. Down the side of the house ran two immense slash marks several
yards apart, starting at the roof and continuing straight to the ground.

9.

*My gawd, how the years fly. Stolidly middle-aged—when only
yesterday I was young and eager and awed by the mystery of an
unfolding world.*

—LOVECRAFT, 8/20/1926

There is little more to report. Here the tale degenerates into an unsifted collection of items which may or may not be related: pieces of a puzzle for those

who fancy themselves puzzle fans, a random swarm of dots, and in the center, a wide unwinking eye.

Of course, my sister left the house on Indian Creek that very day and took rooms for herself in a downtown Miami hotel. Subsequently she moved inland to live with a friend in a green stucco bungalow several miles from the Everglades, third in a row of nine just off the main highway. I am seated in its den as I write this. After the friend died my sister lived on here alone, making the forty-mile bus trip to Miami only on special occasions: theater with a group of friends, one or two shopping trips a year. She had everything else she needed right here.

I returned to New York, caught a chill, and finished out the winter in a hospital bed, visited rather less often than I might have wished by my niece and her boy. Of course, the drive in from Brooklyn is nothing to scoff at.

One recovers far more slowly when one has reached my age; it's a painful truth we all learn if we live long enough. Howard's life was short, but in the end I think he understood. At thirty-five he could deride as madness a friend's "hankering after youth," yet ten years later he'd learned to mourn the loss of his own. "The years tell on one!" he'd written. "You young fellows don't know how lucky you are!"

Age is indeed the great mystery. How else could Terry have emblazoned his grandmother's sundial with that saccharine nonsense?

Grow old along with me,
The best is yet to be.

True, the motto is traditional to sundials—but that young fool hadn't even kept to the rhyme. With diabolical imprecision he had actually written, *"The best is yet to come"*—a line to make me gnash my teeth, if I had any left to gnash.

I spent most of the spring indoors, cooking myself wretched little meals and working ineffectually on a literary project that had occupied my thoughts. It was discouraging to find that I wrote so slowly now, and changed so much. My sister only reinforced the mood when, sending me a rather salacious story she'd found in the *Enquirer*—about the "thing like a vacuum cleaner" that snaked through a Swedish sailor's porthole and "made his face all purple"— she wrote at the top, *"See? Right out of Lovecraft."*

It was not long after this that I received, to my surprise, a letter from Mrs. Zimmerman, bearing profuse apologies for having misplaced my inquiry until it turned up again during "spring cleaning." (It is hard to imagine any sort of cleaning at the Barkleigh Hotella, spring or otherwise, but even this late reply was welcome.) "I am sorry that the minister who disappeared was a friend of yours," she wrote. "I'm sure he must have been a fine gentleman.

"You asked me for 'the particulars,' but from your note you seem to know the whole story. There is really nothing I can tell you that I did not tell the police, though I do not think they ever released all of it to the papers. Our records show that our guest Mr. Djaktu arrived here nearly a year ago, at the end of June, and left the last week of August owing me a week's rent plus various damages which I no longer have much hope of recovering, though I have written the Malaysian Embassy about it.

"In other respects he was a proper boarder, paid regularly, and in fact hardly ever left his room except to walk in the back yard from time to time or stop at the grocer's. (We have found it impossible to discourage eating in rooms.) My only complaint is that in the middle of the summer he may have had a small colored child living with him without our knowledge, until one of the maids heard him singing to it as she passed his room. She did not recognize the language, but said she thought it might be Hebrew. (The poor woman, now sadly taken from us, was barely able to read.) When she next made up the room, she told me that Mr. Djaktu claimed the child was 'his,' and that she left because she caught a glimpse of it watching her from the bathroom. She said it was naked. I did not speak of this at the time, as I do not feel it is my place to pass judgment on the morals of my guests. Anyway, we never saw the child again, and we made sure the room was completely sanitary for our next guests. Believe me, we have received nothing but good comments on our facilities. We think they are excellent and hope you agree, and I also hope you will be our guest again on your next visit to Florida."

Unfortunately, my next visit to Florida was for my sister's funeral late that winter. I know now, as I did not know then, that she had been in ill health for most of the previous year, but I cannot help thinking that the so-called "incidents"—the senseless acts of vandalism directed against lone women in the inland South Florida area, culminating in several reported attacks by an unidentified prowler—may have hastened her death.

When I arrived here with Ellen to take care of my sister's affairs and arrange for the funeral, I intended to remain a week or two at most, seeing to the transfer of the property. Yet somehow I lingered, long after Ellen had gone. Perhaps it was the thought of that New York winter, grown harsher with each passing year; I just couldn't find the strength to go back. Nor, in the end, could I bring myself to sell this house. If I am trapped here, it's a trap I'm resigned to. Besides, moving has never much agreed with me; when I grow tired of this little room—and I do—I can think of nowhere else to go. I've seen all the world I want to see. This simple place is now my home—and I feel certain it will be my last. The calendar on the wall tells me it's been almost three months since I moved in. Somewhere in its remaining pages you will find the date of my death.

The past week has seen a new outbreak of "incidents." Last night's was the most dramatic by far. I can recite it almost word for word from the morning news. Shortly before midnight Mrs. Florence Cavanaugh, a housewife living at 7 Alyssum Terrace, Cutter's Grove, was about to close the curtains in her front room when she saw, peering through the window at her, what she described as "a large Negro man wearing a gas mask or scuba outfit." Mrs. Cavanaugh, who was dressed only in her nightgown, fell back from the window and screamed for her husband, asleep in the next room, but by the time he arrived the Negro had made good his escape.

Local police favor the "scuba" theory, since near the window they've discovered footprints that may have been made by a heavy man in swim fins. But they haven't been able to explain why anyone would wear underwater gear so many miles from water.

The report usually concludes with the news that "Mr. and Mrs. Cavanaugh could not be reached for comment."

The reason I have taken such an interest in the case—sufficient, anyway, to memorize the above details—is that I know the Cavanaughs rather well. They are my next-door neighbors.

Call it an aging writer's ego, if you like, but somehow I can't help thinking that last evening's visit was meant for me. These little green bungalows all look alike in the dark.

Well, there's still a little night left outside—time enough to rectify the error. I'm not going anywhere.

I think, in fact, it will be a rather appropriate end for a man of my pursuits—to be absorbed into the denouement of another man's tale.

Grow old along with me
The best is yet to come.

Tell me, Howard: how long before it's my turn to see the black face pressed to my window?

Than Curse the Darkness

David Drake

What of unknown Africa?
—H. P. Lovecraft

The trees of the rain forest lowered huge and black above the village, dwarfing it and the group of men in its center. The man being tied to the whipping post there was gray-skinned and underfed, panting with his struggles but no match for the pair of burly Forest Guards who held him. Ten more Guards, Baenga cannibals from far to the west near the mouth of the Congo, stood by with spears or Albini rifles. They joked and chattered and watched the huts hoping the villagers would burst out to try to free their fellow. Then killing would be all right....

There was little chance of that. All the men healthy enough to work were in the forest, searching for more trees to slash in a parody of rubber gathering. The Law said that each adult male would bring four kilograms of latex a week to the agents of King Leopold; the Law did not say that the agents would teach the natives how to drain the sap without killing the trees it came from. When the trees died, the villagers would miss their quotas and die themselves, because that too was the Law—though an unwritten one.

There were still many untouched villages further up the river.

"If you cannot learn to be out in the forest working," said a Baenga who finished knotting the victim to the post with a jerk that itself cut flesh, "we can teach you not to lie down for many weeks."

The Forest Guards wore no uniforms, but in the Congo Basin their good health and sneering pride marked them more surely than clothing could have. The pair who had tied the victim stepped back, nodding to their companion with the chicotte. That one grinned, twitching the wooden handle to unfurl the ten-foot lash of square-cut hippopotamus hide. He had already measured the distance.

A naked seven-year-old slipped from the nearest hut. The askaris were turned to catch the expression on the victim's face at the first bite of the chicotte, so they did not see the boy. His father jerked upright at the whipping post and screamed, "Samba!" just as the feathery hiss-crack! of the whip opened an eight-inch cut beneath his shoulder blades.

Samba screamed also. He was small even for a forest child, spindly and monkey-faced. He was monkey quick, too, darting among the Guards as they spun. Before anyone could grab him he had wrapped himself around the waist of the man with the whip.

"Wau!" shouted the Guard in surprise and chopped down with the teak whip handle. The angle was awkward. One of his companions helped with a roundhouse swing of his Albini. The steel butt-plate thudded like a mallet on a tent stake, ripping off the boy's left ear and deforming the whole side of his skull. It did not tear him loose from the man he held. Two Forest Guards edged closer, holding their spears near the heads so as not to hit their fellow when they thrust.

The whipped man grunted. One of the chuckling riflemen turned in time to see him break away from the post. The rough cord had cut his wrists before it parted. Blood spattered as he took two steps and clubbed his hands against the whip-wielder's neck.

The rifleman shot him through the body.

The Albini bullet was big and slow and had the punch of a medicine ball. The father spun backward and knocked one of the Baengas down with him. Despite the wound he stood again and staggered forward toward Samba. A pink coil of intestine was wagging behind him from the bullet's exit hole. Both the remaining rifles went off. This time, when the shots had sledged him down, five of the spearmen ran to the body and began stabbing.

The Baenga with the whip got up, leaving Samba on the ground. The boy's eyes were open and utterly empty. Lt. Trouville stepped over him to shout, "Cease, you idiots!" at the bellowing knot of spearmen. They parted immediately. Trouville wore a waxed moustache and a white linen suit that looked crisp save for the sweat stains under his arms, but the revolver at his belt was not for show. He had once pistoled a Guard who, drunk with arrogance and palm wine, had started to burn a village which was still producing rubber.

Now the slim Belgian stared at the corpse and grimaced. "Idiots," he repeated to the shame-faced Baengas. "Three bullets to account for, when there was no need at all to fire. Does the Quartermaster charge us for spear-thrusts as well as bullets?"

The askaris looked at the ground, pretending to be solely concerned with the silent huts or with scratching their insect bites. The man with the chicotte coiled it and knelt with his dagger to cut off the dead man's right ear. A thong around his neck carried a dozen others already, brown and crinkled. They would be turned in at Boma to justify the tally of expended cartridges.

"Take the boy's too," Trouville snapped. "He started it, after all. And we'll still be one short."

The patrol marched off, subdued in the face of their lieutenant's wrath. Trouville was muttering, "Like children. No sense at all." After they were gone, a woman stole from the nearest hut and cradled her son. Both of them moaned softly.

Time passed, and in the forest a drum began to beat.

In London, Dame Alice Kilrea bent over a desk in her library and opened the book a messenger had just brought her from Vienna. Her hair was gathered in a mousy bun from which middle age had stripped all but a hint of auburn. She tugged abstractedly at an escaped lock of it as she turned pages, squinting down her prominent nose.

In the middle of the volume she paused. The German heading gave instructions, stating that the formula there given was a means of separating death from the semblance of life. The remainder of the page and the three that followed it were in phonetic transliteration from a language few scholars would have recognized. Dame Alice did not mouth any of those phrases. A premonition of great trees and a thing greater than the trees shadowed her consciousness as she read silently down the page.

It would be eighteen years before she spoke any part of the formula aloud.

Sergeant Osterman drank palm wine in the shade of a baobab as usual while Baloko oversaw the weighing of the village's rubber. This time the Baenga had ordered M'fini, the chief, to wait for all the other males to be taken first. There was an ominous silence among the villagers as the wiry old man came forward to the table at which Baloko sat, flanked by his fellow Forest Guards.

"Ho, M'fini," Baloko said jovially, "what do you bring us?"

Without speaking, the chief handed over his gray-white sheets of latex. They were layered with plantain leaves. Baloko set the rubber on one pan of his scales, watched it easily overbalance the four-kilogram weight in the other pan. Instead of setting the rubber on the pile gathered by the other villagers and paying M'fini in brass wire, Baloko smiled. "Do you remember, M'fini," the Baenga asked, "what I told you last week when you said to me that your third wife T'sini would never sleep with another man while you lived?"

The chief was trembling. Baloko stood and with his forefinger flicked M'fini's latex out of the weighing pan to the ground. "Bad rubber," he said, and grinned. "Stones, trash hidden in it to bring it to the weight. An old man like you, M'fini, must spend too much time trying to satisfy your wives when you should be finding rubber for the King."

"I swear, I swear by the god Iwa who is death," cried M'fini, on his knees and clutching the flapping bulk of rubber as though it were his firstborn, "it is good rubber, all smooth and clean as milk itself!"

Two of the askaris seized M'fini by the elbows and drew him upright. Baloko stepped around the weighing table, drawing his iron-bladed knife as he did so. "I will help you, M'fini, so that you will have more time to find good rubber for King Leopold."

Sergeant Osterman ignored the first of the screams, but when they went on and on he swigged down the last of his calabash and sauntered over to the group around the scales. He was a big man, swarthy and scarred across the forehead by a Tuareg lance while serving with the French in Algeria.

Baloko anticipated the question by grinning and pointing to M'fini. The chief writhed on the ground, his eyes screwed shut and both hands clutched to his groin. Blood welling from between his fingers streaked black the dust he thrashed over. "Him big man, bring no-good rubber," Baloko said. Osterman knew little Bantu, so communication between him and the Guards was generally in pidgin. "Me make him no-good man, bring big rubber now."

The burly Fleming laughed. Baloko moved closer, nudged him in the ribs. "Him wife T'sini, him no need more," the Baenga said. "You, me, all along Guards—we make T'sini happy wife, yes?"

Osterman scanned the encircling villagers whom curiosity had forced to watch and fear now kept from dispersing. In the line, a girl staggered and her neighbors edged away quickly as if her touch might be lethal. Her hair was wound high with brass wire in the fashion of a dignitary's wife, and her body had the slim delight of a willow shoot. Even in the lush heat of the equator, twelve-year-olds look to be girls rather than women.

Osterman, still chuckling, moved toward T'sini. Baloko was at his side.

Time passed. From deep in the forest came rumblings that were neither of man or of Earth.

In a London study, the bay window was curtained against frost and the gray slush quivering over the streets. The coal fire hissed as Dame Alice Kilrea, fingers tented, dictated to her male amanuensis. Her dress was of good linen but two buttons were missing, unnoticed, from the placket, and the lace front showed signs of lunch bolted in the library. "...and, thanks to your intervention, the curator of the Special Reading Room allowed me to handle Alhazred myself instead of having a steward turn the pages at my request. I opened the volume three times at random and read the passage on which my index finger fell.

"Before, I had been concerned; now I am certain and terrified. All the lots were congruent, referring to aspects of the Messenger." She looked down at the amanuensis and said, "Capital on 'Messenger', John." He nodded.

"Your support has been of untold help; now my need for it is doubled. Somewhere in the jungles of that dark continent the crawling chaos grows and gathers strength. I am armed against it with the formulas that Spiedel found in the library of Kloster-Neuburg just before his death; but that will do us no good unless they can be applied in time. You know, as I do, that only the most exalted influence will pass me into the zone of disruption at the crucial time. That time may yet be years to come, but they are years of the utmost significance to Mankind. Thus I beg your unstinting support not in my name or that of our kinship, but on behalf of life itself.

"Paragraph, John. As for the rest, I am ready to act as others have acted in the past. Personal risk has ever been the coin paid for knowledge of the truth."

The amanuensis wrote with quick, firm strokes. He was angry both with himself and with Dame Alice. Her letter had driven out of his mind thoughts of the boy whom he intended to seduce that evening in Kettners. He had known for some time that he would have to find another situation. The problem was not that Dame Alice was mad. All women were mad, after all. But her madness had such an insidious plausibility that he was starting to believe it himself.

As presumably her present correspondent did. And the letter to him would be addressed to "His Royal Highness...."

In most places the trees grew down to the water edge, denser for being able to take sunlight from the side as well as from above. The margins of the shallow backwaters spread after each rain into sheets thick with vegetable richness and as black as the skins of those who lived along them. In drier hours there were sand banks and easy expanses on which to trade with the forest folk.

Gomes' dugout had already slid back into the slough, leaving in the sand the straight gouge of its keel centered in the blur of bare footprints. A score of natives still clustered around Kaminski's similar craft, fondling his bolts of bright-patterned cloth or chatting with his paddlers. Then the steamship swung into sight around the wooded headland.

The trees had acted as a perfect muffler for the chuffing engine. With a haste little short of panic, the forest dwellers melted back into concealment. The swarthy Portuguese gave an angry order and his crew shipped their paddles. Emptied of its cargo, the dugout drew only a few inches of water and could, had there been enough warning, have slid up among the tree roots where the two-decked steamer could never have followed.

Throttled down to the point its stern wheel made only an occasional slapping, the government craft edged closer to Gomes. On the Upper Kasai it was a battleship, although its beamy twenty-four meters would have aroused little interest in a more civilized part of the world. Awnings protected the hundreds of askaris overburdening the side rails. The captain was European, a blond, soft-looking man in a Belgian army uniform. The only other white man visible was the non-com behind the Hotchkiss swivel-mounted at the bow.

"Messieurs Gomes and Kaminski, perhaps?" called the officer as the steamship swung to, a dozen yards from the canoe. He was smiling, using his fingertips to balance his weight on the starboard bridge rail.

"You know who we are, de Vriny—damn you," Gomes shot back. "We have our patent to trade and we pay our portion to your Societe Cosmpolite. Now leave us!"

"Pay your portion, yes," de Vriny purred. "Gold dust and gold nuggets. Where do you get such gold, my fine mongrel friends?"

"Carlos, it's all right," called Kaminski, standing in his grounded boat. "Don't become angry—the gentleman is doing his duty to protect trade, that is all." Beneath the sombrero which he had learned to wear in the American Southwest, sweat was boiling off Kaminski. He knew his friend's volcanic temper, knew also the reputation of the blond man who was goading them. Not now! Not on the brink of the success that would gain them entree to any society in the world!

"Trade?" Gomes was shouting. "What do they know about trade?" He shook his fist at de Vriny and made the canoe rock nervously, so that the plump Angolan woman he had married a dozen years before put a calming hand on his leg. "You hold a rifle to the head of some poor black, pay him a ha'penny for rubber you sell in Paris for a shilling fourpence. Trade? There would be no gold coming out of this forest if the tribes didn't trust us and get a fair value for the dust they bring!"

"Well, we'll have to explore that," grinned the Belgian. "You see, your patent to trade was issued in error—it seems it was meant for some Gomez who spelled his name with a 'z'—and I have orders to escort you both back to Boma until the matter can be resolved."

Gomes' broad face went saffron. He began to slump like a snow figure on a sunny day. "They couldn't take away our patent because of a spelling mistake their own clerks made?" he whined, but his words were more of a sick apostrophe than a real question.

The Belgian answered it anyway. "You think not? Don't you know who appoints the judges of our Congo oh-so-Free State? Not Jews or nigger-wenching Portu-gees, I assure you."

Gomes was probably bracing his sagging bulk against the thwart, though he could indeed have been reaching for the Mauser lying across the pack in front of him. Presumably that was what the Baenga thought when he fired the first shot and blew Gomes into the water. Every Forest Guard with a rifle followed in a ragged volley that turned the canoe into a chip dancing on an ornamental fountain. Jets of wood and water and blood spouted upward.

"Christ's blood, you fools!" de Vriny cried. Then, "Well, get the rest of them too!"

Kaminski screamed and tried to follow his paddlers in a race for the tree line, but he was a corpulent man whose boots punched ankle-deep into the soft sand. The natives had no chance either. The Hotchkiss stuttered, knocking down a pair of them as the gunner checked his range. Then, spewing empty cases that hissed as they bounced into the water, the machine gun hosed bullets across the other running men. Kaminski half turned as the black in front of him pitched forward hemorrhaging bright blood from mouth and nose. That desire to see his death coming preserved the trader from it: the bullet that would otherwise have exited through his forehead instead drilled through both upper maxillary bones. Kaminski's eyes popped out as neatly as oysters into a gourmet's silver spoon. His body slapped hard enough to ripple the sand in which it came to rest face up.

The firing stopped. Capsized and sinking, Gomes' shattered dugout was drifting past the bow of the steamer. "I want their packs raised," de Vriny ordered. "Even if you have to dive for them all day. The same with the packs on shore—then burn the canoes."

"And the bodies, master?" asked his Baenga headman.

"Faugh," spat the Belgian. "Why else did the good Lord put crocodiles in this river?"

They did not take Kaminski's ear because it was white and that would attract comment. Even in Boma.

Time passed. Deep in the forest the ground spurted upward like a grapefruit hit by a rifle bullet. Something thicker than a tree bole surged, caught at a nearby human and flung the body, no longer distinguishable as to sex or race, a quarter mile through the canopy of trees. The earth subsided then, but in places the surface continued to bubble as if made of heated tar.

Five thousand miles away, Dame Alice Kilrea stepped briskly out of her solicitors' office, having executed her will, and ordered her driver on to the Nord Deutscher-Lloyd Dock. Travelling with her in the carriage was a valise containing one ancient book and a bundle of documents thick with wax, ribbons, and gold foil—those trappings and the royal signatures beneath. On the seat across from her was the American servant she had engaged only the week before as she closed her London house and discharged the remainder of her establishment. The servant, Sparrow, was a weaselly man with tanned skin and eyes the frosty color of lead cast in too hot a mold. He said little but glanced around frequently; and his fingers writhed as if with separate life.

Occasionally chance would merge the rhythm of mauls and axes splitting wood in a dozen parts of the forest. Then the thunk-thunk-THUNK would boom out like a beast approaching from the darkness. Around their fire the officers would pause. The Baengas would chuckle at the joke of it and let the pounding die away. Little by little it would reappear at each separate group of woodsmen, finally to repeat its crescendo.

"Like children," Colonel Trouville said to Dame Alice. The engineer and two sergeants were still aboard the *Archiduchesse Stephanie*, dining apart from the other whites. Color was not the only measure of class, even in the Congo Basin. "They'll be cutting wood—and drinking their malafou, wretched stuff, to call it palm wine is to insult the word 'wine'—they'll be at it almost till dawn. After a time you'll get used to it. There's nothing, really, to be done, since we can only carry a day's supply of fuel on the steamer. While they of course could find and cut enough dry wood by a reasonable hour each night, when one is dealing with the native 'mind'.... "

De Vriny and Osterman joined in their Colonel's deprecating laughter. Dame Alice managed only a preoccupied smile. During the day, steaming upriver from the Stanley Pool, she had stared at the terrain in which her battle would be joined: heavy forest, here mostly a narrow belt fringing the watercourse but later to become a sprawling, barely penetrable expanse. The trees climbed to the edge of the water and mushroomed over the banks. Dame Alice could imagine that where the stream was less than the Congo's present mile breadth the branches would meet above in laced blackness.

Now at night, blackness was complete even on the lower river. It chilled her soul. The equatorial sunset was not a curtain of ever-thickening gauze but a knifeblade that separated the hemispheres. On this side was death, and neither the laughter of the Baenga askaris nor the goblets of Portuguese wine being drunk around Trouville's campfire could change that.

Captain de Vriny swigged and eyed the circle. He was a man of middle height with the roundedness of a bear, a seeming softness which tended to mask the cruelty beneath. Across from him, Sparrow dragged on the cigarette he had rolled and lit his face orange. The captain smiled. Only because his mistress, the mad noblewoman, had demanded it, did Sparrow sit with the officers. He wore a cheap blue-cotton shirt, buttoned at the cuffs, and denim trousers held up by suspenders. Short and narrow-chested, Sparrow would have looked foolish even without the waist belt and the pair of huge double-action revolvers hanging from it.

Dame Alice was unarmed by contrast. Like the men she wore trousers, hers tucked into low-heeled boots. De Vriny looked at her and, shaping his mocking smile into an expression of friendly interest, said, "It surprises me, Dame Alice, that a woman as well-born and, I am sure, delicate as yourself would want to accompany an expedition against some of the most vicious sub-men on the globe."

Dame Alice lifted the faintly bulbous tip of her nose and said, "It's no matter of wanting, Captain." She eyed de Vriny with mild distaste. "I don't suppose you want to come yourself—unless you like to shoot niggers for lack of better sport? One does unpleasant things because someone must. One has a duty."

"What the Captain is suggesting," put in Trouville, "is that there are no lines of battle fixed in this jungle. A spearman may step from around the next tree and snick, end all your plans—learned though we are sure they must be."

"Quite," agreed Dame Alice, "and so I brought Sparrow here—" she nodded to her servant—"instead of trusting to chance."

All heads turned again toward the little American.

In French, though the conversation had previously been in English to include Sparrow, de Vriny said, "I hope he never falls overboard. The load of iron-mongery he carries will sink him twenty meters through the bottom muck before anyone knows he's gone."

Again the Belgians laughed. In a voice as flat and hard as the bottom of a skillet, Sparrow said, "Captain, I'd surely appreciate a look at your nice pistol there."

De Vriny blinked, uncertain whether the question was chance or if the American had understood the joke of which he had been made the butt. Deliberately, his composure never more than dented, the Belgian unhooked the flap of his patent-leather holster and handed over the Browning pistol. It was small and oblong, its blued finish gleaming like wet sealskin in the firelight.

Sparrow rotated the weapon, giving its exterior a brief scrutiny. He thumbed the catch in the grip and stripped out the magazine, holding it so that the light fell on the uppermost of its stack of small brass cartridges.

"You are familiar with automatic pistols, then?" asked Trouville in some surprise at the American's quick understanding of a weapon rarely encountered on his native continent.

"Naw," Sparrow said, slipping the magazine back home. His fingers moved like those of a pianist doing scales. "It's a gun, though. I can generally figure how a gun works."

"You should get one like it," de Vriny said, smiling as he took the weapon back from Sparrow. "You would find it far more comfortable to carry than those—yours."

"Carry a toy like that?" the gunman asked. His voice parodied amazement. "Not me, Captain. When I shoot a man, I want him dead. I want a gun what'll do the job if I do mine, and these .45s do me jist fine, every time I use'um." Sparrow grinned then, for the first time. De Vriny felt his own hands fumble as they tried to reholster the Browning. Suddenly he knew why the askaris gave Sparrow so wide a berth.

Dame Alice coughed. The sound shattered the ice that had been settling over the men. Without moving, Sparrow faded into the background to become an insignificant man with narrow shoulders and pistols too heavy for his frame.

"Tell me what you know about the rebellion," the Irishwoman asked quietly in a liquid, attractive voice. Her features led one to expect a nasal whinny. Across the fire came snores from Osterman, a lieutenant by courtesy but in no other respect an officer. He had ignored the wine for the natives' own malafou. The third calabash had slipped from his numb fingers, dribbling only a stain onto the ground as the bearded Fleming lolled back in his camp chair.

Trouville exchanged glances with de Vriny, then shrugged and said, "What is there ever to know about a native rebellion? Every once in a while a few of them shoot at our steamers, perhaps chop a concessionaire or two when he comes to collect the rubber and ivory. Then we get the call"—the Colonel's gesture embraced the invisible *Archiduchesse Stephanie* and the dozen Baenga canoes drawn up on the bank beside her. "We surround the village, shoot the niggers we catch, and burn the huts. End of rebellion."

"And what about their gods?" Dame Alice pressed, bobbing her head like a long-necked diving bird.

The Colonel laughed. De Vriny patted his holster and said, "We are God in the Maranga Concession."

They laughed again and Dame Alice shivered. Osterman snorted awake, blew his nose loudly on the blue sleeve of his uniform coat. "There's a new god back in the bush, yes," the Fleming muttered.

The others stared at him as if he were a frog declaiming Shakespeare. "How would you know?" de Vriny demanded in irritation. "The only Bantu words you know are 'drink' and 'woman'."

"I can talk to B'loko, can't I?" the lieutenant retorted in a voice that managed to be offended despite its slurring. "Good ol' Baloko, we been together long time, long time. Better fella than some white bastards I could name.... "

Dame Alice leaned forward, the firelight bright in her eyes. "Tell me about the new god," she demanded. "Tell me its name."

"Don' remember the name," Osterman muttered, shaking his head. He was waking up now, surprised and a little concerned to find himself center of the attention not only of his superiors but also of the foreigner who had come to them in Boma as they readied their troops. Trouville had tried to shrug Dame Alice aside, but the Irishwoman had displayed a patent signed by King Leopold himself.... "Baloko said it but I forget," he continued, "and he was drunk too, or I don' think he would have said. He's afraid of that one."

"What's that?" Trouville interrupted. He was a practical man, willing to accept and use the apparent fact that Osterman's piggish habits had made him a confidant of the askaris. "One of our Baenga headmen is afraid of a Bakongo god?"

Osterman shook his graying head again. Increasingly embarrassed but determined to explain, he said, "Not their god, not like that. The Bakongos, they live along the river, they got their fetishes just like any niggers. But back in the bush, there's another village. Not a tribe; a few men from here, a few women from there. Been getting together one at a time, a couple a year, for Christ... maybe twenty years. They got the new god, they're the ones who started the trouble.

"They say you don' have to pay your rubber to the white men, you don' have to pray to any fetish. Their god gonna come along and eat up everything. Any day now."

Osterman rubbed his eyes blearily, then shouted, "Boy! Malafou!"

A Krooman in breeches and swallow-tailed coat scurried over with another calabash. Osterman slurped down the sweet, brain-stunning fluid in three great gulps. He began humming something meaningless to himself. The empty container fell, and after a time the Fleming began to snore again.

The other men looked at one another. "Do you suppose he's right?" the Captain asked Trouville.

"He could be," the slim Colonel admitted with a shrug. "They might well have told him all that. He's not much better than a nigger himself despite the color of his skin."

"He's right," said Dame Alice, looking at the fire and not at her companions. Ash crumbled in its heart and a knot of sparks clawed toward the forest canopy. "Except for one thing. Their god isn't new, it isn't new at all. Back when the world was fresh and steaming and the reptiles flew above the swamps, it wasn't new either. The Bakongo name for it is Ahtu. Alhazred called it Nyarlathotep when he wrote twelve hundred years ago." She paused, staring down at her hands tented above the thin yellow wine left in her goblet.

"Oh, then you are a missionary," de Vriny exclaimed, glad to find a category for the puzzling woman. Her disgusted glance was her reply. "Or a student of religions?" de Vriny tried again.

"I study religions only as a doctor studies diseases," Dame Alice said. She looked at her companions. Their eyes were uncomprehending. "I…" she began, but how did she explain her life to men who had no conception of devotion to an ideal? Her childhood had been turned inward to dreams and the books lining the cold library of the Grange. Inward, because her outward body was that of an ugly duckling whom everyone knew had no chance of becoming a swan. And from her dreams and a few of the very oldest books had come hints of what it is that nibbles at the minds of all men in the darkness. Her father could not answer or even understand her questions, nor could the Vicar. She had grown from a persistent child into an iron-willed woman who lavished on her fancy energies which her relatives felt would have been better spent on the Church… or, perhaps, on breeding spaniels.

And as she had grown, she had met others who felt and knew what she did.

She looked around again. "Captain," she said simply, "I have been studying certain—myths—for most of my life. I've come to believe that some of them contain truths or hints of truths. There are powers in the universe. When you know the truth of those powers, you have the choice of joining them and working to bring about their coming—for they are unstoppable—or you can fight, knowing there is no ultimate hope for your cause and going ahead anyway. Mine was the second choice." Drawing herself even more rigidly straight, she added, "Someone has always been willing to stand between mankind and Chaos. As long as there have been men."

De Vriny snickered audibly. Trouville gave him a dreadful scowl and said to Dame Alice, "And you are searching for the god these rebels pray to?"

"Yes. The one they call Ahtu."

From the score of firelit glades around them came the thunk-thunk-THUNK of axe and wedge, then the booming native laughter.

"Osterman and de Vriny should have their men in position by now," said the Colonel, pattering his fingertips on the bridge rail as he scanned the wooded shore line. "It's about time for me to land, too."

"Us to land," Dame Alice said. She squinted, straining forward to see the village the Belgian force was preparing to assault. "Where are the huts?" she finally asked.

"Oh, they're set back from the shore some hundreds of meters," Trouville explained offhandedly. "The trees hide them, but the fish weirs—" he pointed out the lines of upright sticks rippling foam tracks down the current— "are a good enough guide. We've stayed anchored here in the stream so that the villagers would be watching us while the forces from the canoes downriver surrounded them."

Muffled but unmistakable, a shot thudded in the forest. A volley followed, drawing with it faint screams.

"Bring us in," ordered the Colonel, tugging at the left half of his mous-tache in his only sign of nervousness.

The *Archiduchesse* grated as her bow nuzzled into the trees, but there was no time now for delicacy. Forest Guards streamed past the Hotchkiss and down the gangplank into the jungle. The gunner was crouched behind the metal shield that protected him only from the front. Tree boles and their shadows now encircled him on three sides.

"I suppose it will be safe enough on the shore," said Trouville, adjusting his harness as if for parade instead of battle. "You can accompany me if you wish—and if you stay close by."

"All right," said Dame Alice as if she would not have come without his permission. Her hand clutched not a pistol but an old black-bound book. "If we're where you think, though, you'll need me very badly before you're through here. Especially if it takes till sunset." She swung down the compan-ionway behind Trouville. Last of all from the bridge came Sparrow, grimy and small and deadly as a shark.

The track that wound among the trunks was a narrow line hammered into the loam by horny feet. It differed from a game trail only in that shoulders had cleared the foliage to greater height. The Baengas strode it with some discomfort—they were a Lower Congo tribe, never quite at home in the up-river jungles. Trouville's step was deliberately nonchalant, while Dame Al-ice tramped gracelessly and gave an accurate impression of disinterest in her physical surroundings. Sparrow's eyes twitched around him as they always did. He carried his hands waist-high and over his belted revolvers.

The clearing was an anticlimax. The score of huts in the center had been protected by a palisade of sorts, but the first rush of the encircling Baengas had smashed great gaps in it. Three bodies, all of them women, lay spilled in the millet fields outside. Within the palisade were more bodies, one of them an askari with a long iron spearhead crosswise through his rib cage. About a hundred villagers, quavering but alive, had been forced together in the compound in front of the chief's beehive hut by the time the force from the steamer arrived. Several huts were already burning, sending up shuddering columns of black smoke.

Trouville stared at the mass of prisoners, solidified by fear into the terrible, stinking apathy of sheep in the slaughtering chute. "Yes…" he murmured appreciatively. His eyes had already taken in the fact that the fetishes which normally stood to the right or left of a well-to-do family's doorway were absent in this village. "Now," he asked, "who will tell me about the new god you worship?"

As black against a darkness, so the new fear rippling across faces already terrified. Near the Belgian stood an old man, face knobbed by a pattern of ritual scarring. He was certainly a priest, though without a priest's usual trappings of feathers and cowrie shells. Haltingly he said, "Lord, l-lord, we have no new gods."

"You lie!" cried Trouville. His gloved fingertip sprang out like a fang. "You worship Ahtu, you lower-than-the-apes, and he is a poor weak god whom our medicine will break like a stick!"

The crowd moaned and surged backwards from the Colonel. The old priest made no sound at all, only began to tremble violently. Trouville looked at the sky. "Lieutenant Osterman," he called to his burly subordinate, "we have an hour or so till sunset. I trust you can get this carrion—" he pointed to the priest— "to talk by then. He seems to know something. As for the rest… de Vriny, take charge of getting the irons on them. We'll decide what to do with them later."

The grinning Fleming slapped Baloko on the back. Each seized one of the priest's arms and began to drag him toward the shade of a baobab tree. Osterman started to detail the items he needed from the steamer and Baloko, enthusiastic as a child helping his father to fix a machine, rattled the list off in translation to a nearby askari.

The evening breeze brought a hint of relief from the heat and the odors, the oily scent of fear and the others more easily identified. Osterman had set an overturned bucket over the plate of burning sulphur to smother it out when it was no longer needed. Reminded by Trouville, he had also covered the brush of twigs he had been using to spread the gluey flames over the priest's genitals. Then, his work done, he and Baloko had strolled away to add a bowl of malafou to the chill. "Thank you, Lieutenant," which was all the praise

Trouville had offered for their success.

The subject of their ministrations—eyes closed, wrists and ankles staked to the ground—was talking. "They come, we let them," he said, so softly and quickly that Trouville had to strain to mutter out a crude translation for Dame Alice. "They live in forest, they not bother our fish. Forest here evil, we think. We feel god there, we not understand, not know him. All right that anybody want, wants to live in forest."

The native paused, turning his head to hawk phlegm into the vomit already pooled beside him. Dame Alice squatted on the ground and riffled the pages of her book unconsciously. She had refused to use the down-turned bucket for a stool. Sparrow paid only scant attention to the prisoner. His eyes kept picking across the clearing, thick and raucous now with Baengas and their leg-shackled prisoners; the men and the trees beyond them. Sparrow's face shone with the frustrated intensity of a man certain of an ambush but unable to forestall it. Shadows were beginning to turn the dust the color of the noses of his bullets.

The priest continued. The rhythms of his own language were rich and firm, reminding Dame Alice that behind Trouville's choppy French were the words of a man of dignity and power—before they had brought him down. "All of them are cut men. First come boy, no have ears. His head look me, like melon that is dropped. Him, he hear god Ahtu calling do what god tell him.

"One man, he not have, uh, manhood. God orders, boy tells him… he, uh, he quickens the ground where Ahtu sleeps.

"One man, he only half face, no eyes… him sees, he sees Ahtu, he tells what becoming, uh, is coming. He—"

The priest's voice rose into a shrill tirade that drowned out the translation. Trouville dispassionately slapped him to silence, then used a rag of bark cloth in his gloved hand to wipe blood and spittle from the fellow's mouth. "There are only three rebels in the forest?" he asked. If he realized that the priest had claimed the third man was white, he was ignoring it completely.

"No, no… many men, a ten of tens, maybe more. Before we not see, not see cut men only now and now, uh, again, in the forest. Now god is ripe and, uh, his messengers.…"

Only a knife edge of sun could have lain across the horizon, for the whole clearing was darkening to burnt umber where it had color at all. The ground shuddered. The native pegged to it began to scream.

"Earthquake?" Trouville blurted in surprise and concern. Rain forest trees have no deep tap roots to keep them upright, so a strong wind or an earth tremor will scatter giants like straw in the threshing yard.

Dame Alice's face showed concern not far from panic, but she wholly ignored the baobab tottering above them. Her book was open and she was rolling out syllables from it. She paused, turned so that the pages opened to the fading sun; but her voice stumbled again, and the earth pitched. It was sucking in under the priest whose fear so gripped him that, having screamed out his breath, he was unable to draw another one.

"Light!" Dame Alice cried. "For Jesus' sake, light!" If Trouville heard the demand against the litany of fear rising from the blacks, guards and prisoners alike, he did not understand. Sparrow, his face a bone mask, dipped into his shirt pocket and came out with a match which he struck alight with the thumb of the hand that held it. The blue flame pulsed above the page, steady as the ground's motion would let the gunman keep it. Its light painted Dame Alice's tight bun as she began again to cry words of no meaning to any of her human audience.

The ground gathered itself into a tentacle that spewed up from beneath the prisoner and hurled him skyward in its embrace. One hand and wrist, still tied to a deep stake, remained behind.

Two hundred feet above the heads of the others, the tentacle stopped and exploded as if it had struck a plate of lightning. Dame Alice had fallen backward when the ground surged, but though the book dropped from her hands she had been able to shout out the last words of what was necessary. The blast that struck the limb of earth shattered also the baobab. Sparrow, the only man able to stand on the bucking earth, was knocked off his feet by the shock wave. He hit and rolled, still gripping the two handguns he had leveled at the after-image of the light-shot tentacle.

Afterwards they decided that the burned-meat odor must have been the priest, because no one else was injured or missing. Nothing but a track of sandy loam remained of the tentacle, spilled about the rope of green glass formed of it by the false lightning's heat.

Colonel Trouville rose, coughing at the stench of ozone as sharp as that of the sulphur it had displaced. "De Vriny!" he called. "Get us one of these devil-bred swine who can guide us to the rebel settlement!"

"And who'll you be finding to guide you, having seen this?" demanded the Irishwoman, kneeling now and brushing dirt from the fallen volume as if more than life depended on her care.

"Seen?" repeated Trouville. "And what have they seen?" The fury in his voice briefly stilled the nightbirds. "They will not guide us because one of them was crushed, pulled apart, burned? And have I not done as much myself a hundred times? If we need to feed twenty of them their own livers, faugh! the twenty-first will lead us—or the one after him will. This rebellion must end!"

"So it must," whispered Dame Alice, rising like a champion who has won a skirmish but knows the real test is close at hand. She no longer appeared frail.

"So it must, if there's to be men on this earth in a month's time."

The ground shuddered a little.

Nothing moved in the forest but the shadows flung by the dancers around the fire. The flames spread them capering across the leaves and tree trunks, distorted and misshapen by the flickering.

They were no more misshapen than the dancers themselves as the light displayed them.

From a high, quivering scaffold of njogi cane, three men overlooked the dance. They were naked so that their varied mutilations were utterly apparent. De Vriny started at the sight of the one whose pale body gleamed red and orange in the firelight; but he was a faceless thing, unrecognizable. Besides, he was much thinner than the plump trader the Belgian had once known.

The clearing was a quarter-mile depression in the jungle. Huts, mere shanties of withe-framed leaves rather than the beehives of a normal village, huddled against one edge of it. If all had gone well, Trouville's askaris were deployed beyond the hut with Osterman's group closing the third segment of the ring. All should be ready to charge at the signal. There would not even be a fence to delay the spearmen.

Nor were there crops of any kind. The floor of the clearing was smooth and hard, trampled into that consistency by thousands of ritual patterns like the one now being woven around the fire. In, out, and around—crop-limbed men and women who hobbled if they had but one foot; who staggered, hunched and twisted from the whippings that had left bones glaring out of knots of scar tissue; who followed by touch the motions of the dancers ahead of them if their own eye-sockets were blank holes.

There was no music, but the voices of those who had tongues drummed in a ceaseless chant: "Ahtu! Ahtu!"

"The scum of the earth," whispered de Vriny. "Low foreheads, thick jaws; skin the color of a monkey's under its hair. Your Mr. Darwin was right about Man's descent from the apes, Dame Alice—if these brutes are, in fact, kin to Man."

"Not my Mr. Darwin," the Irishwoman replied.

The Krooman steward, in loincloth now instead of tailcoat, was behind the three whites with a hissing bull's-eye lantern. Dame Alice feared to raise its shutter yet, though, and instead ran her fingers nervously along the margins of her open book. Three other blacks, armed only with knives, stood by de Vriny as couriers in case the whistle signals were not enough. The rest of the Captain's force was invisible, spread to either side of him along the margin of the trees.

"Don't like this," Sparrow said, shifting his revolvers a millimeter in their holsters to make sure they were free in the leather. "Too many niggers around. Some of 'em are apt to be part of the mob down there, coming back late from a hunt or something. Any nigger comes running up in the dark and I'm gonna let'im hold one."

"You'll shoot no one without my order," de Vriny snapped. "The Colonel may be sending orders, Osterman may need help—this business is going to be dangerous enough without some fool killing our own messengers. Do you hear me?"

"I hear you talking." A stray glimmer of firelight caught the throbbing vein in Sparrow's temple.

Rather than retort, the Belgian turned back to the clearing. After a moment he said, "I don't see this god you're looking for."

Dame Alice's mouth quirked. "You mean you don't see a fetish," she said. "You won't. Ahtu isn't a fetish."

"Well, what kind of damned god is he then?" de Vriny asked in irritation.

The Irishwoman considered the question seriously, then said, "Maybe they aren't gods at all, him and the others... it and the others Alhazred wrote of. Call them cancers, spewed down on Earth ages ago. Not life, surely, not even things—but able to shape, to misshape things into a semblance of life and to grow and to grow and to grow."

"But grow into what, madame?" de Vriny pressed.

"Into what?" Dame Alice echoed sharply. Her eyes flashed with the sudden arrogance of her bandit ancestors, sure of themselves if of nothing else in the world. "Into this earth, this very planet, if unchecked. And we here will know tonight whether they can be checked yet again."

"Then you seriously believe," de Vriny began, sucking at his florid moustache to find a less offensive phrasing. "You believe that the Bakongos are worshipping a creature which would, will, begin to rule the world if you don't stop it?"

Dame Alice looked at him. "Not 'rule' the world," she corrected. "Rather become the world. This thing, this seed awakened in the jungle by the actions of men more depraved and foolish than I can easily believe... this existence, unchecked, would permeate our world like mold through a loaf of bread, until the very planet became a ball of viscid slime hurtling around the sun and stretching tentacles toward Mars. Yes, I believe that, Captain. Didn't you see what was happening last night in the village?"

The Belgian only scowled in perplexity.

A silver note sang from across the broad clearing. De Vriny grunted, then put his long bosun's pipe to his lips and sounded his reply even as Osterman's signal joined it.

The dance broke apart as the once-solid earth began to dimple beneath men's weight.

The Forest Guards burst out of the tree line with cries punctuated by the boom of Albini rifles. "Light!" ordered Dame Alice in a crackling alto, and the lantern threw its bright fan across the book she held. The scaffolding moved, seemed to sink straight into ground turned fluid as water. At the last instant the three figures on it linked hands and shouted, "Ahtu!" in triumph. Then they were gone.

In waves as complex as the sutures of a skull, motion began to extend through the soil of the clearing. A shrieking Baenga, spear raised to thrust into the nearest dancer, ran across one of the quivering lines. It rose across his body like the breaking surf and he shrieked again in a different tone. For a moment his black-headed spear bobbled on the surface. Then it, too, was engulfed with a faint plop that left behind only a slick of blood.

Dame Alice started chanting in a singsong, molding a tongue meant for liquid Irish to a language not meant for tongues at all. A tremor in the earth drove toward her and those about her. It had the hideous certainty of a torpedo track. Sparrow's hands flexed. De Vriny stood stupefied, the whistle still at his lips and his pistol drawn but forgotten.

The three couriers looked at the oncoming movement, looked at each other... disappeared among the trees. Eyeballs white, the Krooman dropped his lantern and followed them. Quicker even than Sparrow, Dame Alice knelt and righted the lantern with her foot. She acted without missing a syllable of the formula stamped into her memory by long repetition.

Three meters away, a saw-blade of white fire ripped across the death advancing through the soil. The weaving trail blasted back toward the center of the clearing like an ant run blown by carbon disulphide.

De Vriny turned in amazement to the woman crouched so that the lantern glow would fall across the black-lettered pages of her book. "You did it!" he cried. "You stopped the thing!"

The middle of the clearing raised itself toward the night sky, raining down fragments of the bonfire that crowned it. Humans screamed—some at the touch of the fire, others as tendrils extruding from the towering center wrapped about them.

Dame Alice continued to chant.

The undergrowth whispered. "Behind you, Captain," Sparrow said. His face had a thin smile. De Vriny turned, calling a challenge. The brush parted and a few feet in front of him were seven armed natives. The nearest walked on one foot and a stump. His left hand gripped the stock of a Winchester carbine; its barrel was supported by his right wrist since there was a knob of ancient scar tissue where the hand should have been attached.

De Vriny raised his Browning and slapped three shots into the native's chest. Bloodspots sprang out against the dark skin like additional nipples. The black coughed and jerked the trigger of his own weapon. The carbine was so close to the Belgian's chest that its muzzle flash ignited the linen of his shirt as it blew him backwards.

Sparrow giggled and shot the native through the bridge of his nose, snapping his head around as if a horse had kicked him in the face. The other blacks moved. Sparrow killed them all in a ripple of fire that would have done justice to a Gatling gun. The big revolvers slammed alternately, Sparrow using each orange muzzle flash to light a target for his other hand. He stopped shooting only when there was nothing left before his guns; nothing save a writhing tangle of bodies too freshly dead to be still. The air was thick with white smoke and the fecal stench of death. Behind the laughing gunman, Dame Alice Kilrea continued to chant.

Pulsing, rising, higher already than the giants of the forest ringing it, the fifty-foot-thick column of what had been earth dominated the night. A spear of false lightning jabbed and glanced off, freezing the chaos below for the eyes of any watchers. From the base of the main neck had sprouted a ring of tendrils, ruddy and golden and glittering over all with inclusions of quartz. They snaked among the combatants as flexible as silk; when they closed, they ground together like millstones and spattered blood a dozen yards up the sides of the central column. The tendrils made no distinction between Forest Guards and the others who had danced for Ahtu.

Dame Alice stopped. The column surged and bent against the sky, its peak questing like the muzzle of a hunting dinosaur. Sparrow hissed, "For the love of God, bitch!" and raised a revolver he knew would be useless.

Dame Alice spoke five more words and flung her book down. The ground exploded in gouts of cauterizing flame.

It was not a hasty thing. Sparks roared and blazed as if the clearing were a cauldron into which gods poured furnaces of molten steel. The black column that was Ahtu twisted hugely, a cobra pinned to a bonfire. There was no heat, but the light itself seared the eyes and made bare flesh crawl.

With the suddenness of a torn puffball, Ahtu sucked inward. The earth sagged as though in losing its ability to move it had also lost all rigidity. At first the clearing had been slightly depressed. Now the center of it gaped like a drained boil, a twisted cylinder fed by the collapsing veins it had earlier shot through the earth.

When the blast came it was the more stunning for having followed a relative silence. There was a rending crash as something deep in the ground gave way; then a thousand tons of rock and soil blew skyward with volcanic power behind them. Where the earth had trembled with counterfeit life, filaments jerked along after the main mass. In some places they ripped the surface as much as a mile into the forest. After a time, dust and gravel began to sprinkle down on the trees, the lighter particles marking the canopy with a long flume down wind while larger rocks pattered through layer after layer of the hindering leaves. But it was only dirt, no different than the soil for hundreds of miles around into which trees thrust their roots and drew life from what was lifeless.

"God damn if you didn't kill it," Sparrow whispered, gazing in wonderment at the new crater. There was no longer any light but that of the hooked moon to silver the carnage and the surprising number of Forest Guards straggling back from the jungle to which they had fled. Some were beginning to joke as they picked among the bodies of their comrades and the dancers.

"I didn't kill anything," Dame Alice said. Her voice was hoarse, muffled besides by the fact that she was cradling her head on her knees. "Surgeons don't kill cancers. They cut out what they can find, knowing that there's always a little left to grow and spread again...."

She raised her head. From across the clearing, Colonel Trouville was stepping toward them. He was as dapper and cool as always, skirting the gouge in the center, skirting also the group of Baengas with a two-year-old they must have found in one of the huts. One was holding the child by the ankles to drain all the blood through its slit throat while his companions gathered firewood.

"But without the ones who worshipped it," Dame Alice went on, "without the ones who drew the kernel up to a growth that would have been... the end of Man, the end of Life here in any sense you or I—or those out there—would have recognized it.... It'll be more than our lifetimes before Ahtu returns. I wonder why those ones gave themselves so wholly to an evil that would have destroyed them first?"

Sparrow giggled again. Dame Alice turned from the approaching Belgian to see if the source of the humor showed on the gunman's face.

"It's like this," Sparrow said. "If they was evil, I guess that makes us good. I'd never thought of that before, is all."

He continued to giggle. The laughter of the Baengas echoed him from the clearing as they thrust the child down on a rough spit. Their teeth had been filed to points which the moonlight turned to jewels.

ଧ ଧ

Jeroboam Henley's Debt

Charles R. Saunders

T he October moon limned the old house and its surrounding copse of trees in a wan white glare. A lowslung black sedan slowly approached the driveway, then turned in. The sound the car's motor made before its driver switched off the ignition was reminiscent of the growl of an impatient beast.

The door on the driver's side opened; when he emerged, it was as though a segment of the shadowy machine had detached itself and assumed the shape of a tall, muscular man. As the driver, whose name was Theotis Nedeau, started up the porch steps, an outside light flared on, illuminating his face. Even in the light, his complexion was of a singularly dusky hue.

With a sharp squeal of hinges, the screen door flew open and a short, rotund man bounded onto the porch to greet his visitor.

"Theotis!" he cried. "It's been so long since you wired from Toronto. My God, I thought something had happened to you...."

About to catch his friend in an impulsive embrace, the smaller man, whose name was Jeremiah Henley, suddenly stepped back. For he recognized the grim set of the dark man's mouth and the glint in his narrowed eyes.

Anticipating Henley's next thought, Nedeau broke his silence.

"I was...delayed...at a gas station outside of Chatham."

Suppressed fury crackled like static electricity in his voice.

"You'd better come in and have a drink, Theotis," Henley suggested.

"Maybe I'd better."

Together, the two men hauled Nedeau's two suitcases out of the trunk of the new-model 1933 Auburn and carried them into the house. Though the suitcases were of similar weight, Henley had to labour with the one he'd chosen, while Nedeau bore his own burden easily. Once again, Henley recalled his friend's phenomenal athletic prowess, how Nedeau had set football records that still stood and had once held his own sparring three rounds with Harry Wills, the black heavyweight even the great Jack Dempsey never dared to meet.

And he remembered a night more than a dozen years ago in Virginia, when he and Nedeau had been stopped by a policeman wanting to know exactly how a couple of "Nigras" had come by such a fine motorcar as the one they were in without having stolen it. Nedeau had flattened the policeman with one blow and they'd fled the state with a posse of cracker cops on their tail all the way up to the gates of the black college they'd been attending.

It had taken virtually all of the Dean of Men's powers of diplomacy to forestall a major racial incident. And an abrupt increase in Howard University's endowment, courtesy of Nedeau's mysteriously moneyed father, had saved Theotis from summary expulsion.

Now, Theotis Nedeau had been "delayed."

Henley shivered a little as he ensconced his friend in an overstuffed chair in the living room. Then he poured two tumblers of bourbon.

"Are Emma and the boys here?" Nedeau asked.

"No," Henley replied. "They're staying with my in-laws in Dresden, north of here. They'll be safe there."

Nedeau nodded somberly. Silence fell between the two seated figures as they sipped their bourbon. They were a study in contrast. Nedeau was black as polished ebony. The immaculate dark suit he wore barely hid the mesomorphic lines of his physique. Henley was of a *café-au-lait* complexion, with a neatly trimmed mustache and carefully pomaded hair. There were lines of worry in his face and deep shadows smudged the skin beneath his eyes. His lounging suit, though expensively tailored, was unpressed.

More than a decade had passed since the former college roommates had seen each other. Even so, they had maintained a regular correspondence. It was Henley's most recent letter, followed by an urgent telegram, that had brought Nedeau more than a thousand miles northward to Ontario....

Nedeau finished his drink, then began to talk in a flat, uninflected tone.

"I had some problems with directions," he said. "Up to a point, the guards at the Niagara Falls border crossing were helpful—after I signed a statement swearing that I won't remain in Canada longer than two weeks."

Henley shook his head. He knew the intensity of Nedeau's race pride, but it was no secret that the Canadian government officially discouraged "coloured immigration". It wasn't Nedeau's pride that was at stake now, though.

"It wasn't difficult to find my way to Toronto, where I wired you to let you know I was coming, and from there to Chatham," Nedeau continued. "But I became confused a few miles west of Chatham. I saw a gas station on the side of the road, and pulled in to ask for directions. Before I could say anything, the attendant said, 'We don't serve your kind here.' When I mentioned that I only wanted directions to Henleyville, he pulled a gun, flashed a deputy's badge and forced me out of my car. He said he was going to arrest me for car theft."

Nedeau's fists clenched.

"He was disappointed to find that all my identification was in order—including my auto registration. But he wasn't done. He asked what I wanted in Henleyville. I told him I intended to visit an old friend. When he asked who the friend was, I was tempted to tell him it was none of his concern. But I wanted to arrive here as quickly as I could. So, I mentioned your name. For a moment, I thought he was going to shoot me. Then, strangely enough, he gave me the directions and walked back into the station without another word."

"That would be Lorne Cooder," Henley murmured half to himself. "I wouldn't be surprised if he paid us a visit tonight. Listen, Theotis, I'm sorry about...."

"Forget it," Nedeau said.

His eyes wandered to the wall above an ornate mantelpiece. There was a large square of wallpaper several shades lighter than the surrounding area, as though a picture that had hung there for a long time had suddenly been removed.

"What happened to the portrait?" Nedeau asked.

Henley started violently. His eyes widened with something akin to terror as he looked at Nedeau. Then Henley remembered their many late-night conversations about his illustrious grandfather—Jeroboam Henley.

Jeroboam Henley was a slave who had escaped to the North of the United States, then assisted fellow runaways in fleeing to sanctuary in Canada via the network of abolitionists known as the "Underground Railroad". Henley himself had finally emigrated from Ohio to Canada in protest against the passage of the Fugitive Slave Law by the U.S. Congress shortly before the start of the Civil War.

Settling in Ontario, Henley built a house and founded a self-contained community of ex-slaves. He had disdained the mass migration of blacks back to the U.S. when slavery was abolished there, and the diminished community he had founded eventually bore his name.

As Jeroboam Henley's grandson, Jeremiah had been something of a celebrity even at Howard, a college replete with the scions of illustrious men of colour. He had told Nedeau of the large portrait of old Jeroboam—who had died before Jeremiah was born—that hung over the mantelpiece of the ancestral home. Thus, it was not surprising that Nedeau remembered it now.

"I burned it," Jeremiah Henley said.

& &

Now, it was Nedeau's turn to express shock, though for him that expression was limited to a raising of his brows followed by an intense, thoughtful gaze.

"Jeremiah," he said, "I think you'd better swallow that drink of yours, pour yourself another, then start from the beginning. I won't be able to help you until I know the whole story."

Nodding jerkily, Henley complied. There was a tremor in his hands as he finished his first drink. When he finished the second, the trembling was gone.

"It began a few weeks ago," he said. "No—even before that. I had trouble sleeping. And when I did sleep, I tossed and yelled so much that Emma took to going downstairs and sleeping on the couch. If it was nightmares, I couldn't remember them. At least, not until *that night*...."

"As usual, I couldn't get to sleep. But I must have dozed off somehow, because the next thing I remember, I was sitting up in bed and Emma wasn't there. I decided to go down to the living room to talk to her. I got out of bed, went down the hall...*but my feet wouldn't let me go down the stairs!* I found myself walking past the children's room, toward the walled-over end of the hall where the stairs to the attic are supposed to be. I tried to stop myself—I had always dreaded that part of the house since my father whipped me within an inch of my life just for asking about it—but my legs wouldn't obey me.

"The closer I got to the end of the hall, the more fear I felt. My eyes were getting used to the dark, but I still wanted to put on the hall lights. I couldn't stop myself from walking in a straight line toward the hidden attic stairs. I decided I must be dreaming—but never before had I known I was dreaming while the dream was still going on.

"When I got to the end of the hall, my hands—of their own accord—pressed against certain sections of the wall. Then the whole wall slid back, not making any sound at all! I'll tell you, Theotis, I've never been more scared in my life than I was then—not even when those crackers chased us out of Virginia. I hadn't even thought of that part of the house since the beating my father gave me. And now I was at the stairs, and my feet were carrying me up into that dark attic....

"Once I got up there, though, it wasn't all that dark. There's a big dormer window in the attic and there weren't any shades to block the moonlight. The place was piled high with boxes, crates and trunks. There were black shadows between the piles. My feet carried me straight toward one of those shadows. I knelt down. My hands reached out. My fingers worked at the fastenings of a small chest I couldn't see. I opened the lid of the chest, reached in and pulled out a thick, leather-bound book of some sort. I went to the light of the window and opened the book. By then, I was in control of my actions—and I knew I wasn't dreaming.

"The moon was full. By its light, I could clearly see the writing in the book. It was a diary—my grandfather's diary."

Henley drew the back of one hand across his brow. The hand came away wet. Silently, Nedeau waited for him to continue.

"It was actually more of a record than a diary. My grandfather kept detailed listings of all the runaway slaves who passed through his 'station' on the Underground Railroad. There were scores of names. Everyone knows Jeroboam Henley helped many of his people to freedom.

"But some of the names were—*crossed out*. I didn't know what that meant until I paged further through the book, and found a special section in the back. The names that had been crossed out earlier were repeated—with monetary values entered next to them. It was like a ledger.

"Suspicion dawned...a sickening suspicion that was confirmed as I read further and understood more fully. With each word I read, a part of me died.

"Not all of the runaways who came to my grandfather's house in Ohio went on to Canada, Theotis. You know what that man was doing? *He was selling his own people to a plantation owner in Louisiana!* Not all of them, mind you. Just the ones who met the plantation owner's specifications. They had to be native African, and by the 1850s, you couldn't find many of those—so my grandfather said.

"He drugged their food, then tied them up and turned them over to the plantation owner's Northern agent, who lived in the town under the guise of a freight operator. The whites paid my grandfather well and they kept his secret. They needed him. He was the only one, other than Harriet Tubman, that the runaways trusted implicitly—*damn him!*

"There were hints in the diary that the plantation owner had some sort of hold over my grandfather. There were also suggestions that the slaves were used as sacrifices to some sort of god or devil named 'Shub-Niggurath.'"

"I don't like the sound of that name," Nedeau interrupted.

"Neither do I!" Henley flared. "But it sure as hell didn't bother my grandfather! All he could think about was the money the plantation owner paid him! Hell, he loved it! The greedy son of a bitch!"

Overcome with emotion, Henley held his face in his hands.

"Damn," Nedeau said softly. "Jeremiah, I'm really sorry to hear that. You must have—"

"That's not all of it!" Henley cried. "There was a final name on the list of the ones my grandfather betrayed. It was an African name...'Gbomi'. He was a witch doctor of some kind, so my grandfather said. When this Gbomi realized he had been drugged, he called down a curse on my grandfather. My grandfather laughed as the African mumbled and slurred in his native tongue while being bound. He took his blood money from the plantation owner's agent and thought no more about Gbomi—not until things began to happen at night in that Ohio town.

"Strange things...a black face appearing in people's windows...cattle, sheep and dogs slaughtered mysteriously, horribly, drained of blood...splayed foot prints leading to my grandfather's house....

"The town turned against my grandfather. The people were stirred up by an element which had always been opposed to his antislavery activities. The plantation owner and his agent soon let my grandfather know that he was of no further use to them. He panicked. He fled to Canada, using his opposition to the Fugitive Slave Law as a smokescreen. But he was really running from Gbomi."

"When I finished with that damnable diary, my eyes were sore from the strain of reading by moonlight. I felt as betrayed as those slaves my grandfather sold. Then the anger came, driving everything else before it. I walked out of that attic. This time, *I* was the one controlling my actions. Enraged as I was, I still managed to step quietly, so as not to awaken my sons.

"I kept walking until I got to the living room. Emma was there, sleeping on the couch. There was a low fire in the fireplace. It got higher when I set my grandfather's diary in the flames. Then I looked over to the mantel and saw his portrait. I took it down and put it in the fireplace, frame and all.

"By the time Emma woke up, both the diary and the portrait were nothing but ashes. Emma looked at the empty wall, then at the fireplace, then at me. And she ran sobbing from the room. She gathered up the boys and left. She thought I was crazy. Maybe I was that night. Maybe I still am....

"It was not long after that night that things began to happen here—things similar to the events that forced Jeroboam Henley out of Ohio. That's why I need you, Theotis. You're the only one who can help me. Don't you see? He's come back. By all that's holy and unholy, Theotis, *he's come back!*"

"Who?" Nedeau asked quietly.

Nonplussed, Henley cried, "What do you mean, 'Who?'"

"Who do you think has come back?" Nedeau pressed. "Gbomi—or your grandfather?"

Before Henley could reply, a sudden crashing sound splintered the short silence. Both men sprang to their feet. The roar of a car motor faded in the distance as Henley and Nedeau rushed to the shattered front window. Henley bent to pick something up from the shards of glass, while Nedeau wrenched the front door open and raced outside. Only a few moments passed before he returned, his face set in a scowl of frustration.

"Couldn't get the bastard's licence number," he muttered.

"I know who it is," Henley said. "Remember, I said we'd get a visit from Lorne Cooder tonight."

Nedeau looked at him. Never before had he heard such bitterness in his friend's tone. Wordlessly, Henley handed Nedeau the red house brick that had been thrown through the window. There was a note attached:

NIGGER—
If your black friend has come to take you out of here, tell him it had better be sooner than later!

The note bore no signature.

"It's come to this," Henley said. "My neighbours show their true colours at last—lily white. It was fine for us back in the old days, when the escaped slaves came up here and the Canadians took them in so that they could fling their 'true adherence to the principles of freedom' in the faces of the Americans. But when slavery was over, we became 'niggers' again. And when something goes wrong...."

"Whoever wrote that note was right in one sense," Nedeau cut in.

"What do you mean?"

"We have no time to lose," Nedeau said as he reached for the handle of one of his suitcases. "Let's go."

"Go where?" Henley asked numbly.

"Upstairs. To the attic."

"After what you just heard about my grandfather, you're still going to help me?"

"Do you think you're to blame for what your grandfather did?"

Henley left the question unanswered.

ȣ ♌

For only the second time in his life, Jeremiah Henley stood in the cobwebbed attic of his ancestral home. Despite Nedeau's presence, Henley was experiencing even more anxiety than he had the night something outside himself had guided him to a secret better left buried with its bearer....

Except for the flicker of a row of three tapers, the attic was shrouded in darkness. Nedeau had covered the single window with a heavy quilt. Henley watched uncertainly while Nedeau carefully arranged the apparatus he had extracted from his suitcase.

Nedeau poured a sackful of sand into a shallow metal tray and spread it evenly across the bottom. From another, smaller sack he poured a fine black powder into a wooden bowl carved with geometric African designs. He took special care not to allow any of the powder to touch his skin.

Henley felt a queer sense of detachment as he observed his friend's preparations. He remembered Nedeau's almost obsessive absorption with African culture back in college, as well as how spitefully Nedeau had been ridiculed for it. All things African had been shunned by Howard students then; even the smattering of Africans attending the college were derided as "Home Boys". More than once, Henley had privately defended Nedeau's affinity for the "Home Boys". Publicly, Nedeau had always been more than capable of defending himself.

Now, Nedeau was a professor in the Howard history department and taught courses in African lore. He had even spent a year in the Gold Coast, a British West African colony. Henley thought of the letters he had received with Gold Coast postage—long, enthusiastic missives full of near-incomprehensible reports of Nedeau's studies of the magic of West African *ju-ju* men....

"I hope this voodoo of yours works," Henley said, for no reason other to break a silence that was becoming intolerable.

Nedeau looked at him. He had removed his coat and shirt, and his bare torso was even more impressive than Henley recalled. It was Nedeau's eyes, however, that caused Henley to recoil in dismay.

"Voodoo!" He spat the word as if it were a curse. "It would take more time than I have to explain to you the difference between that half-baked Haitian superstition and the true magic of Africa."

Scowling, he returned to his preparations. Henley, who remained seated on a dusty trunk, could not suppress a gasp of shock when Nedeau drew a pair of long, white bones from the suitcase.

"Leopard, not human," Nedeau said. "They were given to me by a powerful *malam*—what the ignorant would call a 'witch doctor' or 'ju-ju man'—because I spoke on his behalf in a case brought against him by a District Commissioner. We will need them tonight.

"From the hints I gathered in your letter—confirmed by our conversation downstairs—I would say you are being stalked by a *semando*—a deadsending."

"You mean a…zombie?"

"Worse than that. Your grandfather's enemy must have been a powerful *malam* indeed to have launched a curse that has spanned two generations."

"What is a *semando,* if it isn't a zombie?"

"A *semando* is a dead thing shaped and motivated by the will of the *malam*. The animal killings are typical of a *semando*'s work, for it needs blood to build its potency to the point where it can fulfill its ultimate purpose—vengeance."

Henley shuddered. "How can such a—*thing*—be stopped?"

"With the powder in that bowl. It is *kaliloze,* meaning that it's deadly to any supernatural thing it touches. It will be the only thing that will save us when I summon the *semando* here."

"What?" Henley cried. "Have you gone insane?"

"It's the only way, man. We can't go out to seek the creature; it's a thing of the night and it would be suicidal to attempt to face it in its own element. I must lure it here, where I'll at least have a chance to get to it with the *kaliloze*. And it *will* come. I have only to call it, using this oracle of sand and the bones of power. The *semando* will come, for what it wants is here—you."

"God!" Henley exclaimed. "This is so senseless—unreal! Savage ceremonies *here*, in 1933…."

Nedeau stood up, towering over Henley.

"You asked for my help," he grated. "If you don't want it, say so now. If you do, then you'll keep your mouth shut until this thing is over with."

Henley, well aware of the meaning of his friend's tone, fell silent. He was beginning to fear Theotis Nedeau….

Holding the leopard bones like a pair of drumsticks, Nedeau squatted before the sand-filled tray. Then he began to strike the sand with the bones, beating out a rhythmic pattern that slid and twisted like a serpent of sound through Henley's mind. While he drummed, he chanted, singing a litany in a language Henley hadn't heard before.

Nervously, Henley kept his eyes on Nedeau. Though the attic was unheated, beads of perspiration were forming on Nedeau's bare chest. Reflected candlelight transformed the droplets into shimmering liquid gems. Henley moved his gaze to the sand in the tray. The yellow grains bounced and shifted to the rhythm of the pounding bones. He could almost see *shapes* appearing in the leaping sand—the shapes of graves opening at midnight....

The din of the drumming and the cacophony of the chant seemed an assault on Henley's sanity, inexorably dragging him back to things he did not want to remember and never wanted to know. Just as he was about to shout at Nedeau to stop, a rending crash surmounted the sound of the rite.

Immediately, the drumming ceased. Nedeau's voice fell silent. He sat stock-still, like an ebony carving, his eyes fixed in a set stare at something Henley could not see.

Then the footsteps came. Footsteps that ascended the stairs at a steady, measured pace. Footsteps that grew louder as the thing that made them slowly approached the door of the attic. Footsteps that rose and fell with a squamous, sucking sound....

The footsteps stopped.

"For God's sake, Theotis," Henley shouted. "*It's here!*"

Nedeau did not move.

The attic door banged inward. Dimly, the light from the floor below illuminated the hulking, indistinct silhouette filling the doorway. The figure moved closer, catching the wavering glimmer of the candles.

Henley screamed.

The *semando* was a grotesque, misshapen thing formed of mephitic grave-mud that oozed with each sickening step it took. But it was not the lurching travesty of a body that bulged Henley's eyes and clove his tongue to the roof of his mouth. It was the face.

Crudely molded and distorted as its features were, Henley had seen them before—in the portrait that had hung over the mantelpiece downstairs. It was the face of his grandfather, Jeroboam Henley....

Blunt, malformed fingers reached clawlike for Henley's throat as the *semando* drew nearer. Henley could not move; sheer horror rooted him to his seat.

"*Theotis!*" he shrieked, as if the sheer sound of his terror could halt the advance of the thing with his grandfather's face.

Then a lithe, shadowy form leaped between Henley and the approaching hell-creature. It was Nedeau, cradling the wooden bowl of *kaliloze* powder in his hands. With a swift, smooth motion, Nedeau flung the bowl's contents full into the face of the *semando*.

For a single, timeless moment, the dust hung like a black miasma, enveloping the head of the *semando*. Then it spread across the death-sending's carcass like a swarm of tiny, voracious insects.

The *semando* halted its advance. Its mouth opened, but no sound issued forth. Then the mud began to slough from its form, pooling viscously on the floorboards. Mixed with the malodorous mire was the animal blood that had lent the *semando* its macabre semblance of life. Only a skeleton remained. Then that, too, collapsed, leaving only a tangle of smeared bits of calcium behind.

"You did it, Theotis!" Henley cried, his voice weak with relief. "You destroyed the thing Gbomi sent to kill me."

"It served its purpose," Nedeau said quietly.

"What do you mean?" Henley asked.

Before Henley could move, Nedeau's hands shot out and enclosed the smaller man's throat in a clasp of steel. Henley struggled with a strength born of desperation, but Nedeau held him easily. He tightened his grip, choking off Henley's outcries. But Henley's betrayed, innocent eyes mirrored the man's final question: *Why?*

Nedeau told him.

"I never mentioned much about my family back in Louisiana, Jeremiah. I never told you how we came by our name. 'Nedeau' means 'born of the water' in Creole French. In the Yoruba language of West Africa, the word for 'born of the water' is…'Gbomi.' Gbomi—*my grandfather.* It is Gbomi who has returned, not Jeroboam Henley. Gbomi is *in me.*"

Nedeau's voice was calm and steady, betraying no indication of the effort it took to keep Henley helpless in his grasp. His face was as impassive as a mask.

In a strangled voice, Henley managed to croak, "For…God's sake…Theotis…I'm…your…*friend!*"

Something softened in Nedeau's face then. His eyes blinked; his fingers began to relax…. Then, abruptly, his features contorted. An unholy flame kindled in his eyes. His lips drew back from his teeth in a rictus of sheer hatred. And the voice that issued from Nedeau's throat was not his own. The accent was thick, alien, but the words were as plain as the dates chiseled on a tombstone.

"*Hen-lee…now, you die!*"

Nedeau's fingers constricted. Henley's eyes popped. His tongue protruded. His cries of pain were crushed in his throat. With an abrupt wrench, Nedeau snapped Jeremiah Henley's neck. When his hands opened, a new corpse dropped to the floor beside another, far older one.

Calmly, Nedeau put on his shirt and coat. Before departing the attic, he overturned the still-burning tapers. For a moment, he watched the flames spread among the musty crates and boxes. Then he hurried down the stairs.

ဢ ၒ

The Henley house blazed like a giant pyre against the night sky. Seated in his black sedan, Theotis Nedeau watched the conflagration. He knew the fire would soon be spotted even in this isolated countryside, and the man who had thrown the brick through Henley's window would return before long. By then, Nedeau would be gone, safely and anonymously back across the border while Canadian authorities sorted vainly through the maze of fictitious identification he had provided them.

His face remained expressionless as he remembered an earlier killing...the death in the Gold Coast of a man whose grandfather had sold a *malam* named Gbomi to the captain of a Yankee slave ship so many years ago. The Gold Coast man was innocent...innocent like Jeremiah Henley. Nedeau regretted those deaths.

But there was another man behind the mask of Theotis Nedeau's face... the other who had been there since the day Nedeau participated in a calling-of-the-ancestors rite in the Gold Coast. Though his bones rotted in a secret graveyard in a Louisiana bayou, the spirit of Gbomi had spanned an ocean to join with, and ultimately overwhelm, that of his grandson.

It was Gbomi who taught Nedeau the *malam*'s way: all generations were part of a single continuum, ancestors and descendants all as one. Until the debts of the forebears were paid, they must be borne by the progeny....

One more death remained to be dealt...that of the grandson of the Louisiana slave-owner who had attempted to steal the spirit of an African *malam,* then slain the *malam* as a sacrifice to a god with an unspeakable name. One more death and perhaps then, the relentless shade of Gbomi would be placated. Perhaps then, only Theotis Nedeau would dwell behind the eyes that now turned from the burning house and began to study a road map of Louisiana.

Gbomi would not allow Theotis Nedeau to weep for his friend....

ဢ ၒ

Nethescurial

Thomas Ligotti

The Idol and the Island

I have uncovered a rather wonderful manuscript, the *letter began*. It was an entirely fortuitous find, made during my day's dreary labors among some of the older and more decomposed remains entombed in the library archives. If I am any judge of antique documents, and of course I am, these brittle pages date back to the closing decades of the last century. (A more precise estimate of age will follow, along with a photocopy which I fear will not do justice to the delicate, crinkly script, nor to the greenish black discoloration the ink has taken on over the years.) Unfortunately there is no indication of authorship either within the manuscript itself or in the numerous and tedious papers whose company it has been keeping, none of which seem related to the item under discussion. And what an item it is—a real storybook stranger in a crowd of documentary types, and probably destined to remain unknown.

I am almost certain that this invention, though at times it seems to pose as a letter or journal entry, has never appeared in common print. Given the bizarre nature of its content, I would surely have known of it before now. Although it is an untitled "statement" of sorts, the opening lines were more than enough to cause me to put everything else aside and seclude myself in a corner of the library stacks for the rest of the afternoon.

So it begins: "In the rooms of houses and beyond their walls—beneath dark waters and across moonlit skies—below earth mound and above mountain peak—in northern leaf and southern flower—inside each star and the voids between them—within blood and bone, through all souls and spirits—among the watchful winds of this and the several worlds—behind the faces of the living and the dead…" And there it trails off, a quoted fragment of some more ancient text. But this is certainly not the last we will hear of this all-encompassing refrain!

As it happens, the above string of phrases is cited by the narrator in reference to a certain *presence*, more properly an omnipresence, which he encounters on an obscure island located at some unspecified northern latitude. Briefly, he has been summoned to this island, which appears on a local map under the name of Nethescurial, in order to rendezvous with another man, an archaeologist who is designated only as Dr. N— and who will come to know the narrator of the manuscript by the self-admitted alias of "Bartholomew Gray" (they don't call 'em like that anymore). Dr. N—, it seems, has been occupying himself upon that barren, remote, and otherwise uninhabited isle with some peculiar antiquarian rummagings. As Mr. Gray sails toward the island, he observes the murky skies above him and the murky waters below. His prose style is somewhat plain for my taste, but it serves well enough once he approaches the island and takes surprisingly scrupulous notice of its eerie aspect: contorted rock formations; pointed pines and spruces of gigantic stature and uncanny movements; the masklike countenance of sea-faring cliffs; and a sickly, stagnant fog clinging to the landscape like a fungus.

From the moment Mr. Gray begins describing the island, a sudden enchantment enters into his account. It is that sinister enchantment which derives from a profound evil that is kept at just the right distance from us so that we may experience both our love and our fear of it in one sweeping sensation. Too close and we may be reminded of an omnipresent evil in the living world and threatened with having our sleeping sense of doom awakened into full vigor. Too far away and we become even more incurious and complacent than is our usual state and ultimately exasperated when an imaginary evil is so poorly evoked that it fails to offer the faintest echo of its real and all-pervasive counterpart. Of course, any number of locales may serve as the setting to reveal ominous truths; evil, beloved and menacing evil, may show itself anywhere precisely because it is everywhere and is as stunningly set off by a foil of sunshine and flowers as it is by darkness and dead leaves. A purely private quirk, nevertheless, sometimes allows the purest essence of life's malignity to be aroused only by sites such as the lonely island of

Nethescurial, where the real and the unreal swirl freely and madly about in the same fog.

It seems that in this place, this far-flung realm, Dr. N— has discovered an ancient and long-sought artifact, a marginal but astonishing entry in that unspeakably voluminous journal of creation. Soon after landfall, Mr. Gray finds himself verifying the truth of the archaeologist's claims: that the island has been strangely molded in all its parts, and within its shores every manifestation of plant or mineral or anything whatever appears to have fallen at the mercy of some shaping force of demonic temperament, a genius loci which has sculpted its nightmares out of the atoms of the local earth. Closer inspection of this insular spot on the map serves to deepen the sense of evil and enchantment that had been lightly sketched earlier in the manuscript. But I refrain from further quotation (it is getting late and I want to wrap up this letter before bedtime) in order to cut straight through the epidermis of this tale and penetrate to its very bones and viscera. Indeed, the manuscript does seem to have an anatomy of its own, its dark green holography rippling over it like veins, and I regret that my paraphrase may not deliver it alive. Enough!

Mr. Gray makes his way inland, lugging along with him a fat little travelling bag. In a clearing he comes upon a large but unadorned, almost primitive house which stands against the fantastic backdrop of the island's wartlike hills and tumorous trees. The outside of the house is encrusted with the motley and leprous stones so abundant in the surrounding landscape. The inside of the house, which the visitor sees upon opening the unlocked door, is spacious as a cathedral but far less ornamented. The walls are white and smoothly surfaced; they also seem to taper inward, pyramid-like, as they rise from floor to lofty ceiling. There are no windows, and numerous oil lamps scattered about fill the interior of the house with a sacral glow. A figure descends a long staircase, crosses the great distance of the room, and solemnly greets his guest. At first wary of each other, they eventually achieve a degree of mutual ease and finally get down to their true business.

Thus far one can see that the drama enacted is a familiar one: the stage is rigidly traditional and the performers upon it are caught up in its style. For these actors are not so much people as they are puppets from the old shows, the ones that have told the same story for centuries, the ones that can still be very strange to us. Traipsing through the same old foggy scene, seeking the same old isolated house, the puppets in these plays always find everything new and unknown, because they have no memories to speak of and can hardly recall making these stilted motions countless times in the past. They struggle through the same gestures, repeat the same lines, although in rare moments they may feel a dim suspicion that this has all happened before. How like they are to the human race itself! This is what makes them our perfect representatives—this and the fact that they are hand carved in the image of maniacal victims who seek to share the secrets of their individual torments as their strings are manipulated by the same master.

The secrets which these two Punchinellos share are rather deviously presented by the author of this confession (for upon consideration this is the genre to which it truly belongs). Indeed, Mr. Gray, or whatever his name might be, appears to know much more than he is telling, especially with respect to his colleague the archaeologist. Nevertheless, he records what Dr. N— knows and, more importantly, what this avid excavator has found buried on the island. The thing is only a fragment of an object dating from antiquity. Known to be part of a religious idol, it is difficult to say which part. It is a twisted piece of a puzzle, one suggesting that the figure as a whole is intensely unbeautiful. The fragment is also darkened with the verdigris of centuries, causing its substance to resemble something like decomposing jade.

And were the other pieces of this idol also to be found on the same island? The answer is no. The idol seems to have been shattered ages ago, and each broken part of it buried in some remote place so that the whole of it might not easily be joined together again. Although it was a mere representation, the effigy itself was the focus of a great power. The ancient sect which was formed to worship this power seem to have been pantheists of a sort, believing that all created things—appearances to the contrary—are of a single, unified, and transcendent *stuff*, an emanation of a central creative force. Hence the ritual chant which runs "in the rooms of houses", et cetera, and alludes to the all-present nature of this deity—a most primal and pervasive type of god, one that falls into the category of "gods who eclipse all others", territorialist divinities whose claim to the creation purportedly supersedes that of their rivals. (The words of the famous chant, by the way, are the only ones to come down to us from the ancient cult and appeared for the first time in an ethnographical, quasi-esoteric work entitled *Illuminations of the Ancient World*, which was published in the latter part of the nineteenth century, around the same time, I would guess, as this manuscript I am rushing to summarize was written.) At some point in their career as worshipants of the "Great One God", a shadow fell upon the sect. It appears that one day it was revealed to them, in a manner both obscure and hideous, that the power to which they bowed was essentially evil in character and that their religious mode of pantheism was in truth a kind of *pandemonism*. But this revelation was not a surprise to all of the sectarians, since there seems to have been an internecine struggle which ended in slaughter. In any case, the anti-demonists prevailed, and they immediately rechristened their ex-deity to reflect its newly discovered essence in evil. And the name by which they henceforth called it was Nethescurial.

A nice turn of affairs: this obscure island openly advertises itself as the home of the idol of Nethescurial. Of course, this island is only one of several to which the pieces of the vandalized totem were scattered. The original members of the sect who had treacherously turned against their god knew that the power concentrated in the effigy could not be destroyed, and so they decided to parcel it out to isolated corners of the earth where it could do the least harm. But would they have brought attention to this fact by allowing these widely disseminated burial plots to bear the name of the pandemoniacal god? This is doubtful, just as it is equally unlikely that it was they who built those crude houses, temples of a fashion, to mark the spot where a particular shard of the old idol might be located by others.

So Dr. N— is forced to postulate a survival of the demonist faction of the sect, a cult that had devoted itself to searching out those places which had been transformed by the presence of the idol and might thus be known by their gruesome features. This quest would require a great deal of time and effort for its completion, given the global reaches where those splinters of evil might be tucked away. Known as the "seeking", it also involved the enlistment of outsiders, who in latter days were often researchers into the ways of bygone cultures, though they remained ignorant that the cause they served was still a living one. Dr. N— therefore warns his "colleague, Mr. Gray", that they may be in danger from those who carried on the effort to reassemble the idol and revive its power. The very presence of that great and crude house on the island certainly proved that the cult was already aware of the location of *this* fragment of the idol. In fact, the mysterious Mr. Gray, not unexpectedly, is actually a member of the cult in its modern incarnation; furthermore, he has brought with him to the island—bulky travelling bag, you know—all the other pieces of the idol, which have been recovered through centuries of seeking. Now he only needs the one piece discovered by Dr. N— to make the idol whole again for the first time in a couple millennia.

But he also needs the archaeologist himself as a kind of sacrifice to Nethescurial, a ceremony which takes place later the same night in the upper part of the house. If I may telescope the ending for brevity's sake, the sacrificial ritual holds some horrific surprises for Mr. Gray (these people seem never to realize what they are getting themselves into), who soon repents of his evil practices and is driven to smash the idol to pieces once more. Making his escape from that weird island, he throws these pieces overboard, sowing the cold gray waters with the scraps of an incredible power. Later, fearing an obscure threat to his existence (perhaps the reprisal of his fellow cultists), he composes an account of a horror which is both his own and that of the whole human race.

End of manuscript. *

---

* Except for the concluding lines, which reveal the somewhat extravagant, but not entirely uninteresting, conclusion of the narrator himself.

Now, despite my penchant for such wild yarns as I have just attempted to describe, I am not oblivious to their shortcomings. For one thing, whatever emotional impact the narrative may have lost in the foregoing précis, it certainly gained in coherence: the incidents in the manuscript are clumsily developed, important details lack proper emphasis, impossible things are thrown at the reader without any real effort at persuasion of their veracity. I do admire the fantastic principle at the core of this piece. The nature of that pandemoniac entity is very intriguing. Imagine all of creation as a mere mask for the foulest evil, an absolute evil whose reality is mitigated only by our blindness to it, an evil at the heart of things, existing "inside each star and the voids between them—within blood and bone—through all souls and spirits", and so forth. There is even a reference in the manuscript that suggests an analogy between Nethescurial and that beautiful myth of the Australian aborigines known as the Alchera (the Dreamtime, or Dreaming), a super-reality which is the source of all we see in the world around us. (And this reference will be useful in dating the manuscript, since it was toward the end of the last century that Australian anthropologists made the aboriginal cosmology known to the general public.) Imagine the universe as the dream, the feverish nightmare of a demonic demiurge. O Supreme Nethescurial!

The problem is that such supernatural inventions are indeed quite difficult to imagine. So often they fail to materialize in the mind, to take on a mental texture, and thus remain unfelt as anything but an abstract monster of metaphysics—an elegant or awkward schematic that cannot rise from the paper to touch us. Of course, we do need to keep a certain distance from such specters as Nethescurial, but this is usually provided by the medium of words as such, which ensnare all kinds of fantastic creatures before they can tear us body and soul. (And yet the words of this particular manuscript seem rather weak in this regard, possibly because they are only the drab green scratchings of a human hand and not the heavy mesh of black type.)

But we do want to get close enough to feel the foul breath of these beasts, or to see them as prehistoric leviathans circling about the tiny island on which we have taken refuge. Even if we are incapable of a sincere belief in ancient cults and their unheard of idols, even if these pseudonymous adventurers and archaeologists appear to be mere shadows on a wall, and even if strange houses on remote islands are of shaky construction, there may still be a power in these things that threatens us like a bad dream. And this power emanates not so much from within the tale as it does from somewhere behind it, someplace of infinite darkness and ubiquitous evil in which we may walk unaware.

But never mind these night thoughts; it's only to bed that *I* will walk after closing this letter.

Postscript

Later the same night.

Several hours have passed since I set down the above description and analysis of that manuscript. How naïve those words of mine now sound to me. And yet they are still true enough, from a certain perspective. But that perspective was a privileged one which, at least for the moment, I do not enjoy. The distance between me and a devastating evil has lessened considerably. I no longer find it so difficult to imagine the horrors delineated in that manuscript, for I have known them in the most intimate way. What a fool I seem to myself for playing with such visions. How easily a simple dream can destroy one's sense of safety, if only for a few turbulent hours. Certainly I have experienced all this before, but never as acutely as tonight.

I had not been asleep for long but apparently long enough. At the start of the dream I was sitting at a desk in a very dark room. It also seemed to me that the room was very large, though I could see little of it beyond the area of the desktop, at either end of which glowed a lamp of some kind. Spread out before me were many papers varying in size. These I knew to be maps of one sort or another, and I was studying them each in turn. I had become quite absorbed in these maps, which now dominated the dream to the exclusion of all other images. Each of them focused on some concatenation of islands without reference to larger, more familiar land masses. A powerful impression of remoteness and seclusion was conveyed by these irregular daubs of earth fixed in bodies of water that were unnamed. But although the location of the islands was not specific, somehow I was sure that those for whom the maps were meant already had this knowledge. Nevertheless, this secrecy was only superficial, for no esoteric key was required to seek out the greater geography of which these maps were an exaggerated detail: they were all distinguished by some known language in which the islands were named, different languages for different maps. Yet upon closer view (indeed, I felt as if I were actually journeying among those exotic fragments of land, tiny pieces of shattered mystery), I saw that every map had one thing in common: within each group of islands, whatever language was used to name them, there was always one called Nethescurial. It was as if all over the world this terrible name had been insinuated into diverse locales as the only one suitable for a certain island. Of course there were variant cognate forms and spellings, sometimes transliterations, of the word. (How precisely I saw them!) Still, with the strange conviction that may overcome a dreamer, I knew these places had all been claimed in the name of Nethescurial and that they bore the unique sign of something which had been buried there—the pieces of that dismembered idol.

And with this thought, the dream reshaped itself. The maps dissolved into a kind of mist; the desk before me became something else, an altar of coarse stone, and the two lamps upon it flared up to reveal a strange object now positioned between them. So many visions in the dream were piercingly clear, but this dark object was not. My impression was that it was conglomerate in form, suggesting a monstrous whole. At the same time these outlines which alluded to both man and beast, flower and insect, reptiles, stones, and countless things I could not even name, all seemed to be changing, mingling in a thousand ways that prevented any sensible image of the idol.

With the upsurge in illumination offered by the lamps, I could see that the room was truly of unusual dimensions. The four enormous walls slanted toward one another and joined at a point high above the floor, giving the space around me the shape of a perfect pyramid. But I now saw things from an oddly remote perspective: the altar with its idol stood in the middle of the room, and I was some distance away, or perhaps not even on the scene. Then, from some dark corner or secret door, there emerged a file of figures walking slowly toward the altar and finally congregating in a half-circle before it. I could see that they were all quite skeletal in shape, for they were identically dressed in a black material which clung tightly to their bodies and made them look like skinny shadows. They seemed to be actually bound in blackness from head to foot, with only their faces exposed. But they were not, in fact, faces—they were pale, expressionless, and identical masks. The masks were without openings and bestowed upon their wearers a terrible anonymity, an ancient anonymity. Behind these smooth and barely contoured faces were spirits beyond all hope or consolation except in the evil to which they would willingly abandon themselves. Yet this abandonment was a highly selective process, a ceremony of the chosen.

One of the white-faced shadows stepped forward from the group, seemingly drawn forth into the proximity of the idol. The figure stood motionless, while from within its dark body something began to drift out like luminous smoke. It floated, swirling gently, toward the idol and there was absorbed. And I knew—for was not this my own dream?—that the idol and its sacrifice were becoming one within each other. This spectacle continued until nothing of the glowing, ectoplasmic haze remained to be extracted, and the figure—now shrunken to the size of a marionette—collapsed. But soon it was being lifted, rather tenderly, by another from the group who placed the dwarfish form upon the altar and, taking up a knife, carved deep into the body, making no sound. Then something oozed upon the altar, something thick and oily and strangely colored, though not with any of the shades of blood. Although the strangeness of this color was more an idea than a matter of vision, it began to fill the dream and to determine the final stage of its development.

Quite abruptly, that closed, cavernous room dissolved into an open stretch of land: open yet also cluttered with a bric-a-brac topography whose crazed shapes were all of that single and sinister color. The ground was as if covered with an ancient, darkened mold, and the things rising up from it were the same. Surrounding me was a landscape that might have been of stone and earth and trees (such was my impression) but had been transformed entirely into something like petrified slime. I gazed upon it spreading before me, twisting in the way of wrought iron tracery or great overgrown gardens of writhing coral, an intricate latticework of hardened mulch whose surface was overrun with a chaos of little carvings, scabby designs that suggested a world of demonic faces and forms. And it was all composed in that color which somehow makes me think of rotted lichen. But before I exited in panic from my dream, there was one further occurrence of this color: the inkish waters washing upon the shores of the island around me.

As I wrote a few pages ago, I have been awake for some hours now. What I did not mention was the state in which I found myself after waking. Throughout the dream, and particularly in those last moments when I positively identified that foul place, there was an unseen presence, something I could feel was circulating within all things and unifying them in an infinitely extensive body of evil. I suppose it is nothing unusual that I continued to be under this visionary spell even after I left my bed. I tried to invoke the gods of the ordinary world—calling them with the whistle of a coffee pot and praying before the icon of the electric light—but they were too weak to deliver me from that other whose name I can no longer bring myself to write. It seemed to be in possession of my house, of every common object inside and the whole of the dark world outside. Yes—lurking among the watchful winds of this and the several worlds. Everything seemed to be a manifestation of this evil and to my eyes was taking on its aspect. I could feel it also emerging in myself, growing stronger behind this living face that I am afraid to confront in the mirror.

Nevertheless, these dream-induced illusions now seem to be abating, perhaps driven off by my writing about them. Like someone who has had too much to drink the night before and swears off liquor for life, I have forsworn any further indulgence in weird reading matter. No doubt this is only a temporary vow, and soon enough my old habits will return. But certainly not before morning!

The Puppets in the Park

Some days later, and quite late at night.

Well, it seems this letter has mutated into a chronicle of my adventures Nethescurialian. See, I can now write that unique nomen with ease; furthermore, I feel almost no apprehension in stepping up to my mirror. Soon I may even be able to sleep in the way I once did, without visionary intrusions of any kind. No denying that my experiences of late have tipped the scales of the strange. I found myself just walking restlessly about—impossible to work, you know—and always carrying with me this heavy dread in my solar plexus, as if I had feasted at a banquet of fear and the meal would not digest. Most strange, since I have been loath to take nourishment during this time. How could I put anything in my mouth, when everything looked the way it did? Hard enough to touch a doorknob or a pair of shoes, even with the protection of gloves. I could feel every damn thing squirming, not excluding my own flesh. And I could also see what was squirming beneath every surface, my vision penetrating through the usual armor of objects and discerning the same gushing *stuff* inside whatever I looked upon. It was that dark color from the dream, I could identify it clearly now. Dark and greenish. How could I possibly feed myself? How could I even bring myself to settle very long in one spot? So I kept on the move. And I tried not to look too closely at how everything, *everything* was crawling within itself and making all kinds of shapes inside there, making all kinds of faces at me. (Yet it was really all the same face, everything gorged with that same creeping stuff.) There were also sounds that I heard, voices speaking vague words, voices that came not from the mouths of people I passed on the street but from the very bottom of their brains, garbled whisperings at first and then so clear, so eloquent.

This rising wave of chaos reached its culmination tonight and then came crashing down. But my timely maneuvering, I trust, has put everything right again.

Here, now, are the terminal events of this nightmare as they occurred. (And how I wish I were not speaking figuratively, that I was in fact only in the world of dreams or back in the pages of books and old manuscripts.) This conclusion had its beginning in the park, a place that is actually some distance from my home, so far had I wandered. It was already late at night, but I was still walking about, treading the narrow asphalt path that winds through that island of grass and trees in the middle of the city. (And somehow it seemed I had already walked in this same place on this same night, that this had all happened to me before.) The path was lit by globes of light balanced upon slim metal poles; another glowing orb was set in the great blackness above. Off the path the grass was darkened by shadows, and the trees swishing overhead were the same color of muddied green.

After walking some indefinite time along some indefinite route, I came upon a clearing where an audience had assembled for some late-night entertainment. Strings of colored lights had been hung around the perimeter of this area, and rows of benches had been set up. The people seated on these benches were all watching a tall, illuminated booth. It was the kind of booth used for puppet shows, with wild designs painted across the lower part and a curtained opening at the top. The curtains were now drawn back, and two clownish figures were twisting about in a glary light which emanated from inside the booth. They leaned and squawked and awkwardly batted each other with soft paddles they were hugging in their soft little arms. Suddenly they froze at the height of their battle; slowly they turned about and faced the audience. It seemed the puppets were looking directly at the place I was standing behind the last row of benches. Their misshapen heads tilted, and their glassy eyes stared straight into mine.

Then I noticed that the others were doing the same: all of them had turned around on the benches and, with expressionless faces and dead puppet eyes, held me to the spot. Although their mouths did not move, they were not silent. But the voices I heard were far more numerous than was the gathering before me. These were the voices I had been hearing as they chanted confused words in the depths of everyone's thoughts, fathoms below the level of their awareness. The words still sounded hushed and slow, monotonous phrases mingling like the sequences of a fugue. But now I could understand these words, even as more voices picked up the chant at different points and overlapped one another, saying, "In the rooms of houses… across moonlit skies… through all souls and spirits… behind the faces of the living and the dead."

I find it impossible to say how long it was before I was able to move, before I backed up toward the path, all those multitudinous voices chanting everywhere around me and all those many-colored lights bobbing in the wind-blown trees. Yet it seemed only a single voice I heard, and a single color I saw, as I found my way home, stumbling through the greenish darkness of the night.

I knew what needed to be done. Gathering up some old boards from my basement, I piled them into the fireplace and opened the flue. As soon as they were burning brightly, I added one more thing to the fire: a manuscript whose ink was of a certain color. Blessed with a saving vision, I could now see whose signature was on that manuscript, whose hand had really written those pages and had been hiding in them for a hundred years. The author of that narrative had broken up the idol and drowned it in deep waters, but the stain of its ancient patina had stayed upon him. It had invaded the author's crabbed script of blackish green and survived there, waiting to crawl into another lost soul who failed to see what dark places he was wandering into. How I knew this to be true! And has this not been proved by the color of the smoke that rose from the burning manuscript and keeps rising from it?

I am writing these words as I sit before the fireplace. But the flames have gone out, and still the smoke from the charred paper hovers within the hearth, refusing to ascend the chimney and disperse itself into the night. Perhaps the chimney has become blocked. Yes, this must be the case, this must be true. Those other things are lies, illusions. That mold-colored smoke has not taken on the shape of the idol, the shape that cannot be seen steadily and whole but keeps turning out so many arms and heads, so many eyes, and then pulling them back in and bringing them out again in other configurations. That shape is not drawing something out of me and putting something else in its place, something that seems to be bleeding into the words as I write. And my pen is not growing bigger in my hand, nor is my hand growing smaller, smaller...

See, there is no shape in the fireplace. The smoke is gone, gone up the chimney and out into the sky. And there is nothing in the sky, nothing I can see through the window. There is the moon, of course, high and round. But no shadow falls across the moon, no churning chaos of smoke that chokes the frail order of the earth, no shifting cloud of nightmares enveloping moons and suns and stars. It is not a squirming, creeping, smearing shape I see upon the moon, not the shape of a great deformed crab scuttling out of the black oceans of infinity and invading the island of the moon, crawling with its innumerable bodies upon all the spinning islands of inky space. That shape is not the cancerous totality of all creatures, not the oozing ichor that flows within all things. *Nethescurial is not the secret name of the creation.* It is not in the rooms of houses and beyond their walls... beneath dark waters and across moonlit skies... below earth mound and above mountain peak... in northern leaf and southern flower... inside each star and the voids between them... within blood and bone, through all souls and spirits... among the watchful winds of this and the several worlds... behind the faces of the living and the dead.

I am not dying in a nightmare.

ೞ ೞ

Calamari Curls

Kage Baker

The town had seen better days.

Its best year had probably been 1906, when displaced San Franciscans, fleeing south to find slightly less unstable real estate, discovered a bit of undeveloped coastline an inconvenient distance from the nearest train station.

No tracks ran past Nunas Beach. There wasn't even a road to its golden sand dunes, and what few locals there were didn't know why. There were rumors of long-ago pirates. There was a story that the fathers from the local mission had forbidden their parishioners to go there, back in the days of Spanish rule.

Enterprising Yankee developers laughed and built a road, and laid out lots for three little beach towns, and sold them like hotcakes. Two of the towns vanished like hotcakes at a Grange Breakfast, too; one was buried in a sandstorm and the other washed out to sea during the first winter flood.

But Nunas Beach remained, somehow, and for a brief season there were ice-cream parlors and photographers' studios, clam stands, Ferris wheels, drug stores and holiday cottages. Then, for no single reason, people began to leave. Some of the shops burned down; some of the cottages dwindled into shanties. Willow thickets and sand encroached on the edges. What was left rusted where it stood, with sand drifting along its three streets, yet somehow did not die.

People found their way there, now and then, especially after the wars. It was a cheap place to lie in the sun while your wounds healed and your shell-shock faded away. Some people stayed.

Pegasus Bright, who had had both his legs blown off by a land mine, had stayed, and opened the Chowder Palace. He was unpleasant when he drank and, for that matter, when he didn't, but he could cook. The Chowder Palace was a long, low place on a street corner. It wasn't well lit, its linoleum tiles were cracked and grubby, its windows dim with grease. Still, it was the only restaurant in town. Therefore all the locals ate at the Chowder Palace, and so, too, did those few vacationers who came to Nunas Beach.

Mr. Bright bullied a staff of illegal immigrants who worked for him as waiters and busboys; at closing time they faded like ghosts back to homeless camps in the willow thickets behind the dunes, and he rolled himself back to his cot in the rear of the Palace, and slept with a tire iron under his pillow.

❞ ❟

One Monday morning the regulars were lined up on the row of stools at the counter, and Mr. Bright was pushing himself along the row topping up their mugs of coffee, when Charlie Cansanary said:

"I hear somebody's bought the Hi-Ho Lounge."

"No they ain't, you stupid bastard," said Mr. Bright. He disliked Charlie because Charlie had lost his right leg to a shark while surfing, instead of in service to his country.

"That's what I heard too," said Tom Avila, who was the town's mayor.

"Why would anybody buy that place?" demanded Mr. Bright. "*Look* at it!"

They all swiveled on their stools and looked out the window at the Hi-Ho Lounge, which sat right across the street on the opposite corner. It was a windowless stucco place painted gray, with martini glasses picked out in mosaic tile on either side of the blind slab of a door. On the roof was a rusting neon sign portraying another martini glass whose neon olive had once glowed like a green star against the sunset. But not in years; the Hi-Ho Lounge had never been open in living memory.

"Maybe somebody wants to open a bar," said Leon Silva, wiping egg yolk out of his mustache. "It might be kind of nice to have a place to drink."

"You can get drinks here," said Mr. Bright quickly, stung.

"Yeah, but I mean legally. And in glasses and all," said Leon.

"Well, if you want to go to *those* kinds of places and spend an arm and a leg—" said Mr. Bright contemptuously, and then stopped himself, for Leon, having had an accident on a fishing trawler, only had one arm. Since he'd lost it while earning a paycheck rather than in pursuit of frivolous sport, however, he was less a target for Mr. Bright's scorn. Mr. Bright continued: "Anyway it'll never happen. Who's going to buy an old firetrap like that place?"

"Those guys," said Charlie smugly, pointing to the pair of business-suited men who had just stepped out of a new car and were standing on the sidewalk in front of the Hi-Ho Lounge.

Mr. Bright set down the coffee pot. Scowling, he wheeled himself from behind the counter and up to the window.

"Developers," he said. He watched as they walked around the Hi-Ho Lounge, talking to each other and shaking their heads. One took a key from an envelope and tried it in the padlock on the front door; the lock was a chunk of rust, however, and after a few minutes he drew back and shook his head.

"You ain't never getting in that way, buddy," said Tom. "You don't know beach winters."

The developer went back to his car and, opening the trunk, took out a hammer. He struck ineffectually at the lock.

"Look at the sissy way he's doing it," jeered Mr. Bright. "Hit it *hard*, you dumb son of a bitch."

The padlock broke, however, and the chain dropped; it took three kicks to get the door open, to reveal inky blackness beyond. The developers stood looking in, uncertain. The spectators in the Chowder Palace all shuddered.

"There has got to be serious mildew in there," said Charlie.

"And pipes rusted all to hell and gone," said Mr. Bright, with a certain satisfaction. "Good luck, suckers."

↋ ↊

But the developers seemed to have luck. They certainly had money.

Work crews with protective masks came and stripped out the inside of the Hi-Ho Lounge. There were enough rusting fixtures to fill a dumpster; there were ancient red vinyl banquettes, so blackened with mold they looked charred, and clumped rats' nests of horsehair and cotton batting spilled from their entrails.

When the inside had been thoroughly gutted, the outside was tackled. The ancient stucco cracked away to reveal a surprise: graceful arched windows all along both street walls, and a shell-shaped fanlight over the front door. Stripped to its framing, the place had a promise of airy charm.

Mr. Bright watched from behind the counter of the Chowder Palace, and wondered if there was any way he could sue the developers. No excuses presented themselves, however. He waited for rats to stream from their disturbed havens and attack his customers; none came. When the workmen went up on ladders and pried off the old HI-HO LOUNGE sign from the roof, he was disappointed, for no one fell through the rotting lath, nor did sharp edges of rusted tin cut through any workmen's arteries, and they managed to get the sign down to the sidewalk without dropping it on any passers-by. Worse; they left the neon martini glass up there.

"It *is* going to be a bar," said Leon in satisfaction, crumbling crackers into his chowder.

"Shut up," said Mr. Bright.

"And a restaurant," said Charlie. "My brother-in-law works at McGregor's Restaurant Supply over in San Emidio. The developers set up this account, see. He says they're buying lots of stuff. All top of the line. Going to be a seafood place."

Mr. Bright felt tendrils of fear wrap about his heart and squeeze experimentally. He rolled himself back to his cubicle, took two aspirins washed down with a shot of bourbon, and rolled back out to make life hell for Julio, who had yet to clear the dirty dishes from booth three.

ও ৶

The place opened in time for the summer season, despite several anonymous threatening calls to the County Planning Department.

The new sign said CALAMARI CURLS, all in pink and turquoise neon, with a whimsical octopus writing around the letters. The neon martini glass was repiped a dazzling scarlet, with its olive once again winking green.

Inside was all pink and turquoise too: the tuck-and-roll banquettes, the napkins, the linoleum tiles. The staff, all bright young people working their way through Cal State San Emidio, wore pink and turquoise Hawaiian shirts.

Calamari Curls was fresh, jazzy and fun.

Mr. Bright rolled himself across the street, well after closing hours, to peer at the menus posted by the front door. He returned cackling with laughter.

"They got a *wine list!*" he told Jesus, the dishwasher. "And you should see their *prices!* Boy, have they ever made a mistake opening *here!* Who the hell in Nunas Beach is going to pay that kind of money for a basket of fish and chips?"

Everyone, apparently.

The locals began to go there; true, they paid a little more, but the food was so much better! Everything was so bright and hopeful at Calamari Curls! And the polished bar was an altar to all the mysteries of the perfect cocktail. Worse still, the great radiant sign could be seen from the highway, and passers-by who would never before have even considered stopping to fix a flat tire in Nunas Beach, now streamed in like moths to a porch light.

Calamari Curls had a glowing jukebox. Calamari Curls had karaoke on Saturday nights, and a clown who made balloon animals. Calamari Curls had a special tray with artfully made wax replicas of the mouth-watering desserts on their menu.

And the ghostly little businesses along Alder Street sanded the rust off their signs, spruced up a bit and got some of the overflow customers. After dining at Calamari Curls, visitors began to stop into Nunas Book and News to buy magazines and cigarettes. Visitors peered into the dark window of Edna's Collectibles, at dusty furniture, carnival glass and farm implements undisturbed in twenty years. Visitors poked around for bargains at the USO Thrift Shop. Visitors priced arrowheads and fossils at Jack's Rocks.

But Mr. Bright sat behind his counter and served chowder to an ever-dwindling clientele.

ଛ ଛ

The last straw was the Calamari Curls Award Winning Chowder.

Ashen-faced, Mr. Bright rolled himself across the street in broad daylight to see if it was really true. He faced down the signboard, with its playful lettering in pink-and-turquoise marker. Yes; Award-Winning Chowder, containing not only fresh-killed clams but conch and shrimp too.

And in bread bowls. Fresh-baked on the premises.

And for a lower price than at the Chowder Palace.

Mr. Bright rolled himself home, into the Chowder Palace, all the way back to his cubicle. Julio caught a glimpse of the look on Bright's face as he passed, and hung up his apron and just walked out, never to return. Mr. Bright closed the place early. Mr. Bright took another two aspirin with bourbon.

He put the bourbon bottle back in its drawer, and then changed his mind and took it with him to the front window. There he sat through the waning hours, as the stars emerged and the green neon olive across the street shone among them, and the music and laughter echoed across the street pitilessly.

ଛ ଛ

On the following morning, Mr. Bright did not even bother to open the Chowder Palace. He rolled himself down to the pier instead, and looked for Betty Step-in-Time.

Betty Step-in-Time had a pink bicycle with a basket, and could be found on the pier most mornings, doing a dance routine with the bicycle. Betty wore a pink middy top, a little white sailor cap, tap shorts and white tap shoes. Betty's mouth was made up in a red cupid's bow. Betty looked like the depraved older sister of the boy on the Cracker Jack box.

At the conclusion of the dance routine, which involved marching in place, balletic pirouettes and a mimed sea battle, Betty handed out business cards to anyone who had stayed to watch. Printed on the cards was:

ELIZABETH MARQUES
performance artist
interpretive dancer
transgender shaman

Mr. Bright had said a number of uncomplimentary things about Betty Step-in-Time over the years, and had even sent an empty bottle flying toward his curly head on one or two occasions. Now, though, he rolled up and waited in silence as Betty trained an imaginary spyglass on a passing squid trawler.

Betty appeared to recognize someone he knew on board. He waved excitedly and blew kisses. Then he began to dance a dainty sailor's hornpipe.

"Ahem," said Mr. Bright.

Betty mimed climbing hand over hand through imaginary rigging, pretended to balance on a spar, and looked down at Mr. Bright.

"Look," said Mr. Bright, "I know I never seen eye to eye with you—"

Betty went into convulsions of silent laughter, holding his sides.

"Yeah, okay, but I figure you and I got something in common," said Mr. Bright. "Which would be, we like this town just the way it is. It's a good place for anybody down on his luck. Am I right?

"But *that* place," and Mr. Bright waved an arm at Calamari Curls, "that's the beginning of the end. All that pink and blue stuff—Jesus, where do they think they are, Florida?—that's, whatchacallit, gentrification. More people start coming here, building places like that, and pretty soon people like you and me will be squeezed out. I bet you don't pay hardly any rent for that little shack over on the slough, huh? But once those big spenders start coming in, rents'll go through the roof. You mark my words!"

He looked up into Betty's face for some sign of comprehension, but the bright, blank doll-eyes remained fixed on him, nor did the painted smile waver. Mr. Bright cleared his throat.

"Well, I heard some stories about you being a shaman and all. I was hoping there was something you could do about it."

Betty leaped astride his pink bicycle. He thrust his left hand down before

Mr. Bright's face, making a circular motion with the tip of his left thumb over the tips of his first and second fingers.

"You want to get *paid*?" said Mr. Bright, outraged. "Ain't I just explained how you got a stake in this too?"

Betty began to pedal, riding around and around Mr. Bright in a tight circle, waving bye-bye. On the third circuit he veered away, pulling out a piece of pink Kleenex and waving it as he went.

"All right, God damn it!" shouted Mr. Bright. "Let's do a deal."

Betty circled back, stopped and looked at him expectantly. Glum and grudging, Mr. Bright dug into an inner coat pocket and pulled out a roll of greasy twenties. He began to count them off, slowly and then more slowly, as Betty looked on. When he stopped, Betty mimed laughing again, throwing his head back, pointing in disbelief. Mr. Bright gritted his teeth and peeled away more twenties, until there was quite a pile of rancid cabbage in his lap. He threw the last bill down in disgust.

"That's every damn cent I got with me," he said. "You better be worth it."

Betty swept up the money and went through a routine of counting it himself, licking his thumb between each bill and sweeping his hands out in wide elaborate gestures. Apparently satisfied, he drew a tiny, pink vinyl purse from his bicycle's basket and tucked away the money. Leaning down, he winked broadly at Mr. Bright.

Then he pushed his little sailor cap forward on his brow and pedaled off into the fog.

&z ꙅ

Three days later, Mr. Bright was presiding over a poker game at the front table with Charlie, Leon and Elmore Souza, who had lost both hands in an accident at the fish cannery but was a master at manipulating cards in his prostheses, to such an extent that he won frequently because his opponents couldn't stop staring. Since they were only playing for starlight mints, though, nobody minded much.

Mr. Bright was in a foul mood all the same, having concluded that he'd been shaman-suckered out of a hundred and eighty dollars. He had just anted up five mints with a dip into the box from Iris Fancy Foods Restaurant Supply when he looked up to see Betty Step-in-Time sashaying into the Chowder Palace. His friends looked up to see what he was snarling at, and quickly looked away. A peculiar silence fell.

Betty was carrying a Pee Chee folder. He walked straight up to Mr. Bright, opened the folder with a flourish, and presented it to him. Mr. Bright stared down at it, dumfounded.

"We should maybe go," said Leon, pushing away from the table. Charlie scuttled out the door ahead of him, and Elmore paused only to sweep the star-light mints into his windbreaker pocket before following them in haste.

Betty ignored them, leaning down like a helpful maitre d' to remove a mass of photocopied paper from the folder and arrange it on the table before Mr. Bright.

The first image was evidently from a book on local history. It was a very old photograph, to judge from the three-masted ship on the horizon; waves breaking in the background, one or two bathers in old-fashioned costume, and a couple of little board and batten shacks in the foreground. White slanted letters across the lower right-hand corner read: *Nunas Beach, corner of Alder and Stanford.* Squinting at it, Mr. Bright realized that he was seeing the view from his own front window, a hundred years or more in the past.

Silently Betty drew his attention to the fact that the future site of Calamari Curls was a bare and blasted lot, though evening primrose grew thickly up to its edge.

"Well, so what?" he said. In reply, Betty whisked the picture away to reveal another, taken a generation later but from the same point of view. A building stood on the spot now—and there were the same arched windows, the same fanlight door, above which was a sign in letters solemn and slightly staggering: ALDER STREET NATATORIUM.

"A nata-what?" said Mr. Bright. Betty placed his hands together and mimed diving. Then he gripped his nose, squeezed his eyes shut and sank down, waving his other hand above his head.

"Oh. Okay, it was a swimming pool? What about it?"

Betty lifted the picture. Under it was a photocopied microfilm enlarge-ment, from the *San Emidio Mission Bell* for May 2, 1922. Mr. Bright's reading skills were not strong, but he was able to make out enough to tell that the ar-ticle was about the Alder Street Natatorium in Nunas Beach, which had closed indefinitely due to a horrifying incident two days previous. Possible ergot poi-soning—mass hallucinations—sea-creature—prank by the boys of San Emidio Polytechnic?—where is Mr. Tognazzini and his staff?

"Huh," said Mr. Bright. "Could we, like, blackmail somebody with this stuff?"

Betty pursed his cupid's bow and shook a reproving finger at Mr. Bright. He drew out the next paper, which was a photocopied page from the *Weekly Dune Crier* for April 25, 1950. There were three young men standing in front of the Hi-Ho Lounge, looking arch. The brief caption underneath implied that the Hi-Ho Lounge would bring a welcome touch of sophistication and gray-flannel elegance to Nunas Beach.

"So I guess they boarded the pool over," said Mr. Bright. "Well?"

Quickly, Betty presented the next photocopy. It was an undated article from the *San Emidio Telegraph* noting briefly that the Hi-Ho Lounge was still closed pending the police investigation, that no marihuana cigarettes had been found despite first reports, and that anyone who had attended the poetry reading was asked to come forward with any information that might throw some light on what had happened, since Mr. LaRue was not expected to recover consciousness and Mr. Binghamton and Mr. Cayuga had not been located.

Mr. Bright shook his head. "I don't get it."

Betty rolled his eyes and batted his lashes in exasperation. He shuffled the last paper to the fore, and this was not a photocopy but some kind of astronomical chart showing moon phases. It had been marked all over with pink ink, scrawled notations and alchemical signs, as well as other symbols resembling things Mr. Bright had only seen after a three-day weekend with a case of Ten High.

"What the hell's all this supposed to be?" demanded Mr. Bright. "Oh!... I guess this is… some kind of shamanic thing?"

Betty leaped into the air and crossed his ankles as he came down, then mimed grabbing someone by the hand and shaking it in wildly enthusiastic congratulation. Mr. Bright pulled his hands in close.

"Okay," he said in a husky whisper. He looked nervously around at his empty restaurant. "Maybe you shouldn't ought to show me anything else."

But Betty leaned forward and tapped one image on the paper. It was a smiling full moon symbol. He winked again, and backed toward the door. He gave Mr. Bright a thumbs-up, then made an OK symbol with thumb and forefinger, and then saluted.

"Okay, thanks," said Mr. Bright. "I get the picture."

He watched Betty walking primly away, trundling the pink bicycle. Looking down at the table, he gathered together the papers and stuffed them back in the Pee Chee folder. He wheeled himself off to his cubicle and hid the folder under his pillow, with the tire iron.

Then he rolled around to his desk, and consulted the calendar from Nunas Billy's Hardware Circus. There was a full moon in three days' time.

ଧ ଗ

It was Saturday, and the full moon was just heaving itself up from the eastern horizon, like a pink pearl. Blue dusk lay on Nunas Beach. The tide was far out; salt mist flowed inland, white vapor at ankle level. Mr. Bright sat inside the darkened Chowder Palace, and watched, and hated, as people lined up on the sidewalk outside Calamari Curls.

Calamari Curls was having Talent Nite. The Early Bird specials were served, and senior diners went shuffling back to their singlewides, eager to leave before the Goddamned rock and roll started. Young families with toddlers dined and hurried back to their motels, unwilling to expose little ears to amplified sound.

Five pimply boys set up their sound equipment on the dais in the corner. They were the sons of tractor salesmen and propane magnates; let their names be forgotten. The front man tossed his hair back from his eyes, looked around at the tables crowded with chattering diners, and said in all adolescent sullenness:

"Hi. We're the Maggots, and we're here to shake you up a little."

His bassman leaped out and played the opening of "(I Can't Get No) Satisfaction" with painful slowness, the drummer boy joined in clunk-clunk-clunk, and the front man leaned forward to the mike and in a hoarse scream told the audience about his woes. The audience continued biting the tails off shrimp, sucking down frozen strawberry margaritas and picking at Kona Coffee California Cheesecake.

When the music ended, they applauded politely. The front man looked as though he'd like to kill them all. He wiped sweat from his brow, had a gulp of water.

Betty Step-in-Time wheeled his bicycle up to the door.

"We're going to do another classic," said the front man. "Okay?"

Ka-*chunk!* went the drums. The keyboardist and the lead guitarist started very nearly in sync: Da da da. *Dada. DA DA DA. Dada.*

"*Oh Lou-ah Lou-ah-eh, ohhhh baby nagatcha go waygadda go!*" shouted the front man.

Betty Step-in-Time dismounted. Just outside the restaurant's threshold, he began to dance. It began in time with the music, a modest little kickstep. A few diners looked, pointed and laughed.

"*Nah nah nah nah asaya Lou-ah Lou-ah eh, whooa babeh saya whaygachago!*"

Betty's kickstep increased its arc, to something approaching can-can immodesty. He threw his arms up as he kicked, rolling his head, closing his eyes in abandon. A diner sitting near the door fished around in pockets for a dollar bill, but saw no hat in which to put it.

"*Ah-nye, ah-dah, ah ron withchoo, ah dinkabobsa gonstalee!*" cried the front man. Betty began to undulate, and it seemed a tremor ran through the floor of the building. A tableful of German tourists jumped to their feet, alarmed, but their native companion didn't even stop eating.

"Just an aftershock," he said calmly. "No big deal."

"*Ah rag saga leely, badoom badoom, wha wah badoo, jaga babee!*"

Betty began to dance what looked like the Swim, but so fast his arms and legs blurred the air. The lights dimmed, took on a greenish cast.

"Who's playing with the damn rheostat?" the manager wanted to know.

"Ayah ha Lou-ah Lou-ah eh, whoa ba-bah shongo waygatchago!"

Sweat began to pour from Betty's face and limbs, as his body began to churn in a manner that evoked ancient bacchanals, feverish and suggestive. The green quality of the light intensified. Several diners looked down at their plates of clam strips or chimichangas and stopped eating, suddenly nauseous.

"Ya ya ya ya ah-sha-da Lou-ah Lou-ah he, Nyarlathotep bay-bah weygago!" sang the front man, and he was sweating too, and—so it seemed—dwindling under the green light, and the carefully torn edges of his black raiment began to fray into rags, patterned with shining mold.

Betty's hips gyrated, his little sailor hat flew off, and every curl on his head was dripping with St. Elmo's fire. Several diners vomited where they sat. Others rose in a half-crouch, desperate to find the lavatory doors marked *Beach Bums* and *Beach Bunnies*. Half of them collapsed before they made it. They slipped, stumbled and fell in the pools of seawater that were condensing out of the air, running down the walls.

"Ah Lou-ah Lou-ah eh, ph'nglui mglw'nafh Cthulhu R'lyeh wgah'nagl fhtagn!" wailed the white-eyed thing the front man had become, and his band raised reed flutes to their gills and piped a melody to make human ears bleed, and the mortal diners rose and fought to get out the windows, for Betty was flinging handfuls of seaweed in toward them, and black incense.

The pink and turquoise linoleum tiles by the bandstand popped upward, scattered like hellish confetti, as a green-glowing gas of all corruption hissed forth, lighting in blue flames when it met the air, followed by a gush of black water from the forgotten pool below. The first of the black tentacles probed up through the widening crack in the floor.

Betty sprang backward, grabbed up his sailor hat, leaped on his pink bicycle and pedaled away as fast as he could go, vanishing down the misty darkness of Alder Street.

The neon olive had become an eye, swiveling uncertainly but with malevolence, in a narrow scarlet face.

Watching from across the street, Mr. Bright laughed until the tears poured from his eyes, and slapped the arms of his wheelchair. He raised his bourbon bottle in salute as Calamari Curls began its warping, strobing, moist descent through the dimensions.

ଉ ଉ

He was opening a new bottle by the time gray dawn came, as the last of the fire engines and ambulances pulled away. Tom Avila stood in the middle of the street, in gloomy conference with the pastor of St. Mark's, the priest from Mission San Emidio, and even the rabbi from Temple Beth-El, who had driven in his pajamas all the way over from Hooper City.

Holy water, prayer and police tape had done all they could do; the glowing green miasma was dissipating at last, and the walls and windows of Calamari Curls had begun to appear again in ghostly outline. Even now, however, it was obvious that their proper geometry could never be restored.

Tom shook hands with the gentlemen of God and they departed to their respective cars. He stood alone in the street a while, regarding the mess; then he noticed Mr. Bright, who waved cheerfully from behind his window. Tom's eyes narrowed. He came stalking over. Mr. Bright let him in.

"You didn't have anything to do with this, did you, Peg?" the mayor demanded.

"Me? How the hell could I of? I just been sitting here watching the show," said Mr. Bright. "I ain't going to say I didn't enjoy it, neither. Guess nobody's going to raise no rents around *here* for a while!"

"God damn it, Peg! Now we've got us *another* vortex into a lost dimension, smack in the middle of town this time!" said the mayor in exasperation. "What are we going to do?"

"Beats me," said Mr. Bright, grinning as he offered him the bourbon bottle.

ß ø

But the present became the past, as it will, and people never forget so easily as when they want to forget. The wreck of Calamari Curls became invisible, as passers-by tuned it out of their consciousness. The green olive blinked no more.

Mr. Bright found that the black things that mewled and gibbered around the garbage cans at night could be easily dispatched with a cast-iron skillet well aimed. His customers came back, hesitant and shamefaced. He was content.

And mellowing in his world view too; for he no longer scowled nor spat in the direction of Betty Step-in-Time when he passed him on the pier, but nodded affably, and once was even heard to remark that it took all kinds of folks to make a world, and you really shouldn't judge folks without you get to know them.

ß ø

Jihad over Innsmouth

Edward Morris

cold, black, liquescent fear laps at the edges of my heart as I approach the first gate in the long Caliph's Maze of Airport Security.

Some darker force is trying to sway me unobtrusively away, to make me renege my retainer's oath, cut my losses and run headlong to South America with the dwindling remains of my bank account.

Should I die on my quest, a first-class seat in Paradise awaits me. In my time, I have lived through every hell Shaitan could possibly devise right here on Earth, moving behind newspaper headlines which even Al-Jazeera fears to run. Enquiring minds want to know, but some truths are better left to the darkness at the center of the universe, to be drowned out by the skirlings of the blind piper and his retinue of idiot flute-players.

But the oath I took goes deeper than the contract I signed with the old black man in Oakland last week. It is one our folk call fatwa, and is not to be broken. Come flood or djinn or plague of insects, I will board this plane.

I carry no arms upon my person. I'm simply afraid of Americans.

This is a very hot land for me now. Every time I have to fly, I expect Justice Department agents in sober black suits and Agent Smith shades to surround me, barking on their surveillance headsets that I am under arrest for any one of a thousand occupationally hazardous reasons which I foreswore tabulating long ago.

No minions of the law shew themselves in the crowd. My fear settles back inside me and changes shape. For myself, I merely offer a silent prayer to Allah that my limited human perceptions somehow interpreted the recent stars incorrectly. If not, as the American GI's I 'consult' with, put it, I'll be in a world of shit.

They know they can batten down all the iron hooks of their 'Patriot Act' upon me for any number of 'moving violations.' If he were here, Dad would tell me I'm just being paranoid. But Dad's in Gaza, on a contract of his own.

In any case, your William Burroughs writes that perfect paranoia is perfect awareness. In my line of work, selective application of that idea holds the potential to save one's life. Under that lens, I realize that if They (definition subject to change without notice) felt like taking me out of the game, they could have done it by now. I can only assume I'm still in their good graces and travel at will, until a harsh and bracketed detainment at this pestiferous little airport, followed by an unspecified hitch in the Tombs, wherein New York's Finest would perform upon my habeas corpus certain interrogation methods never proscribed by the Geneva Convention.

I'm afraid of Americans. But I keep forgetting that I'm an American, too. It seems an unlikely thing to forget, but one way or another, I've been a nomad all my life.

Under my real name, Hassan Sabbah al-Gazi (just call me Han, as people have since my sixth-grade year, the year of those ubiquitous *Star Wars* movies), I became a naturalized citizen when I was eleven.

Dad moved us over here from Jerusalem after things got a little tense between himself and a false friend in the Mossad, the Israeli Secret Service. Our people have long sworn that Mossad eat what they kill. But my father, in disappearing, was actually doing the operative a favor (albeit one of a nature that would never hold up in court.) But that's another tale, for another day.

I approach the gate. A petrified-looking Lebanese guy with a chicken chest and a fake badge puffs up in my face at the first metal detector. The Marines have a wonderful idiom for his sort, an "empty uniform". His is hanging on him like a drop-cloth! I stifle a laugh.

"Sir," he barks in heavily-accented English. "Could you please remove your shoes?"

I drop to one knee, hands where he can see them, and do so, handing them up. He inspects them, then looks as though he may presently swallow his chin. As he reaches for his radio, I stay his hand so quickly he doesn't anticipate the motion. Amateur. I address him softly in Arabic.

"Look, effendi, you push on the back and the heel fills up with air." I show him.

He looks again, and groans at my Reebok pump gym sneakers that are probably almost as old as he is. "A thousand pardons, cousin. My boss, you understand, he asks that we—"

I sigh. "Yeah, yeah. You're just doing your job. No worries."

He scutters back to the X-ray conveyor, takes a long look at the screen, and hands me my bag.

"Shalom aleichem, habibi. Safe journey."

I bow with my right hand over my heart. "Asayem aleichem shalom, cousin. Don't work too hard."

"Not possible." He chuckles and waves me through. I start looking for Gate 11.

ॐ ॐ

The thought of hitting Boylston Street in Boston around dinner time makes me salivate. De gustibus est non disputandem, especially after the Swanson frozen fare in first class. From what I hear, the Combat Zone has been strip-mined of most of its red stoplights and dive bars, so further recreation is probably best left out. I wish I had time hit the old MTA Pneumatic Railway tunnels down there and see if there are any new leads for me on the corkboard in the lobby of the other Pickman Gallery.

But there's no time to schmooze with the denizens, let alone the citizens. I am to meet with my contact on Boston Common an hour after we land. Transportation has been arranged. We will drive much further north from there, along a particularly fierce section of the Massachusetts coastline. Most maps have forgotten our destination, simply listing it as an unincorporated township on a dead, played-out reef. But the old brain-cases living on Supplemental Security in Arkham and Kingsport still call it Innsmouth.

Innsmouth. I can taste the word in my throat like raw calamari. My skin goes hot as my sweat goes cold. The word, and the memory of the word, fills my nostrils with the smell of cold boom town gone bust, mine-dumps leaching sulfur into the water table, sad rotting houses covered over with Z-Brick, with living denizens and permanently bolted doors.

The word smells like Kreutzfeld-Jakob's Disease, leprosy, cannibalism and a hundred other kinds of runoff from inbreeding that science does not yet wish to name.

I'm going back. The mere thought makes me better understand, in this moment, the Hakkagure of the ancient Japanese samurai. It is the same with

those of my faith who ply my trade. Behave as though the flesh is dead. Then…
and now more than ever… one does not lose his mind when confronted with
the dark.

In place of fear, my thoughts turn to wrath as Gate 11 looms large, just
down the way a bit on the right. Several screaming children twine around me
like cats for a moment. I consult my watch. I know I'm not late.

Wrath. The denizens of Innsmouth deliberately flout my faith. The
Prophet teaches us that Man evolved from clots of blood. Our learned men of
this age teach also that somewhere between blood clot and H. sapiens sapiens,
we crawled out of the sea. This is not to be doubted.

But Innsmouth follows an infidel faith. Their own Shaitan, whom Islam
has called Dagon since Babylon, has performed a miracle of fish unto any
and every hard-luck sailor dumb or amateur enough to steer his tired old
Downeaster Alexa into the waters off the town's own Devil Reef.

Since the 1920s, decapod mating patterns in that part of the Bay, and
migratory patterns of just about every aquatic species that ever turned a buck,
have climbed steadily with no spike in sight. Of course, the corporate fisheries
were in there first. But the fish are so thick you could practically walk on the
water like Yeshua. Dagon apparently shares and shares alike.

By hypothetical evidence, (which, being based in the supernatural, can
neither be proven or refuted in court) rock-ribbed Protestants in every hamlet
for miles around Innsmouth, are slowly being swayed to the notion that there
might be other fish in the sea. To harvest said fish, their mad TV preacher
boasts, you must devolve back to the blood clot, to drown beneath the waves
of our own DNA, to crawl back to the womb and die.

The Prophet cast out Dagon with all the other false gods. My business
with the debased tornado-bait of Innsmouth is nothing more or less than
jihad. One may work full-time during Ramadan for such a purpose, it is written. I just hope it's over with quickly.

My contact is a rich writer from Bangor, only a few years my junior.
Mr. Bachman is to outfit me with the necessary ordnance and artifacts. Dick
also holds a private pilot's license. All the paperwork has been taken care of
through my Oakland liason.

When did they start calling this section "Business Elite", I wonder? Was
"First Class" too classist for these people? These funny, half-blind, blissfully
oblivious, cell-phone-babbling, off-in-their-own-little-world Americans? It's
their world. We're all just living in it.

Long might some of them live to think so. I sigh, stepping hurriedly on
board. The pilot looks like a whippet with an elaborate mop of gray hair, pre-
scription shades and a thick mustache. He grins a set of teeth like the white

keys on a piano.

"Welcome aboard! Happy holidays!" He briskly shakes my hand. I notice a bead of cocaine-colored snot twinkling just beneath his right nostril. Pilots are all alike. In Arabic, I tell him he's an idiot and he's going to get us all killed. He smiles and nods and herds me in.

I slide up through Coach, glancing at the seat number on my ticket. C-4. Very funny, Boss. You want me blown up that bad, do you? Freak. I can't help but chuckle.

The intercom speakers blare into life, "GOOD MORNING. HAPPY HOLIDAYS." I part the curtain and venture into "Business Elite," my eyes slightly ahead of me.

"FLIGHT 180 WILL BE DEPARTING LAGUARDIA IN JUST A FEW MINUTES. YOUR—"

"Oh, shit." I look down fast. A soccer mom two seats ahead glances back at me like I'm about to pull out a box-cutter. Right now, she's the least of my worries.

We Sufi have a kind of prayer for times like this. No matter what the Creator hands you, be it a hundred dollars or two broken legs, you smile as broadly as you can and say Thank You, Sir, May I Have Another? And you laugh. Thus, the worse something gets, the more important it becomes to deflect it.

But... my God... if... the man... if such he can be termed... who I was hired to find in ...Innsmouth and kill is... seated... right beside me on... this plane?

I committed the photograph to memory before I rolled a hashish spliff with it and smoked it to the head. This is a spot-on match. This is a practical joke. This is...

Why, this is going to be a long flight. I smile, grit my teeth and sit down, trying not to look at him. But to hear him slurp and slobber over that sushi box, sucking on his mucilaginous webby fingers, a green rill of wasabi wending its way down his vestigial chin—

My mind spools out its quiet dossier, calming my restless hands that want to make my shoelaces into garrottes. Reverend Irving Waite, in the name of Allah, the compassionate, the merciful. The false prophet I have been promised ten million U.S. dollars (half up front), and flown all the way from Oakland, to smear from the skin of Space and Time. You can hear about something until the teller is blue in the face.

But seeing it sitting beside you is another matter entirely. He looks something like the jazz singer Mel Tormé, if Mel were to commission a bust of himself as a horror-movie latex appliance by Tom Savini. As the Marines say, he stinks like low tide took a shit in his pants. And then there's the reaction-time thing. Lovely dinner company.

I have been charged to end this creature. At present, I must somehow summon up the ingenuity to sit still for an hour-plus flight and act as though I had no idea who he was. I shove my bag under the seat and give up.

"How's the sushi?" In my head, I'm humming an old family chant to harmonize body functions. My sense of smell cycles down to almost nothing.

Waite's long, peeling head swivels like a newt's. His eyes are all wrong. I knew an autistic kid once, in Jerusalem, a beggar's son, whose eyes were almost that shade of gold. But the cataracts in Waite's eyes (or whatever they really are) make the effect somehow more alarming. The tail of a shrimp hangs from his thick lower lip until he sees me looking and snaps it back.

Most people would assume the black patches are squamous melanoma, flaking and coruscating at the sides of his wattled neck. Said neck, like his head, is home to alarmingly random patches of scraggly nicotine-colored hair.

Anyone would think the Reverend was taking chemotherapy. I know better. He's getting ready to go join the Eternal Family Reunion out on Devil Reef. He's getting ready to grow gills, and use them.

He's getting ready to clot.

"Ehhh." The Rev rumbles back in a voice like a shovel over wet cement. "Tastes…two days… old. I c'd…get better'n this at home." His metabolism is probably so slowed-down by now that he took this long to register my presence.

That's an article of his faith too, you see. With immortality comes icthyic serenity, and thus their human shells are swallowed in Devonian slime. I smile and nod.

"I'll bet you could." The conversation is left dangling.

To the left of us, in C-2, some punk kid is asleep with his shaven head against the window, blocking the view. He's dressed fairly nice for his sort, in an all-black suit with no tie, a rack of hoop earrings and a stud in either nostril. He looks exhausted.

A crewcut flight attendant, who looks and swishes alarmingly like Dr. Smith on the old *Lost In space* show, pops up. "Would you care for a beverage, after we get rolling?"

"Green tea. No sugar."

"Very good, Mr. Sabbah." He blinks at Waite. "And we'll bring your clam juice for you, too, Reverend. I'll check on him," he jerks a thumb at Punkboy, "Later."

Behind and above us, the tastefully-concealed speakers drone on, "PLEASE DISCONTINUE THE USE OF ALL CELL PHONES DURING

THE TAXI PERIOD. FLIGHT ATTENDANTS, CROSS-CHECK AND AISLE CALL, PLEASE."

Waite pushes his sushi box aside. Dr. Smith twinkles it away and flips the old bastard's tray table up for him, trying not to make a face at Waite's personal BO of fish and unknown precious metals. (He does well. Very professional.)

"...Muuhokay." the Reverend replies too late. Dr. Smith is long gone.

Reverend... I shudder in the leather seat as we begin to taxi and the pilot tells us over the loudspeakers that we will be first in line for takeoff. Reverend of what, a shithouse?

I have a whole file cabinet on this fool. He's the titular head of the Esoteric Order of Dagon. No union lobsterman or fisherman on that part of the coast will hear a word spoken against him. His kooky theosophical crossbreeding of Aleister Crowley and L. Ron Hubbard has cranked his books to the top of the *New York Times* best-seller list for weeks on end. Until very recently, his arena "revivals" packed in the faithful deeper than the wildest dreams of Billy Graham.

But Waite isn't on the "revival" circuit any more. He looks like hell in a Bundt pan. I wonder about his game plan. My employer in Oakland, Mistah Thotep-if-you-please, is exactly right. Now's the perfect time to strike, before Waite passes on the racket that he's apparently running by remote control these days.

Two rows behind us, a baby is crying very loudly. Something tells me again that I'm in for a long flight. I could sit still for days, if that's what it takes. I have, in the cold plains of Kyrzgstan and Outer Mongolia and the nearly nameless nightmare countries close to the top of the world, teasing my kills, waiting out every querencia. But give me a chance when we land, and Waite will be going to that great big fish-hatchery in the sky.

I look out the window at the obscenely gibbous moon over the desolate hubbub of Ground Zero, where the World Trade Center towers were, as we ascend above the pollution and the clouds. As always when I see that dry socket in the earth, I do my level best to cry (though the actual act is, in my case, impossible), and beg Allah's forgiveness upon us all. I haven't been able to cry since my last op in Afghanistan. My tears are on the inside.

From somewhere, in-flight Muzak blithely murders the entire Dave Matthews band. I unfold the little screen from my armrest, find my remote, turn it sideways, punch a few buttons and wait for In-Flight Tetris to download, trying not to think about the thing in the seat beside me.

In the name of all that is holy, why isn't Waite on a private jet? He could afford a fleet of Lears with the "donations" from his "crusades"... and oh, how apropos the latter word is.)I could snap his neck right now.

But Innsmouth folk are quite hard to kill by ordinary means. It would take several tries, and attract too much notice. Do I speak from experience? I wish I didn't.

What are the chances that he'd be flying on Christmas, anyway? I'd thought to get a leg up, slip into Innsmouth on Greyhound under cover of night, and get this over with. I could be in the Caymans the next morning smoking ganja on the beach. But Allah has more in store for me than the easy road.

At the front of the cabin, the screen now glows with a brown-and-green map of our journey. The speakers whinge on once more.

"THIS IS YOUR CAPTAIN SPEAKING. WE HAVE LEVELLED OFF AT THIRTY-SEVEN THOUSAND FEET. WINDS ARE AT TEN MILES AN HOUR, VISIBILITY IS MODERATE TO LOW WITH OVERCAST SKIES AND LOW CLOUD COVER. WE WILL BE ARRIVING IN BOSTON IN APPROXIMATELY ONE HOUR'S TIME. PLEASE ENJOY YOUR FLIGHT. HAPPY HOLIDAYS."

Dr. Smith bobs up from the forward flight attendants' area pushing a cart. I set Tetris on level 10, wait again, and bow over the steaming blue earthen mug of tea he hands me. Thankfully, I can't smell the clam juice he sets before Waite, professionally folding the Reverend's tray table down once more and placing the cup there in one quick move. Bleh.

The kid in C-2's awake now. His voice is a throaty rasp. "Excuse me, boss. Next time you come by, could I get a cup of coffee?"

Dr. Smith nods immediately. "We've got French roast, cappucino, and—"

The kid grins an endearing, crooked grin. "Black. In a cup." Dr. Smith nods briskly, and retreats to the next row. The kid shakes his head.

"Well, you can't beat this. They just shoved me in first class. Gotta love PriceLine."

"Ah." I sip my tea, flip the screen down into my armrest and turn it off with the remote. Conversation is always preferable on a long flight." The luck of the draw. Why are you flying on Christmas?"

The kid shrugs. "Why not?"

That's fair, but I'm bored and curious. "Were you in the military?" His hair has the look of being perpetually cut short by choice. I surmise that we could swap soldier-stories the entire flight.

"Nah. They wouldn't take me." He slapped his knee. "Game leg. Unfit For Service. You?"

"A bit. Not in America, though."

Waite is looking at the kid as if he wonders how he might taste. The kid ignores him completely. "Where did you do your service?"

"Mmm. All over the Middle East. I was a consultant, you might say. I'm done with that now, though."

He nods. "My sisters put it like that, too. 'I'm done.' I guess I can understand that. Maybe I'm better off."

"What do you do now?" I ask. Beside him, Waite appears to nod off like a chicken with its head placed beneath its wing.

"I write comic books. Creator-owned projects are going the way of the dinosaur, but... there are all sorts of ways around that."

He names a few he writes for. You'd know them. You'd know his name, too, if you're seriously into that sort of thing. I nod. "Do you know Grant Morrison?" That's just the first name I think of. "I used to read 'Doom Patrol' sometimes, when I could keep up with—"

Dr. Smith passes back by with the kid's coffee. "Here you are, sweetie."

"Thanks. Yeah, I met him once." The kid beams. "What a neat guy. I remember staying up with him 'till four in the morning at the Hyatt in San Francisco talking about whether or not Rod Serling was right and the past really is inviolable."

"Ah—" My compulsive reading pays off sometimes. "Serling must have learned that from Jack Finney. Do you know of him?"

The kid frowns. "Didn't he write *Time and Again*?"

"Yes. Also, a book of short stories called—"

I stop. The back of my neck is alive with a chill. The kid looks unfazed.

"Yeah." He answers the question I didn't ask. "I felt it too. Hmm..."

A visor drops over his face. I know that visor very well, from those strange, strange days in Afghanistan in the eighties before the shit hit the fan and we were airlifted out. I saw it every time I looked in the mirror to shave, back then, on the few cold mornings in Kandahar when anything but a dry shave was available.

I wonder what hell this kid has been through, to heighten his senses like that. "I thought it was just me—" he begins. Then, out of nowhere, Reverend Waite stands up and steps into the aisle. The next few minutes are the only time in my life I've ever been sorry to have been born an Arab.

Things are falling into place, changing, switching perspectives like angles in a haunted house. I will myself to concentrate on what's really here.

There's a choked gurgling sound over the loudspeakers. The plane banks hard right and down. In the row in front of us, a blue-haired old lady with a portable oxygen tank and a tube in her nose screams at the top of her lungs, clutching her chest.

Waite cocks his head at her, his cataracted eyes burning bright. She goes limp in her seat, hands flopping in opposite directions, the life leaving her like the filament breaking in a light bulb, that quick.

The kid shrinks back in his seat, frantically searching his pockets while trying to keep the rest of him still.

"Hey!" The young woman beside her in that row yelps indignantly. "Hey, what did you—" Then I saw her jerk forward and heard her sudden silence. The seat to the old lady's right is empty. The passengers across the aisle are panicking, and simply don't see.

From Coach and Business Elite alike, more screams and herd terror-babble ramp up as the plane began to vibrate. Wild lightning rattles through the seas of clouds outside. Turbulence shakes everything with Loma Prieta-scale force. Tray tables bounce. Drinks spill hither and yon. My tea flies toward the front of the cabin like a rocket-propelled grenade.

I turn around. In the front row of the Coach section, where the curtain has been yanked aside, a young girl with her hair dyed three different Crayola colors claws at her seatbelt, eyes bugging out. Beside her, her boyfriend is still asleep.

A grossly fat yuppie with a Jimmy Carter part in his hair bounces to his feet, brandishing his briefcase and charges me, bellowing, "Dirka dirka, mother fucker!!!" His tie's crooked. His loafers pound the aisle as his seatbelt clattered to the ground.

The only friend of Allah on this plane is sitting perfectly still, yawning. The yuppie observes this phenomenon… and sees Waite standing in the aisle, alive and alight, not a bit groggy at all.

Waite grins with small, sharp teeth. One webbed hand comes up, palm down, fat sushi-gummy fingers splayed. He croaks something that might once have been a word.

The yuppie falls backward into seat D-5, knocking over an old man's martini glass. The old man screams, almost scooting into the lap of a snotty-looking little princess who pushes him away. "No!! Ew, I—Help!"

The yuppie rolls onto the floor, not looking like he wants up. Or like he's breathing. Waite folds his arms. The look on his jowly face says, Next? But the imperious son of a bitch isn't even going to say anything.

My faith teaches that in times of common disaster, every believer is the executor of Allah's law. I'm just waiting for these fools to quit flogging it and play their hand. Once more, the cockpit speakers crackle. For a time, nothing comes out of them.

"Phn'glui mgl'whnaf Cthulhu Ry'leh wgah-naghl fthagn." They're testing the mics. My Dad taught me that, in debased Atlantaean, the phrase was their answer to our Alif lam-mim. This book is not to be doubted.

But they're quoting the *Necronomicon*, not the Koran. The *Necronomicon* is Not To Be Doubted for all the wrong reasons. Even hearing it makes me want to pick up a sword and start cutting heads. Beside me, the kid's playing possum. Smart.

Waite grins, taking a deep breath through the gill-slits in his scabby throat. "Today shalt thou be with us in Paradise," he croaks.

No one on the whole plane has a problem hearing that.

The speakers are still on, ringing with dead silence over the whine of the engines and the rattle of the wings. Every passenger is in panic mode, too confused to really listen.

"Citizens of America, please do not attempt to thwart the Beloved who are now flying this Boeing 767 aircraft." The voice from the speakers is burbling, staticky, full of the wrong inflections.

"There will be one refueling stop over the Bermuda Triangle. Please to remain still and no one will be harmed until cabin is depressurized."

A knot of people, all ages and sexes, attempt to storm the cockpit, taking turns pounding on the door. A similar knot makes for the back, every commuter wanting to be the first one to hide in the lavatory. The flight attendants, Dr. Smith included, attempt to direct traffic and mostly get plowed under. The baby is wailing grand opera. The Devil commands.

"Your government sank the nuclear sub U.S.S. *Burnside* off Devil Reef in Massachusetts and then lied about it in the news. Our people are dying down there. You elected the ones who do this thing to us. Sacrifice must be made to Dagon and Great Ktulu-ili-mo'ku to repay for then. R'lyeh surfaces this night off the Forbidden Atoll. Draw near and know."

Even when I was seventeen, I spoke better English than these guys. I shake my head and move toward the kid, and he pushes me deliberately away with great force. The move is made to look random. He really is playing possum. I take my cue.

The world narrows down for me. There is no one else on that plane but myself and my adversary. A cheap Skilcraft pen has fallen onto the seat from the kid's pocket. I reach for it, not understanding what I see out the window.

It's like the Northern Lights are going on outside just for us, a fantastic rainbow stereopticon flicker-play, a spectral phantasy above the clouds. Mists of unknown hue swirl around the plane, faster and faster. All I can think, over and over, was Kill the head and the body will die…

I take two steps diagonally behind Waite, yank his head back and shove the pen up his nose with a brutal Hapkido palm-strike. The sound the pen makes when it hits cartilage is like a boning knife meeting a rack of lamb. Just for chuckles, I tear out both the Reverend's gills with my bare hands, cutting my palms up quite badly in the process.

I feel his essence surging and lapping around me, seeking to gain a foothold as its body dies. I'm humming a different chant now, focusing my energy into my pelvic floor and pushing the intruder out through my feet.

"No one in my body but me," I snarl. My teeth chop down on each other hard.

Waite slumps to the floor, leaking black ichor all over my gym shoes. But it's not quite Game Over. There's one more infidel on this plane. I smell It. I just hope it doesn't smell me.

Shoving my way through the throng, I reach the cockpit door. It was never completely locked. Fools. I kick it in.

A trembling, scaly thing mans the controls. It looks like it belongs in a carnival jar of formaldehyde. Three extremely leaky bodies in white shirts and gold epaulets clutter the floor. The creature looks hungrily out the window, snuffling up the last of the pilot's cocaine, rolling it around on toothless gums with one webbed finger.

It sees me and gets to its feet. I move on it, then—PONK. The coffeepot connects with its head, and the critter goes down. "God go with us, friend," the punk kid says from beside me in a good accent. The thing starts to get up. The kid kicks it boredly in the head with one Doc Marten boot. It makes a hrrumping noise and goes down again.

"Put your jaw back in place, and blink," he instructs me. For the first time, I really notice how careworn his face was, distantly pondering the terrors it must have witnessed as he speaks again. "I grew up in Arkham. I saw shit like this going on at my high school, man. These guys musta thought they were dealin' with a buncha amateurs. Now you—" He waits.

"I figured you were in some kind of Black Ops, since you didn't have a million war stories for me." His eyes plead. "Can you fly?"

I'm already frowning at the altimeter and sitting down. "Leave that to me."

Doctor Smith pops up behind us, looking relieved, holding a first-aid kit. My bloody hands grip the tiller. All the other flight attendants break into a ragged cheer. Then the passengers began to cheer, too.

I wonder how loudly they'd cheer if they knew my family trade. We've been assassins since the Crusades.

We Sabbah follow the Sufi path. What that means to those with our calling is simply a hunger for clipping spooks. Especially big-money spooks like the one who just got done bleeding cod liver oil all over my sneakers. Then again, for ten million dollars I could buy a lot more gym shoes. C'est la guerre.

Without asking, the kid sits down near the cooling clay of the co-pilot and grabs the radio.

"Mayday, mayday, mayday," he rasps, "This is Flight 180. I have no idea where we are, but we got a good pilot. Tell me what's up..."

My money will be in the bank by the time I land this bird, take three showers and hunt for a bottle of emotional bleach. After that, as I promised myself, I'm done.

At the thought, my tear-ducts decide to start working again.

ಚ ಎ

"So do not become weak, or sad, and you shall triumph if you are indeed believers."

—Koran 3:139

Bad Sushi

Cherie Priest

aku's hand shook.

In it, he held a pinch of wasabi, preparing to leave the condiment as a peaked green dollop beside a damp pile of flesh-colored ginger. He hesitated, even though his fellow chef slapped the kitchen bell once, twice, a third time—and the orders were backing up.

The waitress flashed Baku a frown.

Some small fact was wiggling around in his expansive memory. In the back of his sinuses, he felt a tickle of sulfur. The kitchen in Sonada's smelled like soy sauce and sizzling oil, and frying rice; but Baku also detected rotten eggs.

He smeared the glob of gritty paste onto the rectangular plate before him, and he pushed the neatly-sliced sushi rolls into the pick-up window. The hot yellow smell grew stronger in his nose, but he could work through it. All it took was a little concentration.

He reached for his knives. The next slip in the queue called for a California roll, a tuna roll, and a salmon roll. Seaweed. Rice. Fish meat, in slick, soft slabs. He wrapped it all expertly, without thinking. He sliced the rolls without crushing them and slid them onto the plate.

This is why Sonada's kept Baku, despite his age. He told them he was seventy, but that was a lie by eight years—an untruth offered because his employers were afraid he was too old to work. But American Social Security wasn't enough, and the work at the restaurant wasn't so hard. The hours were not so long.

The other workers were born Americans. They didn't have to take the test or say the pledge, one hand over their hearts.

Baku didn't hold it against them, and the others didn't hold his original nationality against him, either. They might have, if they'd known the uniform he'd once worn. They might have looked at him differently, these young citizens, if they'd known how frantically he'd fired, and how he'd aimed for all the bright blue eyes.

There it was again. The sulfur.

Baku had tripped over a G.I.'s body as he staggered toward the beach at Cape Esperance, but he hadn't thought much of it. He'd been preoccupied at the time—thinking only of meeting the secret transport that would take him out of Guadalcanal. The Emperor had declared the island a lost cause, and an evacuation had been arranged. It had happened under cover of night. The transport had been a crushing rush of thirteen thousand brown-eyed men clamoring for the military ferry. The night had reeked of gunpowder, and body odor, and sulfur, and blood.

Baku thought again of the last dead American he'd seen on Guadalcanal, the man's immobile body just beginning to stink in the sunset. If someone had told him, back in 1942, that in sixty years he'd be serving the dead American's grandchildren sushi rolls…Baku would have never believed it.

He looked at the next slip of lined white and green paper.

Shrimp rolls. More tuna.

Concentrate.

He breathed in the clean, sparse scent of the seafood—so faint it was almost undetectable. If it smelled like more than salt and the ocean, it was going rotten. There were guidelines, of course, about how cold it must be kept and how it must be stored—but the old chef didn't need to watch any thermometers or check any dates. He knew when the meat was good. He knew what it would taste like, lying on top of the rice, and dipped lightly in a small puddle of soy sauce.

One order after another, he prepared them. His knives flashed, and his fingers pulled the sticky rice into bundles. His indefatigable wrists jerked and lurched from counter to bowl to chopping block to plate.

Eventually, with enough repetition and enough concentration, the remembered eggy nastiness left his head.

When his shift was over, he removed his apron and washed his knives.

He dried the knives each in turn, slipping them into a cloth pouch that he rolled up and carried home. The knives belonged to him, and they were a condition of his employment. They were good knives, made of German steel by a company that had folded ages before. Baku would work with no others.

At home that night, he lay in bed and tried to remember what had brought on the flashback. Usually there was some concrete reason—an old military uniform, a glimpse of ribbon that looked like a war medal, or a Memorial Day parade.

What had brought him back to the island?

At home in bed, it was safe to speculate. At home, in the small apartment with the threadbare curtains and the clean kitchen, it was all right to let his mind wander.

Sixty years ago there was a war and he was a young man. He was in the Emperor's army and he went to the South Pacific, and there was an island. The Americans dug in, and forced the Japanese troops to retreat.

They sneaked away at night, from the point at Cape Esperance. Personnel boats had been waiting. "There were thirteen-thousand of us," he breathed to himself in his native tongue. "And we left in the middle of the night, while the Americans slept."

The water had been black and it had been calm, as calm as the ocean ever was. Hushed, hushed, and hushed, the soldiers slogged into the water to meet the transports. In haste and in extreme caution, they had boarded the boats in packs and rows. They had huddled down on the slat seats and listened to the furtive cacophony of oars and small propellers.

He seemed to recall a panic—not his own. Another man, someone badly hurt, in mind and body. The man had stood up in the boat and tried to call out. His nearest neighbor tackled him, pulled him back down into his seat; but the ruckus unsettled the small craft.

Baku was sitting on the outside rail, one of the last men crammed aboard.

When the boat lunged, he lost his balance. Over the side he toppled, and into the water. It was like falling into ink with a riptide. Fear was halted by the fierce wetness, and his instincts were all but exhausted by days of battle. He thought to float, though. He tried to right himself, to roll out of the fetal suspension.

And something had stopped him—hard.

Even after sixty years, the memory of it shocked him—the way the thing had grabbed him by the ankle. The thing that seized him felt like a living cable made of steel. It coiled itself around his leg, one loop, two loops, working its way to a tighter grip with the skill of a python and the strength of something much, much larger.

Inside Baku's vest he carried a bayonet blade made of carbon steel. It was sharp enough to cut paper without tearing it. It was strong enough to hold his weight.

His first thought and first fear was that this was a strange new weapon devised by the Americans; but his second thought was that this was no weapon at all, but a living creature. There was sentience and insistence in the way the thing squeezed and tugged. He curled his body up to pull his hand and his knife closer to the clutching, grasping thing.

And because he was running out of air, he arched his elbow up and tightened his leather-tough wrists. Even then they'd been taut and dense with muscle. He'd grown up beside the ocean, cutting the fish every day, all day, until the Emperor had called for his service and he'd taken up a gun instead.

So it was with strength and certainty that he brought the knife down into the thing that held his leg.

It convulsed. It twitched, and Baku stabbed again. The water went warmer around his ankle, and the terrible grip slackened. Again. A third time, and a fourth. In desperation, he began to saw, unafraid that he would hit his own flesh, and unaware of the jagged injury he created when he did so.

By then his air was so low and he was so frightened, that he might have cut off his whole leg in pursuit of escape. But after several heroic hacks Baku all but severed the living lasso; and at that moment, one of his fellow soldiers got a handful of the back of his shirt. Human hands pulled him up, and out, and over—back into the boat. A faint and final tug at his leg went nearly unnoticed as the last of the thing stretched, split, and tore.

On the floor of the boat Baku gasped and floundered. The other soldiers covered him with their hands, hushing him. Always hushing. The Americans might hear.

He shook and shook—taking comfort in the circle of faces that covered him from above and shut out the star-spangled sky. At last he breathed and the breath was not hard-won.

But he did not feel safe.

Around his leg the leftovers clung. He unwound the ropy flesh from his own quivering limb and the dismembered coil fell to the boat bottom where it twitched, flopped, and lay still.

"What is it?" someone asked. "What is it?" the call was echoed around the boat in quiet voices.

No one wanted to touch it, so no one did until the next day.

Baku stared down at the thing and wondered what it had once belonged to. All he had to judge it by was the lone, partial tentacle, and it did not tell him much. It was a sickly greenish brown and it came with a smell to match—as if it were made of old dung, spoiled crab meat, and salt; and suction pads lined one side, with thorny-looking spines on the other. He did not remember the bite of the spines, but his leg wore the results.

"What is it?" the question came again from one of his fellow soldiers, who poked at the leavings of the peculiar predator with the end of his gun.

"I don't know. Have you ever seen anything like it?"

"Never."

Never before that night had he seen anything like the tentacle. It represented no squid or octopus that Baku knew, and he was born into a family that had fed itself from the water for generations. Baku thought he had seen everything the ocean had to offer, even from the bottom-most depths where the fish had blind-white eyes, and the sand was as fine as flour. But he'd never seen a thing like that, and he would never forget it. The scars on his legs would remind him for the rest of his life, even when he was an old man, and living in America, and lying in bed on a cool spring night... half dozing and half staring at the ceiling fan that slowly churned the air above him.

And it was that smell, and that remembered texture of stubborn rubber, that had reminded him of the sulfur stench at Guadalcanal.

Twice in his life now, he had breathed that nasty, tangy odor and felt a tough cord of flesh resist the push of his knife.

His stomach turned.

The next day at work, Baku wondered if the store manager had noticed anything strange about the sushi. He asked, "Are we getting different meat now? It seemed different yesterday, when I was cutting it for the rolls."

The manager frowned, and then smiled. "I think I know what you mean. We have a new vendor for some of the fish. It's a company from New England, and they carry a different stock from the Gulf Coast company. But they come with very good references, and they cost less money than the others, too. They distribute out of a warehouse downtown, by the pier at Manufacturer's Row."

"I see."

"Was there a problem with the fish?"

Baku was torn.

He did not want to complain. He never liked to complain. The manager was happy with the new vendor, and what would he say? That the octopus meat reminded him of war?

"No," he said. "No problem. I only noticed the change, that's all." And he went back to work, keeping his eyes open for more of the mysterious meat.

He found it in the squid, and in the crab. It lurked amid the pale bits of ordinary fish and seafood, suspicious landmines of a funny smell and a texture that drove him to distraction.

Baku watched for the new vendor and saw him one day driving up in a big white truck with a large "A" painted on the side. He couldn't make out the company's name; it was printed in a small, elaborate script that was difficult to read. The man who drove the truck was a tall, thin fellow shaped like an egg roll. His skin was doughy and hairless.

When he moved the chilled packages of sealed, wrapped food on the dolly, he moved with strength but without hurry. He walked like a sea lion, with a gently lumbering gait—as if he might be more comfortable swimming than walking.

His big, round eyes stared straight ahead as he made his deliveries. He didn't speak to anyone that Baku ever saw, and when he was handed a pen to sign at the clipboard, he looked at it blankly before applying his mark to the proper forms.

"I think he's *challenged*," the Sonada's manager said. "Mentally challenged, you know. Poor man."

"Poor man," Baku agreed. He watched him get into his truck and drive away. He would be back on Tuesday with more plastic-wrapped boxes that emitted fogged, condensed air in tiny clouds around their corners.

And meanwhile, business boomed.

Every night the restaurant was a little more packed, with a few more patrons. Every night the till rang longer, and the receipts stacked higher on the spike beside the register. Every night the waitresses ran themselves more ragged and collected more tips.

By Saturday, Sonada's was managing twice its volume from the week before. By Sunday, people were lined out the door and around the side of the building. It did not matter how long they were told to wait.

They waited.

They were learning an unnatural patience.

Baku took on more hours, even though the manager told him it was not necessary. A new chef was hired to help with the added burden and another would have been helpful, but the kitchen would hold no more workers.

Baku insisted on the extra time. He wanted to see for himself, and to watch the other men who cut the sushi rolls and steamed the sticky rice. He wanted to see if they saw it too—the funny, pale meat the color of a pickle's insides. But if anyone noticed that something was out of order, no one spoke about it. If something was different, something must be good—because business had never been better.

And the old chef knew that one way or another, the strange meat was bringing the customers in.

Even though Sonada's served a broad variety of Asian food, no one ever ordered fried rice anymore, or sesame chicken. Egg rolls had all but vanished from the menu, and Baku couldn't remember the last time beef was required for a dish.

Everyone wanted the sushi, and Baku knew why.

And he knew that something was happening to the regular patrons, the ones who came every night. From the kitchen window that overlooked the lobby he saw them return for supper like clockwork, and with every meal they took, they were changed.

They ate faster, and walked slower. They talked less.

Baku began to stay longer in the kitchen, and he rushed hurriedly to his car at night.

Baku paused his unending slicing, cutting, scooping and scraping to use the washroom. He closed the door behind himself and sighed into the quiet. For the first time all evening, he was alone. Or so he thought.

All the stall doors were open, save the one at the farthest end of the blue-tiled room—which was closed only a little way. From within it, someone flushed.

Out of politeness, Baku pretended not to see that the other man had left the door ajar. He stepped to the nearest sink and washed his hands. He covered them with runny pink soap and took his time building lather, then rinsing under the steamy tap water. He relished the heat.

The kitchen had become so cold in the last week, since the grills were rarely working and the air conditioner was running full-blast. Instead of sporadic warmth from the stoves, the refrigerator door was incessantly opened and closed—bringing fresh meat for the sushi rolls. The chefs handled cold meat, seaweed, and sticky rice for nine hours at a time.

His knuckles never thawed.

But while he stood there, warming his fingers beneath the gushing stream, he noticed the sound of repeated flushing foaming its way into the tiled room. Dampness crept up the sole of Baku's shoe. Water puddled on the floor around his feet. He flipped the sink's chrome lever down, shutting off the water.

He listened.

The toilet's denouement was interrupted before the plumbing could finish its cycle and another flush gurgled. A fresh tide of water spilled out from under the door.

Baku craned his neck to the right, leaning until he could see the square of space between the soggy floor and the bottom of the stall. Filthy gray sneakers stood ankle-deep in overflow. The laces were untied; they floated like the hair of a drowning victim.

"Hello?" Baku called softly. He did not want a response. "Can I help you with something, sir?" His English was heavy, but he was careful with his pronunciation.

He took a cautious step forward, and that small shuffle cleared nearly half the distance between him and the stall door. He took a second step, but he made that one even tinier than the first, and he put out his hand.

The tips of his fingers quivered, as they tapped against the painted metal door. He tried to ask, "Are you all right?" But the words barely whispered out of his throat.

A groan answered him without offering specifics.

He pushed the door.

He found himself staring at a man's hunched back and a sweaty patch of shirt between his shoulder blades. The shirt itself was the beige kind that comes with an embroidered nametag made in dark blue thread. When the man at the toilet turned around, Baku read that the tag said "Peter," but he'd guessed that much already. He knew the shirt. It was the uniform worn by the man who drove the delivery truck each Tuesday, Thursday, and Sunday.

Peter's eyes were blank and watery. They looked like olives in a jar.

The deliveryman seemed to know that his peculiar ritual was being questioned, and he did not care for the interruption. With another petulant groan he half lunged, half tipped forward.

Baku recoiled, pulling the door closed with his retreat.

Peter was thwarted a few seconds longer than he should have been. Perhaps it was only his innate imbecility that made him linger so long with the slim obstacle, but it bought the old chef time to retreat. He slipped first, falling knee-down with a splash, but catching himself on the sink and rising. Back into the hall and past the ice machine he stumbled, rubbing at his knee and shaking from the encounter. It had been too strange, too stupidly sinister.

At the far end of the dining area a big round clock declared the time. For a moment he was relieved. He needed to go home, and if the clock could be believed, he had less than an hour remaining on his shift.

But his relief dissolved as quickly as it had blossomed. The scene beneath the clock was no more reassuring than the one in the bathroom.

Dozens of people were eating in silence, staring down at their plates or their forks. They gazed with the same bland olive eyes, not at each other but at the food. The waitresses and the one lone male waiter lurked by the kitchen window without talking. The cash register did not ring.

Where was the manager? He'd been in and out for days, more out than in. The assistant manager, then. Anyone, really—anyone who was capable of sustaining convincing eye contact would suffice.

Into the kitchen Baku ducked, anticipating an oasis of ordinary people.

He was disappointed. The cooks stood in pockets of inattentive shoe-gazing, except for the two who had made their way back into the refrigerator. From within its chilly depths, Baku heard the sounds of sloppy gnawing.

Was he the only one who'd not been eating the sushi?

He turned just in time to hear the bathroom door creak open. Peter moaned as he made his way into the corridor and then began a slow charge towards the chef.

The grunting, guttural call drew the attention of the customers and the kitchen staff. They turned to see Peter, and then the object of his attention. All faces aimed themselves at Baku, whose insides immediately worked into a tangle.

Two nearby customers came forward. They didn't rise from their seats or fold their napkins, and they didn't put down their forks. Together they stood, knocking their chairs backwards and crashing their thighs against the table, rocking it back and forth. The woman raised her hand and opened her mouth as if she meant to speak, but only warm air and half-chewed sushi fell out from between her lips. Her dinner companion managed a louder sound—like an inflatable ball being squeezed—and the low, flatulent cry roused the remaining customers and the kitchen staff alike. In a clumsy wave, they stumbled towards Baku.

On the counter, he spied the folded roll of his fine German knives. He fired one hand out to snag it; then he tucked it under his arm and pushed the glass door with his elbow.

Behind him the crowd rallied, but it was a slow rally that was impeded by everything in its path. Chairs thwarted them. Counters baffled them.

Baku hurried. Outside the sky was growing dark with a too-early dusk brought on by a cloudy almost-storm. He tumbled into the parking lot and pulled the door shut behind his back.

The bus stop was empty.

The chef froze. He always rode the bus home. Every night. Rain or shine he waited under the small shelter at the corner.

Over his shoulder he watched the masses swarm behind the windows, pushing their hands through the blinds and slapping their palms against the glass. They were slow, but they wouldn't give him time to wait for the 9:30 bus.

He crushed at his knives, taking comfort from their strength wrapped inside the cloth. His knuckles curled around them.

As a young man he'd confronted the ocean with nets and hooks, drawing out food and earning his livelihood. Then he'd been called as a soldier, and he'd fought for his country, and to serve his Emperor. In the years that followed he had put away his bayonet and had taken up the knives of a cook; he had set aside the uniform of war and put on an apron.

But knives like these could be weapons, too.

"I am not too old," he breathed. Behind him, a dozen pairs of hands slapped at the windows, rattling the blinds. Shoulders pummeled at the doors, and the strained puff of a pneumatic hinge told Baku that they were coming. "I am not too old to work. Not too old to cut fish. I am *not* too old to fight."

Peter's delivery vehicle sat open in the parking lot's loading zone. The refrigerated trailer compartment hung open, one door creaking back and forth in the pre-storm breeze. A faint briny smell wafted forth.

Baku limped to the trailer door and took a deep breath of the tepid air. The contents within were beginning to turn.

He slammed the metal door shut and climbed into the cab. He set his knives down on the passenger's seat and closed his own door just as the first wave of angry patrons breached the restaurant door.

At first, he saw no keys. He checked the ignition and the glove box. But when he checked the visor a spare set tumbled down into his lap. He selected the engine key without a tremor and plugged it into the slot. The engine gagged to life, and with a tug of the gearshift, the vehicle rolled forward—pushing aside a pair of restaurant patrons, and knocking a third beneath the van's grille.

Baku did not check to see them in the rearview mirror.

Downtown, to Manufacturer's Row. That's where the manager had said the new meat came from. That's where Baku would go.

He roughly knew the way, but driving was something he'd forgotten about years before. Busses were cheap to ride, and cars were expensive to maintain. This van was tall and top-heavy. It reacted slowly, like a boat. It swayed around corners and hesitated before stopping, or starting, or accelerating.

He drove it anyway.

The streets were more empty than not. The roads were mostly clear and Baku wished it were otherwise. All the asphalt looked wet to him, shining under the streetlamps. Every corner promised a sliding danger. But the van stayed upright, and Baku's inexpert handling bothered no one.

He arrived at the distribution center and parked on the street in front of a sign that said "Loading Zone," and he climbed out of the cab, letting the door hang open. So what if it was noted and reported? Let the authorities come. Let them find him and ask why he had forced his way into the big old building.

At first he thought this as a whim, but then he began to wish it like a prayer. "Let them come."

In his arm he felt a pain, and in his chest there was an uncomfortable tightness from the way he breathed too hard. "Let them bring their guns and their lights. I might need help."

From a sliver of white outlined vertically along the wall, Baku saw that the front door was open.

He put his face against the crack and leaned on his cheekbone, trying to see inside. The space was not enough to peep through, but the opening was big enough to emit an atrocious smell. He lifted his arm and buried his nose in the crook of his elbow. He wedged his shoulder against the heavy slab of the door and pushed. The bottom edge of the sagging door grated on the concrete floor.

Within, the odor might have been overpowering to someone unaccustomed to the smell of saltwater, fish, and the rot of the ocean. It was bad enough for Baku.

Two steps sideways, around the crotchety door, and he was inside.

His shoes slipped and caught. The floor was soaked with something more viscous than saline, more seaweed-brown than clear. He locked his knees and stepped with care. He shivered.

The facility was cold, but not cold enough to freeze his breath. Not quite. Industrial refrigerators with bolted doors flanked one wall, and indoor cranes were parked haphazardly around the room. There were four doors—one set of double doors indicated a corridor or hall. A glance through the other three doors suggested office space; a copy room, a lunch room with tables, and two gleaming vending machines.

Somewhere behind the double doors a rhythmic clanking beat a metal mantra. There was also a mechanical hum, a smoother drone. Finally there came a lumpy buzz like the sound of an out-of-balance conveyor belt.

In his hand, Baku's fist squeezed tightly around his roll of knives.

He unclenched his fingers and opened the roll across his palm. It would do him no good to bring them all sheathed, but he could not hold or wield more than two. So for his right hand, he chose a long, slim blade with a flexible edge made to filet large fish. For his left, he selected a thicker, heavier knife—one whose power came from its weight. The remaining blades he wrapped up, tied, and left in a bundle by the door.

"I will collect you on the way out," he told them.

Baku crept on toward the double doors, and he pushed tentatively at them.

They swayed and parted easily, and the ambient noise jumped from a background tremor to a sharper throb.

The stink swelled too, but he hadn't vomited yet and he didn't intend to, so Baku forced the warning bile back down to whence it had come. He would go toward the smell. He would go toward the busy machines and into the almost frigid interior. His plan was simple, but big: He would turn the building off. All of it. Every robot, light, and refrigerator. There would be a fuse box or a power main.

As a last resort, he might find a dry place to start a fire.

On he went, and the farther his explorations took him, the more he doubted that a match would find a receptive place to spark.

Dank coldness seeped up through his shoes and his feet dragged splashing wakes along the floor. He slipped and stretched out an arm to steady himself, leaning his knuckles on the plaster. The walls were wet, too. He wiped the back of his hand on his pants. It left a trail of slime.

The clank of machines pounded harder, and with it the accompanying smell insinuated itself into every pore of Baku's body, into every fold of his clothing.

But into the heart of the warehouse he walked—one knife in each hand—until he reached the end of the corridor that opened into a larger space—one filled with sharp-angled machines reaching from the floor to the ceiling. Rows of belts on rollers shifted frosty boxes back and forth across the room from trucks to chilled storage. Along the wall were eight loading points with trucks docked and open, ready to receive shipments and disperse them. He searched for a point of commonality, or for some easy spot where all these things must come together for power. Nothing looked immediately promising, so he followed the cables on the ceiling with his eyes, and he likewise traced the cords along the floor. Both sets of lines followed the same path, into a secondary hallway.

Baku shuffled sideways and slithered with caution along the wall and toward the portal where the electric lines all pointed. Once through the portal, Baku found himself at the top of a flight of stairs. Low-power emergency lights illuminated the corridor in murky yellow patches.

It would have to be enough.

When he strained to listen, Baku thought he detected footsteps, or maybe even voices below. He tiptoed towards them, keeping his back snugly against the stair rail, holding his precious knives at the ready.

He hesitated on the bottom stair, hidden in the shadows, reluctant to take the final step that would put him firmly in the downstairs room. There in the basement the sad little emergency lights were too few and far-between to give any real illumination. The humidity, the chill, and the spotty darkness made the entire downstairs feel like night at the bottom of a swimming pool.

A creature with a blank, white face and midnight-black, lidless eyes emerged from inside an open freezer. It was Sonada's manager, or what was left of him.

"You," the thing accused.

Baku did not recoil or retreat. He flexed his fingers around the knife handles and took the last step down into the basement.

"You would not eat the sushi with us. Why?" The store manager was terribly changed without and within; even his voice was barely recognizable. He spoke as if he were talking around a mouthful of seaweed.

Baku circled around the manager, not crossing the floor directly but staying with his back to the wall. The closer he came, the slower he crept until he halted altogether. The space between them was perhaps two yards.

"Have you come now for the feast?" the manager slurred.

Baku was not listening. It took too much effort to determine where one word ended and the next began, and the message didn't matter anyway. There was nothing the manager could say to change Baku's mind or mission.

Beside the freezer with its billowing clouds of icy mist there was a fuse box. The box was old-fashioned; there were big glass knobs the size of biscuits and connected to wiring that was as frayed and thick as shoelaces. It might or might not be the heart of the building's electrical system, but at least it might be *connected* to the rest. Perhaps, if Baku wrenched or broke the fuses, there was a chance that he could short out the whole building and bring the operation to a halt. He'd seen it in a movie he'd watched once, late at night when he couldn't sleep.

If he could stop the electricity for even an hour—he could throw open the refrigerators and freezers and let the seafood thaw. Let it rot. Let it spoil here, at the source.

The manager kept talking. "This is the new way of things. He is coming, for the whole world."

"So this is where it comes?" Baku asked, speaking over the manager. He took a sideways shuffle and brought himself closer to the manager, to the freezer, to the fuse box.

"No. We are not the first."

Baku came closer. A few feet. A hobbled scuffing of his toes. He did not lower the knives, but the manager did not seem to notice.

"Tell me about this. Explain this to me. I don't understand it."

"Yes," the manager gurgled. "Like this." And he turned as if to gesture into the freezer, as if what was inside could explain it all.

Baku jumped then, closing the gap between them. He pushed with the back of his arm and the weight of his shoulder, and he shoved the manager inside the freezer.

The door was a foot thick; it closed with a hiss and a click. Only if he listened very hard could Baku hear the angry protests from within. He pressed his head against the cool metal door and felt a fury of muted pounding on the other side.

When he was comfortable believing that the manager would not be able to interfere, he removed his ear from the door. He turned his attention again to the fuse box, regarding it thoughtfully.

Then, one after the other, the fuzzy white pods of light were extinguished.

Darkness swallowed the stray slivers of light which were left.

The basement fell into perfect blackness.

And the heavy thing that struck Baku in the chest came unseen, unheard, but with all the weight of a sack of bricks.

The shock sent him reeling against the freezer door. He slammed against it and caught himself by jabbing his knives into the concrete floor, the door, and anything else they could snag.

Somewhere nearby the thing regrouped with a sound like slithering sandbags. Baku's ear told him that it must be huge—but was this an illusion of the darkness, of the echoing acoustics? He did not know if the thing could see him, and he did not know what it was, only that it was powerful and deadly.

On the other side of the room Baku's assailant was stretching, lashing, and reaching. Baku flattened his chest against the wall and leaned against it as he tried to rise, climbing with the knives, scraping them against the cement blocks, cutting off flecks and strips of paint that fluttered down into his hair and settled on his eyelashes.

A loud clank and a grating thunk told Baku that his knives had hit something besides concrete. He reached and thrust the knife again. He must be close to the fuse box; he'd only been a few feet away when the lights went out.

The thudding flump that accompanied his opponent's movement sounded louder behind Baku as he struggled to stand, to stab. Something jagged and rough caught at his right hand.

A warm gush soaked his wrist and he dropped that knife. With slippery fingers he felt knobs, and what might have been the edge of a slim steel door panel. He reached for it, using this door to haul himself up, but the little hinges popped under his weight and he fell back down to his knees.

The monstrous unseen thing snapped out. One fat, foul-smelling limb crashed forward, smacking Baku's thighs, sweeping his legs out from underneath him.

His bleeding right hand grazed the dropped knife, but he couldn't grasp it. Holding the remaining blade horizontally in his left hand, Baku locked his wrist. When the creature attacked again, Baku sliced sideways.

A splash of something more gruesome than blood or tar splashed against the side of the face.

He used his shoulder to wipe away what he could. The rest he ignored. The wet and bloody fingers of his right hand curled and fastened themselves on a small shelf above his head.

The thing whipped its bulk back and forth but it was not badly hurt. It gathered itself together again, somewhere off in the corner. If Baku could trust his ears, it was shifting its attack, preparing to come from the side. He rotated his left wrist, moving the knife into a vertical position within his grip. He opened and closed his fingers around it. To his left, he heard the thing coming again.

Baku peered up into the darkness over his head where he knew the fuse box now hung open.

The creature scooted forward.

Baku hauled himself up and swung the fine German steel hard at the box, not the monster—with all the weight he could put behind it. It landed once, twice, and there came a splintering and sparking. Plastic shattered, or maybe it was glass. Shards of debris rained down.

One great limb crushed against Baku and wrapped itself around his torso, ready to crush, ready to break what it found. The man could not breath; there in the monster's grip he felt the thing coil itself, slow but wickedly dense, as if it were filled with wet pebbles.

In the center of the room the beast's bulk shuddered unhappily as it shifted, and shuffled, and skidded. The appendage that squeezed Baku was only one part of a terrible whole.

Before his breath ran out, before his hands grew weak from lost blood and mounting fear, Baku took one more stab. The heavy butcher's blade did not bear downward, but upward and back.

The fuse box detonated with a splattering torrent of fire and light.

For two or three seconds Baku's eyes remained open. And in those seconds he marveled at what he saw, but could have never described. Above and beyond the thunderous explosion of light in his head, the rumbling machines ceased their toil.

The current from the box was such that the old man could not release the knife, and the creature could not release its hold on the old man.

As the energy coursed between them, Baku's heart lay suddenly quiet in his chest, too stunned to continue beating. He marveled briefly, before he died, how electricity follows the quickest path from heaven to earth, and how it passes with pleasure through those things that stand in water.

The Dream of the Fisherman's Wife

John Hornor Jacobs

In the afternoon, when the café and the cobbled lane beside the quay empties until the ships come back in, she stands in her apron among the tables and stares out past the seawall, beyond the rocky shore tangled with bladderwrack and snarls of trawler's nylon nets, to the sea.

Flights of gulls wheel and bank in a grey sky while a trio of boys yell good-natured profanity at each other as they roust an upturned skiff from the shore, flip it, and push it into the foam.

"Maebe, here comes Lancelot from the visitor's bureau," Laura says through the open window, hands full of dishes but standing in the interior dining area. Laura's wide face gleams in the low half-light of the afternoon, and she gives a grin to Maebe that is as playful as it is lurid.

"Now's the time. And he is handsome."

Maebe follows Laura's gaze down the lane, past the bright confections of trinket and t-shirt shops, past the tourists wearing garish shirts adorned with flowers that only bloom under the brighter sun of latitudes thousands of miles away.

The man from the visitor's bureau grins at Maebe and waves. When he gets close enough, he calls her name.

She waits.

He orders a Diet Coke and a salad with grilled chicken and sits with his back to the quay, so he can watch her, watch the way her body moves under her clothes, the heaviness of her hips, the sway of her breasts.

"Sit with me."

"That's not a good idea."

He's blond and lean and has the light, translucent fluff that shows where the razor didn't touch, high on his cheek. He wears white tennis shoes with no socks, khakis, and his collar up in a way that makes her want to cry for his desperation. He's a creature of sun and surf and boarding schools. He loves to sail.

"Sit with me."

Laura grins from inside and shuffles off to dump dishes in the sink. Maebe sits with the man, looking beyond him to the boys and their skiff. They have moved out past the breakers and now the skiff bobs on the great face of sea.

"I love this weather. Gusty. You'll be at the regatta this weekend?"

"No."

"No?"

"Not really interested in sailing."

He smiles as if this is the most amusing thing he's ever heard. He looks at her hand. The one with the wedding-band.

"You've worn that as long as I've known you."

"I was married. It's hard to forget."

He sits, silent, sipping his drink. But he doesn't look upset by her statement, just curious and wanting to let the matter pass, like a cloud scuttling across the face of sun.

But she looks at him and says, "He went down to the sea."

The man smiles, again, at her antiquated way of saying death by drowning.

"Will you meet me tonight?"

Maebe stands and goes into the dim interior of the café and gets his salad. He's still smiling when she places it in front of him and smoothes her apron. She sits again and turns her face back toward the lane, the seawall.

He eats with the exuberance of the young. When he's done, he wipes the corners of his mouth with a napkin and says, "You won't meet me?"

He's asked every day for the last two weeks and Maebe has always replied the same way. "No, thank you. But you're very kind to ask."

The boys in their skiff have disappeared, out beyond everything she knows. The gunmetal clouds shift, and a pillar of sunlight breaks on the surface of the sea, shattering into a million bits. And then it is gone.

It has been too long.

Laura leers at her from inside the café.

"Yes," Maebe says, and takes his hand. "I'd love to see you. Let me give you my address."

៚ ៚

He takes her to a restaurant down the coast and pushes the escargot and coq au vin possibly because he likes it and possibly because he thinks he should. She dips the restaurant's crusty bread into the escargot's garlic butter and it tastes like grease and ashes on her tongue. She shoves the food around on her plate with a fork and drinks expensive wine from an oversized glass.

"Most sailors love the Melges 24 class because of its speed and performance but weekenders love the simplicity. It's so easy to sail." Despite the pomp and ceremony of the French restaurant, he had ordered a beer and drank it from the bottle. He winked at her when the waiter scowled and said, "Hey, it's good beer! Microbrewery."

"So, you go every weekend?" she asks.

"Yah, pair runs. Me and Walter. Have you met him? We've just been sponsored by Trident Sails—I pulled a few strings through the ICVB—so this weekend's regatta means a lot to both of us."

He likes numbers and corporate acronyms. But he is handsome.

He looks at her closely. "The great thing about the Melges is it only takes two crewmemebers." He raises his eyebrows and waggles them at her comically. "So whaddya say?"

She sits in her chair, holding the napkin in her lap, staring at him.

"I'm sorry? What?"

"Sailing. Will you come with me?"

It takes a long moment, but she's confident that the horror washing over her doesn't spill onto her face.

"I'm not good in situations like that."

He grins at her, stabs a bit of chicken with his fork and pops it in his mouth.

"You'd be surprised at how easy it all is." He lowers his eyes. "And I'll be there to guide you the whole time."

"You mean, tonight?"

He nods and his smile is gone, replaced with a nervous expression that is ill-suited to his good looks.

"We pick a star and sail straight on till morning."

The thought of being out on the dark swell of ocean in a boat makes her shudder. His expression crumbles.

"It's cold in here," she says, taking his hand and hoping it explains her goosebumps. "I was thinking maybe we could go back to my place."

ໄ ໑

Before, at the restaurant, he'd been forceful. He ordered for Maebe, and was absolutely adamant that the sommelier was tipped amply. He put his arm around her on the walk back to the car. It made her sad, the role he wanted to play, that picture of modern American manhood. He talked of movies, and school and told jokes that she didn't understand, truly, but she smiled anyway.

But now, at her house, the little bungalow within a stone's throw of the beach, he's unsure of himself. He gulps down the drink she gives him, whiskey, and doesn't quite know what to do with his body in such a small space.

She gives him another drink and he looks at her pictures.

"This your husband?" He holds up an ornate silver frame that had been on the bookcase.

"No. My brother."

"Oh? What does he do?"

"He went down to the sea." She tilts her head at the small cameo on the wall. "There's my husband. Aaron."

The man looks at the photo, her dead husband staring back at him, and he remains there for a long while but eventually, as if he's making a decision, he turns and goes to sit on the sofa, next to Maebe. He drapes his arm over her shoulder, tugging her in, pressing his side against her.

He smells of tallow and whiskey and a whiff of the restaurant they'd just come from so it's not unpleasant when she kisses him. At first it's chaste, a simple pressing of the lips together and she has a moment's worry that he'll go no further, but soon he's exploring her mouth with his tongue, her chest with his hands.

When he's hard, she tugs him by the hand up from the couch into the bedroom.

His naked body bristles and she's fascinated by the perfect triangle of hair on his chest trailing down to his sex. His fingers and tongue feel good on her skin and his cock, pressing so hard against her, feels almost hot to the touch.

But he wants to please her. He traces kisses down to her center, to between her legs. He smiles up at her, his mouth above her most delicate spot, and she cups his face with her hands but eventually lets him go and he splits her open with his tongue.

It has been so long.

When her lips part, it feels like some seal has been broken and the sea is gushing forth past the seawall, flooding the whole world, and she tilts her head back and closes her eyes.

The sensations rise and crest and she feels like she's on a raft lost on the face of the dark, infinitesimal and wave-tossed, while something far below in the unseen depths rises, approaching the surface.

She gasps and locks her fingers in his blond hair. He draws up and away, his face glistening. He's on his knees when he grasps her legs and pulls her toward him. She's wide open when he takes his sex in hand, pausing before her portal.

It has been too long.

He doesn't see the shadow that comes into the bedroom and brings the hammer across the back of his skull with a dull crack. Maebe feels an instant of regret that Laura couldn't have waited a few moments longer.

ଧ ଔ

They go down to the sea, the sisters, dragging the naked man between them. He still breathes but his head is distended and blood darkens his back.

At the shore, Laura withdraws the knife and cuts him, twice, on each side of his genitals, slicing deep into his inner thighs. When the tendons are severed, his legs swing outward, splayed like a frog's legs, and blood pours into the surf.

They drag him as far as they can into the waves.

It's only a short wait for Aaron to come in from the sea. He and his brothers walk slowly, waves crashing around them. They're bloated and lantern-eyed, wrapped in skeins of bladderwrack and luminous in the light coming from the moon.

Aaron opens his mouth and water pours from his sodden lungs and looks at the man bleeding out into the waves. He turns to Maebe, slowly.

"Seabride," he says, his black tongue working like an eel in his mouth. "He comes."

Out beyond the breakers, the ocean rises and Maebe worries that there's been an earthquake calving huge tsunamis to drench the world in darkness. The sea swells and a massive shape broaches the surface and for a vertiginous moment, Maebe thinks that a shelf of land has cracked and been wrenched away from the plate of earth that makes the surface of her world, tipped on end from unstoppable tectonic forces. It rises, spanning miles and miles, up to the sky, blotting out the stars, the moon. She looks down at the man, the man who'd been with her in bed. He'd had a handsome face and kissed her so sweet.

Aaron's eyes blink like yellow lights being shuttered and he takes her hand in his cold, dead one. A tremendous wave crashes into them, pushing Maebe and Laura back a few steps but not swaying the men at all.

Her mouth tastes of salt and blood now and the man from the visitor's bureau is gone, his body carried away on the surf.

"He comes."

They watch the sea rise.

The Doom that Came to Inn/mouth

Brian McNaughton

We need not dust off the history of our nation's dealings with the Indians to find examples of genocide nor even go so far from our doorsteps as Montgomery, Alabama, to see instances of racism. Right here in our own state of Massachusetts, in February of 1928, agents of the U. S. Treasury and Justice Departments perpetrated crimes worthy of Nazi Germany against a powerless minority of our citizens.... When the dust of this jack-booted invasion had settled, no citizens [of Innsmouth, Massachusetts] were found guilty of any crime but the desire to live their peaceful lives in privacy and raise their children in the faith of their fathers. The mass internments and confiscations have never been plausibly explained or legally justified nor has compensation ever been so much as attempted to the innocent victims of this official hooliganism.

—Sen John F. Kennedy,
Commencement Address
to the Class of 1959 at
Miskatonic University,
Arkham, Mass.

Grandma had been a bootlegger, according to a family joke that we didn't share with her when we visited the nursing-home.

I did… once. "Is it true that you got busted by Eliot Ness, Grand-ma?" I asked, wise-ass kid that I was. She started carrying on about "Loch Ness," and getting very worked up, because that place was important to her religion.

"You got a golden crown waiting for you there, Joe, a crown that out-shines the sun," she croaked in her liquid way, a way that nobody but me understood half the time. Even when I got the words, I wasn't always sure what they meant.

My name isn't "Joe," by the way, it's Bob, Bob Smith, but she always got me confused with her brother that she adored, Joe Sargent, long ago passed over. Ignored or even mocked by the bitchy attendants who kept her strapped in her bed, she clung to a pathetic scrap of pride that her brother—or I—used to drive a dinky bus in Massachusetts that connected the Back of Beyond with the Middle of Nowhere.

She thought it was a big deal that he had been allowed to hobnob with "outside folk." Her religion had been dead set against contact with non-believ-ers, and only a few special people were allowed to "swim beyond the school," as she called any travel outside of Innsmouth. She bitterly regretted that she had been forced to swim way beyond the school and, what with one thing and another, never swam back.

Her life was pretty dismal. She was brought up in the strict cult that owned her hometown, not much of a town at its best, but she'd loved it. She never recovered from the shock when the Feds invaded and trashed her birthplace. Mom theorized that it was a Prohibition raid that got out of hand when some deputies recruited from nearby towns grabbed the chance to ex-press their prejudice against Innsmouth people. They roughed them up a lot, I guess, but to hear Grandma tell it, they herded people into cellars and set fire to the houses, then opened up with tommy-guns on anyone who tried to escape. But this was the United States of America, after all, and I was sure she had confused real events with movies about Nazis.

They sent her to a camp in Oklahoma, where she said a lot of people died of "separation from the Great Mother," which meant they missed the ocean. Swimming was a sacrament to these people.

Franklin D. Roosevelt inherited the mess when he came into office in 1932 and was reportedly horrified, although he had bigger problems on his mind at the time. Even though a U.S. Senator from Massachusetts, Marcus Allen Coolidge, tried to prevent or delay their release, the president just closed the camp with as little fuss as possible, leaving the inmates to find their own way home. I guess having a few hundred more bums on the road during the Great Depression seemed preferable to letting J. Edgar Hoover run a concentration camp.

Funny thing about that: Grandma insisted that Hoover had Innsmouth blood, that he had "the look," and that he persecuted his own people because they reminded him of a heritage he rejected, But she was always claiming famous people as "really one of us," Gloria Swanson and Edward G. Robinson, for instance. The only famous person she claimed to be certain about was Albert Fish, a cannibal and serial child-killer who went to the electric-chair in 1936.

She tried to make her way back east by hopping freight-trains, a pretty rough way for a woman to get around, though not all that uncommon in those days. It was not the most direct way to get anywhere, and with stops at jails and hobo-jungles, with detours that took her from Louisiana to Minnesota, she finally gave up when she got to Seattle. It was the wrong side of the continent, she said, but it was near an ocean.

There she met a fisherman named Newman, a bastard who married Grandma for no other reason than the universal superstition that her people had a way with fish. You can say "Innsmouth" to a trawlerman from Norway or Japan and, if he's old enough, you'll get a startled look of recognition, even though he usually doesn't want to talk about it. Newman used to take her along on his boat as a good-luck charm. When he didn't catch anything, he would beat her.

Grandma started to go round the bend after Mom was born, but it was fifteen years before Newman put her away. Mom left home not long after, and I was twelve years old before she made an effort to locate her mother and visit her.

I nagged her into doing it, because I have always been intensely curious about my roots. As far back as I can remember, I felt different from other people. I used to daydream about the magnificent welcome l would get when my real parents—the King and Queen of Mars, maybe—tracked me down. I had night-time dreams of flying, or maybe swimming, through the stupendous galleries of a twilight city like nothing I had even heard about on earth. I believe I had those dreams even before I was exposed to some of Grandma's wilder ravings.

For Mom, the reunion was shattering. "God, she's ugly! And she's crazy as a bedbug." Mom shivered with loathing. "And she smells." She cried all the way home on the bus. Later I would sometimes catch her looking at me in a strange way, as if trying to decide whether I was starting to take after Grandma.

She wanted nothing more to do with her mother. I believed she would have forbidden me to visit her if I asked, so I never asked. Knowing I was different, I learned early to protect my secrets and wriggle around the rules made for other people. In case you think I'm bragging, nobody even suspected me when I finally helped her escape, to say nothing of other things I've managed to get away with. But in those days I got to see Grandma once or twice a month by making up stories or skipping school to walk and hitchhike my way to the nursing-home, which was way out near Issaquah.

I didn't think she was ugly, I thought she was beautiful, so sleek and graceful in her old-fashioned way. Her huge eyes would transfigure her face when she talked about her home and her beliefs and seemed actually to be gazing on the vasty deep. I didn't think she was completely crazy, either, not when her stories raised echoes from my own dreams. As for smelling bad, that was the fault of the attendants, but I would raise hell whenever I went there until they cleaned her up and tended the sores from her restraints. Even when I was a kid, people knew I meant business when I looked at them in a certain way.

Since I was so different from other people, it stood to reason that my religion must be different from theirs, so I embraced Grandma's. I only wish I'd listened harder and understood more, and that Grandma's ordeal hadn't left her so confused. The story about the beautiful princess sleeping under the sea, waiting for me to wake her with the stones and the baptism, fueled my teen-age masturbation fantasies. I hated to consider the possibility that this was all wrong, that Grandma had mixed up her religion with the story of Sleeping Beauty.

Even though I searched every library and old bookshop in Washington and Oregon, even though I wrote dozens of letters to professors and churchmen, I never found any solid information about the beliefs and practices of the Esoteric Order of Dagon. Maybe there just weren't any more Dagonites.

Maybe I was the last one.

"My Grandma's brother used to drive this bus."

The driver glanced at me with annoyance.

"Not *this* bus, I mean, one that traveled the same route between Newburyport and Innsmouth in the old days, before—"

"See that sign? Don't talk to the driver," he said in the flat, Yankee way that reminds me of ducks quacking.

"You still don't much take kindly to Innsmouth folks around here, do you?"

"Sure, we do." At last I got a sort of smile out of him in the rear-view mirror as he added, "Because there ain't any."

I believed him. It was hard to imagine a romantically ruined town and its otherworldly cultists in this wasteland of stripmalls and Dairy Queens, where summer shacks had been converted into year-round homes for people who couldn't afford trailers. In this clutter that had been dumped willy-nilly onto a strangled marshland, you knew you were nearing the sea only when the junked automobiles in the yards gave way to junked boats, when the handwritten, cardboard signs in the windows said LIVE BAIT instead of BEAUTY SALON.

The last of the other passengers had got off at a mall with a K-Mart a few miles back. I had studied them all guardedly for any resemblance to Grandma, or maybe to myself, but they were nothing but long-chinned, quacking Yankees in John Deere hats or pastel hair-rollers. Nobody but me was going all the way to Innsmouth. I would have liked to ask the bus driver if he thought I had "the look," but maybe his attitude said it all.

My own look is pretty damned odd, ever since alopecia hit me like a truck last year. Some people with the disease can brazen it out: yeah, I got no hair, no eyebrows, no eyelashes, this is how I look, so fuck you, Jack. I admire such people, I even like their clean, smooth appearance, but I have spent my lifetime trying to blend in, so that's not my way. Besides, I couldn't have done that even if I'd wanted to, not after the onset of psoriasis a few months later. A perfectly bald head might go unremarked, but a perfectly bald, peeling head draws jeers in the street from children.

One alternative is to use false hair, and that might pass muster if you are rich enough to afford a very good rug and have the skill and patience of a makeup-artist. I wasn't rich. Pop had called himself an entrepreneur, which meant he would start doomed businesses and run them, or get me to run them—like the famous Ice Kween Ice Kreem Co.—until he got bored or they failed. After he died and I sorted out his disastrous affairs, I was left with a second-hand record shop in one of Seattle's more blighted areas, which I hung onto because I thought it would be a good way to find girls. I hadn't realized that it's mostly guys who buy old records. Correction: mostly guys who shoplift them.

A second alternative is to look for miracle cures. The first doctor I consulted had told me the brutal truth, that my hairlessness was hereditary and incurable, tough luck. He was more hopeful but no more helpful about the rash, which he said I would have until it went away. That didn't stop me from going around in my cheap wig, often-crooked eyebrows and ruddled face to every charlatan in the phone book.

None of them helped, but a Dr. Errol, who went to the trouble of asking for my medical and personal history, had heard about Innsmouth. He was up on all the angles of squeezing money out of patients, insurance companies and the government, and he urged me to apply for assistance under the Kennedy-Keaton Act. I didn't imagine it would be as simple as filling out a form and cashing a check, but I was floored by what I did get by registered mail within two days:

> Pursuant to provisions of the Federal Reparations Art of 1962, as amended in 1994, which offers compensation to residents of Innsmouth, MA, or their legal heirs or assigns for actions by agents of the U.S. Government on or about February 14, 1928, et seq., you are required to present yourself to the Field Office of the US. Public Health Service, 291 N Eliot St., Innsmouth, MA 01939-1750. in order to duly process your claim. Failure to appear is punishable by a fine of not more than ten thousand dollars ($10,000) and/or imprisonment for up to five (5) years.

> Food lodging and appropriate clothing will be provided for approximately ten (10) days while you undergo such tests and interviews as are required by law. Additionally, you are permitted to bring any personal effects which may be carried in a case no larger than 40X30x7.62 cm. and weighing no more than 2.3 kg. The importation of photographic equipment, audio or video recording devices, firearms or other weapons, alcohol, tobacco, combustible materials or controlled substances into the Facility is prohibited by law and punishable by a fine of not more than ten thousand dollars ($10,000) and/or imprisonment for up to Five (5) years.

> At the time of your induction into the Facility, you will be required to present your birth certificate, Social Security card and photographic ID (Passport, state driver's license, or Other deemed acceptable by the Examiner), current bank and credit-card statements, along with any documentation in the form of personal letters, diaries, family photographs, etc., that may relevate to your claim. Additionally, it is required that you complete the enclosed Questionnaire, Medical Release Forms and Waiver of Liability and return them, duly signed and notarized, to the above address, postmarked no later than five (5) business days from receipt of this communication.

Failure to comply with this notice or any of its provisions or with any rules, regulations or provisions not explicitized herein, is punishable by a fine of not more than ten thousand dollars ($10,000.00) and/or imprisonment for a period of up to five (5) years.

(signed) I.M. Saltonstall, M.D.
Field Director
Innsmouth Facility
U.S. Public Health Service.

Because I am the way I am, my first thought when I got this horrifying letter was to change my name and make a run for the Fiji Islands. Not only did I vividly recall Grandma's stories about tommy-guns and concentration-camps, I had my own reasons for avoiding government scrutiny. No amount of money was worth this kind of grief.

But.... I had always wanted to visit Innsmouth. I had been held back by the fear of barging in where outsiders were mistrusted. This summons gave me a legitimate reason to visit my ancestral home and question people who might have answers. My clerk could run the record-shop at least as well as I could in my absence, and the government promised in fine print to pay my travel expenses.

I had misgivings about the tone of the summons, but I told myself that was how bureaucrats did things, and I still believed that I wasn't living in the People's Republic of China. I filled out all the forms as honestly as I dared and sent them off. I actually began looking forward to my trip. I would go by bus and see the country. It would be the first real vacation I ever had, and it would be free.

Was it too much to hope that I might at last meet the torpid beauty beneath the sea, Mother Hydra, the Ice Kween who would be woken by my kisses and the special stones?

The jolting of the bus mused me from a half-doze. The road had become narrow and pot-holed, and on either side the marshland reasserted itself. Black little creeks ran through it, with here and there a boat forlornly anchored. I wondered how the owners could get to and from them in the trackless swamp without using other boats, and I laughed silently at the picture of confusion this evoked.

I was shocked to discover the bus-driver studying me sourly in the mirror. I wiped the smile from my face and tried to check my wig and eyebrows without seeming to.

My embarrassment vanished when I realized that the ocean shimmered before me through the windshield. The sight has always stirred profound emotions within me, the nameless but powerful feelings evoked in others by great music or poetry, and this, the Atlantic, the very ocean of my dreams, stirred me as I never had been before. I sat up straighter and wriggled for a better look, wishing the driver were the sort of person who would have let me run forward to gaze out beside him.

Then, in the foreground, I saw the town.

I had assumed it would be not much different from other depressed towns I had glimpsed on the way. Despite hard times and a genuine disaster in the past, the indomitable Yankees would have put a bold face on things and got on with their God-given mission to make money. Seaside real estate was worth something, wherever it might be, and I had half-expected to be affronted by a welter of marinas and condos, with maybe a theme-park, a water-slide and a gauntlet of shack-up motels. In my worst imaginings, the weird charm of the town would have been buried under a Sea-Tac Strip East that stretched all the way to Boston, complete with hookers who quacked like ducks.

I was wrong. The Feds had killed it seventy years ago, and it was still dead. Toward the beach, where you might have expected some rebuilding, the devastation was complete. The burnt-out shells of industrial buildings remained, but the sites of former houses were marked only by free-standing chimneys and clogged cellar-holes.

Just before we reached the bottom of a hill and the oceanfront dropped out of view, I noticed a metallic glimmer stitching the rubble. It looked like a fence topped with razor-wire, separating the seaward ruins from the rest of Innsmouth. Oddly, it looked shiny and new.

After contemptuously scrawling the receipt I required and ignoring my sarcastically cheerful promise to see him in a week or so, the driver dropped me at the Gilman House in Town Square, a once-gracious building in the Georgian mode whose upper windows, like most of the shops in the square, had been boarded up.

The clerk looked like a forlorn refugee from Woodstock who took his style from David Crosby, his tie knotted loosely as if worn under protest. As a further comment on his job and perhaps the town itself, his tie bore a reproduction of Edvard Munch's *The Scream*. He asked suspiciously, "Will you be checking in, Sir?"

"No, I have to stay at the Facility on Eliot Street, but can I check this bag here?"

"That Public Health thing?" His desire to peer closely at me struggled painfully with one to retreat beyond the range of contagion.

You see many people going that way?"

"None at all until lately. Then a couple weeks ago, four or five turned up. And there was a girl last week, Ms. Gilman, just like the hotel, she asked for directions." He added, as if to distinguish her from me and the others, "She was nice."

He put a receipt on the counter beside my ten-dollar bill, which he hadn't picked up.

"Hey, if you see Mr. Marsh out there, ask him what he wants done with his suitcase. We can't hang onto it forever, and I ain't heard a word from him since he left it."

Marsh, Gilman: these were both names from the old days. I was unprepared for a stirring of what you might call nostalgia-by-proxy. I looked away for a moment, and the seedy lobby was dimmed by tears. At last, I would actually get to meet some of *my* people!

"What's chances of getting in a swim before I go?"

"We got no pool. You'd have to go to the Ramada out on 1-A—"

"No, no, I meant in the ocean. Is there anyplace by the beach to change?"

"You don't want to swim in the ocean here. Well, maybe you do, but you can't. Everything east of the Old Square has been off limits since I been here, and that's twenty years come September."

"Off limits?" I'd seen the fence, but still the authoritarian phrase surprised me.

"Didn't you see that burnt-out area? An Air Force plane crashed. Back in the nineteen-fifties, I think it was, a terrible tragedy, wrecked half the town, and it was carrying a bomb they never found. I ain't caught myself glowing in the dark yet, so I guess it's safe enough here, but you don't want to go swimming in nookie-leer waste. That's why you're here for that Public Health thing, ain't you? Children of people who got zapped?"

"I guess," I said, hiding my amusement. "Are any people still living here from the old days? People named Marsh, or Gilman, or Sargent?"

"Some, I think, but you really want to ask Old Lady Waite, she's our local expert. Most of the people in town now are Portuguese, they came here to fish, only they have to go to Marblehead to do it on account of the pollution. But they live here because houses are really cheap."

"Where would I find her?"

"You want to go down Bank Street, that's the second left as you leave the hotel, and you can't miss her house, it's the only one on the river side of the street. Past her house, you hang a left on Adams, and that'll take you into Eliot. But the Facility is a long walk, it's halfway back to Ipswich, and Larry, that's our only cab-driver, he took a fare to Boston this morning and ain't come back yet."

"I don't mind the walk. I'd like to do some sight-seeing."

He withheld comment, even though I knew he wanted to make one.

Leaving the hotel, I happened to glance back through the streaked glass of the door. The clerk hadn't touched my money or my bag before I left, and I now observed him taking the bag from the counter. He had first wrapped his hand in a red bandanna to protect it from germs. Or radiation.

A Portuguese bar at the corner of Bank Street, outside of which a few swarthy loafers muttered about me to one another, marked the apex of Innsmouth's social scene. Beyond that point, the houses on the left side guarded their inhabitants behind drawn shades, lulling them with a varied chorus of air-conditioners. Here and there shadows would stir at windows as I walked up the steep street, but the residents were good at concealing themselves. I saw no one, not even a hand at a drape as it shifted.

Above a picture-postcard falls, the Manuxet grew far more energetic and noisy than any human as it raced between bulkheaded banks, and even frightening. The river had penetrated the ancient pilings to undermine the footway on the right. Gaps yawned in the sidewalk. I'm sure the road was next on its list, then the buttoned-up houses, until it swept all of Innsmouth and then New England out to sea. Its continuous roar, made up of a million gurgles and mutters, was alarmingly loud as it echoed off the blank house-fronts, and I seemed to eavesdrop on a wealth of incomprehensible conversations in a din that threatened at any moment to become clear.

I stayed to the left-hand side, but no one came out, as I half-expected, to glare at me and demand that I account for myself. In the far distance a lonely dog barked an interminable litany of grievances that probably had nothing to do with my return to the seat of my ancestors.

The river roared more loudly, constricted by a granite outcropping of the bank where some scruffy woods and a small cottage, the only house on the river side, clung perilously in a fine, perpetual mist. The house was very old, to judge by the small, lead-filled windows of imperfect glass, and I fancied that its unpainted cedar shakes might have been made with an ax. It was oddly out of proportion, as many old New England houses seem to me, with the single story dwarfed by a bloated chimney and roof.

I knocked, then repeated it before the door opened. I took a step back from a disturbing figure, a tall, slim and impenetrably veiled woman.

"Excuse me, my name is—"

"No, don't tell me. It's *Sargent* isn't it? You could be Joe, just a couple years before he passed over."

And hers could have been my Grandma's voice, either because of a local accent or locally hereditary quirk. Before I even suspected that I might, I burst into tears.

"Alma Sargent was my Grandma, yes, Joe's sister, but my name is Bob Smith," I said when I could speak.

"Bob is a good name, a real Innsmouth name. Come in, Bob."

I was about to sit in a straight chair opposite her rocker when she demanded, "What's that you got in your pocket?"

"Nothing," I mumbled, feeling like a trapped kid.

"Show me! In the name of Mother Hydra!"

She was definitely not a lady I could refuse. I pulled out the three pyramidal chunks of granite that had caught my eye on the way to her house. She studied them closely, then spat on them and held them tight in her gloved hand for a moment as if willing them to reveal their secrets. "These are okay," she said at last, handing them back. "These'll do." She added playfully, "Figure on finding somebody to baptize while you're in town, Bob?"

"Well." I coughed, looked away, wondered if my rash was bad enough today to hide my blushing.

"I see you follow the old ways, that's good. I expect Alma taught you? It's a cryin' shame you can't do the baptizing out on Devil Reef, like Our Lord intended, but the Navy blasted the bejesus out of it in twenty-eight. But if you do it with the right spirit, you can perform a baptism even out in the middle of Kansas."

I had spent sleepless nights struggling with that point of theology, and her words took an enormous weight off my soul.

Before I could thank her, she said, "Love that name! Bob. I do believe I can prophesy a truly glorious future for you. So tell me all about yourself, Bob."

I did. My God! I never thought I could have revealed such secrets to a stranger unless I had gone stark, raving mad, but they just tumbled out. And she accepted them. Instead of ordering me out or screaming for help, Old Lady Waite nodded and murmured… approval. Often I knew that she was smiling gently behind her veil, amused by my account of my clumsy efforts to be true to my heritage, but her amusement was in no way contemptuous.

Even as I spoke so unguardedly, I wondered about the spell she had cast over me. The unfamiliar emotion I felt was as strong as love is reputed to be, but it would be crazy to suppose that I had fallen in love with a woman almost three times my age whose face was veiled. She was in fact concealed completely in dark, old-fashioned clothing, and might have been a mannikin if she hadn't murmured from time to time, if her rocker hadn't moved rhythmically.

I was forced to the conclusion that I felt at home, and that I had never felt that way anywhere, not even in my boyhood home with my own parents. The feeling seemed to be generated by a combination of subtle influences that I didn't perceive until I tried hard to sort them out. Nothing around me, not the spare furniture of colonial design, the home-hooked rugs on the mirror-polished floor with its wide and irregular boards, the huge, unlit fireplace that doubled as an oven with its iron doors, was inconsistent with the eighteenth century, a time that has always seemed more congenial to me. I saw no television set, no tawdry magazines, no brightly-packaged products of mass consumption. I believed that the unlit lamps were fueled by kerosene, for I saw no electrical outlets or wires. Despite the absence of air conditioning, the house was comfortably cool and dank behind its small windows, beaded by the river's mist, and under its huge roof this atmosphere, together with an indefinable odor that came from the woman herself and all she had touched, must have been responsible for my profound sense of comfort.

But none of these factors really explained my feelings as well as my first impression, that I had fallen under a magical spell.

"Alma must have passed over," she said. "I'm surprised she hasn't come by. We were best friends, and I thought she'd just love to tease me about the long time I'm taking."

"It was fourteen years ago when I helped her with the last rites, but it was a long ways off. Puget Sound."

"Oh! Then I expect she'll be by one of these days."

"Actually it was a river that runs into the Sound," I admitted a bit guiltily. I have a deep aversion against speaking the name, but I forced myself: "The Green River."

The name provoked no special reaction. She just said, "Fresh water is okay."

"But pretty swift."

Her laughter was surprisingly youthful. "This river out here is pretty swift, but it doesn't stop old friends from coming to call on me when they're of a mind."

"Do you suppose I could...?"

"Meet them? Sure, why not! How long you plan to be in town? You can stay right here with me, so's not to miss anyone."

"I wish I could, but I came here to take advantage of the federal reparations. I have to stay at—"

"Not the Facility! Oh, my," she groaned. She stopped rocking for the first time since she'd sat down.

"What? What's wrong? The program was sponsored by President Kennedy, and he seemed—"

"He was a friend to our kind, a real true friend. You ever wonder how he happened to survive so long in the ocean, injured as he was, after his PT-boat got sunk? And did you ever see a picture of his daddy's mistress, Gloria Swanson? Those eyes of hers say it all, if you know what to look for. But what he seems mostly now is *dead,* and laws have a way of getting amended. This one got amended with bells on, to say nothing of books and candles. The Facility caught some local folks when they first set up shop, but I saw right through them, and I wanted no part of it. I told that wicked Dr. Saltonstall take his stethoscope and stick it. Fortunately Ramon Medeiros, he's the mayor now, is a good friend to all of us, and he's moving heaven and earth to get that place shut down." She chuckled. "He leaves the sea to me. I'd give Ramon a call right now if I had one of those goddamn telephone machines—"

Someone knocked on the door. It was a loud, peremptory, no-nonsense knock.

"I bet that's not Ed McMahon and Dick Clark, come to make me rich," she said.

"What should I do? Is the back—"

"You don't really suppose they're not out there, too, do you? If you were foolish enough to sign anything you better go, because Uncle Sam is an alligator: dumb as hell and easy to avoid, but once he gets his jaws set, he won't let go. Your best bet is to go along with them now so you don't get hurt, and let me do what I can on the outside."

The sight waiting for me at the door was unnerving, for the heavy-set older man and his grinning, dapper companion bore a skewed likeness to the pitchmen she had named.

"Mr. Smith?" the dapper one said. "We heard you might need a lift to the Facility."

"Want to go for a nice ride, too, Mrs. Waite?" the other one said to the woman standing just behind me. "That would save everybody a lot of hassle."

"You don't know what hassle is, sonny-boy. You'll find out if you do Mr. Smith, here, any harm."

"Harm? We're here to *help* you people, don't you understand? How long do you think you can fuck with the U.S. Government?"

"How deep is the ocean?" she laughed.

"Ed" hummed the tune she had quoted all during the ride. It was proof that spells of a sort really can be cast on others, and I tried to take that as a good omen.

I was unprepared for the Facility, a Victorian fantasy of sooty bricks that managed to look both brutal and whimsical, a bad combination. The high fence around the grounds, capped with broken glass, was part of the original design, but the electronic gate looked brand new. The guard who controlled it was armed. As I was hurried up the front steps, I saw that the new sign over the door only partly concealed the original name in bas-relief:

MANUXET ASYLUM FOR THE INSANE.

The interior corridors were huge and ill-lit, wainscotted in dark wood and smelling of dust, disinfectant and century-old misery. Most alarming was the emptiness. Except for my escort and a few attendants who were trying to avoid notice or look busy, I suspected that I might be the only one here.

This suspicion was born out in the days that followed, but I didn't regret my isolation. The first thing they did was take away my false hair and give me a chemical shower that aggravated my rash. Bald and scabrous, clad in an orange jump-suit, I might have been an imperfectly fashioned android under study by the normally-dressed people and white-uniformed keepers who hustled me here and there to determine where my creation had gone wrong. Under these circumstances, I wanted to meet no one whose opinion might have mattered to me.

Forced to choose the one thing about the Facility I liked least, I would have picked Dr. Isaac Mordecai Saltonstall, the director. A long-faced, long-fingered scarecrow in tweeds, he treated me like a child, or worse. Sometimes when he stared at me blankly over his tented fingers I imagined he was trying to decide whether to have me gassed now or later. At least he didn't quack, but he swallowed his vowels, except for an occasional "a" as broad as a barn door. His diplomas said he had gone to Harvard and identified him, curiously enough, as a psychiatrist.

"The Seattle police questioned you in July of eighty-three and again in September of that year," he asked as he studied my distressingly thick dossier.

This was the first time that subject had come up. I was sorely tempted to babble, but I followed the rule I had observed since arriving: say nothing unless asked a direct question. That had always worked with the police.

"Why do you suppose that was?" he said at last.

"I guess they were being thorough."

"But why you?"

"I was there."

"At the murders?"

That was a low blow, but I took it without flinching. "No, not at the murders!" It seemed reasonable to inject a little anger into my voice. "I drove by the Strip, where many of the girls were abducted, in my ice-cream truck every day. The hookers were my customers, I recognized some of the victims. Maybe the Green River Killer was a customer, too. But it turned out I couldn't help. I was never a *suspect!*"

"No need to get excited," Dr. Saltonstall said: 'We have to be thorough, too. Now your grandmother went missing from the nursing-home not long before the first murder, didn't she?"

"She wandered off, yes."

"You didn't help her *pass over*, did you?"

I tried to conceal my shock at his use of these words with more anger: "What, killed my Grandma? I loved her!"

"That's not what I said."

"Yes, you did. People use euphemisms for dying, like *pass over*. Do you think I helped her commit suicide or something?"

"People do?"

"Other people. I always try to say what I mean. So, do I get my money? When do I get out of here?"

"Do you still have your rocks?"

The previous interviews had covered only medical details. I guess he had been trying to lull my suspicions. Today he was coming at me from all sides, jabbing me where I least expected it.

"Rocks?"

"You had some rocks in your pocket when you came here."

"Oh. Those." I made a show of searching the deep pocket of the jumpsuit. "Yeah."

"Why do you carry rocks in your pocket?"

Better than in my head you know-it-all son of a bitch! "I picked them up in town." I smiled. "Genuine Innsmouth rocks. Souvenirs. I don't know why I do it. If I see an odd-shaped rock or a bird-feather, or, I don't know, an unusual bottle-cap, I pick it up. For luck, I guess."

He wrote something in my dossier. If he had believed me, it was "obsessive-compulsive."

"Where is everybody?" I asked, deciding to go on the offensive. "Do you have a Mr. Marsh here?"

"He left. How do you know him?"

"The clerk at the hotel told me he never returned for his bag. If he left here, why didn't he go back for it?"

He wrote something else: *Have clerk killed?* No, the hotel-clerk was one of their spies. He must have told them I was at Old Lady Waite's house.

"Mr. Marsh left the day you arrived. He probably picked up his bag after you spoke to the clerk."

It pleased me that his lie should be so transparent, but maybe it shouldn't have. Maybe he didn't care if he was believed by a man who would soon follow Mr. Marsh into limbo.

"What about a girl named Gilman?"

"Ondine Gilman? She's here. Haven't you met her?"

"No," I said evenly, "I haven't."

"It's a big place. You're sure to run into her."

It was no surprise at all when I went to enter the cafeteria that evening and saw, for the first time, another person seated at one of the plastic tables. She wore a jump-suit like mine, but she exhibited no pathological symptoms.

I was reluctant to enter, not just because of my appearance but because *I* knew that she or I, or both, was being manipulated by Dr. Saltonstall. I forced myself.

"Ondine Gilman," she responded when I brought a tray to her table and introduced myself.

"Really?"

"What do you mean?"

"Nothing. I heard the name, and I thought... well, I thought Dr. Salton-stall might have planted an impostor."

She laughed. "He makes me paranoid, too."

She tried to avoid looking at me directly, but I stared hard at her. Her blue eyes were large and rather protuberant, but not so much as Grandma's or mine. I saw no hint of extra skin between her fingers, no rash, and certainly no alopecia: her auburn hair was real.

"You don't look like an Innsmouth person," I said.

She grimaced. "I'm not. And since they know I'm not, I wonder why the hell I'm still here!"

She had raised her voice for the benefit of the bored server at the counter, but he continued to look bored.

"It's none of my business—"

"Sure it is, we're in this together. You'd think if they won't let me go home, they'd at least let me have a goddamn cigarette, it's not as if this place is burst-ing at the seams with people whose lungs I can pollute. Why can't I go home?"

The last remark, in her flattest, hardest quack, was also addressed to the server, who retreated to the kitchen without comment.

"I'm sorry," she said.

"If you're not an Innsmouth person—"

"Then why am I here? It's embarrassing. No, it isn't, it's funny, actually.

My father looked sort of like you before he...."

"Passed over?"

She seemed startled. "That was what he said he was going to do, that's the phrase he used. Only he didn't die, he ran away. I never knew why, but maybe I do now."

"Why?"

"He wasn't my father, that's why. They found that out as soon as they took my first blood-test, and then they confirmed it with DNA. My father, Wade Gilman, had Innsmouth parents, but my biological father must've been the mailman or somebody. I never even suspected that until they took the blood-test, but maybe my father suspected it long before, and that's why he left."

She strove for a light tone, but her voice shook. I said, "I'm sorry."

"It's a bitch. I just came here to get some money for art school in Providence, so they lock me up without cigarettes and tell me my mother was screwing around. Have they put you in the tank yet?"

"What's that?"

"They truss you up and dump you in a tank full of water to see how long you can hold your breath. They make damn sure you're not faking, too, they keep you under till you pass out. And they do it again and again. They put me in the tank even after they *knew* I wasn't a Kermie!"

"A what!"

"I'm sorry, that's not nice, I guess. That's what they call Smouthies—Innsmouth people, I mean—in Rowley, where I come from. For Kermit the Frog?"

"Why don't they let you leave?"

"That's *my* question, Dr. Einstein!" Annoyed by the close scrutiny I had given her, she stared back at me and added coldly: "You've got enough problems of your own, I guess."

"There were some other people—applicants—when you came here, weren't there?"

"Oh, yeah, this place was really hopping...." She looked as if she wanted to bite her tongue.

"They looked like me, you mean?"

"No, I meant.... Okay, if that's what you want, they looked like you." She didn't like being put on the defensive, and she stopped trying to hide her contempt for me. "It should have been obvious that I didn't belong."

"What happened to them?

She shrugged. "One day they were gone. We didn't become best friends. Nobody said good-bye. I guess they just took their money and hopped away."

"Did you see them leave?"

"No." She glanced uneasily toward the counter, but we were still alone.

"What's your point?"

"Maybe they didn't leave."

"Huh? Oh, come *on!* You mean they killed them?" Her surprise was overdone. I think she had considered that possibility on her own and was trying to reject it. "But they wouldn't kill me. I'm not like *them!*"

"I guess it was all a terrible mistake," I said mildly. "They'll ask you to promise not to tell anybody that they tortured you, or that all the Kermies disappeared, and let you go. Tomorrow, probably."

"You son of a bitch. Being sarcastic doesn't help."

"Do you want to go? Without waiting for them to tidy up all the paperwork, or whatever it is they say they're doing?"

"Damn. Are you serious? You don't look exactly like a...."

"A knight in shining armor?"

"A man of action, I was going to say."

"My looks are deceptive." This misplaced nitwit had irritated me. Born in an earlier time, she would have egged on the thugs who massacred the detested "Smouthies." My tone was bitter as I added, "Just think of me as the Frog Prince."

"Jesus, don't look at me like that!" She failed to repress a shudder. "I think I believe you."

The second floor of the wing where my room lay had originally comprised four cavernous wards, but the one on the end had been divided with drywall into thirty cubicles under a false ceiling, each barely large enough to contain a single bed, plastic chair and fiberboard writing-desk, all of them bolted in place to discourage their use as weapons. A reproduction of a bland Matisse seascape was similarly bolted to the brick exterior wall. Mine could be considered a first-class accommodation, I suppose, since it shared one of the old madhouse windows, heavily barred and screened, with an adjoining cubicle. Standing on the chair, I had a view of the gatehouse in the distance and, under the window, most of the parking lot.

The door was the most interesting feature of my cell, for it wouldn't have met the security standards of a dollhouse. I believed the lock could be spread with one of the long but sloppily-installed bolts I had extracted from Matisse. I hadn't experimented, though, for fear of marking the door or even splintering it.

Swathed as he was in medical degrees and patrician breeding, I don't think Dr. Saltonstall ever considered that anyone would mistrust him or try to escape his prison. And if they did, his omnipotent drugs would stop them. Every night I had been given a big red capsule that I dutifully swallowed, and every night it knocked me out within ten minutes. Tonight I concealed it under my tongue until I could spit it out.

I lay quietly in my bed for an hour or so until I heard cars starting up, four in succession. I climbed onto the chair and watched as they drove to the gate and were let through. While I watched, the doctor himself strode across the parking lot to his car and left. Two others followed him within the next ten minutes, leaving only one car. When a fat man in uniform trudged from the gatehouse to the main building carrying a brown bag, I was sure the Facility had now shut down for the night.

The gap between the door and the jamb wasn't as wide as I'd thought. I couldn't push the bolt in even when I leaned on it with all my weight. I hesitated to hammer it with the heel of my shoe, but I had no choice. If the guard heard me, I told myself, he would assume I was signalling for help and take his time about responding. I had another bad moment when the cheap bolt I was using as a lever seemed on the verge of bending. Again, I had no choice. I pushed harder. The bolt held and the door sprang open.

I had the freedom of their new, plasterboard corridor, but an insuperable hurdle might remain: the heavy, iron door of the former ward. If they had locked that door—but they hadn't. This was more of the doctor's smug faith in drugs, I supposed.

I prowled along the outer corridor, where the only light glowed in an EXIT sign. I heard tinny voices and laughter as I approached the main stairway, where a broad landing overlooked the lobby. The guard I had seen sat at a desk by the front door, watching television and eating a sandwich. It seemed rather melodramatic not to just stroll naturally across the landing, but I tiptoed.

At the end of the next wing I found another ward converted to cubicles, and it seemed likely that this would be the women's quarters. The first ten doors were unlocked, the rooms empty. When I found the eleventh locked, it seemed likely I would find Ondine Gilman behind it.

This door was just as flimsy as the one on my own cell, and since it opened inward, I believed I could simply kick it open. This worked, but the thunderous crash of the door against the wall made me cringe. I ran to the outer corridor to listen. Minutes passed. I heard nothing except the canned laughter of the television until a human guffaw joined in, testimony that the guard's attention was fully occupied.

I felt confident enough to snap on the light after I had closed the woman's door behind me. She didn't stir.

"Ondine!" I said, and, more loudly, "Miss Gilman!"

Curled on her side, she breathed deeply and evenly. Her breathing didn't change even when I shook her by the shoulder. I stood considering my options for a moment, then lifted her covers and pushed her green hospital gown above her waist. She continued to sleep soundly even when I peeled her underpants down and extricated her feet.

I wasn't displeased by what I saw and touched, but I wished I still had my ice-cream truck. An hour in the locker would have done wonders for her superior attitude. I restored everything as it had been except for the panties, indecent, red ones of the sort favored by roadside whores. After using them to wipe the evidence of my visit from her buttocks, I wadded them into my pocket and turned off the light. She continued to breathe evenly.

I was tempted to try the stones for size, but decided she would keep while I explored the Facility.

The stairs marked as an exit led me down to an unguarded rear door. I stepped outside and savored a warm night that was loud with crickets, frogs and… sirens? I strained my ears, but I couldn't identify the sounds in the distance. They might have been sirens, or even thin screams.

The stairs continued down to the basement, where I knew the medical department was housed. I had been given tests here, but I hadn't suspected its extent. There was a fully equipped operating theater and other rooms that held machines liberally plastered with radiation warnings.

The last room, and the largest, was obviously a morgue. Nevertheless it was a shock to pull out a drawer and find a naked body. And a second. And a third. And…. They were Innsmouth people, every one of them, and they were dead. I couldn't say what had killed them, but they had all been stitched up crudely after autopsies.

My knees wobbled, the room swam, and without further warning I found myself throwing up until my stomach clenched down on itself like a hard, painful, empty fist.

My shock and sickness gave way to fury. I raged down the line, pulling out drawer after drawer. Fifteen of them. Twenty! Someone would pay, someone would pay dearly. These were my people, my own unique, precious people, standing even further above Saltonstall and his henchmen than those butchers fancied they stood above worms. Left to evolve in peace, they would have shed their simian traits and passed over into magnificent beings who would have lived for all time in the glorious kingdom of the Lord. But now, denied all hope of transfiguration, they were just so many dead chimps.

"Father Dagon!" I screamed. "Mother Hydra! Where were you!"

I came at last upon a drawer whose contents shocked me into stillness. Those evil savages had succeeded in meddling with something they couldn't even begin to comprehend. It was the ultimate obscenity, a blasphemy for which no human words exist, and I forced my imperfect tongue to struggle with curses that were more appropriate, but still woefully inadequate to the horror. With drugs, with surgery or radiation, they had forced a Deep One to pass over on dry land.

It was huge, and even in its desiccated state it was beautiful, godlike. My hands fumbled reverently over the dry scales, the pathetically limp crest of spikes that should have stood proud. Sobbing bitterly, I promised a hundred sacrifices, a thousand, a holocaust that would rouse Father Dagon and make the sea rise up to the sky and draw down the moon in its awful wrath.

Stroking the massive chest, I realized that I felt no stitches. I looked closely. I saw no obvious wounds at all. I felt no heartbeat or respiration either, but it was possible, just barely, that he had shut down all his systems hard when faced with the horror of a landlocked metamorphosis. As Grandma was so fond of quoting, "That is not dead which can eternal lie...."

I dashed back to the next room, where I had seen a sink. I looked about for a bucket of some kind, but—better! I smashed the glass case holding a firehose, oblivious to the shrieking alarm this set off, and wrenched the wheel over until the hose came to life like a wrathful dragon, spewing a destructive jet that smashed cases of fiendish instruments and foul drugs open and hurled their contents clattering and crashing through the torture-chambers.

I manhandled it back to the morgue and directed the stream on the ceiling above the Deep One, bouncing down a flood of life-giving water on the poor victim.

I didn't notice when the alarm was silenced. I couldn't understand why the hose suddenly went limp and dry. Then I became aware of the man quacking furiously at the door to the next room.

"Put that down, you goddamn loony! Drop it, asshole, or you are dead meat!"

I had found what I wanted, a human being to absorb the full force of my rage, and I threw the hose aside and stalked toward him.

"Don't you realize what you're doing here!" I screamed. "Don't you know—"

"I know what I'm doing is catching a goddamn Loony who's fucking up the hospital. Stop! Stop right now! This here is a .357 Magnum, shit-head, and it's about to tear out your spine and pin it to the far wall. I am not joking with you."

I stopped. What could I have been thinking of? All hope of escape was lost. Dr. Saltonstall would lock me up tight. More probably he would take no more chances with me, and I would be filling one of these morgue-drawers before lunchtime tomorrow.

"That's better. Assume the position."

I knew what he meant. I turned to the wall, leaning forward to support my weight with my hands on a closed drawer. He strutted up behind me and took great delight in kicking my ankles wider apart.

"Scabby son of an Innsmouth bitch," he snarled, "I'm really hurting to blow your baldy-ass head all over the wall just for laughs, so don't try nothing, you hear? I just want an excuse to blow one of you scum-suckers away. What the hell you got here?"

He had found the rocks I had been saving, which he hurled on the floor. He thrust his hand into my other pocket and extracted Ondine's panties. After a moment of baffled silence, he made a gagging noise of utter loathing.

"You goddamn pervert!" he screamed.

The wall hit me in the face, cracking teeth. I only then became aware of a worse pain where he had hit the back of my head with his gun. I wondered how I had wound up on my knees. They hurt, too.

"Bastard bastard bastard!" he screamed, kicking me in the back as if trying to squash a bug to paste. "You got me to touch your goddamn frogspawn jackoff rag—"

He stopped kicking me. I tried to stop my sobbing and groaning so I could hear what he was saying, though his words were strangely muffled. It sounded as if he were choking. Was it too much to hope that he was dying of apoplexy?

I managed to twist my head around. I couldn't imagine what was happening to him. Most of his face was covered by a wet, black cloth, and he was apparently standing a foot off the floor, his heavy-duty oxfords and white tube-socks jerking spasmodically.

But it was no cloth that covered his face. It was the huge, webbed hand of the dark figure that loomed behind him, the Deep One I had revived.

"Praise Mother Hydra!" I sobbed.

"Praise her name!" a rich, deep, croaking voice responded.

"Sokay, sweetie," I slurred, dumping Ondine Gilman into a lobby chair of the hotel that, most inaccurately, bore her name. "Jus' get us a room, okay?"

"Wha…?Where?"

I leaned forward and, under the pretext of giving her a kiss, pressed her carotid arteries until she lost consciousness again. After changing my *modus operandii* in the Northwest, I had learned that this was every bit as effective as an ice-cream locker for draining the will of baptismal candidates.

"Excuse me, Sir! Just what—oh. It's Mr. Smith, isn't it?"

"Bob. It's good ol' Bob," I said, steering a wayward course for the desk and the clerk I had seen before, the one who had used a bandanna to pick up my bag. He was still wearing his Munch necktie. The image was a deliberate slur against my people.

"What's going on?"

"Celebrash. Celebration. We're outta that damn crazy-house."

"I can see that. What's going on outside, I meant."

I pretended to hear the sirens for the first time. And there were indeed screams, too.

"They're celebratin', I guess." I heard a burst of automatic gunfire.

"God!"he cried, starting from behind the desk.

"Hey, wait. Need a room for me and my sweetie."

"I can't rent you a room, you're drunk. And I'm closing."

"Then gimme my bag," I said. "Left my bag, remember?"

"Oh. Sure. Then will you go?"

"Drunk, huh?"

"Where am I?" Ondine cried.

"'Sokay, honey."

He dumped my bag on the counter, forgetting to protect his precious hand from my contagion in his confused haste. He fretted and fussed as I opened it, and he grew even more flustered at another burst of automatic fire in the distance.

"I'm not really drunk," I said clearly as I pulled the nine-millimeter Browning out of the bag and jacked a Black Talon round into the chamber.

"What?"

"I'm just very different from you, that's all."

I put the bullet right through the Screamer's bald, distorted head and through the clerk's breastbone.

"I'm coming, dear," I told Ondine, and hurried over to deprive her simian brain of yet more oxygen.

I was afraid she might not be able to understand what I was doing after I had stripped her and tied her to the bed in the room I had assigned us, but she came around as good as new. Nobody would have paid attention to her screams and curses over the similar noises in Town Square.

I took all the time I wanted to amuse myself, but it surprised me when dawn broke while I was still thrusting into her. I turned and saw that it was a dawn of floodlights, powerful floodlights from the section of town sealed off by razor-wire. The gunfire had become constant, but it seemed as if fewer guns were in use.

"You fucking bastard!" Ondine sobbed.

"You got part of that right," I grunted, "but I'm the one who's legitimate, remember!"

"Freak!"

I'd had enough of her and her filthy mouth. I pulled out and rummaged among my clothing for the stones. Her screams found surprising new energy as I inserted them in the secret places, but I managed to ignore her as I recited the words. I'm not sure if the words and the procedure are exactly right, since Grandma explained them fully only at the very last, when she had passed over and was in a fearful hurry to rejoin her people, but I have always used them.

I suspect that any human being who reads this account may think that my baptism of forty-eight women between 1982, the year Grandma passed over, and 1984 was somehow excessive. On the contrary, it was based on an exact calculation of the yearly baptisms Grandma was prevented from performing while she was interned in Oklahoma (four), and while she was confined in the nursing-home (forty-four). Despite all the hard work and laborious planning involved, to say nothing of the danger, I wanted to complete Grandma's hecatomb and ensure that she was granted full honor among the Deep Ones as quickly as possible. Don't you think she had suffered long enough and waited long enough already? If you still believe someone should be censured for upsetting the public with such a concentrated flurry of "criminal" activity, you might look to President Herbert Hoover, whose agents disrupted her life and prevented the free exercise of her religion, or to Sidney Newman, my grandfather, who did the same.

It was my turn to scream as the door opened. I recoiled from the figure in black that stood there, but then I saw that it was Old Lady Waite.

"I don't know what you did, Bob," she said admiringly, "but you sure stirred up the Host of the Sea. However," she added as she set a crocheted bag on the bedside table and withdrew a large black book and a butcher-knife, "that's not really the way to go about this business." To Ondine she said, "Hush, now, child, this won't take much longer at all. To baptize your soul we have to separate it from your body. Take heart from the fact that your suffering won't be wasted. Even now your pain and shame are floating out like incense to feed those whose glory you can't even begin to comprehend."

While I watched and listened, she showed me exactly how it should be done.

The flapping roar of helicopters deafened us as we ran through the marsh. They raced toward us, flying barely higher than the reeds. I thought this was the end, but they passed right over us to the town, where they blasted the beach with rockets and cannon-fire.

"They're killing them!" I cried.

"I doubt it," Old Lady Waite said. "The Deep Ones are not stupid, you know. They wanted to destroy the Facility and give the boys in the back room something to chew on, and they've done it. They're long gone by now, taking their dead with them. You'll read in the papers tomorrow how some foreign fishermen got out of line when they thought they saw a sea monster, or maybe a mermaid, and how the dumb state troopers called in an air strike. There's no fun on earth like reading the papers, if you know what to look for."

Whatever the papers might say, our position was untenable. Dr. Salton-stall knew what I'd done in the Northwest, he hadn't just been on a fishing expedition, and he couldn't be the only one who knew. I had made no attempt to hide the remains of Ondine and the hotel clerk. As for Old Lady Waite, she was sure that they would come hunting for any lingering Dagonites in Innsmouth, whatever the papers might say, with her at the head of their list.

She had kept a small sloop ready for just such an emergency, and now it ghosted through the black creek under a small jib while she steered it expertly.

"Where are we going?"

"You mentioned Fiji. It's nice there. There's an island where the Deep Ones mix freely with the people, just like they used to do in Innsmouth. Just like they'll do again here when this blows over and Ramon does what I told him."

"We're going to... to the South Pacific in this?"

"Not we, I'll be passing over before very long at all." She laughed at the horror on my face. "What's the matter, can't you swim?"

"Yes, of course, but—"

"Don't worry. I'll make sure you know how to sail it before I pass over. Then I'll stick by you, or maybe our friends will."

Old Lady Waite—but that was merely the name of her larval shell, soon to be discarded as she assumed the glorious form that I came to know and love, in every sense of those words, as Pth'th-l'yl-l'yth.

It was the magnificent soul of that companion and lover-to-be who had guided me, and who now gestured at the black water. I saw nothing at first, then aglow in the depths, a trail of phosphorescence to one side of the boat. A second followed on the other side. Large, submarine creatures escorted us.

Lost Stars

Ann K. Schwader

Wind driven sleet spattered Obscura Gallery's windows, turning a late November afternoon even gloomier. Sara sighed. Just what she needed, after a long day hanging large-format photographs for tomorrow's meet-the-artist reception.

Shards of Rameses II strewn across Lower Nubia mocked her in black and white. Lost Aegypt was their most important show this year—as her boss kept reminding her. Never mind that she'd already taken off, or that Sara herself should have been home half an hour ago.

So much for attending that women's spirituality meeting tonight. Not that she'd been looking forward to it, but Diane was counting on her... opinion? Support? Reassurance? Her friend hadn't been clear, only anxiously enthusiastic.

Enthusiasm was a big part of Diane's personality, but anxiety wasn't—at least, it hadn't been. They'd fallen out of touch these past few months. Sara had been working a lot of overtime, while Diane whirled through diets, feminist causes, and dead-end relationships at her usual breakneck pace.

In all three departments, she'd been certain each latest discovery was the Real One. Her voice on the phone last night hadn't sounded so unshakable.

She'd just insisted that this new group was unlike anything she'd ever been involved in. More authentic. More *empowering*.

The gallery door's tinkling bell interrupted.

"Oh wow," came a female voice moments later. "Can I borrow your employee discount?"

Sara snorted. "My what?"

Halfway down the tippy ladder, she got her first good look at Diane. Her friend had been struggling with her weight for years without much success. Now the wrists protruding from the sleeves of her loose black sweater were positively bony. Her jeans sagged in the rear, and even her features looked pared down.

"Good God, girl. What diet drugs are you on?"

Diane laughed, but her laugh was thin too.

"Just plain old womanpower—*really* old womanpower." Her eyes lit with secret humor. "It's like we're all tapped into this ancient matriarchal energy source. There's nothing it can't help you do: lose weight, find a job that doesn't suck, get clear of the idiot men in your life."

"Not a problem." The idiot man in Sara's life had left on his own. And not recently, either.

"Sorry." Her friend's smile faded. "I guess what I'm saying is, you've got to try it yourself. Come meet our circle tonight. Meet Sesh'tet ..."

"Who?"

"Our High Priestess, except this isn't Wicca. It's way older, out of Egypt. Like Sesh'tet."

Sara stifled an inward groan. She'd tried women's spirituality groups before, and remained unimpressed. Too much New Age crap. Too much lip service to Sisterhood, with the same bitchy backstabbing afterwards.

But Egypt?

"Come on." Diane grinned. "You know you want to."

The hell of it was, she did. Egyptology was a recent but major hobby. She'd even taken a class last summer, accumulating embarrassing quantities of books and Egyptian jewelry since.

Fingering the ornate silver *ankh* under her collar, she sighed.

"Just let me get these last few straight." Heading for the front door, she locked it and flipped the CLOSED sign around. "You can tell me all about Sesh'tet. What's she working from, anyhow—Isian mysteries?"

"Older."

Something in Diane's tone made Sara frown. "I can't imagine what might be older and still documented, not in that part of the world."

The secret look flashed in her friend's eyes again. "I can."

Sara took a deep breath to quiet her own frustration. Whatever cult Sesh'tet was selling, it obviously resonated at some deep emotional level. Maybe tonight's meeting would show her how to unsnarl Diane from this latest spiritual tangle.

Of course, it might be legit. She'd read about some pretty strange religious survivals, animism and shamans and such. And this was Boulder: People's Republic of Alternative Reality.

"So who made this Sesh'tet a High Priestess? Was it part of an initiation, or what?"

"An initiation in the Valley of the Kings." That proud-confused tone was back in Diane's voice. "She hasn't told us much about it, though. I think she's afraid of the Egyptian government—they're not exactly big on religious freedom."

"Makes sense." A nastier thought occurred to Sara. "Have *you* been initiated yet?"

Diane's chin bobbed down before she could catch herself.

"Don't worry—I won't ask for details."

The secrecy didn't bother her. Mystery cults worked like that. What she deeply didn't like was the idea of initiation after maybe three months. Didn't Wicca require a year and a day?

Of course, this wasn't Wicca. It was far older—or so this Sesh'tet person claimed. Which meant she wouldn't learn a damn thing without meeting Sesh'tet.

Straightening one last photograph, Sara climbed off the ladder and dusted her hands on her chinos. "Ready to go?"

Diane blinked at her. "I thought you weren't… " The corners of her thin mouth twisted. "Egypt snagged you, didn't it?"

It's snagged one of us, anyhow. And I want to understand why.

At least the incense smelled right. Balsam and cedar and something else, ancient and bitter, still thick in the air an hour after tonight's "open" meeting. The one she'd been allowed to sit through before Diane and about a dozen other women left to attend an initiates' circle with Sesh'tet in the basement. The High Priestess didn't always attend open meetings.

Which really fueled Sara's suspicions, since she'd been tonight's only non-initiate.

After another glance at her watch, she debated switching on the overhead light and cracking a couple of windows. She was getting a headache, and she still had no idea of her surroundings. When they'd arrived at the shabby two-story house off Pearl Street, no one had greeted them at the door. Diane had just hurried them both down a pitch-dark hallway, toward candles flickering in some wider space at its far end.

There wasn't enough light to know what kind of space. This might be somebody's made-over living room, or a specially consecrated ritual area. A cluster of guttering candles and tiny brass incense burners occupied an altar at one end of the room, but even that was draped in dark cloth. From the way the walls absorbed the candlelight, they might be draped as well.

Maybe the draperies also accounted for tonight's muted voices. Or maybe not. Even by candlelight, many of the initiates looked —and sounded—unhealthy. A few had racking smokers' coughs. Another used crutches, and still another wore a colorful, tightly wrapped headscarf with no hair or eyebrows showing.

Tonight's leader had urged everyone to remember "our absent sisters" in their meditations through the week. She'd ask Diane later what *absent* meant, but it didn't sound empowering.

The meeting hadn't told her much about Sesh'tet's agenda. There had been readings from something called *The Gate of All Lost Stars*, which sounded Egyptian enough—though the subject matter was odd. If Diane was right about how old this cult was, *Gate* should have echoed the Old Kingdom's Pyramid Texts. It didn't.

She'd heard no references to any solar deity, or to Osiris. The primary god-name had been Ammut-something. Ammutseba, maybe? At least it sounded female—most of the others, she couldn't even guess at. *Nyarlat* and *Assatur* sounded potentially Egyptian; but *Shuddam-El, Karakossa,* and *Shuppnikkurat* were utter mysteries.

They weren't good names to sit alone with in the dark, either: all hard Ks and hissing Ss and weird gutturals that barely sounded human. Not that anybody else had had problems. The smokers coughed worse when they said them, but that's why you didn't smoke.

Light. Oh God, she needed more light.

Sara struggled up from her pile of pillows and headed for the nearest wall, intending to work her way around until she found a switch plate. Surely nobody would have been stupid enough to drape over one—and if they had, she'd rip through and damn the consequences.

Shoving her hand hard against the wall—which was indeed draped heavily—she started groping for a switch. Ks and Ss clicked and hissed in her brain. Her sinuses shriveled with the incense, and cold apprehension traced her spine as her fingers burrowed into the cloth.

Then light appeared somewhere behind her, faint and flickering. Moving closer.

As her fingers closed on the nub of a wall switch at last.

"Sara?"

Diane's voice in the doorway came just as she flipped that switch —and nothing happened. Whirling, she saw Diane cradling a flat clay oil lamp in both hands, staring at her. A second thin figure stood just behind and to the left of her friend.

"Sara, this is Sesh'tet."

Her first impression was of something closer to a bush baby than a woman—a tiny creature with too-large eyes in a narrow dark face. When Sesh'tet stepped past Diane to greet her, her bare feet barely whispered on the hardwood floor.

The clay lamp's additional light didn't help much. Except for her feet, hands, and face, Sesh'tet's whole body was swathed in loose inky fabrics. Where these fell away from wrist or ankle or throat, Sara glimpsed only more formfitting darkness: a turtleneck leotard and dancer's tights, maybe. Islamic modesty meets Martha Graham.

"Welcome, Sara."

The words emerged as an arid whisper between Sesh'tet's lips. Without waiting for an answer, she reached forward and grasped Sara's right hand in both of her own.

"Thanks for letting me come."

She pried the words from some last reserve of politeness, trying to ignore the worst—or at least the weirdest—handshake she'd ever experienced. Sesh'tet's hands felt dry-slippery as snakeskin, and about as warm. Sara was suddenly aware of her own palms sweating terribly... and of the other woman's surprising strength. The tendons in those hands felt like roped steel.

Sesh'tet released her grasp slowly, leaving behind a lingering chill. Sara fought the urge to wipe her hands on her chinos. At least they weren't sweating now—in fact, they felt dry enough to be itchy. Almost painful.

"What do you think, then?" The High Priestess glanced past her to Diane, who stood by with an expression approaching awe.

"I wouldn't have brought her if I didn't think she could... benefit." The last word emerged with shy hesitation. "She's been through some bad times."

Sara scowled at her friend.

"I just came tonight because Egyptology fascinates me." She could feel heat spreading across her cheekbones. "I'm not exactly what you'd call a seeker."

Sesh'tet's bush-baby eyes blinked at her. "Are you sure?"

Before Sara could reply, she dropped something into her hand: a small flat stone lozenge on a braided cord. The lozenge felt deeply engraved on one side.

Diane's expression shifted from awe to disbelief.

"Wear that until our next meeting," Sesh'tet continued. "Next to the skin, preferably. Let it serve as a focus for your own power. A reminder of the strength She holds for all who hunger, whose hearts are aligned with Hers."

With Diane and Sesh'tet both watching, Sara had little choice but to unwind the cord and slip it over her head. The stone pendant slid under her collar to hang between her breasts, just below but touching the *ankh* she already wore. It felt oddly cold, as though no one else had touched it.

"Thanks." What else could she say?

"Be sure to keep your thoughts focused on what you want happening in your life right now," said Sesh'tet. "Focused female energy is very powerful. It may take a day or two, but most of us notice some change right away." The knife-thin lips quirked in a smile. "Diane's already told you how effective this can be, I'm sure."

Diane's own smile filled with nervous relief. "I'll get her a copy of this week's *Gate* readings."

"I think that would help a lot." Sara meant it, too—though not in a seeker's way. Unless or until she could identify the engraving on this amulet, she needed every available clue.

That night she slept badly, her mind churning with random phrases from *The Gate of All Lost Stars*—or rather, her own fevered memories of those readings. Surely *Behold, Ammutseba has devoured the light of the stars, she has eaten their words of power, she has eaten their spirits* wasn't meant literally. All religious writing was rooted in symbolism. References to *devouring the light* (among other things) probably meant the light of truth. To devour was to internalize, so devouring light would be internalizing wisdom or...

She woke up suddenly, bruised where the new amulet had gotten between her chest and a hard corner of the bed.

What the...?

Reaching down to pull the amulet around behind her neck, where her *ankh* already hung quite comfortably, Sara found that the small chilly thing wouldn't budge. It also didn't feel much like stone against her fingers. The polished basalt surface had turned yielding and gummy—almost leechlike.

And it was stuck to her.

Flipping on her bedside lamp, Sara peeled up her t-shirt. The lozenge of greasy blackness was still wedged between her breasts—and pulling at it did no good. When she pried underneath with a thumbnail, though, she heard a miniscule pop of broken suction. Prying harder, tearing skin in the process, she finally got it loose and yanked the braided cord over her head.

Still shuddering, she threw the ugly thing across the room. The movement slid her silver *ankh* around on its chain. When she tried to toss it back behind her, she noticed it wasn't catching the light.

Then the chain broke, and she found herself holding the tarnished ruin of her favorite Egyptian pendant. The mess in her palm looked about a thousand years old, its elaborate hieroglyphs reduced to dust on corroded metal.

Sara folded her fingers around it and got up carefully. Heading for her desk against the far wall, she scrabbled one-handed through its drawers for a clean envelope and spilled the *ankh* into it. Then she laid that on her desktop and flipped on the overhead light.

The new amulet lay in plain sight on the floor where she'd thrown it. She knelt down and prodded it with a finger: cold black stone.

Cold black inscribed stone.

Picking it up by its cord, she put it on her desk and shrugged into her bathrobe. Sleep was no longer an option. Neither was handling this alone. Taking a deep breath, she began by sketching the amulet's design, taking care not to touch it again

After that, she turned on her computer, swallowed her pride, and started a very long e-mail—to the only Egyptologist she knew.

Despite the short notice, Diane was happy to join her at work for lunch next day. She arrived with a bag from the mall's burger joint. While Sara nibbled at raw veggies and yogurt, her friend devoured a large order of fries, a cheeseburger, and a strawberry shake.

Sara wasn't sure whether to be jealous or worried. "Is that the Sesh'tet diet plan?"

Diane grinned and munched another fry.

"That's what's so great about being tapped into all this energy. Once you're focused, dieting doesn't matter. I want to lose weight, so I do."

She pulled a sheaf of papers from her black leather backpack. "There's a lot about focus in this week's readings. I went ahead and photocopied them for you." Her grin faded a little. "You must've really impressed Sesh'tet last night. She doesn't just hand those amulets out, you know."

Sara frowned. "I hope not."

Setting aside her yogurt, she went to her back room desk and returned with two small white boxes. Diane looked puzzled as she handed her the first one.

"What's this junk?"

"My *ankh* I ordered direct from Cairo back in January."

"God." Diane looked sympathetic. "What happened to it?"

"That damn amulet trashed it."

Sara told the story as simply as she could, leaving out the bad dreams and her nagging suspicion that more than a simple chemical reaction was involved. It didn't make sense—not twenty-first century, daylight sense. What had driven her to copy the amulet's design, then send a frantic e-mail to the one expert she knew of, was impossible to explain over lunch.

"I've never had any problem with mine." Diane touched the lump beneath her heavy sweater. "And I've been wearing it nonstop ever since Sesh'tet gave it to me."

"When was that?"

Her friend's expression clouded. "When I got initiated."

And if Sesh'tet had given *her* one right away, what did that mean? There was no kind way to ask. Instead, she handed Diane the second box.

"Well, you can give this one back to her. It's sticky and creepy, and it wrecked my necklace."

Diane frowned. Her chin twitched sideways.

"What do you mean, no? You're the one who dragged me to that meeting!"

"I mean no, you can't give it back. Sesh'tet made it for *you*."

Cold anger knotted in Sara. "Because she knew I'd be there last night?"

"I didn't think you'd mind. Really. Sesh'tet's always asking if we have friends who might benefit from our group—women with, um, life issues. Women who need empowerment..."

"Don't give me that psych crap!"

Even as her temper flared, Sara was sorry. Diane worked in a metaphysical bookstore. It wasn't her fault that she picked up the buzzwords, or that she'd wanted to help a friend. Sara just preferred keeping her private life private.

Including the fact that she hadn't *had* a private life for way too long.

Taking a deep breath, she tried to apologize. Diane listened silently, finishing the last of her fries and wadding her trash into a tidy ball. She didn't look so much offended as preoccupied—or maybe distracted.

Finally, Sara gave up before she got angry again.

"Look, just keep the amulet. Please." Diane handed its box back to her. "I'm sorry it messed up your pendant, but you need to give it another try. I know it sounds weird, but these amulets do help you focus on... well, the energy. Sesh'tet calls them power triggers."

Noticing Sara's dubious frown, she shrugged. "Anyhow, mine started working for me really fast."

Diane shot her lunch trash into the back room wastebasket. Watching her sweater sleeves flap around her arms, Sara felt like screaming.

"Maybe you've lost about *enough* weight," she finally said. "Maybe you don't need any more meetings. Or that amulet. I know you're feeling all empowered, but this Sesh'tet just seems like bad news."

She hoped she didn't sound racist. It wasn't Sesh'tet's Arabic looks that set off her shivers, but the cold reptilian feel of the woman's touch. The way her eyes bulged dark, unaccustomed to the sun.

Diane just looked amused. "You mean her clothes—that whole bundled-up thing?"

"Partly."

"Oh, that's gotten a lot better. When I first started coming to meetings, she was wearing a veil over her whole body. And gloves. She's really loosened up since…"

Diane glanced past her at the wall clock and broke off mid-sentence.

"Since when?"

"Since she's been in this country, I guess." Diane reached for her big duffel coat and backpack. "I've got to run. Visiting hours at the hospital started half an hour ago."

Her expression was so grim, Sara hated to ask.

"It's one of my circle sisters." Diane bit her lip. "She's… not good. Sesh'tet asked me to stop by and drop off the week's readings, maybe pray with her if she was awake."

Her gaze slid away. "Not likely."

When Sara got home that night, she had two messages on her machine. One was from Dr. Stanley, her instructor from last summer's Egyptology course.

The other was a voice she'd never expected to hear again.

"Sara? Sara, pick up if you're there. Please." The speaker hesitated. "OK, either you're gone or you're still pissed at me… but I'm back, and I wanted you to know. That job in Seattle didn't work out. I'm staying at my sister's for now."

Another pause, longer this time.

"I know you've still got her number. If you haven't eaten yet, give me a call and we can go out. Greek or Chinese or whatever you want. I'd like to talk."

Mine started working for me really fast.

Sweat trickled down inside her shirt, stinging the raw spot Sesh'tet's amulet had left. Absently, she scratched it as she played her ex's message again. It sounded unreal. Scripted, though the shadows in every corner of her very empty bedroom didn't care. You wanted who you wanted, and if…

No.

With an effort, she deleted that message and started the other. Martin Stanley sounded older than she remembered. All he'd left was his San Francisco phone number—which she'd asked for in last night's e-mail—and a terse suggestion to use it immediately.

He picked up on the second ring.

"I'm glad you called, Sara." His voice was shaky and exhausted. "I've been... concerned about that information you sent. Ammutseba isn't a name one runs across often in the literature. She's strictly First Intermediate. Very esoteric—fortunately."

Which explained how her own small library had failed her. But "fortunately"? Martin's lectures had never shied away from the controversial, the bloody, or the morbid. He delighted in the details of mummification. When he described the contendings of Set and Horus, eye-gouging and castration figured prominently. So what made Ammutseba different?

"To begin with, she isn't actually Egyptian. Probably a leftover from Stygian cultic practice, though some think she goes back further than that."

"Stygian?"

"A *very* early pre-Egyptian culture. One can't call it a civilization, from the evidence." He laughed mirthlessly. "The only Egyptology program in this country that covers it is Miskatonic's. I did post-grad field work with them in the '70s, on linkages between religious change in the First Intermediate Period and the rise of tomb-robbing."

Sara frowned, fascinated in spite of her own problems. "Sounds, um, esoteric. Did you find anything?"

"More than we'd expected." She heard pages being turned. "Your scan of the amulet's design didn't come through on this end. Could you describe it for me?"

"Three upside-down, five-pointed stars under something like a table. The amulet looks like basalt, but it didn't feel..."

"I know." More pages. "Three is the Egyptian number of plurality—representing many, or any large number. Your table hieroglyph is probably *pet*, sky. The star hieroglyph, *seba*, hardly ever appears inverted. Are you sure?"

"I have the drawing right here." She reached for the amulet's box beside it. "Do you want me to check the original?"

"God, no. Don't touch it." He took a long, unsteady breath. "Sara, are you wearing that amulet?"

"Not now."

There was another silence, punctuated by the thump/shuffle of books being moved.

"OK, Sara," he finally said. "I want you to wrap that amulet up and send it here. I'll e-mail you the address, and I need yours. I'll be sending you some photocopies, plus an old field journal I've got. In the meantime, stay away from that study group."

"It's a women's spirituality circle." How could she have read him so wrong? Despite his flair for the sensational, Martin had never struck her as anything but a mainstream Egyptologist. She'd expected help, not a one-way ticket to Bram Stoker country.

Now he was laughing again, bitterly. "Well it *would* be, wouldn't it? How utterly perfect. Seven Sisters all over again."

He hesitated, his breathing ragged. "Listen, Sara. Ever read Lovecraft's Egyptian stuff? *'Older than Memphis and mankind?'* HPL didn't know the half of it! He'd never walked on those sands at the dark of the moon, under the dying light of murdered stars. He'd never been inside an Old Kingdom tomb, seen what the two-legged jackals left... what they scrawled on burial chamber walls after they'd torn royal mummies apart for the jewels and the gold. Maybe he'd read about it happening, all right—but he didn't know *in whose Name they did it.*"

Reaching for her desk lamp, Sara turned it on and felt a little better. Maybe.

"Martin, this is sounding way too Indiana Jones. My friend Diane—the one who took me to the meeting—isn't a tomb robber, for Godsakes. She's just a New Age feminist who thinks she's tapped into some ancient 'female energy.'"

Martin snorted.

"The poor fool's got it backwards. There's ancient energy, all right... unless I'm very much mistaken... but *it's* tapped into *her.* Her and all the others. This High Priestess Sesh'tet isn't some neo-pagan pretender. She's the genuine article, though I can't think how it happened."

"Diane said something about an initiation in the Valley of the Kings." Sara hesitated, thoroughly confused. "It was kept secret because of the Egyptian government."

"The Egyptian government's notion of evil begins and ends with radical fundamentalist Islam. This particular evil is far older than Mohammed—or even Alhazred."

He paused, and she could hear him gulping water. "All these pagan revivals and survivals.... mix and match spirituality... it's no good, Sara. Not good at all. Traditional 'earth religions' have their dark side—and Kemet's is darker than most because it's so much older. People have no idea... they buy their Mommy Isis statues and little Bast cats and never think about the rest of it. Set chopping up his own brother. Apophis coiled in the Underworld and, God, what the Sphinx was first carved to mimic..."

She heard a rattle of pills, then, and more gulping. More ragged breathing.

"Martin? Are you OK?"

"Just tell me you're going to leave this alone. Send me that amulet—quickly—but leave this 'spirituality group' alone. Leave your friend Diane alone, too. She sounds like a believer, and belief is power. Belief raises power—they knew that, in ancient Memphis. And in the cult-temples of Stygia."

Sara reached for a notepad and wrote the last word down, underlining it twice. "All right," she said. "I won't go to any more circle meetings, and I'll send you the amulet tomorrow."

Martin laughed dryly. "That's a start." The humor drained from his voice. "It's been good talking to you. You take care."

He hung up before she could reply, leaving her alone in her desk lamp's inadequate light. Scrambling to her feet, Sara flipped on the overhead.

Then started digging through drawers for mailing labels.

Next morning, exhausted by broken sleep and worse dreams, she sent Martin the amulet from work. Next day delivery weighed on her conscience, but she couldn't imagine explaining to her boss. After the phone call last night, she'd checked through Diane's photocopies. *The Gate of All Lost Stars* was a creepy piece of work, though it did sound believably Egyptian.

And, indeed, this week's readings were about focus.

For the true intention of Her heart is hidden from the lesser gods of this world, and her aspect is unknown. She is darker than the shadow heart of night, deeper than the Duat. No lesser eye knows her true appearance… none testifies to Her appetites accurately.

She called Diane during her lunch hour, hoping for a little enlightenment—only to be told that her friend had left work early for a doctor's appointment. Not a short one, either, judging by the disapproval in the bookstore owner's voice.

Sara hung up frowning. She couldn't imagine what her friend might need to see a doctor about, though yesterday's lunch suggested an eating disorder. Was she supplementing woman power with bulimia?

The longer the afternoon wore on, the more she worried. Martin was right, unfortunately: Diane was a believer. What she'd latched onto this time almost certainly wasn't good for her. Nor did it seem to be healthy for some of her "sisters"… unless that was sheer coincidence. Had Martin's rant about pre-Dynastic cults done a number on her nerves last night?

She finally decided to swing by Diane's on her way home from work.

A half-familiar smell lingered in the stairwell of the basement apartment. Balsam and cedar and—dust? earth?—plus something else she couldn't place. The first three scents reminded her of the incense from the circle meeting.

The last was... almost reptilian, she'd have said, but garter snakes didn't hang around this late into fall.

Diane answered her knock by peering through the peephole. When she opened her door, she didn't take the chain off immediately.

As Sara reached through to do it for her, she caught a stronger whiff of incense—and a glimpse of burning candles on Diane's altar in one corner of the living room.

"I really do need to talk to you." She slipped inside before Diane could change her mind. "It's important, and it won't take long."

Her friend just shrugged. Her eyes looked red-rimmed, bloodshot, and not too focused. She was holding a nearly empty wine glass.

Sara felt her stomach knotting. Diane almost never drank.

"What's wrong?" she asked, heading for the battered couch. Diane perched on one arm of it, clutching her glass in both hands now. She made no effort to speak, drink, or offer any hospitality—and she looked as though she'd start crying again any second.

Frustrated beyond words, Sara decided to check out her personal altar instead. After last night's phone call, she wasn't in the mood for manners. She needed information—any information—which might clarify Martin's disturbing hints.

It didn't take long to find some.

Depending on the season and Diane's current pagan interests, the small table might hold any combination of votive candles, statuettes—generally goddesses—and found objects. Pride of place tonight went to a dull black bowl holding charcoal and a few nuggets of incense. Incense wasn't Diane's thing. Sara's frown deepened as she examined the bowl itself: a *pet* hieroglyph with three upside-down stars had been incised deeply into one side, then filled with red pigment.

The rest of the table top was crowded with lit votives in wildly assorted holders. "What's this?" she asked, trying to keep her tone light. "Your whole supply?"

Diane nodded.

"Mind if I ask what for?"

"I thought they might help. More light. More energy." She waved feebly toward the little candles, which weren't burning well. "Maybe I haven't got enough."

Sara's stomach clenched. "Enough for what?"

When her friend didn't answer, she returned to the couch and sat down. "Look, I know you've been to the doctor's. Your boss told me. She sounded pretty concerned."

Diane took a gulp of wine. "It was just some tests, OK?"

"What kind of tests?"

Her friend's lips tightened. In the silence, Sara could hear the votives sputtering in their holders, threatening to go out. The bitter incense curled in her nostrils as she grabbed Diane's hand. "*What kind?*"

"Cervical… cancer. Maybe cancer. Maybe just a bad Pap reading."

The way she said it, though, this wasn't the first round of tests. Or even the first doctor. And cervical cancer was nasty even if you caught it early, which Sara was guessing they hadn't. So much for weight loss.

Diane's fingers slipped inside the open neck of her flannel shirt, twisting her amulet's cord. Biting her lip, Sara yanked her friend's hand away.

"Leave that damn thing alone!"

Diane just stared at her, crying. Sara grabbed the braided cord and tried yanking it over her head, cursing again when that didn't work. In a burst of fear and rage, she pulled the shirt open—sending buttons flying—and winced as she saw what lay underneath.

Angry streaks of inflammation fanned out from the top of a black camisole. Her amulet nestled between her breasts, as Sara's had, but it didn't look much like stone. Its slick oily surface pulsed and rippled with each breath Diane took, bulging like a pustule.

Or a leech gorged on blood.

Diane kept crying as Sara wrapped her hand with tissues and tried to pull the thing off. It finally came away with a sharp wet pop, seeping blood and yellow fluid. The underside bristled with writhing cilia.

She yelped and threw it at the door—then ran to crush it underfoot, frowning when her boot heel met something hard rather than squashy. Gritting her teeth, she ground until she heard a brittle snap.

Diane gasped.

"That's done it—I hope." Still using a tissue, Sara gathered the amulet's pieces and crumpled them into it. "I'd pitch this in the outside garbage if I were you."

Diane stared down at the wad on the coffee table. "What *was* that? I mean, it looks OK now, but when you pulled it off…"

"I don't know."

But whatever it was, Sesh'tet made it for you. Your so-empowering High Priestess who worships this Ammutseba thing, this ancient darkness even tomb robbers were probably scared of.

One by one, the altar votives began flickering out. Diane looked up to watch them briefly, then buried her head in her hands.

"I'm sorry," Sara whispered. "I just wish there was something else I could do."

Diane raised her head to stare at her with bloodshot eyes. "You mean that?"

When Sara nodded reluctantly, she dug a photocopy from under some magazines. It showed a crude map and a few driving directions.

"Our circle's doing a healing ritual on the night of the 18th," she said, handing it to her. "Leonids night. Sesh'tet's going to lead it for all of us who have… problems. It's a power raising, so the more women who come, the better."

Sara hesitated. Power raising was common to many traditions—but it wasn't Egyptian.

"It's going to be outside, under the stars. The shooting stars." Diane smiled faintly. "Sesh'tet says they'll be a strong focus for intention and healing. *And the stars are as bread for Her body; even the imperishable stars in the height of the sky are as thousands of bread. For Her restoration she shall swallow up their fires in the night.*'"

Tiny hairs rose on the back of Sara's neck. "Where did you get that?"

"One of the *Gate* readings. Powerful, isn't it?" Her smile faded. "Just tell me you'll come, Sara. Please. For me."

Next day at work was a slow-motion nightmare, haunted by the images of Lost Aegypt. Even the Rameses II photo she'd once been tempted to buy made her shudder. Its chunks of eroded stone in the Nubian desert now resembled a tomb robber's leftovers, some dismembered royal victim whose once-imperishable body now fed jackals.

And beyond those robbers rose something even older and more malevolent. Something which granted worshippers the gift of moonless, starless darkness. The cult of Ammutseba: a name she'd translated as *Devourer of Stars*.

Martin Stanley was right. Some lost gods needed to stay lost.

Sara called the metaphysical bookstore during her lunch hour, only to be told Diane was out sick. She knew she ought to check on her on the way home, but she wasn't nearly ready to face that situation again. Not until she'd read whatever Martin had promised to send her.

The padded envelope with its Next Day stickers was jammed into her apartment's mailbox. She pried it out with difficulty, then took the stairs up two at a time.

Her answering machine was flashing for attention as she walked in.

"Sara? Sara, if you're there, please pick up… OK, here's the deal. I'm still at my sister's and I'd still like to see you. Could you please call me?"

She was tempted. Dinner with her ex (though he hadn't offered dinner this time, she noticed) just might be a good idea. A break from this sick morbid mess Diane had gotten her into. All she had to do was call Martin first, let him know his stuff arrived, and then she could take a little time for *her* life.

With guilty relief, she laid the envelope on her desk and dialed San Francisco.

Somewhere in the static, Martin's phone rang... and kept ringing. She was about to hang up when a younger male voice answered.

"Could I speak with Dr. Martin Stanley, please?"

For several seconds, the unfamiliar voice—Middle Eastern, and very musical—said nothing.

It was too busy stifling grief.

"I'm sorry," she finally broke in, feeling awful. "I'll try back later. I'm a former student of Dr. Stanley's..."

"Are you Sara? Is this about the package you sent him?"

"Actually, about the one he sent me. But I did send him one, too. Did it arrive?"

Only faint, sick laughter replied.

"I'm sorry?"

"Yes, your little box arrived. This morning it arrived. Martin took it to his study to examine it. When I called him for lunch about one o'clock, he didn't come out."

"What's happened?" She knew, suddenly, that something terrible had.

"Martin's dead." The voice took on a cautious tone. "He'd been ill for a long time, but we both thought he was coping well. Then, this afternoon, it... exploded. All over his body, his face... "

"*What's happened?*"

Another, longer hesitation. "Did he ever tell you why he stopped teaching and moved back here?"

"Not really." Though Martin had mentioned something, just before he left, about health problems. There weren't many health problems people wouldn't discuss in Boulder—but she could think of one that might fit these circumstances.

"Ever heard of Kaposi's Sarcoma?" asked the voice. "Connective tissue cancer—very ugly. Dark lesions under the skin, and Martin had them *everywhere* when I found him. Purplish-brown blotches like medieval plague, like his whole body was rotting."

He took a long, shuddering breath. "They aren't sure yet how he died, but his doctor says his lungs were involved—and that he's never seen lesions erupt so rapidly. I mean, Martin had been living with AIDS since... "

Sara felt herself start shaking.

"Please—can you tell me what happened to the box? Did Martin even open it?"

The only response was an agonized flood of Arabic, or maybe Farsi. She got the vague impression that he was cursing someone. Her? Fate?

Ammutseba?

Murmuring condolences, Sara hung up. With one trembling finger, she erased her ex's message—then sat motionless for several minutes at her desk, paralyzed by shock too deep for grief. She knew, as surely as the voice in San Francisco did, that her amulet had killed Martin Stanley. And that Diane's amulet was trying very hard to kill her.

Cilia writhed behind her eyes as she reached for Martin's padded envelope.

The contents hardly seemed worth dying for. Only a worn canvas-bound field journal and one sheaf of photocopies—though several slips of paper and yellowed newspaper clippings protruded from the journal. Blinking back tears she had no time for, Sara opened it carefully.

Journal of: Evelyn Bishop, Valley of the Kings, 1924–25 Season.

Evelyn was a copyist, the daughter of an American excavator working some tomb site in the vicinity of KV 62. That meant they'd caught the aftermath of Howard Carter's discovery... though she couldn't recall anybody else in that area then.

Curious, she flipped through the first few pages. It seemed to be both diary and sketch book, including some watercolors. Evelyn didn't draw maps of the area, however—and she never mentioned the tomb by number.

Instead, she used the same nickname Martin had: Seven Sisters. It didn't take long to see why. Their entire season had been taken up with removing over a dozen mummies from niches cut into the tunnel-like tomb's rock walls. All the mummies so far had been female.

Sara frowned. Aside from a few stockpiles of already-desecrated royals, hidden in the vain hope of protecting them from robbers, multiple entombments weren't common. These women hadn't been re-entombed—or even apparently royal.

Priestesses, Evelyn noted, below a sketch showing one entire wall of niche tombs. *But not Hathor's, or anyone recognizable.* She added a hieroglyphic scrawl after this last: three spiky blobs under some kind of table. In red ink.

Next to the scrawl, a slip of paper bore one word in Martin's handwriting. *Ammut-seba?*

That same glyph turned up all over this sprawling tomb, always in red. Like a good copyist, Evelyn recorded each occurrence, though none of the excavators had any theories. They were also beginning to grumble that this site wasn't even a proper KV tomb.

Too early. And the walls look wrong.

Evelyn added a sketch to illustrate. Where a normal rock-cut tomb had chips and flaws marking door-sill edges, Seven Sisters had what looked like *drippings*—as though something had burned through it, melting rock like wax.

Another slip of paper fluttered to the floor. *Stygian: Shuddam-El*, Martin had written. *Devourer of the Earth (Khemite), or ??? S-E in service to A? Alliance? No wonder tomb robbers 1st Intermed. so hideously effective!*

Sara stared. Martin had called Stygia a "very early" pre-Egyptian culture—which made it just about older than any she could imagine.

Maybe even pre-human?

Of course, this tomb couldn't be pre-human. Evelyn's fragmentary grave-goods list on the following page suggested early Dynastic, with an abrupt cut-off near the end of the First Intermediate period. After that, the tomb had been sealed up (how? *from which side?*) and hidden so well even catalogers never found it.

The only evidence that anyone other than the occupants ever had known its location appeared in a sketch a couple of pages later. Red clay potsherds, as found near the misshapen crack of the tomb's only entrance.

Breaking the Red Pots, Martin's note added helpfully. *Early ritual exorcism—funerary rite?—to destroy malign spirits or?*

The tomb's occupants hadn't been popular in life, either. Several had died by fire, or violence so obvious even mummification couldn't hide it. Evelyn's father expected to find more of the same when he unwrapped his chosen specimen. She would be sketching it, of course, but she confessed to feeling queasy about the assignment.

Queasy didn't begin to describe Sara's own feelings as she read. For a while it was mostly sketches: not mummies, yet, but wall ornamentation. Walls and ceiling. The tomb's main chamber ceiling boasted a strange variant on the Nut-mother of later tombs, her dark form twisted and bloated by cankers which—on closer examination—seemed to be clusters of stars. Another steady stream of stars poured (or was being sucked?) into her gaping mouth.

Gate p. 12, Martin noted. *As highlighted.*

Sure enough, the sheaf of papers was entitled *The Gate of All Lost Stars: A Fragmentary Translation*. She couldn't find a translator's name, and the manuscript looked as though it had been photocopied at least a dozen times. The handwriting was clear enough otherwise, though: tiny neat academic script below meticulously drawn lines of hieroglyphs.

Page twelve had its own heading: Of How She May Come Forth By Night. *Behold, Ammutseba has devoured the light of the stars, she has eaten their words of power, she has eaten their spirits...*

Sara stared at the highlighted passage. Here it was, from *And the stars are as bread for Her body* to *For Her restoration she shall swallow up their fires in the night*. The whole week's reading as Diane had supplied it to her—but how had Martin known? She hadn't quoted it to him on the phone, or in her e-mails.

Turning back to Evelyn's drawing of the Nut-like figure, she found three words written beneath it in faded pencil. *Devourer of Stars.*

And, again, the table-and-three-spiky-blobs glyph. This time, though, the blobs were three upside-down stars. This thing... this diseased, woman-shaped black hole... *was* Ammutseba. And swallowing stars (weren't stars the souls of Kemet's blessed dead?), nourished her.

Allowed her to her come forth by night.

Desperately, Sara dove back into the journal. *Gate* had something to do with the Seven Sisters tomb, and she guessed it might have been found there. But where? She'd seen no mention of papyri found with the mummies, or any tomb texts on the walls.

It took her a month's entries to find out. In the meantime, she came across another of Martin's notes—with the epithet *Daughter of Isfet* (Chaos / Azathoth?)—accompanying a tomb wall sketch with similar hieroglyphs. Copying this bit of art had given Evelyn nightmares.

It's as though we aren't alone here any more. All the mummies... the awful ways some of them died... really starting to wear on me. Father says they found the ideal specimen today, though. A High Priestess, from her regalia, maybe the last one entombed here. Strangled and stabbed and burned...

So the worship of Ammutseba wasn't healthy then, either. Sara flipped forward. Sure enough, Evelyn's father picked this last mummy to unwrap— defying the wishes of his colleagues.

But it's all right, Evelyn noted the next day, *because there's actually writing on some of the bandages. Hieroglyphs. Whole words and phrases and prayers.*

Sure enough, she'd found *Gate*. Skimming ahead, Sara learned that several other mummies were also being unwrapped, in search of more texts. Meanwhile, Evelyn's father continued with his High Priestess.

I'm supposed to start sketching her tomorrow. I don't want to. Her face is... awful, what's left of it. What they did to her...

Besides, I'm nursing Dr. Parker now. He's got a terrible fever and none of the fellaheen will go near him.

She was skimming ahead, noting uneasily that the native workers disappeared from the site soon after, when she came across another sketch. This one was full page and tinted with watercolor, but less detailed than Evelyn's usual.

And something about it was faintly, hideously, familiar.

Readjusting her desk lamp, Sara studied it. She'd seen unwrapped mummies before, in half a dozen books. The look of ancient death had never bothered her. So why did this particular one send cold spiders down her spine?

To start with, it didn't look quite human. The frail woman's face was freakishly narrow, and her leathery eye sockets took up far too much of it. They'd been both rounder and larger than any normal person's. More like a nocturnal animal...

She whispered the name an instant before she read it, penciled below the sketch. *Sesh-tet.*

She's the genuine article, though I can't think how it happened.

The journal slipped from her shaking hands, scattering newspaper clippings like dead leaves. The *Cairo Daily News*, 1925: three brief mentions of a young woman rescued in the Valley of the Kings. Delirious with fever and sunstroke, she'd had nothing with her but a knapsack stuffed with what appeared to be mummy wrappings. Under these, they'd found her field journal—which was fortunate, since her tongue had been too swollen for speech.

She died alone in a charity hospital two days later.

Diane called Sara at work next morning, but only to remind her about the power raising. If she'd heard back from her tests, she wasn't telling—and Sara wasn't asking. She just wanted a few particulars about the ritual site, a recreational area a few miles outside town.

"Good and private, this time of year," Diane assured her. "Unless we get too much cloud cover, it'll be fantastic. Just be sure to set your alarm!"

Sara frowned. "On the weekend?"

"Leonids should be peaking around 3 A.M. Sunday. The 18th, remember? The paper says we've got a good chance at the meteor storm of a lifetime. Sesh'tet's really excited."

For Her restoration she shall swallow up their fires in the night...

"I'm sure she is."

Fighting the urge to warn her, Sara halfway promised to come if she didn't oversleep. Then she hung up, her exhausted mind spinning. After reading Martin's photocopy until dawn, all she knew for sure was that power wouldn't be the only thing raised this Sunday morning. Not if Sesh'tet had her way.

She tried catching up on her sleep that night—hardly her idea of a Friday—then spent Saturday running around madly. The *Gate* translation offered little guidance, and less encouragement. Like other tomb texts, it was a "book" for believers... but not for use in the next world.

Instead, most passages spoke of Ammutseba manifesting in *this* world.

Hail, O ye who open up the ways of night, O guide and guardian in the nameless hours... devourer of the beaten path of stars, She who was the thought of Isfet before the sky was split from the earth... before the Ones Who Were withdrew to their abysses beyond the sky...

That sky was utterly clear when she drove out of Boulder around one on Sunday morning. Sara cut her headlights a mile from the site, praying she wouldn't cause an accident. Faint meteor streaks in the distance tempted her to drive faster—what if the ritual had already started?—but gravel roads weren't quiet at speed.

She inched along impatiently until she spotted the first parked cars. Then, turning off her engine, she waited for her eyes to adjust. In the open field ahead, flashlight beams bobbed and wove in some kind of dance. She watched for a while, then eased her door open. The light sharp wind carried women's voices, raised in a song—chant?—which didn't sound Egyptian at all. Or like any pagan ritual she'd ever attended.

Her spine stiffened as she recognized names and phrases from *The Gate of All Lost Stars*. They were burning incense, too, the same bitter stuff from the circle meeting... and one page of Evelyn Bishop's journal, where she'd smeared yellowish paste from a jar in the tomb.

Grabbing her overstuffed knapsack, she ducked away from her car.

Meteors were streaking above the Flatirons now, more every minute. The chant grew louder. Some of the women were coughing as they chanted, choking on the strange gutturals—or perhaps on the smoke twisting up against the night. They'd marked out their ritual circle with smudge pots.

Stepping carefully on the crisp grass, Sara moved forward until she could recognize people. Diane, of course, her believer's face lifted to the shooting stars. Seven or eight other women—two on crutches, one on blankets on the ground—and, in the center, a tiny figure swathed in darkness.

Sara loosened her pack's drawstring as she slipped it from her shoulders.

It was Sesh'tet's voice, she realized, which rose so clearly over the others—reedy and thin, yet with unmistakable power. Every syllable fell crisp and perfect from her lipless mouth, ringing with adoration.

"Ia! Isfet-daughter! Ammutseba!"

A collective gasp rose from the circle of women. They were all staring into the sky—even Sesh'tet, though she still kept up the chant, soloing now.

Sara noticed nothing at first. Nothing but a thin dark haze, like incense smoke stretched across the night... but too high and far too plentiful for mere smudge pots. The wind wasn't moving it around, either. When one meteor's path crossed into that haze, it flared abruptly and vanished, like a candle flame blown out.

Sesh'tet raised both arms in a wide, triumphant gesture. "*Ia! Ammut-seba!*"

As the others echoed her, the woman on the blankets began moaning. Diane and another circle member hurried toward her, only to be intercepted by their High Priestess.

"She is first to ascend!" Sesh'tet cried. "She is first among us all to live forever!"

From where Sara stood, the stricken woman was doing no such thing. As her moaning changed to whimpering, she lifted herself on her elbows, staring around in shock and agony. Then one thin tendril of whitish... *smoke?* ...seeped from between her parted lips, snaking on the wind toward Sesh'tet.

Sesh'tet inhaled. Another meteor winked out in the thickening mist over-head.

"Ia! First among us all to live forever!"

As her circle sisters took up the cry, the woman on the ground collapsed. Sesh'tet lifted her arms higher, their enfolding dark sleeves slipping back for the first time. The skin underneath, though brown and smooth and perfect, was crisscrossed with some very odd striations. Like bandages.

Wishing she'd brought binoculars, Sara felt her gut clench. What she thought she'd just seen—what the *Gate* translation had predicted in gleeful detail—simply could not be happening. Meanwhile, the Leonids kept raining down just as predicted, a real banner year.

Except that now a lot of them weren't raining *down*. Just vanishing into that body of dark vapor overhead—which was looking more and more like a real body.

The body of Nut-mother, but twisted... corrupted... stretching out across the stars to devour them...

Diane wasn't chanting now. She was screaming. Wrenching her attention from the horror overhead, Sara saw her friend fall to her knees at one edge of the circle. The others spiraled out in their dance without breaking step, leaving her alone at the center with the body sprawled on its blankets.

And with Sesh'tet.

Fishing a lighter from one pocket, Sara reached into her knapsack. The first bottle gurgled in her hand as she lit its rag wick. Barely pausing to aim, she hurled it flaming toward the circle's heart, praying Diane wasn't wearing anything flammable.

Her first throw went wild, catching one of her target's flowing sleeves.

Sesh'tet shrieked and tore the burning cloth away, exposing her right arm to the shoulder. Just above the elbow, that same arm dwindled to a dark twig of leather and bone. Worse, her enveloping hood had slipped back. Above that narrow face with its strange, too-wide eyes, nothing but mummified skin stretched tight over her skull.

"Look at her!" Sara yelled at the others, voice raw with desperation. "She's not human! She was *never* human!"

Their chanting faltered as dancer after dancer—all but Diane, sprawled on the ground now—broke step and stared. Sara lit another bottle. This time, it landed right at Sesh'tet's feet, spattering her with broken glass and flaming fuel.

Without stopping to watch, Sara ignited a third. Sesh'tet shrieked again, gesturing in her attacker's direction with her still-draped arm.

"*She must... not... live!*"

The others hesitated, trembling like aspens in a high wind. Then, in one tight silent pack, they rushed her.

Sara hurled her last missile over their heads and ran as hard as she could. Circling wide, she doubled back toward Diane—and the writhing woman-torch still lifting her hands to the sky. Still calling on the Darkness now stretching Her solidifying mass above their heads, quenching meteors like so many fireworks.

"Isfet-daughter! Ammutseba!"

Diane was on her hands and knees now. Crawling toward the High Priestess, she grabbed a handful of burning hem and yanked with all her strength. Sesh'tet staggered. Still racing to help, Sara stumbled over one of the smudge-pots, shattering it.

Sesh'tet's shriek changed to a high, terrible wailing.

Breaking the Red Pots. These pots weren't red—aside from their distinctive hieroglyphs, anyhow—but they were certainly breakable enough. Sara turned and kicked another pot, then another. Charcoal and incense scattered across a patch of snow and died.

As the pack caught up at last, Sara kicked at more pots and shouted for their help.

"They're making her stronger. They're making that thing in the sky stronger! Get this stuff put out now!"

One or two women grabbed at her, still confused, but the rest started stomping or swatting with crutches. Sara looked around for Diane. She was still dragging at Sesh'tet's robes, her own hands and arms horribly burned. Her lips moved in a profane litany.

It took Sara a moment to realize what Diane was dragging the burning woman toward. Her final missile—unbroken after a bad throw—lay on the ground, still half-full. Releasing her hold on Sesh'tet with one hand, she grabbed for it.

"It's OK," Diane said, grinning at Sara as she raised the smoldering wine bottle. "I'm taking the bitch with me."

Tightening her grip, she smashed it against Ammutseba's priestess.

Somebody ran back for a Land Rover's water jugs, but it didn't matter. Seasoned by thousands of years, Sesh'tet went up in a flaming pillar against the night. The last sound from her dying captor's mouth was a scream of triumph.

Overhead, the dark mist-shape quivered and swirled, coalescing again briefly. Then it dispersed on the wind, accompanied by a few scattered meteors.

"She really was dying anyway," the Rover's owner told Sara softly. "She told us tonight, before the ritual. Those tests…"

Sara turned away. There was a hard, cold lump in her throat, and she didn't want to start thinking about lumps. Maybe she and the others would be all right in the morning.

Maybe that tiny burning pain she'd felt in one breast lately would be gone.

ଧ ଧ

The Oram County Whoosit

Steve Duffy

Maybe for the rest of the welcoming committee it was the proudest afternoon of their lives; I remember it mostly as one of the wettest of mine. We were standing on a platform in Oram, West Virginia, waiting for a train to pull in, and it hadn't stopped raining all day. It wasn't really a problem for everybody else: the mayor had a big umbrella, and his cronies had the shelter of the awning, over by the ticket office. I had my damn hat, was all.

They belonged to the town, you see, and I didn't. I'd been sent down from Washington, like the guest of honour we were all waiting on that day. Our newspaper had sprung for him to travel first-class, having sent me along the afternoon before in a ratting old caboose—to pave the way for his greatness, I guess. Because he was some kind of a great man even then, in newspaper circles at least. Nowadays, you'll find his stories in all the best textbooks, but back then the majority of folks knew Horton Keith mostly from the stuff they read over the breakfast table; which was pretty damn good, don't get me wrong. But then so were my photographs, or so I thought, so why was I the one left outside in the cold and wet like a red-headed stepchild? It's a hell of a life, and no mistake; that's what I was thinking. I was twenty-four back then, in case you hadn't guessed: as old as the century. That didn't feel so old then—but it does now, here on the wrong side of nineteen-eighty. Then again, the century hasn't weathered too well either.

Away down the track a whistle blew, and the welcoming committee spat out their tobacco and gussied themselves up for business. Through the sheets of rain you could barely see the hills above the rooftops, but you felt them pressing in on you: that you did. Row upon row of them, their sides sheer and thickly forested, the tops lost in the dense grey clouds that had lain on the summits ever since I arrived. By now, I was starting to wonder whether there *was* any sort of blue sky up there, or whether mist and rain were the invariable order of the day. Since then I've looked into it scientifically, and what happens is this: the weather fronts blow in off the Atlantic coast, and they scoot across Virginia like a skating rink till they hit the Alleghenies. Then, those fronts get forced up over the mountains by the prevailing winds, and by the time they're coming down the other side, boy, they're dropping like a shot goose. And *then*, the whole bunch of soggy-bottom clouds falls splat on to Oram County, and it rains every goddamn day of the year. Scientifically speaking.

A puff of smoke from round the track, and then the train came into view. The welcoming committee shuffled themselves according to rank and feet above sea-level; one of them dodged off round the side of the station, and hang me for a liar if he didn't come back with a marching band, or the makings of one at least—a tuba, half-a-dozen trumpets, and a big bass drum. The musicians had been waiting someplace under shelter, or so I hoped: if not, then I wasn't going to be standing too close to that tuba when it blew. It might give me a musical shower-bath on top of my regular soaking.

The first man off the train when it pulled in was a Pullman conductor, an imperturbable Negro who looked as if he'd seen this sort of deal at every half-assed station down the line. Next was a nondescript fat man packed tight into a thin man's suit, weighed down by a large cardboard valise. If he looked uncomfortable before, you can bet he looked twice as squirrelly when the band struck up a limping rendition of "Shenandoah" and the mayor bore down on him like a long-lost brother. One look at that, and the poor guy jumped so high I practically lost him in the cloud—his upper slopes, at least. In many ways he was wasted on the travelling-salesman game; he ought to have been trying out for the Olympics over in Paris, France. Instead, he was stuck selling dungarees to miners. Like I said before, it's a hell of a life.

While that little misunderstanding was being cleared up, a few carriages down my man was disembarking, quietly and without any fuss. You may have seen photographs of Horton Keith—you may even have seen *my* photograph of him, which just happens to be the one on the facing-title page of his *Col-*

lected Short Stories—but in many ways he looked more like his caricature. Not a bad-looking man, hell no; that sweep of white hair and the jet-black cookie-duster underneath meant he'd always get recognised, by everyone but the good folk of Oram, West Virginia at any rate. And there was nothing wrong with his features, if you liked 'em lean and hungry-looking. But the hunger was the key, and it came out in the drawings more vividly than in any photo I ever took of him. I never saw a keener man, nor one more likely to stick at it till the job got done. As a hunting acquaintance of mine once put it: "He's a pretty good writer, but he'd have made one hell of a bird-dog."

"Sir?" I presented myself as he stepped down from the train. He looked me up and down and said, "Mister Fenwick?" Subterranean rumble of a voice. I nodded, and tipped the sopping straw brim of my hat. "Good to meet you, sir."

"Nice hat," he said, still taking my measure as he shook my outstretched hand. "Snappy." No hint of a joke in those flinty eyes. It was 1924, for God's sake. *Everyone* wore a straw hat back then.

"I guess it's had most of the snap soaked out of it by now," I said, taking it off and examining it. "We could dry it out, maybe, or else there's a horse back there in town without a tooth in his head, poor bastard. He could probably use it for his supper."

Keith smiled at that. Didn't go overboard or anything; but I think I passed the test. Then, the welcoming committee were upon us.

🙰 🙰

The guest of honour was polite and everything; that is to say, he wasn't outright rude, not to their faces. He shook all their hands, and listened to a few bars more of "Shenandoah" from underneath the mayor's big umbrella. I was fine, I had my snappy straw hat. But then the mayor, a big moose called Kronke, wanted to cart him off in the civic automobile for some sort of a formal reception with drinks, and Keith drew the line at that.

"Gentlemen, it's been a long day, and I need to consult with my colleague here. We'll meet up first thing in the morning, if it's all the same to you." *My colleague.* That was about the nicest thing I'd heard since I'd arrived in Oram County. It did my self-esteem a power of good; better than that, it got me a lift in the mayoral flivver as far as the McEndoe Hotel, which was where Keith and I had rooms.

The McEndoe was a rambling old clapboard palace, one of the few buildings in town that went much above two storeys. It had a view over downtown Oram that mostly comprised wet roofs and running gutters, and inevitably you found your eyes were drawn to the wooded hills beyond, brooding and enigmatic beneath their caps of cloud. Here and there you saw scars running down the hillside, old landslides and abandoned workings. Oram was a mining town, and you weren't likely to forget it; at six in the evening the big siren blew, and soon after a stream of men came shuffling down main street on their way home from the pits. Looking at their sooty exhausted faces from my perch in the window of the hotel smoking lounge as I sipped bootleg brandy from my hip flask, I told myself there were worse things in life than getting my hat a little wet. I might have to work for a living, like these poor lugs.

"It's funny," Keith said, close up behind me. I hadn't heard him come in.

"What?" I guessed he meant peculiar; God knows there was little enough that was comical about the view.

He was staring at the miners as they stumbled by in their filthy denim overalls. "I was up in the Klondike round the time of the gold rush, back in '98," he said. "Dug up about enough gold to fill my own teeth, was all. It was like that with most of the men: I never knew but half-a-dozen fellows who ever struck it rich; I mean really rich. But my God, we were eager sons o' bitches! We'd jump out of our bunks in the morning and run over to those workings, go at it like crazy men all the length of a Yukon summer's day till it got dark, and like as not we'd be singing a song all the way home. And were we singing because we were rich? Had we raised so much as a single grain of gold? No, sir. Probably not." He took a cigar from his inside pocket and examined it critically. I waited for him to carry on his story, if that's what it was.

"Now these fellers," he said, indicating with his cigar: "each and every one of them will have pulled maybe a dozen tons of coal out of that hill today. No question. They found what they were looking for, all right. Found a damn sight more of it than we ever did. But you don't see them singing any songs, do you?" He looked at me, and I realised it wasn't a rhetorical question: he was waiting for an answer. I was sipping my drink at the time, and had to clear my throat more quickly that I'd have liked.

"They're working for the company," I said, as soon as I could manage it. "You fellers were working for yourselves. Man doesn't sing songs when he knows someone else is getting eighty, ninety cents out of every dollar he earns."

"No," agreed Keith. "No, he doesn't. But that's just economics, after all. You know what the main difference is?" I had a pretty good idea, but shrugged, so that he'd go on. "We were digging for gold," he said simply, "and these poor sons-of-bitches ain't. Call a man an adventurer, send him to the top of the world so he's half dead from the frostbite and the typhus and the avalanches, and he's happy, 'cause he knows he might—just might!—strike it rich. Set him to dig coal back home day in, day out for a wage, and he's nothing but a slave. It's the difference between what you dream about, and what you wake up to."

It sounds commonplace when I write it down. That's because you don't hear the way his voice sounded, nor see the animation in his face. I don't know if I can put that into words. It wasn't avaricious, not in the slightest. I never met a man less driven by meanness or greed. It was more as if that gold up in the Klondike represented all the magic and excitement he'd ever found in the world; as if the idea had caught hold of him when he was young and come to stand for everything that was fine and desirable, yet would always remain slightly out of reach, the highest, sweetest apple on the tree. That he kept reaching was what I most admired about him, in the end: that he knew he wasn't ever going to win the prize, and yet still reckoned it was worth fighting for. The Lord loves a trier, they say, but sometimes I think he's got a soft spot for the dreamer, too.

"Well, these fellows here might have been digging for coal," I said, offering him a light, "but seems as if a couple of 'em may have lit on something else, doesn't it?"

"Indeed," said Keith, glancing at me from beneath those jet-black bushy eyebrows before bending to the flame of the match. "Now you mention it, I guess it is kind of time we talked about things." He fished out another stogie and offered it to me.

I sat up straight and gave it my best stab at keen and judicious. Keith probably thought I'd gotten smoke in my eyes.

"What do you think we actually have here, Fenwick?" He honestly sounded as if he wanted to know what I thought. Back in my twenties, that was still pretty much of a novelty.

"Toad in a hole," I said promptly. "There's a hundred of 'em in the newspaper morgue—seems like they pop up every summer, around the time the real news dries up."

"Toad in a hole," said Keith thoughtfully. He gestured with his cigar for me to continue. Emboldened, I did so.

"The same story used to run every year in the papers out West," I said, to show I'd done my homework and wasn't just any old newspaper shutterbug. "Goes like this: some feller brings in a lump of rock split in half, it's got a tiny little hole in the middle. See there, he says? That's where the frog was. Jumped clean out when I split the rock in two, he did. Here he is, look—and he lays down some sorry-looking sun-baked pollywog on the desk. Swears with his hand on his heart: it happened just the way I'm telling you, sir, so help me God. And the editor's so desperate, he usually runs with it." I spread my hands. "That's about the way I see it, Mr. Keith."

Keith nodded. "So you don't believe such a thing could happen?"

"Huh-uh." With all the certainty of twenty-four summers. "Toads just can't live inside rocks. Nothing could. No air. No sustenance." Speaking of sustenance, I offered him a pull on my hip flask. Keith accepted, then said:

"But these miners here—they don't claim to have found a toad exactly, now, do they?" He was watching my face narrowly all the while through a pall of cigar smoke, gauging my reactions.

"No sir. They say they've found a whoosit."

"A whoosit."

"Exactly that. A whoosit, just like P.T. Barnum shows on Broadway. A jackalope. A did-you-ever. An allamagoosalum."

"Jersey devil," said Keith, entering into the spirit of the thing.

"Feegee mermaid," I amplified. "Sewn-up mess of spare parts from the taxidermy shop, monkey head stuck on the back end of a catfish. That's the ticket." I felt pleased we'd nailed the whole business on the head. Maybe we could be back in Washington by this time tomorrow evening.

Keith was nodding still. He showed every sign of agreeing with me, right up until he said—musing aloud it seemed—"So, how does a thing like that get inside a slab of coal, do you suppose, Mr. Fenwick?"

"Well, that's just it. It doesn't, sir." Had I not made myself clear?

"But this one did." His deep-set eyes bored into me, but I held my ground.

"So they say. I guess we'll see for ourselves in the morning, sir."

Unexpectedly, Keith dropped me a wink. "The hell with that. I was thinking we might take a stroll down to the courthouse after dinner and save ourselves a night of playing guessing games. Skip all the foofaraw the mayor's got planned. That is, unless you have plans for the rest of the evening?" A wave of his cigar over sleepy downtown Oram.

I spread my hands, palms up. "What do you know? Clara Bow just phoned to say she couldn't make it."

ଌ ଅ

And so, in the absence of Miss Bow's company, I found myself walking out down the main street of Oram with Horton Keith, headed for the courthouse. We'd passed it in the mayor's car earlier that afternoon; Kronke had told us that was where the whoosit was being kept, under lock and key and guarded by his best men. If the man who was on duty out front when we arrived was one of Kronke's best, then I'd have loved to have seen the ones he was keeping in reserve. He was a dried-up, knock-kneed old codger with hardly a tooth left in his head, and when Keith told him we were the men from Washington come to see the whoosit, he waved us right through. "In there," he said, without bothering to get up off his rocking chair. "What there is of it, anyways."

"What there is of it?" Keith's heavy brows came down.

"Feller who found it, Lamar Tibbs? Had him a dispute with the mine bosses when he brung it up last week. They said, any coal comes out of this shaft belongs to the company, and that's that. Lamar, he says well, thisyer freak of nature ain't made of coal though, is it? Blind man can see that. And they say, naw, it ain't. And Lamar, he says, it's more in the nature of an animal, ain't it? And they say, reckon so. And Lamar says, well, I take about a thousand cooties home out of this damn pit of yourn ever' day, so I reckon this big cootie here can come along for the ride as well. And he up an took it home with 'im." The caretaker cackled with senile glee at Lamar's inexorable logic. I guess it was a rare thing for some poor working stiff to get the better of the company, at that. But more to the point:

"You're saying the whoosit isn't actually in there?"

"No sir. It's over to Peck's Ridge, up at the Tibbs place. Mayor's plannin' to take you there in the automobile, I believe—first thing after the grand civic breakfast."

This was starting to look like a snipe hunt we'd been sent on. Keith jabbed his cigar butt at the courthouse. "So what *have* you got in here?"

"Lump o' coal it came out of," said the caretaker proudly. "Got an exact imprint of the whoosit in it, see? Turn it to the light, you can see everything. Like life."

"Is that right?" Keith said. "Company hung on to the lump of coal, I guess?"

"That they did," agreed the last surviving veteran of the Confederate army. "All the coal comes out of that mine's company coal—them's the rules. Mayor's just holdin' it for safekeeping, is all."

"Exactly so," said Keith. "Well, thankyou, sir." He slipped a dollar into the caretaker's eager hand—assuming it was eagerness that made it tremble so. "Now if you could see your way to showing us where they're keeping it, we'll quit bothering you."

"They got it in the basement," said the caretaker, leaning back in his rocker and expelling a gob of tobacco juice. "Keep goin' down till you can't go down no more, mister, an' that'll do it."

The basement of that courthouse was like a mine itself; you might almost have believed they'd dug the whoosit out right there, in situ. Keith and I came to the bottom of a winding flight of stairs and found ourselves in a damp dripping sort of crawlspace, its farther corners filled with shadows the single electric bulb on the ceiling couldn't hope to reach. The ceiling was low enough that we both had to stoop a little, and most of the floor was taken up with trunks and boxes and filing cabinets full of junk. Thank God we weren't looking for anything smaller than a pork barrel. We'd have been down there all night. As it was, we began on opposite sides of the basement and aimed to get the job done in something under an hour.

"This is annoying," Keith called over his shoulder. "These damn rubes don't realise what they've got a hold of here."

"Toad in a hole," I called back. Keith ignored me.

"This miner fellow—"

"Lamar Tibbs," I sang out in an approximation of the caretaker's Virginian twang.

"—he probably thinks he's sitting on a crock of gold, just like the mayor here and the mining company with their slab of coal. But the two things *apart* don't amount to a hill of beans, and they don't have the sense to see it."

"How so?" I didn't think the whole thing amounted to much, myself.

"Because the one authenticates the other, don't you see? Look here, I'm the authorities, okay? This here's some sort of a strange beast you claim to have found in the middle of a piece of coal. Who's to say it's not a, a, what-d'ye-call-'em—"

"Feegee mermaid."

"Feegee mermaid, exactly." A grunt, as he moved some heavy piece of trash out of the way. "Nothing to make a man suppose it ever saw the inside of a slab of coal—*without the coal to prove it*. The imprint of the beast in the coal goes to corroborate the story, see?"

"Yes, but—" I was going to point out that you didn't find beasts, living or dead, inside slabs of coal anyway, so there was no story there to corroborate, only a tall tale out of backwoods West Virginia. But Keith didn't seem to be interested in that self-evident proposition.

"And it's the same thing with the coal. Suppose there is an imprint of something in there? What good is it without the very thing that *made* that imprint? It's just the work of an few weekends for an amateur sculptor, is all." He bent to his task again, shoving more packing-cases out of the way. "They don't understand," he muttered, almost to himself. "You need the two together."

"Even if you did have the two things, though—" I wasn't letting this one go unchallenged—"it still wouldn't *prove* anything, in and of itself. It might go some way towards the *appearance* of proof—hell, it might even make a good enough story for page eight of the newspaper, I guess. That's your business. I just take the pictures, that's all. But at the end of the day—"

At the end of the day, Keith wasn't listening. I happened to glance in his direction at that moment, and saw as much immediately. He was standing in the far corner of the basement, hands on his hips, staring at something on the floor—from where I was, I couldn't make it out. I called his name. I had to call again, and then a third time, before he even noticed. When he did, he looked up with an odd expression on his face.

"Come over here a second, Fenwick," he called, and his voice sounded slightly strained. "Think I've found something."

I crossed to where he was standing. In that corner the light was so dim I could hardly see Keith, let alone whatever it was he'd found, so the first thing we did was lay ahold of it and drag it to the centre of the basement, right beneath the electric bulb. It was heavy as hell, and we pushed it more than carried it across the packed-mud basement floor.

It was lying inside an open packing-case, all wrapped up in a bit of old tarpaulin. You could see the black gleam of coal where Keith had unwrapped it at one end. "You raise it up," muttered Keith, and again I heard that unusual strain in his voice; "I'll get the tarpaulin off of it."

I laid hold of it and heaved it upright, and Keith managed to get the tarp clear. It was just one half of the slab, as it turned out; its facing piece lay underneath wrapped in more tarpaulin. Stood on its end, the half-slab was roughly the size of a high-back dining chair: it would have weighed a lot more, more than we could have dreamed of shifting, probably, except that it was all hollowed out, as if someone had sawn a barrel in half right down its centre.

The hollow space was nothing more than an inky pool of shadow at first, till I tilted the slab toward the light. Then, its shiny black surfaces gave up their secrets, and the electric light reflected off a wealth of curious detail. I gave a low whistle. Whoever's work this was, he was wasted on Oram. He ought to have been knocking out statues for the Pope in Rome. For it was the finest, most intricately detailed job of carving you ever saw—*intaglio*, I believe they call it, where the sculptor carves in hollows instead of relief. There was even a kind of *trompe l'oeil* effect: as you looked at the shape while turning it slightly, it seemed to stand out in prominence, the strange hollow form suddenly becoming filled-out and real. I'd have to say it was actually a little bit unsettling, for a cheap optical illusion.

"My God." A fellow would have been hard put to recognise Keith's voice. It made me turn from the slab of coal to look at him. He was staring openmouthed at the hollow space at the heart of the slab, with an expression I took at first to be awe. Only later did I come to recognise it as something more like horror.

"It's pretty good at that," I allowed. "The detail…"

"It's exact in every detail," said Keith, in wonderment. "You could use it for a mould, and you'd cast yourself a perfect copy." He shook his head, never taking his eyes off of the coal slab.

"Copy of what, though?" I squinted at the concavity, turned it this way and that to get a sense of it in three dimensions. "It's like nothing I've ever seen—it's a regular whoosit, all right. Are those things supposed to be tentacles, there? Only they've got claws on the end, or nippers or something. And where's its head supposed to be?"

"The head retracts," said Keith, almost as if he was reading it from a book. "Like a slug drawing in on itself."

I stared at him. "Beg your pardon, sir?"

"You said it's like nothing you've ever seen," said Keith. "Well, I've seen it. Or something exactly like it."

"You *have*?" It was all I could think of to say.

Keith nodded. "Let's get out of this damn mausoleum," he said abruptly, turning away from the packing-case and its contents. "I'll tell you up in the real world, where a man can breathe clean air, not this infernal stink." And with that he turned his back and was off, stumping up the wooden steps and out of the basement, leaving me to rewrap and repack the slab of coal as best I could before hastening after him.

I was full of questions, all of them to do with the strange artefact we'd been looking at. I have to confess, the level of realism the unknown sculptor had managed to suggest had impressed me—not to say unnerved me. I mentioned before the optical illusion of solidity conjured out of the void, that sensation of seeing the actual thing, not just the impression it had made. That actually began to get to you after a while. Three-dimensional, I said? Well, maybe so. But the longer you looked at it, the dimensions started to looked wrong somehow; impossible, you might say.

On top of that was Keith's admission that he'd seen the like before. What did he mean by that? And over and above everything… well, Keith was right. We needed to be in the fresh air. Fact was, it stank in that damn basement: I've never known a smell like it. It was as if a bushel of something had gone bad, and been left to fester for an long time.

An awful long time, at that.

ଧ ଥ

Back at the hotel Keith went straightaway up to his room for about an hour, leaving me to pick at my evening meal in the all-but-empty dining room. The smell down in that basement had killed my appetite, pretty much; in the end I pushed my plate aside and went to the smoking lounge. That was where

Keith found me.

He looked better than he had back outside the courthouse, at least. I'd found him leaning against the side of the building, looking as if he was going to be sick: he had that grey clammy cast to his face. I asked him was he all right, and he waved me away. Now, there was a little more colour in him, and his eyes were focussing properly again, not staring off into the middle distance the way they do when a fellow is on the verge of losing his lunch.

"You got any of that brandy left?" he said, taking the chair opposite mine. "Medicinal purposes, you understand."

"You're in luck, as it happens," I said, offering him the flask. "I've just taken an inventory of our medical supplies."

"Good," said Keith, and took a long swallow. His eyes teared up a little, but that was only natural. It had kind of a kick to it, that bathtub Napoleon. You could have used it for rocket fuel.

"Well, then." Keith handed me back the flask. "I believe I owe you a story, Mr. Fenwick. Recompense for leaving you with the baby, down there in the basement."

I waved a hand, which could equally be taken to mean, *no problem, don't trouble yourself about it*, or—as I hoped Keith would read it—*Go on, go on, you interest me strangely*. The reason I waved a hand instead of actually saying either of those things was because I'd just taken a pull on that flask myself, and was temporarily speechless.

Keith settled back in his armchair and crossed his long thin legs. He lit a cigar, having thrown me one over too, and then he told me the following tale in the time it took us to reduce them down to ash.

"I was thirty at the time: a dangerous age, Mr. Fenwick. You'll learn that, soon enough. I was working on the *Examiner* back in San Francisco when gold fever hit up in the Yukon, back in '98. That news came at exactly the right time, so far as I was concerned—a lot of other folks too, among that first wave of prospectors and adventurers. I was missing something, we all were: the frontier had been closed, and all the wild days of excitement out West were over, or so it seemed. For better or for worse, the job of shaping the nation was finished, over and done with, and we'd missed the chance to leave our stamp on it. It felt as if we'd all been running West in search of something—something magical and unique, that would make real men out of us—only once we'd gotten there, it had already set sail out of the Golden Gate, and there was no way we could follow. The Gay Nineties, you say? I tell you, there were folks dying in the street in San Francisco. Hunger, want; maybe nothing more than heartbreak.

"So you can bet we jumped at the chance to go prospecting, away up in the frozen wastes. That was a new frontier, sure enough: maybe the last frontier, and we weren't about to miss it. So we piled on to those coffin-ships out of Frisco and Seattle, hundreds of us at a time; stampeders, we called ourselves. There was about as much thinking went into it as goes into a stampede.

"The Canucks wouldn't let you into the country totally unprepared, though. You had to have a ton of goods, supplies and suchlike, else they'd stop you at the docks. So that took some getting together; eleven hundred pounds of food, plus clothing and equipment, horses to carry it with, that sort of thing. I was travelling light—reckoned to hire sled-dogs up in Canada—but even so, my goods took some lugging at the wharf.

"So we sailed North. A thousand miles out of Seattle we made the Lynn Canal, which was where every one of us bold prospectors had to make his first big decision. Where was he going to disembark? 'Cause there were two trails, see, up to Dawson and the gold-fields, six hundred miles due north. You could take the easy route, avoiding all the big mountains—that was Skagway and the White Pass. The other route started in Dyea, and it took in the Chilkoot Pass, leading on to the lakes. Even us greenhorns knew about the Chilkoot by that time.

"A lot of folk chose Skagway, but I never heard anything good about that town. In Indian it's "the place where a fair wind never blows", which pretty much sums it up, I guess. Leave it to the Indians to know which way the wind blows. Soapy Smith's gang ran the town—he was an old-time con-artist out of Georgia, and he knew a hundred ways to pick the pockets of every rube that staggered down the gangplank. Twenty-five cents a day wharf rates on each separate piece of goods. Lodging-houses where they fleeced you on the way in and the way out. Saloons and whorehouses; casinos with rigged wheels and marked cards. Portage fees. Tolls all the way along the trail—and bandits too, armed gangs and desperadoes, hand in glove with the 'official escorts', like as not. No sir: I chose Dyea, which was not a hell of a lot more salubrious, but at least you didn't have Soapy's hand in your britches all the while.

There was ice all over the boat as it hove into Dyea. It looked like a ghost ship, and I guess we were a sorry-enough looking bunch of ghosts as we stumbled off. The mountains came right down to the outskirts of town; took us two weeks of hard going to climb as far as Sheep Camp, at the base of the Chilkoot. I tell you: there were lots of men took one look at that mountainside and gave it up on the spot, stayed on in camp and made a living for themselves as best they could. You couldn't call them the stupid ones, not really. A thousand feet from base to summit, sheer up and down, straight as a beggar can spit? Any sane man would have turned round and said okay, my mistake, beg your pardon.

"We were obliged to stay in Sheep Camp for the best part of March, till the pass came navigable. Bad weather, and the worst kind of terrain; even the Indian guides wouldn't touch it in those conditions. It was just before spring thaw, and the weather was ornery in the extreme. Minus sixty-five one night, by the thermometer in Lobelski's General Store. It stayed light from nine-thirty in the morning to just before four in the afternoon. The rest of it was pitch dark and endless cold.

"They were building kind of a hoisting-gear up the Chilkoot, the tramway they called it, but I never saw it finished. I hauled my goods up there, the old fashioned way. I could have paid the Indians to do it for me, a dollar a pound, but I didn't have two thousand dollars to spare. That was why I was bound for the Yukon in the first place. So I hauled every last case up that mountain side, forty trips in all. I was raw from the chafing of the ropes on my shoulders, and I was nigh on crippled by the exhaustion and the cold—but I managed it. Somehow. Don't ask me how. It'd kill me now if I tried it.

"Truth is, I don't know how it didn't kill me back then. Fifteen hundred toe-holds in the ice, up a trail no more than two feet wide. Take a step to left and right, and you were in the powder stuff, loose and treacherous. If a man slipped, it was all up with him; you never saw him again. That pass was filled with the bodies of good men.

"Anyway! Come April I was over the Chilkoot and heading toward Dawson, a mere five hundred and fifty miles off. The trail led along Lake Linde-man and Lake Bennett: if you waited for the thaw, the sheer volume of melt coming down off the mountains turned the rivers into rapids. If you went early, like I did, it was just a question of praying the ice wouldn't break. You put it out of your mind, till it came time to camp at night and you'd hear the ice creaking and groaning below you. We rigged up the sleds with sails, and the wind used to push us along at a fine clip. All we had to do was trust in the Lord and watch out for the cracks.

"The lakes weren't properly clear of ice till the end of May, and by that time we bold sled-skaters were already in Dawson, just six months after we'd first set out to strike it rich. Dawson was a stumpy, scroungy kind of town at the bend of the river, set on mudflats and made of nothing much but mud, or so it seemed. Five hundred people lived there as a rule: gold fever pushed that up to twelve thousand by the start of the year, thirty thousand by that sum-mer's end. It was a breeding ground for typhoid—I stayed clear of the place, except when I made my victualling run once a week.

"I was working my claim south-east of Dawson city, out among the dried-up river beds. That was where I got my crash-course in mining—a year earlier, I'd have thought you just scuffed around in the dirt with the toe of your boot till you turned up some nuggets. Not in Yukon territory. You had to dig your way down to the pastry, we called it, the layers where the gold lay, through forty, fifty feet of rock and frost-hard river muck; hard going? Yes, sir. You broke your back on nothing more than a hunch and a hope. After that, all you had was the comradeship of your fellows and the one chance in a hundred thousand your claim would pay out big. I almost came to value the one more than the other, because when the chips were down you could rely on the comradeship at least.

"So, all through that summer I dug away in the dried-up beds, till it came autumn, and time to make another big decision. The last boat out of Dawson sailed on September the sixteenth, and a lot of fellows I knew were on it, the ones who'd struck it rich and the ones who'd simply had enough. I didn't fall into either camp: I waved that boat away from the landing, and made my plans to stay on through the winter. Plenty did: the proud and foolish ones like me, who couldn't quite bring themselves to admit defeat and go home with only a few grains of gold in their pokes; the optimists, who couldn't believe that the best was over, that the juicy lodes were already worked out and the rest only dry holes; and worst of all the hard core, the ones who'd caught it worst of all, who had no place left for them back in the real world. Quite a bunch.

"I remember one evening in that October of '98, standing up on the banks outside my camp and looking out over the dry gulches. Some of the fellows were burning fires at their workings, trying to melt the frost so the digging would go easier. It lit up all that strange alien landscape, like lanterns shining out in the gloom, and the way the woodsmoke smell drifted up across the bluffs... I could have stayed there for the rest of my life, or so I told myself. I sat and watched those fires till it got full dark, anyway, and later on that night I saw the aurora for the first time, the Northern lights, flickering green and magical in the moonless sky.

"The week after, it began to snow for real, and I had to strike camp and head back for Dawson. Some didn't; some stayed out on the flats, and that's where the story really begins.

"I must've been back in Dawson a couple of months, because it was nigh on Christmas when we got word from out on the workings that they'd found something strange—not gold, which would have been strange enough by that time, but something weird, something the likes of which nobody had ever seen. At least, that's what Sam Tibbets told us, when he come in to Dawson for supplies. It was the three Tibbets brothers worked the claim, along with a half-dozen other fellows all hailed from Maine: they were a syndicate, all for one and one for all. They hadn't found a lot of gold—hardly enough for one man to retire on, let alone nine—but Sam reckoned if the worst came to the worst, they could always go into the exhibition business with this thing they'd dug up out of the frost. 'It's a new wonder of the world, or maybe the oldest one of all,' I can hear him saying it, hunkered down by the stove in the saloon with the frost melting in his mustache and the steam rising off his coat; 'I reckon it must 'a turned up late for last boarding on the ark, or else Noah threw it overboard on account of its looks.'

"'What d'you mean?' I asked him.

"'Aw, Horton, you never saw such a cretur as this,' he said earnestly—he was straight-ahead and simple, was Sam Tibbets. He was one of the original ice-skaters from back on the lakes in the spring: I liked him a lot. 'It's like an ugly dried-up old thing the size of one of them barrels there—' he pointed at a hogshead in the corner—'and about that same shape, 'cept maybe it comes to sort of a narrow place up top. It's got long thin arms, only dozens of 'em, all around, and there's nippers on the end, same as a lobster? I swear there ain't never been such a confusion. Wait till we haul it back out of here, come the thaw. They'll pay a dime a head back in Frisco just to clap eyes on it, I tell you!'

"It was a plan at that, and if nothing else it made me mighty curious to take a look at this thing, whatever it was. The way Sam told it, they'd been digging through the frozen subsoil when they turned it up: he thought it must have gotten caught in the river away back, stuck in the mud and froze up when the winter came. How deep was it, I asked him, thinking the deeper it lay, the older it must be; 'bout twenty feet, he reckoned.

"'So it's dead, then, this thing?' That was Cy Perrette, who was not the smartest man in the Yukon territory, not by a long chalk. He was staring at Sam Tibbets like a dog listening to a sermon.

"'It better be,' said Sam. 'It's been buried in the earth since Abraham got promoted to his first pair of long pants, ain't it?' Men started laughing all through the saloon, and pretty soon Sam had a line of drinks set down before him. Dawson folks appreciated a good tale, see: something to take their minds off the cold and dark outside, and the endless howling winds. I remember the aurora was particularly strong that night; when I staggered out of the saloon and the cold knocked me sober, there it was, fold upon fold, glowing and rippling from horizon to horizon. I remember thinking, that's what folk mean when they say 'unearthly'. Something definitively not of this planet, something more to do with the heavens than the earth.

"Come morning there was quite a little gang of us, all bent on following Sam Tibbets back to his camp for a look-see at the eighth wonder. Sam was agreeable, said he'd waive our admission fees just this once, on account of the circumstances, and we set off towards the workings. It was a cheerful excursion; the sleds were always lighter when you had company along the trail.

"Sam broke into a run when we reached the banks of the river bed; wanted to welcome us to the site of their discovery, I suppose, like any showman would. He clambered up a snowdrift; then, when he reached the top, he stopped, and even from down below I thought he looked confused. He let go his sled; it slithered down the bank and I had to look sharp, else it'd have taken me off at the shins. 'Sam!' I called him, but he didn't look round. I scrambled up after him, cussing him for a clumsy oaf and the rest of it; then I saw what he'd seen, and the words got choked off in my throat.

"Straight away you could see something was wrong. Sam and his partners had built themselves a cabin by the workings, nothing fancy, but solid enough to take whatever the Yukon winter could throw at it, they'd thought. Now, one end of that cabin was shivered all to pieces. The logs were snapped and splintered into matchwood, just exactly as if someone had fired a cannonball at it. Only the cannon would have had to be on the inside of the cabin, not the outside: there was wreckage laying on the ground for a considerable distance, all radiating out and away from the stoved-in part.

"That wasn't the worst part, though. In amongst the wreckage you could see the snow stained red, and there was at least one body mixed in with the blown-out timber. I saw it straight away; I know Sam had too, because he turned around and looked at me as I grabbed his arm, and I could hear this high sort of keening noise he was making, like some kind of machine that's slipped its gears, about to break itself to pieces. That was the purest, most fundamental sound of grief I ever heard coming out of a human being. I've never forgotten it to this day.

"My first thought as we began running down the banks was: dynamite. Plenty of the miners used it to start off an excavation, or to clear whatever obstructions they couldn't dig around. It wasn't unusual for a camp such as this to have a few sticks laying around in case of emergencies. Now, if you got careless...? You understand what I'm saying. That was my first assumption, anyway. It lasted until I got in amongst the wreckage.

"Dynamite couldn't account for it, was all. It couldn't have left cups and bottles standing on the table, and still blown a hole in the cabin wall big enough to drive a piled-up dogsled through. It wouldn't have left a man's body intact inside its clothes, and taken his head clean off at the neck. And it couldn't have done to that head... the things I saw done to the head of poor Bob Gendreau. Put it this way: my second assumption was bears; them, or some other wild animal. Bears roused too soon from their hibernation, hungry and enraged, coming on the camp and smashing it all to pieces. But again, when you looked at all the evidence, that didn't sit right either.

"There was a side of bacon hanging on the wall still; bears would have taken that. And they wouldn't have stopped at knocking off the head of Bob Gendreau; that's not where the sustenance lies, and all a bear ever looks for is sustenance. Whatever took Bob's head off, then mauled it so his own mother wouldn't have known it; that thing wasn't doing what it did out of blind animal instinct, nor yet the need for nourishment. That thing was doing what it did because it wanted to—because it liked it, maybe. Some say man is the lord of all creation because he's the only creature blessed with reason; others, that he's set apart from the rest of the beasts because he takes pleasure in killing, and there's no other animal does that. But up in that cabin I learned different. Now, I believe there's at least one other creature on this planet that draws satisfaction from its kills, and not just a square meal. I got my first inkling of that when I saw what was left of Harvey Tibbets.

"He was jammed into an unravaged corner of the cabin. It looked as if he'd been trying to dig clean through the packed-mud floor; there was a hole in the ground at his feet, and his fingers were all bloodied and torn. You could see that, because of the way he was laying; hunkered down on his haunches, facing out towards the room, for all the world like a Moslem when he prays to Mecca. His forehead was touching the earth, and his arms were stretched out in supplication. His hands were clenched in the dirt, still clutching two last handfuls of it even in death. There was no mistaking it: he'd been begging whatever had passed through that cabin to spare him. Begging it for mercy.

"And whatever it was had looked down upon him as he crouched grovelling in his corner; listened to his screams, I guess. And had it granted him mercy? I don't know. I can't speak as to its motivations. What it *had* done, was sever both his hands, cut 'em clear off at the wrists. Remember before, when I said he appeared to have been digging in the dirt, trying to escape? Both his hands were still there, torn-up and bloody like I said. And he was kneeling down with his arms outstretched; you remember that. But in between the stumps at the end of his forearms and the tattered beginnings of his wrists, there was nothing but a foot of blood-soaked earth. Whatever had killed him had cut off both his hands, and watched him bleed out on the floor while he begged it still for mercy. Now what sort of a creature does that sound like to you?

"Indians, was what some of the men thought; Indians touched with the windigo madness. But how could any man, crazy or sane, have knocked an entire gable end out of the cabin that way? There was an Indian with us, one of the portageurs, a quiet, dark-complected fellow named Jake: he wouldn't come within ten yards of the devastation, but he told me it wasn't any of his kin. 'Not yours either,' he said after a pause, and I asked him what he meant by it.

"He took me aside and pointed in the snow. There was a mess of our prints, converging on the cabin so that the ground outside the blasted-out place was practically trampled bare. All around the snow was practically virgin still, and Jake showed me the only thing that sullied it. A single set of tracks, leading from the cabin and headed away north, down along the gulch. I say leading from the cabin, mostly because there wasn't anything in the cabin could have made those prints, living or dead. If it wasn't for that, then I don't know that I could have told you what direction whatever made the prints was travelling in. They weren't regular footmarks, you see, and they were all wrong in their shape, in their arrangement—in their number, even. And the weirdest thing about them? They stopped dead about fifty yards out. A step, then another, then nothing but the undisturbed snow, as far as the eye could see.

"Later on, once the shock of it had passed, I asked Jake what could have made those prints, and he told me an old legend of his people, about the time before men walked these northern wastes, when it was just gods and trolls and ogres.

"Back then, he said, there were beings come down from the sky, and they laid claim to the Earth for a long season of destruction. They were like pariahs between the stars, these beings: not even the Old Ones, the gods without a worshipper, could bear to have them near. They were cast out in the end, as well as the Old Ones could manage it: but the story goes that some of them escaped exile by burrowing down into the earth and waiting their time, till some cataclysm of the planet might uncover them. They could wait: nothing on Earth could kill them, you see. They couldn't die in this dimension. They would only sleep, through geologic ages of the planet, till something disturbed them and they came to light once more.

"That was the legend: I got it out of Jake later that same day, when the party had split up and we were searching all the low land around the arroyo. The mood of the party was shocked and unforgiving: something had done this to our friends, and we were bound to avenge them the best we could. The trail of footprints had given some of the fellows pause for thought, but I think most of them just took the prints as simple evidence of something they could go after, and didn't reflect too much on what could have made them. If they'd stopped and thought it through, I doubt whether any one of them would have been prepared to do what we ended up doing that night: lying in ambush and waiting for the culprit to come back to the cabin.

"The reasoning—so far as it went—was, if it's an animal, it'll come back where there's food. If it's a man, it'll come back because that's what murderers do: revisit the scene of the crime. Pretty shaky logic, I know, but the blood of the party was up. We were really just looking for trouble, and we damn near found it, too.

"As night fell we set up an ambuscade in the ruins of the cabin. We'd buried the bodies by then, of course, but inside the cabin still felt bad; stank, too, like something had lain dead in there all through the summer, and not just a few hours in the bitter icy cold. We had the stove going: we had to, else we'd have froze to death. We had guards at all the windows, and a barricade at the wrecked end of the cabin. It didn't matter what direction trouble might be coming at us from, we had it covered. Or so we thought.

"God, we were so cold! The wind died down soon after dark, and that probably saved us all from the hypothermia. Still it was like a knife going through you, that chill, and you had to get up and move around every so often, just to prove to yourself you were still alive. We passed around a bottle of whiskey we found among the untouched provisions, and waited.

"All across the wide northern sky there was a glow, cold and mysterious, as far removed as you could imagine from the world of men and their paltry little hopes and fears. The aurora was so vivid that night, you might have read a newspaper by it. All the better to see whatever's coming, we thought; at least it can't creep up on us and take us unawares, not in this light.

"Somewhere in the very pit of the night, just when the body's at its weariest and wants only to drop down and sleep, an uncanny sort of stillness fell across the snowed-up river bed. What was left of the wind dropped entirely, and the only sound beneath the frozen far-off stars seemed to come from the creaking of the stove round which we sat, the cracking and spitting of the logs that burned inside it. A few of us looked round at each other; all of us felt it now, the heightened expectation, the heightened fear. Without words, as quietly as we could, we moved away from the stove and took up our places at the barricade.

"I remember—so clearly!—how it felt, crouching behind that mess of planks and packing-cases, waiting to see what might show its head above the snow-banks. A couple of times I thought I saw something, away out beyond the bounds of night vision. Even under the greenish radiance of the aurora I couldn't be sure: *was* that something moving? *Could* it be? One time Joe McRudd discharged his rifle, and scared us all to hell. 'Sorry,' he mouthed, when we'd all regained our senses. He cleared his throat. 'Thought I saw sump'n creepin' round out there.'

"'Save your ammo,' grunted Sam Tibbets, not even bothering to look at poor Joe. 'Keep your nerve.' That was all. Directly after that it was upon us.

"It came from the only direction we hadn't reckoned on: overhead. There was a thump on the roof of the cabin, and then a splintering as the boards were wrenched off directly above our heads. It caused a general confusion: everyone jumped and panicked, and no-one really knew what was happening. Joe McRudd's rifle went off again; some of the other fellows shot as well, I don't know what at. Before I could react, Sam Tibbets was snatched up from alongside me—something had him fast around the head and was dragging him off of his feet, up towards the hole in the roof.

"I grabbed him around the waist, but it was no use: I felt my own feet lifting clear of the floor as Sam was hoisted ever upward. He was trying to call out, but whatever had snatched him was laying tight hold around the whole of his head and neck, and all I could hear was a muffled roar of anger and pain—fear, too, I guess. It was as if he was being lynched, hung off a high bough and left to swing there while he throttled. I called to the rest of them to help, to hang on to us: a couple of them laid ahold of my legs and heaved, and for a moment we thought we had him. Then there came an awful sound, like something out of a butcher's shop, and suddenly we were all sprawled on the floor of the cabin, with Sam Tibbets' headless body lying dead weight on top of us.

"I don't remember exactly how the next few seconds panned out. All I remember was being soaked with Sam's blood: the heat of it, the force with which it gushed from his truncated neck, the bitter metallic stink. The fellows told me afterwards that I was screaming like a banshee on my hands and knees, but I know I wasn't the only one. Jake the Indian brought me out of it: he dragged me away from the shambles in the middle of the room and slapped me a couple times till I quit bawling. As if coming round from a dream I goggled at him slack-mouthed; then I came to myself in a dreadful sort of recollection. Before he could stop me, I'd grabbed the big hunting-knife from its scabbard at his waist and pushed him out of the way.

"By climbing up on top of the hot stove, I just about managed to reach the hole in the roof. I had Jake's knife between my teeth like the last of the Mohicans; I was covered all over in Sam Tibbets' blood, and I was filled with the urge to vengeance, nothing else. I hoisted myself up so my head and shoulders were through the hole. With my elbows planted on the snow-covered shingles, I looked around.

"It was crouched by the farther end of the roof like a big old sack of guts, mumbling on something. Sam's head. I made some sort of a noise, and it looked up: I mean, the thick squabby part on top of it suddenly grew long like an elephant's trunk, and one furious red eye glared out at me from its tip. The noise it made: good God, I never heard the like. It damn near deafened me, even out in the open; it went ringing through my head like the last trump.

"Some part of its belly opened itself up, and Sam Tibbets' head was gone with a terrible sucking crunch. Then all those tentacles that fringed the trunk suddenly came to life, writhing and flailing like a stinging jellyfish. One of them caught in my clothing—I slashed out at it with Jake's knife, but I might as well have tried to cut a steel hawser. It had me fast; it was like being caught in a death-hold. The thing let rip a revolting sort of belch, and started to haul me in, and I had just enough time to feel the entire sum of my courage vanish in a wink as fear, total and absolute, rushed in to fill up every inch of my being. It's a hell of a thing, to lose all self-respect that way: to know that the last thing you'll feel before death is nothing but abject, craven panic. God, let me die like a man, I prayed, as the thing dragged me up out of the hole towards its gulping maw—that glaring gorgon's eye—

"It was Jake down below contrived to save my life. He grabbed me by the ankles and swung on them like a church bell, and there came a sharp rip as my coat came to pieces at the seams. It didn't have proper hold of me, only by the fabric, you see: that was what saved me, that and the Chinee tailor back in San Francisco who'd scrimped on the thread when he put that old pea-coat together. I went sliding back through the hole on the roof, while the thing struggled to regain its balance on the icy shingles. It let out another of those blood-freezing hollers, and then I was laying on top of Jake, in amidst all of the blood and the panic down below.

"All of the breath had gotten knocked out of me by the fall, and the same for Jake, who was underneath me, remember. The two of us were pretty much hors de combat for a while; plus, I dare say I wouldn't have been much use even with breath in my lungs, not after the jolt I'd took up on the roof. I was aware that the rest of the fellows were running round like crazy, firing into the rafters and yelling fit to raise Cain. For myself, right then, I figured old Harvey Tibbets'd had the best idea, digging himself a hole—or trying to. I knew if it wanted to come down and try conclusions, we none of us stood a chance in hell, guns or no guns. I thought it was all up with us still, and to this day I don't know why it wasn't.

"Because after a while, in amongst all the raving and the letting-off of guns and the war-whoops and hollers and what have you, it gradually dawned on the fellows that there was no movement from up on the roof. Nothing coming through the hole at us, no fresh attack; no sound of creaking timbers, even—though I doubt we'd have heard it, we were making so much noise ourselves. In the end a couple of men ran outside to look up on the roof: nothing there, they yelled, and I thought to myself, no, of course not. It won't show itself so easy. I figured it had only gone to earth for a while, that it would pick us off one by one when we weren't expecting it.

"Then one of them happened to look upwards—I mean straight up, towards the sky. What he saw up there made him let out such a shout, it brought us all out of that broke-up shambles of a cabin. We joined him out in the snow: I remember us all standing there, staring up into the heavens as if God in all his glory was coming down and the final judgement was upon us.

"Silhouetted against the wraithlike flux of the aurora, the thing was ascending into the night sky. It had wings, but they didn't seem to be lifting it, or even bearing its weight; it was as if it simply rose through the air the way a jellyfish rises through the water. That sound—that eldritch piercing howl—echoed all across the wide expanse of the landscape, from mountain to lakeshore, through all the sleeping trees, and I swear every beast that heard it must have trembled in its lair; must have whined and cowered and crept to the back of its cave and prayed to whatever rough gods had made it, *Lord, let this danger pass.*

"Up it rose, till we could hardly make it out against the green-wreathed stars. Then, there came one last throb of phosphorescence, bright as day—and it was as if a circuit burned out, somewhere in the sky. The aurora vanished, simple as that; and in the brief interval while our eyes adjusted to the paler starlight, I believe we all screamed, like children pitched headlong into the dark.

"As soon as we could see what we were doing again, we lost no time in getting out of that hateful place. Without waiting to bury our dead—poor Sam Tibbets—we beat a retreat back to Dawson, and there was never a band of pilgrims more relieved to see the sun come up. It shone off the frozen river in bright clean rainbows of ice; it showed us the dirty old log cabins we called home, and we wept with joy at the sight. Exhausted as I was, and scared too, and bewildered at all I'd seen, I believed we might be safe at last. Until the night came; that first night, and all the other nights that followed through that long Canadian winter.

"The nights were bad, you see. I took to sleeping in the daytime, when I could, and once it got dark I'd sit with Jake and the rest of the men in a private room at the back of one of the saloons, playing cards and drinking through to sun-up, very deliberately not talking about what we'd been through that evening. I was never really any good after that; not till I made it out of Dawson with the first thaw. Another season of that, and I'd have ended up a rummy in the streets of Skagway, telling tall tales for the price of a pint of hooch. Some of the men had heard of a fresh strike in Alaska, up on the shale banks at Nome—me, I'd lost heart, and could only think of getting home to San Francisco, where such things as we'd seen up on the roof of the cabin couldn't be. Or that's what I thought back then. What do *you* think, Mr. Fenwick?"

ଧ ଧ

For a second I thought he just wanted me to pass judgement on his tale—to say *yes, I believe you*, or *hang on a minute, are you sure about that?* Then I realised the import of his words. "You mean that thing down in the basement, don't you?" I said, slowly, almost reluctantly, and he nodded. I opened my mouth, but nothing came out, and after a moment or two I shut it again.

"It looks every inch a match," Keith said, through his hands. He sighed, and leaned back in his chair, staring up at the nicotine-yellow ceiling. "It was like some sort of damnable optical illusion—didn't you get that?—the longer you looked at that black void, the more it seemed as if the creature was projected into the empty space." With hands that trembled hardly at all, he lit up another cigar.

"A thing can't come to life after so long," I asserted, without a fraction of the confidence that had illuminated Keith's entire narrative. "Nothing of this earth—" and there I stopped, remembering what the Indian had had to say on that subject.

"—Could last so long trapped inside a layer of coal," finished Keith, helpfully. "It's bituminous coal hereabouts; laid down during the Carboniferous age. That's, what? Three hundred million years ago, give or take a few million. Imagine the world back then, Fenwick: the way it looked, the way things were all across the land. Dense humid forests; sodden bogs and peat swamps. The stink of rot, of decomposition; of new life forming, down amongst the muck and the decay. The first creatures had just crawled up out of the warm slimy seas, lizards and snails and molluscs, is all. Trilobites and dragonflies. Nothing much bigger than a crawdad. God, they would have been lords of the earth, Fenwick! They could still be now, if—" He broke off, and his hands went once more to his thin eager face. "If enough of them got turned up." His voice was muffled somewhat, but in another way it was remarkably clear—clear-headed, at least.

"Three hundred million years." I was having trouble with the concept—you could say that. Yes, you could certainly say that the concept was troubling me. "You're saying that a thing—a thing—"

"Not of this earth," put in Keith helpfully.

"Whatever—could keep alive for so long, under such incredible pressure; no air, no sustenance… why, it's fantastic."

"It's fantastic, all right," said Keith, and for the first time there was a hint of impatience in his deep even voice. "I thought I made it clear this wasn't a tale you'd hear every day. But look at the facts. These miners here—they didn't find a fossil, a chunk of rock! No more than the Tibbets found a fossil up there in the Klondike. Set aside your preconceptions, Fenwick. I had to. Look at the facts."

"That's just what I aim to do," I said. "Tomorrow, when we get a look at this damn stupid whoosit of theirs."

And on that note, though with a deal more talk thereafter, we agreed to leave it; and I went up to bed with a head full of questions and misgivings. The brandy helped me get off to sleep, in the end. If I dreamed, I'm glad to say I don't remember it. And in any case—

There are many less-than-pleasant ways to be woken from even the most fitful of slumbers, I guess: but let the voice of experience assure you that there's no more absolute way of rousing a fellow than the sound of a monstrous siren going off in what sounds like the next room down the corridor. I was practically thrown out of bed and into the corridor, where I bumped into Keith. He was already dressed; or more probably hadn't been to bed yet.

"Accident at the mine," I croaked. By this time I'd managed to remember where the hell I was, or just about.

"Maybe," was all Keith would say. "Get your pants on, newspaperman."

By the time we made it out into the street people were milling around in their nightshirts, asking each other was there trouble up to the mine. For a while no-one seemed to know, and everyone expected the worst; then, we saw the Mayor's Ford barrelling down main street, and Keith practically flung himself in the way of it. Before Kronke or any of his stooges could complain, we were scrambling into the rumble seat and pumping them for information.

"Had us a report of some trouble, up on Peck's Ridge," was all Kronke would say. He looked grey with panic; the flesh practically hung off his face.

"Peck's Ridge?" We'd heard that place name before, of course. "Isn't that where Lamar Tibbs lives?" The mayor didn't answer at first; Keith leaned forwards and gripped his shoulder. "Tibbs? The man who found the creature?"

"Up near there," Kronke said, shaking loose his arm. He tried to regain some of his mayoral authority: "'Tain't rightly speaking none of your business anyways, mister—"

"Drop that," Keith said impatiently. "Drop that straightaway, or else I'll make sure you come across as the biggest hick in all creation when the story makes it into the papers. How's that gonna play with the voters come election time, Mr. Kronke?"

The two men stared angrily at each other, but there was only ever going to be one winner of that contest. After a second Kronke told his chauffeur "Drive on," and we were off, away down main street heading out of town, up into the hill country.

That was some drive, all right. The middle of the night, and not a light showing in all that desolate stretch; only the headlamps of the car on the ribbon of road ahead. Trees crowding close to the track, and between their ghostly lit-up trunks only the blackness of the forest. Overhead, a canopy of branches, and no starlight, no sliver of the moon; it felt as if we were going down into the ground as much as climbing, as if we'd entered some miner's tunnel lined with wooden props, heading clear down to the Carboniferous.

Alongside me on the rumble, Keith sat, hands clenched on the back of the seat in front. He was willing the automobile on, it seemed to me, the way a jockey nurses a horse along in the home straight. His old man's mop of hair showed up very white in the near darkness, but that didn't fool me any: underneath it all was still the dreamer he'd always been and would remain, the thirty-year-old who'd walked out on his safe job with Mr. Hearst and headed up North to the Klondike on nothing more than a notion and a chance. Hero worship? I should say so.

Maybe seven or eight miles out of town, we saw light up ahead: fire. The Ford swung round and down a trail so narrow, the branches plucked at our sleeves and we had to cover our faces from their lash, and then we came out into a natural dip between two high sides of hills, with a farmhouse and outbuildings down the bottom of the hollow. All hell was breaking loose down there.

People were running back and forth between the main house and the outhouses, the farthest of which was well ablaze. You could hear the screams of animals trapped in the sheds; I couldn't be sure there weren't the cries of people in there too.

Before we even came to a halt, an old man in biballs came running up, crying out unintelligibly. "Was it you phoned?" Kronke bellowed at him above the tumult. Whether he expected any answer, I don't know. It was clear the fellow was raving mad, for the time being at least. Keith passed him over to Kronke's buddies, who were very pointedly not setting foot outside the automobile, and beckoned me follow him down towards the house. Kronke hung back, unwilling to leave the safety of the car; why he'd even bothered coming out there in the first place was hard to say. Perhaps he thought it was his chance to get the whoosit back, on behalf of the mining company. Perhaps—I think this is not unlikely, myself—perhaps there was always some sort of a trip planned for that night, Kronke and a few men armed with pistols, up to Peck's Ridge on company business. Well, they might have had a chance at that, I guess; had things only panned out just a little differently.

Down by the sheds Keith managed to get a hold of one of the people fighting the fire; a teenager, no more, in a plaid shirt and patched drawers.

"What's going on here?" he yelled.

"They're trapped!" the kid hollered back, his eyes round with panic. "Uncle Jesse and Uncle Vern! In there! They were a-watchin' over it!"

"Watching over what?" The kid tried to shake free, but Keith had him tight. "Were they keeping guard? What over?"

"Over Pap's thing!" The kid made to break loose again, without success. "That what Pap found, down to the mine! Lemme go, mister—"

"Your pap Lamar Tibbs?" Keith was implacable. I felt for the youngster, I did. But I wanted to know as well.

The kid nodded, and Keith had one more question. "Where is he?"

"*I don't know!*" screamed the boy. "*I DON'T KNOW!*" Keith was so shocked at the ferocity of it, the sheer volume, that he let him go. The kid stood there for a second, surprised himself I guess, then shook himself all over like a dog coming out of the creek and ran off towards the burning barn. We followed on behind.

Some of the men had formed a chain, and were passing buckets of water up from the pump. The fellows nearest the door were emptying the buckets into the smoke and flames; Keith brushed straight past them and was inside before anyone could stop him. I went to follow him, but one of the men in the doorway grabbed me. "It's gonna come down!" he yelled in my ear: I was just about to holler after Keith when he appeared through the smoke, coughing and staggering. "It's not in there," he wheezed, soon as he could talk. Then there came a mighty creaking and splintering, and we all sprang back as the roof collapsed in a roaring billow of sparks.

"It's gone," Keith insisted, as we stood and watched the barn burn out from a safe distance. "But it was there, though." I was about to ask him what he meant, how he could have known that, when a stocky little man came running up from the house shouting, and interrupted me.

"You see anything of Vern and Jesse in there, mister?" His face was blackened, eyes white and staring; I learned later they'd dragged him out of the barn once already, half-dead from the smoke. "It's my brothers—I'm Lamar Tibbs."

Keith nodded. The man was about to ask the next, the obvious, question, but I guess Keith's expression told him what he wanted to know. Tibbs' own features crumpled up, and he bowed his head.

After a little while he said: "It all up with them?" Keith nodded again. "Fire?"

"Before the fire," Keith said. The miner looked up, and he went on: "They were over in the far corner. They weren't burned any." I think he meant it kindly; that was the way Tibbs took it, not knowing any better then. But Keith's eyes were flinty hard, and I for one had my misgivings.

"Was it that thing caused it?" Tibbs' voice was all but inaudible. "That thing I brung up from the mine?"

"I believe so." Keith's voice sounded calm enough, the more so if you couldn't take a cue from his face. "It's not there any more: it looks to have busted out the back before the roof went."

That got Tibbs' attention. "You sure?"

"Can't be certain that's the way it got out," said Keith, picking his words with care. "It wasn't in there when the roof fell in, though—that, I'm sure of."

Tibbs looked hard at Keith, who stared levelly back at him. What he saw seemed to make his mind up. "Wait there, mister," he said shortly, and started back towards the house. Over his shoulder, he shouted: "You in the mood for a dawg hunt?"

I began to say something, but Keith stopped me with a upraised hand. "What about you, Mr. Fenwick? You in the mood for a dawg hunt, sir?"

What could I say? Understanding that no matter what, Keith would go through with it, I nodded miserably. Then there was no more time to think: Tibbs was running back from the house with three of the mangiest, meanest-looking yaller hounds you ever saw in your life. The chase was on.

The dogs picked up a trail directly we got round the back of the barn. They shivered uncontrollably—as if they were passing peach pits, as Keith memorably put it later that same night—and set off at a good fast clip into the trees. Tibbs had them on the end of a short leash, and it was all he could do to keep up the pace. Keith loped along after him, and I brought up the rear. A few of Tibbs' relatives from back in the yard joined in—thankfully, they'd thought to bring along lanterns. There were a half-dozen of us in all.

"I thought it was a goner," panted Tibbs from up in front. He'd pegged Keith for a straight shooter more or less from the beginning, that was clear: I suppose it was watching Keith dive straight into that burning barn had done it. I doubt it came easy for him to trust anyone much, outside of his extended family circle, but he damn near deferred to Horton Keith. "We'd been blastin' on the big new seam, see: I swung my hammer at a big ol' chunk of coal fell out the roof, 'bout the size of a barrel—the fall must 'a cracked it some, 'cause one lick from me was all it took. That chunk split wide open like a hick'ry nut, clean in two—an' there it was, the whoosit, older than Methuselah. Fitted in there like a hand inside a glove, it did."

"I know," Keith wheezed. He was keeping up pretty good, for a man well into his fifties, but Tibbs was setting a punishing pace. "Seen it—back at the courthouse."

"You seen that? You seen the coal? Then you got a pretty good idea what we brung back here." *He's got a better idea than that, maybe*, I thought to myself, but I didn't say anything. For one thing, I doubt my aching lungs would have let me—nor yet my growing panic, which I was only just managing to keep in check.

"Anyhow, it was deader'n Abel slain by Cain—I'll swear to that, an' these men here'll back me up. You never seen a thing so dried out an' wrinkled—nor so ugly, neither. Jesus Christ, it made me sick to look at it!—but it was my prize, an' I swore it was goin' to make me a rich man. Me an' all my kin—" He choked up at that, and we none of us pressed him; we ran on, was all, with the rustling thud of our footfalls through the brush warning the whole forest of our approach, probably.

The dogs were still straining hard after the scent, when all of a sudden they stopped and gathered round something underfoot, down by a little stand of dwarf sumac. I thought it was a rock at first: I couldn't see through the bodies of the hounds. It was Tibbs' cry that made me realise what it *might* be—that, and the story Keith had told me not half-a-dozen hours previously, rattling round my mind the way it had been ever since.

Tibbs couldn't pick it up, that roundish muddy thing the dogs had found. That was left to Horton Keith: he lifted it just a little, enough for one of the other men in the party to gasp and mutter "Jesse." Tibbs repeated the name a few times to himself, while Keith replaced the thing the way he found it and straightened up off his haunches. Then Tibbs gave it out in a howl that made the dogs back off, cower on their bellies in the leaf-rot as if they'd been whipped. I swear that sound went all the way through me. I hear it still, when I think about that night. It's bad, and I try not to do it too much, mostly because the next thing I think of is what I heard next—what we all heard, the sound that made us snap up our heads and turn in the direction of our otherworldly quarry.

You'll probably remember that Keith had already taken a stab at describing that sound. If you go back and look what he said, you'll see he compared it to the last trump, and all I can say is, standing out there in the middle of the forest, looking at each other in the lantern light, we all of us knew exactly what he meant. It turned my guts to water: I damn near screamed myself.

It was so close; that was the thing. Just by the clarity and lack of muffling you could tell it wasn't far off—five, maybe ten score of paces on through the trees, somewhere just over the next ridge. Tibbs got his senses back soonest of us all, or maybe he was so far gone then that sense had nothing to do with it: he was off and running, aiming to close down those hundred yards or so and get to grips with whatever cut down his brothers and took a trophy to boot. The dogs almost tripped him up; they were cowering in the dirt still, and there was no budging them. He flung down the leash and left them there.

It was Keith started after him, of course. And once Keith had gone, I couldn't not go myself. Then the rest of then followed on; all of which meant we were pretty strung out along the track. It may have saved Keith's life, that arrangement.

I heard Tibbs up ahead, cursing and panting; then, I heard a strange sort of a whizzing noise. I once stood at a wharf watching a cargo ship being unloaded, and one of the hawsers broke on the winching gear. The noise it made as it lashed through the air; that was what I heard. Whip-crack, quick and abrupt; and then I didn't hear Tibbs any more.

What I thought I heard was the sound of rain, pattering on the leaves and branches. I even felt a few drops of it on my face. Then one of the men in the rear caught up and shone his lantern up ahead. It lit first of all on Keith as he staggered back, hand to his mouth. Then, it lit on Tibbs.

At first it seemed like some sort of conjuror's trick. He was staggering too, like a stage drunk, only there was something about his head... At first your brain refused to believe it. Your eyes saw it, but your brain reported back, no, it's a man; men aren't made that way. It's a trick they do with mirrors; a slather of stage blood to dress it up, that's all. Then, inevitably, Tibbs lost his balance and fell backwards. Once he was down it became easier to deal with, in one way—easier to look at and trust your own eyes, at any rate. At last, you could look at it and see what there was to be seen. Which was this: from the neck up, Tibbs' head was gone.

I said you could look at it; not for long, though. Instead I turned to Keith, who was pressed back up against a tree trunk, still with his hand to his mouth. He saw me, and he tried to speak, shaking his head all the while, but he couldn't find the words.

Then we both heard it together: a rustling in the branches above our head, the sound of something dropping. We both looked up at about the same time, and that was how I managed to spring back, and so avoid the thing hitting me smack on the crown of my head. It hit the ground good and hard, directly between the two of us: the soft mud underfoot took all the bounce off it, though. It rolled half of the way over, then stopped, so you couldn't really see its features. There was no mistaking it, though, even in the shaky lanternlight; I'd been looking at the back of Tibbs' head only a moment ago, hadn't I?

A dreadful realisation dawned in Keith's eyes, and he looked back up. Instinctively I followed suit. I guess we saw about the same thing, though Keith had the experience to help him evaluate it. It was like this:

The branches were close-meshed overhead, with hardly any night sky visible in between. What you could see was tinted a sickly sort of greenish hue: the way modern city streetlights will turn the night a fuzzy, smoky orange, and block out all the stars. Through the treetops, something was ascending. I'd be a liar if I said I could recognise it; there was just no way to tell, not with all those shaking, rustling branches in the way. All I got was a general impression of size and shape; enough for me to stand in front of that slab of coal in the courthouse basement the next day and say, yeah, it could have been; I guess. Keith was with me, and so far as he was concerned it was a deal more straight-forward; but as I say, he had the benefit of prior acquaintance.

Up it went, up and up, till it broke clear of the canopy, and we had no way of knowing where to look. The sky gave one last unnatural throb of ghoulish green, as if it was turning itself inside out; and it was over. All that was left was the bloody carnage down below: Lamar Tibbs' body, that we dragged between us back to the farmhouse, and the bodies of his brothers covered up with a tar-paulin. One entire generation of a family, wiped out in the course of a night.

What with the weeping and the wailing of the relatives, and the never-ending questions—most of them from that fat fool Kronke, who hadn't even the guts to leave his damn automobile—that business up on Peck's Ridge took us clear through dawn and into the afternoon of the next day to deal with. It stayed with us a good while longer than that, though; in fact, it's never really gone away. Ask either of my wives, who will surely survive me through having gotten rid of me, as soon as was humanly possible. They'll tell you how I used to come bolt upright in the middle of a nightmare, hands flailing desperately above my head, screaming at the ghosts of trees and branches, babbling about a sky gone wrong. Ask them how often it happened, and what good company I was in the days and weeks that followed. Yes, you could say it's stayed with me, my three days down in Oram County.

ཞ ཞ

I knew Keith for a dozen more years in all: right up till the time he set off with the rest of the Collins Clarke archaeological party for the headwaters of the Amazon, and never came back. Missing, presumed dead, all fifteen men and their native bearers; nothing was ever found of them, no overflights could even spot their last camp. Keith was well into his sixties by then, but there was never any question that he'd be joining the expedition, once he'd heard the rumours—the ruins up above Iquitos on the Ucayali, the strange carvings of beasts no-one had ever seen before. He'd done his preparation in the library at Miskatonic with Clarke himself, cross-referencing the Indian tales with certain books and illustrations—and with that slab of coal from the Oram County courthouse, one-half of which had made its way into the cabinets of the University's Restricted Collection. There was no stopping him: he was convinced he was on the right track at last. "But why put yourself in their way again?" I asked him. "With all you know; after all you've seen?" He never answered me straight out; there's only his last telegram, sent from Manaus, which I like to think holds, if not an answer, then a pointer at least, to the man and to the nature of his quest.

Dear Fenwick (it said): *Finally found someplace worse than Skagway. And they say there's no such thing as progress. We set off tomorrow on our snipe hunt, not a moment too soon for all concerned. Wish you were here—on the strict understanding that we're soon to be somewhere else. With all best wishes from the new frontier, Your friend, Horton Keith.*

෫ ෨

The Crawling Sky

Joe R. Lansdale

(1)
WOOD TICK

Wood Tick wasn't so much as town as it was a wide rip in the forest. The Reverend Jebediah Mercer rode in on ebony horse on a coolish autumn day beneath an overcast sky of humped up, slow-blowing, gunmetal-gray clouds; they seemed to crawl. It was his experience nothing good ever took place under a crawling sky. It was an omen, and he didn't like omens, because, so far in his experience, none of them were good.

Before him, he saw a sad excuse for a town: A narrow clay road and a few buildings, not so much built up as tossed up, six altogether, three of them leaning South from Northern winds that had pushed them. One of them had had a fireplace of stone, but it had toppled, and no one had bothered to rebuild it. The stones lay scattered about like discarded cartridges. Grass, yellowed by time, had grown up through the stones, and even a small tree had sprouted between them. Where the fall of the fireplace had left a gap was a stretch of fabric, probably a slice of tent; it had been nailed up tight and it had turned dark from years of weather.

In the middle of the town there was a wagon with wooden bars set into it and a flat heavy roof. No horses. Its axel rested on the ground giving the wagon a tilt. Inside, leaning, the Reverend could see a man clutching at the bars, cursing at a half dozen young boys who looked likely to grow up to be ugly men, were throwing rocks at him. An old man was sitting on the precarious porch of one of the leaning buildings, whittling on a stick. A few other folks moved about, crossing the street with the enthusiasm of the ill, giving no mind to the boys or the man in the barred wagon.

Reverend Mercer got off his horse and walked it to a hitching post in front of the sagging porch and looked at the man who was whittling. The man had a goiter on the side of his neck and he had tied it off in a dirty sack that fastened under his jaw and to the top of his head and was fastened under his hat. The hat was wide and dropped shadow on his face. The face needed concealment. He had the kind of features that made you wince; one thing God could do was he could sure make ugly.

"Sir, may I ask you something?" the Reverend said to the whittling man.

"I reckon."

"Why is that man in that cage?"

"That there is Wood Tick's jail. All we got. We been meaning to build one, but we don't have that much need for it. Folks do anything really wrong, we hang 'em."

"What did he do?"

"He's just half-witted."

"That's a crime?"

"If we want it to be. He's always talkin' this and that, and it gets old. He used to be all right, but he ain't now. We don't know what ails him. He's got stories about haints and his wife done run off and he claims a haint got her."

"Haints?"

"That's right."

Reverend Mercer turned his head toward the cage and the boys tossing rocks. They were flinging them in good and hard, and pretty accurate.

"Having rocks thrown at him can not be productive," the Reverend said.

"Well, if God didn't want him half-witted and the target of rocks, he'd have made him smarter and less directed to bullshit."

"I am a man of God and I have to agree with you. God's plan doesn't seem to have a lot of sympathy in it. But humanity can do better. We could at least save this poor man from children throwing rocks."

"Sheriff doesn't think so."

"And who is the sheriff."

"That would be me. You ain't gonna give me trouble are you?"

"I just think a man should not be put behind bars and have rocks thrown at him for being half-witted."

"Yeah, well, you can take him with you, long as you don't bring him back. Take him with you and I'll let him out."

The Reverend nodded. "I can do that. But, I need something to eat first. Any place for that?"

"You can go over to Miss Mary's, which is a house about a mile down from the town, and you can hire her to fix you somethin'. But you better have a strong stomach."

"Not much of a recommendation."

"No, it's not. I reckon I could fry you up some meat for a bit of coin, you ready to let go of it."

"I have money."

"Good. I don't. I got some horse meat I can fix. It's just on this side of being good enough to eat. Another hour, you might get poisoned by it."

"Appetizing as that sounds, perhaps I should see Miss Mary."

"She fixes soups from roots and wild plants and such. No matter what she fixes, it all tastes the same and it gives you the squirts. She ain't much to look at neither, but she sells out herself, you want to buy some of that."

"No. I am good. I will take the horse meat, long as I can watch you fry it."

"All right. I'm just about through whittling."

"Are you making something?"

"No. Just whittlin'."

"So, what is there to get through with?"

"Why my pleasure, of course. I enjoy my whittlin'."

🐍 🐍

The old man who gave the Reverend his name as if he had given up a dark secret, was called Jud. Up close, Jud was even nastier looking than from the distance of the hitching post and the porch. He had pores wide enough and deep enough in his skin to keep pooled water and his nose had been broken so many times it moved from side to side when he talked. He was missing a lot teeth, and what he had were brown from tobacco and rot. His hands were dirty and his fingers were dirtier yet, and the Reverend couldn't help but wonder what those fingers had poked into.

Inside, the place leaned and there were missing floor boards. A wooden stove was at the far end of the room, and a stove pipe wound out of it and went up through a gap in the roof that would let in rain, and had, because the stove was partially rusted. It rested heavy on the worn flooring. The floor sagged and it seemed to the Reverend that if it experienced one more rotted fiber, one more termite bite, the stove would crash through. Hanging on hooks on the wall there were slabs of horse meat covered in flies. Some of the meat looked a little green and there was a slick of mold over a lot of it.

"That the meat you're talkin' about?"

"Yep," Jud said, scratching at his filthy goiter sack.

"It looks pretty green."

"I said it was turnin'. Want it or not?"

"Might I cook it myself?"

"Still have to pay me."

"How much?"

"Two bits."

"Two bits, for rancid meat I cook myself."

"It's still two bits if I cook it."

"You drive quite the bargain, Jud."

"I pride myself on my dealin'."

"Best you do not pride yourself on hygiene."

"What's that? That some kind of remark?"

Reverend Mercer pushed back his long black coat and showed the butts of his twin revolvers. "Sometimes a man can learn to like things he does not on most days care to endure."

Jud checked out the revolvers. "You got a point there, Reverend. I was thinkin' you was just a blabber mouth for God, but you tote them pistols like a man whose seen the elephant."

"Seen the elephant I have. And all his children."

The Reverend brushed the flies away from the horse meat and found a bit of it that looked better than rest, used his pocket knife to cut it loose. He picked insects out of a greasy pan and put the meat in it. He put some wood in the stove and lit it and got a fire going. In short time the meat was frying. He decided to cook it long and cook it through, burn it a bit. That way, maybe he wouldn't die of stomach poisoning.

"You have anything else that might sweeten this deal?" the Reverend asked.

"It's the horse meat or nothin'."

"And in what commerce will you deal when it turns rancid, or runs out?"

"I've got a couple more old horses, and one old mule. Somebody will have to go."

"Have you considered a garden?"

"My hand wasn't meant to fit a hoe. It gets desperate, I'll shoot a squirrel or a possum or a coon or some such. Dog ain't bad you cook 'em good."

"How many people reside in this town?"

"About forty, forty-one if you count Norville out there in the box. But, way things look, considerin' our deal, he'll be leavin'. Sides, he don't live here direct anyway."

"That number count in the kids?"

"Yeah, they all belong to Mary. They're thirteen and on down to six years. Drops them like turds and don't know for sure whose the daddy, though there's one of them out there that looks a mite like me."

"Bless his heart," the Reverend said.

"Yeah, reckon that's the truth. Couple of 'em have died over the years. One got kicked in the head by a horse and the other one got caught up in the river and drowned. Stupid little bastard should have learned to swim. There was an older girl, but she took up with Norville out there, and now she's run off from him."

ɮ ꙅ

When the meat was as black as a pit and smoking like a rich man's cigar, Reverend Mercer discovered there were no plates, and he ate it from the frying man, using his knife as a utensil. It was a rugged piece of meat to wrestle and it tasted like the ass end of a skunk. He ate just enough to knock the corners off his hunger, then gave it up.

Jud asked if he were through with it, and when the Reverend said he was, he came over picked up the leavings with his hands and tore at it like a wolf.

"Hell, this is all right," Jud said. "I need you on as a cook."

"Not likely. How do people make a living around here?"

"Lumber. Cut it and mule it out. That's a thing about East Texas, plenty of lumber."

"Some day there will be a lot less, that is my reasoning."

"It all grows back."

"People grow back faster, and we could do with a lot less of them."

"On that matter, Reverend, I agree with you."

ɮ ꙅ

When the Reverend went outside with Jud to let Norville loose, the kids were still throwing rocks. The Reverend picked up a rock and winged it through the air and caught one of the kids on the side of the head hard enough to knock him down.

"Damn," Jud said. "That there was a kid."

"Now he's a kid with a knot on his head."

"You're a different kind of Reverend."

The kid got up and ran, holding his hand to his head squealing.

"Keep going you horrible little bastard," Reverend Mercer said. When the kid was gone, the Reverend said, "Actually, I was aiming to hit him in the back, but that worked out quite well."

They walked over to the cage. There was a metal lock and a big padlock on the thick wooden bars. Reverend Mercer had wondered why the man didn't just kick them out, but then he saw the reason. He was chained to the floor of the wagon. The chain fit into a big metal loop there, and then went to his ankle where a bracelet of iron held him fast. Norville had a lot of lumps on his head and his bottom lip was swollen up and he was bleeding all over.

"This is no way to treat a man," Reverend Mercer said.

"He could have been a few rocks shy of a dozen knots, you hadn't stopped to cook and eat a steak."

"True enough," the Reverend said.

(2)
NORVILLE'S STORY: THE HOUSE IN THE PINES

The sheriff unlocked the cage and went inside and unlocked the clamp around Norville's ankle. Norville, barefoot, came out of the cage and walked around and looked at the sky, stretching his back as he did. Jud sauntered over to the long porch and reached under it and pulled out some old boots. He gave them to Norville. Norville pulled them on, then came around the side of the cage and studied the Reverend.

"Thank you for lettin' me out," Norville said. "I ain't crazy, you know. I seen what I seen and they don't want to hear it none."

"Cause you're crazy," Jud said.

"What did you see?" the Reverend asked.

"He starts talkin' that business again, I'll throw him back in the box," Jud said. "Our deal was he goes with you, and I figure you've worn out your welcome."

"What I've worn out is my stomach," Reverend Mercer said. "That meat is backing up on me."

"Take care of your stomach problems somewhere else, and take that crazy sonofabitch with you."

"Does he have a horse?"

"The back of yours," Jud said. "Best get him on it, and you two get out."

"Norville," the Reverend said, "Come with me."

"I don't mind comin'," Norville said, walking briskly after the Reverend.

Reverend Mercer unhitched his horse and climbed into the saddle. He extended a hand for Norville, helped him slip up on the rear of the horse. Norville put his arms around Reverend Mercer's waist. The Reverend said, "Keep the hands high or they'll find you face down outside of town in the pine straw."

"You stay gone, you hear?" Jud said, walking up on the porch.

"This place does not hold much charm for me, Sheriff Jud," Reverend Mercer said. "But, just in case you should over value your position, you do not concern me in the least. It is this town that concerns me. It stinks and it is worthless and should be burned to the ground."

"You go on now," Jud said.

"That I will, but at my own speed."

The Reverend rode off then, glancing back, least Jud decide to back shoot. But it was a needless concern. He saw Jud go inside the shack, perhaps to fry up some more rancid horse meat.

They rode about three miles out of town, and Reverend Mercer stopped by a stream. They got down off the horse and let it drink. While the horse quenched its thirst, the Reverend removed the animal's saddle, then he pulled the horse away from the water least it bloat. He took some grooming items out of a saddle bag and went to work, giving the horse a good brushing and rub down.

Norville plucked a blade of grass and put it in his mouth and worked it around, found a tree to sit under, said, "I ain't no bowl of nuts. I seen what I seen. Why did you help me anyway? For all you know I am a nut."

"I am on a mission from God. I do not like it, but it is my mission. I'm a hunter of the dark and a giver of the light. I'm the hammer and the anvil. The bone and the sinew. The sword and the gun. God's man who sets things right. Or at least right as God sees them. Me and him, we do not always agree. And let me tell you, he is not the God of Jesus, he is the God of David, and the angry city killers and man killers and animal killers of the Old Testament. He is constantly jealous and angry and if there is any plan to all this, I have yet to see it."

"Actually, I was just wantin' to know if you thought I was nuts."

"It is my lot in life to destroy evil. There is more evil than there is me, I might add."

"So...You think I'm a nut, or what?"

"Tell me your story."

"If you think I'm a nut are you just gonna leave me?"

"No. I will shoot you first and leave your body...Just joking. I do not joke much, so I'm poor at it."

The Reverend tied up the horse and they went over and sat together under the tree and drank water from the Reverend's canteen. Norville told his story.

🙠 🙢

"My daddy, after killin' my mother over turnip soup, back in the Carolinas, hitched up the wagon and put me in my sister in it and come to Texas."

"He killed your mother over soup?"

"Deader than a rock. Hit her upside the head with a snatch of turnips."

"A snatch of turnips? What in the world is a snatch of turnips?"

"Bunch of them. They was on the table where she'd cut up some for soup, still had the greens one 'em. He grabbed the greens, and swung them turnips. Must have been seven or eight big ole knotty ones. Hit her upside the head and knocked her brain loose I reckon. She died that night, right there on the floor. Wouldn't let us help her any. He said God didn't want her to die from getting hit with turnips, he'd spare her."

"Frankly, God is not all that merciful...You seen this? You father hitting your mother with the turnips?"

"Yep. I was six or so. My sister four. Daddy didn't like turnips in any kind of way, let alone a soup. So he took us to Texas after he burned down the cabin with mama in it, and I been in Texas ever since, but mostly over toward the middle of the state. About a year ago he died and my sister got a bad cough and couldn't get over it. Coughed herself to death. So I lit out on my own."

"I would think that is appropriate at your age, being on your own. How old are you. Thirty?"

"Twenty-six. I'm just tired. So I was riding through the country here, living off the land, squirrels and such, and I come to this shack in the woods and there weren't no one livin' there. I mean I found it by accident, cause it wasn't on a real trail. It was just down in the woods and it had a good roof on it, and there was a well. I yelled to see anyone was home, and they wasn't, and the door pushed open. I could see hadn't nobody been there in a long time. They had just gone off and left it. It was a nice house, and had real glass in the windows, and whoever had made it had done good on it, cause it was put together good and sound. They had trimmed away trees and had a yard of sorts.

"I started livin' there, and it wasn't bad. It had that well, but when I come up on it for a look, I seen that it had been filled in with rocks and such, and there wasn't no gettin' at the water. But there was a creek no more than a hundred feet from the place, and it was spring fed and I was right at the source. There was plenty of game, and I had a garden patch where I grew turnips and the like."

"I would have thought you would have had your fill of turnips in all shapes and forms."

"I liked that soup my mama made. I still remember it. Daddy didn't have no cause to do that over some soup."

"Now we are commanding the same line of thought."

"Anyway, the place was just perfect. I started to clean out the well. Spendin' a bit of time each day pullin' rocks out of it. In the meantime, I just used the spring down behind the house, but the well was closer, and it had a good stone curbin' around it, and I thought it would be nice if it was freed up for water. I wouldn't have to tote so far.

"Meanwhile, I discovered the town of Wood Tick. It isn't much, as you seen, but there was one thing nice about it, and every man in that town knew it and wanted that nice thing. Sissy. She was one of Mary's daughters. The only one she knew who her father was. A drummer who passed through and sold her six yards of wool and about five minutes in a back room.

"Thing is, there wasn't no real competition in Wood Tick for Sissy. That town has the ugliest men you ever seen, and about half of them have goiters and such. She was fifteen and I was just five years older, and I took to courtin' her."

"She was nothing but a child."

"Not in these parts. Ain't no unusual thing for men to marry younger girls, and Sissy was mature."

"In the chest or in the head?"

"Both. So we got married, or rather, we just decided we was married, and we moved out to that cabin."

"And you still had no idea who built it, who it belonged to?"

"Sissy knew, and she told me all about it. She said there had been an old woman who lived there, and that she wasn't the one who built the house in the first place, but she died there, and then a family ended up with the land, squatted on it, but after a month, they disappeared, all except for the younger daughter who they found walkin' the road, talkin' to herself. She kept sayin' 'It sucked and it crawled' or some such. She stayed with Mary in town who did some doctorin', but wasn't nothing could be done for her. She died. They said she looked like she aged fifty years in a few days when they put her down.

"Folks went out to the house but there wasn't nothin' to be found, and the well was all rocked in. Then another family moved in, and they'd come into town from time to time, and then they didn't anymore. They just disappeared. In time, one of the townspeople moved in, a fellow who weaved ropes and sold hides and such, and then he too was gone. No sign as to where. Then there was this man come through town, a preacher like you, and he ended up out there, and he said the house was evil, and he stayed on for a long time, but finally he'd had enough and came into town and said the place ought to be set afire and the ground plowed up and salted so nothing would grow there and no one would want to be there."

"So he survived?"

"He did until he hung himself in a barn. He left a note said: I seen too much."

"Concise," the Reverend said.

"And then I come there and brought Sissy with me."

"After all that, you came here and brought a woman as well. Could it be, sir, that you are not too bright?"

"I didn't believe all them stories then."

"But you do now?"

"I do. And I want to go back and set some thing straight on account of Sissy. That's what I was tryin' to tell them in town, that somethin' had happened to her, but when I told them what, wouldn't nobody listen. They just figured I was two nuts shy a squirrel's lunch and throwed me in that damned old cage. I'd still have been there wasn't for you. Now, you done good by me, and I appreciate it, and I'd like you to ride me over close to the house, you don't have to come up on it, but I got some business I want to take care of."

"Actually, the business you refer to is exactly my business."

"Haints and such?"

"I suppose you could put it that way. But please, tell me about Sissy. About what happened."

Norville nodded and swigged some water from the canteen and screwed the cap on. He took a deep breath and leaned loosely against the tree.

"Me and Sissy, we was doin' all right at first, makin' a life for ourselves. I took to cleanin' out that old well. I had to climb down in it and haul the rocks up by bucket, and some of them was so big I had to wrap a rope around them and hook my mule up and haul them out. I got down real deep, and still didn't reach water. I come to where it was just nothin' but mud, and I stuck a stick down in the mud, and it was deep, and there really wasn't anymore I could do, so I gave it up and kept carrying water from the spring. I took to fixin' up some rotten spots on the house, nailin' new shingles on the roof. Sissy planted flowers and it all looked nice. Then, of a sudden, it got so she couldn't sleep nights. She kept sayin' she was sure there was somethin' outside, and that she'd seen a face at the window, but when I got my gun and went out, wasn't nothin' there but the yard and that pile of rocks I'd pulled out of the well. But the second time I went out there, I had the feelin' someone was watching, maybe from the woods, and my skin started to crawl. I ain't never felt that uncomfortable. I started back to the house, and then I got this idea that I was bein' followed. I stopped and started to look back, but I couldn't bring myself to do it. Just couldn't. I felt if I looked back I'd see somethin' I didn't want to see. I'm ashamed to say I broke and ran and I closed the door quickly and locked it, and outside the door I could hear somethin' breathin'.

"From then on, by the time it was dark, we was inside. I boarded up all the windows from the inside. In the day, it seemed silly, but when night come around, it got so we both felt as if something was moving around and around the house, and I even fancied once that it was on the roof, and at the chimney. I built a fire in the chimney quick like, and kept one going at night, even when it was hot, and finally, I rocked it up and we cooked outside durin' the day and had cold suppers at night. Got so we dreaded the night. We were frightened out of our gourds. We took to sleepin' a few hours in the day, and I did what I could to tend the garden and hunt for food, but I didn't like being too far from the house or Sissy.

"Now, the thing to do would have been to just pack up and leave. We talked about it. But the house and that land was what we had, even if it was just by squatter's rights, and we thought maybe we were being silly, except we got so it wasn't just a feelin' we had, or sounds, we could smell it. It smelled like old meat and stagnant water, all at once. It floated around the house at night, through them boarded windows and under the front door. It was like it was getting' stronger and bolder.

"One mornin' we came out and all the flowers Sissy had planted had been jerked out of the ground, and there was a dead coon on the doorstep, its head yanked off."

"Yanked off?"

"You could tell from the way there was strings of meat comin' out of the neck. It had been twisted and pulled plumb off, like a wrung chicken neck, and from the looks of it, it appeared someone, or something, had sucked on its neck. Curious, I cut that coon open. Hardly had a drop of blood in it. Ain't that somethin'?"

"That's something all right."

"Our mule disappeared next. No sign of it. We thought it over and decided we needed to get out, but we didn't know where to go and we didn't have any real money. Then one mornin' I come out, and on the stones I'd set in front of the house for steps, there was a muddy print on them. It was a big print and it didn't have no kind of shape I could recognize, no kind of animal, but it had toes and a heel. Mud trailed off into the weeds. I got my pistol and went out there, but didn't find nothin'. No more prints. Nothin'.

That night I heard a board crack at the bedroom window, and I got up with a gun in my hand. I seen that one of the boards I'd nailed over the window outside had been pulled loose, and a face was pressed up against the glass. It was dark, but I could see enough cause of the moonlight, and it wasn't like a man's face. It was the eyes and mouth that made it so different, like it had come out of a human mold of some sort, but the mold had been twisted or dropped or both, and what was made from it was this…This thing. The face was as pale as a whore's butt, and twisted up, and its eyes were blood red and shone at the window as clear as if the thing was standin' in front of me. I shot at it, shatterin' an expensive pane of glass, and then it was gone in the wink of that pistol's flare.

"I decided it had to end, and I told Sissy to stick, and I gave her the pistol, and I took the fire wood axe and went outside and she bolted the door behind me. I went on around to the side of the house, and I thought I caught sight of it, a nude body, maybe, but with strange feet. Wasn't nothin' more than a glimpse of it as it went around the edge of the house and I ran after it. I must have run around that damn house three times. It acted like it was a kid playin' a game with me. Then I saw somethin' white that at first I couldn't imagine was it, because it seemed like a sheet being pulled through the bedroom window I'd shot out.

"You mean it was wraith like…A haint, as you said before?"

Norville nodded. "I ran to the door, but it was bolted of course, way I told Sissy to do. I ran back to the window and started using the axe to chop out the rest of the boards, knocked the panes and the frame out, and I crawled through, pieces of glass stickin' and cuttin' me.

"Sissy wasn't there. But the pistol was on the floor. I dropped the axe and snatched it up, and then I heard her scream real loud and rushed out into the main room, and there I seen it. It was chewin'…You got to believe me, preacher. It had spread its mouth wide, like a snake, and it had more teeth in its face than a dozen folk, and teeth more like an animal, and it was bitin' her head off. It jerked its jaws from side to side, and blood went everywhere. I shot at it. I shot at it five times and I hit it five times.

"It didn't so much as make the thing move. I might as well have been rubbin' its belly. It lifted its eyes and looked at me, and…As God is my witness, it spat out what was left of poor Sissy's head, and slapped its mouth over her blood pumpin' neck, and went to suckin' on it like a kid with a sucker.

"I ain't ashamed to admit it, my knees went weak. I dropped the pistol and ran and got the axe. When I turned, it was on me. I swung that axe, and hit it. The blade went in, went in deep…and there wasn't no blood, didn't spurt a drop. Thing grabbed me up and flung me at the window, and damned if I didn't go straight through it and land out on my back, on top of some of them rocks I'd pulled out of the well. It flowed through that window like it was water, and it come at me. I rolled over and grabbed one of the rocks and flung it and hit that thing square in its bony chest. What five shots from a pistol and a hack from an axe couldn't do, the rock did.

"Monster yelled like the fire of hell had been shoved down its throat, and it ran straight away for the well faster than I've ever seen anything move, its body twistin' in all directions, like it was going to come apart, or like the bones was shiftin' inside of it. It ran and dove into the well and I heard it hit the mud below.

"I climbed back through the window, rushed into the main room, tryin' not to look at poor Sissy's body, and I got the double barrel off the mantle and lit and lantern and went back outside through the front door with the lantern in one hand, the shotgun in the other.

"First I held the lantern over the well, got me a look, but didn't see nothin' but darkness. I bent over the curbin' and lowered the lantern in some, fearin' that thing might grab me. The sides of the well were covered with a kind of slime, and I could see the mud down below, and if the thing had gone into it, there wasn't no sign now accept a bit of a ripple.

"I hid out in the woods. I went back the next mornin' and got Sissy's body and buried it out back of the place, and then before it was dark, I boarded up all the windows good and locked the door and I got the shotgun and sat with it all night in the middle of the big room. I knew it wouldn't do me no good, but that was all I had. Me and that shotgun.

"But didn't nothin' bother me, though I could hear it and smell it movin' around outside the house. Come morning, I was brave enough to go out, and Sissy's body had been pulled from the grave and gnawed on. I reckon animals could have done it in the night, but I didn't think so. I buried her again, this time deep, and mounded up dirt and packed it down. I cut some sticks and tied a cross together and stuck that up, then I walked into town and told my story. They didn't even think I was a murderer. They didn't question if I might have killed Sissy, which is what I thought they might do. They locked me up for bein' a crazy, and wasn't no one cared enough to come and see if her body was at the cabin or not. They wasn't interested. I done taken Sissy off and wasn't no man wanted her back now that she had been with me, which considerin' the kind of women they was usually with didn't make no sense, but then there ain't much about Wood Tick that does make sense.

"And then you come along, and you know the rest from there."

(3)

THE THING DOWN THERE

The sun was starting to slant to the West, but there was still plenty of daylight left when they arrived on horseback. The house was built of large logs and it looked solid. The chimney appeared sound. The shingles well cut and nailed down tight. It was indeed a good cabin and the Reverend understood the attraction it held for those who passed by.

Norville slipped off the back of the horse and hurried around behind the cabin. After the Reverend tied up his horse, he too went out back. Norville stood over an empty grave, the cross turned over and broken. Norville and the Reverend stood there for a long moment.

Norville fell to his knees. "Oh, Jesus. I should have taken her off somewhere else. He's done come and got her."

"It is done now," Reverend Mercer said. "Stand up, man. None of this does any good. Let's look around."

Norville stood up, but he looked ready to collapse. "Buck up, man," Reverend Mercer said. "We have work to do."

No sight or parcel of the body was found. The Reverend went to the well and bent over and looked down. It was deep. He took out a match and struck it on the curbing and dropped it down the shaft, watched the little light fall. The match hissed out in the mud below.

"Do you believe me," Norville said, standing back from the well a few paces. "I do."

"What can I do?"

"Whatever you do, you will not do alone. I will be here with you."

"Kind of you, Reverend, but what can you do?"

"At the moment, I'm uncertain. Let's look inside the house."

The cabin, though not huge, had two rooms. A small bedroom and a large main room with a kitchen table and a rocked in fireplace and some benches and a few chairs. There was blood on the floor and on a rug there, and on the walls and even on the ceiling. The Reverend paused at the rocked up fireplace. He bent down and looked at the rocks. "Did you notice a lot of these rocks have a drawing in them?"

"What now?"

"Look here." Reverend Mercer touched his finger to one of the stones. There was a strange drawing on it, a stick figure with small symbols written around it in a circle. "It's on a lot of the rocks, and my guess is, if you were to pull the ones without visible symbols free, you could turn them over and the marks would be on the other side. They came from inside the well, correct?"

"Nearly all of them. It's a very deep well."

"As I have seen. Did you not notice the marks?"

"Guess I was so anxious to get those rocks out of there I didn't."

"It is only visible if you're looking for it?"

"And you were?"

"I was looking for anything. This is my business. When you said you hit this thing with a rock and it fled after shooting it and hitting it with an axe had no effect, I started to wonder. I believe these are symbols of protection."

The Reverend began walking about the house. He looked under the bed and at the walls and checked nooks and crannies. He bounced himself on the floor to test the boards. He stood looking down at the blood-stained rug for awhile. He picked up the edge of the rug and saw there were a series of short boards that didn't extend completely across the floor.

Sliding the rug aside, the Reverend used his knife and stuck it under the edge of one of the boards and pried it up. There was a space beneath and a metal box was in the space. The Reverend removed a few more boards so he could get a good look at the box. It had a padlock on it.

"Find the axe," the Reverend said.

Norville went outside and got the axe and brought it back. It was a single edge, and the Reverend turned the flat side down and swung and knocked the lock off with one sure blow. He opened the box. Inside was a book.

"Why would someone put a book under lock and key?" Norville said.

The Reverend went to the table and sat on the long bench next to it. Norville sat on the other side. The Reverend opened the book and studied it. He looked up after a moment, said, "Whoever built this house originally, their intentions for us were not good."

"Us?" Norville said. "How would they, whoever that is, know we would be here?"

"Not you and I. Us as in the human race, Norville. They, meaning the ones who possess this book, called THE BOOK OF DOCHES. The ones who find it or buy it or kill to possess it, always believe they will make some pact with the dark ones, the ones darker than our God, much darker, and they believe that if they allow these dark ones to break through they will be either its master or its trusted servant. The latter is sometimes possible, but the former, never. And in the end, a trusted servant is easily replaced."

"What are you talkin' about?" Norville said.

"There are monsters on the other side of the veil, Norville. A place you and I can't see. These things want out. Books like this contain spells to free them, and sometimes the people who possess the book want to set them free for rewards. Someone has already set one of them free."

"The sucking thing?"

"Correct," the Reverend said, shaking the book. "Look at the pages. See. The words and images on the pages are hand printed? The pages, feel them."

Norville used his thumb and finger to feel.

"Its cloth."

"Flesh. Human flesh is what the book says."

Norville jerked his hand back. "You can read this hen scratch?"

"Yes. I read a translation of it long ago, taught myself to understand the original symbols."

"You have the same book?"

"Had. One of them got away from me, the one adapted into English. The other I destroyed."

"How did it get away from you?"

"That's not important to us today. Whoever built this house may have brought this copy here. But their plans didn't work out. They released something, one of the minor horrors, and that minor horror either chased them off, or did to them what they did to your poor Sissy. This thing they called up. The place where it is from is wet, and therefore it takes to the well. And it is hungry. Always hungry. A minor being, but a nasty one."

"But if this beast is on the other side, as you call it, why would anyone bring it here?"

"Never underestimate the curiosity and stupidity and greed of man, Norville."

"If the book set this thing free, then burn the book."

"Not a bad idea, but I doubt that would get rid of anything. In fact, I might do better to study the book. My guess is whoever first brought the book, loosed the creature. They then decided they had made a mistake, made the marks of power on the stones and sealed the thing in the well where it preferred to reside—it liked the dampness, you see. And then, someone, like you, took the rocks from the well and the thing was let loose. One of the other survivors, the preacher for example, may have figured out enough to seal the thing back in the well. And then you let it out again."

"Then we can seal it back up," Norville said.

The Reverend shook his head. "Then someone else will open the well."

"We can destroy the well curbing, put the rocks in, build a mound of dirt over all of it."

"Still not enough. That leaves the possibility of it being opened up in the future, if only by accident. No. This thing, it has to be destroyed. Listen here. It's light yet. Take my horse and walk it and take off its saddle, and then bring it inside where it will be safer."

"The house?"

"Since when are you so particular? I do not want to leave the horse for that thing to kill. If it must have the horse or us, then it will have to come and get the lot of us."

"All right then."

"Bring in my saddle and all that goes with it. And those rocks from the well. Only the rocks from the well. Start bringing them in by the pile."

"Aren't there enough here in the fireplace?"

"They are in use. One may cause this thing to flee, but that doesn't mean one will destroy it. I have other plans. Do it, Norville. Already the sun dips deep and the dark is our first enemy."

When the horse was inside and the stones were stacked in the middle of the floor, the Reverend looked up from the book, said, "Place the stones in a circle around us. A large circle. Make a line of them across the back of this room and put the horse against the wall behind them. Give him plenty of room to get excited. Hobble him and put on his bridle and tie him to that nail in the wall, the big one."

"And what exactly will you be doin'?"

"Reading," the Reverend said. "You will have to trust me. I'm all that is between you and this thing."

Norville went about placing the stones.

It was just short of dark when the stones were placed in a circle around the table and a line of them had been made behind that from wall to wall, containing the tied up horse.

Reverend Mercer looked up from the book. "You are finished?"

Noville said, "Almost. I'll board up the bedroom window. Not that it matters. He can slip between some small spaces. But it will slow it down."

"Leave it as is, and leave the door to the bedroom partially cracked."

"You're sure?"

"Quite."

The Reverend placed one of the rocks on the table, removed the bullets from his belt and took his knife and did his best to copy the symbols in small shapes on the tips of his ammunition. The symbols were simple, a stick man with a few twists and twirls around it. It took him an hour to copy it onto twelve rounds of ammunition.

Finished, he loaded six rounds in each of his revolvers.

"Shall I light the lamp?" Norville asked.

"No. You have an axe and a shotgun lying about. We may have need for both. Recover them, and then come inside the ring of stones."

(4)
THE ARRIVAL

While they waited, sitting cross-legged on the floor inside the circle of stones, the Reverend carved the symbols on the rocks onto the blade of the axe. He thought about the shotgun shells, but it wouldn't do any good to have the symbols on the shells and not on the load, and since the shotgun shot pellets, that was an impossible task.

Lying the axe between them, the Reverend handed the shotgun to Norville. "The shotgun will be nothing more than a shotgun," he said. "And it may not kill the thing, but it will be a distraction. You get the chance, shoot the thing with it, otherwise, sit and do not, under any circumstances, step outside this circle. The axe I have written symbols on and it may be of use."

"Are you sure this circle will keep him out?"

"Not entirely."

Norville swallowed.

ʁ ℘

They sat and they listened and the hours crept by. The Reverend produced a flask from his saddle bags. "I keep this primarily for medicinal purposes, but the night seems a little chill, so let us both have one short nip, and one short nip only."

The Reverend and Norville took a drink and the flask was replaced. And no sooner was it replaced, than a smell seeped into the house. A smell like a charnel house and a butcher shop and an outhouse all balled into one.

"It's near," Norville said. "That's its smell."

The Reverend put a finger to his lips to signal quiet.

There were a few noises on the outside of the house, but they could have been most anything. Finally there came a sound in the bedroom like wet laundry plopping to the floor.

Norville looked at the Reverend.

Reverend Mercer nodded to let him know he too had heard it, and then he carefully pulled and cocked his revolvers.

The room was dark, but the Reverend had adjusted his eye sight and could make out shapes. He saw that the bedroom door, already partially cracked open, was slowly moving. And then a hand, white and puffy like the leaves of an orchid, appeared around the edge of the door, and fingers, long and stalk like, extended and flexed, and the door moved and a flow of muddy water slid into the room along the floor.

The Reverend felt Norville move beside him, as if to rise, and he reached out and touched his shoulder to steady him.

The door opened more, and then the thing slipped inside the main room. It moved strangely, as if made of soft candle wax. It was dead white of flesh, but much of the skin was filthy with mud. It was neither male nor female. No genitals; down there it was a smooth as a well-washed river rock. It was tall, with knees that swung slightly to the sides when it walked, and there was an odd vibration about it, as if it were about to burst apart in all directions. The head was small. Its face was mostly a long gash of a mouth. It had thin slits for eyes and a hole for a nose. At the ends of its willowy legs were large flat feet that splayed out in shapes like claw-tipped four-leaf clovers.

Twisting and winding, long stepping, and sliding, it made its way forward until it was close to the Reverend and Norville. It leaned forward and sniffed. The hole that was its nose opened wider as it did, flexed.

It smells us, thought the Reverend. Only fair, because we certainly smell it.

And then it opened its dripping mouth and came at them in a rush.

As it neared the stones, it was knocked back by an invisible wall, and then there came something quite visible where it had impacted, a ripple of blue fulmination. The thing went sliding along the floor on its belly in its own mud and goo.

"The rocks hold," the Reverend said, and it came again. Norville lifted the shotgun and fired. The pellets went through the thing and came rattling out against the wall on the other side. The hole made in its chest did not bleed, and it filled in rapidly, as if never struck.

Reverend Mercer stood up and aimed one of his pistols, and hit the thing square in the chest, and this time the wound made a sucking sound and when the load came out on the other side, goo and something dark went with it. But it didn't stop the creature. It hit the invisible wall again, bellowed and fell back. It dragged its way around the circle toward the horse, tied behind the line of stones. The terrified horse reared and snapped its reins as if they were nonexistent. The horse went thundering across the line, and then across the circle of stones, causing them to go spinning left and right, and along came the thing, entering the circle through the gap.

The Reverend fired again. The thing jerked back and squealed like a pig. Then it sprang forward again, grabbed the Reverend by the throat and sent him flying across the room, slamming into the side of the frightened horse.

Norville swung the shotgun around and fired right into the thing's mouth, but it was like the thing was swallowing gnats. It grabbed the gun barrel used it to sling the clutching Norville sliding across the floor, collecting splinters until he came up against the bedroom door, slamming it shut.

It started forward, but it couldn't step out of the circle. Not that way. It wheeled to find the exit the horse had made, and as it did, Reverend Mercer, now on his feet, fired twice and hit the thing in the back, causing it to stagger through the opening and fall against the line of rocks that had been there to protect the horse. Its head hit the rocks and the creature cried out, leaping to its feet with a move that seemed boneless and without use of muscle. Its forehead bore a sizzling mark the size of the rock.

"Get back inside the circle," the Reverend said. "Close it off."

Norville waited for no further instruction. He bolted and leaped into the circle and began to clutch at the displaced stones. The Reverend put his right leg forward and threw back his coat by bending his left hand behind him; he pointed the revolver and took careful aim, fired twice.

Both shots hit. One in the head, one in the throat. They had their effect. The horror splattered to the floor with the wet laundry sound. But no sooner had it struck the ground, then it began to wriggle along the floor like a grub worm in a frying pan; it came fast and furious and grabbed the Reverend's boot, and came to spring upright in front of the Reverend with that strange manner it had of moving.

Reverend Mercer cracked it across the head with his pistol, and it grabbed at him. The Reverend avoided the grab and struck out with his fist, a jab that merely annoyed the thing. It spread its jaws and filled the air with stink. The Reverend drew his remaining pistol and fired straight into the hole the thing used for a nose, causing it to go toppling backward along the floor gnashing its teeth into the lumber.

Reverend Mercer ran and leaped into the circle.

When he turned to look, the monster was sliding up the wall like some kind of slug. It left a sticky trail along the logs as it reached the ceiling and crawled along that with the dexterity of an insect.

The horse had finally come to a corner and stuck its head in it to hide. The thing came down on its back, and its mouth spread over the horse's head, and the horse stood up on its hind legs and its front legs hit the wall, and it fell over backward, landing on the creature. It didn't bother the thing in the least. It grabbed and twisted the horse over on its side as if it were nothing more than a feather pillow. There was a crunch as the monster's teeth snapped bones in the horse's head. The horse quit moving, and the thing began to suck, rivulets of blood spilling out from the corners of its distended mouth.

The Reverend jammed his pistol back into its holster, bent and grabbed the axe from the floor and leaped out of the circle. The thing caught sight of the Reverend as he came, rolled off the horse and leaped up on the wall and ran along it. As the Reverend turned to follow its progress, it leaped at him.

Reverend Mercer took a swing. The axe hit the fiend and split halfway through its neck, knocking it back against the wall, then to the floor. Its narrow eyes widened and showed red, and then it came to its feet in its unique way, though more slowly than before, and darted for the bedroom door.

As it reached and fumbled with the latch, the Reverend hit the thing in the back of the head with the axe, and it went to its knees, clawed at the lumber of the door, causing it to squeak and squeal and come apart, making a narrow slit. It was enough. The thing eased through it like a snake. The Reverend jerked the door open to see it going through the gap in the window. He dropped the axe and jerked the pistol and fired and struck the thing twice before it went out through the breach and was gone from sight.

Reverend Mercer rushed to the window and looked out. The thing was staggering, falling, rising to its feet, staggering toward the well. The Reverend stuck the pistol out the window, resting it on the frame, and fired again. It was a good shot in the back of the neck, and the brute went down.

Holstering the revolver, rushing to grab the axe, the Reverend climbed through the window. The monster had made it to the well by then, crawling along on its belly, and just as it touched the curbing, the Reverend caught up with it, brought the spell-marked axe down on its already shredded head as many times as he had the strength to swing it.

As he swung, the sun began to color the sky. He was breathing so hard he sounded like a blue norther blowing in. The sun rose higher and still he swung, then he fell to the ground, his chest heaving.

When he looked about, he saw the thing was no longer moving. Norville was standing nearby, holding one of the marked rocks.

"You was doin' so good, I didn't want to interrupt you," Norville said.

The Reverend nodded, breathed for a long hard time, said, "Saddle bags. If this is not medicinal. I do not know what is."

A few moments later, Norville returned with the flask. The Reverend drank first, long and deep, and then he gave it to Norville.

When his wind was back, and the sun was up, the Reverend chopped the rest of the monster up. It had already gone flat and gushed clutter from its insides that were part horse bones, gouts of blood, and unidentifiable items that made the stomach turn; its teeth were spread around the well curbing, like someone had dropped a box of daggers.

They burned what would burn of the beast with dried limbs and dead leaves, buried the teeth and the remainder of the beast in a deep grave, the bottom and top and sides of it lined with the marked rocks.

When they were done chopping and cremating and burying the creature, it was late afternoon. They finished off the flask, and that night they slept in the house, undisturbed, and in the morning, they set fire to the cabin using the BOOK OF DOCHES as a starter. As it burned, the Reverend looked up. The sky had begun to change, finally. The clouds no longer crawled.

They walked out, the Reverend with the saddle bags over his shoulder, Norville with a pillow case filled with food tins from the cabin. Behind them, the smoke from the fire rose up black and sooty and by night time it had burned down to glowing cinders, and by the next day there was nothing more than clumps of ash.

ຂ ຜ

The Fairground Horror

Brian Lumley

The funfair was as yet an abject failure. Drizzling rain dulled the chrome of the dodgem-cars and stratojets; the neons had not even nearly achieved the garishness they display by night; the so-called "crowd" was hardly worth mentioning as such. But it was only 2:00 p.m. and things could yet improve.

Had the weather been better—even for October it was bad—and had Bathley been a town instead of a mere village, then perhaps the scene were that much brighter. Come evening, when the neons and other bright naked bulbs would glow in all the painful intensity of their own natural (unnatural?) life, when the drab gypsyish dollies behind the penny-catching stalls would undergo their subtle, nightly metamorphosis into avariciously enticing Loreleis—then it *would* be brighter, but not yet.

This was the fourth day of the five when the funfair was "in town."

It was an annual—event? The nomads of Hodgson's Funfair had known better times, better conditions and worse ones, but it was all the same to them and they were resigned to it. There was, though, amid all the noisy, muddy, smelly paraphernalia of the fairground, a tone of incongruity. It had been there since Anderson Tharpe, in the curious absence of his brother, Hamilton, had taken down the old freak-house frontage to repaint the boards and canvas with the new and forbidding legend: TOMB OF THE GREAT OLD ONES.

Looking up at the painted gouts of "blood" that formed the garish legend arching over a yawning, scaly, dragon-jawed entranceway, Hiram Henley frowned behind his tiny spectacles in more than casual curiosity, in something perhaps approaching concern. His lips silently formed the ominous words of that legend as if he spoke them to himself in awe, and then he thrust his black-gloved hands deeper into the pockets of his fine, expensively tailored overcoat and tucked his neck down more firmly into its collar.

Hiram Henley had recognized something in the name of the place—something which might ring subconscious warning bells in even the most mundane minds—and the recognition caused an involuntary shudder to hurry up his back. "The Great Old Ones!" he said to himself yet again, and his whisper held a note of terrible fascination.

Research into just such cycles of myth and aeon-lost legend, while ostensibly he had been studying Hittite antiquities in the Middle East and Turkey, had cost Henley his position as Professor of Archaeology and Ethnology at Meldham University. "Cthulhu, Yibb-Tstll, Yog-Sothoth, Summanus—the Great Old Ones!" Again an expression of awe flitted across his bespectacled face. To be confronted with a… a *monument* such as this, and in such a place…

And yet the ex-professor was not too surprised; he had been alerted to the contents of Anderson Tharpe's queer establishment, and therefore the fact that the owner had named it thus was hardly a matter of any lasting astonishment. Nevertheless Henley knew that there were people who would have considered the naming of the fairground erection, to say nothing of the presence of its afore-hinted *contents,* blasphemous. Fortunately such persons were few and far between—the Cult of Cthulhu was still known only to a minority of serious authorities, to a few obscure occult investigators, and a scattered handful of esoteric groups—but Hiram Henley looked back to certain days of yore when he had blatantly used the university's money to go in search of just such items of awesome antiquity as now allegedly hid behind the demon-adorned ramparts of the edifice before him.

The fact of the matter was that Henley had heard how this Tomb of the Great Old Ones held within its monster-daubed board-and-canvas walls relics of an age already many millions of years dead and gone when Babylon was but a sketch in the mind's eye of Architect Thathnis III. Figures and fragments, hieroglyphed tablets and strangely scrawled papyri, weird greenstone sculptings and rotting, worm-eaten tomes: Henley had reason to believe that many of these things, if not all of them, existed behind the facade of Anderson Tharpe's horror house.

There would also be, of course, the usual nonconformities peculiar to such establishments—the two-headed foetus in its bottle of preservative, the five-legged puppy similarly suspended, the fake mummy in its red- and green-daubed wrappings, the great fruit ("vampire") bats, hanging shutter-eyed and motionless in their warm wire cages beyond the reach of giggly, shuddering women and morbidly fascinated men and boys—but Hiram Henley was not interested in any of these. Nevertheless, he sent his gloved right hand awkwardly groping into the corner of his overcoat pocket for the silver coin which alone might open for him the door to Tharpe's house of horror.

Hiram Henley was a slight, middle-aged man. His thin figure, draped smotheringly in the heavy overcoat, his balding head and tiny specs through which his watery eyes constantly peered; his gloved hands almost lost in huge pockets, his trousers seeming to hang from beneath the hem of his overcoat and partly, not wholly, covering the black patent leather shoes upon his feet; all made of him a picture which was conspicuously odd. And yet Hiram Henley's intelligence was patent; the stamp of a "higher mind" was written in erudite lines upon his brow. His were obviously eyes which had studied strange mysteries, and his feet had gone along strange ways; so that despite any other emotion or consideration which his appearance might ill-advisedly call to mind, still his shrunken frame commanded more than a little respect among his fellow men.

Anderson Tharpe, on the other hand, crouching now upon his tiny seat in the ticket-booth, was a tall man, well over six feet in height but almost as thin and emaciated as the fallen professor. His hair was prematurely grey and purposely grown long in an old-fashioned scholarly style, so that he might simulate to the crowd's satisfaction a necessary erudition; just such an erudition as was manifest in the face above the slight figure which even now pressed upon his tiny window, sixpence clutched in gloved fingers. Tharpe's beady eyes beneath blackly hypnotic brows studied Hiram Henley briefly, speculatively, but then he smiled a very genuine welcome as he passed the small man a ticket, waving away the sixpence with an expansive hand.

"Not *you*, sir, indeed no! From a gent so obviously and sincerely interested in the mysteries within—from a man of your high standing"—again the expansive gesture—"why, I couldn't accept money from you, sir. It's an honour to have you visit us!"

"Thank you," Henley dryly answered, passing myopically into the great tent beyond the ticket booth. Tharpe's smile slowly faded, was replaced by a look of cunning. Quickly the tall man pocketed his few shillings in takings, then followed the slight figure of the ex-professor into the smelly sawdust-floored "museum" beyond the canvas flap.

In all, a dozen people waited within the big tent's main division. A pitifully small "crowd." But in any case, though he kept his interest cleverly veiled, Tharpe's plans involved only the ex-professor. The tall man's flattery at the ticket booth had not all been flannel; he had spotted Henley immediately as the very species of highly educated fly for which his flypaper—in the form of the new and enigmatic legend across the visage of the one-time freakhouse— had been erected above Bathley Moor.

There had been, Tharpe reflected, men of outwardly similar intelligence before at the Tomb of the Great Old Ones; and more than one of them had told him that certain of his *artifacts*—those items which he kept, as his brother had kept them before him, in a separately enclosed part of the tent—were of an unbelievable antiquity. Indeed, one man had been so affected by the very sight of such ancientness that he had run from Tharpe's collection in stark terror, and he had never returned. That had been in May, and though almost six months had passed since that time, still Tharpe had come no closer to an understanding of the mysterious objects which his brother Hamilton had brought back with him from certain dark corners of the world; objects which, early in 1961, had caused him to kill Hamilton in self-defence.

Anderson had panicked then—he realized that now—for he might easily have come out of the affair blameless had he only reported Hamilton's death to the police. For a long time the folk of Hodgson's Funfair had known that there was something drastically wrong with Hamilton Tharpe; his very sanity had been questioned, albeit guardedly. Certainly Anderson would have been declared innocent of his brother's murder—the case would have gone to court only as a matter of formality—but he had panicked. And of course there had been… complications.

With Hamilton's body secretly buried deep beneath the freakhouse, the folk of the fairground had been perfectly happy to believe Anderson's tale of his brother's abrupt departure on yet another of his world-spanning expeditions, the like of which had brought about all the trouble in the first place.

Now Anderson thought back on it all…

He and his brother had grown up together in the fairground, but then it had been their father's property, and "Tharpe's Funfair" had been known throughout all England for its fair play and prices. Wherever the elder Tharpe had taken his stalls and sideshows—of which the freak-house had ever been his personal favourite—his employees had been sure of good crowds. It was only after old Tharpe died that the slump started.

It had had much to do with young Hamilton's joy in old books and fancifully dubious legends; his lust for travel, adventure, and *outre* knowledge. His first money-wasting venture had been a "treasure-hunting" trip to the islands of the Pacific, undertaken solely on the strength of a vague and obviously fake map. In his absence—he had gone off with an adventurous and plausible rogue from the shooting gallery—Anderson looked after the fair. Things went badly, and all the Tharpes got out of Hamilton's venture were a number of repulsively carved stone tablets and one or two patently aboriginal sculptings, not the least of which was a hideous, curiously winged octopoid idol. Hamilton placed the latter obscenity in the back of their caravan home as being simply too fantastic for display to an increasingly mundane and sceptical public.

The idol, however, had a most unsettling effect upon the younger brother. He was wont to go in to see the thing in the dead of night, when Anderson was in bed and apparently asleep. But often Anderson was awake, and during these nocturnal visits he had heard Hamilton *talking* to the idol. More disturbingly, he had once or twice dimly imagined that he heard something talking back! Too, before he went off again on his wanderings in unspoken areas of the great deserts of Arabia, the sensitive, mystery-loving traveller had started to suffer from especially bad nightmares.

Again, in Hamilton's absence, things went badly. Soon Anderson was obliged to sell out to Bella Hodgson, retaining only the freak-house as his own and his prodigal brother's property. A year passed, and another before Hamilton once more returned to the fairground, demanding his living as before but making little or no attempt to work for his needs. There was no arguing, however, for the formerly sensitive younger brother was a changed, indeed a saturnine, man now, so that soon Anderson came to be a little afraid of him.

And quite apart from the less obvious alterations in Hamilton, other changes were much more apparent; changes in habit, even in appearance. The most striking was the fact that now the younger Tharpe constantly wore a shaggy black toupee, as if to disguise his partial premature baldness, which all of the funfair's residents knew about anyway and which had never caused him the least embarrassment before. Also, he had become so reticent as to be almost reclusive; keeping to himself, only rarely and reluctantly allowing himself to be drawn into even the most trivial conversations.

More than this: there had been a time prior to his second long absence when Hamilton had seemed somewhat enamored of the young, single, dark-eyed fortune-teller, "Madame Zala"—a Gypsy girl of genuine Romany ancestry—but since his return he had been especially cool towards her, and for her own part she had been seen to cross herself with a pagan sign when he had happened to be passing by. Once he had seen her make this sign, and then he had gone white with fury, hurrying off to the freak-house and remaining there for the rest of that day. Madame Zala had packed up her things and left one night in her horse-drawn caravan without a word of explanation to anyone. It was generally believed that Hamilton had threatened her in some way, though no one ever took him to task over the affair. For his own part, he simply averred that Zala had been "a charlatan of the worst sort, without the ability to conjure a puff of wind!"

All in all the members of the funfair fraternity had been quick to find Hamilton a very changed man, and towards the end there had been the afore-mentioned hints of a brewing madness...

On top of all this, Hamilton had again taken up his nocturnal visits to the octopoid idol, but now such visits seemed less frequent than of old. Less frequent, perhaps, but they nevertheless heralded much darker events; for soon Hamilton had installed the idol within a curtained and spacious corner of the tent, in the freak-house itself, and he no longer paid his visits alone...

Anderson Tharpe had seen, from his darkened caravan window, a veritable procession of strangers—all of them previous visitors to the freak-house, and always the more intelligent types—accompanying his brother to the tent's nighted interior. But he had never seen a one come out! Eventually, as his younger brother became yet more saturnine, reticent, and secretive, Anderson took to spying on him in earnest—and later almost wished that he had not. In the months between, however, Hamilton had made certain alterations to the interior of the freak-house, partitioning fully a third of its area to enclose the collection of rare and obscure curiosities garnered upon his travels. At that time Anderson had been puzzled to distraction by his brother's firm refusal to let his treasures be viewed by any but a chosen few of the freak-house's patrons: those doubtfully privileged persons who later accompanied him into the private museum never again to leave.

Of course, Anderson finally reasoned, the answer was a simple as it was fantastic: somewhere upon his travels Hamilton had learned the arts of murder and thievery, arts he was now practicing in the freak-house. The bodies? These he obviously buried, to leave behind safely lodged in the dark earth when the fair moved on. But the money... what of the money? For money—or rather its lack—patently formed the younger brother's motive. Could he be storing his booty away, against the day when he would go off on yet another of his foolish trips to foreign places? Beside himself that he had not been "cut in" on the profits of Hamilton's dark machinations, Anderson determined to have it out with him; to catch him, as it were, red-handed.

And yet it was not until early in the spring of 1961 that Anderson finally managed to "overhear" a conversation between his brother and an obviously well-to-do visitor to the freak-house. Hamilton had singled out this patently intelligent gentleman for attention, inviting him back to the caravan during a break in business. Anderson, knowing most of the modus operandi by now and aware of the turn events must take, positioned himself outside the caravan where he could eavesdrop.

He did not catch the complete conversation, and yet sufficient to make him aware at last of Hamilton's expert and apparently unique knowledge in esoteric mysteries. For the first time he heard uttered the mad words Cthulhu and Yibb-Tstll, Tsathoggua and Yog-Sothoth, Shudde-M'ell and Nyarlathotep, discovering that these were names of monstrous "gods" from the dawn of time. He heard mention of Leng and Lh'yib; Mnar, Ib and Sarnath; R'lyeh and "red-litten" Yoth; and knew now that these were cities and lands ancient even in antiquity. He heard descriptions and names given to manuscripts, books, and tablets—and here he started in recognition, for he knew that some of these aeon-old writings existed amid Hamilton's treasures in the freakhouse—and among others he heard the strangely chilling titles of such works as the *Necronomicon,* the *Cthaat Aquadingen,* the *Pnakotic Manuscripts* and the *R'lyehan Texts.* This then formed the substance of Hamilton's magnetism: his amazing erudition in matters of myth and time-lost lore.

When he perceived that the two were about to make an exit from the caravan, Anderson quickly hid himself away behind a nearby stall to continue his observations. He saw the flushed face of Hamilton's new confidante, his excited gestures; and, at a whispered suggestion from the pale-faced brother, he finally saw that gentle man nodding eagerly, wide-eyed in awed agreement. And after the visitor had gone, Anderson saw the look that flitted briefly across his brother's features: a look that hinted of awful triumph, nameless emotion—and, yes, purest evil!

But it was something about the face of the departed visitor—that rounded gentleman of obvious substance but doubtful future which caused Anderson the greatest concern. He had finally recognized that face from elsewhere, and at his first opportunity he sneaked a glance through some of the archaeological and anthropological journals which his brother now spent so much time reading. It was as he had thought: Hamilton's prey was none other than an eminent explorer and archaeologist; one whose name, Stainton Gamber, might even be higher in the lists of famous adventurers and discoverers but for a passion for wild-goose expeditions and safaris. Then he grew even more worried, for plainly his brother could not go on forever depleting the countryside of eminent persons without being discovered.

That afternoon passed slowly for Anderson Tharpe, and when night came he went early to his bed in the caravan. He was up again, however, as soon as he heard his brother stirring and the hushed whispers that led off in the direction of the freak-house. It was as he had known it would be, when for a moment pale moonlight showed him a glimpse of Hamilton with Stainton Gamber.

Quickly he followed the two to the looming canvas tent, and in through the dragon-jawed entranceway, but he paused at the doorflap to the partitioned area to listen and observe. There came the scratch of a match and its bright, sudden flare, and then a candle flickered into life. At this point the whispering recommenced, and Anderson drew back a pace as the candle began to move about the interior of Hamilton's museum. He could hear the hushed conversations quite clearly, could feel the tremulous excitement in the voice of the florid explorer:

"But these are—*fantastic!* I've believed for years now that such relics must exist. Indeed, I've often brought my reputation close to ruin for such beliefs, and now... young man, you'll be world famous. Do you realize what you have here? Proof positive that the Cult of Cthulhu did exist! What monstrous worship—what hideous rites! Where, *where* did you find these things? I must know! And this idol—which you say is believed to invoke the spirit of the living Cthulhu himself! Who holds such beliefs? I know of course that Wendy-Smith—"

"*Hah!*" Hamilton's rasping voice cut in. "You can keep all your Wendy-Smiths and Gordon Walmsleys. They only scraped the surface. I've gone inside—and *outside!* Explorers, dreamers, mystics—mere dabblers. Why, they'd *die*, all of them, if they saw what I've seen, if they went where I've been. And none of them have ever dreamed what I *know!*"

"But why keep it hidden? Why don't you open this place up, show the world what you've got here, what you've achieved? Publish, man, publish! Why, together—"

"Together?" Hamilton's voice was darker, trembling as he suddenly snuffed the candle out. "Together? Proof that the Cult of Cthulhu *did* exist? Show it to the world? Publish?" His chuckle was obscene in the dark, and Anderson heard the visitor's sharp intake of breath. "The world's not ready, Gamber, and the stars are not right! What you would like to do, like many before you, is alert the world to *Their* one-time presence, the days of *Their* sovereignty which might in turn lead to the discovery that *They are here even now!* Indeed Wendy-Smith was right, too right, and where is Wendy-Smith now? No, no—*They* aren't interested in mere dabblers, except that such are dangerous to *Them* and must be removed! *Ia; R'lyeh!* You are no true dreamer, Gamber, no believer. You're not worthy of membership in the Great Priesthood. You're... dangerous! Proof? I'll give you proof. Listen, and *watch*—"

Hearing his brother's injunction, the secret listener would have paid dearly to see what next occurred. A short while earlier, just before Hamilton had snuffed out the candle, Anderson had managed to find a hole in the canvas large enough to facilitate a fair view of the partitioned area. He had seen a semicircle of carved stone tablets, with the octopoid idol presiding atop or seated upon a throne-like pedestal. Now, in the dark, his view-hole was useless. He could still listen, however, and now Hamilton's voice came strange and vibrant, though still controlled in volume—in a chant or invocation of terrible cadence and rhythmic disorder. These were not words the younger Tharpe uttered but unintelligible *sounds,* a morbidly insane agglutination of verbal improbabilities which ought never to have issued from a human throat at all! And as the invocation ceased, to an incredulous gasping from the doomed explorer, Anderson had to draw back from his hole lest he become visible in the glow of a green radiance springing up abruptly in the centre of Hamilton's encircling relics.

The green glow grew brighter, filling the hidden museum and spilling emerald beams from several small holes in the canvas. This was no normal light, for the beams were quite alien to anything Anderson had ever seen before; the very light seemed to writhe and contort in a slow and loathsomely languid dance. Now Anderson found himself again a witness, for the shadows of Hamilton and his intended victim were thrown blackly against the wall of canvas. There was no requirement now to "spy" properly upon the pair; his view of the eerie drama could not have been clearer. The centre of the radiance seemed to expand and shrink alternatively, pulsing like an alien heart of light. Hamilton stood to one side, his arms flung wide in terrible triumph; Stainton Gamber cowered, his hands up before his face as if to shield it from some unbearable heat—or as if to ward off the unknown and inexplicable!

Anderson's shadow-view of the terrified explorer was profile, and he was suddenly astonished to note that while the man appeared to be screaming horribly he could hear nothing of the screams! It was as if Anderson had been stricken deaf. Hamilton, too, was now plainly vociferous; his throat moved in crazed cachinnations and his thrown-back head and heaving shoulders plainly announced unholy glee—but all in stark silence! Anderson knew now that the mad green light had somehow worked against normal order, annulling all sound utterly and thereby hiding in its emerald pulsings the final act in this monstrous shadow-play. As the core pulsated even faster and brighter, Hamilton moved quickly after the silently shrieking explorer, catching him by the collar of his jacket and swinging him sprawling into the core itself!

Instantly the core shrank, sucking in upon itself and dwindling in a moment to a ball of intense brightness. But where was the explorer? Horrified, Anderson saw that now *only one shadow remained faintly outlined upon the canvas—that of his brother."*

Quickly, weirdly, paling as they went, the beams of green light withdrew. Sound instantly returned, and Anderson heard his own harsh breathing. He stilled the sound, moving back to his spy-hole to see what was happening. A faint green glow with a single bright speck of a core remained within the semi-circle; and now Hamilton bowed to this dimming light and his voice came again, low and tremulous with emotion:

Iä, naflhgn Cthulhu R'lyeh mglw'nafh,
Eha'ungl wglw hflghglui ngah'glw,
Engl Eha gh'eehf gnhugl,
Nhflgng uh'eha wgah'nagl hfglufh—
U'ng Eha'ghglui Aeeh ehn'hflgh…
That is not dead which can eternal lie,
And with strange aeons even death may die.

No sooner had Hamilton ceased these utterly alien mouthings and the paradoxical couplet that completed them, and while yet the green glow continued to dim and fade, than he spoke again, this time all in recognizable English. Such was his murmured modulation and deliberate spacing of the spoken sequences that his hidden brother immediately recognized the following as a translation of what had gone before:

Oh, Great Cthulhu, dreaming in R'lyeh,
Thy priest offers up this sacrifice,
That thy coming be soon
And that of thy kindred dreamers.
I am thy priest and adore thee…

It was only then that the full horror of what he had seen—the cold-blooded, premeditated murder of a man by either some monstrous occult device or a foreign science beyond his knowledge—finally went home to Anderson Tharpe, and barely managing to stifle the hysterical babble he felt welling in his throat, he took an involuntary step backwards… to collide loudly with a cage of great bats.

Three things happened then in rapid succession before Anderson could gather his wits to flee. All trace of the green glow vanished in an instant, throwing the tent once more into complete darkness; then in contrast, confusing the elder brother, the bright interior lights blinked on; finally, as he sought to recover from his confusion, Hamilton appeared through the partition's canvas door, his eyes blazing in a face contorted in fury!

"You!" Hamilton spat, striding to Anderson's side and catching him fiercely by the collar of his dressing gown. "How much have you seen?"

Anderson twisted free and backed away. "I… I saw it all, but I had guessed as much some time ago. Murder—and you my brother!"

"Save your sanctimony," Hamilton sneered. "If you've known so much for so long, then you're as much a murderer as I am! And anyway"—his eyes seemed visibly to glaze and take on a faraway look—"it wasn't murder, not as you understand it."

"Of course not." Now it was Anderson's turn to sneer. "It was a—a 'sacrifice'—to this so-called "god" of yours, Great Cthulhu! And were the others all sacrifices, too?"

"All of them," Hamilton answered with a nod, automatically, as in a trance.

"Oh? And where's the money?"

"Money?" The faraway look went out of the younger Tharpe's eyes immediately. "What money?"

Anderson saw that this was no bluff; his brother's motive had not been personal gain, at least not in a monetary sense. Which in turn meant—

Had those rumours and unfriendly whispers heard about the stalls and sideshows—those hints of a looming madness in his brother—had they been more than mere guesswork, then? Surely he would have known. As if in answer to his unspoken question, Hamilton spoke again—and listening to him Anderson believed he had his answer:

"You're the same as all the others, Anderson—you can't see beyond the length of your greedy nose. Money? Pah! You think that *They* are interested in wealth? *They* are not; neither am I. *They* have a wealth of aeons behind *Them; the* future is *Theirs…*." Again his eyes seemed to glaze over.

"Them? Who do you mean?" Anderson asked, frowning and backing farther away.

"Cthulhu and the others. Cthulhu and the Deep Ones, and *Their* brothers and kin forever dreaming in the vast vaults beneath. *Iä, R'lyeh, Cthulhu fhtagn!*"

"You're quite—mad!"

"You think so?" Hamilton quickly followed after him, pushing his face uncomfortably close. "I'm mad, am I? Well, perhaps, but I'll tell you something: when you and the others like you are reduced to mere cattle, before the Earth is cleared off of life as you know it, a trusted handful of priests will guard the herds for Them—and I shall be a priest among priests, appointed to the service of Great Cthulhu Himself!" His eyes burned feverishly.

Now Anderson was certain of his brother's madness, but even so he could see a way to profit from it. "Hamilton," he said after a moment's thought, "worship whatever gods you like and aspire to whatever priesthood—but don't you see we have to live? There could be good money in this for both of us. If only—"

"No!" Hamilton hissed. "To worship Cthulhu is enough. Indeed, it is *all*. That, in there"—he jerked his head, indicating the enclosed area behind him—"is His temple. To offer up sacrifices while yet chinking of oneself would be blasphemous, and when He comes I shall not be found wanting!" His eyes went wide and he trembled.

"You don't know Him, Anderson. He is awful, awesome, a monster, a god! He is sunken now, drowned and dead in deep R'lyeh, but His death is a sleeping death and He will awaken. When the scars are right we chosen ones will answer the Call of Cthulhu, and R'lyeh will rise up again to astound a reeling universe. Why, even the Gorgons were His priestesses in the old world! And you talk to me of money." Again he sneered, but now his madness had a firm grip on him and the sneer soon turned to a crafty smile.

"And you're helpless to do anything, Anderson, for if you breathe a word I'll swear you were in on it—that you helped me from the start! And as for bodies, why, there are none. They are gone to dreaming Cthulhu, through the light He sends me when I cry out to Him in my darkness. So you see, nothing could ever be proved…"

"Perhaps not, but I don't think it would take much to have you, well, *put away!*" Anderson quietly answered. The barb went straight home. A look of terror crossed Hamilton's face and, plainly aware of his own mental infirmity, he visibly paled.

"Put me away? But you wouldn't. If you did, I wouldn't be able to worship, to sacrifice, and—"

"But there's no need to worry about it," Anderson cut him off. "I won't have you put away. Just see things my way, show me how you dissolve them in that green light of yours—I mean, in, er, dreaming Cthulhu's light—and then we'll carry on as before, except that there"ll be money—"

"No, Anderson," the other refused almost gently, "it can't work like that. You could never believe—not even if I showed you proof of my priesthood, which hides beneath this false head of hair that I'm obliged to wear, the very Mark of Cthulhu—and I can't worship as you suggest. I'm sorry." There was an insane sadness in his face as he drew out a long knife from its sheath inside his jacket. "I use this when they're stronger than me," he explained, "and when they're liable to fight. Cthulhu doesn't care for it much because he likes them alive initially and whole, but—" His knife hand flashed up and down.

Only Anderson's speed saved him, for he turned quickly to one side as the blade flashed down toward his breast. Then their wrists were locked and they staggered to and fro, Hamilton frothing at the mouth and trying to bite, while Anderson grimly struggled for dear life. The madman seemed to have the strength of three normal men, and soon they fell to the ground, a thrashing heap that rolled blindly in through the flap of the canvas door to Hamilton's "temple."

There it was that finally the younger brother's toupee came away from his head in the silent struggle—and in a burst of strength engendered of sheer loathing Anderson managed to turn the knife inward and drive it to the madman's heart. He was quick then to be on his feet and away from the thing that now lay twitching out its life upon the sawdust floor—the thing that had been his brother—which now, where the top of Hamilton's head had been, *wore a cap of writhing white worms of finger thickness, like some monstrous sea-anemone sucking vampirishly at the still-living brain!*

Later, when morning came, even had there been someone in whom he might safely confide, Anderson Tharpe could never have related a detailed or coherent account of the preceding hours of darkness. He recalled only the general thread of what had passed; frantic snatches of the fearful activity that followed upon the hideous death of his brother. But first there had been that half hour or so of waiting—of knowing that at any moment, attracted perhaps by strange lights or sounds, someone might just enter the tent and find him with Hamilton's body—but he had been *obliged* to wait for he could not bring himself to touch the corpse. Not while the stubby white tentacles of its head continued to writhe! Hamilton died almost immediately, but his monstrous crown had taken much longer…

Then, when the loathsome—parasite?—had shuddered into lifeless rigidity, he had gathered together his shattered nerves to dig a deep grave in the soft earth beneath the sawdust. That had been a gruesome task with the lights turned down and Cthulhu's stone effigy casting a tentacled shadow over the fearful digger. Anderson later remembered how soft the ground had been— and wet when it ought to have been dry in the weatherproof tent—and he recalled a powerful smell of deep ocean, of aeons-old slime and rotting seaweeds; an odour he had known on occasion before, and always after one of Hamilton's "sacrifices." The connection had not impressed itself upon his mind as anything more than mere coincidence before, but now he knew that the smell came with the green light, as did that strange state of soundlessness.

In order to clear what remained of the fetor quickly—having tamped down the earth, generally "tidied up" and removed all traces of his digging— he opened and tied back the canvas doors of the tent to allow the night air a healthy circulation. But even then, having done everything possible to hide the night's horror, he was unable to relax properly as daylight had crept up and the folk of the funfair began to wake and move about.

When finally Hodgson's Funfair had opened at noon, Anderson had something of a shaky grip on himself, but even so he had found himself drenched in cold sweat at the end of each oratorical session with the crowds at the freak-house. His only moments of relaxation came between shows. The worst time had been when a leather-jacketed teenager peered through the canvas inner door to the partitioned section of the tent; and Anderson had nearly knocked the youth down in his anxiety to steer him away from the place, though no trace remained of what had transpired there.

On reflection, it amazed Anderson that his fight with his brother had not attracted someone's attention, and yet it had not. Even the fairground's usually vociferous watchdogs had remained silent. And yet those same dogs, since Hamilton's return from his travels abroad, had seemed even more nervous, more given to snapping and snarling than ever before. Anderson could only tell himself that the weird "silent state" which had accompanied the green light must have spread out over the entire fairground to dissipate slowly, thus disarming the dogs. Or perhaps they had sensed something else, remaining silent out of fear...? Indeed, it appeared his second guess was correct, for he discovered later that many of the dogs had whimpered the whole night away huddled beneath the caravans of their masters...

Two days later the funfair packed up and moved on, leaving Hamilton Tharpe's body safely buried in an otherwise empty field. At last the worst of Anderson's apprehensions left him and his nerves began to settle down. To be sure his jumpiness had been marked by the folk of the funfair, who had all correctly (though for the wrong reasons) diagnosed it as a symptom of anxiety about his crazy, bad-lot brother. So it was that as soon as Hamilton's absence was remarked upon, Anderson was able simply to shrug his shoulders and answer: "Who knows? Tibet, Egypt, Australia—he's just gone off again—said nothing to me about it—could be anywhere!" And while such inquiries were always politely compassionate, he knew that in fact the inquirers were greatly relieved that his brother had "just gone off again."

Another six weeks went by, with regular halts at various villages and small towns, and during that time Anderson managed to will himself to forget all about his brother's death and his own involvement—all, that is, except the nature of that parasitic horror which had made itself manifest upon Hamilton's head. That was something he would never forget, the way that awful anemone had wriggled and writhed long after its host was dead. Hamilton had called the thing a symbol of his priesthood—in his own words: "The Mark of Cthulhu"—but in truth it could only have been some loathsomely malignant and rare form of cancer, or perhaps a kind of worm or fluke like the tapeworm. Anderson always shuddered when he recalled it, for it had looked horribly *sentient* there atop Hamilton's head; and when one thought about the *depth* at which it might have been rooted...

No, the insidious gropings of that horror within Hamilton's brain simply did not bear thinking about, for that had obviously been the source of his insanity. Anderson in no way considered himself weak to shudder when thoughts as terrible as these came to threaten his now calm and controlled state of mind, and when the bad dreams started he at once lay the blame at the feet of the same horror.

At first the nightmares were vague shadowy things, with misty vistas of rolling plains and yawning, empty coastlines. There were distant islands with strange pinnacles and oddly angled towers, but so far away that the unknown creatures moving about in those island cities were mere insects to Anderson's dreaming eyes. And for this he was glad. Their shapes seemed in a constant state of flux and were not pleasant. They were primal shapes, from which the dreamer deduced that he was in a primal land of aeons lost to mankind. He always woke from such visions uneasy in mind and deflated in spirit.

But with the passing of the months into summer the dreams changed, becoming visually sharper, clearer in their insinuations, and actually frightening as opposed to merely disturbing. Their scenes were set (Anderson somehow knew) deep in the dimly lighted bowels of one of the island cities, in a room or vault of fantastic proportions and awe-inspiring angles. Always he kneeled before a vast octopoid idol... except that on occasion it was *not* an idol but a living, hideously intelligent Being!

These dreams were ever the worst, when a strange voice spoke to him in words that he was quite unable to understand. He would tremble before the towering horror on its throne-like pedestal—a thing one hundred times greater in size than the stone morbidity in the freak-house—and, aware that he only dreamed, he would know that it, too, was asleep and dreaming. But its tentacles would twine and twist and its claws would scrabble at the front of the throne, and then the voice would come...

Waking from nightmares such as these he would know that they were engendered of hellish memory—of the night of the green glow, the deep-ocean smell, and the writhing thing in his brother's head—for he would always recall in his first waking moments that the awful alien voice had used sounds similar to those Hamilton had mouthed before the green light came and after it had taken the florid explorer away. The dreams were particularly bad and growing worse as the year drew to a close, and on a number of occasions the dreamer had been sure that slumbering Cthulhu was about to stir and wake up!

And then, himself waking up, all the horror would come back to Anderson, to be viewed once more in his mind's eye in vivid clarity; and knowing as he did that his brother too had been plagued by just such dreams prior to his second long absence from the fairground, Anderson Tharpe was a troubled man indeed. Yes, they *had* been the same sort of nightmares, those dreams of Hamilton's; hadn't he admitted that "Cthulhu comes to me in dreams?" And had the dreams themselves not heralded the greater horrors?

And yet, in less gloomy mood, Anderson found himself more and more often dwelling upon Hamilton's weird murder weapon, the pulsating green light. He was by no means an ignorant man, and he had read something of the recent progress in laser technology. Soon he had convinced himself that his brother had used an unknown form of foreign science to offer up his mad "sacrifices to Cthulhu." If only he could discover how Hamilton had done it…

But surely science such as that would require complex machinery? It was while pondering this very problem that Anderson hit upon what he believed must be the answer: whatever tools or engines Hamilton had used, they must be hidden in the octopoid idol, or perhaps built into those ugly stone tablets which had formed a semicircle about the idol. And perhaps, like the electric-eye beams which operated the moving floors and blasts of cool air in the fairground's Noah's Ark, Hamilton's chanted "summons" had been nothing more than a resonant trigger to set the hidden lasers or whatever to working. The smell of deep ocean and residual dampness must be the natural aftermath of such processes, in the same way that carbon monoxide and dead oil are the waste from petrol engines and the smell of ozone is attendant to electrical discharges.

The tablets, the idol too, still stood where they had stood in the time before the horror—the only change was that now the canvas partition was down and Hamilton's ancient artifacts were on display with the other paraphernalia of the freak-house—but just suppose Anderson were to arrange them *exactly* as they had been before, and suppose further that he could discover how to use that chanted formula. What then? Would he be able to summon the green light? If so, would he be able to use it as he had tried to convince Hamilton it should be used? Perhaps the answer lay in his dead brother's books…

Certainly that collection of ancient tomes, now slowly disintegrating in a cupboard in the caravan, were full of hints of just such things. It was out of curiosity at first that Anderson began to read those books, or at least what he *could* read of them! Many were not in English but in Latin or archaic German, and at least one other was in ciphers the like of which Anderson had only ever seen on the stone tablets in the freak-house.

There were among the volumes such tides as Peery's *Notes on the* Cthaat Aquadingen, and a well thumbed copy of the same author's *Notes on the* Necronomicon; while yet another book, handwritten in a shaky script, purported to be the *Necronomicon* itself, or a translation thereof, but Anderson could not read it for its characters were formed of an unbelievably antiquated German.

Then there was a large envelope full of yellowed loose leaves, and Hamilton had written on the envelope that this was "Ibn Shoddathua's Translation of the Mum-Nath Papyri." Among the more complete and recognizable works were such titles as *The Golden Bough* and Miss Margaret Murray's *The Witch-Cult in Western Europe,* but by comparison these were light reading.

During December and to the end of January, all of Anderson's free time was taken up in studying these works, until finally he became in a limited way something of an authority on the dread Cthulhu Cycle of Myth. He learned of the Elder Gods, benign forces or deities that existed "in peace and glory" near Betelgeuse in the constellation Orion; and of the powers of evil, the Great Old Ones! He read of Azathoth, bubbling and blaspheming at the center of infinity—of Yog-Sothoth, the "all-in-one and one-in-all", a god-creature coexistent in all time and conterminous with all space—of Nyarlathotep, the messenger of the Great Old Ones—of Hastur the Unspeakable, hell-thing and "Lord of the Interstellar Spaces"—of fertile Shub-Niggurath, "the black goat of the woods with a thousand young"—and, finally, of Great Cthulhu himself, an inconceivable evil that seeped down from the stars like cosmic pus when Earth was young and inchoate.

There were, too, lesser gods and beings more or less obscure or distant from the central theme of the Mythos. Among these Anderson read of Dagon and the Deep Ones; of Yibb-Tstll and the Gaunts of Night; of the Tcho-Tcho people and the Mi-Go; of Yig, Chaugnar Faugn, Nyogtha, and Tsathoggua; of Atlach-Nacha, Lloigor, Zhar, and Ithaqua; of burrowing Shudde-M'ell, flaming Cthugha, and the loathsome Hounds of Tindalos.

He learned how—for practicing abhorrent rites—the Great Old Ones were banished to prisoning environs where, ever ready to take possession of the Earth again, they live on eternally. Cthulhu, of course, having featured prominently in his brother's madness—now supposedly lying locked in sunken R'lyeh beneath the waves, waiting for the stars to "come right" and for his minions, human and otherwise, to perform those rites which would once more return him as ruler of his former surface dominions—held the greatest interest for Anderson.

And the more he read, the more he became aware of the fantastic *depth* of his subject—but even so he could hardly bring himself to admit that there was anything of more than passing interest in such "mumbo-jumbo." Nevertheless, on the night of the second of February, 1962, he received what should have been a warning: a nightmare of such potency that it did in fact trouble him for weeks afterwards, and particularly when he saw the connection in the *date* of this visitation. It had been Candlemas, of course, which would have had immediate and special meaning to anyone with even the remotest schooling in the occult. Candlemas, and Anderson Tharpe had dreamed of basaltic submarine towers of titanic proportions and nightmare angles; and within those basalt walls and sepulchers, he had known that loathly Lord Cthulhu dreamed his own dreams of damnable dominion...

This had not been all. He had drifted in his dreams *through* those walls to visit once more the inner chambers and kneel before the sleeping god. But it had been an unquiet sleep the Old One slept, in which his demon claws scrabbled fitfully and his folded wings twitched and jerked as if fighting to spread and lift him up through the pressured deeps to the unsuspecting world above! Then, as before, the voice had come to Anderson Tharpe—but this time it had spoken in English!

"Do you seek," the voice had asked in awesome tones, *"to worship Cthulhu? Do you presume to His priesthood? I can see that YOU DO NOT, and yet you meddle and seek to discover His secrets? Be warned: it is a great sin against Cthulhu to destroy one of His chosen priests, and yet I see that you have done so. It is a sin, too, to scorn Him; but you have done this also. And it is a GREAT sin in His eyes to seek to use His secrets in any way other than in His service—AND THIS, TOO, YOU WOULD DO! Be warned, and live. Live and pray to your weak god that you are destroyed, in the first shock of the Great Rising. It were not well for you that you live to reap Cthulhu's wrath!"*

The voice had finally receded, but its sepulchral mind-echoes had barely faded away when it seemed to the paralyzed dreamer that the face tentacles of slumbering Cthulhu reached out, groping malignantly in his direction where he knelt in slime at the base of the massive throne!

At that a distant howling sprang up, growing rapidly louder and closer; and as the face tentacles of the sleeping god had been about to touch him, so Tharpe came screaming awake in his sweat-drenched bed to discover that the fairground was in an uproar. All the watchdogs, big and small, chained and roaming free alike, were howling in unison in the middle of that cold night. They seemed to howl at the blindly impassive stars, and their cries were faintly answered from a thousand similarly agitated canine throats in the nearby town!

The next morning speculation was rife among the showmen as to what had caused the trouble with the dogs, and eventually, on the evidence of certain scraps of fur, they put it down to a stray cat that must have got itself trapped under one of the caravans to be pulled to pieces by a Great Dane. Nevertheless, Anderson wondered at the keen senses and interpretation of the dogs in the local town that they had so readily taken up the unnatural baying and howling...

During the next fortnight or so Anderson's slumbers were mercifully free of nightmares, so that he was early prompted to continue his researches into the Cthulhu Cycle of Myth. This further probing was born partly of curiosity and partly (as Anderson saw it) of necessity; he yet hoped to be able to employ gainfully his brother's mysterious green light, and his determination was bolstered by the fact that takings of late had been dismal. So he once more closed off the previously partitioned area of the tent, and his spare-time studies now became equally divided between Hamilton's books of occult lore and a patient examination of the hideous idol and carved tablets. He discovered no evidence of hidden mechanical devices in the queer relics, but nevertheless it was not long before he found his first real clue towards implementing his ambition.

It was as simple as this: he had earlier noted upon the carved tops of the stone tablets a series of curiously intermingled cuneiform and dot-group hieroglyphs, two distinct sets to each stone. This could not be considered odd in itself, but finally Anderson had recognized the pattern of these characters and knew that they were duplicated in the handwritten *Necronomicon;* and more, there were translations of that work into at least two other languages, one of them being the antiquated German in which the bulk of the book was written.

Anderson's knowledge of German, even in its modern form, was less than rudimentary, and thus he enlisted the aid of old Hans Moller from the hoopla stall. The old German's eyesight was no longer reliable, however, and his task was made no easier by the outmoded form in which the work was written; but at last, and not without Anderson's insistent urging, Moller was able to translate one of the sequences first into more modern German (in which it read: *Gestorben ist nicht, was fur ewig ruht, und mit unbekannten Aonen mag sogar der Tod noch sterben),* and then into the following rather poor English: "It is not dead that lies still forever; Death itself dies with the passing of strange years."

When he heard the old German speak these words in his heavy accent, Anderson had to stifle the gasp of recognition which welled within him. This was nothing less than a variation of that paradoxical couplet with which his brother had once terminated his fiendish "sacrifice to Cthulhu!"

As for the other set of symbols from the tablets, frustration was soon to follow. Certainly the figures were duplicated in the centuried book, appearing in what Anderson at first took to be a code of some sort, but they had not been reproduced in German. Moller—while having not the slightest inkling of Anderson's purpose with this smelly, evil old book—finally suggested to him that perhaps the letters were not in code at all, that they might simply be the symbols of an obscure foreign language. Anderson had to agree that Moller could well be right; in the yellowed left-hand margin of the relevant page, directly opposite the frustrating cryptogram, his brother had long ago written: "Yes, but what of the *pronunciation?*"

Hamilton had done more than this: he had obligingly dated his patently self-addressed query, and the surviving Tharpe brother saw that the jotting had been made prior to the fatal second period of travel in foreign lands. Who could say what Hamilton might or might not have discovered upon that journey? Without a doubt he had been in strange places. And he had seen and done strange things to bring back with him that hellish cancer growth sprouting in his brain.

Finally Anderson decided that this jumbled gathering of harsh and unpronounceable letters—be it a scientific process or, more fancifully, a magical evocation—must indeed be the formula with which a clever man might call forth the green light in his dead brother's "Temple of Cthulhu." He thanked old Hans and sent him away, then sat in his caravan poring over the ancient book, puzzling and frowning long into the evening; until, as darkness fell, his eyes lit with dawning inspiration...

And so over the period of the next few days the freak-house suffered its transition into the Tomb of the Great Old Ones. During the same week Anderson visited a printer in the local town and had new admission tickets printed. These tickets, as well as bearing the new name of the show and revised price of admission, now carried upon the reverse the following cryptic instruction:

Any adult person desiring to speak with the proprietor of the *Tomb of the Great Old Ones* on matters of genuine occult phenomena or similar manifestations, or on subjects relating to the Great Old Ones, R'lyeh, or the Cthulhu Cycle of Myth, is welcome to request a private meeting.

Anderson Tharpe: Prop.

The other members of the fairground fraternity were not aware of this offer of Anderson's—nor of his authority, real or assumed, in such subjects to be able to make such an offer—until after the funfair moved into its next location, and by that time they too had discovered his advance advertising in the local press. Of course, Bella Hodgson had always looked after advance publicity in the past, but she could hardly be offended by Anderson's personal efforts toward this end. Any good publicity he devised and paid for himself could only go towards attracting better crowds to the benefit of the funfair in general.

And within a very short time Anderson's plan started to bear fruit, when at last his desire for a higher percentage of rather more erudite persons among his show's clientele began to be realized. His sole purpose, of course, had been to attract just such persons in the hope that perhaps one of them might provide the baffling pronunciation he required, an *acoustical* translation of the key to call up the terrible green glow.

Such authorities must surely exist; his own brother had become one in a comparatively short time, and others had spent whole lifetimes in the concentrated study of these secrets of elder lore. Surely, sooner or later, he would find a man to provide the answer, and then the secrets of the perfect murder weapon would be his. When this happened, then Anderson would test his weapon on the poor unfortunate who handed him the key, and in this way he would be sure that the secret was his alone. From then on… oh, there were many possibilities…

Through early and mid-April Anderson received a number of inquisitive callers at his caravan: some of them cranks, but at least a handful of genuinely interested and knowledgeable types. Always he pumped them for what they knew of the elder mysteries in connection with the Cthulhu Cycle, especially their knowledge in ancient tongues and obscure languages, and twice over he was frustrated just when he thought himself on the right track. On one occasion, after seeing the tablets and idol, an impressed visitor presented him with a copy of Walmsley's *Notes on Deciphering Codes, Cryptograms, and Ancient Inscriptions;* but to no avail, the work itself was too deep for him.

Then, towards the end of April, in response to Anderson's continuous probing, a visitor to his establishment grudgingly gave him the address of a so-called "occult investigator", one Titus Crow, who just might be interested in his problem. Before he left the fairground this same gentleman, the weird artist Chandler Davies, strongly advised Tharpe that the whole thing were best forgotten, that no good could ever come of dabbling in such matters—be it serious study or merely idle curiosity—and with that warning he had taken his leave.

Ignoring the artist's positive dread of his line of research, that same afternoon Anderson wrote to Titus Crow at his London address, enclosing with his letter a copy of the symbols and a request for information concerning them; possibly a translation or, even better, a workable pronunciation. Impatiently then, he watched the post for an answer, and early in May was disappointed to receive a brief note from Crow advising him, as had Davies, to give up his interest in these matters and let such dangerous subjects alone. There was no explanation, no invitation regarding further correspondence; Crow had not even bothered to return the cryptic paragraph so painstakingly copied from the *Necronomicon*.

That night, as if to substantiate the double warning, Anderson once more dreamed of sunken R'lyeh, and again he kneeled before slumbering Cthulhu's throne to hear the alien voice echoing awesomely in his mind. The horror on the throne seemed more mobile in its sleep than ever before, and the voice in the dream was more insistent, more menacing:

"You have been warned, AND YET YOU MEDDLE! While the Great Rising draws ever closer and Cthulhu's shadow looms, still you choose to search out His secrets for your own use! This night there will be a sign; ignore it at your peril, lest Cthulhu bestir Himself up to visit you personally in dreams, as He has aforetime visited others!"

The following morning Anderson rose haggard and pale to learn of yet more trouble with the fairground's dogs, duplicating in detail that Candlemas frenzy of three months earlier. The coincidence was such as to cause him more than a moment's concern, and especially after reading the morning's newspapers.

What was it that the voice in his dream had said of "a sign?"—a warning which he should only ignore at his peril? Well, there had been a sign, many of them, for the night had been filled with a veritable plethora of weird and inexplicable occurrences—strange stirrings among the more dangerous inmates of lunatic asylums all over the country, macabre suicides by previously normal people—a magma of madness climaxed, so far as Anderson Tharpe was concerned, by second-page headlines in two of the national newspapers to the effect that Chandler Davies had been "put away" in Woodholme Sanatorium. The columns went on to tell how Davies had painted a monstrous *G'harne Landscape,* which his outraged and terrified mistress had at once set fire to, thus bringing about in him an insane rage from which he had not recovered. More: a few days later came the news via the same papers that Davies was dead!

If Anderson Tharpe had been in any way a sensitive person, and his evil ambition less of an obsession—had his *perceptions* not been dulled by a lifetime of living close to the anomalies of the erstwhile freak-house—then perhaps he might have recognized the presence of a horror such as few men have ever known. Unlike his brother, however, Anderson was coarse-grained and not especially imaginative. All the portents and evidences, the hints and symptoms, and accumulating warnings were cast aside within a few short days of his nightmare and its accompanying manifestations, when yet again he turned to his studies in the hope that soon the secret of the green light would be his.

From then on the months passed slowly, while the crowds at the Tomb of the Great Old Ones became smaller still despite all Anderson's efforts to the contrary. His frustration grew in direct proportion to his dwindling assets, and while his continued advance advertising and the invitation on the reverse of his admission tickets still drew the occasional crank occultist or curious devotee of the macabre to his caravan, not one of them was able to further his knowledge of the Cthulhu Cycle or satisfy his growing obsession with regard to that enigmatic and cryptical "key" from the handwritten *Necronomicon.*

Twice as the seasons waxed and waned he approached old Hans about further translations from the ancient book, even offering to pay for the old German's services in this respect, but Hans simply was not interested. He was too old to become a *Dolmetscher,* he said, and his eyes were giving him trouble; he already had enough money for his simple needs, and anyway, he did not like the *look* of the book. What the old man did not say was that he had seen things in those yellowed pages, on that one occasion when already he had looked into the rotting volume, which simply did not bear translation! And so again Anderson's plans met with frustration.

In mid-October the now thoroughly disgruntled and morose proprietor of the Tomb of the Great Old Ones looked to a different approach. Patently, no matter how hard he personally studied Hamilton's books, he was not himself qualified to puzzle out and piece together the required information. There were those, however, who had spent a lifetime in such studies, and if he could not attract such as these to the fairground—why, then he must simply send the problem to them. True, he had tried this before, with Titus Crow; but now, as opposed to cultists, occultists, and the like, he would approach only recognized authorities. He spent the following day or two tracking down the address of Professor Gordon Walmsley of Goole, a world-renowned expert in the science of ciphers, whose book, *Notes on Deciphering Codes, Cryptograms, and Ancient Inscriptions,* had now been in his possession for almost seven months. That book was still far too deep and complicated for Anderson's fathoming, but the author of such a work should certainly find little difficulty with the piece from the *Necronomicon.*

He quickly composed a letter to the professor, and as October grew into its third week he posted it off. He was not to know it, but at that time Walmsley was engaged in the services of the Buenos Aires Museum of Antiquities, busily translating the hieroglyphs on certain freshly discovered ruins in the mountains of the Aconcaguan Range near San Juan. Anderson's letter did eventually reach him, posted on from Walmsley's Yorkshire address, but the professor was so interested in his own work that he gave it only a cursory glance. Later he found that he had misplaced it, and thus, fortunately, the scrap of paper with its deadly invocation passed into obscurity and became lost forever.

Anderson meanwhile impatiently waited for a reply, and along with the folk of the fairground prepared for the Halloween opening at Bathley, a town on the northeast border. It was then, on the night of the twenty-seventh of the month, that he received his third and final warning. The day had been chill and damp, with a bitter wind blowing off the North Sea, bringing a dankly salt taste and smell that conjured up horrible memories for the surviving Tharpe brother.

On the morning of the twenty-eighth, rising up gratefully from a sweat-soaked bed and a nightmare the like of which he had never known before and fervently prayed never to know again, Anderson Tharpe blamed the horrors of the night on yesterday's sea wind with its salty smells of ocean; but even explained away like this the dream had been a monstrous thing.

Again he had visited sunken R'lyeh—but this time there had been a vivid *reality* to the nightmare lacking in previous dreams. He had known the terrible, bone-crushing pressures of that drowned realm, had felt the frozen chill of its black waters. He had tried to scream as the pressure forced his eyes from their sockets, and then the sea had rushed into his mouth, tearing his throat and lungs and stomach as it filled him in one smashing column as solid as steel. And though the horror had lasted only a second, still he had known that there in the ponderous depths his *disintegration* had taken place before the throne of the Lord of R'lyeh, the Great Old One who seeped down from the stars at the dawn of time. He had been a sacrifice to Cthulhu...

ᘒ ᘓ

That had been four days ago, but still Tharpe shuddered when he thought of it. He put it out of his mind now as he ushered the crowd out of the tent and turned to face the sole remaining member of that departing audience. Tharpe's oratory had been automatic; during its delivery he had allowed his mind to run free in its exploration of all that had passed since his brother's hideous death, but now he came back to earth. Hiram Henley stared back at him in what he took to be scornful disappointment. The ex-professor spoke:

"'The Tomb of the Great Old Ones', indeed! Sir, you're a charlatan!" he said. "I could find more fearsome things in *Grimm's Fairy Tales,* more items of genuine antiquarian interest in my aunt's attic. I had hoped your—show—might prove interesting. It seems I was mistaken." His eyes glinted sarcastically behind his tiny spectacles.

For a moment Tharpe's heart beat a little faster, then he steadied himself. Perhaps this time...? Certainly the little man was worth a try. "You do me an injustice, sir—you wound me!" He waxed theatrical, an ability with which he was fluent through his years of showmanship. "Do you really believe that I would openly *display* the archaeological treasures for which this establishment was named?—I should put them out for the common herd to ogle, when not one in ten thousand could even recognize them, let alone appreciate them? Wait!"

He ducked through the canvas doorflap into the enclosed area containing Hamilton's relics, returning a few seconds later with a bronze miniature the size of his hand and wrist. The thing looked vaguely like an elongated, eyeless squid. It also looked—despite the absence of anything even remotely mundane in its appearance—utterly evil! Anderson handed the object reverently to the ex-professor, saying: "What do you make of that?" Having chosen the thing at random from the anomalies in his dead brother's collection, he hoped it really was of "genuine antiquarian interest."

His choice had been a wise one. Henley peered at the miniature, and slowly his expression changed. He examined the thing minutely, then said, "It is the burrower beneath, Shudde-M'ell, or one of his brood. A very good likeness, and ancient beyond words. Made of bronze, yet quite obviously it predates the Bronze Age!" His voice was suddenly soft. "Where did you get it?"

"You *are* interested, then?" Tharpe smiled, incapable of either admitting or denying the statements of the other.

"Of course I'm interested." Henley eagerly nodded, a bit too eagerly, Tharpe thought. "I... I did indeed do you a great injustice. This thing is *very* interesting! Do you have... more?"

"All in good time." Tharpe held up his hands, holding himself in check, waiting until the time was ripe to frame his own all-important question. "First, who are you? You understand that *my—possessions—are* not for idle scrutiny, that—"

"Yes, yes, I understand," the little man cut him off. "My name is Hiram Henley. I am—at least I was—Professor of Archaeology and Ethnology at Meldham University. I have recently given up my position there in order to carry out private research. I came here out of curiosity, I admit; a friend gave me one of your tickets with its peculiar invitation. I wasn't really expecting much, but—"

"But now you've seen something that you would never have believed possible in a place like this. Is that it?"

"Indeed it is. And you? Who are you?"

"Tharpe is my name, Anderson Tharpe, proprietor of this"—he waved his hand deprecatingly—"establishment."

"Very well, Mr. Tharpe," Henley said. "It's my own good fortune to meet a man whose intelligence in my own chosen field patently must match my own—whose possessions include items such as this." He held up the heavy bronze piece and peered at it again for a moment. "Now, will you show me—the rest?"

"A glimpse, only a glimpse," Tharpe told him, aware now that Henley was hooked. "Then perhaps we can trade?"

"I have nothing with which to trade. In what way do you mean?"

"Nothing to trade? Perhaps not," Tharpe answered, holding the canvas door open so that his visitor might step into the enclosed space beyond, "but then again... how are you on ancient tongues and languages?"

"Languages were always my—" The ex-professor started to answer, stepping into the private place. Then he paused, his eyes widening as he gazed about at the contents of the place. "Were always my—" Again he paused, reaching out his hands before him and moving forward, touching the ugly idol unbelievingly, moving quickly to the carved tablets, staring as if hypnotized at the smaller figurines and totems. Finally he turned a flushed face to Tharpe. His look was hard to define; partly awed, partly-accusing?

"I didn't steal them, I assure you," Tharpe quickly said.

"No, of course not," Henley answered, "but... you have the treasures of the aeons here!"

Now the tall showman could hold himself no longer. "Languages," he pressed. "You say you have an understanding of tongues? Can you translate from the ancient to the modern?"

"Yes, most things, providing—"

"How would you like to *own* all you see here?" Tharpe cut him off again.

Henley reached out suddenly palsied hands to take Tharpe by the forearms. "You're... joking?"

"No." Tharpe shook his head, lying convincingly. "I'm not joking. There is something of the utmost importance to my own line of—research. I need a translation of a fragment of ancient writing. Rather, I need the *original* pronunciation. If you can solve this one problem for me, all this can be yours. You can be... part of it."

"What is this fragment?" the little man cried. *"Where* is it?"

"Come with me."

"But—" Henley turned away from Tharpe, his gloved hands again reaching for those morbid items out of the aeons.

"No, no." Tharpe took his arm. "Later—you'll have all the time you need. Now there is this problem of mine. But later, tonight, we'll come back in here, and all this can be yours..."

The ex-professor voluntarily followed Tharpe out of the tent to his caravan, and there he was shown the handwritten *Necronomicon* with its cryptic "key."

"Well," Tharpe demanded, barely concealing his agitation, "can you read it as it was written? Can you *pronounce* it in its original form?"

"I'll need a little time," the balding man mused, "and privacy; but I think... I'll take a copy of this with me, and as soon as I have the answer—"

"When? How long?"

"Tonight."

"Good. I'll wait for you. It should be quiet here by then. It's Halloween and the fairground is open until late, but they'll all be that much more tired…" Tharpe suddenly realized that he was thinking out loud and quickly glanced at his visitor. The little man peered at him strangely through his tiny specs; *very* strangely, Tharpe thought.

"The people here are—superstitious," he explained. "It wouldn't be wise to advertise our interest in these ancient matters. They're ignorant and I've had trouble with them before. They don't like some of the things I've got."

"I understand," Henley answered. "I'll go now and work through the evening. With luck it won't take too long. Tonight—shall we say after midnight?—I'll be back." He quickly made a copy of the characters in the old book, then stood up. Tharpe saw him out of the caravan with an assumed, gravely thoughtful air, thanking him before watching him walk off in the direction of the exit; but then he laughed out loud and slapped his thigh, quickly seeking out one of the odd-job boys from the stratojet thrill ride.

An hour later—to the amazement of his fellow showmen, for the crowd was thickening rapidly as the afternoon went by—Anderson Tharpe closed the Tomb of the Great Old Ones and retired to his caravan. He wanted to practice himself in the operation of the tape recorder which he had paid the odd-jobber to buy for him in Bathley.

This final phase of his plan was simple; necessarily so, for of course he in no way intended to honour his bargain with Henley. He *did* intend to have the little man read out his pronunciation of the "key" and to record that pronunciation in perfect fidelity—but from then on…

If the pronunciation were imperfect, then of course the "bargain" would be unfulfilled and the ex-professor would escape with his life and nothing more; but if the invocation worked…? Why, then the professor simply could not be allowed to walk away and talk about what he had seen. No, it would be necessary for him to disappear into the green light. Hamilton would have called it a "sacrifice to Cthulhu."

And yet there had been something about the little man that disturbed Anderson; something about his peering eyes, and his eagerness to fall in with the plans of the gaunt showman. Tharpe thought of his dream of a few days past, then of those other nightmares he had known, and shuddered; and again he pondered the possibility that there had been more than met the eye in his mad brother's assertions. But what odds? Science or sorcery, it made no difference, the end result would be the same. He rubbed his hands in anticipation.

Things were at last looking up for Anderson Tharpe…

At midnight the crowd began to thin out. Watching the people move off into the chill night, Anderson was glad it had started to rain again, for their festive Halloween mood might have kept them in the fairground longer, and the bright lights would have glared and the music played late into the night. Only an hour later all was quiet, with only the sporadic patter of rain on machines and tents and painted roofs to disturb the night. The last wetly gleaming light had blinked out and the weary folk of the fairground were in their beds. That was when Anderson heard the furtive rapping at his caravan door, and he was agreeably surprised that the ever-watchful dogs had not heralded his night-visitor's arrival. Possibly it was too early for them yet to distinguish between comers and goers.

As soon as he was inside Henley saw the question written on Tharpe's face. He nodded in answer: "Yes, yes, I have it. It appears to be a summons of some sort, a cry to vast and immeasurably ancient powers. Wait, I'll read it for you—"

"No, no—not here!" Tharpe silenced him before he could commence. "I have a tape recorder in the tent."

Without a word the little man followed Tharpe through the dark and into the private enclosure containing those centuried relics which so plainly fascinated him. There Tharpe illumined the inner tent with a single dim light bulb; then, switching on his tape recorder, he told the ex-professor that he was now ready to hear the invocation.

And yet now Henley paused, turning to face Tharpe and gravely peering at him from where he stood by the horrible octopoid idol.

"Are you—sure?" the little man asked. "Are you sure you want me to do this?" His voice was dry, calm.

"Eh?" Anderson questioned nervously, terrible suspicions suddenly forming in his mind. "Of course I'm sure—and what do you mean, 'do this?' Do what?"

Henley shook his head sadly. "Your brother was foolish not to see that you would cause trouble sooner or later!"

Tharpe's eyes opened wide and his jaw fell slack. "Police!" he finally croaked. "You're from the police!"

"No such thing," the little man calmly answered. "I am what I told you I was—and something more than that—and to prove it…"

The sounds Henley uttered then formed an exact and fluent duplication of those Tharpe had heard once before, and shocked as he was that this frail outsider knew far too much about his affairs, still Tharpe thrilled as the inhuman echoes died and there formed in the semicircle of grim tablets an expanding, glowing greenness that sent out writhing beams of ghostly luminescence. Quickly the tall man gathered his wits. Policeman or none, Hiram Henley had to be done away with. This had been the plan in any case, once the little man—whoever he was—had done his work and was no longer required. And he had done his work well. The invocation was recorded; Anderson could call up the destroying green light any time he so desired. Perhaps Henley had been a former colleague of Hamilton's, and somehow he had come to learn of the younger Tharpe's demise? Or was he only guessing! Still, it made no difference now.

Henley had turned his back on Anderson, lifting up his arms to the hideous idol greenly illuminated in the light of the pulsating witchfire. But as the showman slipped his brother's knife from his pocket, so the little man turned again to face him, smiling strangely and showing no discernible fear at the sight of the knife. Then his smile faded and again he sadly shook his head. His lips formed the words, "No, no, my friend," but Anderson Tharpe heard nothing; once more, as it had done before, the green light had cancelled all sound within its radius.

Suddenly Tharpe was very much afraid, but still he knew what he must do. Despite the fact that the inner tent was far more chill even than the time of the year warranted, sweat glistened greenly on Anderson's brow as he moved forward in a threatening crouch, the knife raised and reflecting emerald shafts of evilly writhing light. He lifted the knife higher still as he closed with the motionless figure of the little man—*and then Hiram Henley moved!*

Anderson saw what the ex-professor had done and his lips drew back in a silent, involuntary animal snarl of the utmost horror and fear. He almost dropped the knife, frozen now in midstroke, as Henley's black gloves fell to the floor and the thick white worms twined and twisted hypnotically where his fingers ought to have been!

Then—more out of nightmare dread and loathing than any sort of rational purpose, for Anderson knew now that the ex-professor was nothing less than a Priest of Cthulhu—he carried on with his interrupted stroke and his knife flashed down. Henley tried to deflect the blow with a monstrously altered hand, his face contorting and a shriek forming silently on his lips as one of the warmish appendages was severed and fell twitching to the sawdust. He flailed his injured hand and white ichor splashed Tharpe's face and eyes.

Blindly the frantic showman struck again and again, gibbering mindlessly and noiselessly as he clawed at his face with his free hand, trying to wipe away the filthy white juice of Henley's injured hybrid member. But the blows were wild and Hiram Henley had stepped to one side.

More frantically yet, insanely, Tharpe slashed at the greenly pulsating air all about him, stumbling closer to the core of the radiance. Then his knife struck something that gave like rotting flesh beneath the blow, and finally, in a short-lived revival of confidence, he opened stinging eyes to see what he had hit.

Something coiled out of the green core, something long and capering, greyly mottled and slimy! It was a tentacle—a *face*-tentacle, Tharpe knew—twitching spasmodically, even as the hand of a disturbed dreamer might twitch.

Tharpe struck again, a reflex action, and watched his blade bite through the tentacle unhindered, as if through mud—*and then saw that trembling member solidifying again where the blade had sliced!* His knife fell from palsied hands then, and Tharpe screamed a last, desperate, silent scream as the tentacle moved more purposefully!

The now completely sentient member wrapped its tip about Tharpe's throat, constricting and jerking him forwards effortlessly into the green core. And as he went the last things he saw were the eyes in the vast face; the hellish eyes that opened briefly, saw and recognized him for what he was—a sacrifice to Cthulhu!

Quickly then, as the green light began its withdrawal and sound slowly returned to the tent, Hiram Henley put on his gloves. Ignoring as best he could the pain his injury gave him, he spoke these words:

Oh, Great Cthulhu, dreaming in R'lyeh,
Thy priest offers up this sacrifice,
That Thy coming be soon,
And that of Thy kindred dreamers.
I am Thy priest and adore Thee...

And as the core grew smaller yet, he toppled the evil idol into its green center, following this act by throwing in the tablets and all those other items of fabled antiquity until the inner tent was quite empty. He would have kept all these things if he dared, but his orders—those orders he received in dreams from R'lyeh—would not allow it. When a priest had been found to replace Hamilton Tharpe, then Great Cthulhu would find a way to return those rudimentary pillars of His temple!

Finally, Henley switched off the single dim light and watched the green core as it shrank to a tiny point of intense brightness before winking out. Only the smell of deep ocean remained, and a damp circle in the dark where the sawdust floor was queerly marked and slimy....

Some little time later the folk of the fairground were awakened by the clamour of a fire engine as it sped to the blaze on the border of the circling tents, sideshows and caravans. Both Tharpe's caravan and The Tomb of the Great Old Ones were burning fiercely. Nothing was saved, and in their frantic toiling to help the firemen the nomads of the funfair failed to note that their dogs again crouched timid and whimpering beneath the nighted caravans. They found it strange later, though, when they heard how the police had failed to discover anything of Anderson Tharpe's remains.

The gap that the destruction of the one-time freak-house had left was soon filled, for "Madame Zala", as if summoned back by the grim work of the mysterious fire, returned with her horse and caravan within the week. She is still with Hodgson's Funfair, but known to anyone with even the remotest schooling in the occult, she is sometimes seen crossing herself with an obscure and pagan sign…

Cinderlands

Tim Pratt

Close to the end:

Dexter West woke to the sound of claws skittering on hardwood floors above him, thinking in a muzzy, sleep-headed way that the upstairs neighbors must have gotten a dog, even though dogs weren't allowed, and now the horrible noise was going to keep him up all night. But as he sat up in bed he remembered there was no upstairs here. He'd moved out of the apartment building into a house of his own. After turning on the lamp, he went into the walk-in closet, where the noise—the *scuttling*—seemed loudest. A heating duct ran along the ceiling, and he pressed his ear to the metal and listened to the click and patter of tiny claws rushing along inside.

Was it… rats? Rats in the ducts? Rats in the walls?

He banged hard on the duct with his fist, and the scuttling stopped.

"I'll get a cat," he said aloud. "I need the company anyway."

He went back to bed, and dreamed of digging holes in his back yard. Holes filled with squirming, black-furred rats the size of kittens. Holes that went down forever.

ზ ∅

Earlier:

Dexter crouched beneath the toxic fruit trees in his grassless back yard, turning over black earth with the spade he'd taken from the old man, and every shovelful revealed worse things:

clumps of cinders and the dust of ashes;

rusting nails, practically dripping tetanus;

wickedly-curved shards of brown glass;

bullets of various sizes, crusted with dirt;

and a foot or so down, fragments of black-stone statuary, showing here the partial orbit of a life-sized eye, there a broken mouth filled with crude triangular teeth, here a tiny hand with six fingers, all clawed.

Dexter looked toward the unmended fence again and said, "What do you mean, this used to be the cinderlands?"

But the old man next door was gone.

ზ ∅

Earlier still:

Dexter moved in the early spring of his thirty-fifth year. The houses on either side of his own were boarded up, and the neighborhood had the appearance of a mouth filled with missing teeth: empty lots and empty houses outnumbered the inhabited three-to-one. But he didn't mind. After living among noisy neighbors, the silence and solitude surrounding his new life as a homeowner seemed a blessing.

The faded yellow house at 65 Mumford Street was a sprawling one-story affair with additions of varying vintages sprouting from all sides. He loved the labyrinthine interior, despite its many flaws: sagging air ducts from an abandoned remodel, a roof shedding shingles, cracked linoleum. It was still a bargain at the bank's price. The original owner had died, and the dissolute heirs had run the place as a sort of commune—one bank official leaned close and whispered "cult," though she wouldn't elaborate. When the heirs vanished and stopped paying the mortgage, the bank seized the property.

Dexter paid cash, using a little of his settlement money from the case against the city. A year before he'd been attacked and beaten by police on his way to work, a case of mistaken identity—he resembled an escaped serial arsonist who'd recently burned down an officer's home. Even after buying the house he had more than enough money to take time off to fix up the place. He was sure the neighborhood would get better, justifying the investment—the recession couldn't last forever—but in the meantime, he'd enjoy the quiet.

The back yard was full of fruit trees, shading the earth so deeply that no grass could grow, and he spent the evenings under the branches drinking beer and watching the wind stir the leaves, body aching pleasantly from painting, and sanding, and hammering, and laying tile. After so many years teaching history to high school students who barely seemed to care about what had happened to them yesterday, it was refreshing to work with his hands and see the measurable progress of that work each day.

As the trees began to blossom, he looked forward to the fruit—lemon, plum, crab-apple, cherry. He decided to plant some tomatoes in the yard, and choosing between the two spots where sunlight actually touched the ground when a voice from beyond the broken side fence said, "I wouldn't put roots down here if I were you." An old man dressed in a faded white suit of archaic cut leaned on a walkingstick and smiled affably from beneath a broad-brimmed straw hat.

"I didn't realize anyone lived over there."

"At my age I don't come out often," the man said. "Only when the weather is just exactly right. Saw you in that spot of sun. Thinking of gardening? Don't. The soil's poison."

Dexter frowned. "The trees seem healthy."

"Things might grow, but there's so much… oh, lead, and mercury, and who knows what else in the dirt, I wouldn't eat any of it. Plant in containers if you must, though even then…" He shook his head. "The air's bad, too. This whole area used to be the cinderlands."

"I guess I could get the soil tested for lead—"

"No need for all that trouble." The old man reached into his suit and, improbably, drew out a spade with a gleaming blade. "Just dig down a little, you'll see."

"Okay." Dexter had liked his neighbors better when they didn't exist, but he took the spade, and dug… and found sharp, pointy, broken things, though the bits of statuary were the most disturbing. "What do you mean, this used to be the cinderlands?" The old man didn't answer, and when Dexter went to the fence, he was gone, and the yard over there was as derelict as ever, the house just as uninhabited-looking as before.

ᙇ ᙘ

Later:

Dexter decided not to start a garden after all, and when the trees put forth fruit, he knew he'd made the right choice. The lemons were small, and while they were yellow, it was less the yellow of cartoon suns and more the yellow of jaundiced skin or nicotine-stained teeth. The plums seemed to rot rather than ripen, dripping off the branches in slimy clumps. The cherries were hard, and shriveled like shrunken heads, while the crab-apples grew so huge and fast they split their skins—and the inside of every apple was home to vast numbers of worms... possibly, he thought, of a kind unknown to science.

ᔕ ᔕ

A bit later still:

Dexter came home from the hardware store, unlocked both deadbolts—it paid to be safe, since thieves weren't above stripping the copper from any property, inhabited or not—and stepped inside to find unmistakable evidence of intrusion. There were scraps of paper scattered on the floor, covered with peculiar geometric diagrams, and muddy footprints, and in the middle of his living room floor: a straw hat with a crushed crown. The back door stood open, and there were marks on the ground, as if something heavy had been dragged toward the vine-covered back fence, but the trail vanished there.

He went to the neighbor's house and pounded on the door, but no one answered, and when he peered through the windows he saw only empty rooms full of dust. He called the police to tell them he'd had an intruder, but when he gave his name, the dispatcher paused, said, "Dexter *West*? The guy who sued the city? The reason, my bosses tell me, I didn't get a raise this year?"

"Ah—no?" he said.

The dispatcher laughed. "We'll send someone right over. You just sit and wait. Be sure to call us if your house catches fire, too—lots of my friends are firemen, and you know as well as anyone there are arsonists around." The dispatcher hung up.

No one ever came. Dexter was astounded to realize he'd managed to personally anger and alienate the bureaucracy of a city—an institution normally so vast and impersonal that it was wholly unconcerned with individuals. In a way, it was quite an accomplishment.

ᔕ ᔕ

Very near the end:

The scuttling in the ducts continued all summer, increasing until even pounding on the metal failed to make any difference. Dexter spent the deep darkness of the nights awake and listening, and slept through the heat of the days. Work on the house ceased. He only went to the hardware store to acquire rat poison—hadn't he read somewhere that heart medication and rat poison worked on the same principle, by thinning the blood?—and scattered the poison throughout all the secret places in the house: the odd-sized storage rooms, some inexplicably painted red; the little cubbyholes filled with dusty blue glass bottles; the low cabinets with their strangely-angled, cramped interiors. He never saw rat droppings or nibbled wires, but the noises every night told a different tale.

Dexter got a cat, a sleek black one from a shelter that came already equipped with the peculiar name "Ninja-Man," but the animal was dead within days. He was never sure why—maybe it had gotten into the poison, but he preferred to think it had possessed some undiagnosed heart defect or other hidden flaw.

Dexter buried the animal in the yard, deep, though not as deep as he'd intended—about two feet down he began to find things that looked suspiciously like knife blades made of flaked stone, and then fragments of bones that suggested his cat wasn't the first thing to be buried here in the cinderlands. He chose to dig no deeper.

ໄ ໄ

Just before the end:

When the scuttling crescendoed just after three am, he decided to smash the ducts. They weren't even connected to anything— just remnants of a past tenant's attempt to modernize the place with central heat and air. He'd left them in this long because he thought he might install such amenities himself someday, but the noise was overwhelming, worse tonight than ever. He hadn't slept well for weeks, convinced he heard not just rats but also human footsteps and voices, either in the next room, or in the back yard, or in the upstairs apartment which he intermittently forgot didn't actually exist.

He picked up his wrecking bar and began smashing at the ducts, leaving dents and little else, until he finally struck a seam in the metal and caused a plate to pop loose and gape open downward like a sprung trap door.

Dark shapes spilled forth from the duct like a greasy black flood, fur and wriggling noses and tails, and he fell back against the wall, clutching his steel bar, terrified the rats—dozens! scores! hundreds!—would attack him. But they kept running, through his open bedroom door, into the hallway, toward the kitchen and the back door. He imagined his house filled, infested, overrun by rats—

But they weren't rats. Or they weren't *entirely* rats.

He'd seen a program on television once about parasitic wasps. They attacked cockroaches, injected venom into their tiny roach brains, and took control of the insects, driving them like six-legged golf carts into their nests, where the roaches became paralyzed incubators for wasp eggs.

Something similar had been done to these rats. There were glistening greenish-black growths on their necks and heads, foreign tissue sometimes obscuring their eyes, sometimes extending down their backs to their tails. The growths looked wet, and they pulsed, and they might have been a sort of fungus or horrible external tumor...

Except for the eyes. Every growth had a single, marble-sized blue eye somewhere on its mass, gazing backward. The eyes blinked and moved in unison, as if they were parts of the same organism, temporarily separated.

Dexter dropped his wrecking bar and fled, and since he could only flee through the door— the same door the rats were pouring through, endlessly, how could there be so many?—he tried to *leap* through the door over the flood. He leapt well, but the leap had to end, and he came down in his bare feet among the rats. They squealed and twisted and rushed away from him. He lost his footing and stumbled through the dark hall, toward the kitchen—

—where his back door stood open, the rats and their passengers racing through the opening and away. Dexter stared through the door, into the yard, unable to comprehend what he was seeing.

The human eye and brain have ways of coping with size and distance. Objects seen up close appear larger, and as those objects move farther away, they appear to shrink, growing ever smaller as they recede into the distance. So the great ship that looms large as a building while you're standing on the dock becomes a tiny speck of blackness as it vanishes over the distant horizon.

The rats were exactly the opposite. They looked normal-sized up close, but as they streamed into his yard, getting farther away, they seemed to become *larger*, until—in violation of all laws of nature and perspective—they were easily the size of cars by the time they reached the back fence, the eyes on their backs as big as tires, all staring not *at* him, but past him. Just before they should have crashed into the fence, the enormous rats vanished, as if they'd turned a corner that didn't exist... or fallen into a deep, hidden hole.

Dexter stood aside, staring down at the rats as they fled, afraid to lift his gaze again to witness their impossible growth. After a long time—it seemed like hours, though it couldn't have been so long, surely?—the scuttling in the ducts ended, and the final few rats disappeared into the back yard. He watched the last ones go, growing from rat-sized when they left the house, to dog-sized when they were halfway across the yard, to pony-sized and bigger still as they reached the fence... until, finally, the last one vanished.

He released a breath he hadn't realized he was holding. He shut his door, engaged the locks, and only then asked himself—how had the door opened? Had the press of the rats somehow shoved it wide? Maybe the old man who didn't *actually* live next door had been there to open the door for the creatures. Or maybe—

Something in his bedroom thumped, like a great weight hitting the floor.

Frozen by the back door, listening, Dexter suddenly wondered: what were the rats running from? He had no doubt the creatures were fleeing, either in terror or under orders from the staring growths on their backs. Dexter couldn't imagine where they'd originally come from; certainly not within his walls. Nor could he tell where they were going. They were simply… passing through. Whether his house was along some mysterious right-of-way or merely a hastily-chosen detour, he couldn't know, but he was sure of one thing: this was an escape route.

So what, exactly, were the creatures escaping *from*?

Another thump, this one louder, and Dexter began to open the locks, his fingers clumsy, his hands slick with sweat, the thought scuttling and skittering in his mind as insistently as the claws of a thousand fleeing rats: *run, run, run.*

The last locked turned. The door yawned open. The trees in the back yard rustled in the wind, and the old man from next door—now hatless—leaned on his walkingstick by the back fence, face lost in shadow, and shook his head.

Dexter sprinted from the house, but the back fence seemed to get smaller as he ran, and the old man seemed farther away with every step, and Dexter realized, before he fell—before something fell *upon* him, radiating ancient, indifferent heat—that he'd never reach the corner or hole or exit in time. That he was too small, and the world, and all the things in it, were just too big.

ဢ ဢ

Lord of the Land

Gene Wolfe

The Nebraskan smiled warmly, leaned forward, and made a sweeping gesture with his right hand, saying, "Yes indeed, that's exactly the sort of thing I'm most interested in. Tell me about it, Mr. Thacker, please."

All this was intended to keep old Hop Thacker's attention away from the Nebraskan's left hand, which had slipped into his left jacket pocket to turn on the miniature recorder there. Its microphone was pinned to the back of the Nebraskan's lapel, the fine brown wire almost invisible.

Perhaps old Hop would not have cared in any case; old Hop was hardly the shy type. "Waul," he began, "this was years an' years back, the way I hear'd it. Guess it'd have been in my great granpaw's time, Mr. Cooper, or mebbe before."

The Nebraskan nodded encouragingly.

"There's these three boys, an' they had an old mule, wasn't good fer nothin' 'cept crowbait. One was Colonel Lightfoot—course didn't nobody call him colonel then. One was Creech an' t'other 'un..." The old man paused, fingering his scant beard. "Guess I don't rightly know. I *did* know. It'll come to me when don't nobody want to hear it. He's the one had the mule."

The Nebraskan nodded again. "Three young men, you say, Mr. Thacker?"

"That's right, an' Colonel Lightfoot, he had him a new gun. An' this other 'un—he was a friend of my grandpaw's or somebody—he had him one everybody said was jest about the best shooter in the county. So this here Laban Creech, he said *he* wasn't no bad shot hisself, an' he went an' fetched his'un. He was the 'un had that mule. I recollect now.

"So they led the ol' mule out into the medder, mebbe fifty straddles from the brake. You know how you do. Creech, he shot it smack in the ear, an' it jest laid down an' died, it was old, an' sick, too, didn't kick or nothin'. So Colonel Lightfoot, he fetched out his knife an' cut it up the belly, an' they went on back to the brake fer to wait out the crows."

"I see," the Nebraskan said.

"One'd shoot, an' then another, an' they'd keep score. An' it got to be near to dark, you know, an' Colonel Lightfoot with his new gun an' this other man that had the good 'un, they was even up, an' this Laban Creech was only one behind 'em. Reckon there was near to a hundred crows back behind in the gully. You can't jest shoot a crow an' leave him, you know, an' 'spect the rest to come. They look an' see that dead 'un, an' they say, Waul, jest look what become of him. I don't calc'late to come anywheres near *there*."

The Nebraskan smiled. "Wise birds."

"Oh, there's all kinds of stories 'bout 'em," the old man said.

"Thankee, Sarah."

His granddaughter had brought two tall glasses of lemonade; she paused in the doorway to dry her hands on her red-and-white checkered apron, glancing at the Nebraskan with shy alarm before retreating into the house.

"Didn't have a lick, back then." The old man poked an ice cube with one bony, somewhat soiled finger. "Didn't have none when I was a little 'un, neither, till the TVA come. Nowadays you talk 'bout the TVA an' they think you mean them programs, you know." He waved his glass. "I watch 'em sometimes."

"Television," the Nebraskan supplied.

"That's it. Like, you take when Bud Bloodhat went to his reward, Mr. Cooper. Hot? You never seen the like. The birds all had their mouths open, wouldn't fly fer anything. Lot two hogs, I recollect, that same day. My paw, he wanted to save the meat, but 'twasn't a bit of good. He says he thought them hogs was rotten 'fore ever they dropped, an' he was 'fraid to give it to the dogs, it was that hot. They was all asleepin' under the porch anyhow. Wouldn't come out fer nothin'."

The Nebraskan was tempted to reintroduce the subject of the crow shoot, but an instinct born of thousands of hours of such listening prompted him to nod and smile instead.

"Waul, they knowed they had to git him under quick, didn't they? So they got him fixed, cleaned up an' his best clothes on an' all like that, an' they was all in there listenin', but it was terrible hot in there an' you could smell him pretty strong, so by an' by I jest snuck out. Wasn't nobody payin' attention to *me*, do you see? The women's all bawlin' an' carryin' on, an' the men thinkin' it was time to put him under an' have another."

The old man's cane fell with a sudden, dry rattle. For a moment as he picked it up, the Nebraskan glimpsed Sarah's pale face on the other side of the doorway.

"So I snuck out on the stoop. I bet it was a hundred easy, but it felt good to me after bein' inside there. That was when I seen it comin' down the hill t'other side of the road. Stayed in the shadow much as it could, an' looked like a shadow itself, only you could see it move, an' it was always blacker than what they was. I knowed it was the soul-sucker an' was afeered it'd git my ma. I took to cryin', an' she come outside an' fetched me down the spring fer a drink, an' that's the last time anybody ever did see it, far's I know."

"Why do you call it the soul-sucker?" the Nebraskan asked.

"'Cause that's what it does, Mr. Cooper. Guess you know it ain't only folks that has ghosts. A man can see the ghost of another man, all right, but he can see the ghost of a dog or a mule or anythin' like that, too. Waul, you take a man's, 'cause that don't make so much argyment. It's his soul, ain't it? Why ain't it in Heaven or down in the bad place like it's s'possed to be? What's it doin' in the haint house, or walkin' down the road, or wherever 'twas you seen it? I had a dog that seen a ghost one time, an' that'n was another dog's, do you see? *I* never did see it, but he did, an' I knowed he did by how he acted. What was it doin' there?"

The Nebraskan shook his head. "I've no idea, Mr. Thacker." "Waul, I'll tell you. When a man passes on, or a horse or a dog or whatever, it's s'pposed to git out an' git over to the Judgment. The Lord Jesus Christ's our judge, Mr. Cooper. Only sometimes it won't do it. Mebbe it's afeared to be judged, or mebbe it has this or that to tend to down here yet, or anyhow reckons it does, like showin' somebody some money what it knowed about. Some does that pretty often, an' I might tell you 'bout some of them times. But if it don't have business an' is jest feared to go, it'll stay where 'tis—that's the kind that haints their graves. They b'long to the soul sucker, do you see, if it can git 'em. Only if it's hungered it'll suck on a live person, an' he's bound to fight or die." The old man paused to wet his lips with lemonade, staring across his family's little burial plot and fields of dry cornstalks to purple hills where he would never hunt again. "Don't win, not particular often. Guess the first 'un was a Indian, mebbe. Somethin' like that. I tell you how Creech shot it?"

"No you didn't, Mr. Thacker." The Nebraskan took a swallow of his own lemonade, which was refreshingly tart. "I'd like very much to hear it."

The old man rocked in silence for what seemed a long while. "Waul," he said at last, "they'd been shootin' all day. Reckon I said that. Fer a good long time anyhow. An' they was tied, Colonel Lightfoot an' this here Cooper was, an' Creech jest one behind 'em. 'Twas Creech's time next, an' he kept on sayin' to stay fer jest one more, then he'd go an' they'd all go, hit or miss. So they stayed, but wasn't no more crows 'cause they'd 'bout kilt every crow in many a mile. Started gittin' dark fer sure, an' this Cooper, he says, Come on, Lab, couldn't nobody hit nothin' now. You lost an' you got to face up.

"Creech, he says, waul, 'twas my mule. An' jest 'bout then here comes somethin' bigger'n any crow, an' black, hoppin' 'long the ground like a crow will sometimes, do you see? Over towards that dead mule. So Creech ups with his gun. Colonel Lightfoot, he allowed afterwards he couldn't have seed his sights in that dark. Reckon he jest sighted 'longside the barrel. 'Tis the ol' mountain way, do you see, an' there's lots what swore by it.

"Waul, he let go an' it fell over. You won, says Colonel Lightfoot, an' he claps Creech on his back, an' let's go. Only this Cooper, he knowed it wasn't no crow, bein' too big, an' he goes over to see what 'twas. Waul, sir, 'twas like to a man, only crooked legged an' wry neck. 'Twasn't no man, but like to it, do you see? Who shot me? it says, an' the mouth was full of worms. Grave worms, do you see?

"Who shot me? An' Cooper, he said Creech, then he hollered fer Creech an' Colonel Lightfoot. Colonel Lightfoot says, boys, we got to bury this. An' Creech goes back to his home place an' fetches a spade an' a ol' shovel, them bein' all he's got. He's shakin' so bad they jest rattled together, do you see? Colonel Lightfoot an' this Cooper, they seed he couldn't dig, so they goes hard at it. Pretty soon they looked around, an' Creech was gone, an' the soul-sucker, too."

The old man paused dramatically. "Next time anybody seed the soul-sucker, 'twas Creech. So he's the one I seed, or one of his kin anyhow. Don't never shoot anythin' without you're dead sure what 'tis, young feller."

Cued by his closing words, Sarah appeared in the doorway. "Supper's ready. I set a place for you, Mr. Cooper. Pa said. You sure you want to stay? Won't be fancy."

The Nebraskan stood up. "Why, that was very kind of you, Miss Thacker."

His granddaughter helped the old man rise. Propped by the cane in his right hand and guided and supported by her on his left, he shuffled slowly into the house. The Nebraskan followed and held his chair.

"Pa's washin' up," Sarah said. "He was changin' the oil in the tractor. He'll say grace. You don't have to get my chair for me, Mr. Cooper, I'll put on till he comes. Just sit down."

"Thank you." The Nebraskan sat across from the old man.

"We got ham and sweet corn, biscuits, and potatoes. It's not no company dinner."

With perfect honesty the Nebraskan said, "Everything smells wonderful, Miss Thacker."

Her father entered, scrubbed to the elbows but bringing a tang of crankcase oil to the mingled aromas from the stove. "You hear all you wanted to, Mr. Cooper?"

"I heard some marvelous stories, Mr. Thacker," the Nebraskan said.

Sarah gave the ham the place of honor before her father. "I think it's truly fine, what you're doin', writin' up all these old stories 'fore they're lost."

Her father nodded reluctantly. "Wouldn't have thought you could make a livin' at it, though."

"He don't, Pa. He teaches. He's a teacher." The ham was followed by a mountainous platter of biscuits. Sarah dropped into a chair. "I'll fetch our sweet corn and potatoes in just a shake. Corn's not quite done yet."

"O Lord, bless this food and them that eats it. Make us thankful for farm, family, and friends. Welcome the stranger 'neath our roof as we do, O Lord. Now let's eat." The younger Mr. Thacker rose and applied an enormous butcher knife to the ham, and the Nebraskan remembered at last to switch off his tape recorder.

Two hours later, more than filled, the Nebraskan had agreed to stay the night. "It's not real fancy," Sarah said as she showed him to their vacant bedroom, "but it's clean. I just put those sheets and the comforter on while you were talkin' to Grandpa." The door creaked. She flipped the switch.

The Nebraskan nodded. "You anticipated that I'd accept your father's invitation."

"Well, he hoped you would." Careful not to meet his eye, Sarah added, "I never seen Grandpa so happy in years. You're goin' to talk to him some more in the mornin'? You can put the stuff from your suitcase right here in this dresser. I cleared out these top drawers, and I already turned your bed down for you. Bathroom's on past Pa's room. You know. I guess we seem awful country to you, out here."

"I grew up on a farm near Fremont, Nebraska," the Nebraskan told her. There was no reply. When he looked around, Sarah was blowing a kiss from the doorway; instantly she was gone.

With a philosophical shrug, he laid his suitcase on the bed and opened it. In addition to his notebooks, he had brought his wellthumbed copy of *The*

Types of the Folktale and Schmit's *Gods before the Greeks*, which he had been planning to read. Soon the Thackers would assemble in their front room to watch television. Surely he might be excused for an hour or two? His unexpected arrival later in the evening might actually give them pleasure. He had a sudden premonition that Sarah, fair and willow-slender, would be sitting alone on the sagging sofa, and that there would be no unoccupied chair.

There was an unoccupied chair in the room, however; an old but sturdy-looking wooden one with a cane bottom. He carried it to the window and opened Schmit, determined to read as long as the light lasted. Dis, he knew, had come in his chariot for the souls of departed Greeks, and so had been called the Gatherer of Many by those too fearful to name him; but Hop Thacker's twisted and almost pitiable soul-sucker appeared to have nothing else in common with the dark and kingly Dis. Had there been some still earlier deity who clearly prefigured the soul-sucker? Like most folklorists, the Nebraskan firmly believed that folklore's themes were, if not actually eternal, for the most part very ancient indeed. *Gods before the Greeks* seemed well indexed.

Dead, their mummies visited by An-uat, 2.

The Nebraskan nodded to himself and turned to the front of the book.

An-uat, Anuat, "Lord of the Land (the Necropolis)," "Opener to the North." Though frequently confused with Anubis, to whom he lent his form, it is clear that An-uat the jackal-god maintained a separate identity into the New Kingdom period. Souls that had refused to board Ra's boat (and thus to appear before the throne of the resurrected Osiris) were dragged by An-uat, who visited their mummies for this purpose, to Tuat, the lightless, demon-haunted valley stretching between the death of the old sun and the rising of the new. An-uat and the less threatening Anubis can seldom be distinguished in art, but where such distinction is possible, An-uat is the more powerfully muscled figure. Van Allen reports that An-uat is still invoked by the modern (Moslem or Coptic) magicians of Egypt, under the name Ju'gu.

The Nebraskan rose, laid the book on his chair, and strode to the dresser and back. Here was a five-thousand-year-old myth that paralleled the soul-sucker in function. Nor was it certain by any means that the similarity was merely coincidental. That the folklore of the Appalachians could have been influenced by the occult beliefs of modern Egypt was wildly improbable, but by no means impossible. After the Civil War the United States Army had imported not only camels but camel drivers from Egypt, the Nebraskan reminded himself; and the escape artist Harry Houdini had once described in lurid detail his imprisonment in the Great Pyramid. His account was undoubtedly highly colored—but had he, perhaps, actually visited Egypt as an extension of some European tour? Thousands of American servicemen must have passed through Egypt during the Second World War, but the soul-sucker tale was clearly older than that, and probably older than Houdini.

There seemed to be a difference in appearance as well; but just how different were the soul-sucker and this Ju'gu, really? An-uat had been depicted as a muscular man with a jackal's head. The soulsucker had been....

The Nebraskan extracted the tape recorder from his pocket, rewound the tape, and inserted the earpiece.

Had been "like to a man, only crooked-legged an' wry neck." Yet it had not been a man, though the feature that separated it from humanity had not been specified. A doglike head seemed a possibility, surely, and An-uat might have changed a good deal in five thousand years.

The Nebraskan returned to his chair and reopened his book, but the sun was already nearly at the horizon. After flipping pages aimlessly for a minute or two, he joined the Thackers in their living room.

Never had the inanities of television seemed less real or less significant. Though his eyes followed the movements of the actors on the screen, he was in fact considerably more attentive to Sarah's warmth and rather too generously applied perfume, and still more to a scene that had never, perhaps, taken place: to the dead mule lying in the field long ago, and to the marksmen concealed where the woods began. Colonel Lightfoot had no doubt been a historical person, locally famous, who would be familiar to the majority of Mr. Thacker's hearers. Laban Creech might or might not have been an actual person as well. Mr. Thacker had—mysteriously, now that the Nebraskan came to consider it—given the Nebraskan's own last name, Cooper, to the third and somewhat inessential marksman.

Three marksmen had been introduced because numbers greater than unity were practically always three in folklore, of course; but the use of his own name seemed odd. No doubt it had been no more than a quirk of the old man's failing memory. Remembering *Cooper*, he had attributed the name incorrectly.

By imperceptible degrees, the Nebraskan grew conscious that the Thackers were giving no more attention to the screen than he himself was; they chuckled at no jokes, showed no irritation at even the most insistent commercials, and spoke about the dismal sitcom neither to him nor to one another.

Pretty Sarah sat primly beside him, her knees together, her long legs crossed at their slender ankles, and her dishwater-reddened hands folded on her apron. To his right, the old man rocked, the faint protests of his chair as regular, and as slow, as the ticking of the tall clock in the corner, his hands upon the crook of his cane, his expression a sightless frown.

To Sarah's left, the younger Mr. Thacker was almost hidden from the Nebraskan's view. He rose and went into the kitchen, cracking his knuckles as he walked, returned with neither food nor drink, and sat once more for less than half a minute before rising again.

Sarah ventured, "Maybe you'd like some cookies, or some more lemonade?"

The Nebraskan shook his head. "Thank you, Miss Thacker; but if I were to eat anything else, I wouldn't sleep."

Oddly, her hands clenched. "I could fetch you a piece of pie."

"No, thank you."

Mercifully, the sitcom was over, replaced by a many-colored sunrise on the plains of Africa. There sailed the boat of Ra, the Nebraskan reflected, issuing in splendor from the dark gorge called Tuat to give light to mankind. For a moment he pictured a far smaller and less radiant vessel, black-hulled and crowded with the recalcitrant dead, a vessel steered by a jackal-headed man: a minute fleck against the blazing disk of the African sun. What was that book of von Däniken's? *Ships*—no, *Chariots of the Gods*. Spaceships nonetheless—and that was folklore, too, or at any rate was quickly passing into folklore; the Nebraskan had encountered it twice already.

An animal, a zebra, lay still upon the plain. The camera panned in on it; when it was very near, the head of a huge hyena appeared, its jaws dripping carrion. The old man turned away, his abrupt movement drawing the Nebraskan's attention.

Fear. That was it, of course. He cursed himself for not having identified the emotion pervading the living room sooner. Sarah was frightened, and so was the old man—horribly afraid. Even Sarah's father appeared fearful and restless, leaning back in his chair, then forward, shifting his feet, wiping his palms on the thighs of his faded khaki trousers.

The Nebraskan rose and stretched. "You'll have to excuse me. It's been a long day."

When neither of the men spoke, Sarah said, "I'm 'bout to turn in myself, Mr. Cooper. You want to take a bath?"

He hesitated, trying to divine the desired reply. "If it's not going to be too much trouble. That would be very nice."

Sarah rose with alacrity. "I'll fetch you some towels and stuff."

He returned to his room, stripped, and put on pajamas and a robe. Sarah was waiting for him at the bathroom door with a bar of Zest and half a dozen towels at least. As he took the towels the Nebraskan murmured, "Can you tell me what's wrong? Perhaps I can help."

"We could go to town, Mr. Cooper." Hesitantly she touched his arm. "I'm kind of pretty, don't you think so? You wouldn't have to marry me or nothin', just go off in the mornin'."

"You are," the Nebraskan told her. "In fact, you're very pretty; but I couldn't do that to your family."

"You get dressed again." Her voice was scarcely audible, her eyes on the top of the stairs. "You say your old trouble's startin' up, you got to see the doctor. I'll slide out the back and 'round . Stop for me at the big elm."

"I really couldn't, Miss Thacker," the Nebraskan said.

In the tub he told himself that he had been a fool. What was it that girl in his last class had called him? A hopeless romantic. He could have enjoyed an attractive young woman that night (and it had been months since he had slept with a woman) and saved her from... what? A beating by her father? There had been no bruises on her bare arms, and he had noticed no missing teeth. That delicate nose had never been broken, surely.

He could have enjoyed the night with a very pretty young woman—for whom he would have felt responsible afterward, for the remainder of his life. He pictured the reference in The Journal of American Folklore: "Collected by Dr. Samuel Cooper, U. Neb., from Hopkin Thacker, 73, whose granddaughter Dr. Cooper seduced and abandoned."

With a snort of disgust, he stood, jerked the chain of the white rubber plug that had retained his bathwater, and snatched up one of Sarah's towels, at which a scrap of paper fluttered to the yellow bathroom rug. He picked it up, his fingers dampening lined notebook filler.

Do not tell him anything grandpa told you. A woman's hand, almost painfully legible.

Sarah had anticipated his refusal, clearly; anticipated it, and coppered her bets. *Him* meant her father, presumably, unless there was another male in the house or another was expected—her father almost certainly.

The Nebraskan tore the note into small pieces and flushed them down the toilet, dried himself with two towels, brushed his teeth and resumed his pajamas and robe, then stepped quietly out into the hall and stood listening.

The television was still on, not very loudly, in the front room. There were no other voices, no sound of footsteps or of blows. What had the Thackers been afraid of? The soul-sucker? Egypt's mouldering divinities?

The Nebraskan returned to his room and shut the door firmly behind him. Whatever it was, it was most certainly none of his business. In the morning he would eat breakfast, listen to a tale or two from the old man, and put the whole family out of his mind.

Something moved when he switched off the light. And for an instant he had glimpsed his own shadow on the window blind, with that of someone or something behind him, a man even taller than he, a broad-shouldered figure with horns or pointed ears.

Which was ridiculous on the face of it. The old-fashioned brass chandelier was suspended over the center of the room; the switch was by the door, as far as possible from the windows. In no conceivable fashion could his shadow—or any other—have been cast on that shade. He and whatever he thought he had glimpsed would have to have been standing on the other side of the room, between the light and the window.

It seemed that someone had moved the bed. He waited for his eyes to become accustomed to the darkness. What furniture? The bed, the chair in which he had read—that should be beside the window where he had left it—a dresser with a spotted mirror, and (he racked his brain) a nightstand, perhaps. That should be by the head of the bed, if it were there at all.

Whispers filled the room. That was the wind outside; the windows were open wide, the old house flanked by stately maples. Those windows were visible now, pale rectangles in the darkness. As carefully as he could he crossed to one and raised the blind. Moonlight filled the bedroom; there was his bed, here his chair, in front of the window to his left. No puff of air stirred the leaf-burdened limbs.

He took off his robe and hung it on the towering bedpost, pulled top sheet and comforter to the foot of the bed, and lay down. He had heard something—or nothing. Seen something—or nothing. He thought longingly of his apartment in Lincoln, of his sabbatical—almost a year ago now—in Greece. Of sunshine on the Saronic Gulf…

Circular and yellow-white, the moon floated upon stagnant water. Beyond the moon lay the city of the dead, street after narrow street of silent tombs, a daedal labyrinth of death and stone. Far away, a jackal yipped. For whole ages of the world, nothing moved; painted likenesses with limpid eyes appeared to mock the empty, tumbled skulls beyond their crumbling doors.

Far down one of the winding avenues of the dead, a second jackal appeared. Head high and ears erect, it contemplated the emptiness and listened to the silence before turning to sink its teeth once more in the tattered thing it had already dragged so far. Eyeless and desiccated, smeared with bitumen and trailing rotting wrappings, the Nebraskan recognized his own corpse.

And at once was there, lying helpless in the night-shrouded street. For a moment the jackal's glowing eyes loomed over him; its jaws closed, and his collarbone snapped....

The jackal and the moonlit city vanished. Bolt upright, shaking and shaken, he did not know where. Sweat streamed into his eyes.

There had been a sound.

To dispel the jackal and the accursed sunless city, he rose and groped for the light switch. The bedroom was—or at least appeared to be—as he recalled it, save for the damp outline of his lanky body on the sheet. His suitcase stood beside the dresser; his shaving kit lay upon it; *Gods before the Greeks* waited his return on the cane seat of the old chair.

"You must come to me."

He whirled. There was no one but himself in the room, no one (as far as he could see) in the branches of the maple or on the ground below. Yet the words had been distinct, the speaker—so it had seemed—almost at his ear. Feeling an utter fool, he looked under the bed. There was nobody there, and no one in the closet.

The doorknob would not turn in his hand. He was locked in. That, perhaps, had been the noise that woke him: the sharp click of the bolt. He squatted to squint through the old-fashioned keyhole. The dim hallway outside was empty, as far as he could see. He stood; a hard object gouged the sole of his right foot, and he bent to look.

It was the key. He picked it up. Somebody had locked his door, pushed the key under it, and (possibly) spoken through the keyhole.

Or perhaps it was only that some fragment of his dream had remained with him; that had been the jackal's voice, surely.

The key turned smoothly in the lock. Outside in the hall, he seemed to detect the fragrance of Sarah's perfume, though he could not be sure. If it had been Sarah, she had locked him in, providing the key so that he could free himself in the morning. Whom had she been locking out?

He returned to the bedroom, shut the door, and stood for a moment staring at it, the key in his hand. It seemed unlikely that the crude, outmoded lock would delay any intruder long, and of course it would obstruct him when he answered—

Answered whose summons?

And why should he?

Frightened again, frightened still, he searched for another light. There was none: no reading light on the bed, no lamp on the nightstand, no floor lamp, no fixture upon any of the walls. He turned the key in the lock, and after a few seconds' thought dropped it into the topmost drawer of the dresser and picked up his book.

Abaddon. The angel of destruction dispatched by God to turn the Nile and all its waters to blood, and to kill the first-born male child in every Egyptian family. Abaddon's hand was averted from the Children of Israel, who for this purpose smeared their doorposts with the blood of the paschal lamb. This substitution has frequently been considered a foreshadowing of the sacrifice of Christ.

Am-mit, Ammit, "Devourer of the Dead." This Egyptian goddess guarded the throne of Osiris in the underworld and feasted upon the souls of those whom Osiris condemned. She had the head of a crocodile and the forelegs of a lion. The remainder of her form was that of a hippopotamus, Figure l. Am-mit's great temple at Henen-su (Herakleopolis) was destroyed by Octavian, who had its priests impaled.

An-uat, Anuat, "Lord of the Land (the Necropolis)," "Opener to the North." Though frequently confused with Anubis—

The Nebraskan laid his book aside; the overhead light was not well adapted to reading in any case. He switched it off and lay down.

Staring up into the darkness, he pondered An-uat's strange title, Opener to the North. Devourer of the Dead and Lord of the Land seemed clear enough. Or rather Lord of the Land seemed clear once Schmit explained that it referred to the necropolis. (That explanation was the source of his dream, obviously.) Why then had Schmit not explained Opener to the North? Presumably because he didn't understand it either. Well, an opener was one who went before, the first to pass in a certain direction. He (or she) made it easier for others to follow, marking trails and so on. The Nile flowed north, so Anuat might have been thought of as the god who went before the Egyptians when they left their river to sail the Mediterranean. He himself had pictured An-uat in a boat earlier, for that matter, because there was supposed to be a celestial Nile. (Was it the Milky Way?) Because he had known that the Egyptians had believed there was a divine analog to the Nile along which Ra's sun-boat journeyed. And of course the Milky Way actually was—really is in the most literal sense—the branching star-pool where the sun floats....

The jackal released the corpse it had dragged, coughed, and vomited, spewing carrion alive with worms. The Nebraskan picked up a stone fallen from one of the crumbling tombs, and flung it, striking the jackal just below the ear.

It rose upon its hind legs, and though its face remained that of a beast, its eyes were those of a man. "This is for you," it said, and pointed toward the writhing mass. "Take it, and come to me."

The Nebraskan knelt and plucked one of the worms from the reeking spew. It was pale, streaked, and splotched with scarlet, and woke in him a longing never felt before. In his mouth, it brought peace, health, love, and hunger for something he could not name.

Old Hop Thacker's voice floated across infinite distance: "Don't never shoot anythin' without you're dead sure what 'tis, young feller."

Another worm and another, and each as good as the last.

"We will teach you," the worms said, speaking from his own mouth. "Have we not come from the stars? Your own desire for them has wakened, Man of Earth."

Hop Thacker's voice: "Grave worms, do you see?"

"Come to me."

The Nebraskan took the key from the drawer. It was only necessary to open the nearest tomb. The jackal pointed to the lock.

"If it's hungered, it'll suck on a live person, an' he's bound to fight or die."

The end of the key scraped across the door, seeking the keyhole.

"Come to me, Man of Earth. Come quickly."

Sarah's voice had joined the old man's, their words mingled and confused. She screamed, and the painted figures faded from the door of the tomb.

The key turned. Thacker stepped from the tomb. Behind him his father shouted, "Joe, boy! Joe!" And struck him with his cane. Blood streamed from Thacker's torn scalp, but he did not look around.

"Fight him, young feller! You got to fight him!"

Someone switched on the light. The Nebraskan backed toward the bed.

"Pa, DON'T!" Sarah had the huge butcher knife. She lifted it higher than her father's head and brought it down. He caught her wrist, revealing a long raking cut down his back as he spun about. The knife, and Sarah, fell to the floor.

The Nebraskan grabbed Thacker's arm. "What is this!"

"It is love," Thacker told him. "That is your word, Man of Earth. It is love." No tongue showed between his parted lips; worms writhed there instead, and among the worms gleamed stars.

With all his strength, the Nebraskan drove his right fist into those lips. Thacker's head was slammed back by the blow; pain shot along the Nebraskan's arm. He swung again, with his left this time, and his wrist was caught as Sarah's had been. He tried to back away; struggled to pull free. The high old-fashioned bed blocked his legs at the knees.

Thacker bent above him, his torn lips parted and bleeding, his eyes filled with such pain as the Nebraskan had never seen. The jackal spoke: *"Open to me."*

"Yes," the Nebraskan told it. "Yes, I will." He had never known before that he possessed a soul, but he felt it rush into his throat.

Thacker's eyes rolled upward. His mouth gaped, disclosing for an instant the slime-sheathed, tentacled thing within. Half falling, half rolling, he slumped upon the bed.

For a second that felt much longer, Thacker's father stood over him with trembling hands. A step backward, and the older Mr. Thacker fell as well—fell horribly and awkwardly, his head striking the floor with a distinct crack. "Grandpa!" Sarah knelt beside him.

The Nebraskan rose. The worn brown handle of the butcher knife protruded from Thacker's back. A little blood, less than the Nebraskan would have expected, trickled down the smooth old wood to form a crimson pool on the sheet.

"Help me with him, Mr. Cooper. He's got to go to bed." The Nebraskan nodded and lifted the only living Mr. Thacker onto his feet. "How do you feel?"

"Shaky," the old man admitted. "Real shaky."

The Nebraskan put the old man's right arm about his own neck and picked him up. "I can carry him," he said. "You'll have to show me his bedroom."

"Most times Joe was just like always." The old man's voice was a whisper, as faint and far as it had been in the dream-city of the dead. "That's what you got to understand. Near all the time, an' when—when he did, they was dead, do you see? Dead or near to it. Didn't do a lot of harm."

The Nebraskan nodded.

Sarah, in a threadbare white nightgown that might have been her mother's once, was already in the hall, stumbling and racked with sobs.

"Then you come. An' Joe, he made us. Said I had to keep on talkin' an' she had to ask you fer supper."

"You told me that story to warn me," the Nebraskan said. The old man nodded feebly as they entered his bedroom . "I thought I was bein' slick. It was true, though, 'cept 'twasn't Cooper, nor Creech neither."

"I understand," the Nebraskan said. He laid the old man on his bed and pulled up a blanket.

"I kilt him didn't I? I kilt my boy Joe."

"It wasn't you, Grandpa." Sarah had found a man's bandana, no doubt in one of her grandfather's drawers; she blew her nose into it. "That's what they'll say."

The Nebraskan turned on his heel. "We've got to find that thing and kill it. I should have done that first." Before he had completed the thought, he was hurrying back toward the room that had been his.

He rolled Thacker over as far as the knife handle permitted and lifted his legs onto the bed. Thacker's jaw hung slack; his tongue and palate were thinly coated with a clear glutinous gel that carried a faint smell of ammonia; otherwise his mouth was perfectly normal.

"It's a spirit," Sarah told the Nebraskan from the doorway. "It'll go into Grandpa now, 'cause he killed it. That's what he always said."

The Nebraskan straightened up, turning to face her. "It's a living creature, something like a cuttlefish, and it came here from—" He waved the thought aside. "It doesn't really matter. It landed in North Africa, or at least I think it must have, and if I'm right, it was eaten by a jackal. They'll eat just about anything, from what I've read. It survived inside the jackal as a sort of intestinal parasite. Long ago, it transmitted itself to a man, somehow."

Sarah was looking down at her father, no longer listening. "He's restin' now, Mr. Cooper. He shot the old soul-sucker in the woods one day. That's what Grandpa tells, and he hasn't had no rest since, but he's peaceful now. I was only eight or 'bout that, and for a long time Grandpa was 'fraid he'd get me, only he never did." With both her thumbs, she drew down the lids of the dead man's eyes.

"Either it's crawled away—" the Nebraskan began.

Abruptly, Sarah dropped to her knees beside her dead parent and kissed him.

When at last the Nebraskan backed out of the room, the dead man and the living woman remained locked in that kiss, her face ecstatic, her fingers tangled in the dead man's hair. Two full days later, after the Nebraskan had crossed the Mississippi, he still saw that kiss in shadows beside the road.

ଷ ଷ

To Live and Die in Arkham

Joseph S. Pulver, Sr.

Arkham. A nice upscale college town. Just the right shops and bars and restaurants, grills, and cafes, if you have Money—a name helps too. If you don't, there's the other side of town—the side always twitching with things from the inside of Midnight. The city fathers and the police call it, The Downside. Drugs, and cheap street whores workin' the dreamless corners by pool halls and gin joints and open sewers the city fathers call abandoned buildings where the homeless hide and hungry eyes that will take your cigarettes and your wallet and your watch and your life if you can't walk fast enough or if you're a plain John Q. Citizen who is not supposed to be roamin' the cold blocks. That's the side Albert Bergin had come to. He needed something done and this was the place to find fixers and doers of just about anything, if you have the money or the juice. $200 just for the name and directions to the door. Like anyone needs them, you just follow the rot. But Professor Bergin wasn't looking for some tail or blow... He had a task that needed to be performed, he called it an old score, and for that he needed someone who knew The Game and how it's played on The Bottom.

"You want him tits-up maggot food. What'd he do? Fuck yer wife while you were at some *sin*-posium fucking your secretary in the ass?" Will laughed. His 9 didn't.

"He is in possession of an article of mine and I want it back."

"Can't blame a hound for not returnin' good pussy. Can ya, Fuckhead? She give good head?"

"I'm not married." Professor Albert Bergin sat rail straight. No smile.

"With that face and that gut I'm not surprised. They got this thing called walking nowdays. Ya might try it. Maybe you'll meet some fat bitch who wants a mercy fuck?"

"Could we skip the... *bullshit*?"

"Ah. Now yer talkin'. Get yer thing and get it back to you and kill the fuck—Just like that... *That's hard cash*. You prepared to soak me in it?"

"I have money."

"I can see that, but are you willing to part with it? Your jones itch that much?"

"If need be."

"It need be."

"How much?"

"Details, then you get the bill. If you can pay, I play. If you can't. You've wasted my expensive time and you pay in *other ways*. Or you can lay a grand on me right this fuckin' minute and blow. Pick a door, fuckhead."

"I will pay 25,000 dollars."

"You'll pay what I tell you... If I do it. And I get half upfront. Now, get on with it."

"Professor Daniel Washington..."

Will skipped his regular info gathering. Spreading around cash would be a waste with these bookworm types. He'd follow the guy for a day or two and sit outside his house and see what he did at night. Besides, once Professor Washington showed up on a slab and the cops started digging, Will's name would pop up as a person of interest if he inquired about Washington's name or the address. Better to keep this as far under the radar as he could.

All the prim and proper Miskatonic U crowd had their paper reps and little else, he figured. An old boys and ignored pussies clique, who at the end of the day wanted what everyone else wanted, they just took a deep breath and stayed hush-hush about it.

"Sinful Suzie" Jaymes, 5' 6", 109 lbs., Green/Blonde, 38D [so her doctor said after cashing her check for 10 grand]-25-36, she was a favorite of lawyers, investment suits, and bookworms. Will hit the The Treasure Chest looking for Suzie. They'd been on and off half a dozen times in the past few years and the straights really lost it for her. She came on like a librarian turned feral and if you had the cash she had the ass, many of her clients said it could start a revolution, or she had any other part your kink required.

Lap dances in your home. Blow jobs in your car. Bubble baths or spankings in hotel rooms, you pick it she pretty much did it, just so as you paid up before the ride.

Will bought her a drink and asked if either Washington or Bergin were on her dick list. Washington was a no go to both the name and the photo, but Bergin was known. Some of the girls said he was heavy handed. A real Mr. Wham-BAM!. He'd spread around some big money to cover the scars he'd left on a couple of girls.

"He's been in here sniffing around, but never looked at me. Never looked at any of the girls with big tits. Likes 'em skinny and young I hear. Your mark is a hardcore power-tripper. No fuckin', only head. You peel, dance around a little, and give. He gets. You've met the type."

Will had. Fuckin' pussy scumbags. They'd bounce a woman around—fists or whatever else was handy when they popped, but didn't have the balls to even talk hard to other men. Fit his assessment of Bergin.

He left her a C-note and told her he'd call her.

He hit the street. Time to circle the target's nest and see how to play this out.

Will got all the formal paperwork on the S. French Hill St. property of Daniel Washington from the bureaucracy first then cased the house. Two floors, open access from the back and sides, and a botanical garden's worth of trees and deep, tall scrubs all around. Almost the perfect place for a quick and quiet in and out.

1 P.M. Sunny. A model afternoon on a model street. He walked up the steps and rang the doorbell. He had his line ready should need arise. Waited. Played it casual. Looked in windows—bookcases and bookcases and bookcases. Suppressed a laugh examining the lock.

It's a wonder these idiots have indoor plumbing.

Assholes, so deep into their books and lectures and papers they didn't know how to lock up and lock down properly. Not that it really mattered, no one wanted to rob these academic types, their houses were full of books and books and books—like anyone was going to pay good money for Professor Hilary Shitfart's Memoirs of Some Dead Old Fuck From East Boring as Hell or Sir Ralph Fuckface's A Case Study of the Glories of 28 Quiet Sundays in Solitude, and art crap you couldn't pawn easily, not in New England. No expensive TVs, no DVD players, no iPods, bullshit laptops, and next to no jewelry. And tryin' to dump big heavy antiques in this part of the state was a sure fire 3 to 5, the way the Staties were all over the market. Fuck robbin' 'em, they spent their whole lives in their minds.

Tomorrow night. If he was home. If he was alone…

Will rang the bell. Daniel Washington answered. Will's gun backed the older man up.

"Sit yer fuckin' ass in that chair and don't say a word. When I ask you a question, you answer, then shut the fuck up. Got it?"

"Yes." Thin, weak, frightened as his eyes. "Good. If you move or talk you die."

Washington nodded.

Will looked around the room… He froze. There was a photograph of his mother on the mantle and one on the desk. Expensive frames. Dusted though most of the other things in the room were not.

"Where did you get the pictures?"

"I had them taken nearly thirty years ago."

"Why?"

"I was going to ask Seton to marry me."

His mother's name on the lips of this stranger. The gun was moving right to left. Finger and trigger hungry to talk.

"Keep talking."

"Do you know her?"

"I ask the fucking questions, Asshole."

"I was a student at M. U. Seton worked in the diner on Boundary near St. Mary's. We were in love."

"What happened?"

"Why are you so interested? Did you—"

"I said, *I ask the questions.*"

"There was a terrible—She died."

"I know that."

Daniel Washington looked at the man. He had her eyes. Her coloring. Could this somehow be her child?

How could he be?

"If you want to live you'll tell me everything you can about you and her. Start right fucking now."

"We were young and in love. I was a poor student working my way through my second year at M. U. We dated for almost a year. One night on her way home from work she was savagely attacked near Hangman's Hill. Beaten, raped, and horribly scarred by her attacker. I went to the hospital several times to see her, but she wouldn't see me. A nurse told me her face was horrible to look at."

Will remembered her face, and the black veil she hid it under. He'd been four, maybe five. Remembered coming out of his bedroom in the small flat and seeing her crying before the mirror. He'd screamed. She closed the bathroom door.

"Two weeks after the attack I received a letter from Seton saying telling me to leave her alone. I went to her rooming house but her landlady said she'd moved away. I couldn't find her... Back then I had very limited resources. Several years later I heard she died. That's about all I know."

Will knew the back end of her story. She scrubbed floors for a living. Drank gin straight from the bottle. And tried to never touch him. She didn't abuse him, but she couldn't stand to touch him. She didn't like to talk to him either. When he was eight she slit her wrists in the tub with a broken gin bottle and he went to the orphanage. After that he went to jail and back to jail and back to jail... From the age of eight until seventeen days after his twenty-fourth birthday he was locked up.

And sitting before him was the only link to his past he'd every met. Ever heard of. He was here for money not to face his past. Will tried to keep his nights full and avoid solitude or any point in time where his mother's ghost would sit across the table or at his elbow and watch him. It was like surf, rising, a great weight pulling him from his mental steeping stones toward... Outside. The zone of stark, lonely dunes no drug could cure, no woman could kiss away.

What the fuck is this shit?

"I said everything." The rules are simple the 9 said. "And I meant *everything.*"

A delicate, hollow blind man lost in the echo of a love song frightened to death by evil, Daniel Washington went down in the dark place of cold rain better left undisturbed.

"Back then I had nothing but her smile and my dream. She gave me so much love, made me so very happy, then they told me she was... When she wouldn't talk to me, see me, I searched for details. When you take Valentine's Day from a man he seeks redemption. For me it was in facts."

All the horror came out. Fact after fact. The ones carved in stone and the ones his heart knew but could not prove.

"I own a gun, but have never had the guts to shoot him."

"Who?"

"I can prove nothing."

"Give me the fucking name."

Daniel Washington was trying to make sense of this, but couldn't get his mind around it. All these years he'd been faithful to her memory and now this man he thought might be her son was going to kill him. How? Why?

"The fucking name."

"Albert Bergin raped her. Left her for dead."

Will tried to catch his breath. He'd sat in a room face to face with the monster that had killed his mother and sent him into the tombs.

The two men in the room were stone. Outside the world in an episode of cursed sensations. In a distant valley, naked, raped, no roof or sky, only despair... And anger. Crawling from the labyrinths of heart and mind. Claws bared. Hate sharpened and raw. Hate and claws becoming the everywhere. The red wind screamed the monster's name.

The gun lowered. Eyes choking back tears.

"I can't be completely certain it was him."

The room the contract was written in was in Will's mind. The face, he studied it and studied it. Took it apart. Something about that face. The set of the jaw. The nose... It was like... Looking in a mirror.

The gun almost slipped from his hand. Will had never known a single fact about his father until this minute. Now he knew too much.

"Look at me. Can you see him in my face? Do I look like him?"

Daniel Washington strained to see through his tears. And it was there.

"Exactly how old are you?"

Will told him. Washington's expression told him the final fact.

"Your jaw, your nose—he's your father. You're the product of—"

"Rape."

The air was almost too solid to breathe.

"Can I tell you something?"

"Sure."

"Albert Bergin and I were rivals in school. We were both studying the same subject. I was a better student and quicker. Our professors favored me. I know Bergin disliked me and was jealous... Everyone knew how in love I was. I think he raped your mother to unseat me. If I stumbled in my studies he could catch up, maybe surpass me. He destroyed her because of professional jealousy. I always knew he had a black heart, but... I can't believe I never saw this before. Guess I've always thought he was drunk or something and lost his temper."

"But why do you think it was him?"

"Once in the library he was a little drunk. He was reading the newspaper. He had this, almost triumphant, grin on his face. I don't know, the cat that ate the canary, maybe? It was pleased with itself, and evil. Cold. *It was very cold.* And I thought I heard him say, 'She should have shut up.' When he got up he left the paper and I went over and looked at the article he had been reading. It was about your mother and the rape. I should have went after him and killed him. I went to the police but they didn't believe me. A friend of his family was the investigator on the case and thought because we were rivals in school I was trying to tarnish him."

Will wanted to be out in the cool night air. Running. Running from the photos, running to someplace where he could get a drink and his bearings.

"I'm not here for the reason you think. Bergin sent me to get something and bring it to him. *And to kill you.*"

"What are you to get for him."

"A book. Faded red leather with a scorpion-like emblem on the cover."

"The Navarre. It all makes perfect sense. We both studied philosophy, religion, and metaphysics back then. Do you believe in magic or the super-natural?"

"No."

"I do. And so does Bergin. That's what we pursued in our studies."

"Ghosts and shit?"

"No. More like a little-known religious belief. There is a race of terrible beings who once savaged the universe. Somehow they were imprisoned, await-ing a time when they would be free. We tried to separate myth from fact regarding these entities. As a believer I have always sought to understand as much as I can to keep them imprisoned, if that's possible. Bergin had a jeal-ous nature and was power hungry. His lust led him to dark places and darker studies. The book he wants is said to contain rituals and spells to free these otherworldly beings."

"Like bring the things here? He wants to tear the roof off Hell and let these monsters out?"

"Yes."

"That's fucked up."

"I'm going to kill him."

"No you're not. My mother, he owes me for her. And for *my life.*"

"Then let me have some retribution too. Your gun is too merciful. I know a way."

"I'm listening."

Daniel Washington stood, he seemed dry, a faded summertime photo-graph, and walked to a bookcase. The ghost hand, now off its knees, deliber-ate, pushed a hidden button and a door opened. There sat a book and what looked like a rusty iron can.

"Take these items to him."

"Is that the book?"

"It's an exact copy. The real one is locked up."

"And that thing."

"Something he will think is one thing, but it is something entirely different."

"What does he think it is?"

"He will think it holds magical vapors which grant vision. A mage who studied the things Bergin and I have studied once said, *'Great Cthulhu sleeps in his house and shapes the dream of what shall be, dead Cthulhu waits dreaming.'* Based on an incorrect translation, Bergin believes with these vapors he'll be able to see into the dreams of this being."

"Shit's poison. Ain't it?"

"Something far worse."

"You sure he'll be dead?"

"Yes. Certain."

"What do I do?"

"Just give him this and leave."

"Huh?"

"Tell him I'm dead and give him this copy of the book—tell him it's the only one you found. Tell him as compensation you picked this up, thinking it might interest him. Tell him you saw the sigil and it being the same as the one on the cover of the book you thought they might be related in some fashion. Then leave. *Do not stay there.* You do not want to be in the house when he opens this."

"Why? Is it going to blow up?"

"Something like that."

"I'll be back."

Will rang the bell. Albert Bergin answered. Will's gun backed the older man up.

"There's your shit. Where's my money?"

The 9 was heat-soaked stone ready for blood. Bergin knew it.

"He's dead?"

"No, Fuckhead. I put him on a plane to Vegas with a blonde. Yes. Dead as yer grandmother's pussy. My money—now!"

"Of course. I just want to see the book first."

"Then look."

Bergin opened the backpack.

"This is not it."

"It's all I could find. The thing on the cover looks like you said it did. You said it was written in French. That looks like fucking French to me. And there's no fucking doubt it's old. The fucking thing's falling apart. The old fuck was crying before I shot him, said it was a copy. Look at that can-thing I grabbed while I was there."

Bergin removed the object from the bag. If a demon could be delighted with an unexpected present, his eyes said he was.

"This is… Navarre's. How? Where was this?"

"With the book. It's got the same logo thing on it as the book. Figured they went together or something. Now where's my money."

Bergin began to open the container.

"Fuck that! You ain't openin' that fucking thing while I'm here. I seen shows on TV about when they opened those old tombs in Egypt and I ain't breathin' in any old germs that would lay my ass over in Potter's Field. You can wait 'til I count my money and leave."

Bergin sat the container on his desk.

"It's all there. Count it. And leave."

Will picked up the brown manila envelope and began counting.

"We're square. You have fun with yer fuckin' shit there and forget my name and that you ever saw me." Will leveled the 9 at him. "You understand?"

"Yes."

And Will was gone.

Bergin's hands opened the vessel containing Navarre's Vapors. Coughed. His hands burned. Cold and shadows came into the room…

Tentacles of yellow/greenish curling smoke. A burnt odor. The sound of roaring fire in howling wind and a great grinding. Albert Bergin has It in his hands and It has him in its hands…

Will had been locked up in labyrinths and abysses for years and years, passed from hand to hand by creatures with demonic faces and demonic hearts of utter blackness. Cast into a life of Hell by the demonic hands of his father. Will heard a scream inside the house. Remembered the first time he'd screamed when the creatures had him in their hands…

Will remembered some bookworm in a bar once saying something about the child is the father to the man. He wasn't sure just what the guy meant by it, but he knew his take on it. "Just returning the lesson, Daddy."

The real world in slow motion. Will lit a cigarette. Starting walking away from Back. "Who says that's just the way it is? I've never hit a woman or sold dope to kids." *Never killed anybody that didn't have it coming.* "Maybe I still have options."

He took a drag off his smoke. The sun was out. He started walking toward Daniel Washington's house…

The Shallows

John Langan

Il faut cultiver notre jardin.

—Voltaire, *Candide*

"I could call you Gus," Ransom said.

The crab's legs, blue and cream, clattered against one another. It did not hoist itself from its place in the sink, though, which meant it was listening to him. Maybe. Staring out the dining room window, his daily mug of instant coffee steaming on the table in front of him, he said, "That was supposed to be my son's name. Augustus. It was his great-grandfather's name, his mother's father's father. The old man was dying while Heather was pregnant. We…I, really, was struck by the symmetry: one life ending, another beginning. It seemed a duty, our duty, to make sure the name wasn't lost, to carry it forward into a new generation. I didn't know old Gus, not really; as far as I can remember, I met him exactly once, at a party at Heather's parents' a couple of years before we were married."

The great curtain of pale light that rippled thirty yards from his house stilled. Although he had long since given up trying to work out the pattern of its changes, Ransom glanced at his watch. 2:02…pm, he was reasonably sure. The vast rectangle that occupied the space where his neighbor's green-sided house had stood, as well as everything to either side of it, dimmed, then filled with the rich blue of the tropical ocean, the paler blue of the tropical sky. Waves chased one another towards Ransom, their long swells broken by the backs of fish, sharks, whales, all rushing in the same direction as the waves, away from a spot where the surface of the ocean heaved in a way that reminded Ransom of a pot of water approaching the boil.

(Tilting his head back, Matt had said, *How far up do you think it goes? I don't know*, Ransom had answered. Twenty feet in front of them, the sheet of light that had descended an hour before, draping their view of the Pattersons' house and everything beyond it, belled, as if swept by a breeze. *This is connected to what's been happening at the poles, isn't it?* Matt had squinted to see through the dull glare. *I don't know*, Ransom had said, *maybe. Do you think the Pattersons are okay?* Matt had asked. *I hope so*, Ransom had said. He'd doubted it.)

He looked at the clumps of creamer speckling the surface of the coffee, miniature icebergs. "Gus couldn't have been that old. He'd married young, and Heather's father, Rudy, had married young, and Heather was twenty-four or -five…call him sixty-five, sixty-six, tops. To look at him, though, you would have placed him a good ten, fifteen years closer to the grave. Old… granted, I was younger, then, and from a distance of four decades, mid-sixty seemed a lot older than it does twenty years on. But even factoring in the callowness of youth, Gus was not in good shape. I doubt he'd ever been what you'd consider tall, but he was stooped, as if his head were being drawn down into his chest. Thin, frail: although the day was hot, he wore a long-sleeved checked shirt buttoned to the throat and a pair of navy chinos. His head…his hair was thinning, but what there was of it was long, and it floated around his head like the crest of some ancient bird. His nose supported a pair of horn-rimmed glasses whose lenses were white with scratches; I couldn't understand how he could see through them, or maybe that was the point. Whether he was eating from the paper plate Heather's uncle brought him or just sitting there, old Gus's lips kept moving, his tongue edging out and retreating."

The coffee was cool enough to drink. Over the rim of the mug, he watched the entire ocean churning with such force that whatever of its inhabitants had not reached safety were flung against one another. Mixed among their flailing forms were parts of creatures Ransom could not identify, a forest of black needles, a mass of rubbery pink tubes, the crested dome of what might have been a head the size of a bus.

He lowered the mug. "By the time I parked my car, Gus was seated near the garage. Heather took me by the hand and led me over to him. Those white lenses raised in my direction as she crouched beside his chair and introduced me as her boyfriend. Gus extended his right hand, which I took in mine. Hard...his palm, the undersides of his fingers, were rough with calluses, the yield of a lifetime as a mechanic. I tried to hold his hand gently...politely, I guess, but although his arm trembled, there was plenty of strength left in his fingers, which closed on mine like a trap springing shut. He said something, *Pleased to meet you, you've got a special girl, here,* words to that effect. I wasn't paying attention; I was busy with the vice tightening around my fingers, with my bones grinding against one another. Once he'd delivered his pleasantries, Gus held onto my hand a moment longer, then the lenses dropped, the fingers relaxed, and my hand was my own, again. Heather kissed him on the cheek, and we went to have a look at the food. My fingers ached on and off for the rest of the day."

At the center of the heaving ocean, something forced its way up through the waves. The peak of an undersea mountain, rising to the sun: that was still Ransom's first impression. Niagaras poured off black rock. His mind struggled to catch up with what stood revealed, to find suitable comparisons for it, even as more of it pushed the water aside. Some kind of structure—structures: domes, columns, walls—a city, an Atlantis finding the sun, again. No—the shapes were off: the domes bulged, the columns bent, the walls curved, in ways that conformed to no architectural style—that made no sense. A natural formation, then, a quirk of geology. No—already, the hypothesis was untenable: there was too much evidence of intentionality in the shapes draped with seaweed, heaped with fish brought suffocating into the air. As the rest of the island left the ocean, filling the view before Ransom to the point it threatened to burst out of the curtain, the appearance of an enormous monolith in the foreground, its surface incised with pictographs, settled the matter. This huge jumble of forms, some of which appeared to contradict one another, to intersect in ways the eye could not untangle, to occupy almost the same space at the same time, was deliberate.

Ransom slid his chair back from the table and stood. The crab's legs dinged on the stainless steel sink. Picking up his mug, he turned away from the window. "That was the extent of my interactions with Gus. To be honest, what I knew of him, what Heather had told me, I didn't much care for. He was what I guess you'd call a functioning alcoholic, although the way he functioned... he was a whiskey-drinker, Jack Daniel's, Jim Beam, Maker's Mark, that end of the shelf. I can't claim a lot of experience, but from what I've seen, sour mash shortcuts to your mean, your nasty side. That was the case with Gus, at least. It wasn't so much that he used his hands—he did, and I gather the hearing in Rudy's left ear was the worse for it—no, the whiskey unlocked the cage that held all of Gus's resentment, his bitterness, his jealousy. Apparently, when he was younger, Rudy's little brother, Jan, had liked helping their mother in the kitchen. He'd been something of a baker, Jan; Rudy claimed he made the best chocolate cake you ever tasted, frosted it with buttercream. His mother used to let him out of working with his father in the garage or around the yard so he could assist her with the meals. None of the other kids—there were six of them—was too thrilled at there being one less of them to dilute their father's attention, especially when they saw Gus's lips tighten as he realized Jan had stayed inside again.

"Anyway, this one night, Gus wandered into the house after spending the better part of the evening in the garage. He passed most of the hours after he returned from work fixing his friends' and acquaintances' cars, Hank Williams on the transistor radio, Jack Daniel's in one of the kids' juice glasses. In he comes, wiping the grease off his hands with a dishtowel, and what should greet his eyes when he peers into the refrigerator in search of a little supper but the golden top of the cherry pie Jan made for the church bake sale the next day? Gus loves cherry pie. Without a second thought, he lifts the pie from the top shelf of the fridge and deposits it on the kitchen table. He digs his clasp-knife out of his pants-pocket, opens it, and cuts himself a generous slice. He doesn't bother with a fork; instead, he shoves his fingers under the crust and lifts the piece straight to his mouth. It's so tasty, he helps himself to a second, larger serving before he's finished the first. In his eagerness, he slices through the pie tin to the table. He doesn't care; he leaves the knife stuck where it is and uses his other hand to free the piece.

"That's how Jan finds him when he walks into the kitchen for a glass of milk, a wedge of cherry pie in one hand, red syrup and yellow crumbs smeared on his other hand, his mouth and chin. By this age—Jan's around twelve, thirteen—the boy has long-since learned that the safest way, the only way, to meet the outrages that accompany his father's drinking is calmly, impassively. Give him the excuse to garnish his injury with insult, and he'll take it.

"And yet, this is exactly what Jan does. He can't help himself, maybe. He lets his response to the sight of Gus standing with his mouth stuffed with half-chewed pie flash across his face. It's all the provocation his father requires. *What?* he says, crumbs spraying from his mouth.

"*Nothing*, Jan says, but he's too late. Gus drops the slice he's holding to the floor, scoops the rest of the pie from the tin with his free hand, and slaps that to the floor, as well. He raises one foot and stamps on the mess he's made, spreading it across the linoleum. Jan knows enough to remain where he is. Gus brings his shoe down on the ruin of Jan's efforts twice more, then wipes his hands on his pants, frees his knife from the table, and folds it closed. As he returns it to his pocket, he tells Jan that if he wants to be a little faggot and wear an apron in the kitchen, that's his concern, but he'd best keep his little faggot mouth shut when there's a man around, particularly when that man's his father. Does Jan understand him?

"*Yes, pa*, Jan says.

"*Then take your little faggot ass off to bed*, Gus says.

"What happened next," Ransom said, "wasn't a surprise; in fact, it was depressingly predictable." He walked into the kitchen, deposited his mug on the counter. "That was the end of Jan's time in the kitchen. He wasn't the first one outside to help his father, but he wasn't the last, either, and he worked hard. The morning of his eighteenth birthday, he enlisted in the Marines; within a couple of months, he was on patrol in Vietnam. He was cited for bravery on several occasions; I think he may have been awarded a medal. One afternoon, when his squad stopped for a rest, he was shot through the head by a sniper. He'd removed his helmet...to tell the truth, I'm not sure why he had his helmet off. He survived, but it goes without saying, he was never the same. His problems...he had trouble moving, coordinating his arms and legs. His speech was slurred; he couldn't remember the names of familiar objects, activities; he forgot something the second after you said it to him. There was no way he could live on his own. His mother wanted Jan to move back home, but Gus refused, said there was no way he was going to be saddled with an idiot who hadn't known enough to keep his damn helmet on. Which didn't stop him from accepting the drinks he was bought when Jan visited and Gus paraded him at the V.F.W.."

Behind him, a pair of doors would be opening on the front of a squat stone box near the island's peak. The structure, whose rough exterior suggested a child's drawing of a Greek temple, must be the size of a cathedral, yet it was dwarfed by what squeezed out of its open doors. While Ransom continued to have trouble with the sheer size of the thing, which seemed as if it must break a textbook's worth of physical laws, he was more bothered by its speed. There should have been no way, he was certain, for something of that mass to move that quickly. Given the thing's appearance, the tumult of coils wreathing its head, the scales shimmering on its arms, its legs, the wings that unfolded into great translucent fans whose edges were not quite in focus, its speed was hardly the most obvious detail on which to focus, but for Ransom, the dearth of time between the first hint of the thing's shadow on the doors and its heaving off the ground on a hurricane-blast of its wings confirmed the extent to which the world had changed.

(*What was that?* Matt had screamed, his eyes wide. *Was that real? Is that happening?* Ransom had been unable to speak, his tongue dead in his mouth.)

Like so many cranes raising and lowering, the cluster of smaller limbs that rose from the center of the crab's back was opening and closing. Ransom said, "I know: if the guy was such a shit, why pass his name on to my son?" He shrugged. "When I was younger—at that point in my life, the idea of the past…of a family's past, of continuity between the present and that past, was very important to me. By the time Heather was pregnant, the worst of Gus's offenses was years gone by. If you wanted, I suppose you could say that he was paying for his previous excesses. He hadn't taken notice of his diabetes for decades. If the toes on his right foot hadn't turned black, then started to smell, I doubt he ever would have returned to the doctor. Although…what that visit brought him was the emergency amputation of his toes, followed by the removal of his foot a couple of weeks later. The surgeon wanted to take his leg, said the only way to beat the gangrene that was eating Gus was to leap ahead of it. Gus refused, declared he could see where he was headed, and he wasn't going to be jointed like a chicken on the way. There was no arguing with him. His regular doctor prescribed some heavy-duty antibiotics for him, but I'm not sure he had the script filled.

"When he returned home, everyone said it was to die—which it was, of course, but I think we all expected him to be gone in a matter of days. He hung on, though, for one week, and the next, and the one after that. Heather and her mother visited him. I was at work. She said the house smelled like spoiled meat; it was so bad, she couldn't stay in for more than a couple of minutes, barely long enough to stand beside Gus's bed and kiss his cheek. His lips moved, but she couldn't understand him. She spent the rest of the visit outside, in her mother's truck, listening to the radio."

Ransom glanced out the window. The huge sheet of light rippled like an aurora, the image of the island and its cargo gone. He said, "Gus died the week after Heather's visit. To tell the truth, I half-expected him to last until the baby arrived. Heather went to the wake and the funeral; I had to work. As it turned out, we settled on Matthew—Matt, instead."

His break was over. Ransom exited the kitchen, turned down the hallway to the front door. On the walls to either side of him, photos of himself and his family, his son, smiled at photographers' prompts years forgotten. He peered out one of the narrow windows that flanked the door. The rocking chair he'd left on the front porch in a Quixotic gesture stood motionless. Across the street, the charred mound that sat inside the burned-out remains of his neighbor's house appeared quiet. Ransom reached for the six-foot pole that leaned against the corner opposite him. Careful to check that the butcher knife duct-taped to the top was secure, he gripped the improvised spear near the tape and unlocked the door. Leveling the weapon, he stepped back as the door swung in.

In two months of maintaining the ritual every time he opened any of the doors into the house, Ransom had yet to be met by anything. The precaution was one on which his son had insisted; the day of his departure north, Matt had pledged Ransom to maintaining it. With no intention of doing so, Ransom had agreed, only to find himself repeating the familiar motions the next time he was about to venture out to the garden. Now here he was, jabbing the end of the spear through the doorway to draw movement, waiting a count of ten, then advancing one slow step at a time, careful not to miss anything dangling from the underside of the porch roof. Once he was satisfied that the porch was clear, that nothing was lurking in the bush to its right, he called over his shoulder, "I'm on my way to check the garden, if you'd like to join me."

A chorus of ringing announced the crab's extricating itself from the sink. Legs clicking on the wood floors like so many tap shoes, it hurried along the hall and out beside him. Keeping the spear straight ahead, he reached back for one of the canvas bags piled inside the door, then pulled the door shut. The crab raced down the stairs and to the right, around the strip of lawn in front of the house. Watching its long legs spindle made the coffee churn at the back of his throat. He followed it off the porch.

Although he told himself that he had no desire to stare at the remnants of his neighbor, Adam's, house—it was a distraction; it was ghoulish; it was not good for his mental health—Ransom was unable to keep his eyes from it. All that was left of the structure were fire-blackened fragments of the walls that had stood at the house's northeast and southwest corners. Had Ransom not spent ten years living across the road from the white, two-storey colonial whose lawn had been chronically overgrown—to the point he and Heather had spoken of it as their own little piece of the rainforest—he could not have guessed the details of the building the fire had consumed. While he was no expert at such matters, he had been surprised that the flames had taken so much of Adam's house; even without the fire department to douse it, Ransom had the sense that the blaze should not have consumed this much of it. No doubt, the extent of the destruction owed something to the architects of the shape the house's destruction had revealed.

(*There's something in Adam's house*, Matt had said. The eyes of the ten men and woman crowded around the kitchen table did not look at him. *They've been there since before…everything. Before the Fracture. I've heard them moving around outside, in the trees. We have to do something about them.*)

About a month after they had moved into their house, some ten years ago, Ransom had discovered a wasps' nest clinging to a light on the far side of the garage. Had it been only himself, even himself and Heather, living there, he would have been tempted to live and let live. However, with an eight year old factored into the equation, one whose curiosity was recorded in the constellations of scars up his arms and down his legs, there was no choice. Ransom called the exterminator and the next day, the nest was still. He waited the three days the woman recommended, then removed the nest by unscrewing the frosted glass jar to which it was anchored. He estimated the side stoop the sunniest part of the property; he placed the nest there to dry out. His decision had not pleased Heather, who was concerned at poison-resistant wasps emerging enraged at the attack on their home, but after a week's watch brought no super wasps, he considered it reasonable to examine it with Matt. It was the first time he had been this near to a nest, and he had been fascinated by it, the grey, papery material that covered it in strips wound up and to the right. Slicing it across the equator had disclosed a matrix of cells, a little less than half of them chambering larvae, and a host of motionless wasps. Every detail of the nest, he was aware, owed itself to some physiological necessity, evolutionary advantage, but he'd found it difficult to shake the impression that he was observing the result of an alien intelligence, an alien aesthetics, at work.

That same sensation, taken to a power of ten, gripped him at the sight of the structure that had hidden inside Adam's house. Its shape reminded him of that long-ago wasps' nest, only inverted, an irregular dome composed not of grey pulp but a porous substance whose texture suggested sponge. Where it was not charred black, its surface was dark umber. Unlike the house in which it had grown up, Ransom thought that the fire that had scoured this dwelling should have inflicted more damage on it, collapsed it. In spots, the reddish surface of the mound had cracked to reveal a darker substance beneath, something that trembled in the light like mercury. Perhaps this was the reason the place was still standing. What had been the overgrown yard was dirt baked and burnt brittle by the succession of fires. At half a dozen points around the yard, the large shells of what might have been lobsters—had each of those lobsters stood the size of a small pony—lay broken, split wide, the handles of axes, shovels, picks spouting from them.

(Matt had been so excited, his cheeks flushed in that way that made his eyes glow. The left sleeve of his leather jacket, of the sweatshirt underneath it, had been sliced open, the skin below cut from wrist to shoulder by a claw the size of a tennis racket. He hadn't cared, had barely noticed as Ransom had washed the wound, inspected it for any of the fluid [blood?] that had spattered the jacket, and wrapped it in gauze. Outside, whoops and hollers of celebration had filled the morning air. *You should have come with us*, Matt had said, the remark less a reproach and more an expression of regret for a missed opportunity. *My plan worked. They never saw us coming. You should have been there.* Despite the anxiety that had yet to drain from him, pride had swelled Ransom's chest. Maybe everything wasn't lost. Maybe his son... *Yes, well*, Ransom had said, *someone has to be around to pick up the pieces.*)

Ransom continued around the front lawn to what they had called the side yard, a wide slope of grass that stretched from the road up to the treeline of the rise behind the house. If the wreckage across the street was difficult to ignore, what lay beyond the edge of the yard compelled his attention. Everything that had extended north of the house: his next door neighbor, Dan's red house and barn, the volunteer fire station across from it, the houses that had continued on up both sides of the road to Wiltwyck, was gone, as was the very ground on which all of it had been built. As far ahead as Ransom could see, to either side, the earth had been scraped to bare rock, the dull surface of which bore hundred-yard gouges. Somewhere beyond his ability to guesstimate, planes of light like the one on the other side of his house occulted the horizon. Ransom could not decide how many there were. Some days he thought at least four, staggered one behind the other; others he was certain there was only the one whose undulations produced the illusion of more. Far off as the aurora(e) was, its sheer size made the figures that occasionally filled it visible. These he found it easier to disregard, especially when, as today, they were familiar: a quartet of tall stones at the top of a rounded mountain, one apparently fallen over, the remaining three set at irregular distances from one another, enough to suggest that their proximity might be no more than a fluke of geology; from within the arrangement, as if stepping down into it, an eye the size of a barn door peered and began to push out of. Instead, he focused on the garden into which he, Matt, and a few of his neighbors had tilled the side yard.

While Ransom judged the crab capable of leaping the dry moat and clambering up the wire fence around the garden, it preferred to wait for him to set the plank over the trench, cross it, and unlock the front gate. Only then would it scuttle around him, up the rows of carrots and broccoli, the tomatoes caged in their conical frames, stopping on its rounds to inspect a leaf here, a stalk there, tilting its shell forward so that one of the limbs centered in its back could extend and take the object of its scrutiny in its claw. In general, Ransom attributed the crab's study to simple curiosity, but there were moments he fancied that, prior to its arrival in his front yard the morning after Matt's departure, in whatever strange place it had called home, the crab had tended a garden of its own.

Latching but not locking the gate behind him, Ransom said, "What about

Bruce? That was what we called our dog…the only dog we ever had. Heather picked out the name. She was a huge Springsteen fan. The dog didn't look like a Bruce, not in the slightest. He was some kind of weird mix, Great Dane and Greyhound, something like that. His body…it was as if the front of one dog had been sewed to the back of another. He had this enormous head—heavy jowls, brow, huge jaws—and these thick front legs, attached to a skinny trunk, back legs like pipe cleaners. His tail—I don't know where that came from. It was so long it hung down almost to his feet. I kept expecting him to tip over, fall on his face. I wanted to call him Butch, that or something classical, Cerberus. Heather and Matt overruled me. Matt was all in favor of calling him Super Destroyer, or Fire Teeth, but Heather and I vetoed those. Somehow, this meant she got the final decision, and Bruce it was."

The beer traps next to the lettuce were full of the large red slugs that had appeared in the last week. One near the top was still moving, swimming lazily around the PBR, the vent along its back expanding and contracting like a mouth attempting to speak. The traps could wait another day before emptying; he would have to remember to bring another can of beer with him, tomorrow. He said, "Heather found the dog wandering in the road out front. He was in pretty rough shape: his coat was caked with dirt, rubbed raw in places; he was so thin, you could've used his ribs as a toast rack. Heather was a sucker for any kind of hard case; she said it was why she'd gone out with me, in the first place. Very funny, right? By the time Matt stepped off the schoolbus, she'd lured the dog inside with a plateful of chicken scraps (which he devoured), coaxed him into the downstairs shower (after which, she said, he looked positively skeletal), and heaped a couple of old blankets into a bed for him. She tried to convince him to lie down there, and he did subject the blankets to extensive sniffing, but he refused to allow Heather out of his sight. She was…at that point, she tired easily—to be honest, it was pretty remarkable that she'd been able to do everything she had—so she went out to the front porch to rest on the rocking chair and wait for Matt's bus. When she did, the dog—Bruce, I might as well call him that; she'd already settled on the name—Bruce insisted on accompanying her. He plopped down beside her, and remained there until Matt was climbing the front steps. I would have been worried…concerned about how Bruce would react to Matt, whether he'd be jealous of Heather, that kind of thing. Not my wife: when Matt reached the top of the stairs, the dog stood, but that was all. Heather didn't have to speak to him, let alone grab his collar."

The lettuces weren't ready to pick, nor were the cabbages or broccoli. A few tomatoes, however, were sufficiently red to merit plucking from the plants and dropping into the canvas bag. The crab was roaming the top of the garden, where they'd planted Dan's apple trees. Ransom glanced over the last of the tomatoes, checked the frames. "That collar," he said. "It was the first thing I noticed about the dog. Okay, maybe not the first, but it wasn't too long before it caught my eye. This was after Matt had met me in the driveway with the news that we had a guest. The look on his face…he had always been a moody kid—Heather and I used to ask one another, *How's the weather in Mattsville?*—and adolescence, its spiking hormones, had not improved his temperament. In all fairness, Heather being sick didn't help matters, any. This night, though, he was positively beaming, vibrating with nervous energy. When I saw him running up to the car, my heart jumped. I couldn't conceive any reason for him to rush out the side door that wasn't bad: at the very best, an argument with his mother over some school-related issue; at the very worst, another ambulance ride to the hospital for Heather."

A blue centipede the size of his hand trundled across the dirt in front of him. He considered spearing it, couldn't remember if it controlled any of the other species in the garden. Better to err on the side of caution—even now. He stepped over it, moved on to the beans. He said, "Matt refused to answer any of my questions; all he would say was, *You'll see.* It had been a long day at work; my patience was frayed to a couple of threads and they weren't looking any too strong. I was on the verge of snapping at him, telling him to cut the crap, grow up, but something, that grin, maybe, made me hold my tongue. And once I was inside, there was Heather sitting on the couch, the dog sprawled out beside her, his head in her lap. He didn't so much as open an eye to me.

"For the life of me, I could not figure out how Heather had gotten him. I assumed she had been to the pound, but we owned only the one car, which I'd had at work all day. She took the longest time telling me where the dog had come from. I had to keep guessing, and didn't Matt think that was the funniest thing ever? It was kind of funny…my explanations grew increasingly bizarre, fanciful. Someone had delivered the dog in a steamer trunk. Heather had discovered him living in one of the trees out front. He'd been packed away in the attic. I think she and Matt wanted to hear my next story."

Ransom had forgotten the name of the beans they had planted. Not green beans: these grew in dark purple; although Dan had assured him that they turned green once you cooked them. The beans had come in big, which Dan had predicted: each was easily six, seven inches long. Of the twenty-five or thirty that were ready to pick, however, four had split at the bottom, burst by gelid, inky coils that hung down as long again as the bean. The ends of the coils raised towards him, unfolding petals lined with tiny teeth.

"Shit." He stepped back, lowering the spear. The coils swayed from side to side, their petals opening further. He studied their stalks. All four sprang from the same plant. He swept the blade of the spear through the beans dangling from the plants to either side of the affected one. They dinged faintly on the metal. The rest of the crop appeared untouched; that was something. He adjusted the canvas bag onto his shoulder. Taking the spear in both hands, he set the edge of the blade against the middle plant's stem. His first cut drew viscous green liquid and the smell of spoiled eggs. While he sawed, the coils whipped this way and that, and another three beans shook frantically. The stem severed, he used the spear to loosen the plant from its wire supports, then to carry it to the compost pile at the top of the garden, in the corner opposite the apple trees. There was lighter fluid left in the bottle beside the fence; the dark coils continued to writhe as he sprayed them with it. The plant was too green to burn well, but Ransom reckoned the application of fire to it, however briefly, couldn't hurt. He reached in his shirt pocket for the matches. The lighter fluid flared with a satisfying *whump*.

The crab was circling the apple trees. Eyes on the leaves curling in the flames, Ransom said, "By the time Heather finally told me how Bruce had arrived at the house, I'd been won over. Honestly, within a couple of minutes of watching her sitting there with the dog, I was ready for him to move in. Not because I was such a great dog person—I'd grown up with cats, and if I'd been inclined to adopt a pet, a kitten would have been my first choice. Heather was the one who'd been raised with a houseful of dogs. No, what decided me in Bruce's favor was Heather, her...demeanor, I suppose. You could see it in the way she was seated. She didn't look as if she were holding herself as still as possible, as if someone were pressing a knife against the small of her back. She wasn't relaxed—that would be an overstatement—but she was calmer.

"The change in Matt didn't hurt, either." Ransom squeezed another jet of lighter fluid onto the fire, which leapt up in response. The gelid coils thrashed as if trying to tear themselves free of the plant. "How long had that boy wanted a dog...By now, we'd settled into a routine with Heather's meds, her doctors' visits—it had settled onto us, more like. I think we knew...I wouldn't say we had given up hope; Heather's latest tests had returned better than expected results. But we—the three of us were in a place we had been in for a long time and didn't know when we were going to get out of. A dog was refreshing, new."

With liquid pops, the four coils burst one after the other. The trio of suspect beans followed close behind. "That collar, though..." Bringing the lighter fluid with him, Ransom left the fire for the spot where the affected plant had been rooted. Emerald fluid thick as honey topped the stump, slid down its sides in slow fingers. He should dig it out, he knew, and probably the plants to either side of it, for good measure, but without the protection of a pair of gloves, he was reluctant to expose his bare skin to it. He reversed the spear and drove its point into the stump. Leaving the blade in, he twisted the handle around to widen the cut, then poured lighter fluid into and around it. He wasn't about to risk dropping a match over here, but he guessed the accelerant should, at a minimum, prove sufficiently toxic to hinder the plant from regrowing until he could return suitably protected and with a shovel.

There was still the question of whether to harvest the plants to either side. Fresh vegetables would be nice, but prudence was the rule of the day. Before they'd set out for the polar city with Matt, his neighbors had moved their various stores to his basement, for safe keeping; it wasn't as if he were going to run out of canned food anytime soon. Ransom withdrew the spear and returned to the compost, where the fire had not yet subsided. Its business with the apple trees completed, the crab crouched at a safe remove from the flames. Ransom said, "It was a new collar, this blue, fibrous stuff, and there was a round metal tag hanging from it. The tag was incised with a name, 'Noble,' and a number to call in case this dog was found. It was a Wiltwyck number. I said, *What about the owner? Shouldn't we call them?*

"Heather must have been preparing her answer all day, from the moment she read the tag. *Do you see the condition this animal is in?* she said. *Either his owner is dead, or they don't deserve him.* As far as Heather was concerned, that was that. I didn't argue, but shortly thereafter, I unbuckled the collar and threw it in a drawer in the laundry room. Given Bruce's state, I didn't imagine his owner would be sorry to find him gone, but you never know.

"For five days, Bruce lived with us. We took turns walking him. Matt actually woke up half an hour early to take him out for his morning stroll, then Heather gave him a shorter walk around lunchtime, then I took him for another long wander before bed. The dog tolerated me well enough, but he loved Matt, who couldn't spend enough time with him. And Heather...except for his walks, he couldn't bear to be away from her; even when we had passed a slow half-hour making our way up Main Street, Bruce diligently investigating the borders of the lawns on the way, there would come a moment he would decide it was time to return to Heather, and he would leave whatever he'd had his nose in and turn home, tugging me along behind him. Once we were inside and I had his leash off, he would bolt for wherever Heather was—usually in bed, asleep—and settle next to her."

He snapped the lighter fluid's cap shut and replaced it beside the fence. The crab sidled away along the rows of carrots and potatoes on the other side of the beans and tomatoes. Ransom watched it examine the feathery green tops of the carrots, prod the potato blossoms. It would be another couple of weeks until they were ready to unearth; though after what had happened to the beans, a quick check was in order. "On the morning of the sixth day, Bruce's owner arrived, came walking up the street the same way his dog had. William Harrow: that was the way he introduced himself. It was a Saturday. I was cooking brunch; Matt was watching TV; Heather was sitting on the front porch, reading. Of course, Bruce was with her. September was a couple of weeks old, but summer was slow in leaving. The sky was clear, the air was warm, and I was thinking that maybe I'd load the four of us into the car and drive up to the Reservoir for an afternoon out."

On the far side of the house, the near curtain of light, on which he had watched the sunken island rise for the twentieth, the thirtieth time, settled, dimmed. With the slow spiral of food coloring dropped into water, dark pink and burnt orange spread across its upper reaches, a gaudy sunset display that was as close as the actual sky came to night, anymore. A broad concrete rectangle took up the image's lower half. At its other end, the plane was bordered by four giant steel and glass boxes, each one open at the top. To the right, a single skyscraper was crowned by an enormous shape whose margins hung over and partway down its upper storeys. Something about the form, a handful of scattered details, suggested an impossibly large toad.

The first time Ransom had viewed this particular scene, a couple of weeks after Matt and their neighbors had embarked north, a couple of days after he had awakened to the greater part of Main Street and its houses gone, scoured to gray rock, he had not recognized its location. *The polar city?* Only once it was over and he was seated on the couch, unable to process what he had been shown, did he think, *That was Albany. The Empire State Plaza. Those weren't boxes: they were the bases of the office buildings that stood there. Fifty miles. That's as far as they got.*

He was close enough to the house for its silhouette to block most of the three figures who ran onto the bottom of the screen, one to collapse onto his hands and knees, another to drop his shotgun and tug a revolver out of his belt, the third to use his good hand to drag the blade of his hatchet against his jeans' leg. The crab paid no more attention to the aurora's display than it ever did; it was occupied withdrawing one of the red slugs from a beer trap. Ransom cleared his throat. "Heather said she never noticed William Harrow until his work boots were clomping on the front stairs. She looked up from her book, and there was this guy climbing to meet her. He must have been around our age, which is to say, late thirties. Tall, thin, not especially remarkable looking one way or the other. Beard, mustache…when I saw the guy, he struck me as guarded; to be fair, that could have been because he and Heather were already pretty far into a heated exchange. At the sound of the guy's feet on the stairs, Bruce had stood; by the time I joined the conversation, the dog was trembling.

"The first words out of Harrow's mouth were, *That's my dog.* Maybe things would have proceeded along a different course…maybe we could have reached, I don't know, some kind of agreement with the guy, if Heather hadn't said, *Oh? Prove it.* Because he did; he said, *Noble, sit,* and Bruce did exactly that. *There you go,* Harrow said. I might have argued that that didn't prove anything, that we had trained the dog to sit, ourselves, and it was the command he was responding to, not the name, but Heather saw no point in ducking the issue. She said, *Do you know what shape this animal was in when we found him? Were you responsible for that?* and the mercury plummeted.

"Matt came for me in the kitchen. He said, *Mom's arguing with some guy. I think he might be Bruce's owner.*

"*All right,* I said, *hold on.* I turned off the burners under the scrambled eggs and home fries. As I was untying my apron, Matt said, *Is he gonna take Bruce with him?*

"*Of course not,* I said.

"But I could see…as soon as I understood the situation, I knew Bruce's time with us was over, felt the same lightness high in the chest I'd known sitting in the doctor's office with Heather a year and half before, that seems to be my body's reaction to bad news. It was…when Matt—when I…"

From either end of the plaza, from between two of the truncated buildings on its far side, what might have been torrents of black water rushed onto and over the concrete. There was no way for the streams to have been water: each would have required a hose the width of a train, pumps the size of houses, a score of workers to operate it, but the way they surged towards the trio occluded by the house suggested a river set loose from its banks and given free rein to speed across the land. The color of spent motor oil, they moved so fast that the objects studding their lengths were almost impossible to distinguish; after his initial viewing, it took Ransom another two before he realized that they were eyes, that each black tumult was the setting for a host of eyes, eyes of all sizes, shapes, and colors, eyes defining strange constellations. He had no similar trouble identifying the mouths into which the streams opened, tunnels gated by great cracked and jagged teeth.

Ransom said, "Heather's approach…you might say that she combined shame with the threat of legal action. Harrow was impervious to both. As far as he was concerned, the dog looked fine, and he was the registered owner, so there was nothing to be worried about. *Of course he looks good,* Heather said, *he's been getting fed!*

"If the dog had been in such awful shape, Harrow wanted to know, then how had he come all the way from his home up here? That didn't sound like a trip an animal as severely-abused as Heather was claiming could make.

"He was trying to get as far away as he could, she said. Had he been in better condition, he probably wouldn't have stopped here.

"This was getting us nowhere—had gotten us nowhere. *Look*, I said. *Mr. Harrow. My family and I have become awfully attached to this dog. I understand that you've probably spent quite a bit on him. I would be willing to reimburse you for that, in addition to whatever you think is fair for the dog.* Here I was, pretty much offering the guy a blank check. Money, right? It may be the root of all evil, but it's solved more than a few problems.

"William Harrow, though…he refused my offer straight away. Maybe he thought I was patronizing him. Maybe he was trying to prove a point. I didn't know what else to do. We could have stood our ground, insisted we were keeping Bruce, but if he had the law on his side, then we would only be delaying the inevitable. He could call the cops on us, the prospect of which made me queasy. As for escalating the situation, trying to get tough with him, intimidate him…that wasn't me. I mean, really."

With the house in the way, Ransom didn't have to watch as the trio of dark torrents converged on the trio of men. He didn't have to see the man who had not risen from his hands and knees scooped into a mouth that did not close so much as constrict. He didn't have to see the man with the pistol empty it into the teeth that bit him in half. And he did not have to watch again as the third figure—he should call him a man; he had earned it—sidestepped the bite aimed at him and slashed a groove in the rubbery skin that caused the behemoth to veer away from him. He did not have to see the hatchet, raised for a second strike, spin off into the air, along with the hand that gripped it and most of the accompanying arm, as the mouth that had taken the man with the pistol sliced away the rest of the third man. Ransom did not have to see any of it.

(At the last moment, even though Ransom had sworn to himself he wouldn't, he had pleaded with Matt not to leave. *You could help me with the garden,* he had said. *You'll manage,* Matt had answered. *Who will I talk to?* Ransom had asked. *Who will I tell things to? Write it all down,* Matt had said, *for when we get back.* His throat tight with dread, Ransom had said, *You don't know what they'll do to you.* Matt had not argued with him.)

Its rounds of the garden completed, the crab was waiting at the gate. Ransom prodded the top of a carrot with the blunt end of the spear. "I want to say," he said, "that, had Heather been in better health, she would have gone toe-to-toe with Harrow herself... weak as she was, she was ready to take a swing at him. To be on the safe side, I stepped between them. *All right*, I said. *If that's what you want to do, then I guess there isn't any more to say.* I gestured at Bruce, who had returned to his feet. From his jeans pocket, Harrow withdrew another blue collar and a short lead. Bruce saw them, and it was like he understood what had happened. The holiday was over; it was back to the place he'd tried to escape. Head lowered, he crossed the porch to Harrow.

"I don't know if Harrow intended to say anything else, but Heather did. Before he started down the stairs with Bruce, Heather said, *Just remember, William Harrow: I know your name. It won't be any difficulty finding out where you live, where you're taking that dog. I'm making it my duty to watch you—I'm going to watch you like a hawk, and the first hint I see that you aren't treating that dog right, I am going to bring the cops down on you like a hammer. You look at me and tell me I'm lying.*

"He did look at her. His lip trembled; I was sure he was going to speak, answer her threat with one of his own...warn her that he shot trespassers, something like that, but he left without another word.

"Of course Heather went inside to track down his address right away. He lived off Main Street, on Farrell Drive, a cul-de-sac about a quarter of a mile that way." Ransom nodded towards the stone expanse. "Heather was all for walking up there after him, as was Matt, who had eavesdropped on our confrontation with Harrow from inside the front door. The expression on his face...It was all I could do to persuade the two of them that chasing Harrow would only antagonize him, which wouldn't be good for Bruce, would it? They agreed to wait a day, during which time neither spoke to me more than was absolutely necessary. As it turned out, though, Heather was feeling worse the next day, and then the day after that was Monday and I had work and Matt had school, so it wasn't until Monday evening that we were able to visit Farrell Drive. To be honest, I didn't think there'd be anything for us to see.

"I was wrong. William Harrow lived in a raised ranch set back about fifty yards from the road, at the top of a slight hill. Ten feet into his lawn, there was a cage, a wood frame walled and ceilinged with heavy wire mesh. It was maybe six feet high by twelve feet long by six feet deep. There was a large dog house at one end with a food and water dish beside it. The whole thing... everything was brand new. The serial numbers stenciled on the wood beams were dark and distinct; the mesh was bright; the dog house—the dog house was made out of some kind of heavy plastic, and it was shiny. Lying half-in the dog house was Bruce, who, when he heard us pull up, raised his head, then the rest of himself, and trotted over to the side of the cage, his tongue hanging out, his tail wagging.

"Heather and Matt were desperate to rush out of the car, but none of us could avoid the signs, also new, that lined the edge of the property: NO TRESPASSING, day-glo orange on a black background. Matt was all for ignoring them, a sentiment for which Heather had not a little sympathy. But—and I tried to explain this to the two of them—if we were going to have any hope of freeing Bruce, we had to be above reproach. If there were a record of Harrow having called the police on us, it would make our reporting him to the cops appear so much payback. Neither of them was happy, but they had to agree, what I was saying made sense.

"All the same, the second we were back home, Heather had the phone in her hand. The cop she talked to was pretty agreeable, although she cautioned Heather that as long as the dog wasn't being obviously maltreated, there wasn't anything that could be done. The cop agreed to drive along Farrell the next time she was on patrol, and Heather thanked her for the offer. When she hung up the phone, though, her face showed how satisfied she was with our local law enforcement."

Beyond the house, the scene at the Empire State Plaza had faded to pale light. Finished checking the carrots and potatoes, Ransom crossed to the gate. The crab backed up to allow him to unlatch and swing it in. As the crab hurried out, he gave the garden a final look over, searching for anything he might have missed. Although he did not linger on the apple trees, they appeared quiet.

On the way back around the yard, the crab kept pace with him. Ransom said, "For the next month, Heather walked to Farrell Drive once a day, twice when she was well enough. During that time, Bruce did not leave his cage. Sometimes, she would find him racing around the place, growling. Other times, he would be leaping up against one wall of the pen and using it to flip himself over. As often as not, he would be lying half-in the doghouse, his head on his paws. That she could tell—and believe you me, she studied that dog, his cage, as if his life depended on it (which, as far as she was concerned, it did)—Harrow kept the pen tidy and Bruce's dishes full. While she was careful not to set foot on the property, she stood beside it for half an hour, forty-five minutes, an hour. One afternoon, she left our house after lunch and did not return till dinner. When Bruce heard her footsteps, he would stop whatever he was doing, run to the nearest corner of the cage, and stand there wagging his tail. He would voice a series of low barks that Heather said sounded as if he were telling her something, updating the situation. *No change. Still here.*

"She saw Harrow only once. It was during the third-to-last visit she made to Bruce. After a few minutes of standing at the edge of the road, talking to the dog, she noticed a figure in the ranch's doorway. She tensed, ready for him to storm out to her, but he remained where he was. So did Heather. If this guy thought he could scare her, he had another thing coming. Although she wasn't feeling well, she maintained her post for an hour, as did Harrow. When she turned home, he didn't move. The strange thing was, she said to me that night, that the look on his face—granted, he wasn't exactly close to her, and she hadn't wanted him to catch her staring at him, but she was pretty sure he'd looked profoundly unhappy."

The crab scrambled up the stairs to the porch. His foot on the lowest step, Ransom paused. "Then Heather was back in the hospital, and Matt and I had other things on our minds beside Bruce. Afterwards...not long, actually, I think it was the day before the funeral, I drove by William Harrow's house, and there was the cage, still there, and Bruce, still in it. For a second, I was as angry as I'd ever been; I wanted nothing more than to stomp the gas to the floor and crash into that thing, and if Bruce were killed in the process, so be it. Let Harrow emerge from his house, and I would give him the beating I should have that September morning.

"I didn't, though. The emotion passed, and I kept on driving."

Ransom climbed the rest of the stairs. At the top, he said, "Matt used to say to me, *Who wants to stay in the shallows their whole life?* It was his little dig at his mother and me, at the life we'd chosen. Most of the time, I left his question rhetorical, but when he asked it that afternoon, I answered him; I said, *There are sharks in the shallows, too.* He didn't know what to make of that. Neither did I." Ransom went to say something more, hesitated, decided against it. He opened the door to the house, let the crab run in, followed. The door shut behind them with a solid *thunk*.

At the top of the garden, dangling from the boughs of the apple trees there, the fruit that had ripened into a score, two, of red replicas of Matt's face, his eyes squeezed shut, his mouth stretched in a scream of unbearable pain, swung in a sudden breeze.

For Fiona

♌ ♉

The Men from Porlock

Laird Barron

September, 1923

Darkness lay stone heavy as men roused, drawn from inner night by the tidal pull of blood, the weight of bones sagging outward through their flesh. Floorboards groaned beneath the men who shuffled and stamped like dray horses in the gloom of the bunkhouse. Star glow came through chinks in slat siding. Someone had lighted the stove and smoke drifted among the bunks, up to the rafters. It had rained during the night and the air was ghastly damp. Expelled breath gathered on the beams and dripped steadily; condensation oozing as from stalactites of a limestone cave. The hall reeked with the stench of a bunker: creosote and sweat, flatulence and rotten teeth and the bitter tang of ashes and singed tobacco.

Miller hunched nearly double at the long, rough-hewn pine table and ate lumpy dick and molasses for breakfast. He scooped it with a tin spoon from a tin pan blackened and scarred from a thousand fires and the abuses of a thousand spoons. When he'd done, he wiped his mustache on the sleeve of his long johns and drank black coffee from a tin cup, the last element of his rural dining set.

489

His hands were dirty and horned with calluses from Swede saw and felling axe. He'd broken them a few times over the years and his knuckles were swollen as walnuts. He couldn't make a tight fist with the left hand; most mornings his fingers froze into a crab claw barely fit to manage his Willie, much less hook an axe handle. At least he was young—most of the old timers were missing fingers, or had been busted up in a hundred brutal ways—from accidents to fistfights to year after year of the slow, deadly attrition from each swing of mattock or axe. Olsen the Swede (first among the many Swedes west of the Rockies) got his leg shattered by a chain as a kid and hopped around the camp with his broadhead axe for a crutch. His archrival Sven the Norwegian (first among innumerable logger Norwegians south of Norway) lost his teeth and an ear while setting chokers back in the Old World—setting chokers was dog's work no matter what country. Even Manfred the German, known and admired for his quick reflexes, had once been tagged by an errant branch; his skull was soft in places and hairless as if he'd survived a fire, and one eye drooped much lower than the other. Lately Manny had climbed the ladder to donkey puncher. A man wasn't likely to be injured while running a donkey; if anything went wrong he'd be mangled, mutilated and killed with a minimum of suffering.

One of the Poles, a rangy, affable fellow named Kasper, frequently asked Miller if he planned to get out before he got his head lopped off, or his legs snapped, or was cut in half by a whip-cracking choker cable, or ended up with a knife stuck in his ribs during a saloon brawl. Perhaps Miller was as pigheaded as most men his age and addicted to the security of quick money in a trade few wanted and fewer escaped?

As for himself, Kasper claimed to be cursed rather than stubborn—madness ran through his blood and yoked him to cruel labor, the wages of sin committed by an overweening ancestor in the dim prehistory of Eastern Europe. The Pole wrote poems and stories by lamplight, although his English translations were so poor it would've been difficult to know exactly how to rate his poetry. Miller wasn't keen for the art of letters, although he possessed a grudging admiration for those who were clever with words. His own grandmother had studied overseas as a girl. After she shipped back to the U.S., she kept her diaries in Latin to confound nosy relatives. She showed them to Miller when he visited her home in Illinois—grandma filled up seventy-five of the slim, clothbound tomes, a minor library.

Today, Kasper sat on the long form far from Miller, another bleary shade among jostling elbows and grinding jaws. Miller was fine with that arrangement—all day yesterday the Pole worked with him on an eight-foot saw, a misery whip, to take down an old monster cedar. He knew, as did everyone else,

Miller was among the loose contingent of veterans inhabiting Slango Camp.

The Pole confided: *My oldest brother was shot by a sniper along the Rheine. He was killed with one of those fucking German "mousers"—the big rifles they shoot with. Our family lives in Warszawa and only found out what happened because one of my brother's comrades was with him when it happened and relayed the bad news and mailed home his personal effects. The Legiony sent my brother home in a simple box. I guess there was some confusion at the train depot because so many plain wooden boxes filled up the freight cars and the boxes had serial numbers instead of names. The people in charge of these things mixed up the manifest lists, so my family and the other families had to pry apart the boxes to figure out who was inside each one. They didn't send an official death notice until several weeks after the funeral, which I could not attend. I could not afford to travel home for a funeral. My little sister and cousin died last year. Cholera. It is very bad back home, the cholera. I couldn't go to her funeral, either. They buried her in our village. My brother was buried in another village because that is where my father's people come from. All the men in our family are buried there. Probably not me, that would be too expensive, but my other brothers, certainly. None of them are interested in coming to America. They are happy in Polska.*

This monologue had come at Miller over the course of many hours and became intelligible to his ear only after the third or fourth cycle. He grunted nominal responses where necessary. Finally, after they toppled the tree and prepared to call it a day, he effectively ended the conversation by unplugging his canteen and dumping its contents over his head until steam lifted from him. He'd looked the Pole in the eye and said, *At least they found enough of him to pack in a box. That's a pretty good deal if you think about it.*

Slango was small as camps went—two bunkhouses, the filing house, courtesy car, company store, a couple of storage sheds; no electricity, no indoor plumbing, nothing fancy. Bullhead & Co. played fast and loose, a shoestring operation one or two notches above a gyppo outfit. The owner and his partners ran the offices from distant Seattle and Olympia and rumor had it they'd eventually be swallowed up by Weyerhaeuser or another giant.

According to some, Bullhead himself visited once the prior year and stayed for several days in the Superintendent's car on the company engine, *John Henry.* This surprised Miller; Slango Camp lay entrenched in the rugged foothills of Mystery Mountain, a heavily forested region of the Olympic Range. The camp was a good sixteen miles from the main rail line, and from there another eighteen miles from the landing at Bridgewater Junction. The spur to Slango Camp plunged through a temperate jungle of junk hemlock, poplar and skinny evergreens, peckerwood, so-called, and nearly impassable underbrush—seas of devil's club, blackberry brambles, and alder. The loggers spanned the many gullies and ravines with hastily chopped junk trees to support rickety track. It seemed improbable anybody, much less a suit, would visit such a Godforsaken place unless they had no other choice.

Miller stowed his kit and dressed in his boots and suspenders and heavy jacket. The initial sullen mutters of exhausted men coalesced and solidified around him and evolved into crude, jocular banter fueled by food and coffee and the fierce comradery of doomed souls. He'd seen it in the trenches in France between thudding barrages of artillery, the intermittent assaults by German infantry who stormed in with their stick grenades and "mousers" as Kasper said, and finally, hand to hand, belly to belly in the sanguine mud of shoulder-width tunnel walls, their bayonets and knives. He seldom made sense of those days—the mortar roars, the fumaroles from incendiary starbursts boiling across the divide, eating the world; the frantic bleats of terrorized animals, and boys in their muddy uniforms, their blackened helmets like butcher's pots upended to keep the brains in until the red, shearing moment came to let them out.

He went into the cold and wet. Light filtered through the trees. Mist seeped from the black earth and coiled in screens of brush and branches and hung in tatters like remnant vapors of dry ice. Men drifted, their chambray coats and wool sock hats dark blobs in the gathering white. Even as he shivered off that first clammy embrace of morning fog, mauls began to smash spikes and staples into the planed logs laid alongside the edges of the camp. Axes clanged from the depths of the forest, ringing from metal-tough bark. The bull gang paid cables from the iron bulk of the donkey engine. The boys shackled the cable to the harnesses of a six oxen team and drove them, yipping and hollering, into the mist that swallowed the skidder trail—a passage of corduroy spearing straight through the peckerwood and underbrush, steadily ascending the mountain flank where the big timber lay ripe for the slaughter.

"Miller!" McGrath the straw boss gestured to him from the lee of the company store. McGrath was one of the old boys who haunted logging camps everywhere—sinewy and grizzled and generally humorless; sharp-eyed as a blackbird and possessed of the false merriment of one as well. He was Superintendent Barrett's foreman, the voice and the fist of his authority. Plug tobacco stained the corners of his mouth. Veins made ridges and valleys in his forehead and neck and the backs of his leathery hands. A lot of the men regarded him with antipathy, if not naked hatred. But that was the compact between peasants and overseers since the raising of the Pyramids.

Miller acknowledged the dynamic and accepted the state of things with equanimity. He actually felt a bit sorry for the boss, saw in the scarred and taciturn and blustering foreman the green youth who'd been ragged raw and harrowed by the elders of his day, exactly the same as every other wet-behind-the-ears kid, discerned that those scars had burrowed in deeper than most would ever know.

"Miller, boy!"

"Yes, sir."

"Been here, what—two weeks?"

"I guess that's right, sir." Really it was closer to six weeks since he'd signed on in Bridgewater and road the train to Slango with a half dozen other new hands.

"Huh. Two whole weeks and we ain't had us a jaw. I guess we jawin' now. You a good shot, boy?"

"I dunno about that, sir."

McGrath grinned to spit chaw and rubbed his mouth. "You was a rifle-man in the Army, wasn't you? A sniper? That's what I hear. You a real keener."

"Yes sir." Miller looked at his feet. One of the men, probably Rex or Ha-gen, had talked. A group of them went hunting white tails a couple of Sun-days back. They'd been skunked all day and taken to passing around one of the bottles of rotgut hooch Gordy Thompson kept stashed in his footlocker, and swapping lies about the battles they'd fought and the women they'd fucked and who was the lowest of the lowdown mutts in Slango, which boiled down to McGrath or Superintendent Barret, of course, and who wouldn't like to toe the line if it meant a shot at one of those bastards.

The party was heading toward camp to beat darkness when Rex, the bar-rel-chested brute from Wenatchee, proffered a drunken wager nobody could peg a stump he marked by a pinning it with an empty cigarette pack some two hundred yards from their position. Like an idiot, Miller casually opined he could nail a stump from at least twice that distance. Everybody was three sheets to the wind; rowdy wagers were laid. Dosed on whiskey or not, Miller's hands remained steady. He fired five rounds from the British Enfield he'd car-ried home from the Front, rapidly jacking the bolt action to eject each shell and chamber the next bullet—eight of ten rounds in a pattern that obliterated the illustration of a horse and carriage. Floyd Hagen covered the wreckage with a silver dollar as the men murmured and whistled amongst themselves.

"Where you from?"

"Utah."

"You live in the hills, then? You a Mormon?"

"No sir, I'm not a Mormon. My people are Catholic."

"Yeah? I figure everybody in Utah for a Mormon. They run the regular folks out on rails is what I hear."

"Well, I don't know what they do in Salt Lake, sir. We were raised Catholic. The Mormons left us alone."

"But your people lived in the hills, din't they?"

"That's so."

"What I thought. You a hillbilly, I seen it straight away. Me too. North Carolina, Blue Ridges. We know all about squirrel stew, an' opossum pie, ain't that right? You got opossum in Utah, don't you, boy?"

Behind Miller's left eye the world cracked and vomited blood—red sky limning a benighted prairie of scrub and slick pebbles like the scales on the spine of the Ouroboros. In the seam of the horizon a jackrabbit flew from rock to rock.

"That Po-lack said you shot a bunch of Huns in the war. That right, boy? You pick off some Huns?" McGrath grinned and spat again, sent a withering stream of acid against the plank skirting of the shack. "Nah, don't worry about that. My grandpappy was in Antietam and he didn't talk about it none either. They's a photographer comin' in on the *John Henry*. Be here this weekend. Cookie wants a couple nice bucks for supper. I'm thinkin' you, Horn, Ruark, Bane, and Stevens can take the day off, go git us some meat. Oh, and Calhoun. He smashed his thumb the other day. Cain't hold an axe, but maybe he kin skin with his good hand, huh? Useless as teats onna boar 'round here."

"A photographer." That meant a distraction of the highest order, surpassed only by visits from upper management. This outside scrutiny also meant the bosses would be bigger pricks than usual.

"Some greenhorn named Chet Goul-ee-ay. Goddamned Frenchies. The Supe says we gotta squire him around, wipe his ass an' sich. Put on the dog an' pony show."

"I'm in the cedar stand with Ma today." Miller raised his head to follow a jay as it skimmed the roof and landed on a moss-bearded shake. A camp robber. The bird fluffed its gray feathers and watched him and the straw boss.

"I ain't sendin' Ma with you. He cain't shoot worth shit. That I know."

"Somebody's got to pack the meat downhill."

"Okay. Take him too. Seven, that's a good number, anyhow. Maybe you boys'ill get lucky."

Miller went to the bunkhouse and fetched his frame pack and rifle and slipped a knife into his belt. He stuck some shells into his jacket pockets and helped himself to biscuits and beans from the cook shack. There were four cooks. Two stout, no-nonsense types, and two doughty women renowned for their severity and parsimony with seasonings. The dour quartet bossed around a squad of bottle washers and scullery maids. The chief cook, Angus Clemson grudgingly handed over the vittles, grumping that he hadn't been given prior notice of this raid upon his stores. Leftovers were the best he could do—and Miller had best be damned grateful for the courtesy.

The impromptu expedition took some time to organize and it was nearly midday before the other men had gathered the necessary supplies and were ready to venture forth.

Calhoun, Horn, and Ma met him in the yard. Calhoun was a tall lad; hard-bitten and deadly serious. His left thumb was wrapped in a bandage. Despite his youth and hard bark, he'd proved meticulously groomed and well-spoken. Ma was shorter, and wide as a mattock handle across the shoulders. His hair hung long and oily over a prodigious brow and his eyes shone dull yellow. He spoke seldom and when he did, his Welsh slur rendered him largely unintelligible. His raw strength was the stuff of legend. He could walk off with three hundred pounds of cable looped over his shoulders as if it were nothing. He'd once grabbed a planed log that took three men to move and hoisted it overhead with a grunt and a groan before heaving it onto a pile; on another legendary occasion he singlehandedly dragged a cast iron camp stove of at least a quarter ton out of the mud before other men could finish harnessing the mules. Ma wasn't challenged to many arm wrestling or Indian wrestling matches.

Thaddeus Horn, a rawboned youngster raised in the finest Kentucky backwater tradition, wore a coonskin cap slick with grease and dirt, declared it had been in his family for three generations. Flattened and hideously bleached and hopping with bugs as the cap appeared to be, Miller scarcely doubted the assertion. The youth packed a massive Springfield rifle that could've been a relic from the days of the Texas Revolution, or a buffalo gun Sam Houston might've fired over the ramparts of the Alamo—although Cullen Ruark swore by his Big Fifty and Moses Bane scoffed good-naturedly and bragged *his* antique Rigby could knock down a small tree if he cut loose both barrels at once.

Miller asked Horn if he'd seen Stevens or the others. The kid waved toward the hills, said he figured the trio decided to hightail it before the straw boss changed his mind and sent them all back to hacking at trees.

They hiked up out of camp, slogging through the wastes and ruins of a vast swath of clear-cut land. The near slopes were littered with shorn stumps and orange sheaves of bark. The sundered loam oozed sap and water like a great open wound. Bombs might've caused such devastation, or perhaps Proteus himself rose from the depths to rip loose the skin of the ancient mountain, peeled it away to bare the granite bones.

Bane, Ruark, and Stevens awaited them at the boundary where deep forest began. Three pack-mules were tethered nearby, munching on weeds. Ruark was a wiry galoot. His snow-white beard touched the middle button of his leather vest. Nobody knew much about Ruark—he didn't say two words on any given day, but he swung an axe like a fiend from Hell. Moses Bane was another old-timer, hair just as snowy, yet even shaggier. He was also much fleshier than Ruark and scarred around the eyes and nose and almost as bull-ishly powerful as Ma. A lot of the younger hands called him Grampa Moses. He was a bit more talkative than his pal Ruark, especially after he'd gotten a snootful. It was said the duo served in the Spanish-American War as scouts. Neither spoke of it, however.

Both men were loaded like Sherpas—, bedrolls, ropes, and hooch jugs; rifles, single shot pistols, axes, skinning knives, and God knew what all. Miller felt weary from simply looking at the old boys.

Stevens lounged on the butt of a deadfall and smoked an Old Mill from a bashed pack he stuffed in his front pocket. He rested a lever action Winchester across his knees. A few years older than Miller and almost handsome after a rough fashion. His hair was dark and shaggy and fell near the collar of his canvas vest. Some said Stevens was the best topper at Slango; he certainly clambered up trees with the speed and agility of a raccoon.

Miller privately disdained this popular assessment—if the man was *that* good McGrath wouldn't have turned him loose to poach deer, visiting photographer or not. Bullhead & Co. ran entirely too close to the margin—Superintendent Barret had announced a few days beforehand that the home office expected to see the Slango region logged and its timber on rail flats by Valentine's Day. This produced a few sniggers and wisecrack asides about Paul and Babe signing on to right the ship. Neither Barret nor McGrath laughed and it was plain to see Slango would be upping stakes or folding its tents by midwinter.

"Boys," Stevens said.

"Whatch ya got there?" Horn eyed a glass jug in the weeds by Stevens' boot.

"Hooch," Stevens said.

"Well, guddamn, I seen that," Horn said. "Ma got some, too. Regular heathen firewater. Right, Ma?"

Ma ignored them, his attention fixed on a mosquito growing fat with blood on his misshapen thumb knuckle. The stupid intensity of the Welshman's fascination made Miller slightly sick to his stomach.

"Yeh," Stevens said. "May not bag us a deer, but we gonna get shit-drunk tryin'." He picked up the jug and put it in a burlap bag. He tied the bag to his pack and slipped the pack over his shoulders and began trudging into the woods.

"Okay!" Horn followed him, the Springfield slung loosely over his shoulder. Ma went close behind them and Miller hung slightly back to avoid being slashed across the face by sprung branches. The sun had burned through the overcast, but its rays fell weak and diffuse here in the cool, somber vault of the forest. The air lay thick and damp as if they'd shuffled into the belly of a crypt.

None of them was familiar with the environs beyond Slango. However, Stevens had borrowed a topographical map from the Superintendent's car and they decided to follow the ridges above Fordham Creek. The surveyors who'd originally explored the area had noted a sizable deer population in the hinterlands upstream. Eschewing a group council, Bane and Ruark silently moved ahead of the group to cut for sign.

The old growth trees were enormous. These were the elders, rivals to the Redwood Valley sequoias that predated Christ, the Romans, everything but the wandering tribes of China and Persia. Crescents of white fungus bit into slimy folds of bark and laddered toward the canopy. Leaves had begun to drop and the ground was slimy with their brown and yellow husks. Vast mushroom beds, fleshy and splendorous, lay in shallow grottos of root and rock. Horn tromped across one in childish glee. Hooting and cackling, he grabbed Ma by the arm and the pair jigged in the pall of green smoke. Horn had been drinking heavily, or so Miller hoped. He dreaded to think the boy was so simple and maniacal as a matter of inbreeding.

Birds and squirrels chattered from secret perches and Horn abruptly blasted his rifle at a roosting ptarmigan as the group negotiated a steep defile of a dry stream bed. Leaves and wood exploded and it was impossible to determine whether the bird flew away or was blown to bits. The unexpected boom caused Stevens and Miller to drop to their knees. Horn staggered from the recoil and lost his footing on the slippery rocks. He slid ass over teakettle down the slope and crashed into some brambles. The mules skittered free and bolted into the brush and it required a good half hour to recapture them.

Steven scowled at the boy. He gained his feet and hesitated as if contemplating violence. Then he laughed and unlimbered his jug and had a pull. Afterward, he handed the jug to Miller. Miller took a snort of the sweet, dark whiskey and lost his breath for a few seconds. Stars shot through his vision. "Careful, sonny boy. That'll curl your toes—my Daddy makes it himself. Finest Californee awerdenty you're likely to sample in this lifetime."

Miller would've agreed if his voice hadn't been burned to ash in his throat.

Bane and Ruark emerged from the undergrowth and reported they'd located a large hollow not far below the chaparral and possibly that supply of deer meat the boss so badly desired. Spoor was plentiful at least. There were several high vantages and effecting a killing field shouldn't prove difficult. If all went well, the party would bag their prizes and return safely to Slango by tomorrow night.

The expedition made camp within a tiny clearing in the lee of a slab of rock jutting from the hillside. The outcropping loomed, thick with tufts of moss and lichen. They gathered wood and built a bonfire and sawed rounds from a log to seat themselves in the glare of the flames. The men stuck their hands near the fire. It was bitter cold. Each evening the snowline crept lower, dragging its veil of white dust.

Darkness blotted out the landscape. Embers streamed through notches in the canopy and swirled among the stars. Stoic, brooding Ma unpacked his fiddle and sawed a lively jig for the boys, who clogged in time while tending the mules and cooking supper. The Welshman's expression remained remote and dull as ever. His hands moved like mechanisms that operated independently of his brutish mind, or as though plucked and maneuvered by the strings of a muse. Idiocy and genius were too often part and parcel of a man. Miller grinned and tapped his toe to the rhythm, however, the ever watchful segment of his brain that took no joy in anything wondered how far the light and music penetrated into the black forest, how far their shouts and hoots echoed along gullies and draws. And his smile faded.

Supper was roasted venison, Indian bread, and coffee, a couple of fingers of moonshine in the dregs for dessert. Conversation and fiddle-accompaniment ebbed and for a while everyone fell into reverie, heads cocked toward the whispering wind as it brushed the treetops. Night birds warbled and small creatures rustled in the leaves.

"They's stories 'bout these parts," Bane said with an abruptness that caught Miller off guard. Bane and Ruark had laid out an array of knives, tomahawks, and sundry accessories for oiling and sharpening. Ruark hefted an Arkansas Toothpick, turning it this way and that so it gleamed in the firelight. Bane painstakingly stroked a whetstone across the edge of his felling axe. A lump of chaw bulged his cheek. "Legends, guess ya might say." It was no secret how much 'Grandpa Moses' loved to spin a yarn. His companions immediately paid heed, leaning closer toward where he sat, white hair and beard wild and snarled, little orange sparks shooting as he rasped his axe.

Horn became agitated. "Aww, dontcha go on, old man. No call for that kinda talk while we're hunkered here in the woods at night. No sir, no sir."

Stevens guffawed. "What's a matter, kid? Your mama put the fright in you back in Kentucky?"

"Hush yer mouth 'bout my mama."

"Easy, kid. Don't get your bristles up."

Miller didn't speak, yet misgiving nagged him. He'd dwelt among the Christian devout as well as the adherents of mystical traditions. There were those who believed to speak of a thing was to summon it into the world, to lend it form and substance, to imbue it with power. He wasn't sure how to feel about such theories. However, something within him, perhaps the resident animal, empathized with the kid's fear. Mountain darkness was a physical weight pressing down and it seemed to *listen*.

Bane paused to gaze into the darkness that encroached upon the circle of the cheery blaze. Then he looked Stevens dead in the eye. "I knew this Injun name o' Ravenfoot back to Seattle who come from over Storm King Mountain way. Klallam Injun. His people have hunted this neck o' the woods afore round eyes ever hollowed canoes. He told me an' I believe the red man knows his stuff."

"Who'd believe an Injun about anything?" Stevens said. "Superstitious bastards."

"Yeah. An' what tickled yer fancy to speak up now?" Horn said, his tone still sour and fearful. Ma squatted near him, head lowered, digging into the dirt with a knife. Miller could tell the brute was all ears, though.

"That map of your'n," Bane said to Stevens.

"What the hell are you chinnin" about? The map? Now that don't make any kind of sense." Stevens took the map from his pocket, unrolled it and squinted.

"Where'd you get that?" Miller said, noting the paper's ragged border. "Tear it from a book?"

"I dunno. McGrath gave it to me. Prolly he got it from the Supe."

Now Bane's eyes widened. "My grand pappy was a right reverend and a perfessor. Had lots o' books lyin' 'round the house when I was a sprat."

"You can *read*, Moses?" Calhoun spoke from where he reclined with the wide brim of his hat pulled low. The men chuckled, albeit nervously.

"Oh, surely," Bane said. "I kin read, an' also write real pretty when I take a notion."

"Recites some nice poetry, too," Ruark said without glancing up from whetting his knife. "I'm partial to the Shakespeare." These were the first and only words he'd uttered all day.

"But Grand pappy was a dyed in the wool educated feller. He took the Gospel Word to them heathens in Eastern Europe an' the jungles of Africa, an' some them islands way, way down in the Pacific. Brought back tales turn yer hair white."

"Aha, that's what happened to your hair!" Stevens said. "Here I thought you was just old."

Bane laughed, then spat. "Yeh, so I am, laddio. This is a haunted place. Explorers wandered 'round Mystery Mountain in the 1840s. Richies in the city, newspapermen mostly, financed 'em. Found mighty peculiar things, they say. Burial mounds 'an cliffside caves with bodies in 'em like the Chinee do. A few o' them explorers fell on hard luck an' got kilt, or lost. Some tried to pioneer and disappeared, but onea 'em, a Russian, came back an' wrote hisself a book. An pieces o' that book wound up in another one, a kind o' field guide. Looks like a *Farmer's Almanac*, 'cept black with a broken circle on the cover. I seen that page afore. Ain't too many copies o' that guide not what got burned. My mama was a child o' God and hated it on account o' its pagan blasphemy, documentin' heathen rites an' sich. Grand pappy showed me in secret. He weren't a particularly devout feller after he finished spreadin' the Lord's Word. Had a crisis o' faith, he said."

"Well, what did the Russkie find?" Calhoun said.

"Don't recall, 'xactly." Bane leaned the axe against his knee and sighed. "Ruins, mebbe. Mebbe he lied, 'cause ain't nobody backed his claims. He was a snake oil salesman, I reckon. They run him outta the country."

"I think," Miller said, "that's an amazing coincidence, your ending up on this hunt. Could be you're pulling our legs."

"Mebbe. But I ain't. God's truth."

" *Arri, arri.*" Ma scowled and stabbed at the ground. His voice was thick as cold mush.

"Sounds like Ma thinks that redskin mumbo-jumbo rubbed off on you," Stevens said. "Why'n blue blazes did you volunteer to come along if this place is lousy with bad medicine?"

"Hell, son. McGrath done volunteered me."

"Have at it, then." Calhoun raised his hat with one finger. "What's so spooky about Mystery Mountain?"

"Besides the burial mounds and the cave crypts, and them disappeared explorers," Stevens said with a smirk.

"Oh, they's a passel o' ghosts an' evil spirits, an' sich," Bane said, again glancing into the night. "Demons live in holes in the ground. Live in the rocks and sleep inside big trees in the deep forest where the sun don't never shine. Ravenfoot says the spirits sneak up in the dark an' drag poor sleepin' sods to Hell."

"Hear that, Thad?" Stevens nodded at Horn. "Best sleep with one eye open."

"I hearda one," Ruark said, and his companions became so quiet the loudest noise was the pop and sizzle of burning sap. He spat on his whetstone and continued sharpening the knife. "Y'all remember the child's tale Rumpel-stiltskin? The king ordered the miller's daughter to spin straw to gold or die, an' a little man, a dwarf, came to her an' said he'd do the job if'n she promised him her firstborn child? Done deal an' she didn't get her head chopped off."

"They got themselves hitched and made a bunch of papooses," Stevens said. "Everybody heard that story."

"How'n hell that dwarf spin straw to gold?" Horn said. He took a swig of hooch and belched.

"Magic, you jackass," Calhoun said.

"Lil' fucker was the spawn o' Satan, that's how," Bane said.

"The king made her his queen an' everthin' was hunkum-bunkum for a while," Ruark said. "Then, o' course, along comes baby an' who shows up to collect his due? She convinces him to give her until the dark o' the moon to guess his name an' call off the deal. So bein' a cantankerous cuss, the feller agrees. He knows his name is so odd she hasn't a snowball's chance in hell o' sussing it out." He paused and finally looked up from his work and slowly met the wondering gaze of each man riveted to his words. "But that ol' girl *did* cotton to the jig. She sent messengers to the four corners o' the land, their only mission to gather a list o' names. One o' them men reported a queer sight he'd spied in a deep, dark mountain valley. The scout saw a mighty fire below and who danced 'round that blaze but a pack o' demons led by the little gold-spinner hisself. The dwarf cackled an' capered, boasting that his name was Rumpelstiltskin. He was mad as a wet hen when the queen turned the tables later on. He stomped a hole in the palace floor an' fell into the earth. That was the end o' him."

"That's a pretty happy ending, you ask me," Miller said as he pondered the incongruity of camping in the remote mountains with a company of dog-faced loggers and listening to one of them butcher the Rumpelstiltskin fairytale.

"Well, that part about the demons jumpin' 'round the fire an' calling up the forces o' darkness, some say they seen similar happenins in these hills. They say if'n you creep along the right valley in the dead o' night 'round the dark o' the moon you'll hear 'em singin' an' chantin'."

"Hear who?" Calhoun said.

Ruark kind of smiled and shook his head and said no more.

"I'm turnin' in," Horn said and jumped to his feet. "Ain't listenin' to a bit more o' this nonsense. No siree Bob." He stomped a few feet away and rolled out his blanket and climbed under it so only the crown of his cap and the bar-rel of his rifle were showing.

"Too bad your mama ain't here to tuck you in and sing a lullaby," Stevens called.

"Told you to shuddup 'bout my mama," Horn said.

Calhoun chucked a stick of wood, bounced it off the kid's head. That broke the mood and everybody guffawed, and soon the company crawled into their blankets to catch some shuteye.

& &

Miller roused with an urge to piss. A moment later he lay frozen, listening to the faint and unearthly strains of music. Initially, he thought it the continuation of dream he'd had of sitting in the balcony of a fancy court while the queen in her dress and crown entertained a misshapen dwarf who wore a curious suit and a plumed hat, while in the background Ruark narrated in a thick accent, but no, this music was real enough, although it quavered at the very edge of perception. An orchestra of woodwinds and strings buoyed a choir singing in a foreign tongue. This choir's harmony rose and fell with the swirls of wind, the creaking of the sea of branches in the dark above him. He couldn't tell how far off the singers might be. Sound traveled strangely in the wild, was all the more tricky in the mountains.

"Ya hear that?" Calhoun said. Miller could barely make out the gleam of his eyes in the light of the coals. The young man's whisper was harsh with fear. "The hell is that?"

"The wind, maybe," Miller said after a few moments passed and the music faded and didn't resume. The sky slowly lightened to pearl with tinges of red. He rose and ventured into the brush, did his business and wiped his hands with dead leaves and fir needles. Ruark was moving around by the time Miller returned. The old logger kindled the fire and put on coffee and biscuits. That drew the others, grumbling and muttering, from their bedrolls.

No one mentioned anything about voices or music, not even Calhoun, so Miller decided to keep his own counsel lest they think him addled. This was desolate country and uninhabited but for the occasional trapper. He'd heard the wind and nothing else. Soon, he pushed the mystery aside and turned his thoughts toward the day's hunt.

Breakfast was perfunctory and passed without conversation. The party struck camp and headed northwest, gradually climbing deeper into the folds of Mystery Mountain. Sunlight reached fingers of gold through the canopy and cast a tiger stripe pattern over the shrubbery and giant ferns and the sweating boles of the trees. The pattern rippled as leaves rippled and shifted in a way that might hypnotize a man if he stared at it too hard. Miller blinked away the stupor and trudged along until they crested a bluff and found the wide, irregular bog Bane had spoken of the previous evening. The fellow had been correct—there was deer sign everywhere. The party fanned out in pairs and settled behind screens of brush to wait.

Miller dropped one as it entered the field at the edge of his weapon's effective range, while Stevens, Bane, and Ruark each bagged one in the middle ground. Unfortunately, Horn's lone shot merely injured his prey and it darted into the woods, forcing him, Ma, and Calhoun to pursue.

By noon three bucks were skinned and quartered. The men loaded the mules and strapped smaller cuts to their own packs and prepared to set off for Slango. Ma, Horn, and Calhoun remained in the forest pursuing the wounded buck.

"Damnation," Bane said, shading his eyes against the sun. "We gonna be travelin' in the dark as it is. Those green-hands dilly-dally much longer an' it's another biv-oo-ack tonight."

"Hell with that. We don't hoof it back by sundown McGrath will have our hides, sure as the Lord made little green apples." Stevens unplugged the moonshine and had a swig. His face shone with sweat from the skinning and toting. "Here's what I propose. Miller, you and Ruark take the mules and skedaddle back to Slango. Me and Bane will go round up our wayward friends and catch you two down the trail. Let's get a move on, eh?"

Miller swatted at the clouds of swarming gnats and flies. A rifle boomed in the middle distance. Again after a long interval, and a third time. A universal signal of distress. That changed everything. Stevens, Bane, and Ruark frantically shucked the meat and hot-footed in the direction of the gunshots. Miller spent several minutes dumping the saddlebags from the mules and tethering them near a waterhole before setting after his comrades. He moved swiftly, bent over to follow their tracks and broken branches they'd left in their wake. He drew the Enfield from its scabbard and cradled the rifle to his breast.

Into the forest. And gods, the trees were larger than ever there along a shrouded ridge that dropped into a deep gulf of shadows and mist. He was channeled along a trail that proved increasingly treacherous. Water streamed from upslope, digging notches through moss and dirt into the underlying rock. In sections the dirt and vegetation were utterly stripped to exposed plates of slick stone, veined red with alkali and the bloody clay of the earth. The trees were so huge, their lattice of branches so tight, it became dim as a shuttered vault, and chilly enough to see faint vapors of one's breath.

The game trail cut sharply into the hillside and eventually passed through a thick screen of saplings and devil's club and leveled into a marshy clearing. A handful of boulders lay sunken into the moss and muck around the trunks of three squat cottonwood trees. Surprisingly enough, there were odds and ends of human habitation carelessly scattered—rusted stovetops and empty cans, rotted wooden barrels and planed timber, bits of old shattered glass and bent nails. Either the site of a ruined house, long swallowed by the earth, or a dumping ground. The rest of the men gathered at the rim of the hollow nearest a precipitous drop into the valley. Fast moving water rumbled from somewhere below.

Horn lay on his back, his boots propped on the body of the fallen buck. Ma and Calhoun were nowhere in evidence. Miller took it all in for a few moments. He finally shouldered his rifle and had a sip of water from his canteen. "He hurt?" He jerked his thumb at Horn. The boy's coonskin cap had flown off and his long, greasy hair was a bird nest of leaves and twigs. A black and blue lump swelled above his eye.

"Nah, he ain't hurt," Stevens said. "Are ya, kid? He's okay. Got the wind knocked outta him is all. Tripped over a damn root and busted his skull. He'll be right as rain in a minute. Won't ya, kid?"

Horn groaned and covered his eyes with his arm.

"He's affrighted," Bane said, and spat. The grizzled logger clutched his rifle in one hand and a tomahawk in the opposite. His knuckles were white. He kept moving his eyes.

"Afraid of what?" Miller said, surveying the area. He didn't like the feel of the place, its dankness, the malformed cottonwoods, the garbage. He also disliked the fact Calhoun and Ma weren't around.

Stevens and Bane glanced at each other and shrugged. Stevens squatted by Horn and patted his arm almost tenderly. "Wanna slug of this fine awerdenty, kid? Where'd those other boys get to, eh?" He helped Horn get seated upright, then held the jug for him while the kid had pull.

Ruark scowled and ambled to the drop and stared down into the valley. The water thumped and so did Miller's heart. He tilted his head and stared through the opening above the clearing, regarded the brilliant blue-gold sky. Cloudless, immaculate. Already the sun was low against the peaks. Dark came early in the mountains. The sun seemed peculiar—it blurred and flames radiated from its core and its rim blackened like a coal.

Horn coughed and wiped his mouth on his wool sleeve. "Yeh, tripped an' smacked muh noggin'. Weren't no stob, though. No sir. They's a snare yonder. Prolly more where that come from." He pointed and Bane went and examined the spot.

Bane whistled and said, "He ain't blowin' smoke. Step light, boys. We ain't alone."

"Bushwhackers," Ruark said, turning with predatory swiftness to regard his comrade.

"Ain't no bushwhackers." Stevens rose and swiped at the gathering flies with his hat. "We maybe got us a trapper tucked into that park down there. That's what we got."

"Shit." Bane lifted a piece of thin rope, its long end snaking off through the underbrush. He coiled in the slack and gave it a yank. A bell clanged nearby and Bane threw the rope and jumped back as if scalded. "Shit!"

"Yeh, shit!" Ruark said and stepped away from the ridgeline. He had his Sharps in hand now.

Miller said, "Thad, where's Cal and Ma?"

Horn still appeared confused from the blow to his head, but the grave faces of his companions sobered him a bit. "Din't see on account I was woozy for a spell. Heard 'em jawin' with somebody that come up on us. Cal said to hang on, they'd be right back."

"You act a mite nervous. Something else happen?"

The boy hesitated. "Din't much care for the sound of whoever they was that jawed with Cal an' Ma. Not 'tall. Sounded right wicked."

"The hell does that mean?" Stevens said.

Horn shrugged and pulled on his cap.

"Shitfire!" Bane said, and spat.

"How long ago?" Miller said. He thought of hiding in the trenches during the war, scanning the gloom for signs of the enemy creeping forward. He'd learned, as did most men of violence, to recognize the scent of imminent peril. At that moment the scent was very strong indeed.

"I reckon half an' hour ago. I blacked out for a while. Them shots snapped me outta it."

Before the boy had finished speaking, Bane and Ruark slipped away to the edge of the clearing, cutting for sign. Ruark whistled and everyone but Horn hustled over. Just beyond a deadfall he'd found a well-beaten footpath. Their missing comrades had passed this way, and so had at least two others. Bane swore and cut a plug of chaw and jammed it in his mouth. He swore again, and spat. The four held a brief discussion and decided there might be trouble ahead so caution was advised. Miller would help Horn back to camp while the rest went on to find Calhoun and Ma. Horn got to his feet and joined them, visibly shaking off his unsteadiness. "Like hell. Ma is my boy. I'm goin'."

"Fine," Stevens said. "Moses, you lead the way." And the men proceeded along the path single file. The going was much easier than before as the path lay a few feet from the ridgeline and the hills, while steep, were much gentler than before.

Ten minutes later they came to a fork at the base of a dead red cedar. The bole of the cedar would've required four or five men to link hands to span its girth. It had sheared off at about the eighty foot mark. One fork of the trail continued along the ridge; the other descended into the valley, which was still mostly hidden by forest. Boot-prints went both directions, but Bane and Ruark were confident there friends had travelled in the valley. Bane sniffed the air, then gestured downward. "Wood smoke."

"Sure enough," Miller said just then winding the tang of smoke. They'd proceeded only a few paces when he happened to look back and stopped with a hiss of warning to his companions.

"What is it?" Stevens said.

"That tree," Miller said, indicating a blaze mark on the downhill face of the big dead cedar—a stylized ring, broken on the sinister side. The symbol was roughly four feet across and gouged in a good three inches. Someone had daubed it in a thick reddish paint, now bled and mostly absorbed by the wood. It appeared petrified with age. Some inherent quality of the ring caused Miller's flesh to crawl. The light seemed to dim, the forest to close in.

Nobody said anything. Stevens produced a small spy glass and swept the area. He muttered and tossed the glass to Bane. Bane looked around. He passed it to Ruark. Finally he swore and handed the glass back. Stevens in turn let Miller have a go. Stevens said, "I make out three more—there, there, and there." He was correct. Miller spotted the other trees scattered along the hillside. Each was huge and dead, and each bore the weird glyph.

"I seen that mark afore," Bane said in a reverential whisper.

"That book," Miller said and Bane grunted. Miller asked for Stevens' jug, hooked the handle with his pinky, mountain man fashion, and took a long, stout pull of the whiskey until black stars shot across his vision. Then he gasped for air and helped himself to another, healthier swig.

"Jaysus," Stevens said when he finally retrieved his hooch. He shook the jug with a sad, amazed expression as if not quite comprehending how this could've happened to his stock.

"I don't cotton to this 'tall," Horn said. He rubbed the goose egg on his forehead. He was flour-pale.

"I'm with the pup," Bane said. He spat. Ruark grunted agreement. He too spat a gob of Virginia Pride into the shrubbery.

Stevens crept up to the cedar and studied it intently, ran his fingers over the rough bark. He said, "Damn it all! Boys, lookee here." As everyone clustered around he showed them how a great chunk of bark was separate from the tree. The slab of bark was as tall as three men, narrowing to a sharp peak. The outline, as of a door, was clear once they discerned it against the pattern. The bark door was hinged with sinew on one side.

"Whata ya reckon it is?" Horn said, backing away.

Watching Stevens trace the panel in search of a catch caused Miller's anxiety to sharpen. The light was fading and far too early in the afternoon. The sun's edge was being rapidly eaten by a black wave, creating a broken ring of fire and shadow. This phenomenon juxtaposed with the broken ring carved in the tree. Miller said, "Don't boys! Just leave it!"

Stevens muttered his satisfaction at locating the catch. Bane and Stevens pulled the wooden panel three quarters of the way open and then stopped, bodies rigid as stone. From his vantage Miller couldn't make out much of the hollow, gloomy interior, but the other two men stood with their necks craned and Bane moaned, low and aggrieved as a fellow who'd been stabbed in the gut. "Sweet Lord in heaven!" Stevens said.

Miller took several broad steps to join them at the portal. He gazed within and saw—

—Something squirmed and uncoiled, a darker piece of darkness, and resolved into—

—His vision clouded violently and he staggered, was steadied by Ruark while Bane and Stevens sealed the panel, ramming it closed with their shoulders. They spun, faces white, wearing expressions of fear that were terrible to behold in men of such stern mettle.

"Good gawd, lookit the sky," Horn said. The moon occulted the sun and the world became a shadowy realm where every surface glowed and bloomed with a queer bluish-white light. Every living thing in the forest held its breath.

"Jaysus Mother Mary!" Ruark said, breaking the spell. "Jaysus Mother Mary Christ Almighty!"

And the men scrambled, tripped and staggered, grasping at branches to keep their footing. The eclipse lasted four minutes at most. The group reached the bottom as the moon and the sun slid apart and the world brightened by degrees. The valley was narrow and ran crookedly north and south. There were falls to the north and a small, shallow river wound its way through sandbars and intermittent stands of cottonwood and fallen spars and uprooted trunks.

A rustic village lay one hundred seventy or so yards distant upon the opposite side of the valley behind a low palisade of vertical logs—a collection of antique cottages and bungalows that extended as far as the middle heights of the terraced hillside. Several figures moved among the buildings, tending to chickens, hanging clothes. Stevens passed the scope around and it was confirmed that a handful of women were the only visible inhabitants.

Miller had marched similar villages in the European countryside where the foundations might be centuries old, perhaps dated from Medieval times. To encounter such a place here in the wilds of North America was incomprehensible. This town was wrong, utterly wrong, and the valley one of the hidden places of the world. He'd never heard a whisper of the community and only God knew why people would dwell in secret. Perhaps they belonged to a religious sect that had fled persecution and wished to follow their faith in peace. He thought of the dreadful music from the previous night, the ominous drums, the blackening sun, and was not reassured.

Away from the central portion of the community loomed a stone tower with a crenellated parapet surmounted by a turret of shiny clay shingles that narrowed to a spike. The tower rose to a height of four stories, dominating the village and was constructed of bone-white stone notched at intervals by key-hole windows. The broken ring symbol had been painted in black ochre to the left of every window and upon the great ironbound oak doors at the tower's base. As with the symbol of the ring carved into the tree on the hillside, some combination of elements imbued the tower with menace that struck a chord deep inside Miller. His heart quickened and he looked over his shoulder at the way they'd come.

"Be dark soon," Stevens said. He also cast a furtive backward glance. Long shadows spread over the rushes and the open ground before them. The bloody sun hung a finger's breadth above the peaks and the sky was turning to rust. "These folks may be dangerous. Keep your guns ready."

Horn snatched at Bane's sleeve. "What'd y'all see back there?"

"Shut it, boy. Ain't gonna leave this valley goin' that direction. Nothin' more to tell."

"Yeah, shut it," Ruark said and gave the kid a shove to get him moving.

ଊ ଌ

The company forded the river where it rushed shin deep, and moved to the village and passed through the open gate of the palisade after Stevens hailed the occupants. A dozen women of various ages paused in their chores and silently regarded the visitors. The women wore long, simple dresses of a distinctly Quaker style and dour bonnets and kerchiefs. They appeared well-fed and clean. Their teeth were white. Several of them immediately repaired to the central structure, a kind of longhouse. Most of the others went into the smaller houses. One of the younger girls smiled furtively at Miller. Obviously she was simple. Her dress was cut low and revealed her buxom curves, her belly swollen with child and Miller blushed and turned his head away. Chickens pecked in the weeds. A couple of goats wandered around, and a small pack of mutts approached, yipping and snaffling at the men's legs.

A brawny matron with gray hair stepped forward to greet the company, and she too offered a friendly smile. "Hello, strangers. Welcome." Her accent and mannerisms seemed off-kilter, indefinably foreign.

"Beggin' your pardon, Ma'am." Stevens doffed his hat, clutched it nervously. "Our apologies to intrude and all, but we're on the trail of a couple old boys who belong to our group. We're hopin' you might've seen 'em." His voice shook and he and Bane continued to cast worried glances over their shoulders. For his part, Miller had spent the past few minutes convincing himself he'd seen a coon or porcupine in the dead tree. Maybe a drowsing black bear.

To further distract and calm his galloping imagination, he studied the lay of the land. The houses were made of smoothed rocks and mortared stone and the windows were tiny and mostly without glass, protected from the elements by means of thick drapes and shutters. The dirt paths were grooved and hardened to iron with age. The hillside climbed steeply through trees and undergrowth, although its face was mostly rock. A cave mouth opened beneath an overhang. He'd thought perhaps some eccentric industrialist had possibly created a replica of a medieval town and transplanted its citizens, but the closer he inspected it, the more its atmosphere seeped into him, and he understood this was something far stranger.

The matron apparently observed the tension among the loggers. She said, "Dear gentlemen, ye have nothing to fear. Be at peace."

"We're not afraid, Missus," Miller said. He used a gruff tone because the woman unnerved and unsettled him with her odd accent, her antiquated primness, the manner in which she cocked her head like a living doll. How the whites of her eyes were overcome by black. "But we *are* in a powerful hurry."

"The men will soon return from the gathering and ye shall treat with them. Until then, please rest." The matron waved them toward some benches near the statue of a figure in robes, two children of equally indeterminate sex crouched at its feet. The statue was defaced by weather and green mold. One grotesquely elongated hand stretched forth as if to part a curtain to reveal some dark mystery. The children's necks were cruelly bent, tongues distended, spines humped and exposed as if flayed by a butcher's knife. The larger figure's dangling hand caressed their bowed heads. "Girls, see to fetching our guests pie and lemonade." The two younger women disappeared into the longhouse, as did the one who'd smiled at Miller. They moved with the ponderous grace of soon-to-be mothers.

Miller wondered if all of the girls were with child and wished he'd paid more attention. It seemed important. He said to the matron, "How did you come to build this village? It's not on any maps."

"Isn't it?" the woman said and for an instant her smile became sly as a predator of the wood. "Our hamlet is very old and was carried across the sea by our founders when Sir Raleigh still served the Queen's pleasure. This is a place of worship, of communion and far, far from wicked civilizations of men.

The nights are long in this valley. The days are gloomy. It is perfect."

Stevens wrung his hat and fidgeted. "If you don't mind, Ma'am, we need to locate our friends and be on our way before the sun goes down. Could you kindly point the way? Tracks show they come through here."

"You saw them, of course," Miller said. He decided what it was about the woman's speech that bothered him: Her voice was hoarse, the cadences unbalanced, her intonation stilted because she wasn't accustomed to speaking and hadn't been for a long time.

"Aye, she seen 'em alright," Bane said, mouth set in a grim line. "Prolly one o' you wenches that lured em' here."

The matron kept smiling. Her hands trembled. "Our husbands will be home anon. Mayhap they have seen your companions." She turned and walked into the longhouse. The door closed and then came the unmistakable clunk of a bar dropping.

Bane shook his head and spat. He broke apart his Rigby and checked the load and clacked the breech into place again.

"Well, this ain't good," Stevens said.

Horn said, "What we aimin' to do?" He moved to shuck his pack and Ruark frowned and told him to leave it be.

"Gonna find Cal and Ma. That's what. And leave your goddamned pack on. We have to make tracks in a hurry you wanna be all the way up shit crick with no paddle?" Stevens clapped his hat on. "Stick our noses in every last house. Kick in the doors if we have to. Let's make it quick. Daylight is burnin'."

Miller and Bane teamed to search the cottages on the south side; Stevens, Horn, and Ruark took the north. It went fast. Miller took the lead, busting through the doors and making a brief sweep of the interiors. The women inside calmly waited, speaking not a word to the trespassers—and indeed, many were pregnant. Each house was small and dim, but there weren't many places to hide. Most were neat and well-ordered, not untoward in any obvious way. Simple furnishings, albeit archaic. Oil lamps and candles, fireplaces that doubled as ovens. A paltry selection of books on rude shelves. This last detail struck him as truly odd.

He said to Bane, "Not one Bible. You ever see this many houses without a copy or two of the good book lying around?" Bane shrugged and allowed as he hadn't witnessed that particular phenomenon either.

Both parties finished within a few minutes and regrouped in the square. Everyone was sweating from running up the hill to check the half dozen houses perched there. Miller mentioned the lack of holy literature. Stevens said, "Yeh, mighty peculiar. Where are the kids? You seen any?"

"Gudamn!" Horn said. "Brats should be crawlin' underfoot, chasin' the chickens, screamin' bloody murder. Somethin' shore as hell ain't right."

"Mebbe they inside the big house," Ruark said. "Or that tower."

"Well, we gotta check that house," Miller said although the idea made him unhappy. The thought of searching the tower was even worse—it curved out of joint, angles distorted, and the sight made his head queer, his stomach ill. Not the tower if there were any other way.

Horn appeared stricken. "Hold on there, fellas. Them women ain't gonna hold Cal or Ma. No sir. We barge in there an' git shot, some might say we had it comin'."

"Yeh, I reckon," Stevens said. "You can stay out here and keep watch if you're afraid of the ladies. Them husbands gonna be walkin' in on us any minute. Who knows how many of them old boys'll show."

"Plenty, you kin wager," Bane said.

Miller kicked the door. "Solid as a stump," he said. Ruark spat and unlimbered his axe, as did Bane a moment later. The pair stood shoulder to shoulder chopping at the door and it crashed inward after a few blows. The men piled into the house, blinking against the smoky dimness. The sole light came from what seeped through window notches and a guttering fire in the hearth. The murk made hazy blobs of the long table, the counter and barrels stacked in threes here and there. The peak roof vaulted to a height of fifteen or so feet, supported by a massive center beam and a series of angled joists that met the wall at about chin level. Meat hooks, pots and pans, coils of rope, cured ham, and strings of sausage swayed and rustled with each gentle exhalation from the hearth.

Of the women there was no sign, but Ma was present.

Miller almost cried out when he beheld what had been done to the Welshman, and Stevens hollered loud enough to bust an eardrum. Miller didn't blame him. Ma sat Indian style, naked in the middle of the floor, blood thick as pudding around his legs, in his lap. His belly was sliced wide and a quivering rope of purple innards was strung several feet above him and looped through a large eyebolt suspended from a chain. The intestines traveled down again like a pulley cable and wrapped around a wooden turnstile. The turnstile had been cranked repeatedly and its gory yarn oozed and leaked. Most of the rest of Ma's guts were slopped across his thighs, or floating in the grue. His slack jaw drooled. He gave his comrades a glassy eyed nod not much different than his usual.

"Oh, god, Ma!" Stevens said. "What'd they do to you, hoss?"

Horn stuck his head in to see what the commotion was all about and shrieked to beat the band, so Ruark swatted him with his hat and drove him outside. Right then the matron ghosted from the gloom in the corner and hacked Bane's shoulder with a cleaver. He yelled and smacked her in the jaw with the butt of his Rigby and she sprawled.

Blood trickled from the matron's lips. The injury did not diminish her, rather imbued her with an aura of savagery and mania that caused the men to flinch as one might from a wounded beast. Her eyes were so very large and dark and they gleamed with tears of rage and exultation. She whispered with the intimacy of a lover, "Did ye see what's waiting for ye in the trees?"

"Where's our other man?" Miller strode over to the matron and leveled his rifle at her. "I'll blow a damned hole in your kneecap, Missus. See if I won't."

"No need for that. The handsome lad is in the tower. They gave us the fat one for sport. It amuses them to watch us practice cruelty."

Miller walked around Ma and the coagulating lake of blood. He grasped the ring of a trapdoor and pulled. Several of the women were huddled like goats in a root cellar. They gasped and held each other.

"See him?" Stevens said.

Miller slammed the trapdoor and shook his head.

Bane cussed as Ruark pulled the cleaver free of his shoulder with a gristly crunch. Miller fashioned a tourniquet. The entire left side of Bane's buckskin jacket was soaked through and dripping. Horn shouted. Everyone ran to the windows. Twilight lay upon the world and a disjointed chain of lamps bobbed in the purple dark, descending the switchback trail on the other side of the valley. Miller said, "Either we fort up, or we run for it."

Stevens said, "Trapped like rats in here. Roof is made of wood. They could burn us alive."

"Not with they women in here," Bane said through gritted teeth.

"You want to spend the night in here with them?" Miller said.

"Yeh, never mind."

"We could take this one as a hostage," Stevens said halfheartedly.

"Piss on that," Miller said. "Who knows what she'll chop off next time."

"Ye should flee into the hills," the matron said. "The horrors ye will soon meet...flee, good hunters. Or make an end of each other with your guns and knives. T'will be a merciful death in comparison."

"Shut up before I kill you," Miller said. The matron stopped talking at once.

"What about Ma?" Stevens said.

"He's gone," Bane said. "Worst way a man kin go. Gutted like a pig."

"We cain't leave him."

"Naw, we cain't." Ruark drew his flintlock pistol. He walked over and laid the barrel against the back of Ma's head and squeezed the trigger. For Miller, in that moment the past five years of his life were erased and he side slipped through time and space into a muddy trench in France, shells and bodies exploding. He had never left, never escaped.

Stevens aimed his rifle at the matron. He lowered it. "Don't have the sand to shoot no woman. Let's git, boys."

Ruark said, "Won't make it far in these woods in the dark."

Stevens said, "We head for the tower and fetch Cal. See what happens."

The Matron said, "Yes! Yes! Go into the house of the Master! He'll greet ye with a glad smile and open arms!"

"Quiet yerself, hag," Stevens said, menacing her with his rifle butt. "C'mon, boys. Let's find poor Cal before the villains make stew of him." There was grudging acquiescence to this plan and the men withdrew from the longhouse and its horrors.

Miller went to the palisade gate and shouldered the Enfield, aimed at the string of lights and blasted several rounds in rapid succession. One of the approaching lamps burst, the rest were doused momentarily. A howl of pain rose from the field. Miller reloaded in a hurry. He ran for the tower where his companions were gathered near its double doors. Something fluttered to his left—a coat tail disappearing behind a pile of neatly stacked firewood. He knew they'd been had. While the villagers waving lanterns on the flats played decoy, others had crept along in a flanking action. He dropped to a knee and swung his rifle around.

"Ambush!" Bane hollered as a dozen or more men in coats and top hats sprang from behind sheds, cottages, hay bales, seemingly everywhere. Pitchforks, hatchets, and knives, edges gleaming and glinting; a couple carried blunderbusses, bulkier and older than even Ruark's. Those guns cracked and spat fire. Puffs of sulfurous white smoke boiled and seethed.

Ten feet away Bane let loose both barrels of the Rigby with a clap of thunder that sounded as if Archangel Michael himself had descended from Heaven to smite the good Lord's enemies. The muzzle flash lit up the tower courtyard like a rocket explosion. A villager was cut in half and a section of the cottage wall behind him caved in, stomped by an elephant. The other loggers loosed a fusillade in a murderous fireworks display.

Night vision spoiled by the alternating glare and shadow, Miller struggled to find targets. He didn't have the opportunity to draw a bead, but simply emptied the Enfield as fast as he could work the bolt. Most of his bullets clattered off stone or ripped furrows into the earth. However, he shot one bearded brute between the eyes as the man charged with an upraised hatchet, and drilled another in the back as the fellow stood motionless as if uncertain how to join the fray.

The cottage that Bane had perforated with his gun caught fire. Flames leaped into the sky. Glass tinkled as it fractured. The fire spread to another house, then another, and in less than thirty seconds, the combatants were struggling by the red blaze of a circle in hell. Ruark swung his axe and lopped a villager's head. The head floated past Miller and into the blaze. Bane screamed and laughed, his beard splattered with blood. He pressed a man's face against a flaming timber and held it there until flesh popped and sizzled. Horn dropped his rifle and turned to run. An older gent in a stovepipe hat knocked him down and skewered him with a pitchfork. The pitchfork went in with a meaty thunk and a clink as the tines bit through into the dirt. Horn grabbed the handle and wrestled for dear life and the man grunted, planted his boot against Horn's groin, and pried loose the pitchfork and raised it to stick him again. Then Ruark's axe whapped the back of the villager's skull and turned it to jelly and the man collapsed facedown, legs twitching. Stevens' rifle boomed once, twice, and he cursed and drew a knife and sidled in tight with his companions. Miller was empty. He picked up a severed hand and forearm and threw it in a man's face then shoulder-blocked him to the ground and methodically clubbed him to death with his rifle butt. Sweat and grease and flying drops of blood soaked him. Miller's arms were weak and he could scarcely raise them at the end. A blast of heat from the burning houses seared his cheeks and ignited the tips of his hair. The smell of roasting flesh was strong.

The remaining villagers routed, fleeing through the flames and the rolling black smoke. Bane, still braying mad laughter, chucked a tomahawk. It sank into a man's backside. The man yelped and stumbled. Bane whooped and said, "Run, ya fuckin' dogs!" And he barked.

"There's reinforcements yonder!" Stevens and Ruark grasped Horn under the arms and dragged him to his feet. The lad gasped and fainted.

Rifles thundered near the front gate. A musket ball kicked dirt near Miller's foot." "Follow me, boys!" He led the charge up the hill and into the cave along a twisting path illuminated by the hellish conflagration. Storming the tower was out of the question—he suspected it would burn to the ground soon enough. Regardless, anyone trapped inside would be smoked out or broiled alive.

The cave mouth opened into a low-ceilinged area with a sandy floor and natural outcroppings that served as adequate cover. The men quickly repurposed empty barrels and busted timbers to fashion a makeshift barricade at the entrance. After they'd finished effecting hasty fortifications, Stevens passed around the remnants of his bottle. He said, "We're in it deep. Killed us a few, but I count twenty, maybe more. Prolly mad as hornets over what we done."

"Learn us somethin' we don't know, boy," Bane said. Between blood loss and one too many belts of rotgut to kill the pain, he slurred, listing precariously until Ruark helped him sit against the wall.

Below, several houses were utterly consumed in the inferno and the fire made a sound like rushing wind. Sparks ignited the lower branches of nearby trees. The smoke had become so thick it proved difficult to discern the movements of the villagers. Men darted about with buckets, presumably hurling dirt and water on the flames. Miller went flat and laid the Enfield across his rolled jacket. He waited, inhaled, partially exhaled, and squeezed the trigger. A lucky shot—a villager's arms flew from his sides and he toppled and lay in the dirt, one hand extended into a burning pile of wood, and soon his clothes smoked and flames licked over them. The rest of the villagers made themselves scarce. The fire spread swiftly after that.

Horn moaned and twisted on the ground. He prayed for Jesus, Mary, and God. Miller helped Ruark peel aside the boy's shirt and slid his hand under his body and felt around. The tines had indeed gone clean through and Horn leaked like a sieve. It wouldn't be long. He caught Ruark's glance and shook his head slightly. Ruark spat. "Boy didn't even fire that peashooter o' his. Bastards."

Horn cried for his mama.

"Hush," Stevens said, striking a match and lighting a lamp he'd found on a peg. He hung the lamp from a support timber in the back of the cave where it constricted to a narrow passage that descended into absolute darkness. Miller couldn't determine the purpose of the cave; although moderately carved and shored, it wasn't a mine. Occult symbols had been chalked upon the walls. Stick figures bowed and scraped, dwarfed by what appeared to be a huge bundle of twigs. Not twigs—worms, or something squiggly like worms.

Huddled around the lamp, the loggers resembled characters from some gothic fable; resurrection men leaning on spades at midnight in a swampy graveyard. By that primitive oil lamplight, the company was a horrific, blood-soaked mess. They piled their packs and sundries in the middle of the floor and counted ammunition and rations. Wounds were appraised: Bane's hacked shoulder would be the death of him without medicine. Ruark had gotten hit in the belly; the hole was about the size of a bean and welled purple and it bubbled when he took a breath. The black powder ball was still inside, although the old logger shrugged and spat and said he felt fine as frog's hair. Stevens revealed nasty punctures in his thigh and ribs, a vicious slash across his breast. Only Miller had survived the melee unscathed.

"What? None of that blood you're covered in is yours? Not even a scratch, you lucky bastard!" Stevens threw back his head and laughed as Ruark helped wind strips of cloth around his torso to staunch the bleeding.

Miller didn't say anything. He'd never taken more than a few bumps and bruises, the occasional cut from flying shrapnel, during the war, had literally walked through the apocalypse at Belleau Wood untouched.

Stevens made a firepot by slathering bear grease in a tin cup and lighting a strip of cloth for a wick. He and Ruark proposed to scout the tunnel and make certain nobody was sneaking along their back-trail. That left with Miller with the kid, who was unconscious and raving, and Bane, who appeared to also have one foot in the grave.

The wait proved short, however. Stevens and Bane reappeared, wide-eyed as horses who'd been spooked by fire. Ruark tossed loose timber and small rocks in the tunnel opening. Stevens reported that the caves stretched on and on, and branched every few paces. In his estimation, anybody damn fool enough to venture into that labyrinth would be wandering for eternity.

After a long, whispered conference, it was decided the men would wait until daylight and then make a run for Slango. There was no telling when or if McGrath might deign to send a search party, so it was safest to assume they were on their own. Watches were set with Ruark taking the first as he allowed he couldn't sleep anyhow. He snuffed the lamp and the firepot and they settled in to wait.

Stevens said, "Ever wonder what Rumpelstiltskin wanted with a kid?"

Miller pulled his hat down and tried to relax. An eldritch white radiance illuminated the cave and it was just him and Horn; everyone else melted and vanished. Mist flowed from the passage and curled over the pile of packs, swirled over Horn's chest and around Miller's knees. Horn stared. His face was gray, suspended in the mist. He said, "C'mon, tell me true. What'd y'all see in that tree? What was hidin' up in there?"

"Worms," Miller said. He wasn't certain if this was accurate. The memory slipped and slithered and changed when he tried to examine it closely. A fibrous network of slimy roots, or worms, or a mass of tendrils squirming in the moist dark of the mighty cedar bole. "They had faces." *Demons sleep in holes in the ground. Live in the rocks, sleep inside a big ol' trees in the deep forest where the sun don't never shine.*

"Oh." Horn nodded. "I dunno what the little man in the story wanted with the child, but I kin tell ya the villagers give their babies to their friends inside the trees… inside this mountain. The sons an' daughters of Ol' Leech. An' I kin tell ya what the people of Ol' Leech do with 'em."

"I'd rather you didn't."

"Jist shut yer eyes an' look inside. We so close, ya kin see their god. He's sleepy like a bear in winter. Dreamin' of his people. Dreamin' of us here in the daylight, too. But he's wakin' up. Be creepin' out a his den pretty soon, I reckon."

"Save it, kid."

"He loves his people. Loves us too, in a different way." Horn's smile was shrewd and cruel. He opened his mouth and inhaled the peculiar light and Miller's dreams became confused. He dreamt of falling through the mountain, through the entire Earth, and into the sky, accelerating like a bullet until the light of the sun dwindled to a pinprick. He crashed through the icy, blood-black surface of a strange moon and drifted weightless in its hollow core. The cavern was rank and humid and dark as pitch. He floated over crags and canyons and forests of clabbered flesh and fungus, his body carried upon the updrafts of a warm, gelatinous sea. At the center of this sea a mountain range shuddered and stirred. The colossus writhed and uncoiled with satanic majesty, aroused by the whine of flea wings. It whispered to him.

 કજ ⍣

Miller awoke to Calhoun begging for help.

Calhoun cried from the direction of the tower. He called them by name in a tone of anguish and his voice carried. He began screaming the screams of a man partially buried alive or hung in barbed wire or swollen with mustard gas. Miller lay in the shadows, watching the dying light of the fires shiver across the wall of the cave. Calhoun kept screaming and they all pretended not to hear him.

 કજ ⍣

Still later and after night settled in as tight as a blindfold, Stevens shook Miller. "Somethin's wrong."

"Oh, jumpin' Jaysus," Ruark said and moments later lighted the firepot. Miller would've cursed the old man for revealing their position, except he saw the cause of alarm—Horn was gone, spirited away from under their noses. Drips and drabs of blood smeared into the tunnel, into the blackness. "Them sonsabitches snatched Thad!"

As if in response to the light, a faint, ghostly moan echoed up the passage from great subterranean depths. *Help me, boys. Help me.* At least that's what it sounded like to Miller. The distance and acoustics could've made wind whistling through chimneys of rock resemble almost anything.

"Lordy, Lordy," Bane said. He was a frightful sight; gore limed his beard and jacket. He might've been a talking corpse. "That's the boy."

"Ain't him," Stevens said.

"The kid is done for," Miller said. His eyes watered and he struggled to keep his voice even. "Whoever's hooting down that tunnel is no friend of ours."

"They're right, Moses," Ruark said. "This an ol' Injun trick. Make a noise of a wounded friend an draw ya in." He ran his thumb across his throat with an exaggerated flourish. "Ya should know it, hoss. That boy is daid."

"Lookit all the blood," Stevens said.

Bane shoved a plug of tobacco into his mouth and chewed with his eyes closed. His flesh was papery and his eyelids fluttered the way a man's do when he's caught in a terrible dream. He resembled the photographs of dead outlaws in open coffins displayed on frontier boardwalks. He spat. "Yeh, an' lookit me. Still kickin'."

Help me. Help me. The four of them froze like woodland animals, heads inclined toward the dim cries, the cold, cold draft.

"Ain't him," Stevens repeated, but mostly to himself.

Bane stood. He leaned against the wall, the barrel of his Rigby nosing the sand. He nodded to Ruark. "You comin'?"

Ruark spat. He lifted the firepot and led the way.

Bane said, "Alrightee, boys. Take care." He tapped his hat and limped after his comrade. Their shadows swayed and jostled, and their light grew smaller and seeped into the mountain and was gone.

The others sat in the dark for a long time, listening. Miller heard faint laughter, a snatch of Bane singing "John Brown's Body," and then only the fluting of the wind in the rocks.

"Oh, hell," Stevens said when the silence between them had gone on for an age. "You was in the war."

"You weren't?"

"Uh-uh. My father worked for the post office. He fixed my card so's I wouldn't get conscripted."

"Wish I'd thought of that," Miller said.

"You seen the worst of it. Any chance we kin get out a this with our skins?"

"Nope."

There was another long pause. Stevens said, "Want a smoke?" He lighted two Old Mills and passed one to Miller. They smoked and listened, but there was nothing to hear except for the wind, the rustle of branches outside. Stevens said, "He weren't dragged. The kid crawled away."

"How do you figure? He was pretty much dead."

"*Pretty much* ain't the same thing, now is it? I heard 'em talkin' to him, whisperin' from the dark. Only heard bits. Didn't need more…they told him to come ahead. An' he did."

"Must've been persuasive," Miller said. "And you didn't raise the alarm."

"Hard to explain. Snake-bit, frozen stiff. It was like my body fell asleep yet I could hear what was goin' on. I was piss-scared."

Miller smoked his cigarette. "I don't blame you," he said.

"I got my senses back after a piece. Kid was long gone by then. Whoever they are, he went with 'em."

"And now Moses and Ruark are with them too."

"I didn't tell the whole truth about what we saw in the tunnel."

"Is that so."

"Didn't seem much point carryin' on. Not far along the trail it opens into a cavern. Dunno how big; our light couldn't touch but the edges of the walls and the ceilin'. There were drops into plain ol' nothin' an' more passages twistin' every which way. But we stopped only a few steps into the cavern. A pillar rose high as the light could reach. Broad at the base like a pyramid and made of rocks all slippery an' shiny from drippin' water. Except, the rocks weren't just rocks. There were skeletons cemented in between. Prolly hundreds an' hundreds. Small things. There was a hole at eye level. Smooth as the bore of my gun and about the size of my fist. Pure black, solid, glistenin' black that threw the light from our torch back at us. We didn't peep too close on account of the skeletons before we turned tail and ran. Saw one thing as we turned to haul our asses… That hole had widened enough I could a jumped in and stood tall. It made a sound that traveled from somewhere farther and deeper than I want a think about. Not the kind a sound you hear, but the kind you feel in your bones. Felt kinda bad and good at once. I could tell Ruark liked it. Oh, he was afraid, but compelled, I guess you'd say."

"Well," Miller said after consideration, "I can see why you might've kept that to yourself."

"Yeh. I wish them ol' coons had stayed back. Maybe we could a blasted our way out with their guns and ours."

Miller didn't think so. "Maybe. Catch some shut eye. Sunup in a couple hours."

Stevens rolled over and set his hat over his face and didn't move again. Miller watched the stars fade.

ꝁ ꝁ

They left the cave at dawn and descended the hill into the ruins of the village. Ashes turned in the breeze. The tower stood, although scorched and blackened. Its double doors were sprung, wood smoldering, hinges melted. Smoke curled from the gap. Many of the surrounding houses had burned to their foundations. Gray dust lay over everything. Corpses were stacked near the longhouse and covered with a canvas tarp to keep the birds away. Judging from height and width of the collection, at least fifteen bodies were piled beneath the tarp awaiting burial. Twenty-five to thirty men and women combed the charred wreckage. Their hands and faces were filthy with the gray dust. Some stared hatefully at the pair, but none spoke, none raised a hand.

Miller and Stevens trudged through the village and onward, following the river south as it wended through the valley. With every step, Miller's shoulders tightened as he awaited the inevitable musket ball to shear his spine. Early in the afternoon, they climbed a bluff and rested for the first time.

After Stevens caught his breath, he said, "I don't understand. Why they'd let us live?" He removed his hat and peered through the trees, searching for signs of pursuit.

"Did they?" Miller said. He didn't look the way they'd come, instead studying the forest depths before them, tasting the damp and the rot and the cold. He thought of his dream of flying into the depths of space, of the terrible darkness between the stars and what ruled there. "We've got nowhere to hide. I had to guess, I'd guess they're saving us for something very special."

So, they continued on and arrived at the outskirts of Slango as the peaks darkened to purple. Nothing remained of the encampment except for abandoned logs and mucky, flattened areas, and a muddle of footprints and drag marks. Every man, woman, and mule was gone. Every piece of equipment likewise vanished. The railroad tracks had been torn up. In a few months forest would reclaim all but the shorn slopes, erasing any evidence Slango Camp ever stood there.

"Shit," Stevens said without much emotion. He hung his hat on a branch and wiped his face with a bandanna.

"Hello, lads," A man said, stepping from behind a tree. He was wide and portly and wore a stovepipe hat and an immaculate silk suit. His handlebar mustache was luxuriously waxed and he carried a blackthorn cane in his left hand. A dying ray of sun glowed upon the white, white skin of his face and neck. "I am Dr. Boris Kalamov. You have caused me a tremendous amount of trouble." He gestured at the surroundings. "This is not our way. We prefer peaceful coexistence, to remain unseen and unheard, suckling like a hagfish, our hosts none the wiser, albeit dimly cognizant through the persistent legends and campfire tales which please us and nourish us as much as blood and bone. To act with such dramatic flourish goes against our code, our very nature. Alas, certain of my brethren were taken by a vengeful mood what with you torching the village of our servants." He *tisked* and wagged a finger that seemed to possess too many joints.

Miller didn't even bother to lift his rifle. He was focused upon the nightmare taking shape in his mind. "How now, Doctor?"

Stevens was more optimistic, or just doggedly belligerent. He jacked a round into the chamber of his Winchester and sighted the man's chest.

Dr. Kalamov smiled and his mouth dripped black. "You arrived at a poor time, friends. The black of the sun, the villagers' holiest of holy days when they venerate the Great Dark and we who call it home. Their quaint and superstitious ceremony at the dolmen cut short because of your trespass. Such an interruption merits pain and suffering. O' Men from Porlock, it shan't end well for you."

Stevens glanced around, peering into the shadows of the trees. "I figured you didn't come for tea, fancy pants. What I want a know is what happens next."

"You will dwell among my people, of course."

"Where? You mean in the village?"

"No, oh, no, no, not the village with *your* kind, the cattle who breed our delicacies and delights. No, you shall dwell in the Dark with *us*. Where the rest of your friends from this lovely community were taken last night while you two cowered in the cave. You're a wily and resourceful fellow, Mr. Stevens, as are most of your doughty woodsmen kin. We can make use of you. Wonderful, wonderful use."

"Goodbye, you sonofabitch," Stevens said, cocking the hammer.

"Not quite," Dr. Kalamov said. "If we can't have you, we'll simply make do with your relatives. Your father still works for the post office in Seattle, does he not? And your sweet mother knits and has supper ready when he gets home to that cozy farmhouse you grew up in near Green Lake. Your little brother Buddy working on the railroad in Nevada. Your nephews Curtis and Kevin are riding the range in Wyoming. So many miles of fence to mend, so little time. Very dark on the prairie at night. Perhaps you would rather we visit them instead."

Stevens lowered his rifle, then dropped it in the mud. He walked to the doctor and stood beside him, slumped and defeated. Dr. Kalamov patted his head. The doctor's hand was large enough to have encompassed it if he'd wished, and his nails were as long as darning needles. He flicked Stevens' ear and it peeled loose and plopped wetly in the bushes. Stevens clapped his hand over the hole and screamed and fell to his knees, blood streaming between his fingers. Dr. Kalamov smiled an avuncular smile and tousled the man's hair. He pushed a nail through the top of Stevens' skull and wiggled. Stevens fell silent, his face slack and dumb as Ma's had ever been.

"Reckon I'll decline your offer," Miller said. He drew his pistol and weighed it in his hand. "Go ahead and terrorize my distant relations. Meanwhile, I think I'll blow my brains out and be shut of this whole mess."

"Don't be hasty, young man," Dr. Kalamov said. "I've taken a shine to you. You're free to leave this mountain. There's a lockbox in the roots of that tree. The company payroll. Take it, take a new name. And when you're old, be certain to tell of the horrors that you've seen…horrors that will infest your dreams from today until the day you die. We'll always be near you, Mr. Miller." He doffed his hat and bowed. Then he grasped Stevens by the collar and bundled him under one arm and into the gathering gloom.

The lockbox was where the man had promised and it contained a princely sum. Miller stuffed the money in a sack as the sun went down and darkness fell. When he'd finished packing the money he buried his head in his arms and groaned.

"By the way, there are two minor conditions," Dr. Kalamov said, leering from behind a stump. The flesh of his face hung loose as if it were a badly slipping mask. His eyes were misaligned, his mouth a bleeding black slash that extended to his ears. He had no teeth. "You're a virile lad. Be certain to spawn oodles and oodles of babies—I must insist on that point. We'll be observing, so do your best, my boy. There is also the matter of your firstborn…"

Miller had nearly pissed himself at Dr. Kalamov's reappearance. He forced his throat to work. "You're asking for my child."

Dr. Kalamov chuckled and drummed his claws on the wood. "No, Mr. Miller. I jest. Although, those wicked old fairytales are jolly good fun, speaking such primordial truths as they do. Be well, be fruitful." He scuttled backward and then lifted vertically into the shadows, a spider ascending its thread, and was gone.

𝄢 𝄡

Years later, Miller married a girl from California and settled in a small farming town. He worked as a gunsmith. His wife gave birth to a boy. After the baby arrived he'd often lie awake at night and listen to the house settle and the mice scratch in the cupboards. When the baby cried, Miller's wife would go into the nursery and soothe him with a lullaby. Miller strained to hear the words, for it was the deep silences that unnerved him and caused his heart to race.

There was a willow tree in the yard. It cast a shadow through the window. As his wife crooned to the baby in the nursery, Miller watched the shadow branches ripple upon the dull white oval of wall. On the bad nights, the branches twitched and narrowed and writhed like tendrils worming their way through fissures in the plaster toward the bed and his sweating, paralyzed form.

One morning he went to the shed and fetched an axe and chopped the tree down. The first tree he'd felled since his youth. The willow was very old and very large and the job lasted until lunchtime.

The center was semi-rotten and hollow, and when the tree crashed to earth the bole partially split and gushed pulp. Something heavy and multi-segmented shifted and retracted inside the trunk. Water gurgled from the wound with a wheeze that almost sounded like someone muttering his name. He dumped kerosene over everything and struck a match. The neighbors gathered and watched the blaze, and though they gossiped amongst themselves, no one said a word to him. There'd been rumors.

His wife came to the door with the baby in her arms. Her expression was that of a person who'd witnessed a dark miracle and knew not how to reconcile the fear and wonder of the revelation.

Miller stood in the billowing smoke, leaning on his axe, eyes reflecting the lights of hell.

ꝛ ꝼ

Acknowledgments

This book would not have been possible without the hard work, support, and encouragement of the entire Night Shade Books team: Jason Williams, Jeremy Lassen, Tomra Palmer, Dave Palumbo, Amy Popovich, Allison Stumpf, and Liz Upson. Thanks, I couldn't have picked a better bunch of folks to work with.

To the editors and anthologists I've had the pleasure and privilege of working with over the last few years—John Joseph Adams, Scott Connors, Ellen Datlow, Marty Halpern, Ron Hilger, John Klima, Tim Pratt, Jonathan Strahan, and Ann and Jeff VanderMeer—Thanks, it's been a Master Class. Thanks to all of those who helped out, made story suggestions, or offered advice while I was putting this anthology together, particularly John Betancourt, Matthew Carpenter, Stephanie Hartman, Jill Henderson, Michael Lee, Barbara Roden, Mike Roth, and Jerad Walters. Thanks as well to Obrotowy, for his outstanding cover art (*Iä! Cthulhu!*), Claudia Noble, for her breathtaking design, and Allan Kausch, for his copyediting prowess. Thanks also to all the authors whose work appears within these pages, and to Grandpa Theobald—Howard Phillips Lovecraft—for inspiring those authors.

Special thanks to my wife, Jennifer, for her patience as this anthology drove me to the brink of madness… *and beyond!* To my parents, for raising me in a house filled with books. And to Maddie the Shih-Tzu, the best listener an editor could have.

Copyright Acknowledgments

About the Editor

Ross E. Lockhart is the managing editor of Night Shade Books. A lifelong fan of supernatural, fantastic, speculative, and weird fiction, he holds degrees in English from Sonoma State University (BA) and San Francisco State University (MA). He lives in an old church in Petaluma, CA, with his wife Jennifer, hundreds of books, and a small, ravenous dog that he believes may be one of the Elder Gods. *The Book of Cthulhu* is his first anthology.